W.i.t.c.h.

Will Irma Taranee Cornelia Hay Lin

Part VI.
Ragorlang
Volume 1

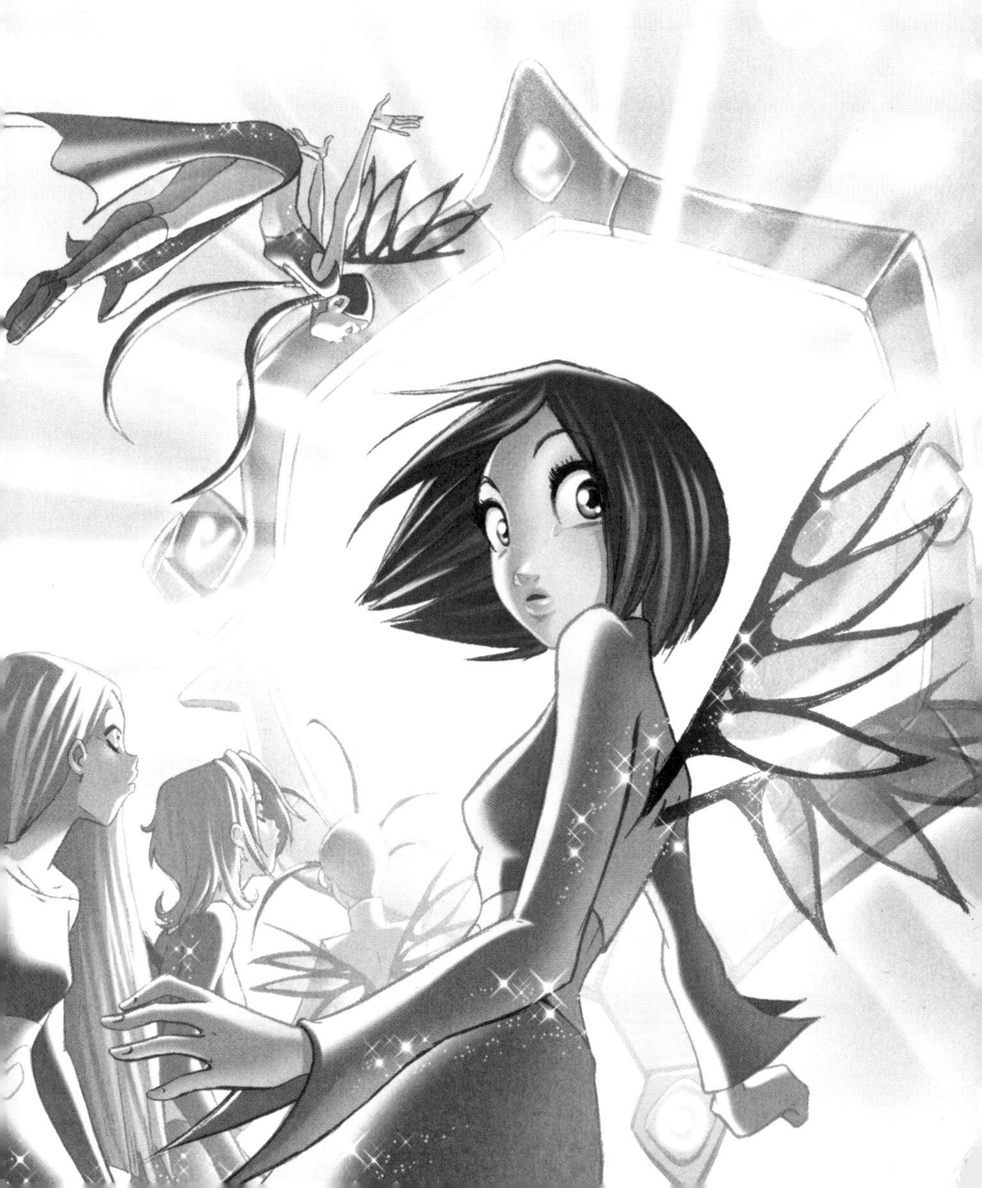

W.i.t.c.h

Will　Irma　Taranee　Cornelia　Hay Lin

Part VI.
Ragorlang
Volume 1

CONTENTS

64

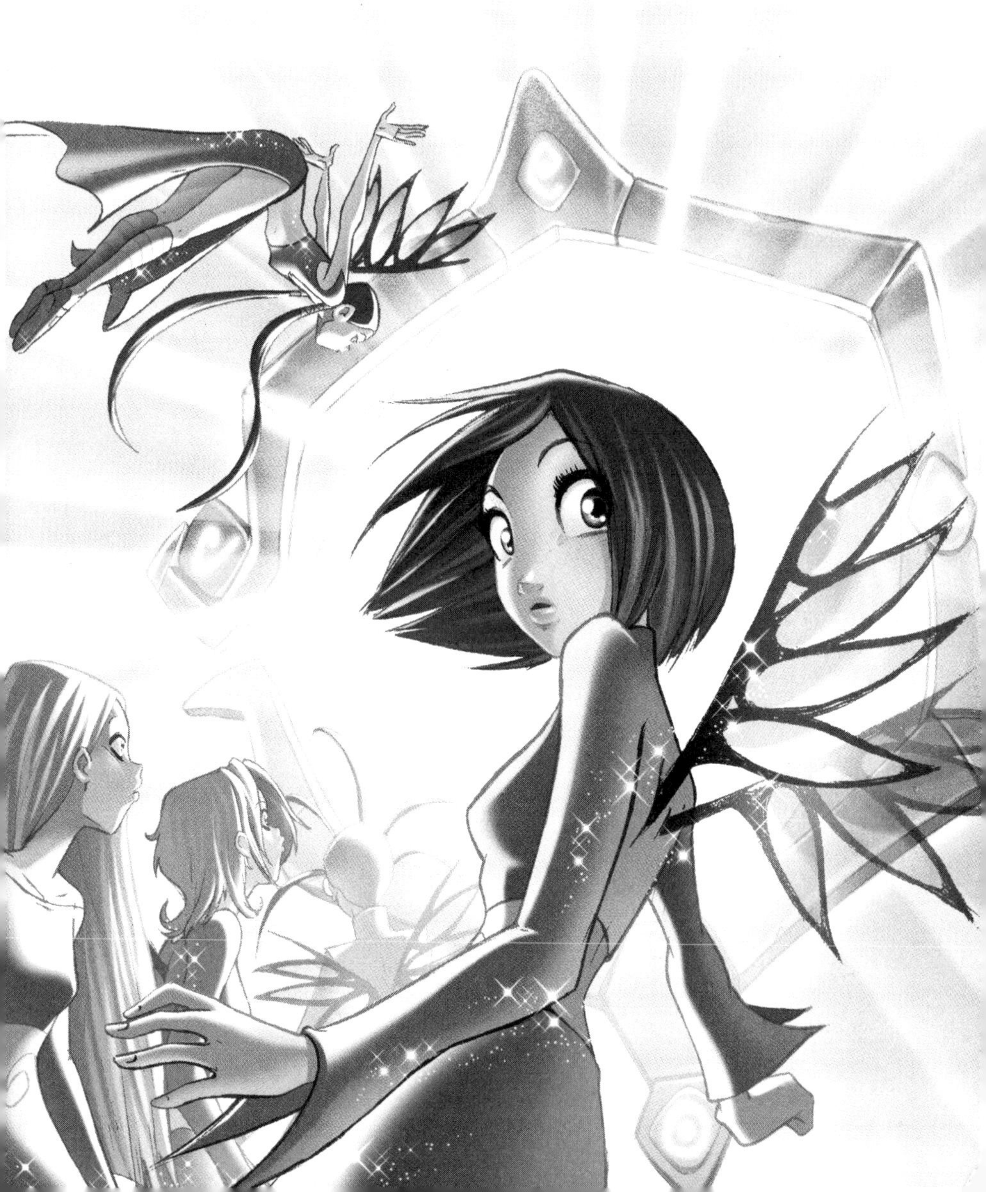

The Screaming Man

"That creature is like a man's shadow..."

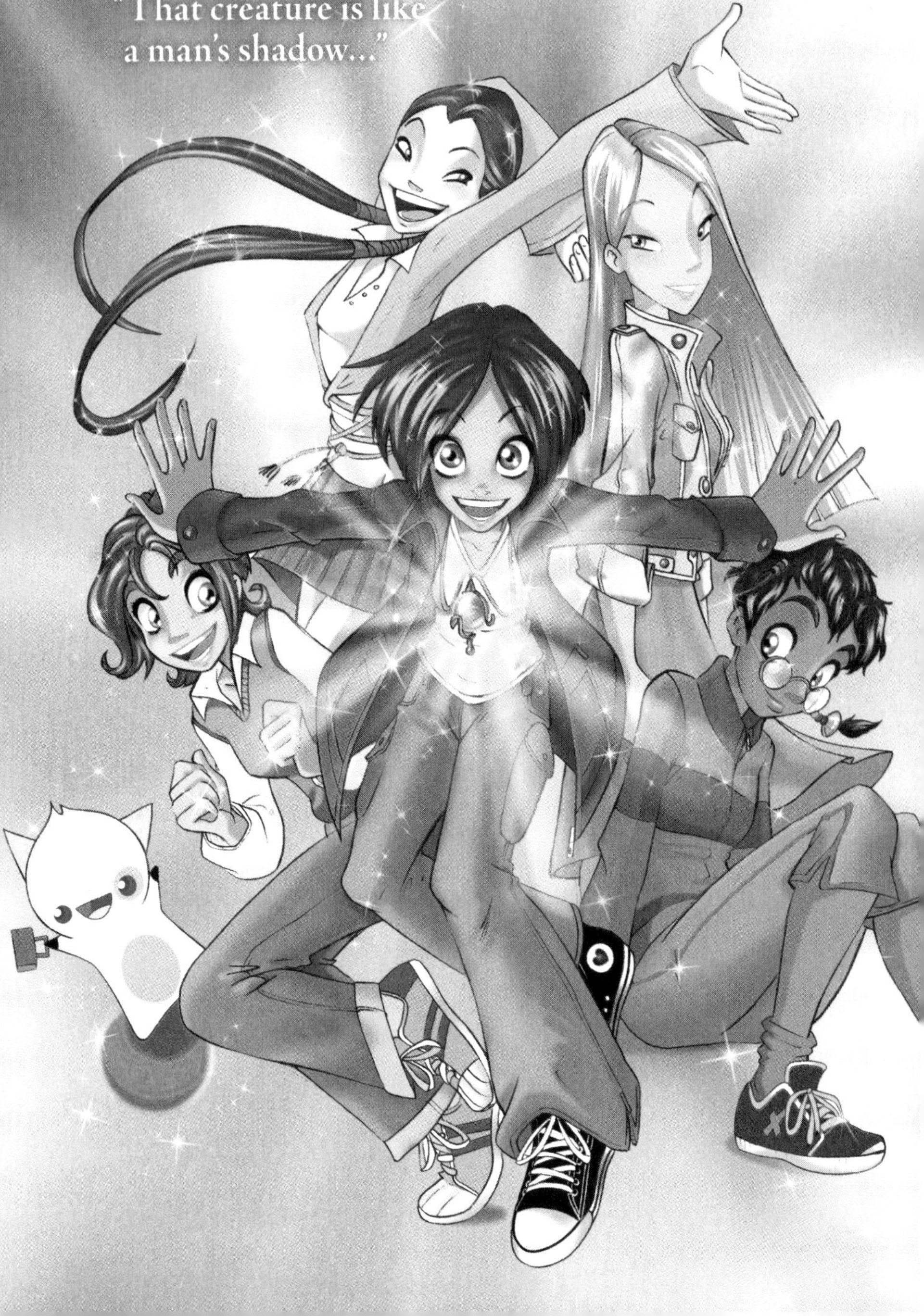

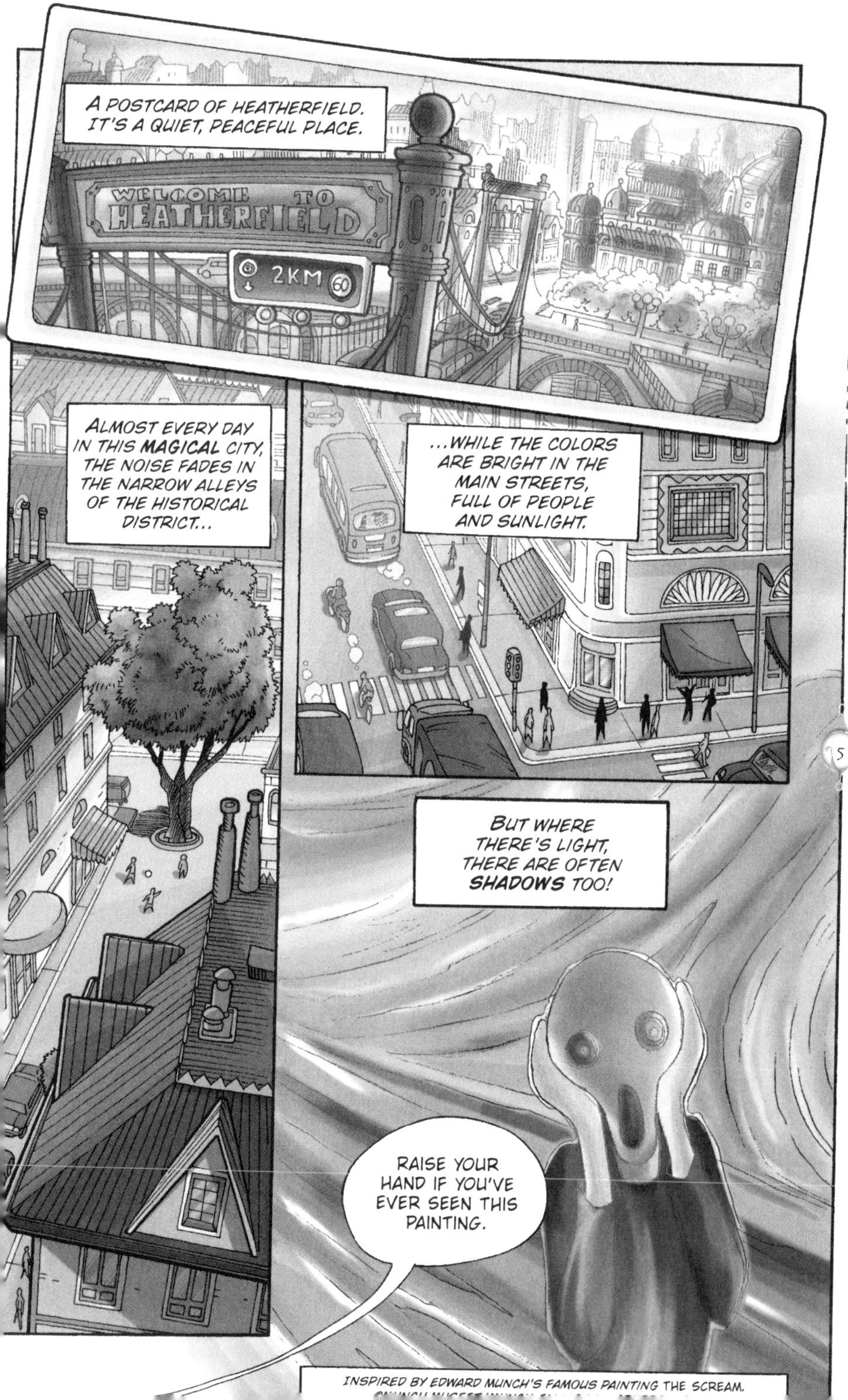
A POSTCARD OF HEATHERFIELD. IT'S A QUIET, PEACEFUL PLACE.
WELCOME TO HEATHERFIELD
2KM
60
ALMOST EVERY DAY IN THIS MAGICAL CITY, THE NOISE FADES IN THE NARROW ALLEYS OF THE HISTORICAL DISTRICT...
...WHILE THE COLORS ARE BRIGHT IN THE MAIN STREETS, FULL OF PEOPLE AND SUNLIGHT.
BUT WHERE THERE'S LIGHT, THERE ARE OFTEN SHADOWS TOO!
RAISE YOUR HAND IF YOU'VE EVER SEEN THIS PAINTING.
INSPIRED BY EDWARD MUNCH'S FAMOUS PAINTING THE SCREAM.

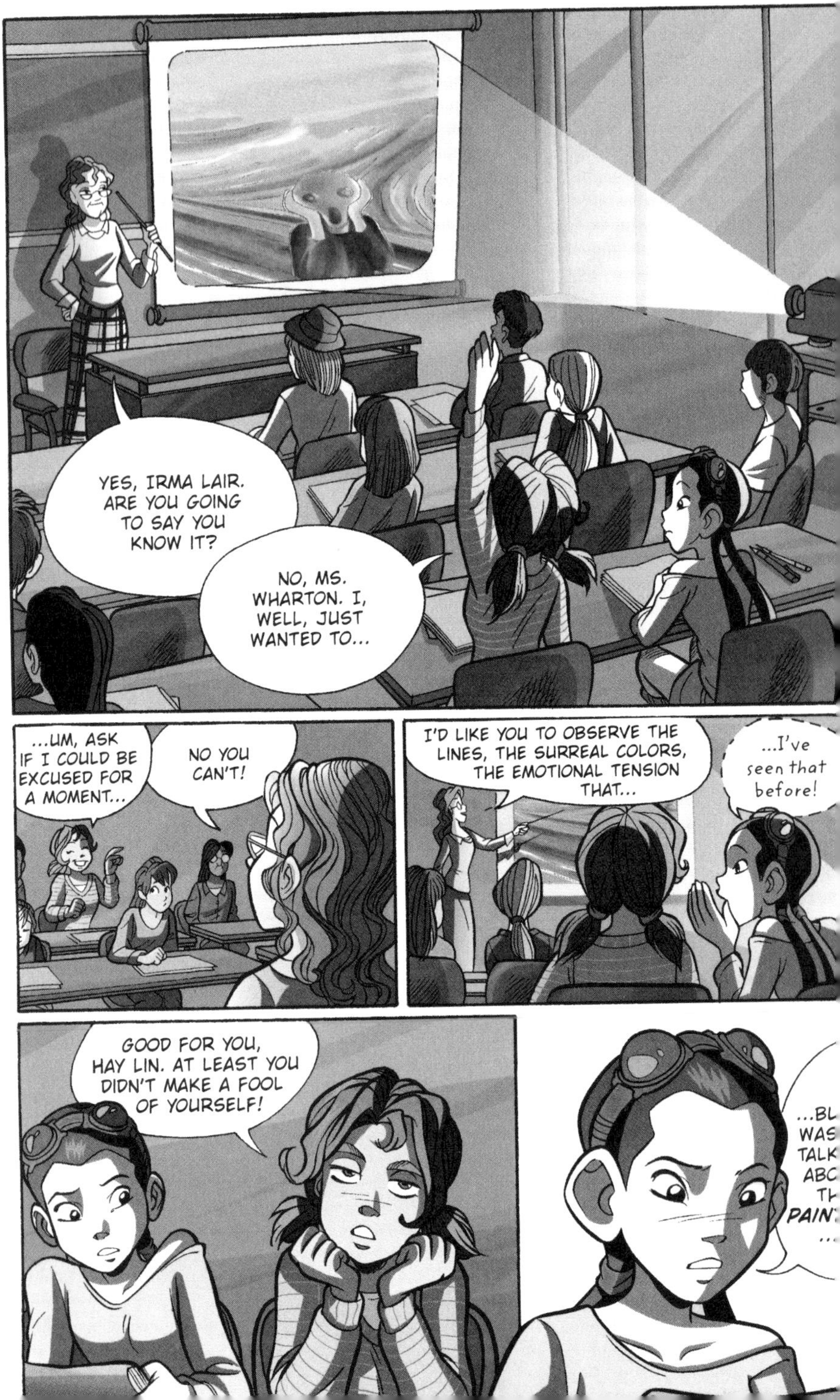
YES, IRMA LAIR. ARE YOU GOING TO SAY YOU KNOW IT?
NO, MS. WHARTON. I, WELL, JUST WANTED TO...
...UM, ASK IF I COULD BE EXCUSED FOR A MOMENT...
NO YOU CAN'T!
I'D LIKE YOU TO OBSERVE THE LINES, THE SURREAL COLORS, THE EMOTIONAL TENSION THAT...
...I've seen that before!
GOOD FOR YOU, HAY LIN. AT LEAST YOU DIDN'T MAKE A FOOL OF YOURSELF!
...BL
WAS
TALK
ABC
TH
PAIN
...

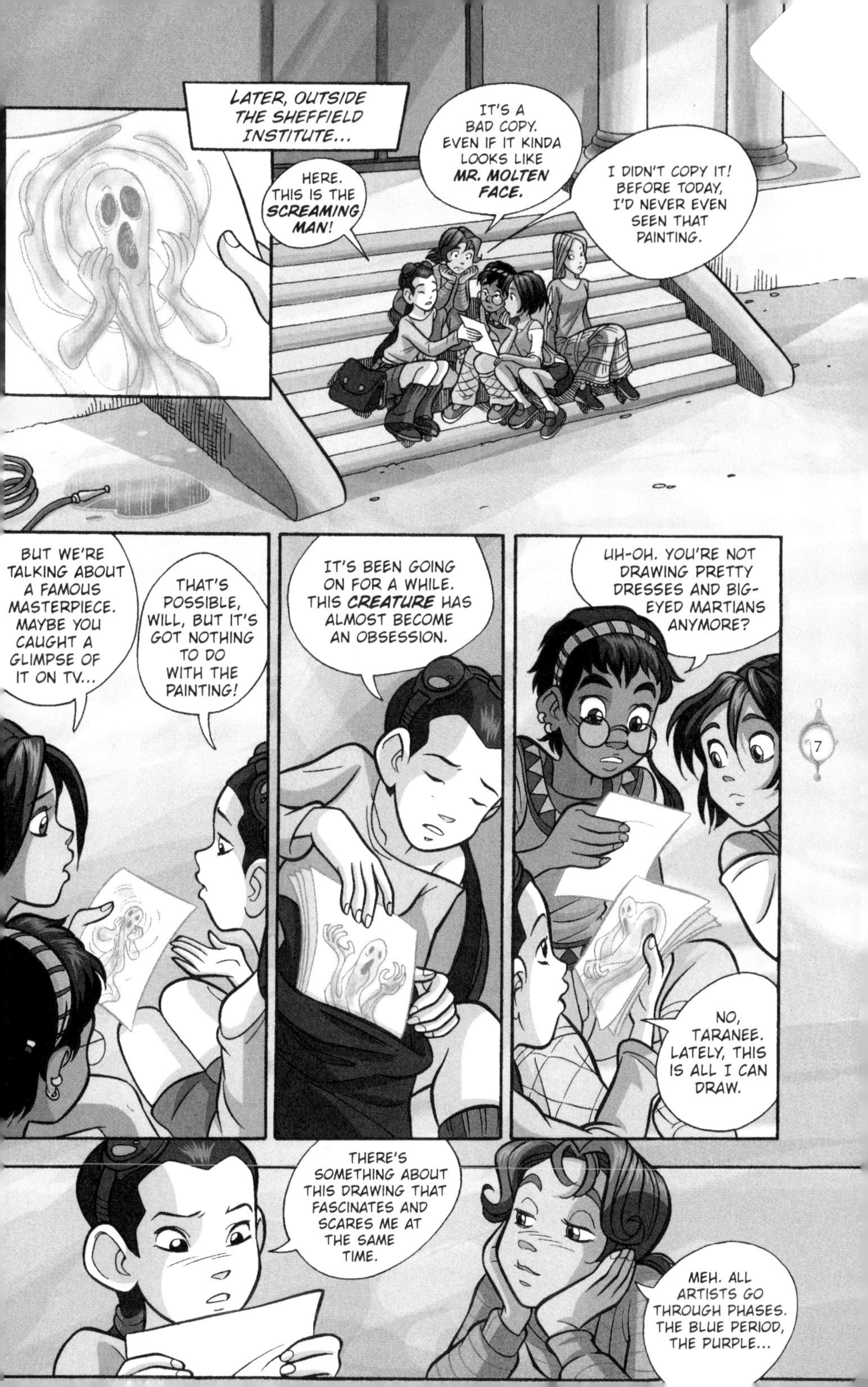
LATER, OUTSIDE THE SHEFFIELD INSTITUTE...
HERE. THIS IS THE SCREAMING MAN!
IT'S A BAD COPY. EVEN IF IT KINDA LOOKS LIKE MR. MOLTEN FACE.
I DIDN'T COPY IT! BEFORE TODAY, I'D NEVER EVEN SEEN THAT PAINTING.
BUT WE'RE TALKING ABOUT A FAMOUS MASTERPIECE. MAYBE YOU CAUGHT A GLIMPSE OF IT ON TV...
THAT'S POSSIBLE, WILL, BUT IT'S GOT NOTHING TO DO WITH THE PAINTING!
IT'S BEEN GOING ON FOR A WHILE. THIS CREATURE HAS ALMOST BECOME AN OBSESSION.
UH-OH. YOU'RE NOT DRAWING PRETTY DRESSES AND BIG-EYED MARTIANS ANYMORE?
NO, TARANEE. LATELY, THIS IS ALL I CAN DRAW.
THERE'S SOMETHING ABOUT THIS DRAWING THAT FASCINATES AND SCARES ME AT THE SAME TIME.
MEH. ALL ARTISTS GO THROUGH PHASES. THE BLUE PERIOD, THE PURPLE...

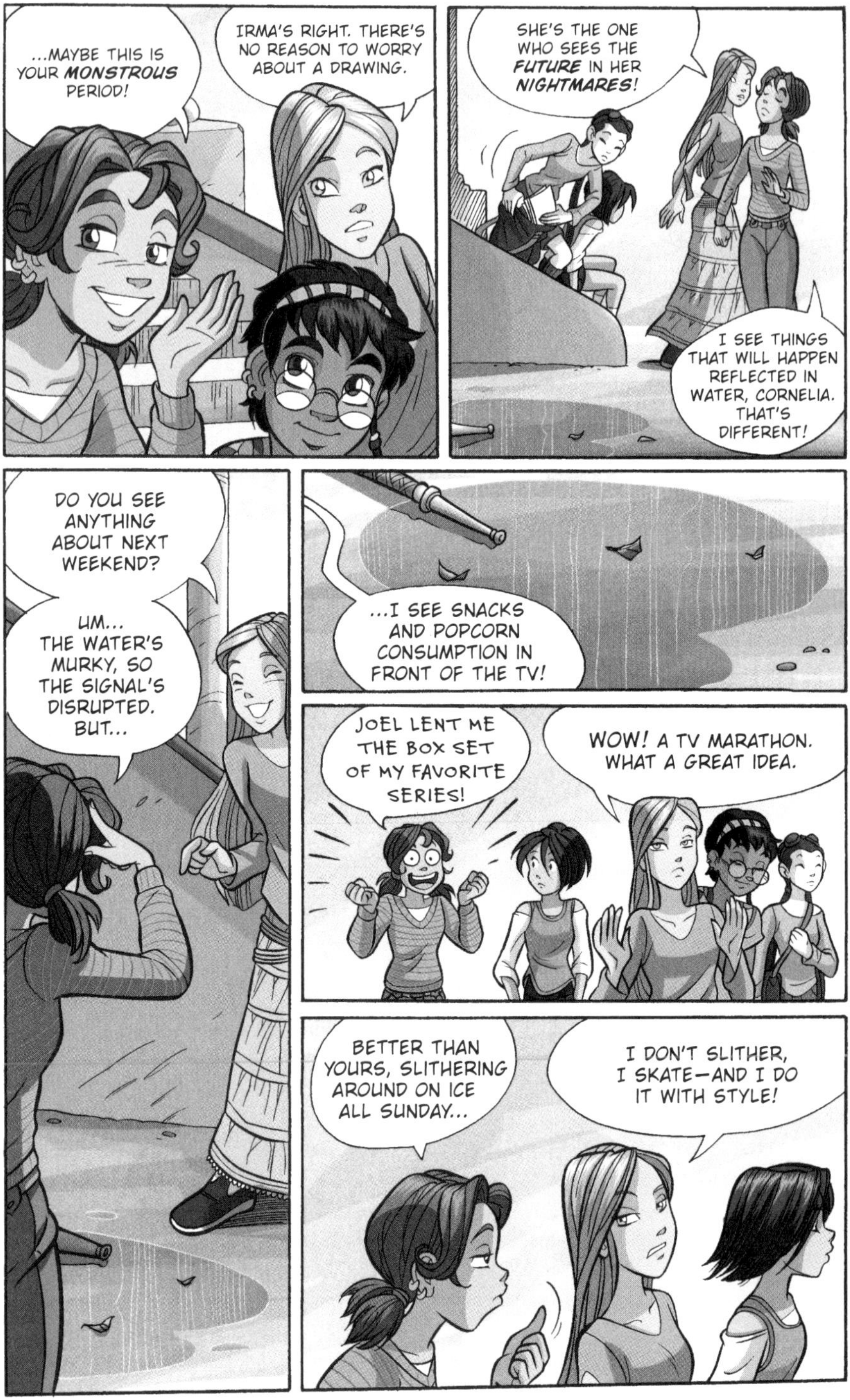

...MAYBE THIS IS YOUR **MONSTROUS** PERIOD!
IRMA'S RIGHT. THERE'S NO REASON TO WORRY ABOUT A DRAWING.
SHE'S THE ONE WHO SEES THE **FUTURE** IN HER **NIGHTMARES**!
I SEE THINGS THAT WILL HAPPEN REFLECTED IN WATER, CORNELIA. THAT'S DIFFERENT!
DO YOU SEE ANYTHING ABOUT NEXT WEEKEND?
UM... THE WATER'S MURKY, SO THE SIGNAL'S DISRUPTED. BUT...
...I SEE SNACKS AND POPCORN CONSUMPTION IN FRONT OF THE TV!
JOEL LENT ME THE BOX SET OF MY FAVORITE SERIES!
WOW! A TV MARATHON. WHAT A GREAT IDEA.
BETTER THAN YOURS, SLITHERING AROUND ON ICE ALL SUNDAY...
I DON'T SLITHER, I SKATE—AND I DO IT WITH STYLE!

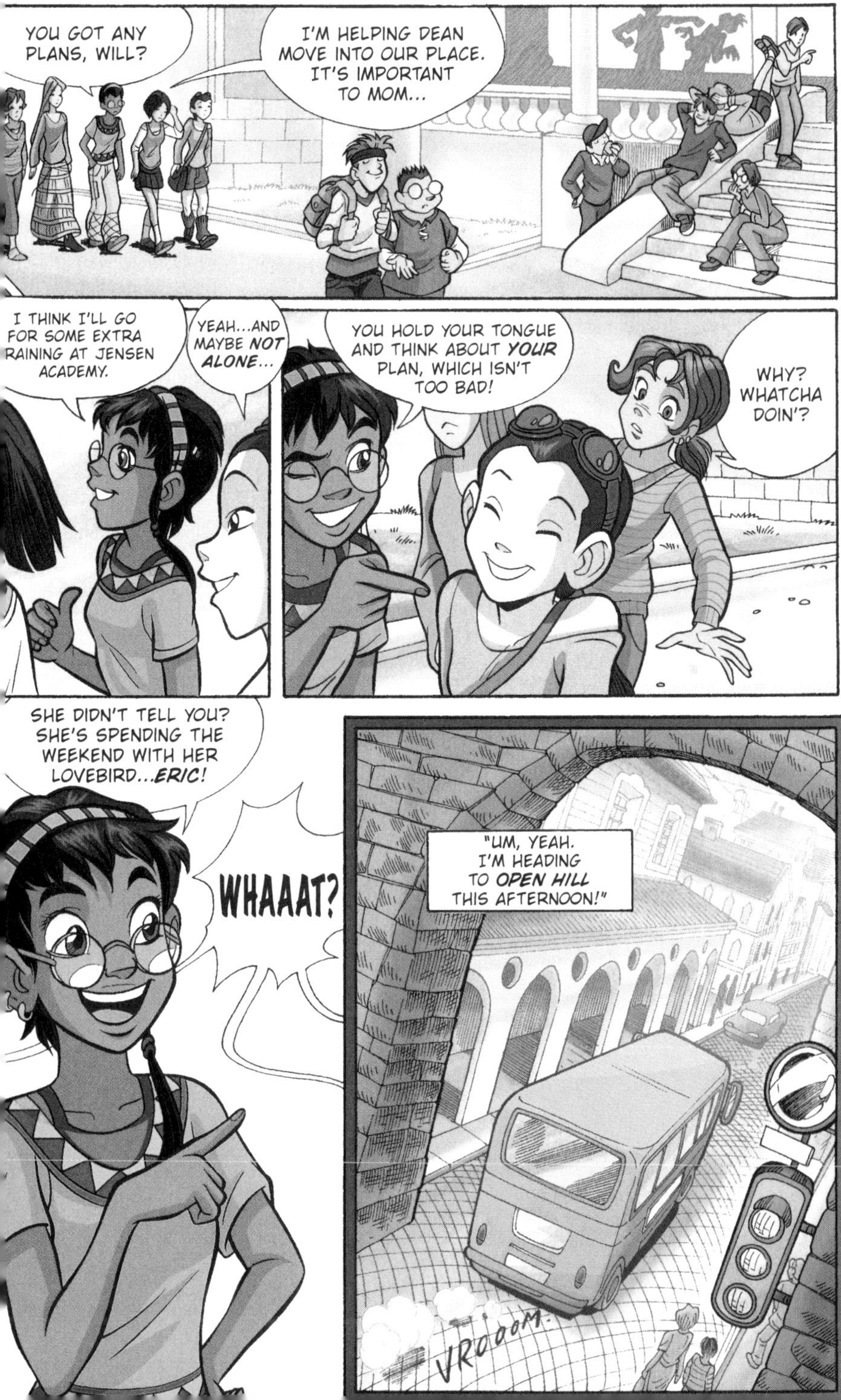

YOU GOT ANY PLANS, WILL?
I'M HELPING DEAN MOVE INTO OUR PLACE. IT'S IMPORTANT TO MOM...
I THINK I'LL GO FOR SOME EXTRA RAINING AT JENSEN ACADEMY.
YEAH...AND MAYBE **NOT ALONE**...
YOU HOLD YOUR TONGUE AND THINK ABOUT **YOUR** PLAN, WHICH ISN'T TOO BAD!
WHY? WHATCHA DOIN'?
SHE DIDN'T TELL YOU? SHE'S SPENDING THE WEEKEND WITH HER LOVEBIRD...**ERIC**!
WHAAAT?
"UM, YEAH. I'M HEADING TO **OPEN HILL** THIS AFTERNOON!"
VROOOM.

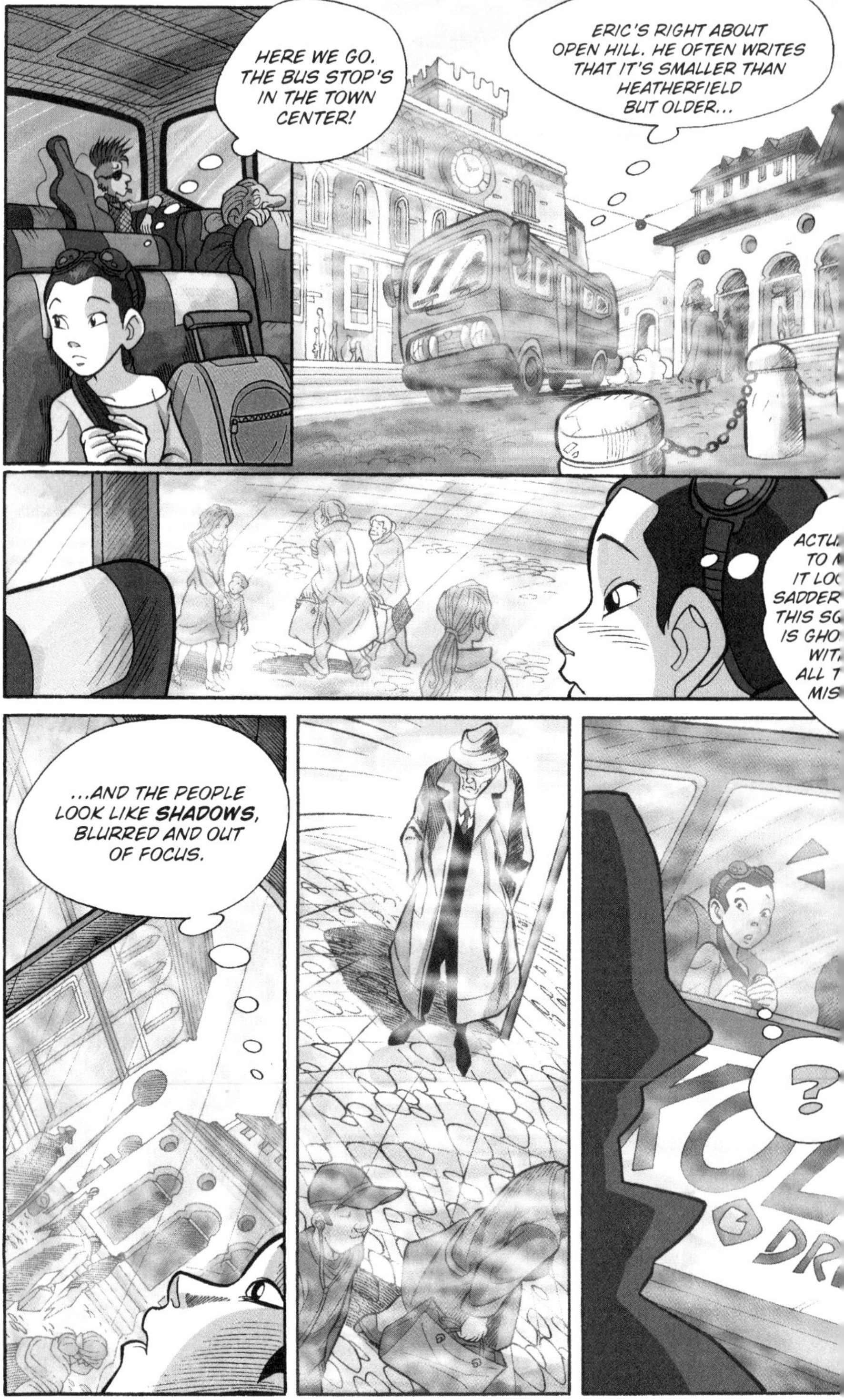
HERE WE GO. THE BUS STOP'S IN THE TOWN CENTER!
ERIC'S RIGHT ABOUT OPEN HILL. HE OFTEN WRITES THAT IT'S SMALLER THAN HEATHERFIELD BUT OLDER...
ACTU TO M IT LOO SADDER THIS SC IS GHO WIT ALL T MIS
...AND THE PEOPLE LOOK LIKE **SHADOWS**, BLURRED AND OUT OF FOCUS.
?

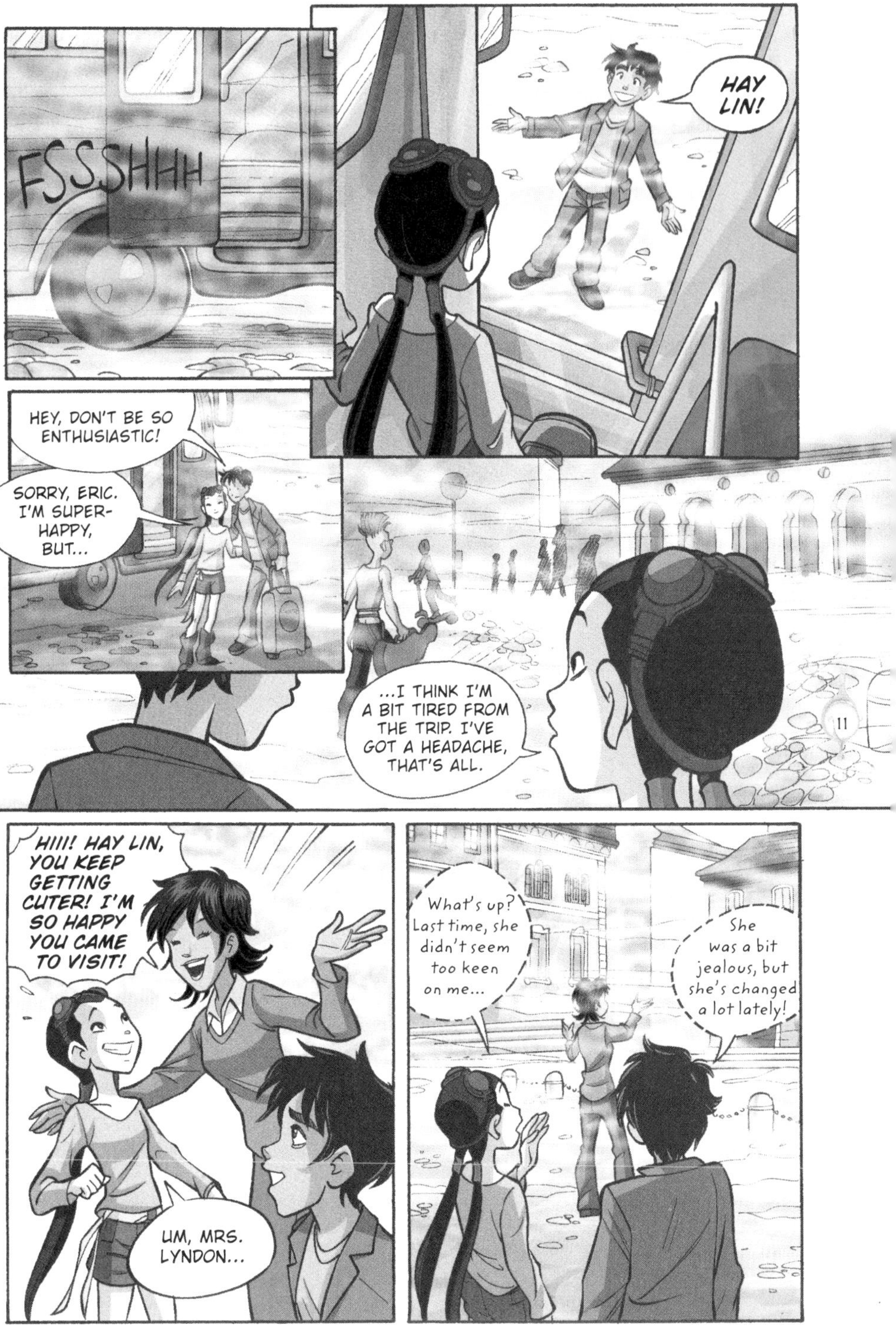
FSSSHHH
HAY LIN!
HEY, DON'T BE SO ENTHUSIASTIC!
SORRY, ERIC. I'M SUPER-HAPPY, BUT...
...I THINK I'M A BIT TIRED FROM THE TRIP. I'VE GOT A HEADACHE, THAT'S ALL.
HIII! HAY LIN, YOU KEEP GETTING CUTER! I'M SO HAPPY YOU CAME TO VISIT!
UM, MRS. LYNDON...
What's up? Last time, she didn't seem too keen on me...
She was a bit jealous, but she's changed a lot lately!

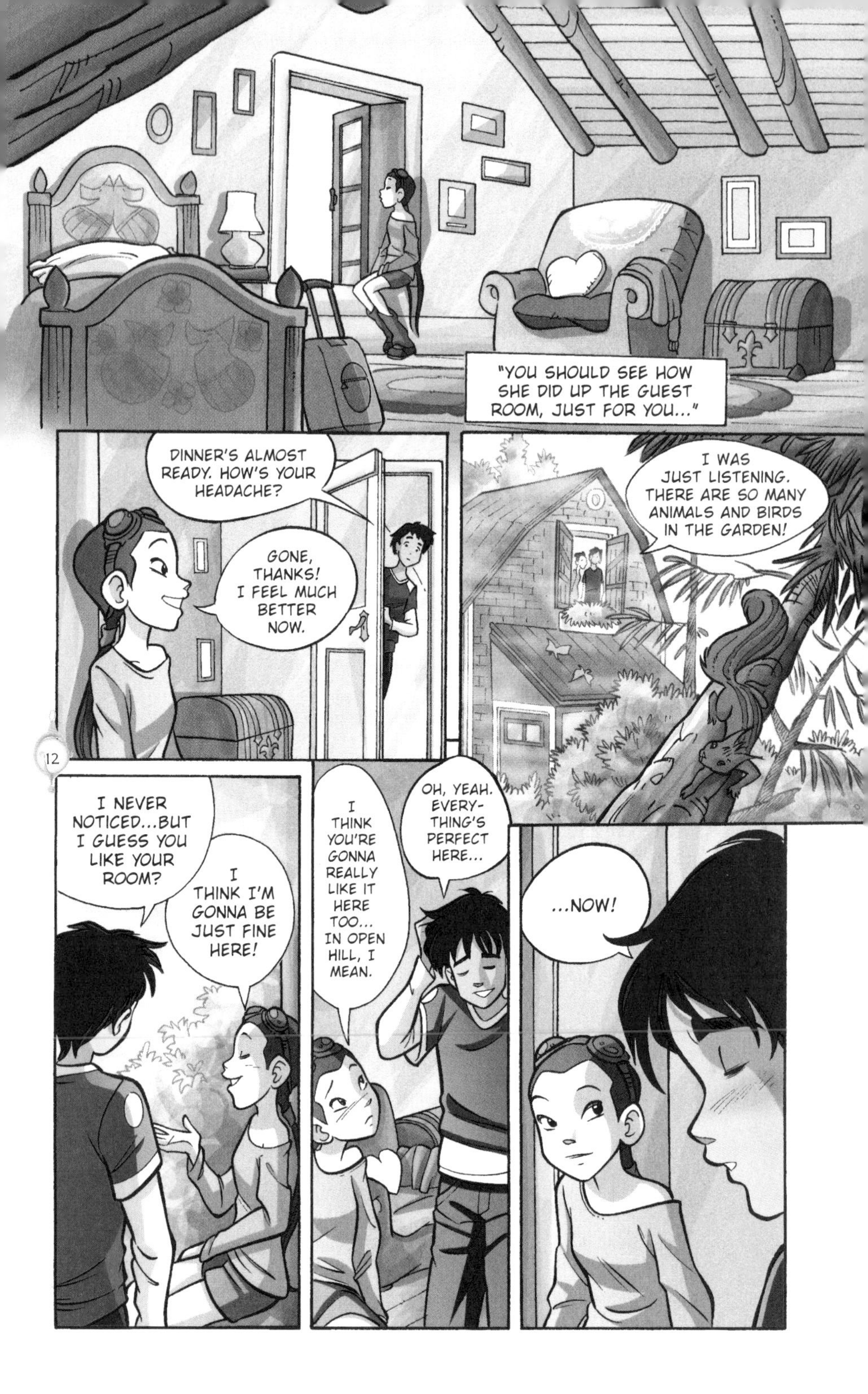
"YOU SHOULD SEE HOW SHE DID UP THE GUEST ROOM, JUST FOR YOU..."
DINNER'S ALMOST READY. HOW'S YOUR HEADACHE?
GONE, THANKS! I FEEL MUCH BETTER NOW.
I WAS JUST LISTENING. THERE ARE SO MANY ANIMALS AND BIRDS IN THE GARDEN!
I NEVER NOTICED...BUT I GUESS YOU LIKE YOUR ROOM?
I THINK I'M GONNA BE JUST FINE HERE!
OH, YEAH. EVERY-THING'S PERFECT HERE...
I THINK YOU'RE GONNA REALLY LIKE IT HERE TOO... IN OPEN HILL, I MEAN.
...NOW!

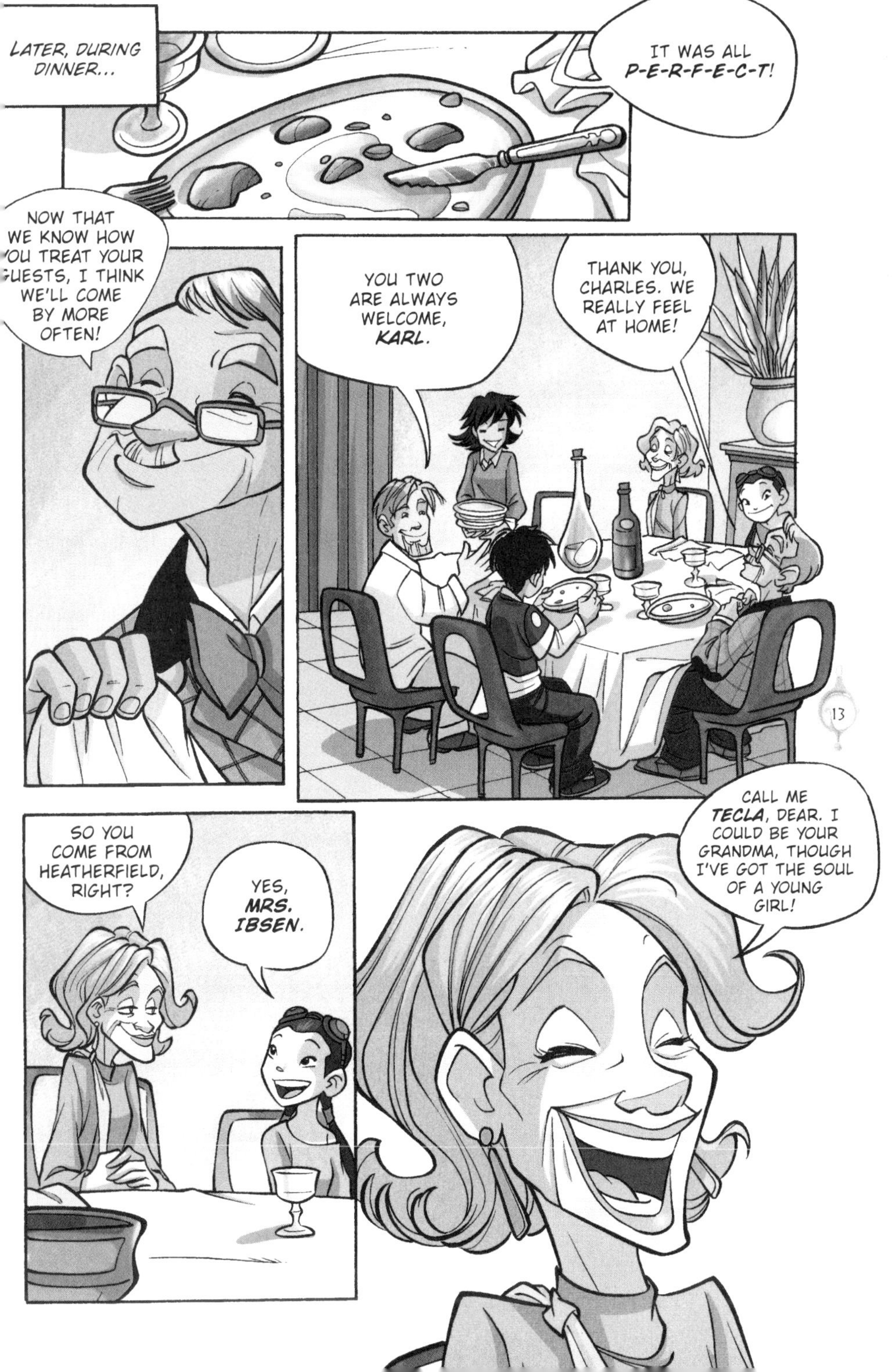
LATER, DURING DINNER...
IT WAS ALL P-E-R-F-E-C-T!
NOW THAT WE KNOW HOW YOU TREAT YOUR GUESTS, I THINK WE'LL COME BY MORE OFTEN!
YOU TWO ARE ALWAYS WELCOME, KARL.
THANK YOU, CHARLES. WE REALLY FEEL AT HOME!
SO YOU COME FROM HEATHERFIELD, RIGHT?
YES, MRS. IBSEN.
CALL ME TECLA, DEAR. I COULD BE YOUR GRANDMA, THOUGH I'VE GOT THE SOUL OF A YOUNG GIRL!

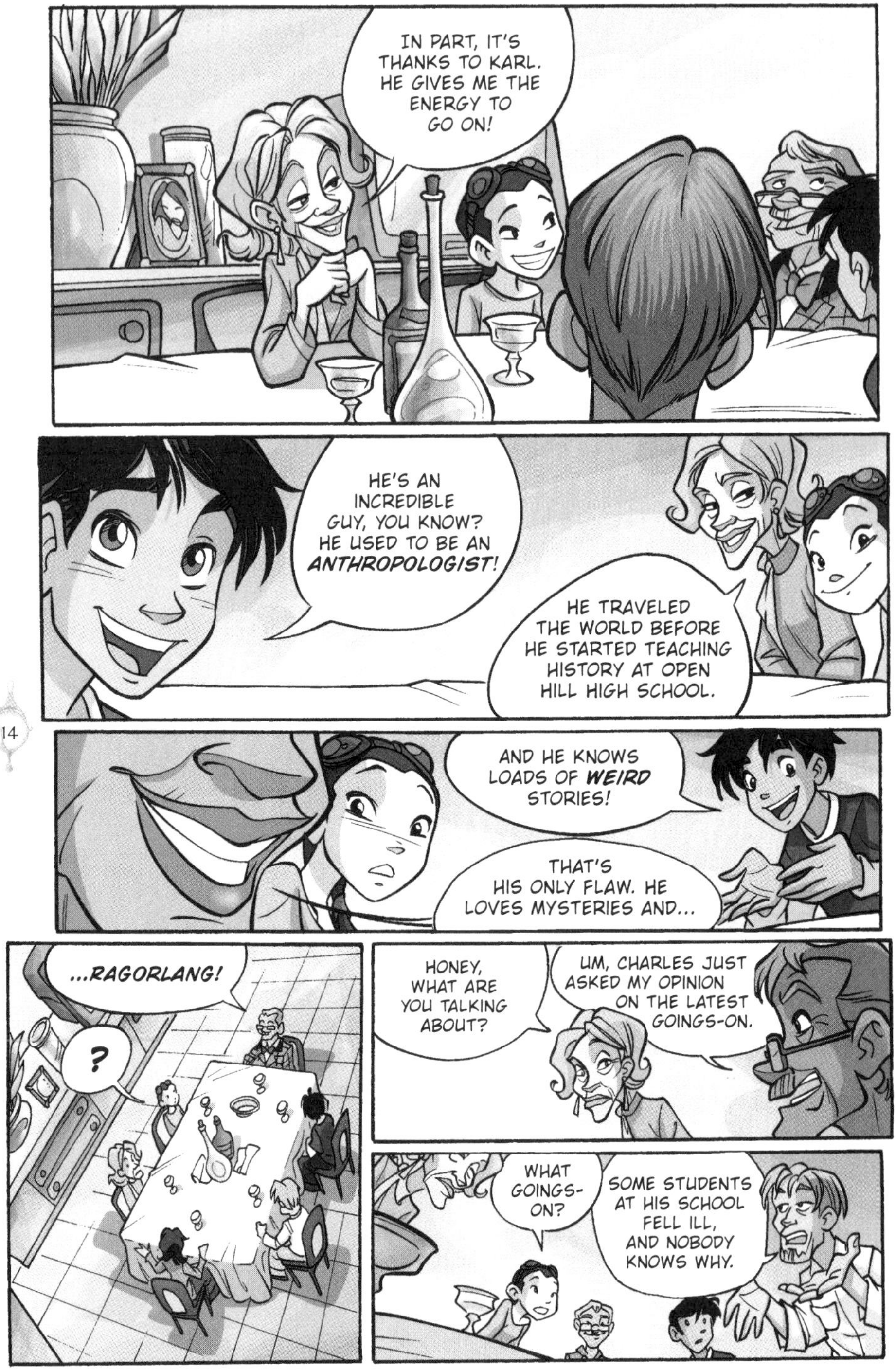
IN PART, IT'S THANKS TO KARL. HE GIVES ME THE ENERGY TO GO ON!
HE'S AN INCREDIBLE GUY, YOU KNOW? HE USED TO BE AN ANTHROPOLOGIST!
HE TRAVELED THE WORLD BEFORE HE STARTED TEACHING HISTORY AT OPEN HILL HIGH SCHOOL.
AND HE KNOWS LOADS OF WEIRD STORIES!
THAT'S HIS ONLY FLAW. HE LOVES MYSTERIES AND...
...RAGORLANG!
?
HONEY, WHAT ARE YOU TALKING ABOUT?
UM, CHARLES JUST ASKED MY OPINION ON THE LATEST GOINGS-ON.
WHAT GOINGS-ON?
SOME STUDENTS AT HIS SCHOOL FELL ILL, AND NOBODY KNOWS WHY.

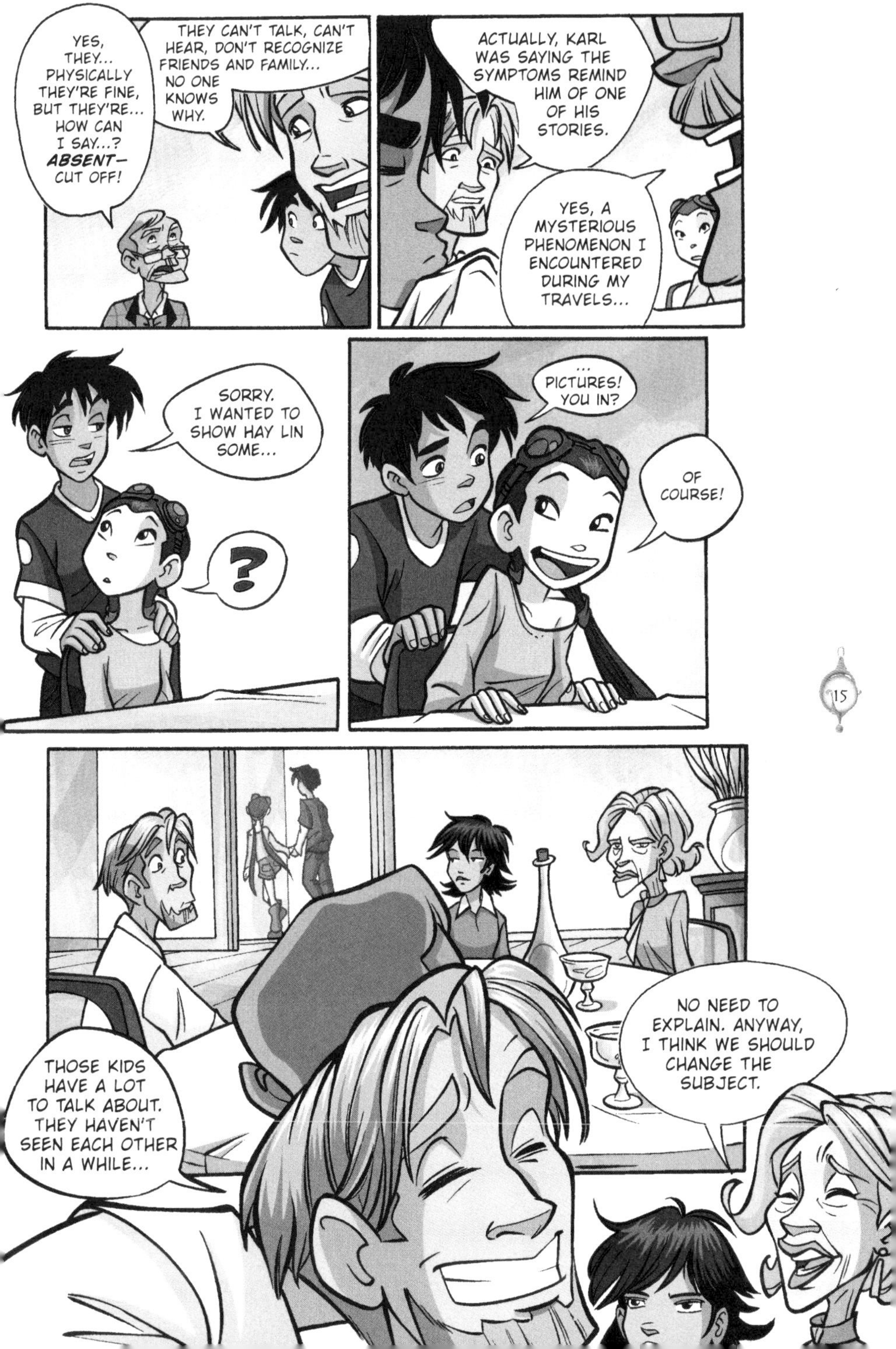

YES, THEY... PHYSICALLY THEY'RE FINE, BUT THEY'RE... HOW CAN I SAY...? ABSENT— CUT OFF!
THEY CAN'T TALK, CAN'T HEAR, DON'T RECOGNIZE FRIENDS AND FAMILY... NO ONE KNOWS WHY.
ACTUALLY, KARL WAS SAYING THE SYMPTOMS REMIND HIM OF ONE OF HIS STORIES.
YES, A MYSTERIOUS PHENOMENON I ENCOUNTERED DURING MY TRAVELS...
SORRY. I WANTED TO SHOW HAY LIN SOME...
?
... PICTURES! YOU IN?
OF COURSE!
THOSE KIDS HAVE A LOT TO TALK ABOUT. THEY HAVEN'T SEEN EACH OTHER IN A WHILE...
NO NEED TO EXPLAIN. ANYWAY, I THINK WE SHOULD CHANGE THE SUBJECT.

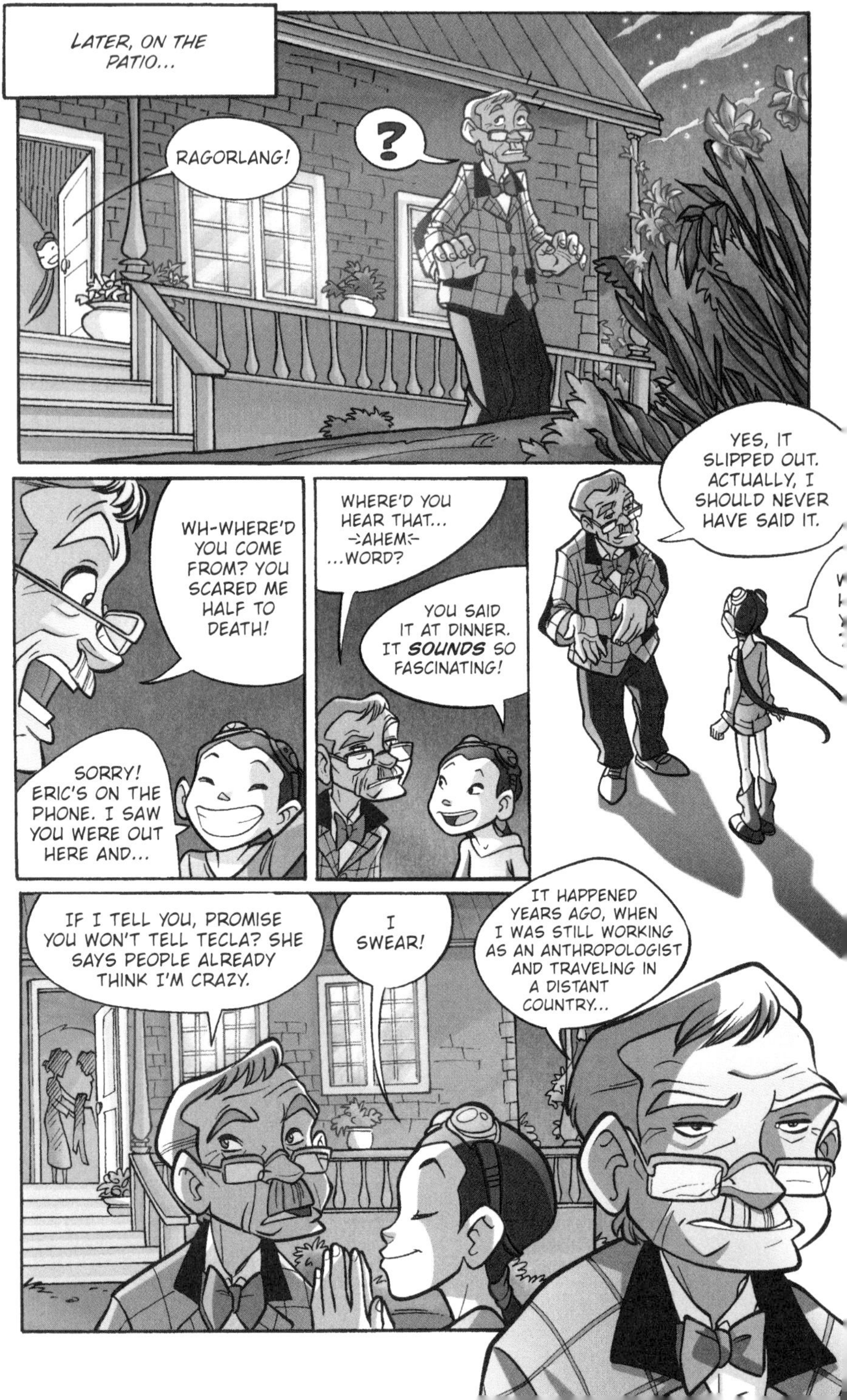

LATER, ON THE PATIO...
RAGORLANG!
?
WH-WHERE'D YOU COME FROM? YOU SCARED ME HALF TO DEATH!
SORRY! ERIC'S ON THE PHONE. I SAW YOU WERE OUT HERE AND...
WHERE'D YOU HEAR THAT... AHEM ...WORD?
YOU SAID IT AT DINNER. IT SOUNDS SO FASCINATING!
YES, IT SLIPPED OUT. ACTUALLY, I SHOULD NEVER HAVE SAID IT.
IF I TELL YOU, PROMISE YOU WON'T TELL TECLA? SHE SAYS PEOPLE ALREADY THINK I'M CRAZY.
I SWEAR!
IT HAPPENED YEARS AGO, WHEN I WAS STILL WORKING AS AN ANTHROPOLOGIST AND TRAVELING IN A DISTANT COUNTRY...

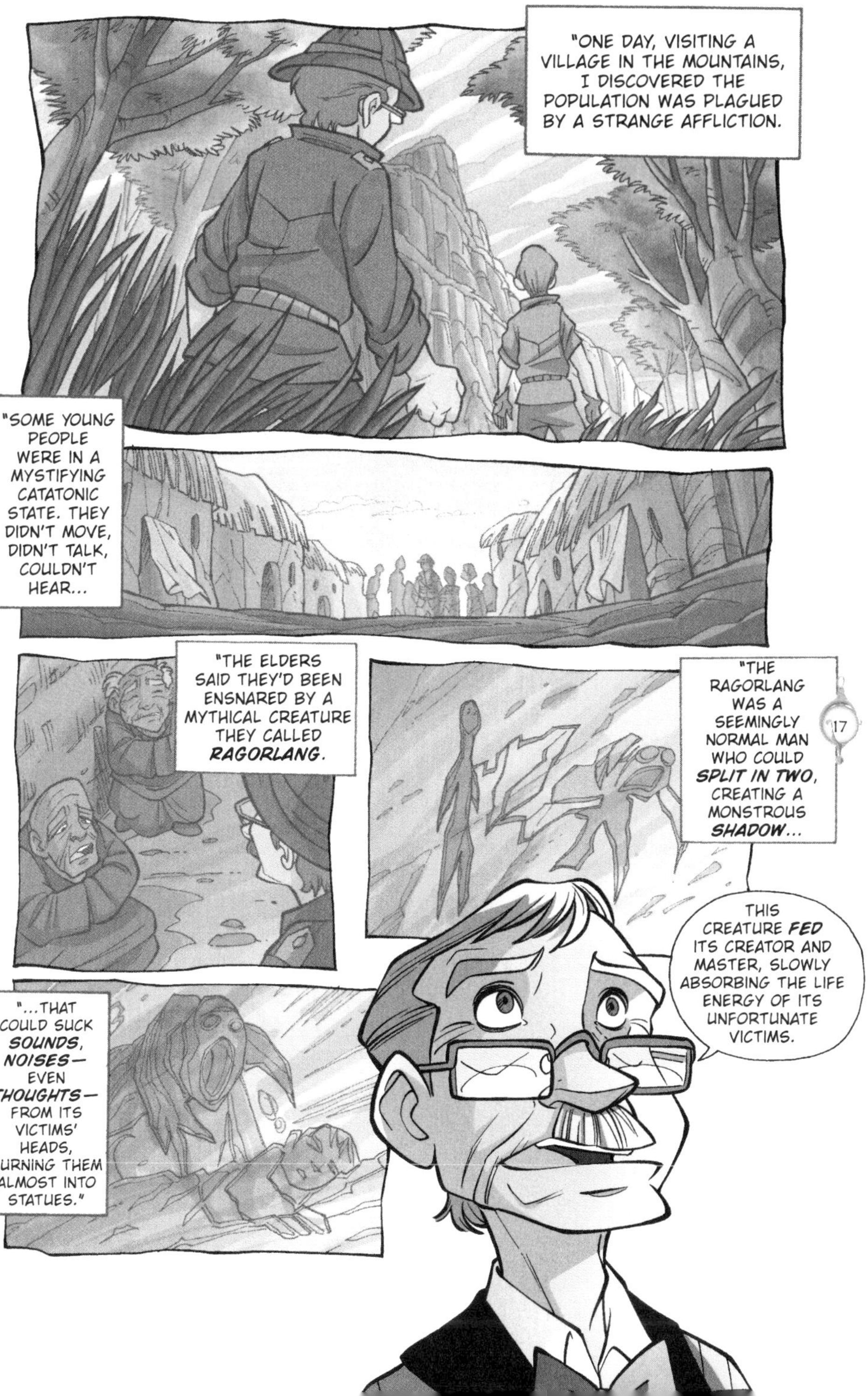
"ONE DAY, VISITING A VILLAGE IN THE MOUNTAINS, I DISCOVERED THE POPULATION WAS PLAGUED BY A STRANGE AFFLICTION.
"SOME YOUNG PEOPLE WERE IN A MYSTIFYING CATATONIC STATE. THEY DIDN'T MOVE, DIDN'T TALK, COULDN'T HEAR...
"THE ELDERS SAID THEY'D BEEN ENSNARED BY A MYTHICAL CREATURE THEY CALLED ***RAGORLANG***.
"THE RAGORLANG WAS A SEEMINGLY NORMAL MAN WHO COULD ***SPLIT IN TWO***, CREATING A MONSTROUS ***SHADOW***...
"...THAT COULD SUCK ***SOUNDS, NOISES***—EVEN ***THOUGHTS***—FROM ITS VICTIMS' HEADS, TURNING THEM ALMOST INTO STATUES."
THIS CREATURE ***FED*** ITS CREATOR AND MASTER, SLOWLY ABSORBING THE LIFE ENERGY OF ITS UNFORTUNATE VICTIMS.

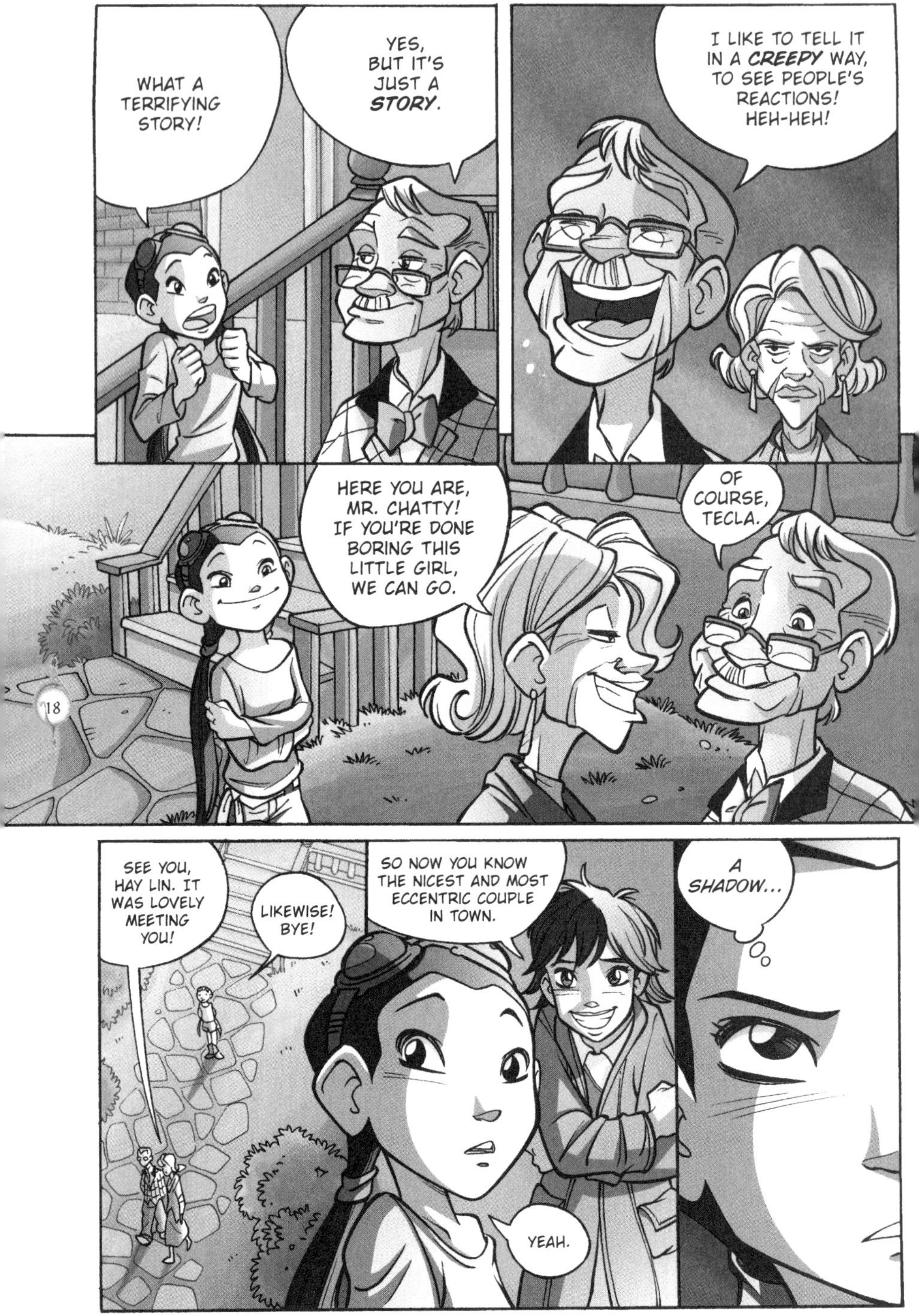
WHAT A TERRIFYING STORY!
YES, BUT IT'S JUST A **STORY**.
I LIKE TO TELL IT IN A **CREEPY** WAY, TO SEE PEOPLE'S REACTIONS! HEH-HEH!
HERE YOU ARE, MR. CHATTY! IF YOU'RE DONE BORING THIS LITTLE GIRL, WE CAN GO.
OF COURSE, TECLA.
SEE YOU, HAY LIN. IT WAS LOVELY MEETING YOU!
LIKEWISE! BYE!
SO NOW YOU KNOW THE NICEST AND MOST ECCENTRIC COUPLE IN TOWN.
YEAH.
A SHADOW...

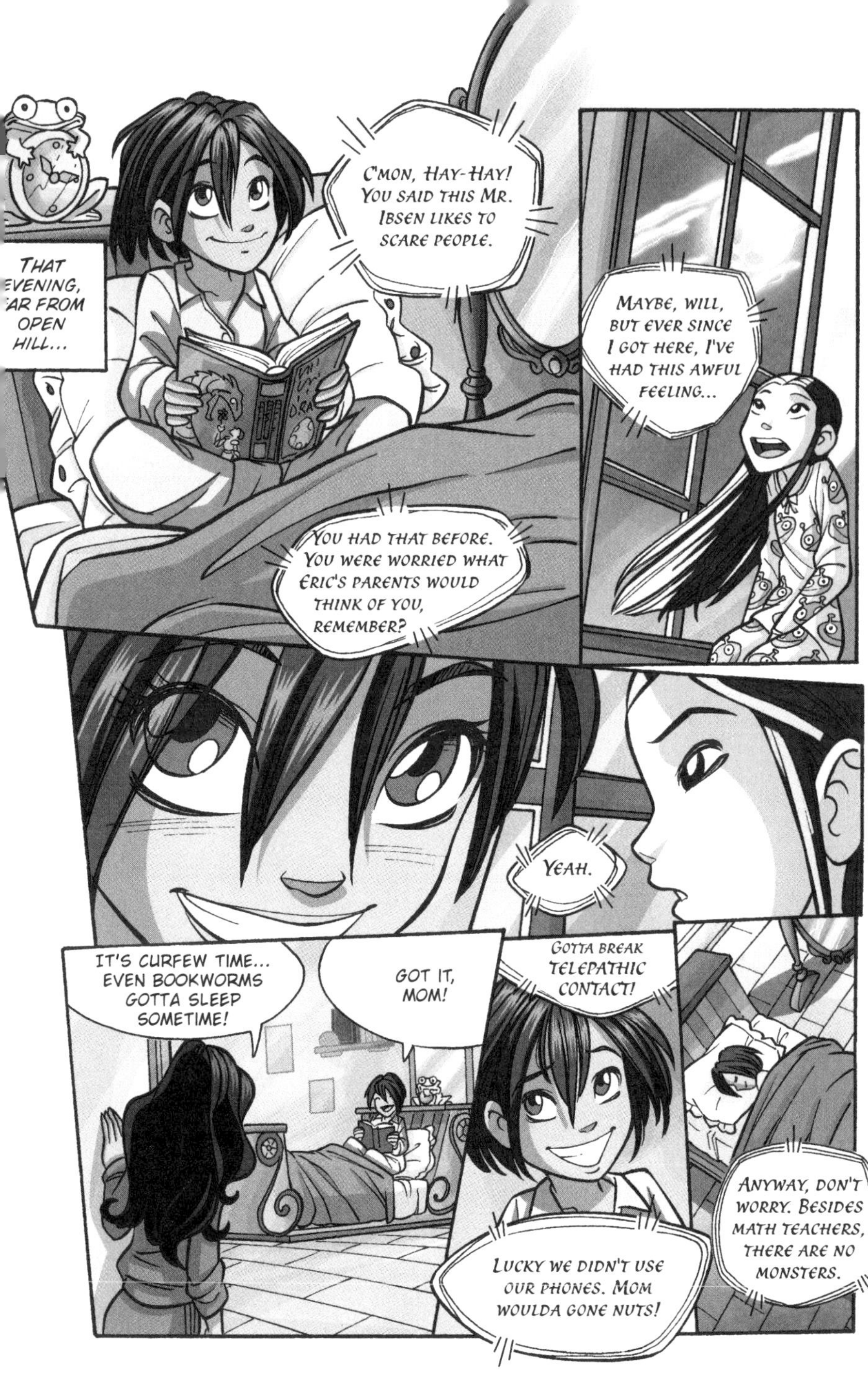

THAT EVENING, FAR FROM OPEN HILL...
C'MON, HAY-HAY! YOU SAID THIS MR. IBSEN LIKES TO SCARE PEOPLE.
MAYBE, WILL, BUT EVER SINCE I GOT HERE, I'VE HAD THIS AWFUL FEELING...
YOU HAD THAT BEFORE. YOU WERE WORRIED WHAT ERIC'S PARENTS WOULD THINK OF YOU, REMEMBER?
YEAH.
IT'S CURFEW TIME... EVEN BOOKWORMS GOTTA SLEEP SOMETIME!
GOT IT, MOM!
GOTTA BREAK TELEPATHIC CONTACT!
LUCKY WE DIDN'T USE OUR PHONES. MOM WOULDA GONE NUTS!
ANYWAY, DON'T WORRY. BESIDES MATH TEACHERS, THERE ARE NO MONSTERS.

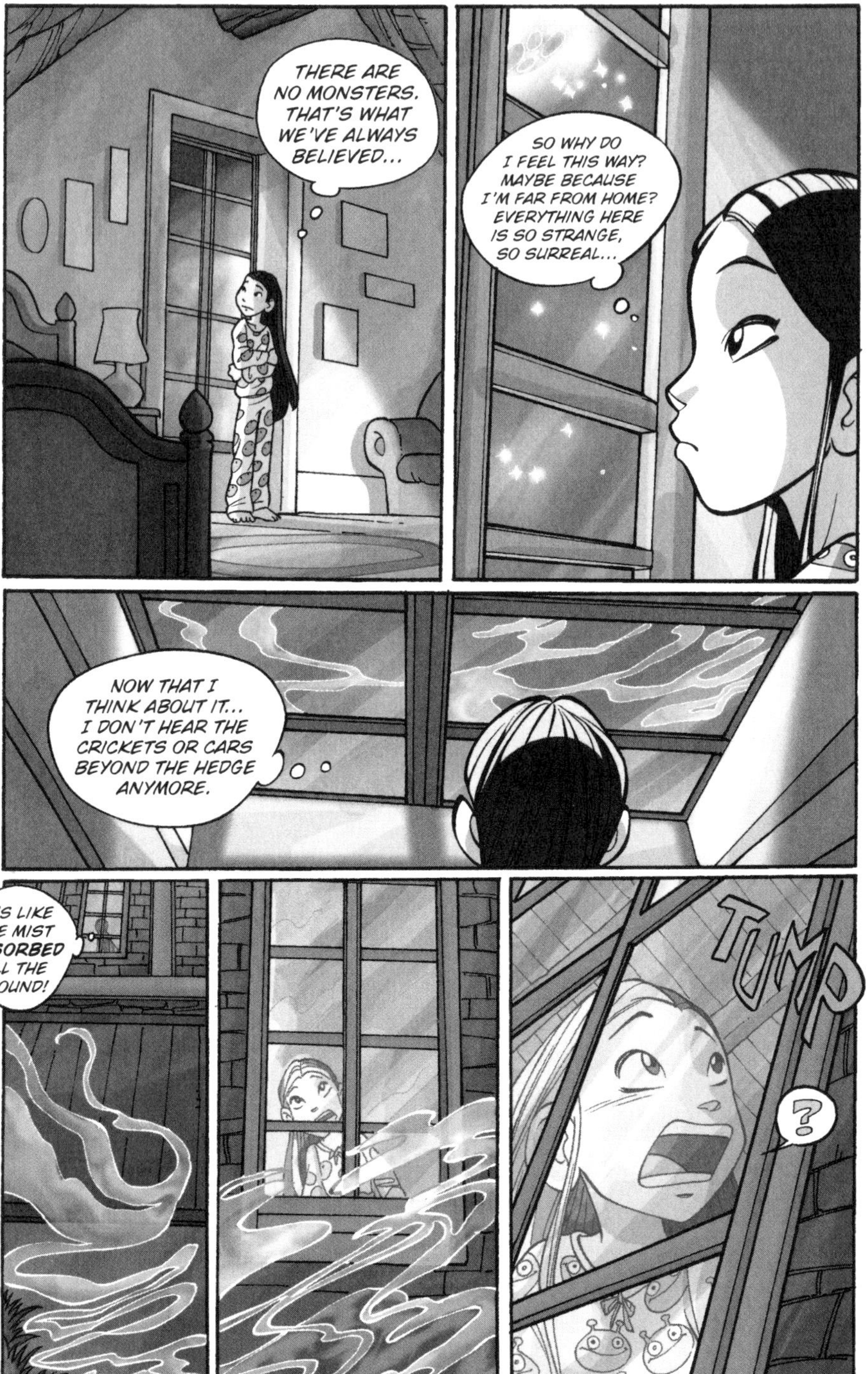
THERE ARE NO MONSTERS. THAT'S WHAT WE'VE ALWAYS BELIEVED...
SO WHY DO I FEEL THIS WAY? MAYBE BECAUSE I'M FAR FROM HOME? EVERYTHING HERE IS SO STRANGE, SO SURREAL...
NOW THAT I THINK ABOUT IT... I DON'T HEAR THE CRICKETS OR CARS BEYOND THE HEDGE ANYMORE.
IT'S LIKE THE MIST **ABSORBED** ALL THE SOUND!
TUMP
?

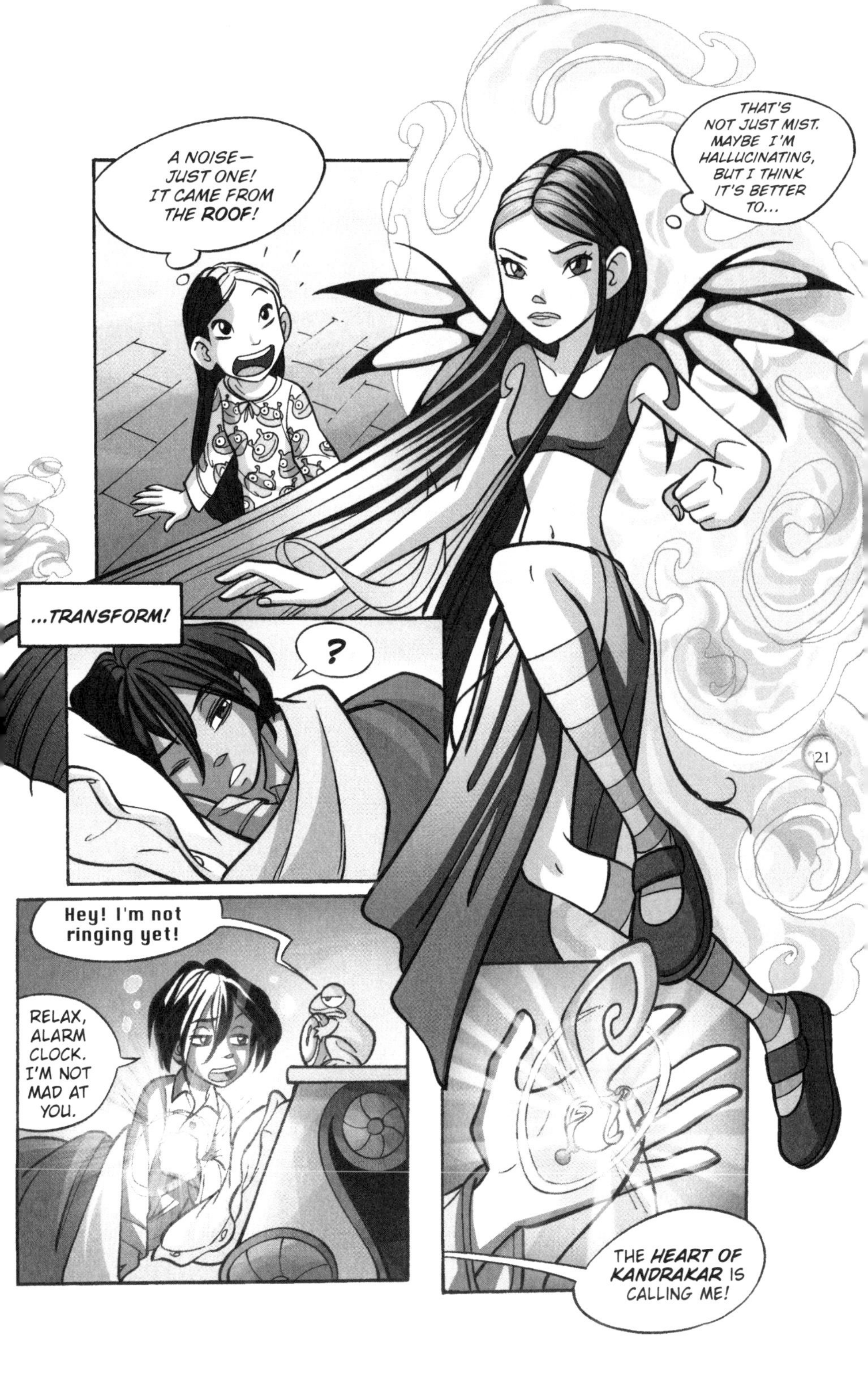
A NOISE— JUST ONE! IT CAME FROM THE ROOF!
THAT'S NOT JUST MIST. MAYBE I'M HALLUCINATING, BUT I THINK IT'S BETTER TO...
...TRANSFORM!
?
Hey! I'm not ringing yet!
RELAX, ALARM CLOCK. I'M NOT MAD AT YOU.
THE HEART OF KANDRAKAR IS CALLING ME!

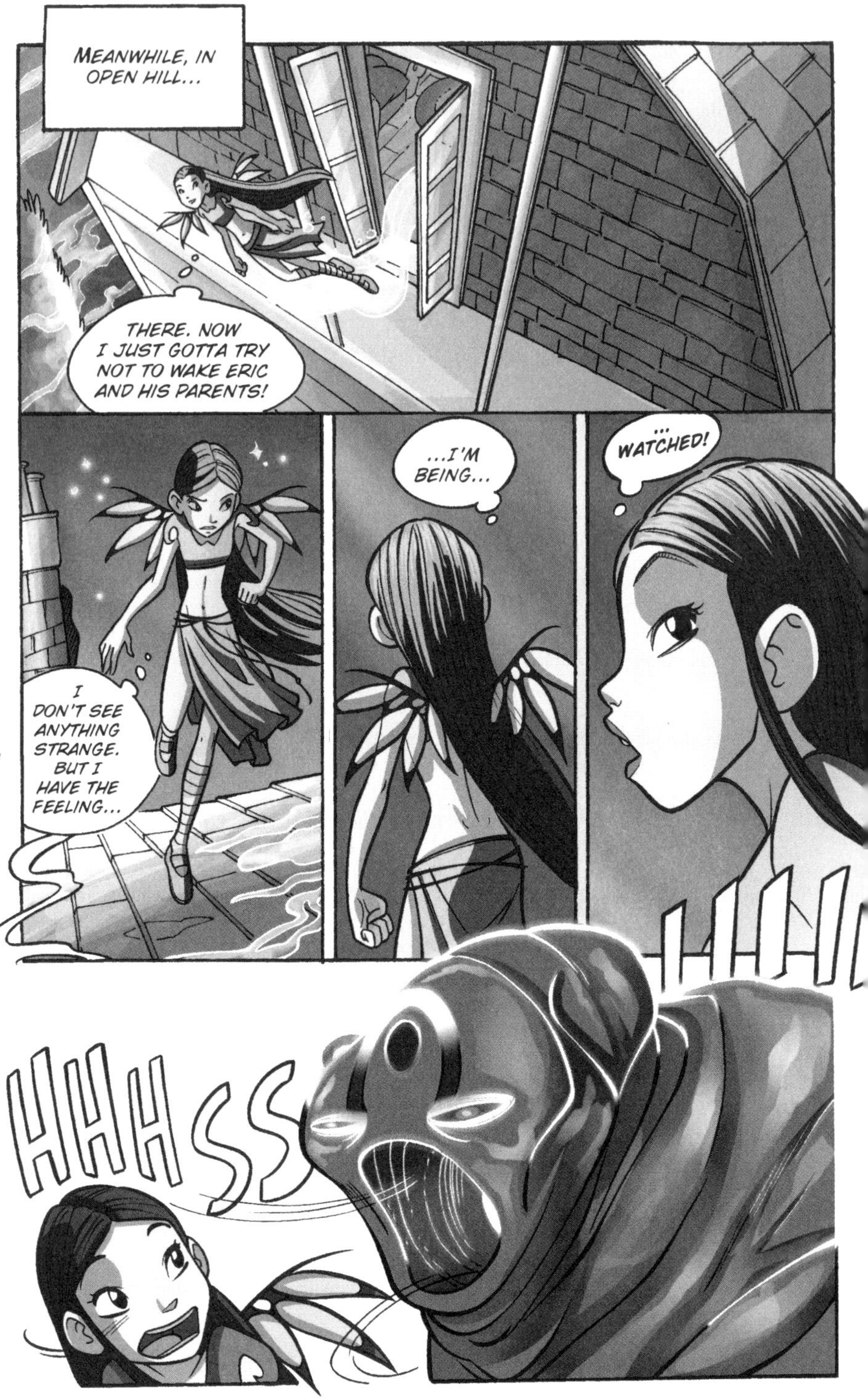
MEANWHILE, IN OPEN HILL...
THERE. NOW I JUST GOTTA TRY NOT TO WAKE ERIC AND HIS PARENTS!
I DON'T SEE ANYTHING STRANGE. BUT I HAVE THE FEELING...
...I'M BEING...
...WATCHED!
HHHSSS

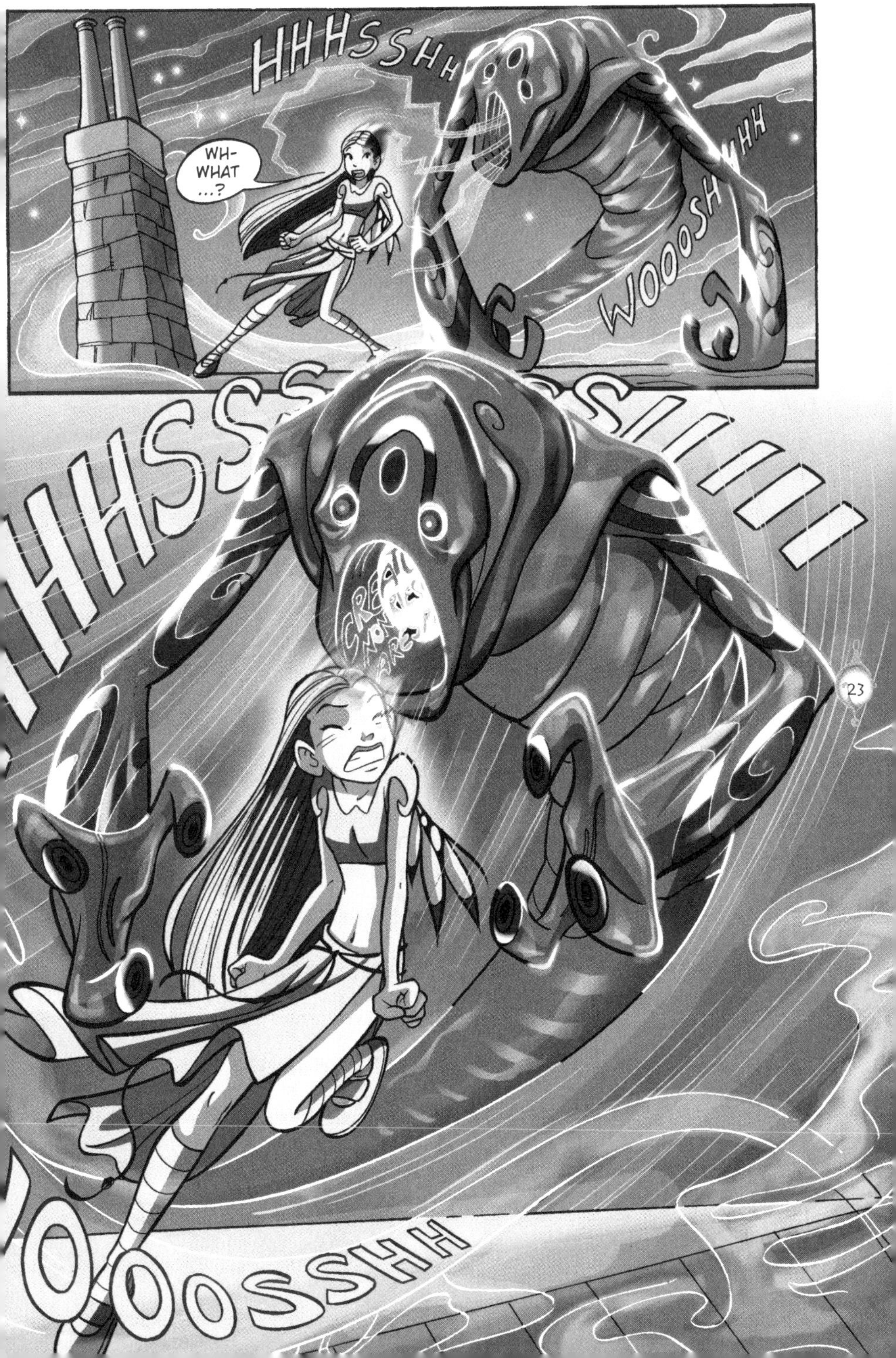
HHHSSHH
WH- WHAT ...?
WOOOSHHHH

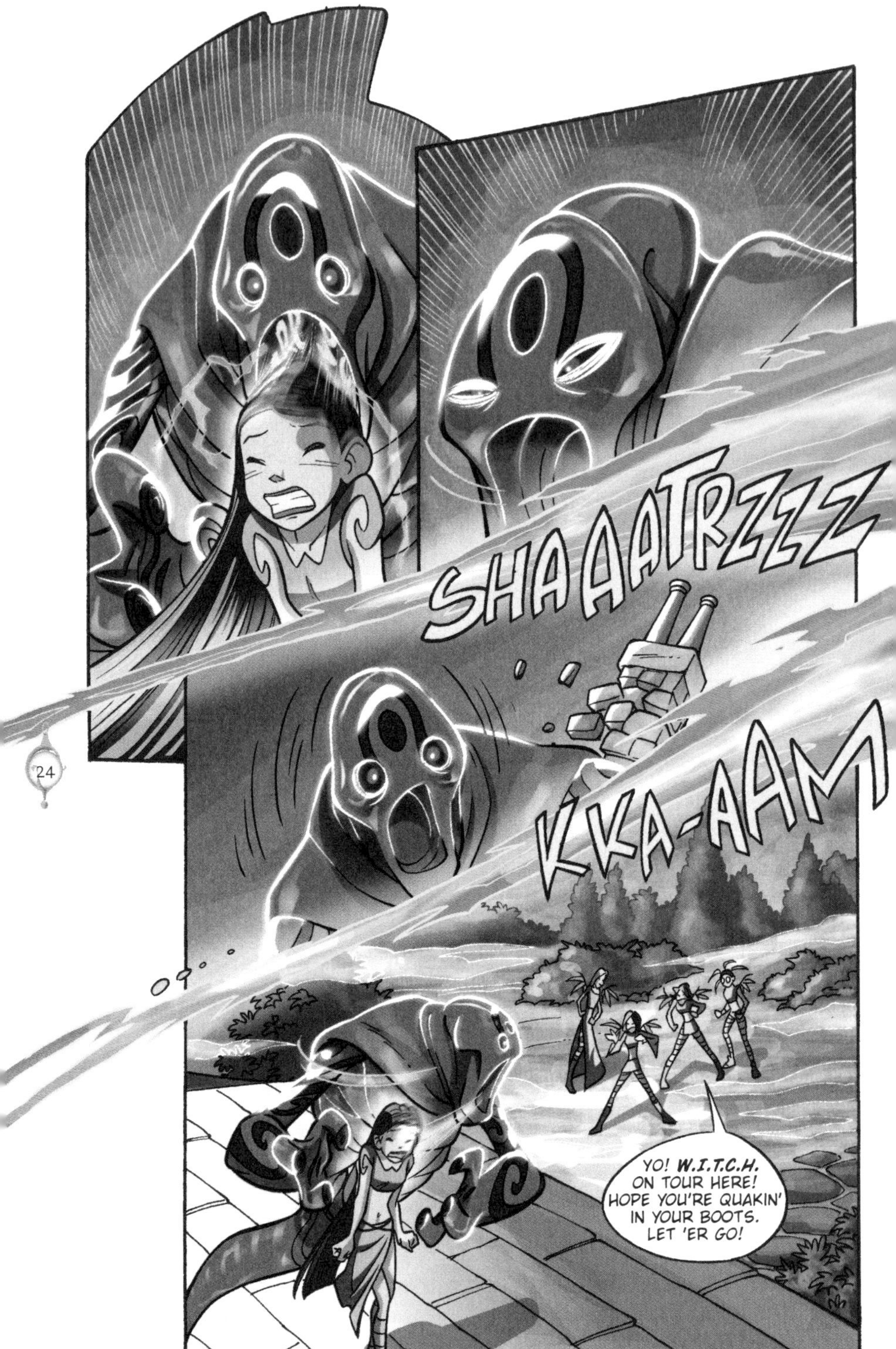
SHAAATRZZZ
KKA-AAM
YO! W.I.T.C.H. ON TOUR HERE! HOPE YOU'RE QUAKIN' IN YOUR BOOTS. LET 'ER GO!

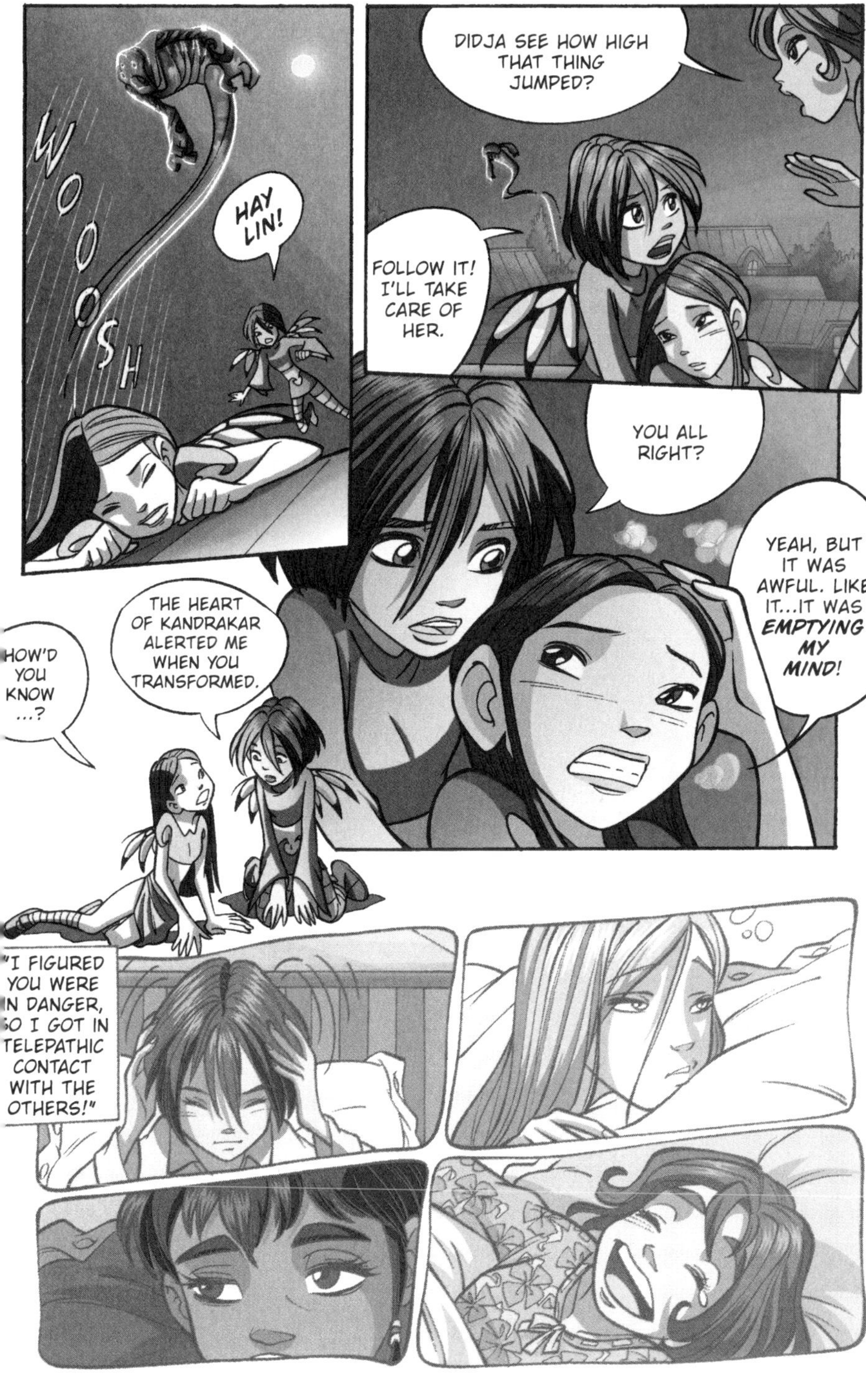
WOOOSH
HAY LIN!
DIDJA SEE HOW HIGH THAT THING JUMPED?
FOLLOW IT! I'LL TAKE CARE OF HER.
YOU ALL RIGHT?
YEAH, BUT IT WAS AWFUL. LIKE IT...IT WAS EMPTYING MY MIND!
THE HEART OF KANDRAKAR ALERTED ME WHEN YOU TRANSFORMED.
HOW'D YOU KNOW ...?
"I FIGURED YOU WERE IN DANGER, SO I GOT IN TELEPATHIC CONTACT WITH THE OTHERS!"

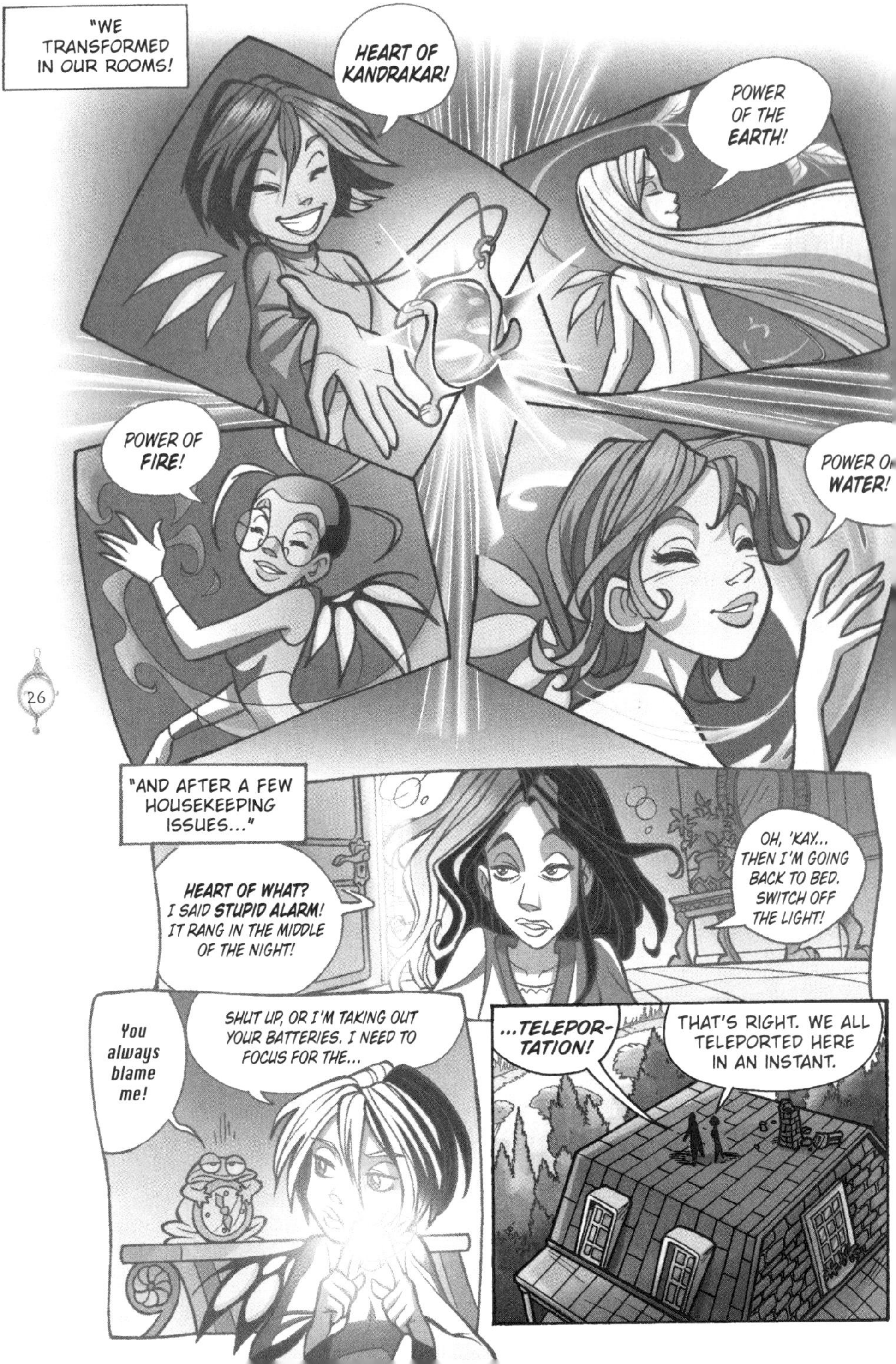

"WE TRANSFORMED IN OUR ROOMS!
HEART OF KANDRAKAR!
POWER OF THE EARTH!
POWER OF FIRE!
POWER OF WATER!
"AND AFTER A FEW HOUSEKEEPING ISSUES..."
HEART OF WHAT? I SAID STUPID ALARM! IT RANG IN THE MIDDLE OF THE NIGHT!
OH, 'KAY... THEN I'M GOING BACK TO BED. SWITCH OFF THE LIGHT!
You always blame me!
SHUT UP, OR I'M TAKING OUT YOUR BATTERIES. I NEED TO FOCUS FOR THE...
...TELEPORTATION!
THAT'S RIGHT. WE ALL TELEPORTED HERE IN AN INSTANT.

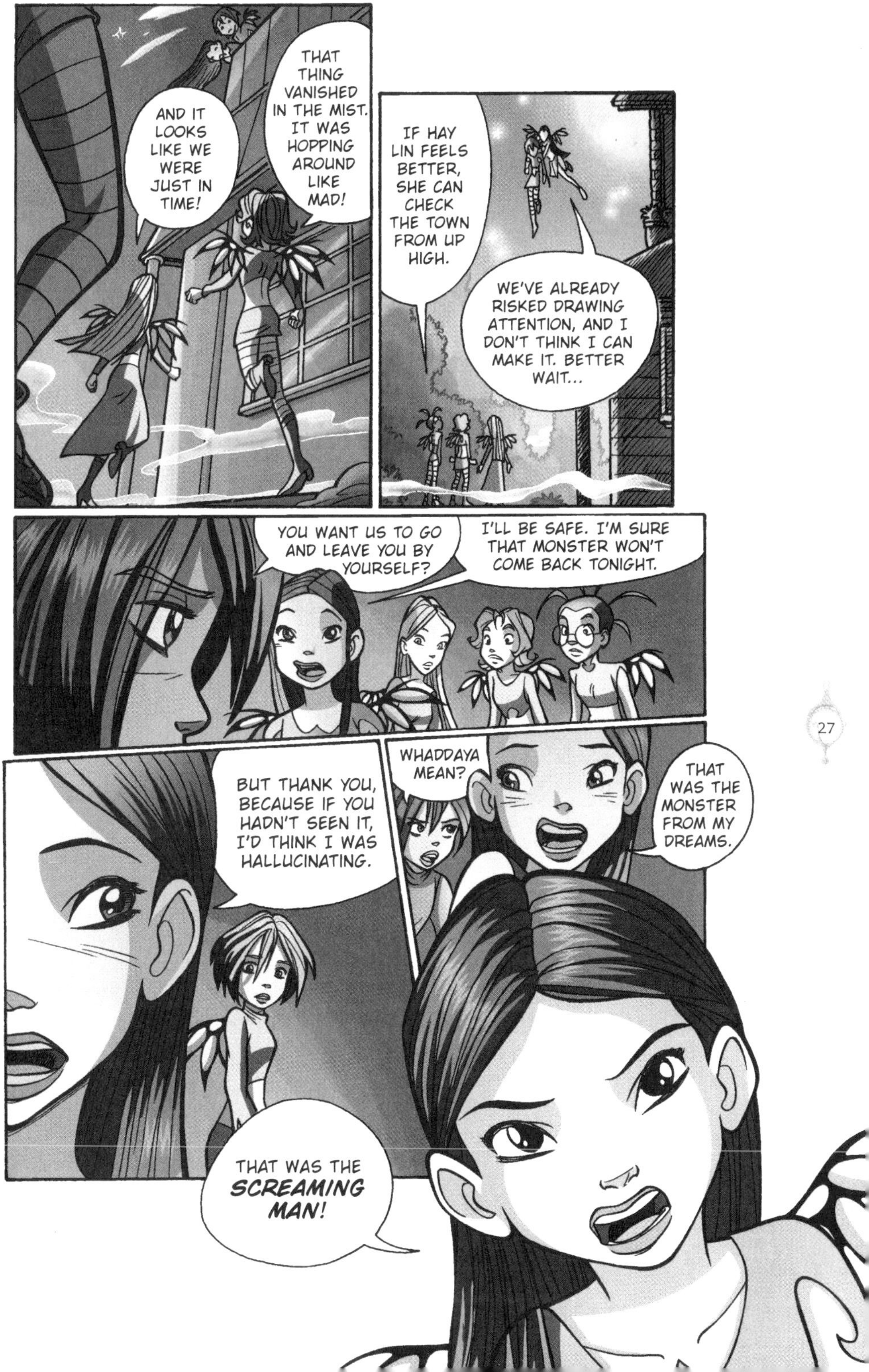
THAT THING VANISHED IN THE MIST. IT WAS HOPPING AROUND LIKE MAD!
AND IT LOOKS LIKE WE WERE JUST IN TIME!
IF HAY LIN FEELS BETTER, SHE CAN CHECK THE TOWN FROM UP HIGH.
WE'VE ALREADY RISKED DRAWING ATTENTION, AND I DON'T THINK I CAN MAKE IT. BETTER WAIT...
YOU WANT US TO GO AND LEAVE YOU BY YOURSELF?
I'LL BE SAFE. I'M SURE THAT MONSTER WON'T COME BACK TONIGHT.
BUT THANK YOU, BECAUSE IF YOU HADN'T SEEN IT, I'D THINK I WAS HALLUCINATING.
WHADDAYA MEAN?
THAT WAS THE MONSTER FROM MY DREAMS.
THAT WAS THE **SCREAMING MAN!**

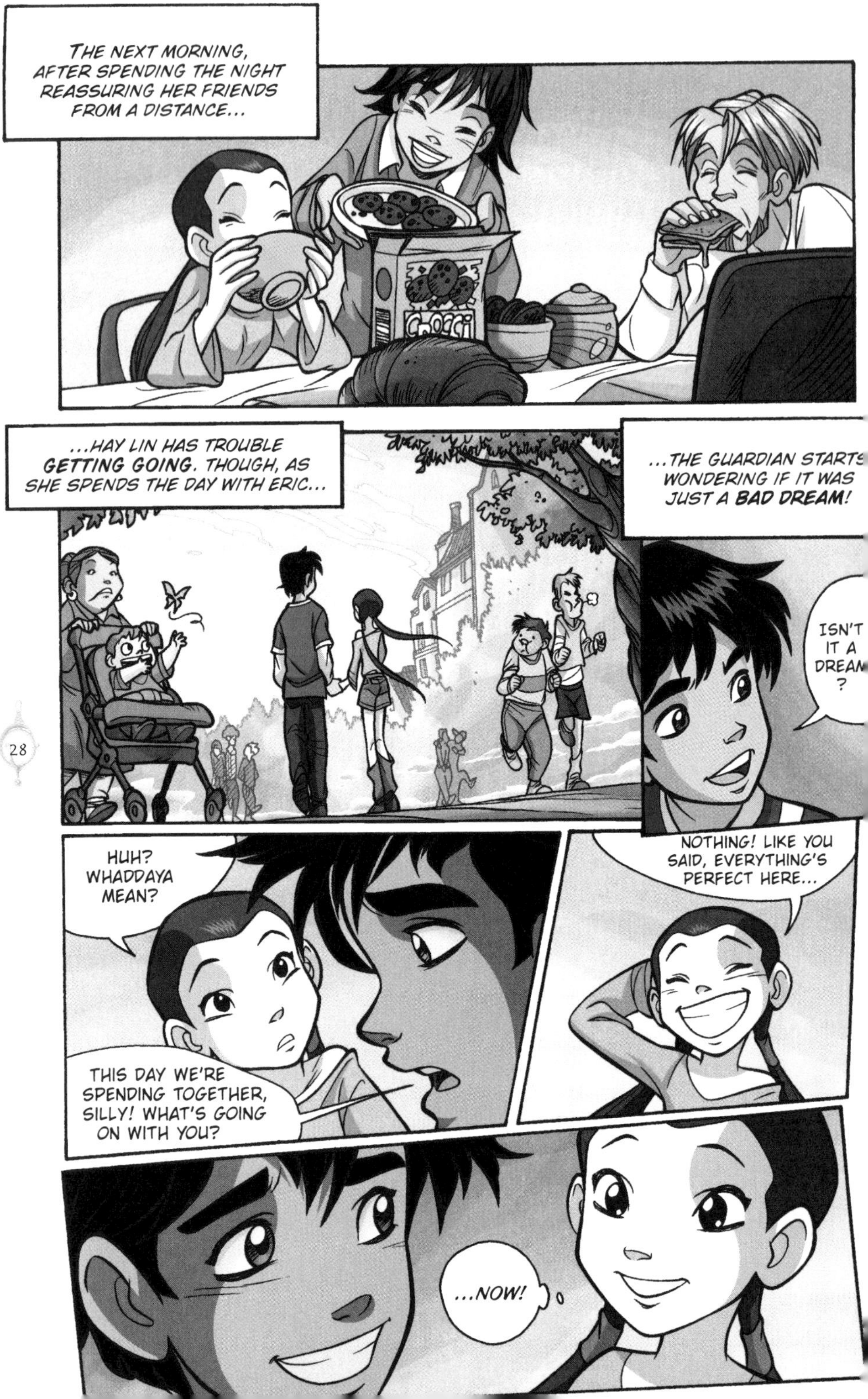
THE NEXT MORNING, AFTER SPENDING THE NIGHT REASSURING HER FRIENDS FROM A DISTANCE...
...HAY LIN HAS TROUBLE GETTING GOING. THOUGH, AS SHE SPENDS THE DAY WITH ERIC...
...THE GUARDIAN STARTS WONDERING IF IT WAS JUST A BAD DREAM!
ISN'T IT A DREAM?
HUH? WHADDAYA MEAN?
THIS DAY WE'RE SPENDING TOGETHER, SILLY! WHAT'S GOING ON WITH YOU?
NOTHING! LIKE YOU SAID, EVERYTHING'S PERFECT HERE...
...NOW!

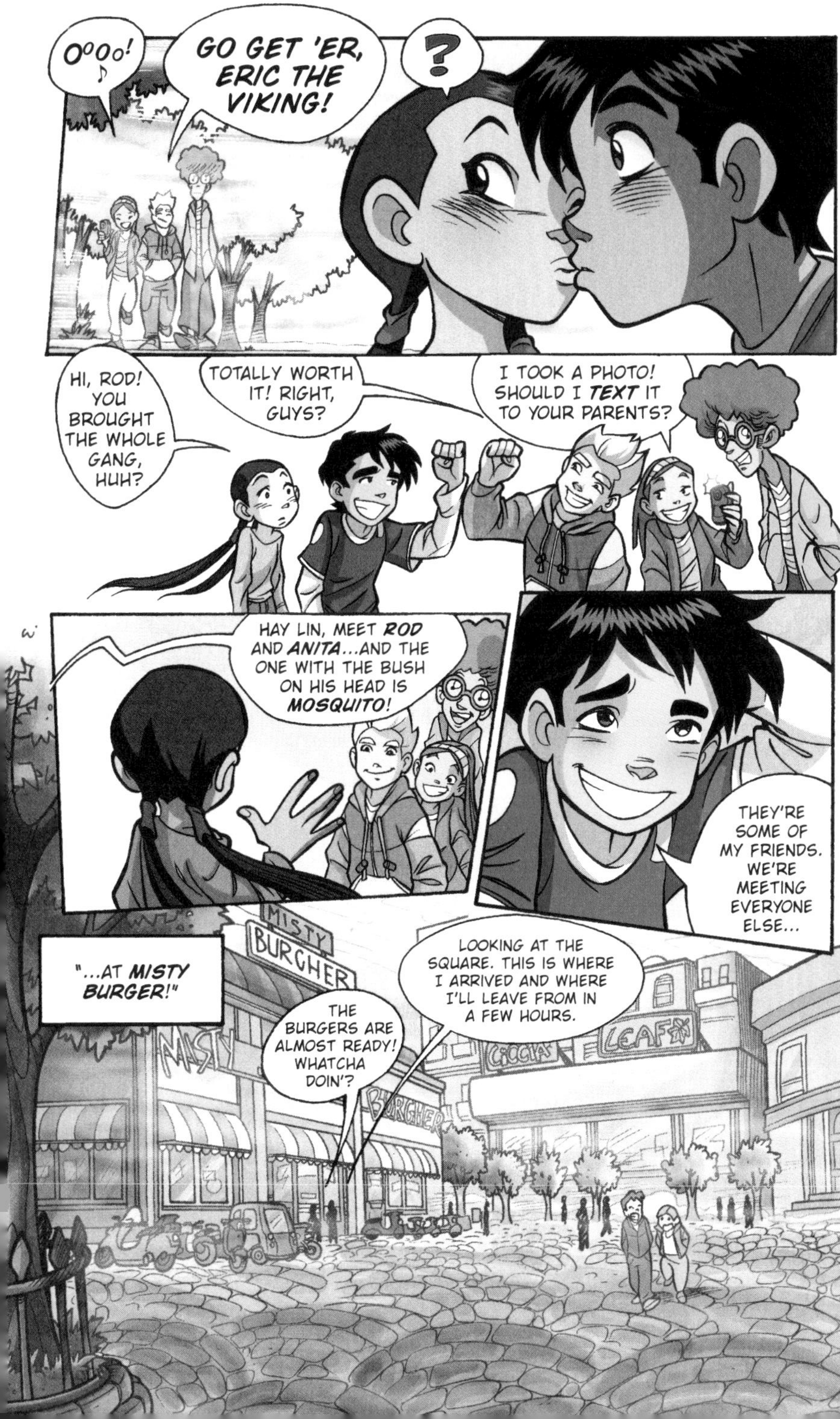
OOOO!
GO GET 'ER, ERIC THE VIKING!
?
HI, ROD! YOU BROUGHT THE WHOLE GANG, HUH?
TOTALLY WORTH IT! RIGHT, GUYS?
I TOOK A PHOTO! SHOULD I TEXT IT TO YOUR PARENTS?
HAY LIN, MEET ROD AND ANITA...AND THE ONE WITH THE BUSH ON HIS HEAD IS MOSQUITO!
THEY'RE SOME OF MY FRIENDS. WE'RE MEETING EVERYONE ELSE...
"...AT MISTY BURGER!"
MISTY BURGHER
LOOKING AT THE SQUARE. THIS IS WHERE I ARRIVED AND WHERE I'LL LEAVE FROM IN A FEW HOURS.
THE BURGERS ARE ALMOST READY! WHATCHA DOIN'?
LEAF

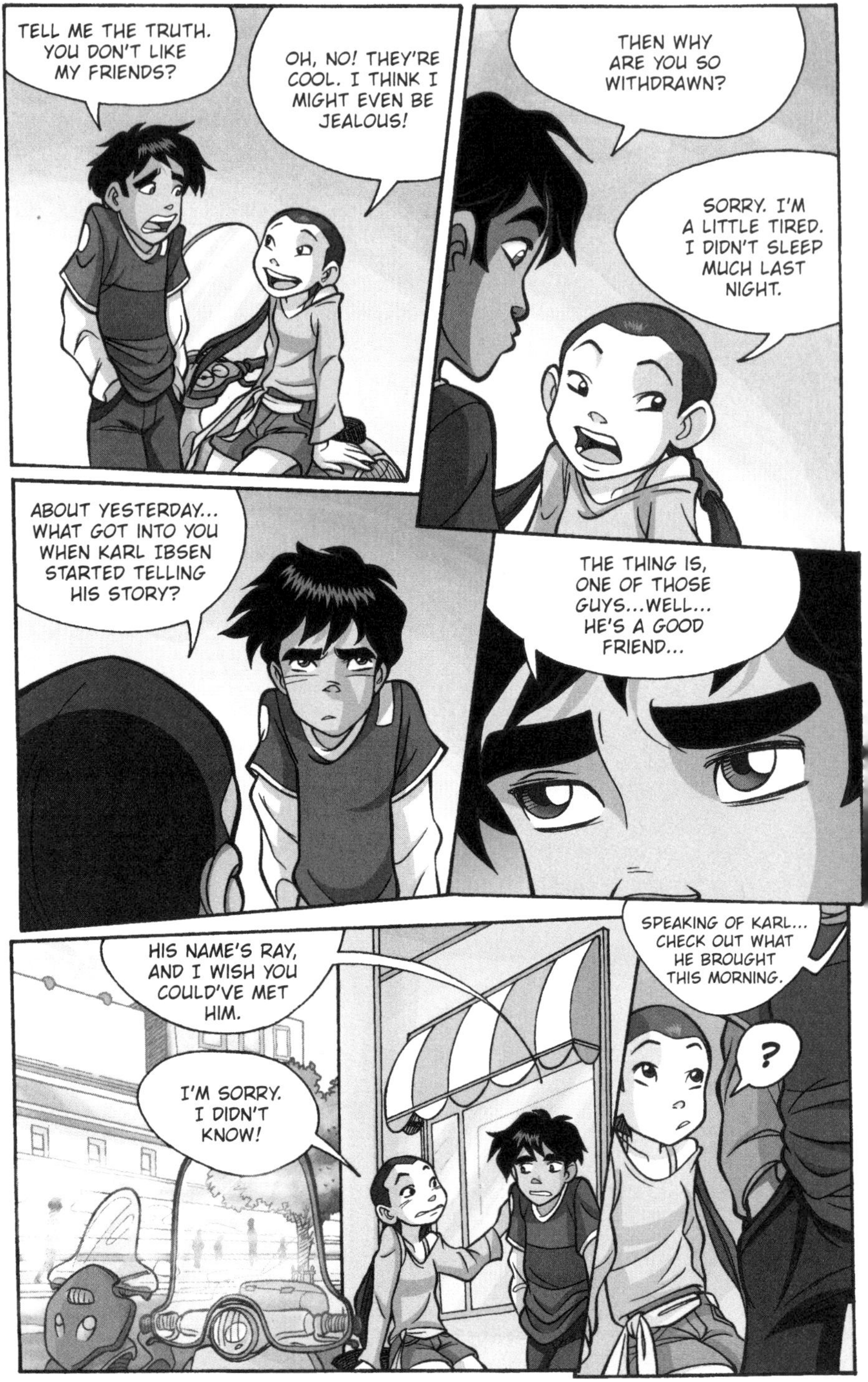
TELL ME THE TRUTH. YOU DON'T LIKE MY FRIENDS?
OH, NO! THEY'RE COOL. I THINK I MIGHT EVEN BE JEALOUS!
THEN WHY ARE YOU SO WITHDRAWN?
SORRY. I'M A LITTLE TIRED. I DIDN'T SLEEP MUCH LAST NIGHT.
ABOUT YESTERDAY... WHAT GOT INTO YOU WHEN KARL IBSEN STARTED TELLING HIS STORY?
THE THING IS, ONE OF THOSE GUYS...WELL... HE'S A GOOD FRIEND...
HIS NAME'S RAY, AND I WISH YOU COULD'VE MET HIM.
I'M SORRY. I DIDN'T KNOW!
SPEAKING OF KARL... CHECK OUT WHAT HE BROUGHT THIS MORNING.
?

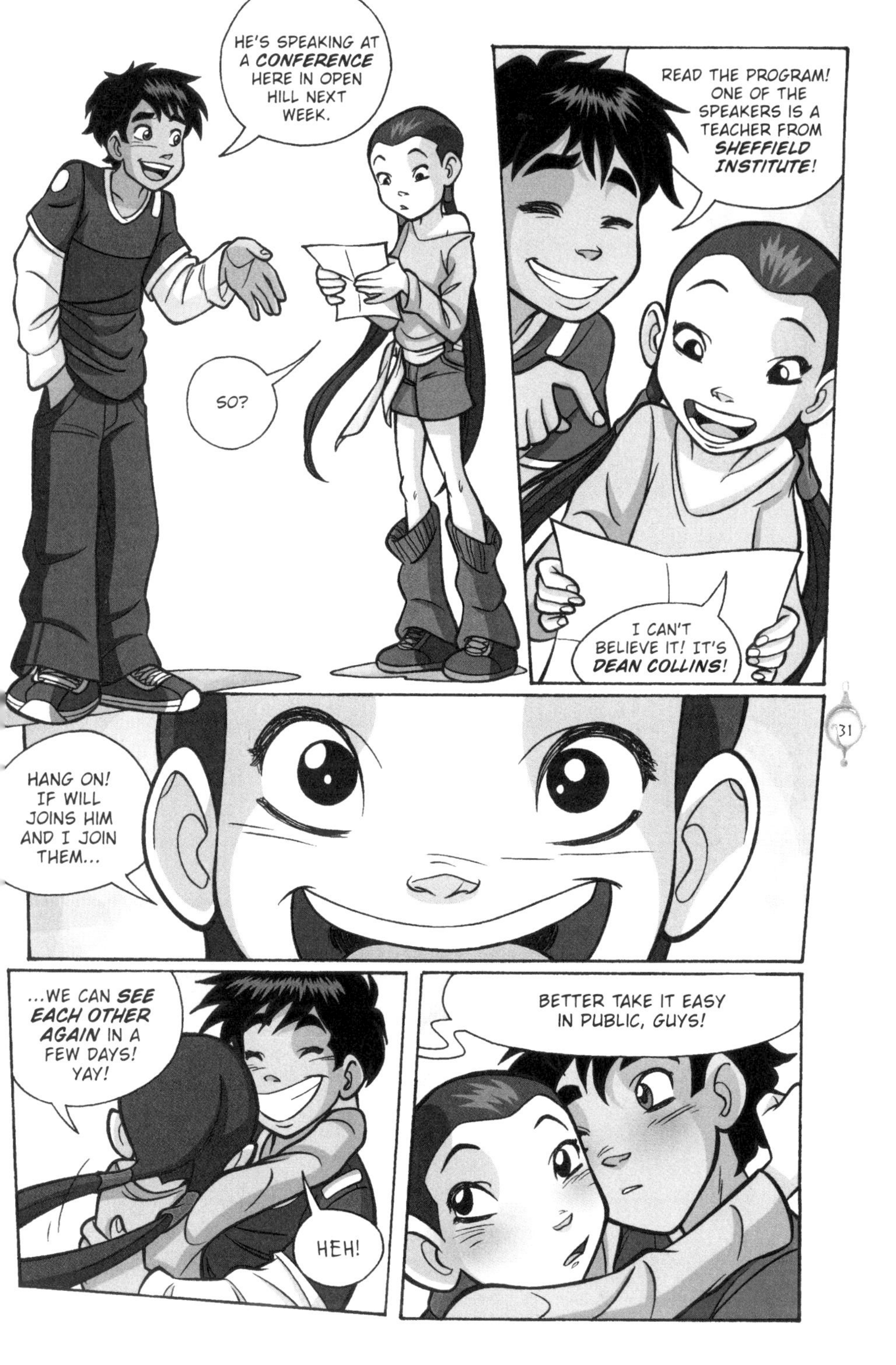
HE'S SPEAKING AT A CONFERENCE HERE IN OPEN HILL NEXT WEEK.
SO?
READ THE PROGRAM! ONE OF THE SPEAKERS IS A TEACHER FROM SHEFFIELD INSTITUTE!
I CAN'T BELIEVE IT! IT'S DEAN COLLINS!
HANG ON! IF WILL JOINS HIM AND I JOIN THEM...
...WE CAN SEE EACH OTHER AGAIN IN A FEW DAYS! YAY!
HEH!
BETTER TAKE IT EASY IN PUBLIC, GUYS!

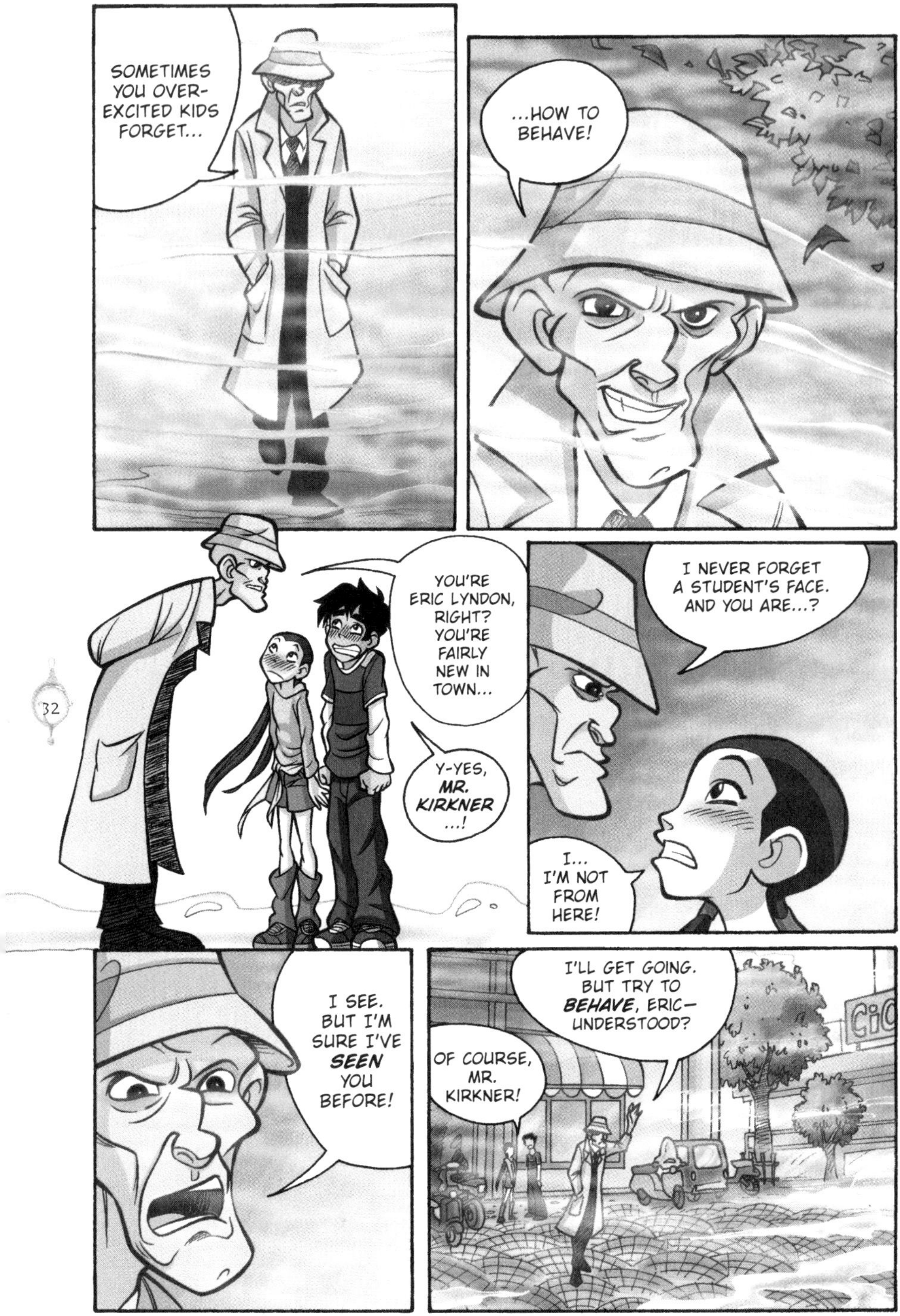
SOMETIMES YOU OVER-EXCITED KIDS FORGET...
...HOW TO BEHAVE!
YOU'RE ERIC LYNDON, RIGHT? YOU'RE FAIRLY NEW IN TOWN...
Y-YES, **MR. KIRKNER** ...!
I NEVER FORGET A STUDENT'S FACE. AND YOU ARE...?
I... I'M NOT FROM HERE!
I SEE. BUT I'M SURE I'VE **SEEN** YOU BEFORE!
I'LL GET GOING. BUT TRY TO **BEHAVE**, ERIC—UNDERSTOOD?
OF COURSE, MR. KIRKNER!
CIO

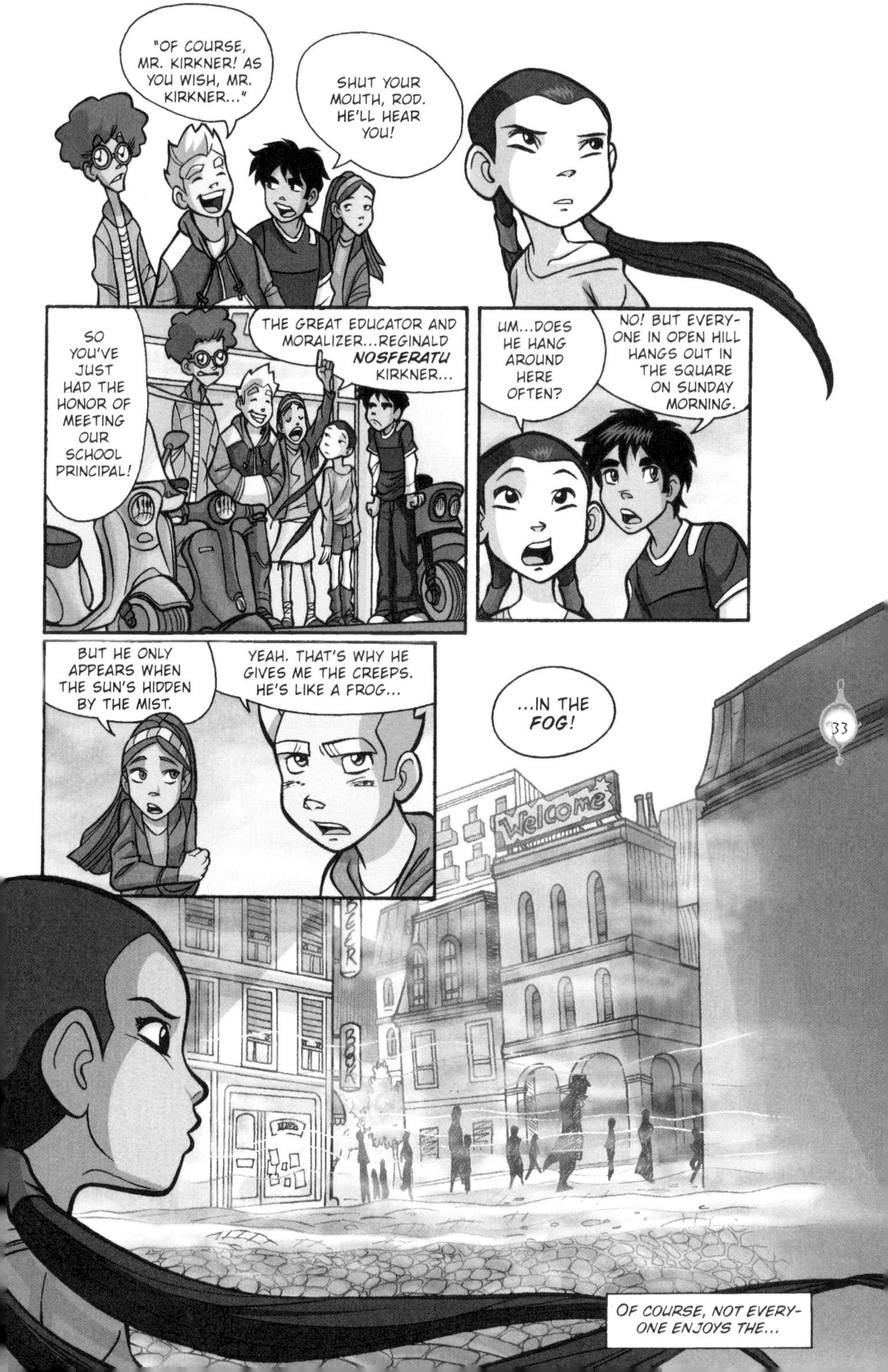
"OF COURSE, MR. KIRKNER! AS YOU WISH, MR. KIRKNER..."
SHUT YOUR MOUTH, ROD. HE'LL HEAR YOU!
SO YOU'VE JUST HAD THE HONOR OF MEETING OUR SCHOOL PRINCIPAL!
THE GREAT EDUCATOR AND MORALIZER...REGINALD NOSFERATU KIRKNER...
UM...DOES HE HANG AROUND HERE OFTEN?
NO! BUT EVERY-ONE IN OPEN HILL HANGS OUT IN THE SQUARE ON SUNDAY MORNING.
BUT HE ONLY APPEARS WHEN THE SUN'S HIDDEN BY THE MIST.
YEAH. THAT'S WHY HE GIVES ME THE CREEPS. HE'S LIKE A FROG...
...IN THE FOG!
Welcome
BEER
BOOK
OF COURSE, NOT EVERY-ONE ENJOYS THE...

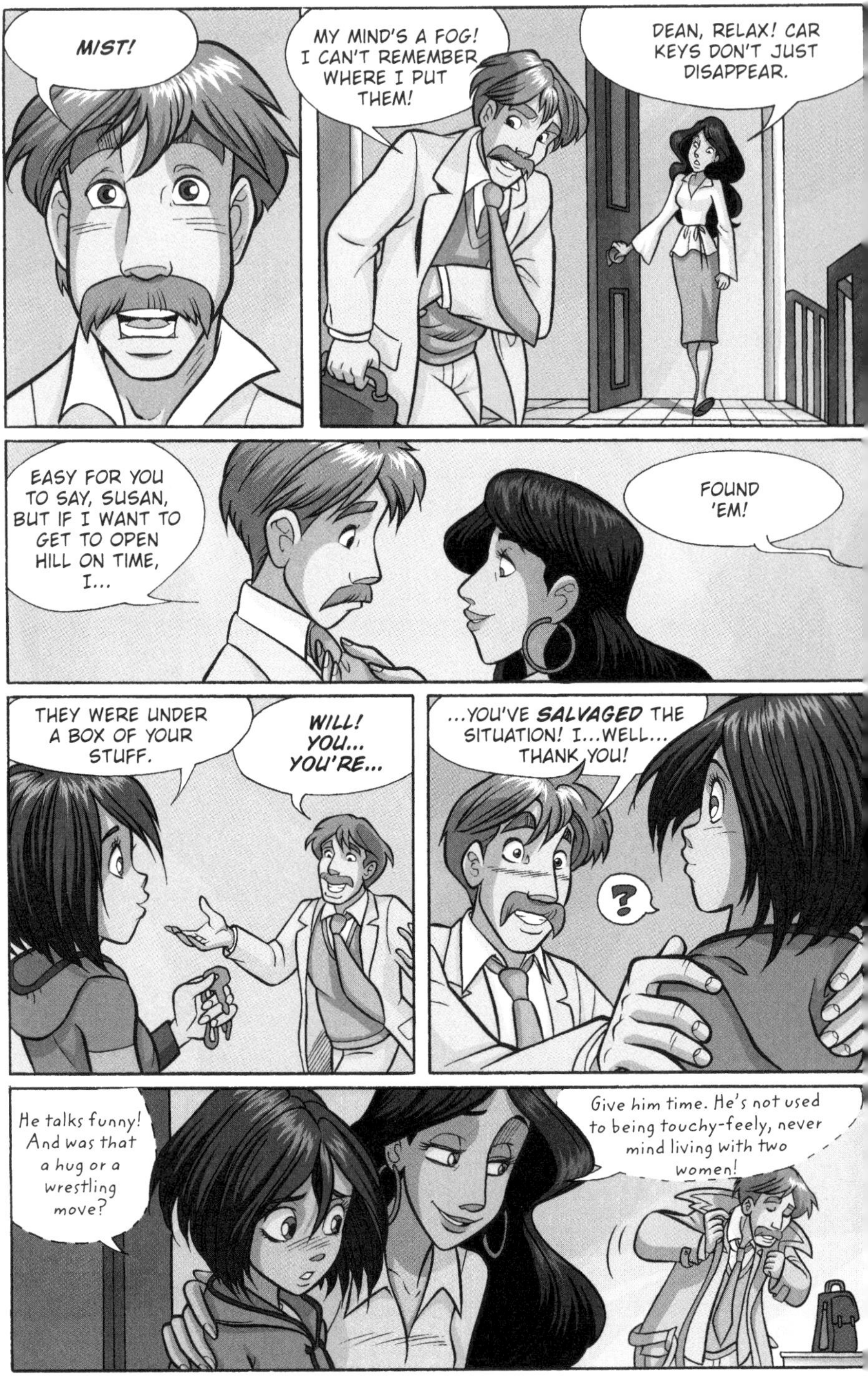

MIST!
MY MIND'S A FOG! I CAN'T REMEMBER WHERE I PUT THEM!
DEAN, RELAX! CAR KEYS DON'T JUST DISAPPEAR.
EASY FOR YOU TO SAY, SUSAN, BUT IF I WANT TO GET TO OPEN HILL ON TIME, I...
FOUND 'EM!
THEY WERE UNDER A BOX OF YOUR STUFF.
WILL! YOU... YOU'RE...
...YOU'VE SALVAGED THE SITUATION! I...WELL... THANK YOU!
?
He talks funny! And was that a hug or a wrestling move?
Give him time. He's not used to being touchy-feely, never mind living with two women!

34

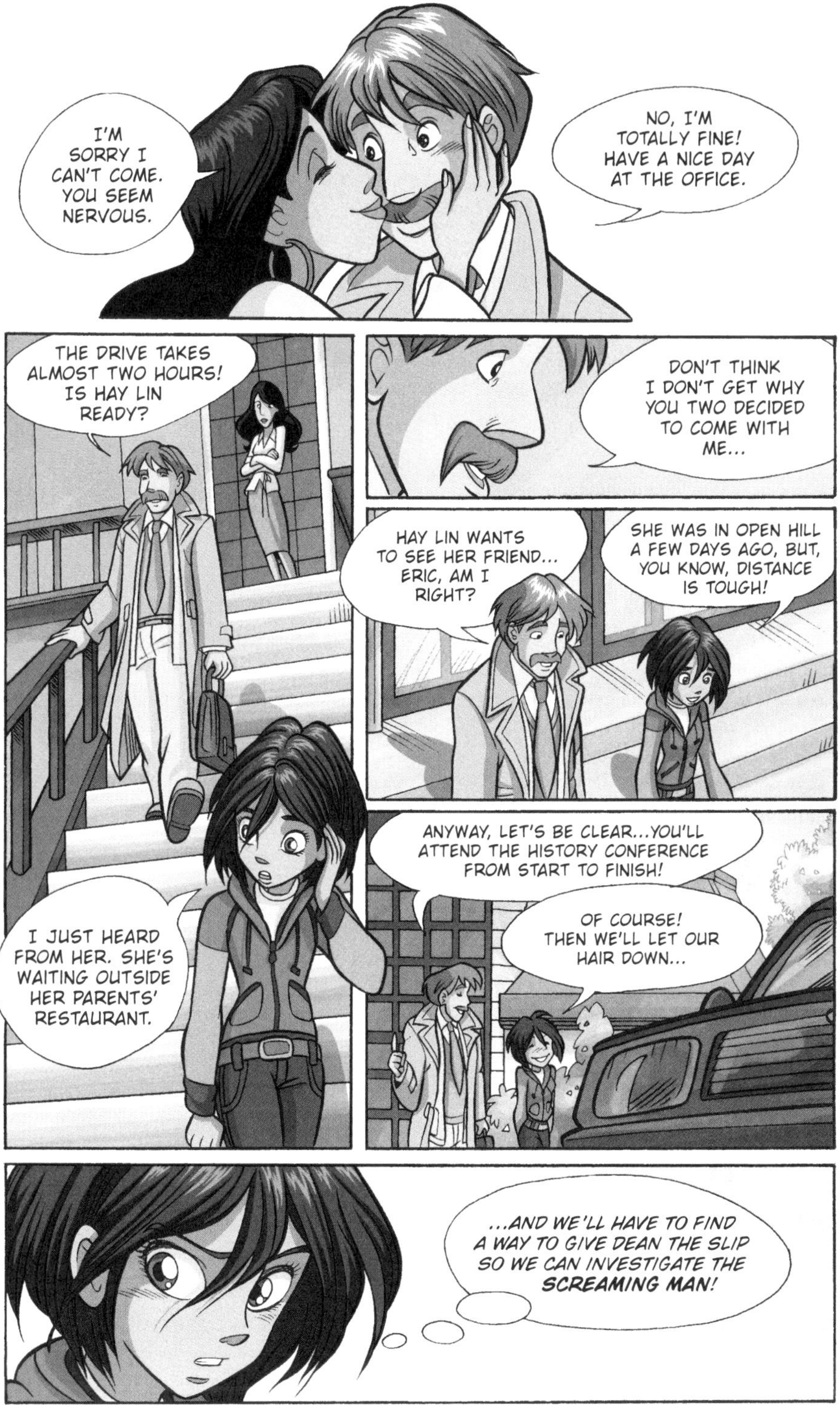
I'M SORRY I CAN'T COME. YOU SEEM NERVOUS.
NO, I'M TOTALLY FINE! HAVE A NICE DAY AT THE OFFICE.
THE DRIVE TAKES ALMOST TWO HOURS! IS HAY LIN READY?
DON'T THINK I DON'T GET WHY YOU TWO DECIDED TO COME WITH ME...
HAY LIN WANTS TO SEE HER FRIEND... ERIC, AM I RIGHT?
SHE WAS IN OPEN HILL A FEW DAYS AGO, BUT, YOU KNOW, DISTANCE IS TOUGH!
I JUST HEARD FROM HER. SHE'S WAITING OUTSIDE HER PARENTS' RESTAURANT.
ANYWAY, LET'S BE CLEAR...YOU'LL ATTEND THE HISTORY CONFERENCE FROM START TO FINISH!
OF COURSE! THEN WE'LL LET OUR HAIR DOWN...
...AND WE'LL HAVE TO FIND A WAY TO GIVE DEAN THE SLIP SO WE CAN INVESTIGATE THE **SCREAMING MAN!**

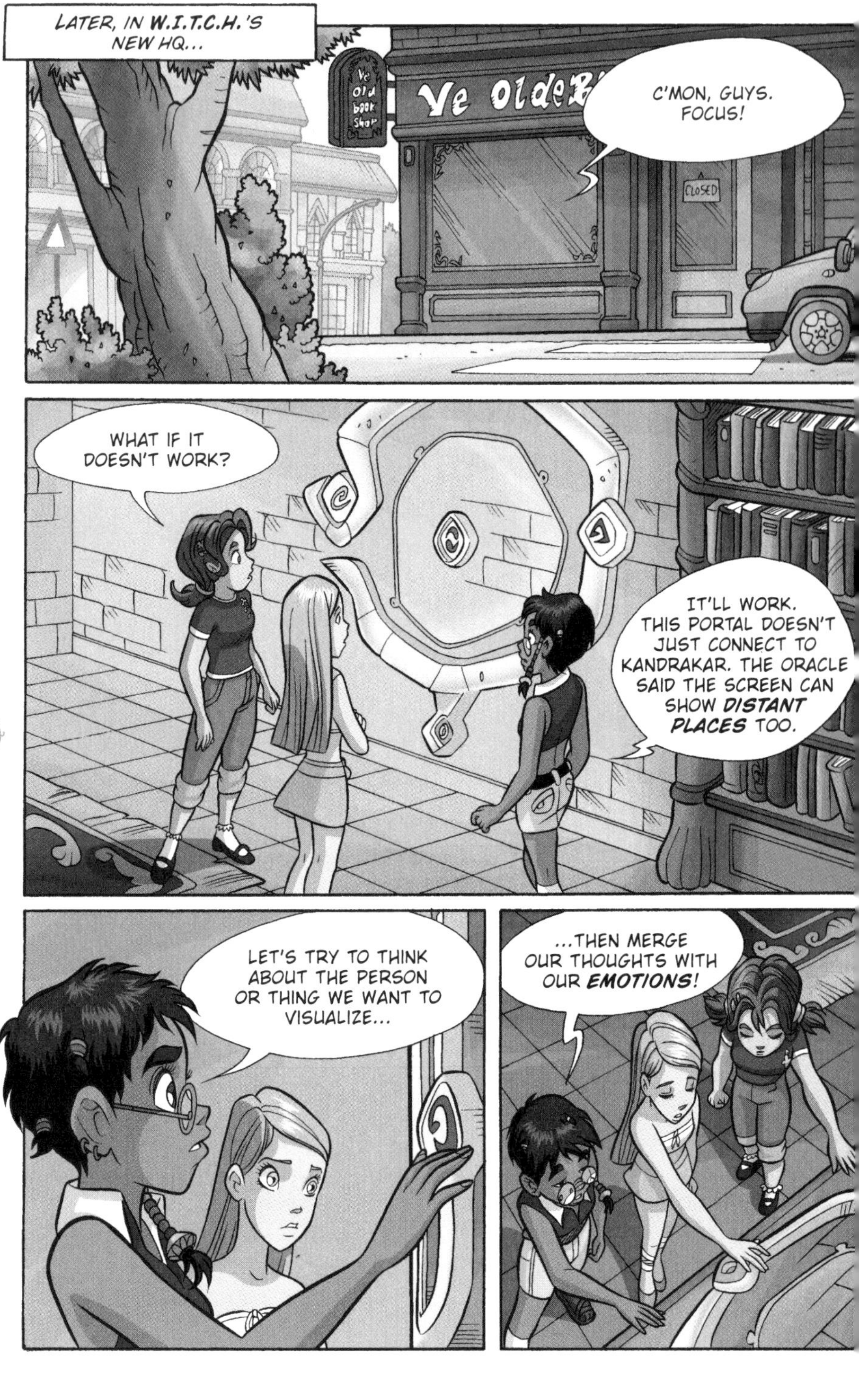
LATER, IN W.I.T.C.H.'S NEW HQ...
Ye Old book Shop
Ye OldeB
C'MON, GUYS. FOCUS!
CLOSED
WHAT IF IT DOESN'T WORK?
IT'LL WORK. THIS PORTAL DOESN'T JUST CONNECT TO KANDRAKAR. THE ORACLE SAID THE SCREEN CAN SHOW ***DISTANT PLACES*** TOO.
LET'S TRY TO THINK ABOUT THE PERSON OR THING WE WANT TO VISUALIZE...
...THEN MERGE OUR THOUGHTS WITH OUR ***EMOTIONS***!

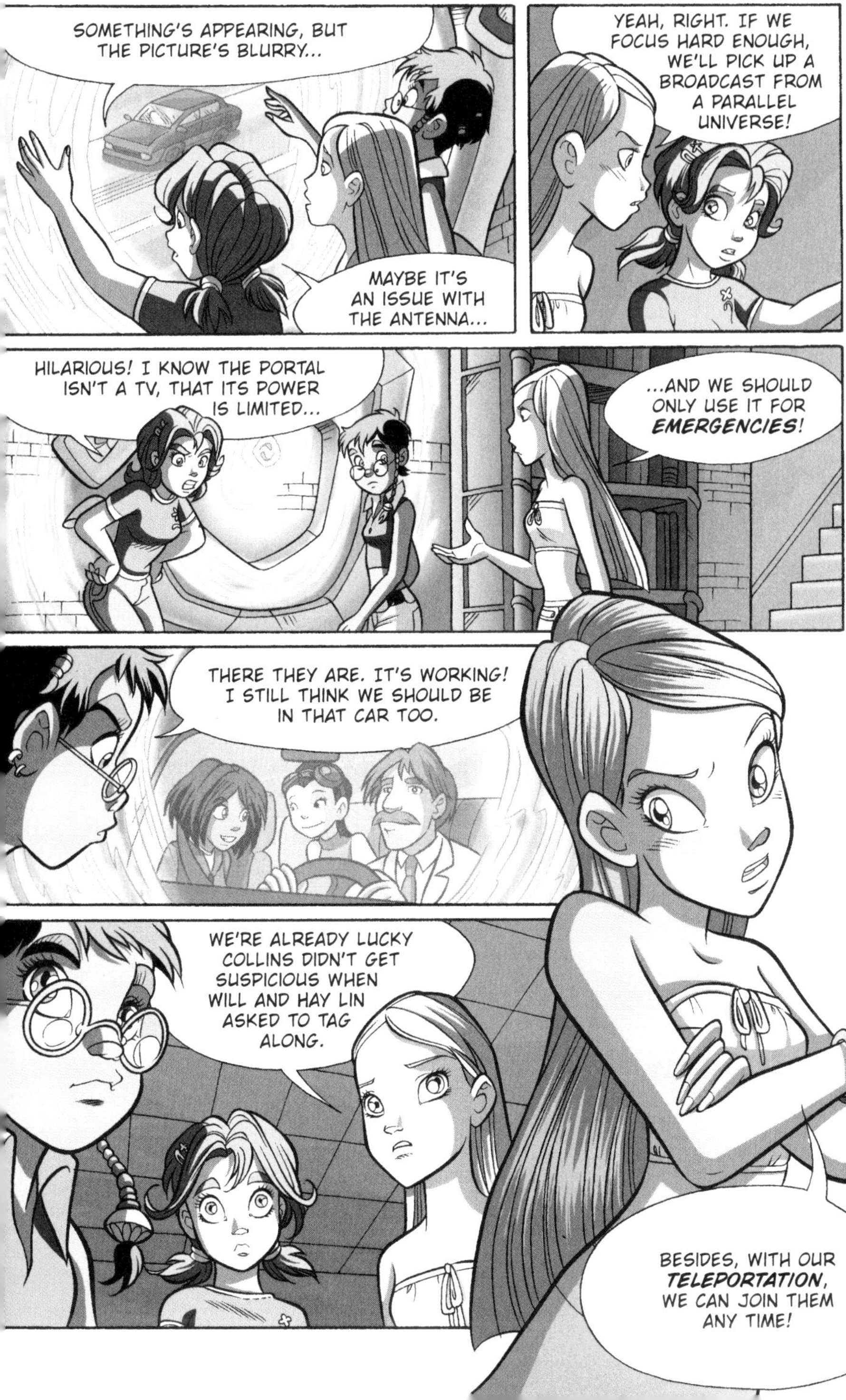
SOMETHING'S APPEARING, BUT THE PICTURE'S BLURRY...
MAYBE IT'S AN ISSUE WITH THE ANTENNA...
YEAH, RIGHT. IF WE FOCUS HARD ENOUGH, WE'LL PICK UP A BROADCAST FROM A PARALLEL UNIVERSE!
HILARIOUS! I KNOW THE PORTAL ISN'T A TV, THAT ITS POWER IS LIMITED...
...AND WE SHOULD ONLY USE IT FOR ***EMERGENCIES***!
THERE THEY ARE. IT'S WORKING! I STILL THINK WE SHOULD BE IN THAT CAR TOO.
WE'RE ALREADY LUCKY COLLINS DIDN'T GET SUSPICIOUS WHEN WILL AND HAY LIN ASKED TO TAG ALONG.
BESIDES, WITH OUR ***TELEPORTATION***, WE CAN JOIN THEM ANY TIME!

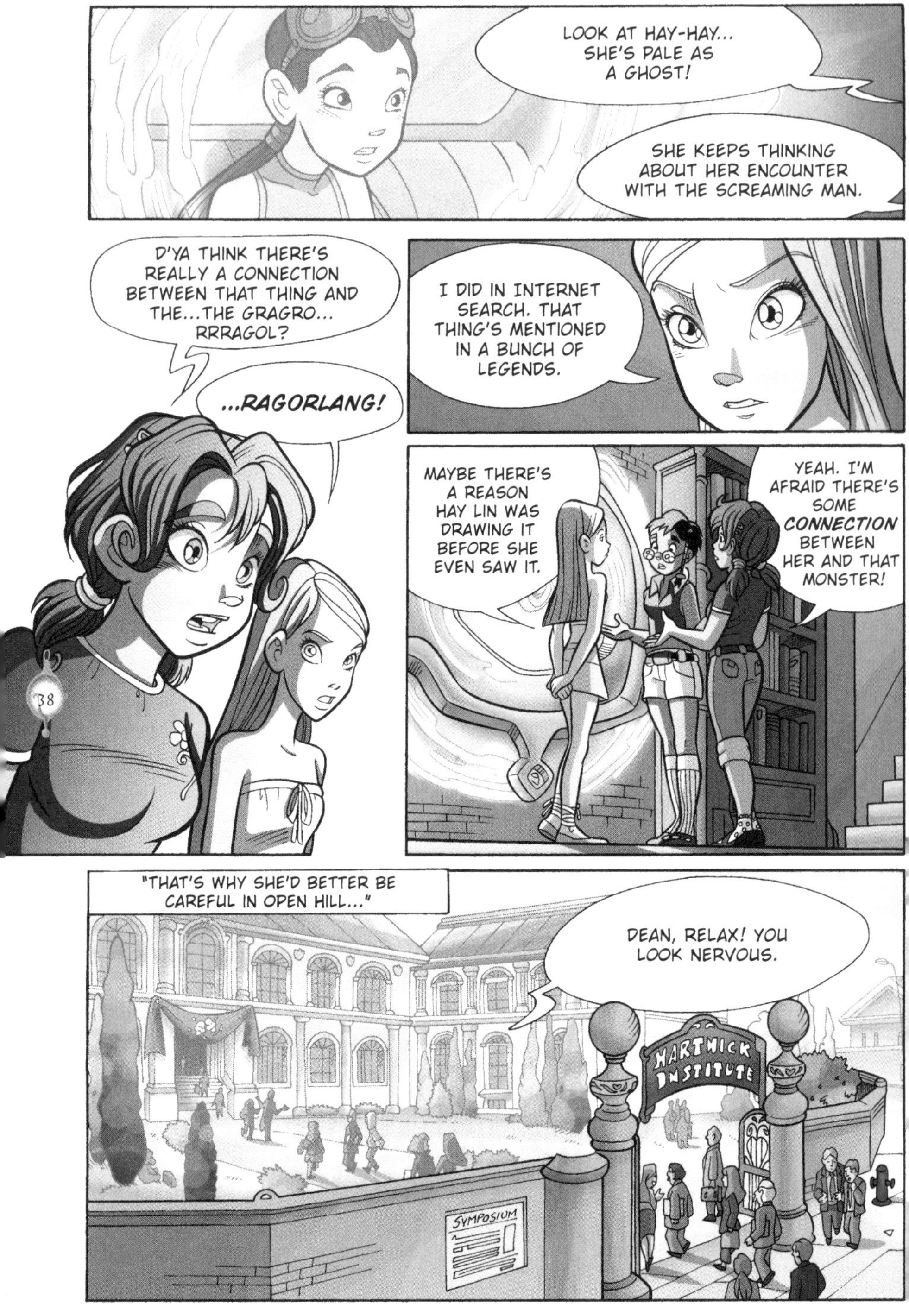

LOOK AT HAY-HAY... SHE'S PALE AS A GHOST!
SHE KEEPS THINKING ABOUT HER ENCOUNTER WITH THE SCREAMING MAN.
D'YA THINK THERE'S REALLY A CONNECTION BETWEEN THAT THING AND THE...THE GRAGRO... RRRAGOL?
...RAGORLANG!
I DID IN INTERNET SEARCH. THAT THING'S MENTIONED IN A BUNCH OF LEGENDS.
MAYBE THERE'S A REASON HAY LIN WAS DRAWING IT BEFORE SHE EVEN SAW IT.
YEAH. I'M AFRAID THERE'S SOME CONNECTION BETWEEN HER AND THAT MONSTER!
"THAT'S WHY SHE'D BETTER BE CAREFUL IN OPEN HILL..."
DEAN, RELAX! YOU LOOK NERVOUS.
HARTWICK INSTITUTE
SYMPOSIUM

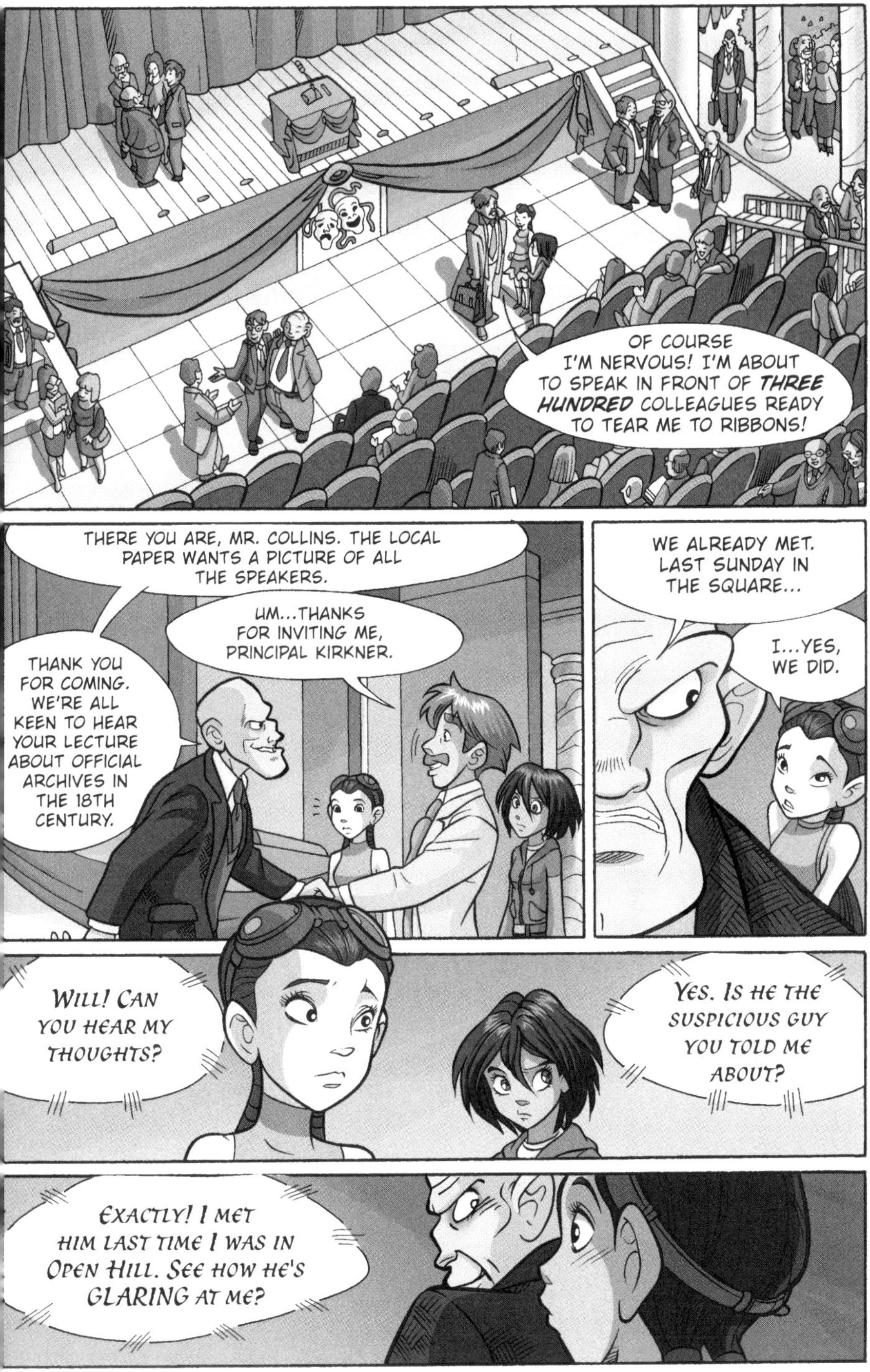
OF COURSE I'M NERVOUS! I'M ABOUT TO SPEAK IN FRONT OF THREE HUNDRED COLLEAGUES READY TO TEAR ME TO RIBBONS!
THERE YOU ARE, MR. COLLINS. THE LOCAL PAPER WANTS A PICTURE OF ALL THE SPEAKERS.
UM...THANKS FOR INVITING ME, PRINCIPAL KIRKNER.
THANK YOU FOR COMING. WE'RE ALL KEEN TO HEAR YOUR LECTURE ABOUT OFFICIAL ARCHIVES IN THE 18TH CENTURY.
WE ALREADY MET. LAST SUNDAY IN THE SQUARE...
I...YES, WE DID.
WILL! CAN YOU HEAR MY THOUGHTS?
YES. IS HE THE SUSPICIOUS GUY YOU TOLD ME ABOUT?
EXACTLY! I MET HIM LAST TIME I WAS IN OPEN HILL. SEE HOW HE'S GLARING AT ME?

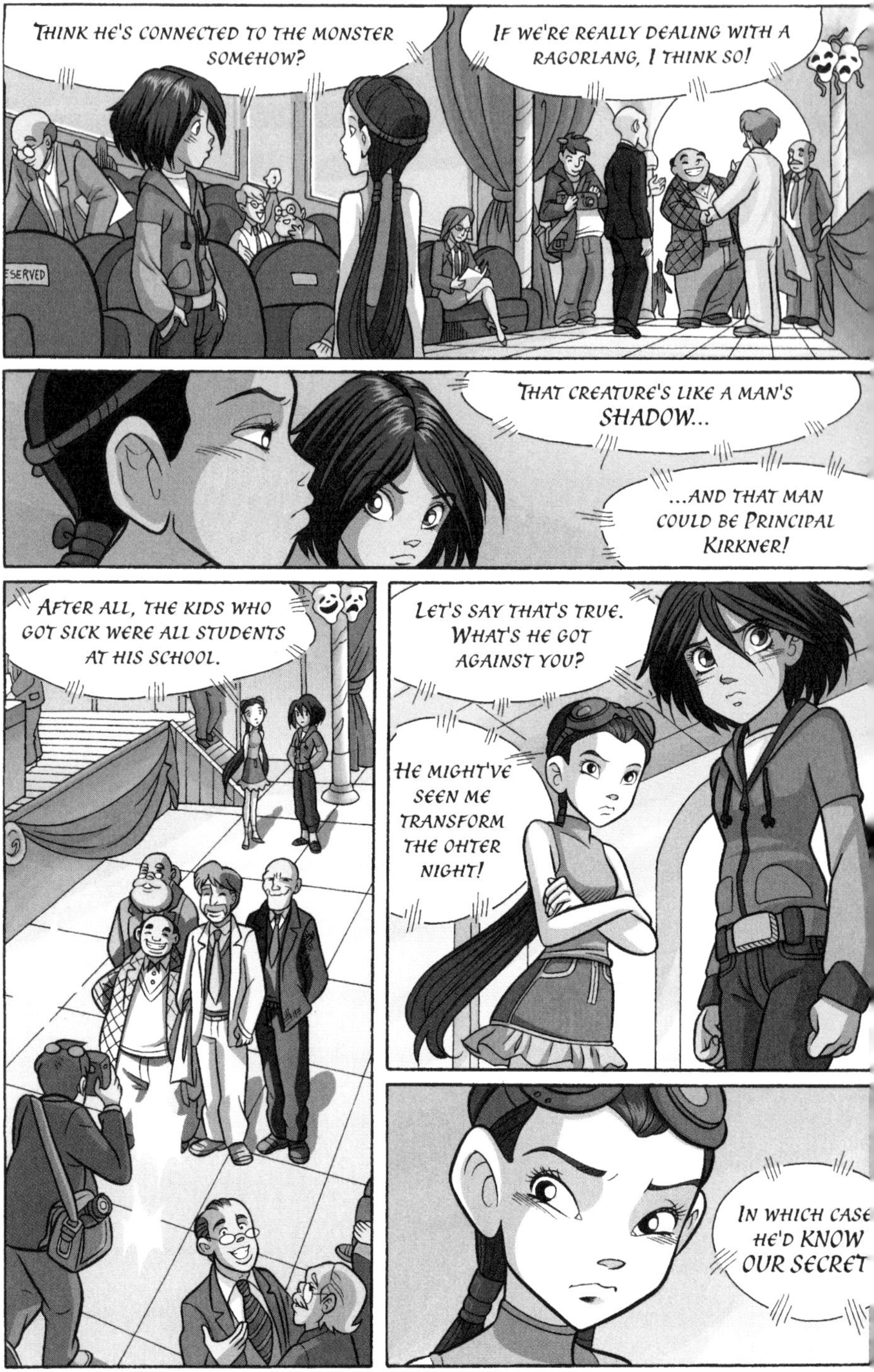
THINK HE'S CONNECTED TO THE MONSTER SOMEHOW?
IF WE'RE REALLY DEALING WITH A RAGORLANG, I THINK SO!
RESERVED
THAT CREATURE'S LIKE A MAN'S SHADOW...
...AND THAT MAN COULD BE PRINCIPAL KIRKNER!
AFTER ALL, THE KIDS WHO GOT SICK WERE ALL STUDENTS AT HIS SCHOOL.
LET'S SAY THAT'S TRUE. WHAT'S HE GOT AGAINST YOU?
HE MIGHT'VE SEEN ME TRANSFORM THE OHTER NIGHT!
IN WHICH CASE HE'D KNOW OUR SECRET

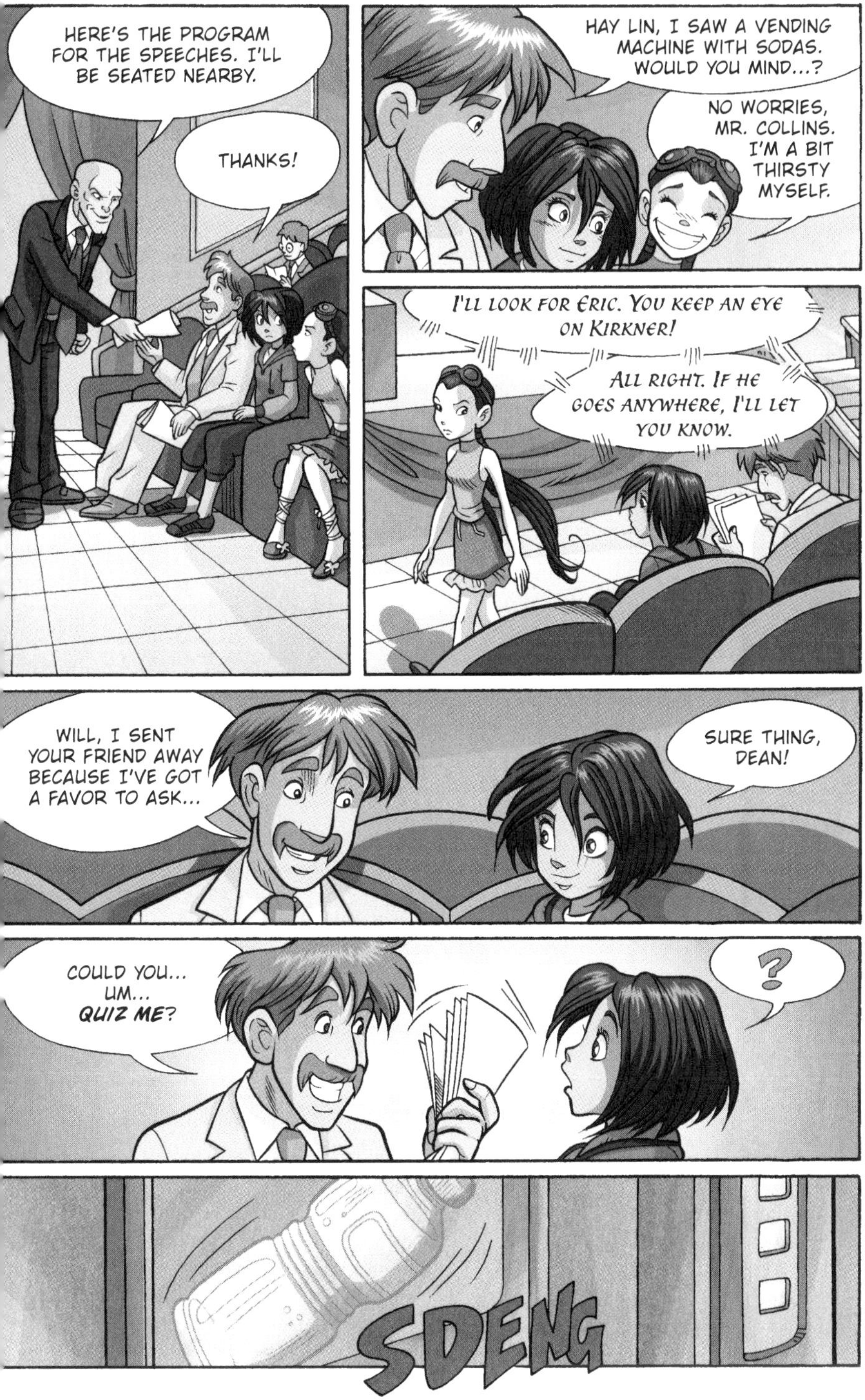
HERE'S THE PROGRAM FOR THE SPEECHES. I'LL BE SEATED NEARBY.
THANKS!
HAY LIN, I SAW A VENDING MACHINE WITH SODAS. WOULD YOU MIND...?
NO WORRIES, MR. COLLINS. I'M A BIT THIRSTY MYSELF.
I'LL LOOK FOR ERIC. YOU KEEP AN EYE ON KIRKNER!
ALL RIGHT. IF HE GOES ANYWHERE, I'LL LET YOU KNOW.
WILL, I SENT YOUR FRIEND AWAY BECAUSE I'VE GOT A FAVOR TO ASK...
SURE THING, DEAN!
COULD YOU... UM... QUIZ ME?
?
SDENG

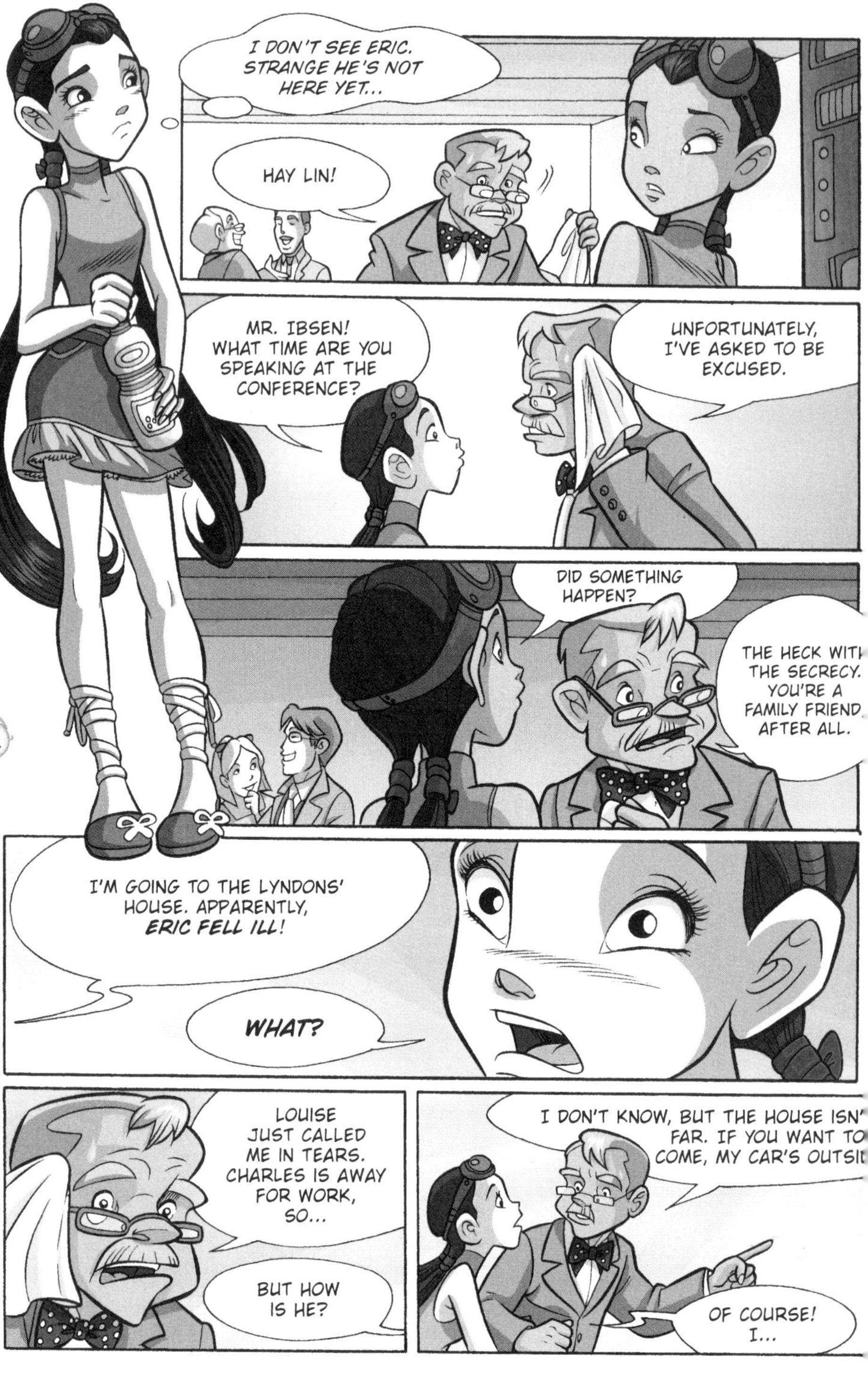
I DON'T SEE ERIC. STRANGE HE'S NOT HERE YET...
HAY LIN!
MR. IBSEN! WHAT TIME ARE YOU SPEAKING AT THE CONFERENCE?
UNFORTUNATELY, I'VE ASKED TO BE EXCUSED.
DID SOMETHING HAPPEN?
THE HECK WITH THE SECRECY. YOU'RE A FAMILY FRIEND AFTER ALL.
I'M GOING TO THE LYNDONS' HOUSE. APPARENTLY, ERIC FELL ILL!
WHAT?
LOUISE JUST CALLED ME IN TEARS. CHARLES IS AWAY FOR WORK, SO...
BUT HOW IS HE?
I DON'T KNOW, BUT THE HOUSE ISN' FAR. IF YOU WANT TO COME, MY CAR'S OUTSI
OF COURSE! I...

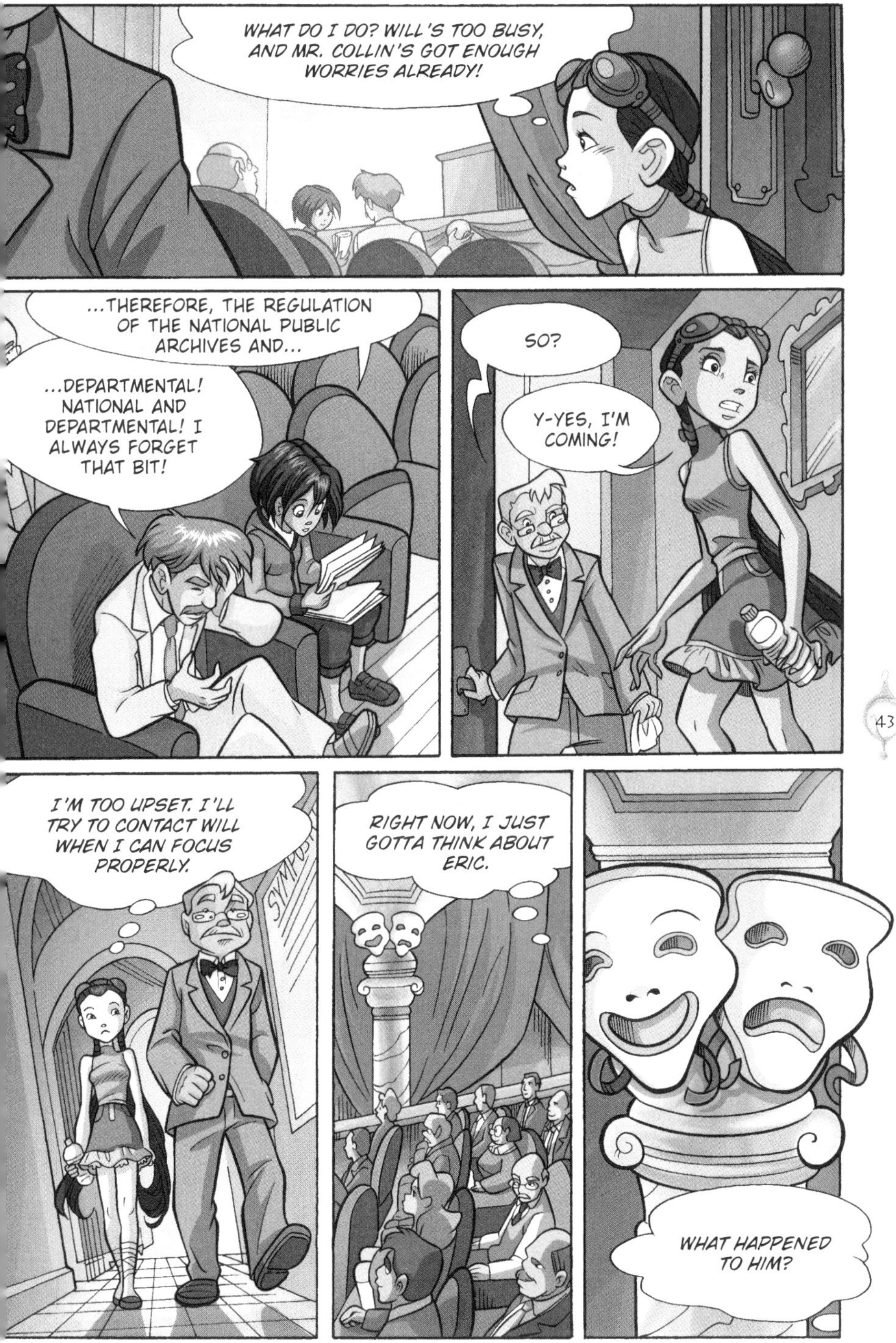
WHAT DO I DO? WILL'S TOO BUSY, AND MR. COLLIN'S GOT ENOUGH WORRIES ALREADY!
...THEREFORE, THE REGULATION OF THE NATIONAL PUBLIC ARCHIVES AND...
...DEPARTMENTAL! NATIONAL AND DEPARTMENTAL! I ALWAYS FORGET THAT BIT!
SO?
Y-YES, I'M COMING!
I'M TOO UPSET. I'LL TRY TO CONTACT WILL WHEN I CAN FOCUS PROPERLY.
RIGHT NOW, I JUST GOTTA THINK ABOUT ERIC.
WHAT HAPPENED TO HIM?

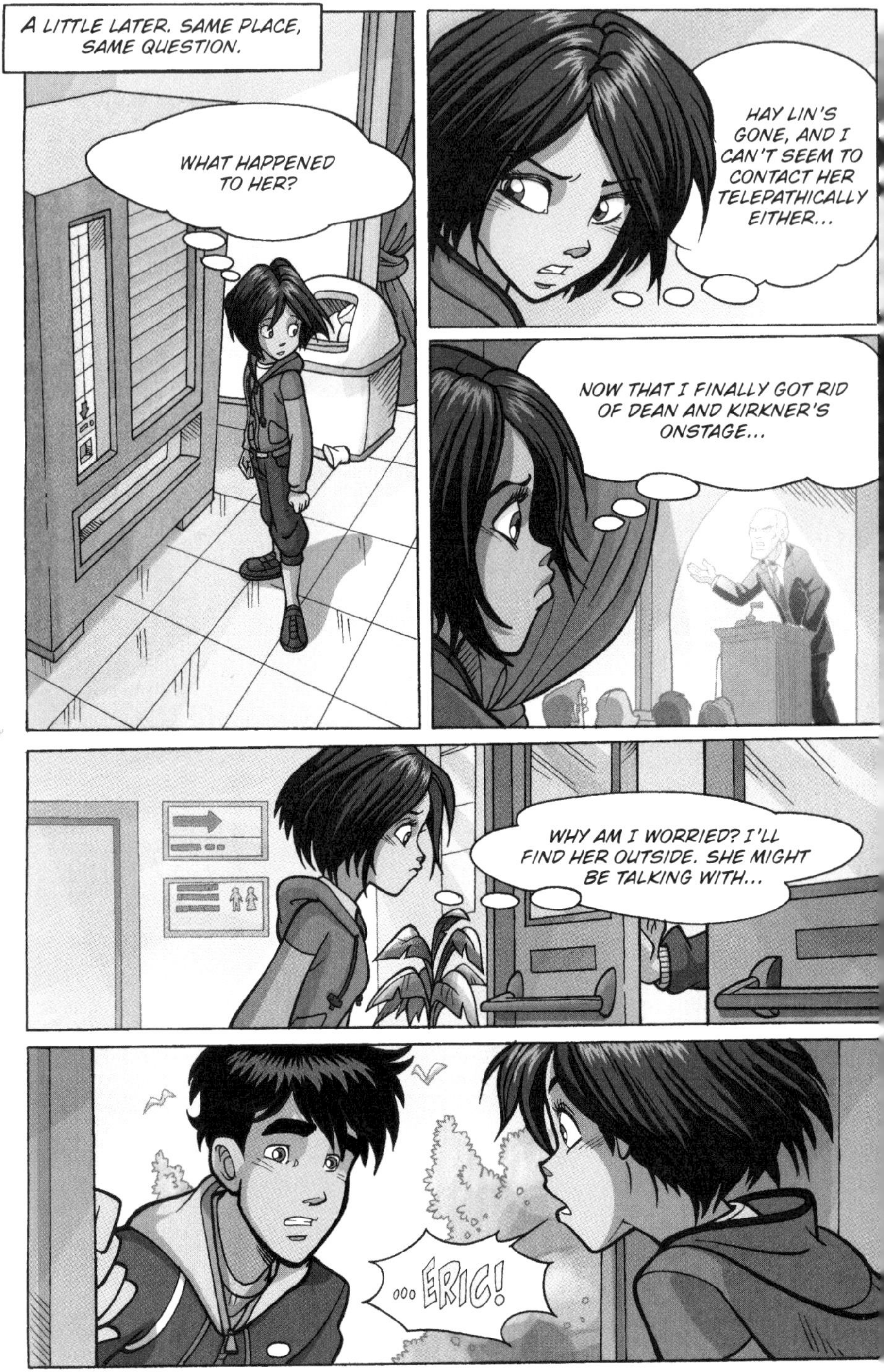
A LITTLE LATER. SAME PLACE, SAME QUESTION.
WHAT HAPPENED TO HER?
HAY LIN'S GONE, AND I CAN'T SEEM TO CONTACT HER TELEPATHICALLY EITHER...
NOW THAT I FINALLY GOT RID OF DEAN AND KIRKNER'S ONSTAGE...
WHY AM I WORRIED? I'LL FIND HER OUTSIDE. SHE MIGHT BE TALKING WITH...
...ERIC!

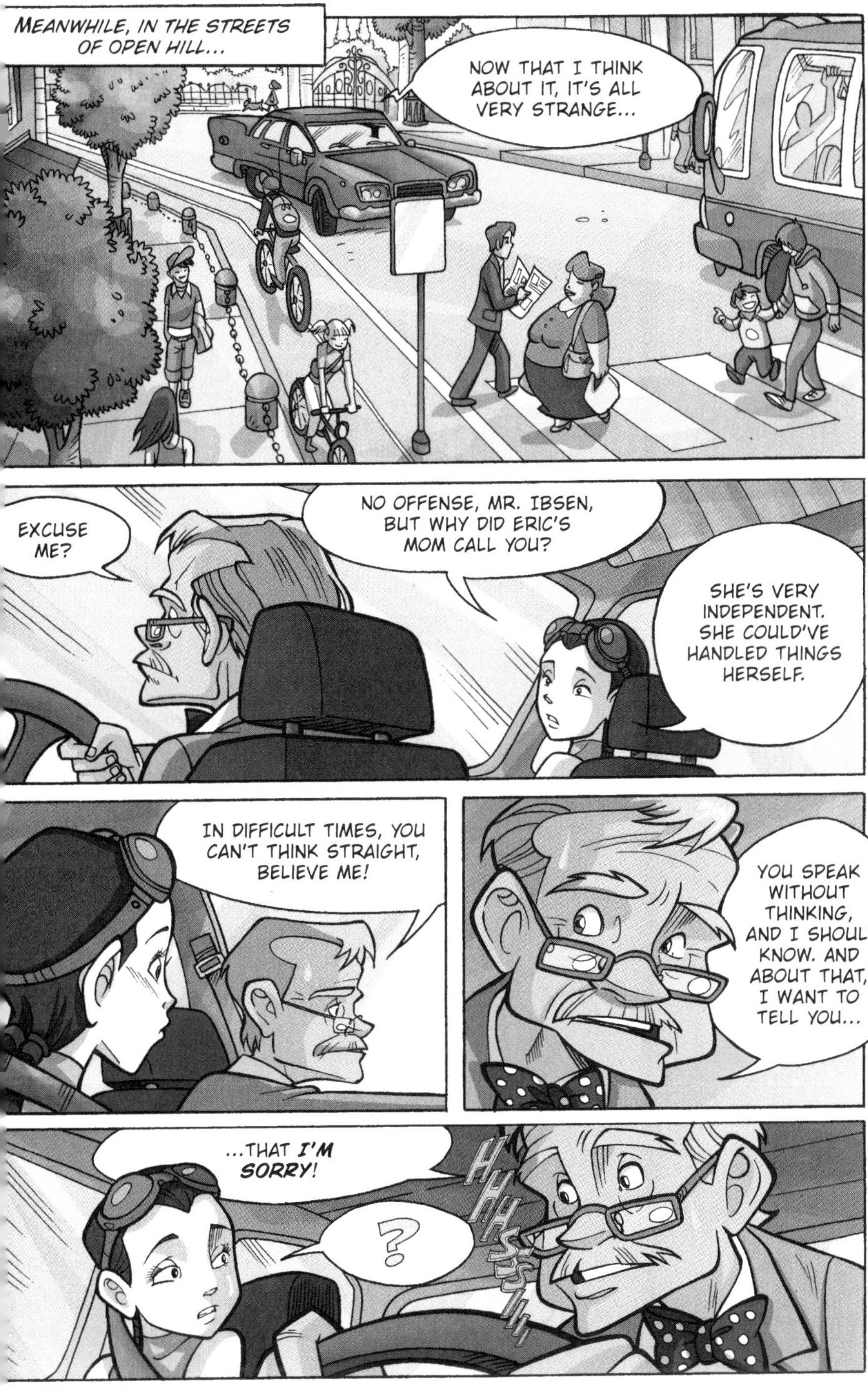
MEANWHILE, IN THE STREETS OF OPEN HILL...
NOW THAT I THINK ABOUT IT, IT'S ALL VERY STRANGE...
EXCUSE ME?
NO OFFENSE, MR. IBSEN, BUT WHY DID ERIC'S MOM CALL YOU?
SHE'S VERY INDEPENDENT. SHE COULD'VE HANDLED THINGS HERSELF.
IN DIFFICULT TIMES, YOU CAN'T THINK STRAIGHT, BELIEVE ME!
YOU SPEAK WITHOUT THINKING, AND I SHOULD KNOW. AND ABOUT THAT, I WANT TO TELL YOU...
...THAT I'M SORRY!
?
HHHSSHH

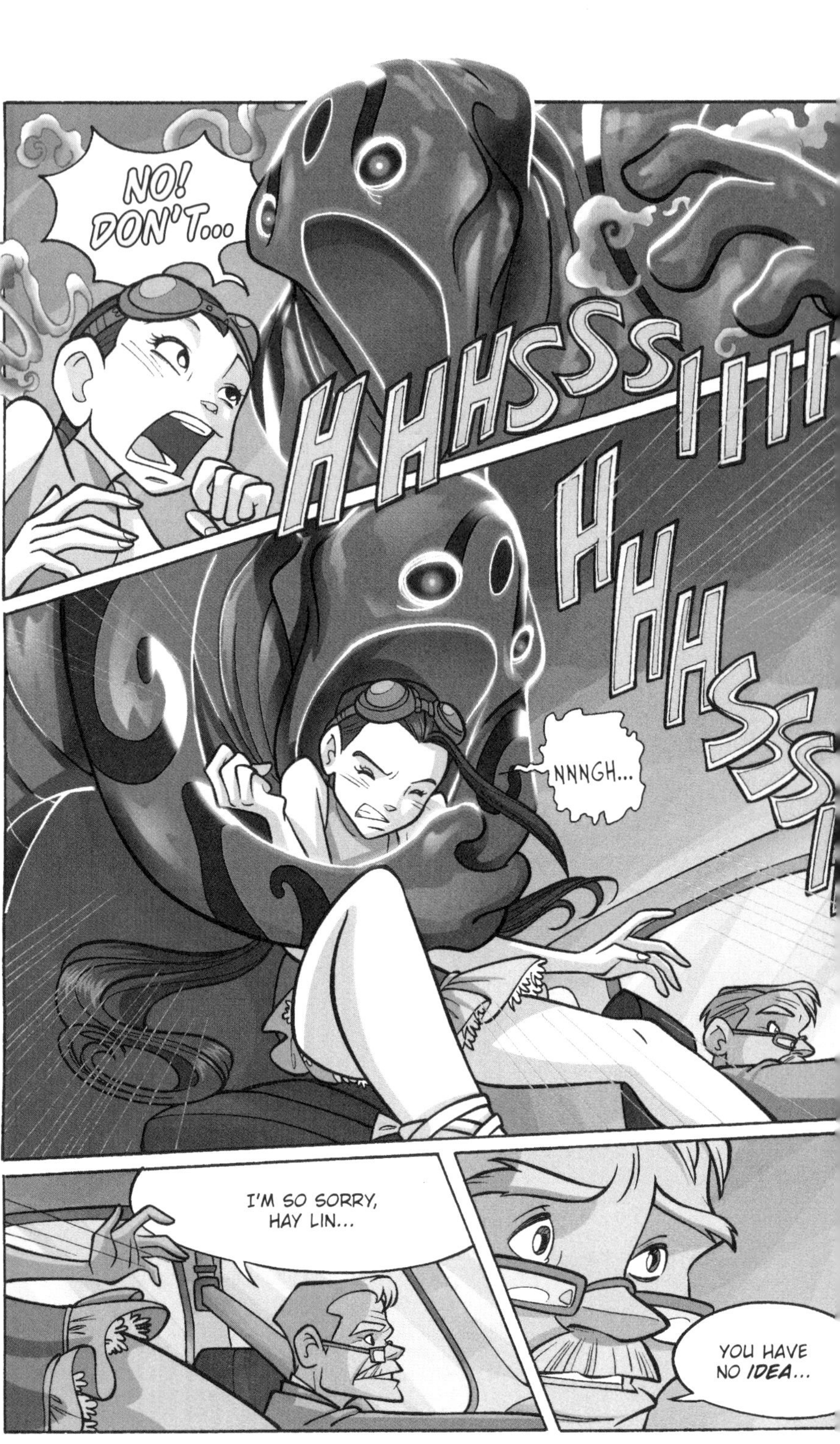
NO! DON'T...
HHHSSSIIII
HHHHSSSSI
NNNGH...
I'M SO SORRY, HAY LIN...
YOU HAVE NO *IDEA*...

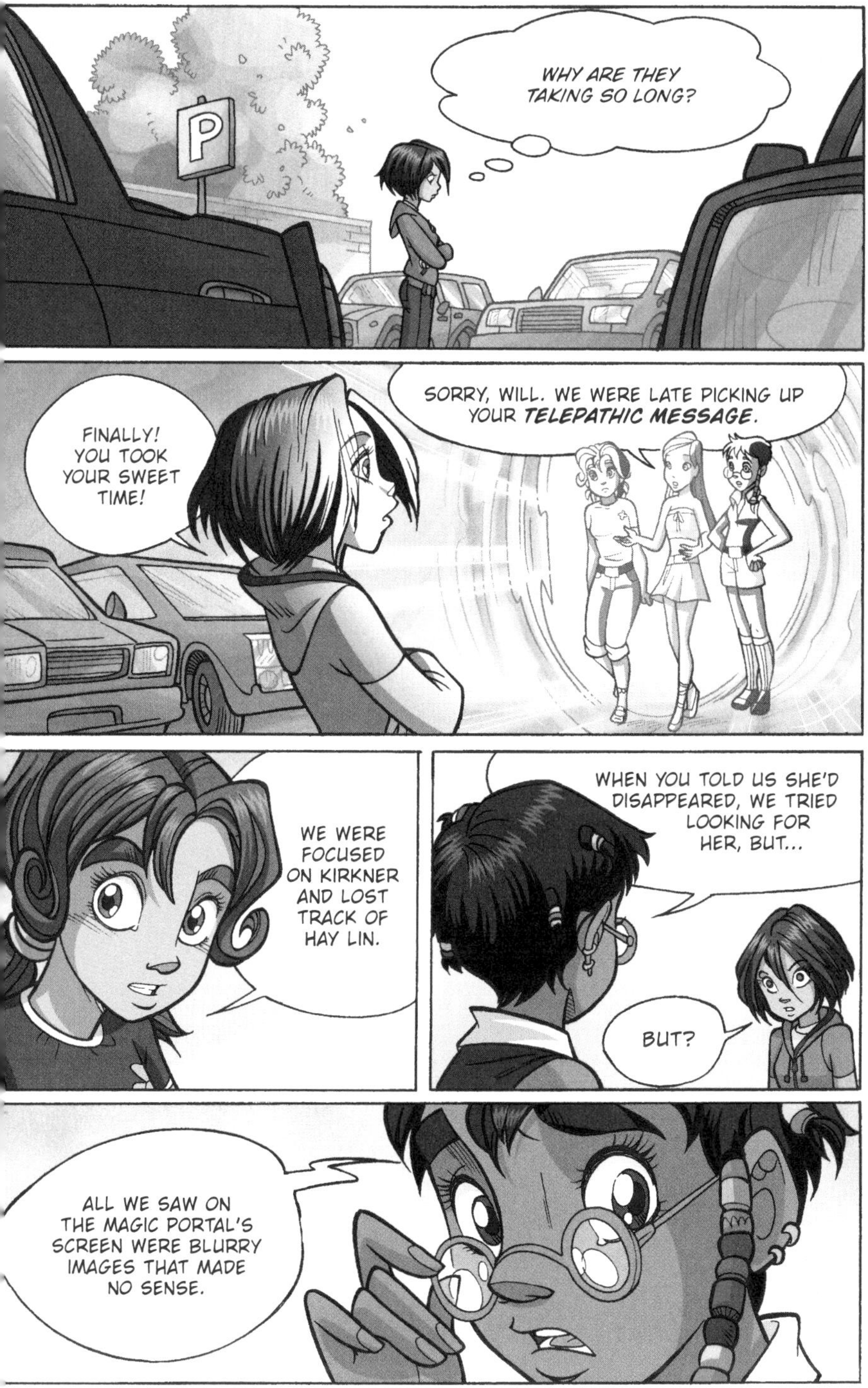
WHY ARE THEY TAKING SO LONG?
FINALLY! YOU TOOK YOUR SWEET TIME!
SORRY, WILL. WE WERE LATE PICKING UP YOUR TELEPATHIC MESSAGE.
WE WERE FOCUSED ON KIRKNER AND LOST TRACK OF HAY LIN.
WHEN YOU TOLD US SHE'D DISAPPEARED, WE TRIED LOOKING FOR HER, BUT...
BUT?
ALL WE SAW ON THE MAGIC PORTAL'S SCREEN WERE BLURRY IMAGES THAT MADE NO SENSE.

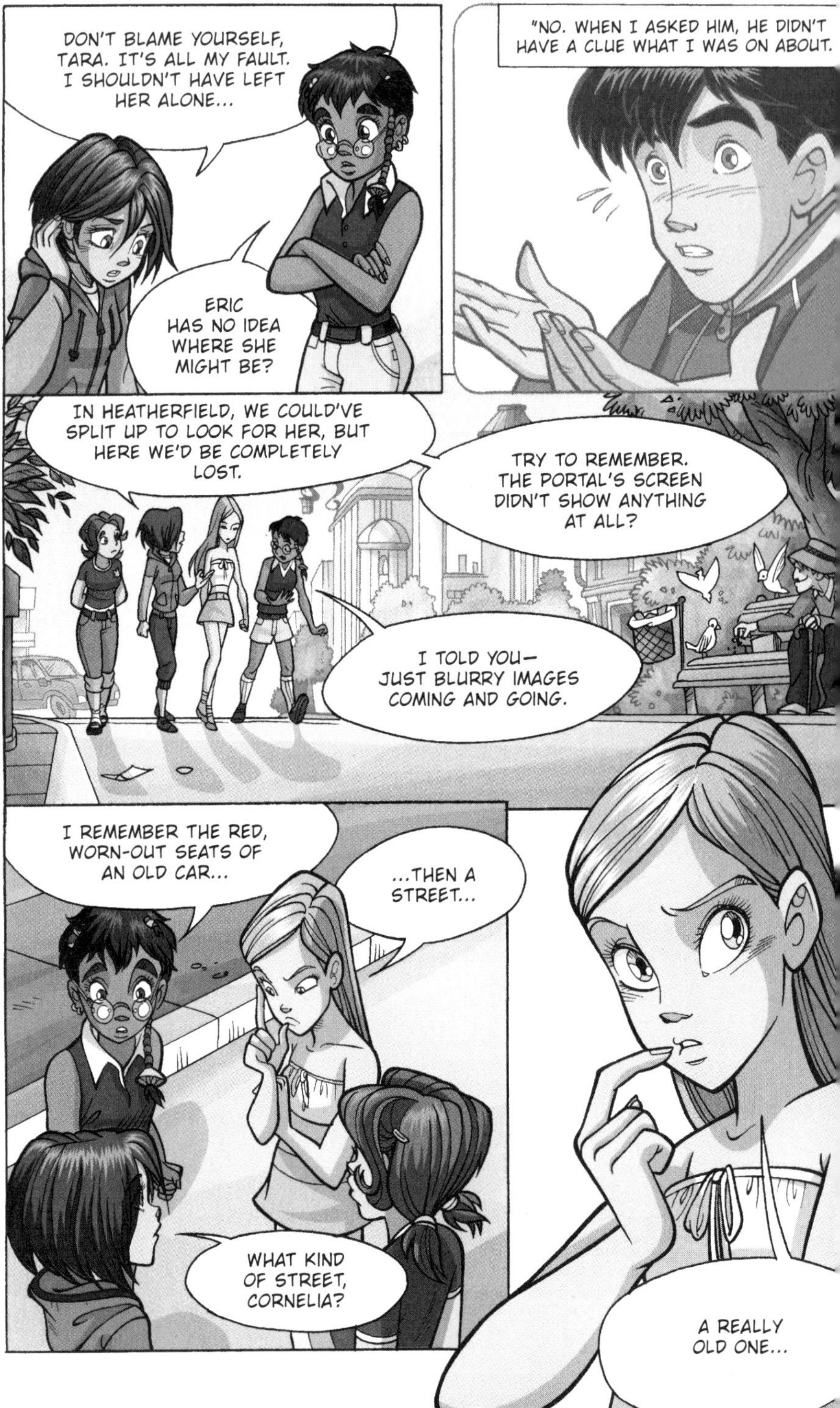
DON'T BLAME YOURSELF, TARA. IT'S ALL MY FAULT. I SHOULDN'T HAVE LEFT HER ALONE...
ERIC HAS NO IDEA WHERE SHE MIGHT BE?
"NO. WHEN I ASKED HIM, HE DIDN'T HAVE A CLUE WHAT I WAS ON ABOUT.
IN HEATHERFIELD, WE COULD'VE SPLIT UP TO LOOK FOR HER, BUT HERE WE'D BE COMPLETELY LOST.
TRY TO REMEMBER. THE PORTAL'S SCREEN DIDN'T SHOW ANYTHING AT ALL?
I TOLD YOU— JUST BLURRY IMAGES COMING AND GOING.
I REMEMBER THE RED, WORN-OUT SEATS OF AN OLD CAR...
...THEN A STREET...
WHAT KIND OF STREET, CORNELIA?
A REALLY OLD ONE...

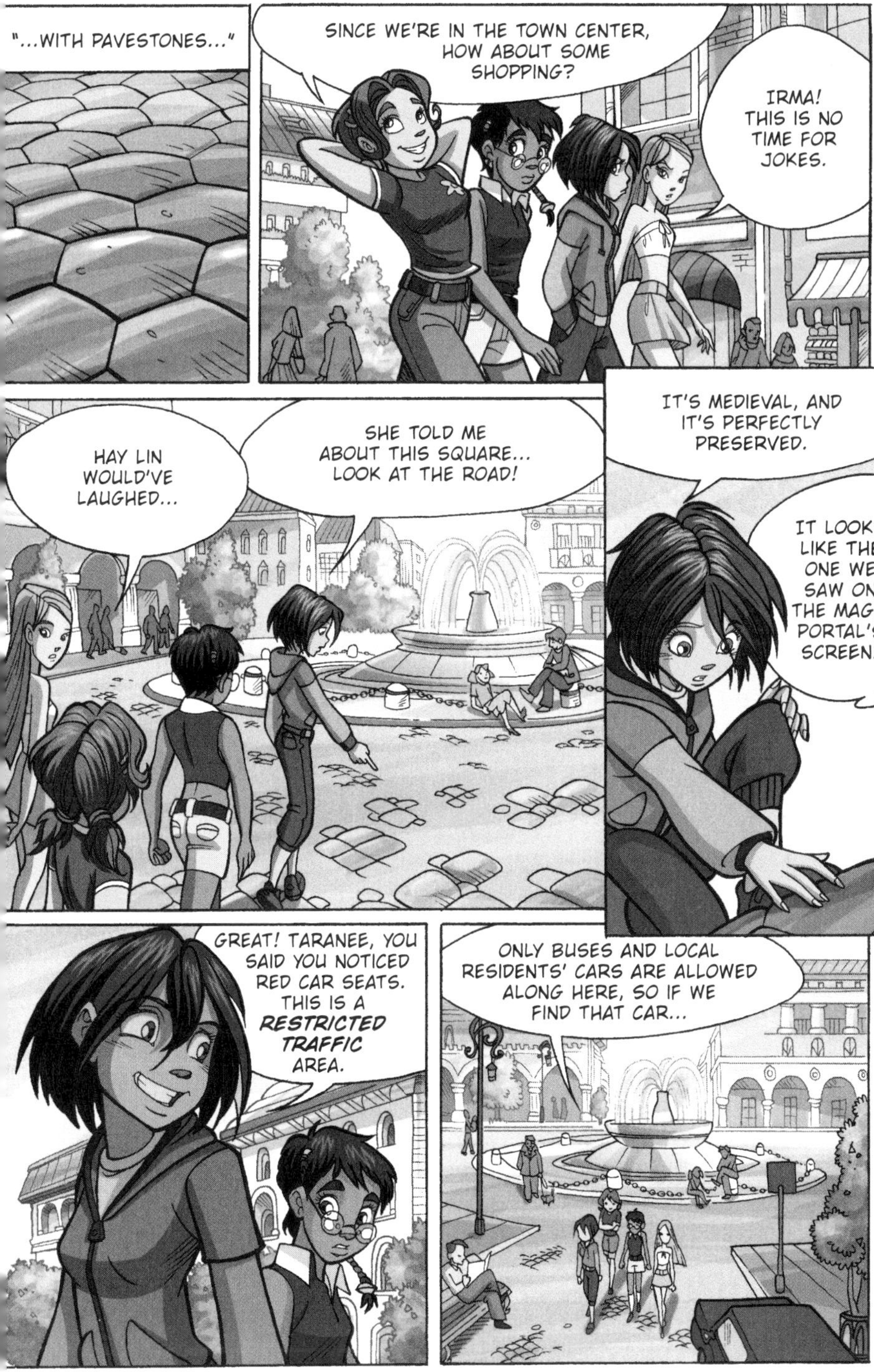
"...WITH PAVESTONES..."
SINCE WE'RE IN THE TOWN CENTER, HOW ABOUT SOME SHOPPING?
IRMA! THIS IS NO TIME FOR JOKES.
HAY LIN WOULD'VE LAUGHED...
SHE TOLD ME ABOUT THIS SQUARE... LOOK AT THE ROAD!
IT'S MEDIEVAL, AND IT'S PERFECTLY PRESERVED.
IT LOOKS LIKE THE ONE WE SAW ON THE MAGIC PORTAL'S SCREEN!
GREAT! TARANEE, YOU SAID YOU NOTICED RED CAR SEATS. THIS IS A *RESTRICTED TRAFFIC* AREA.
ONLY BUSES AND LOCAL RESIDENTS' CARS ARE ALLOWED ALONG HERE, SO IF WE FIND THAT CAR...

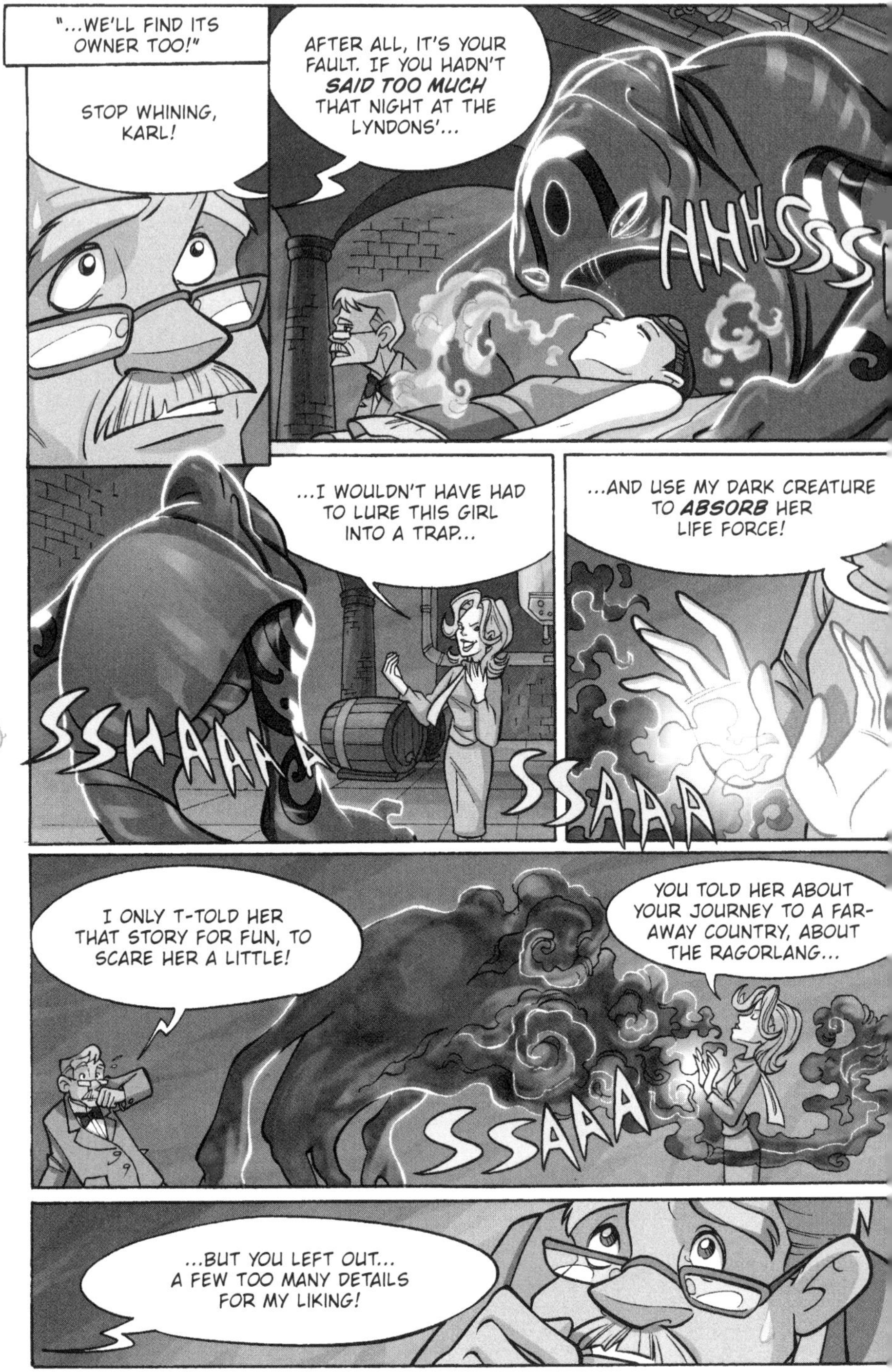
"...WE'LL FIND ITS OWNER TOO!"
STOP WHINING, KARL!
AFTER ALL, IT'S YOUR FAULT. IF YOU HADN'T *SAID TOO MUCH* THAT NIGHT AT THE LYNDONS'...
HHHSSS
...I WOULDN'T HAVE HAD TO LURE THIS GIRL INTO A TRAP...
SSHAAAA
...AND USE MY DARK CREATURE TO *ABSORB* HER LIFE FORCE!
SSAAA
I ONLY T-TOLD HER THAT STORY FOR FUN, TO SCARE HER A LITTLE!
YOU TOLD HER ABOUT YOUR JOURNEY TO A FAR-AWAY COUNTRY, ABOUT THE RAGORLANG...
SSAAA
...BUT YOU LEFT OUT... A FEW TOO MANY DETAILS FOR MY LIKING!

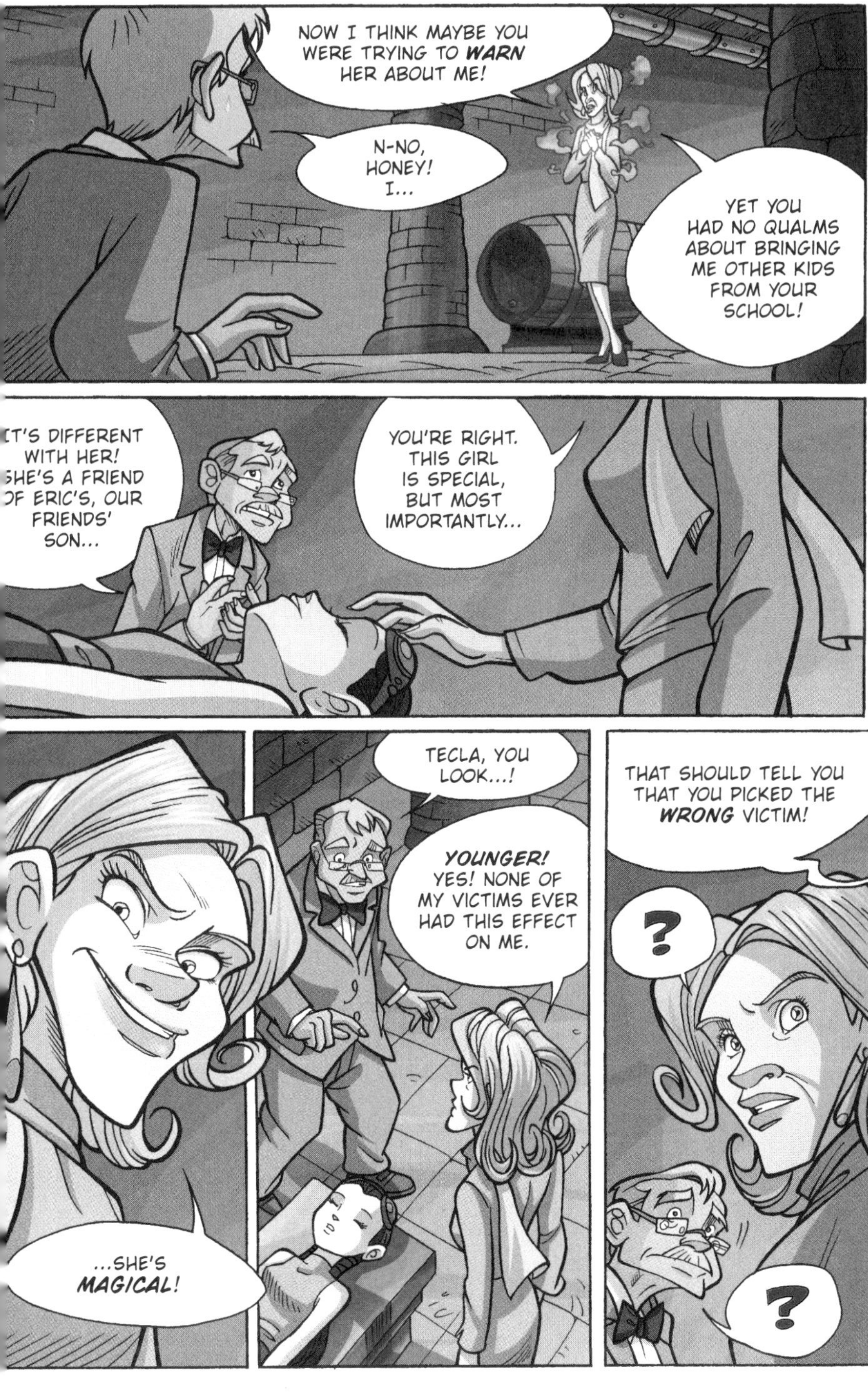
NOW I THINK MAYBE YOU WERE TRYING TO WARN HER ABOUT ME!
N-NO, HONEY! I...
YET YOU HAD NO QUALMS ABOUT BRINGING ME OTHER KIDS FROM YOUR SCHOOL!
IT'S DIFFERENT WITH HER! SHE'S A FRIEND OF ERIC'S, OUR FRIENDS' SON...
YOU'RE RIGHT. THIS GIRL IS SPECIAL, BUT MOST IMPORTANTLY...
...SHE'S MAGICAL!
TECLA, YOU LOOK...!
YOUNGER! YES! NONE OF MY VICTIMS EVER HAD THIS EFFECT ON ME.
THAT SHOULD TELL YOU THAT YOU PICKED THE WRONG VICTIM!
?
?

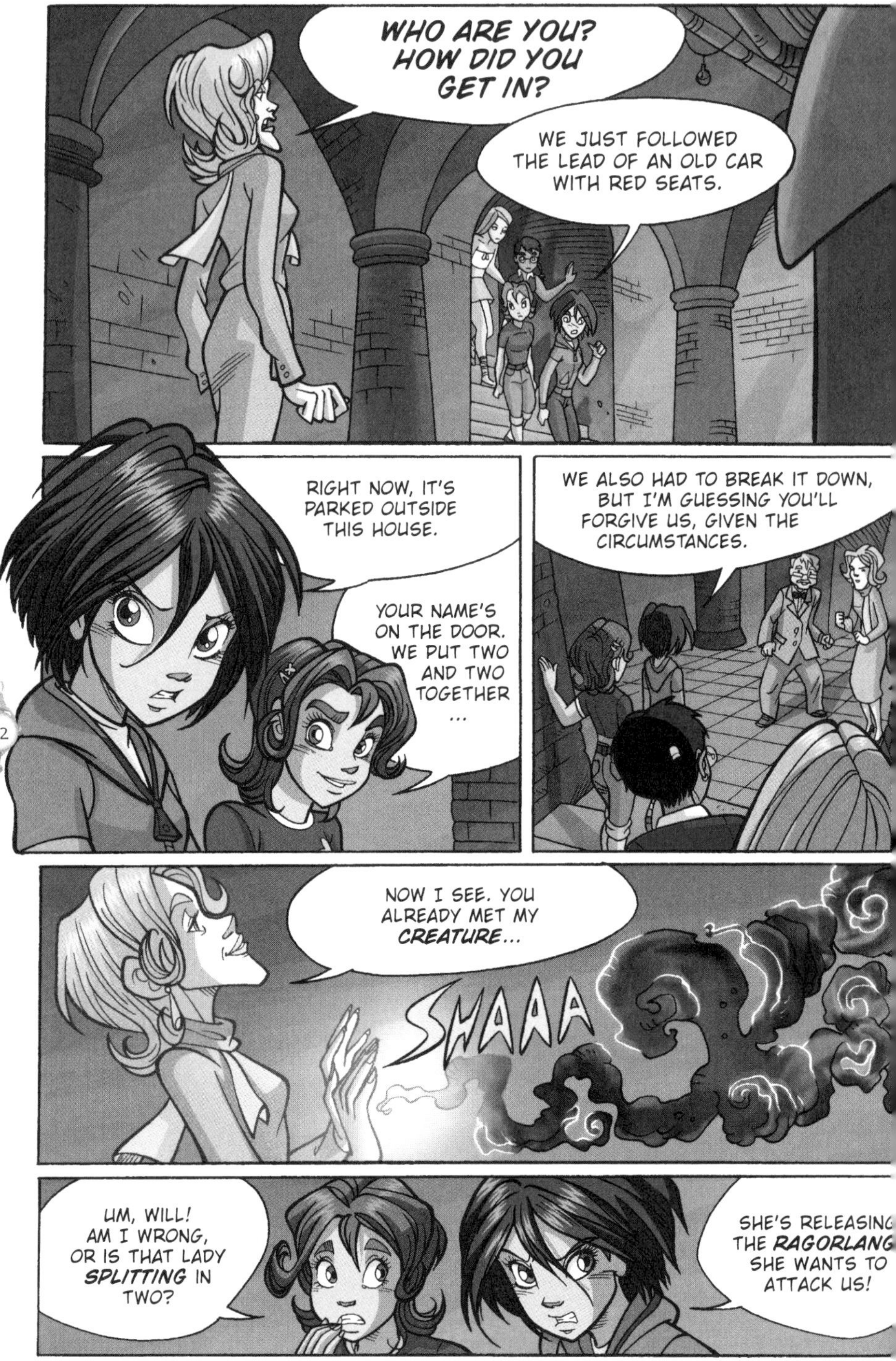
WHO ARE YOU? HOW DID YOU GET IN?
WE JUST FOLLOWED THE LEAD OF AN OLD CAR WITH RED SEATS.
RIGHT NOW, IT'S PARKED OUTSIDE THIS HOUSE.
YOUR NAME'S ON THE DOOR. WE PUT TWO AND TWO TOGETHER ...
WE ALSO HAD TO BREAK IT DOWN, BUT I'M GUESSING YOU'LL FORGIVE US, GIVEN THE CIRCUMSTANCES.
NOW I SEE. YOU ALREADY MET MY CREATURE...
SHAAA
UM, WILL! AM I WRONG, OR IS THAT LADY SPLITTING IN TWO?
SHE'S RELEASING THE RAGORLANG SHE WANTS TO ATTACK US!

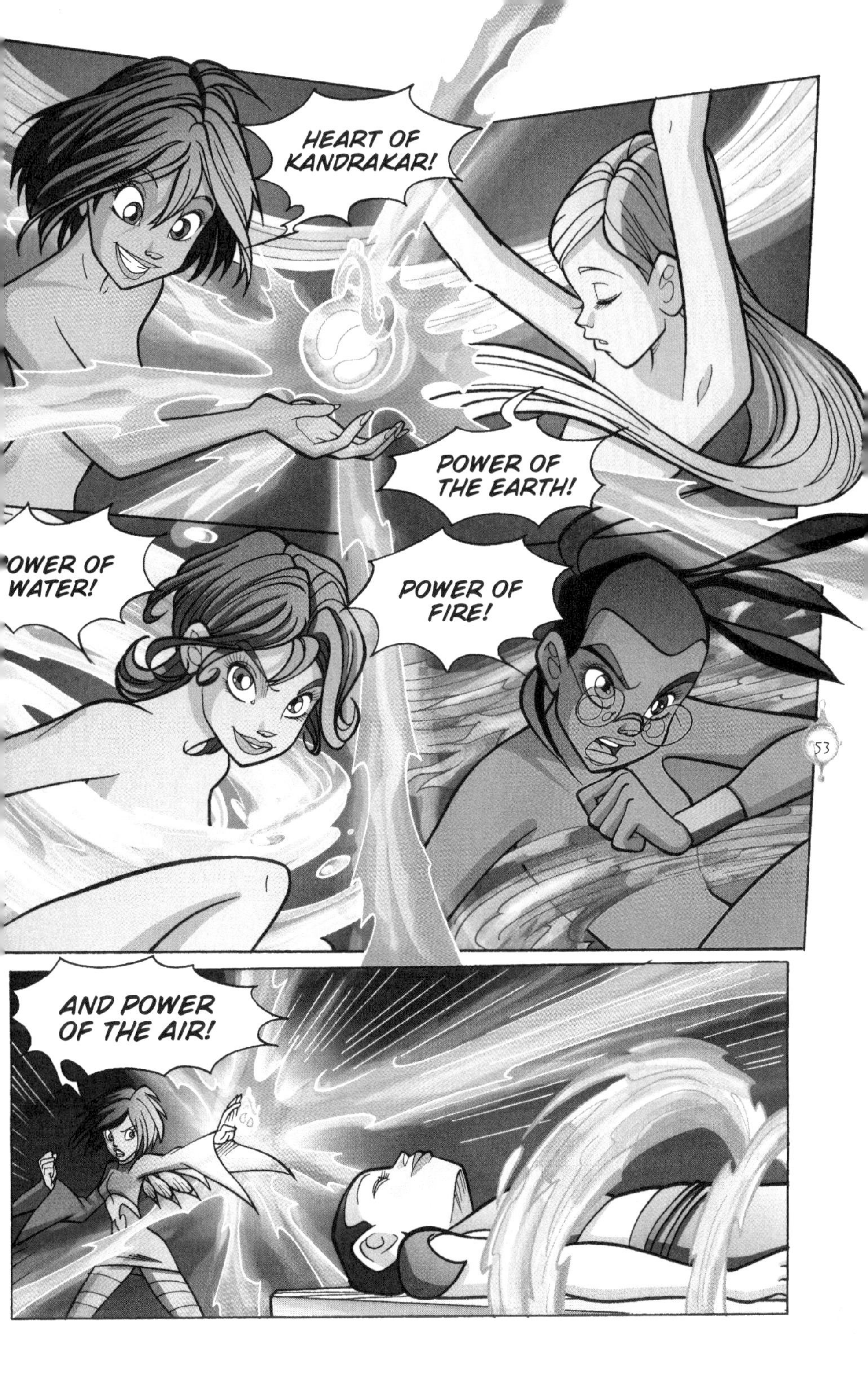
HEART OF KANDRAKAR!
POWER OF THE EARTH!
POWER OF FIRE!
OWER OF WATER!
AND POWER OF THE AIR!

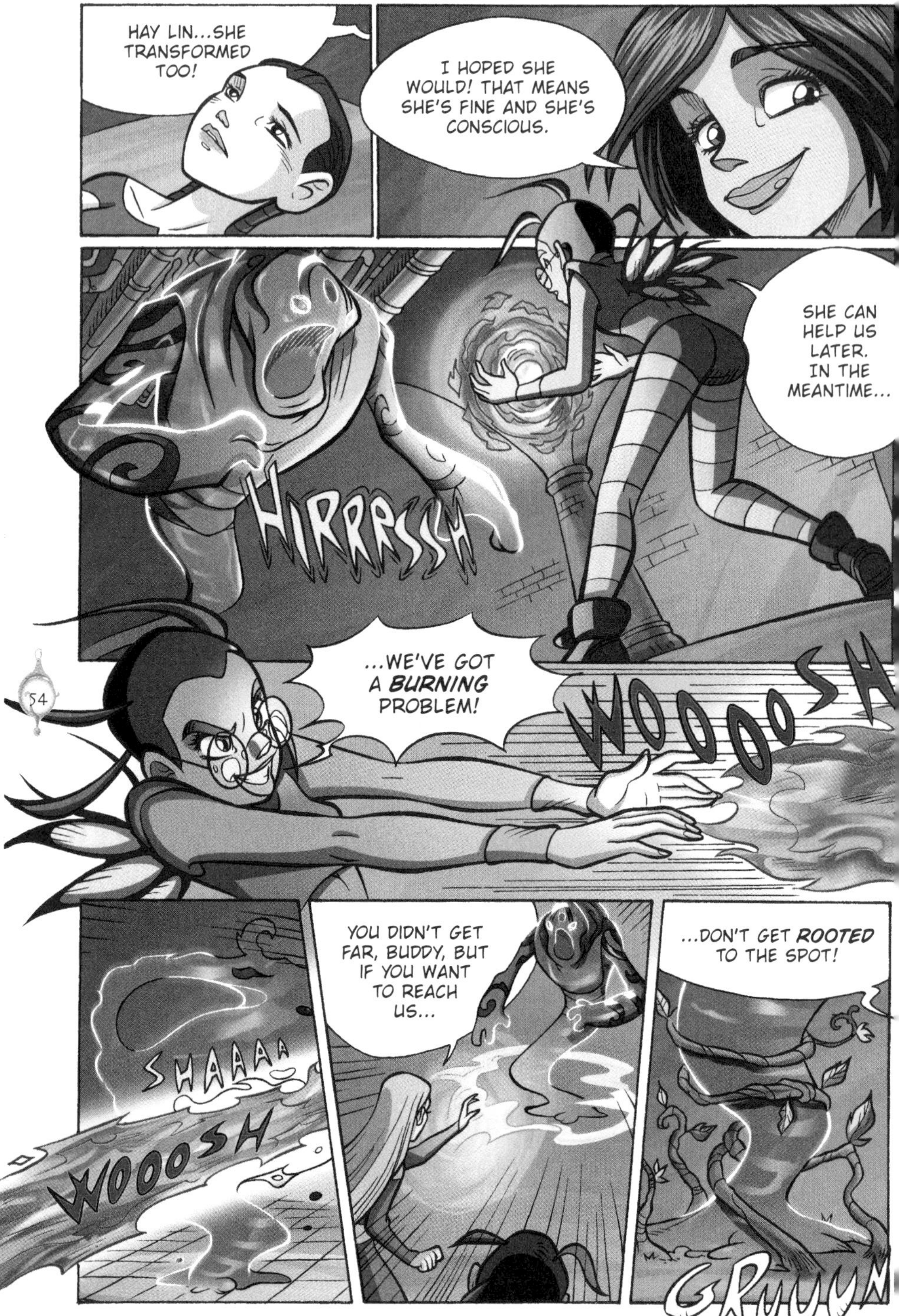
HAY LIN...SHE TRANSFORMED TOO!
I HOPED SHE WOULD! THAT MEANS SHE'S FINE AND SHE'S CONSCIOUS.
SHE CAN HELP US LATER. IN THE MEANTIME...
HIRRRSSSH
...WE'VE GOT A **BURNING** PROBLEM!
WOOOOSH
SHAAAA
WOOOSH
YOU DIDN'T GET FAR, BUDDY, BUT IF YOU WANT TO REACH US...
...DON'T GET **ROOTED** TO THE SPOT!
GRUUUN

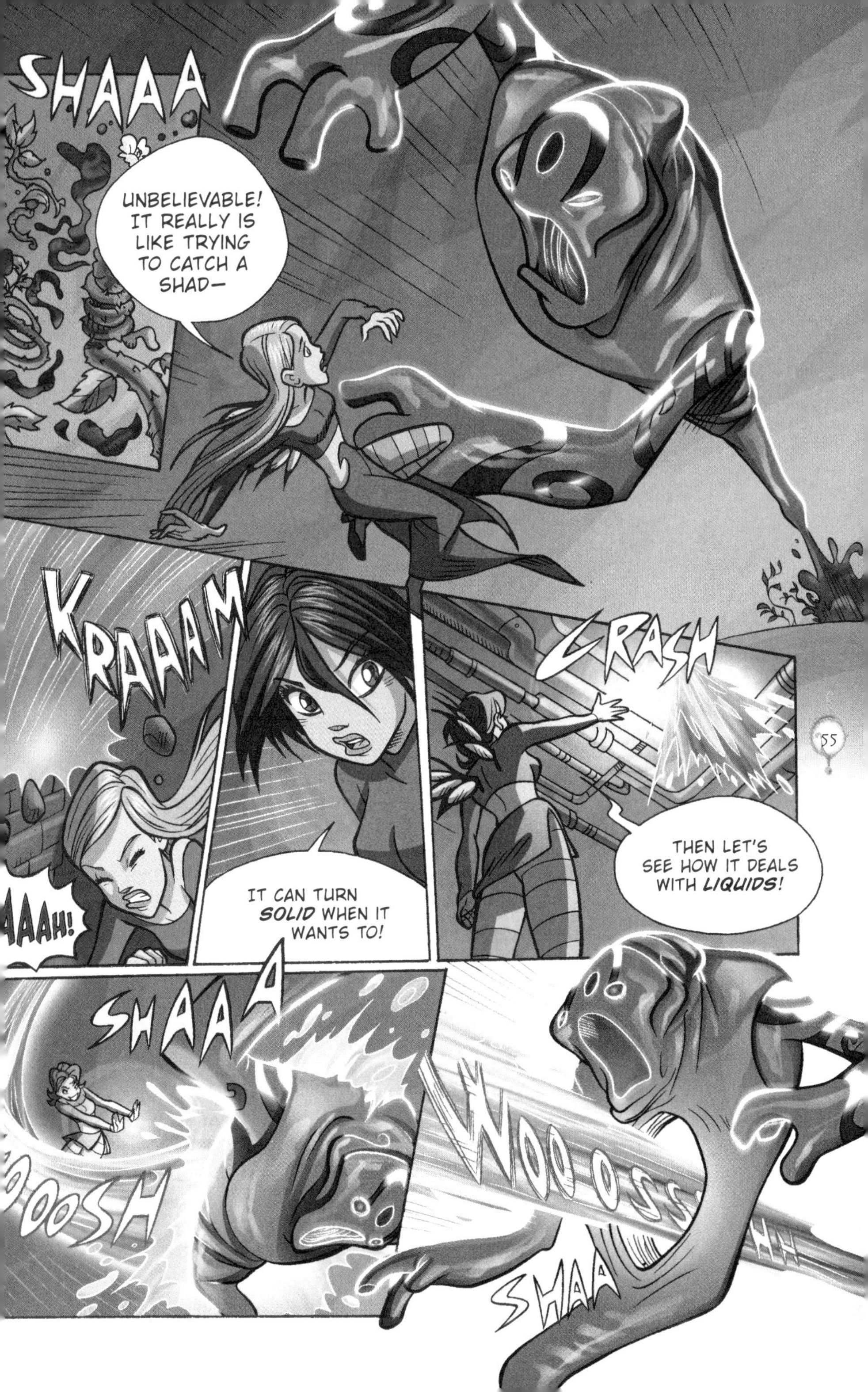
SHAAA
UNBELIEVABLE! IT REALLY IS LIKE TRYING TO CATCH A SHAD—
KRAAAM
AAAH!
IT CAN TURN SOLID WHEN IT WANTS TO!
CRASH
THEN LET'S SEE HOW IT DEALS WITH LIQUIDS!
SHAAA
WOOOSH
WOOOSSSHH
SHAA

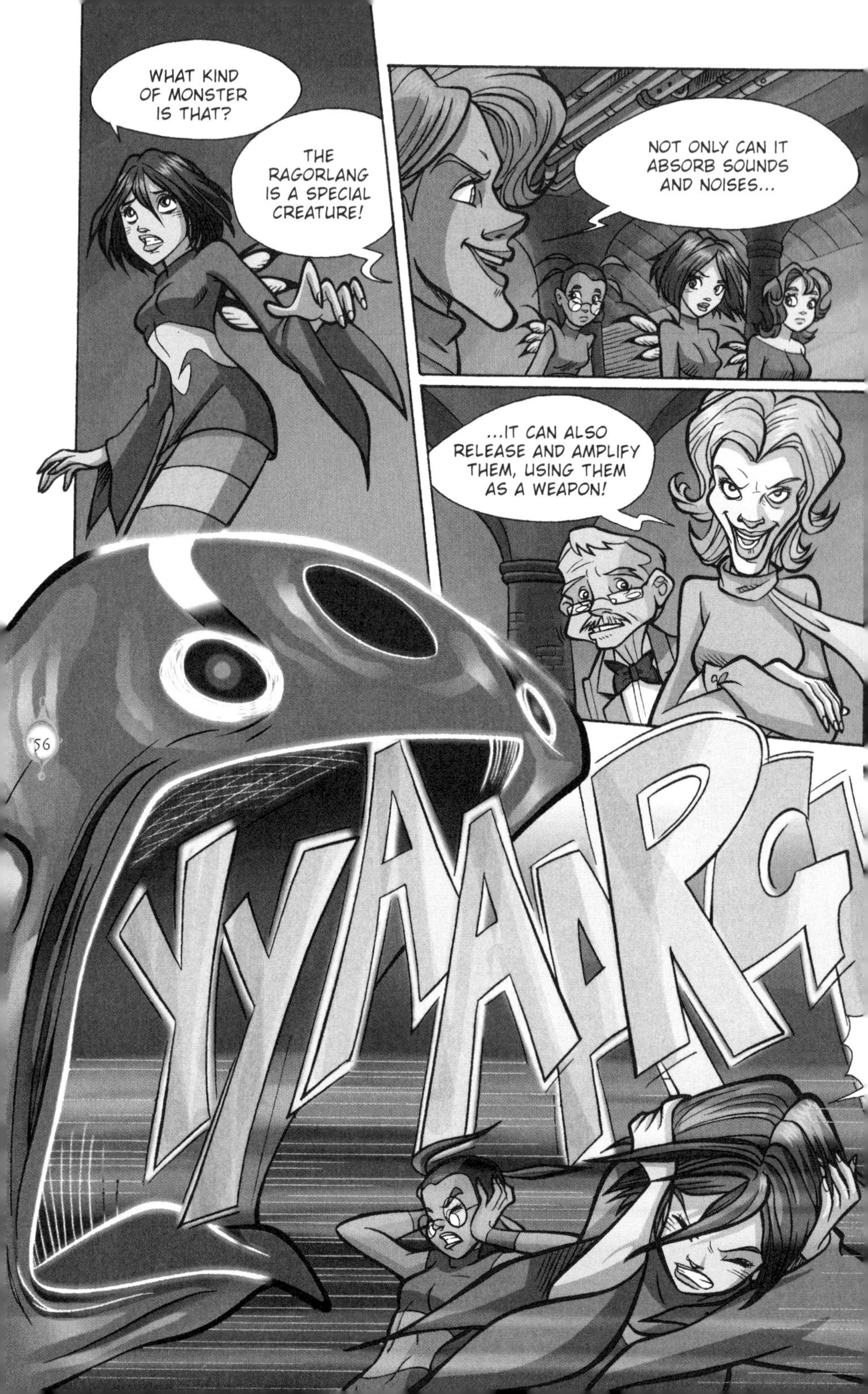
WHAT KIND OF MONSTER IS THAT?
THE RAGORLANG IS A SPECIAL CREATURE!
NOT ONLY CAN IT ABSORB SOUNDS AND NOISES...
...IT CAN ALSO RELEASE AND AMPLIFY THEM, USING THEM AS A WEAPON!
YYAARG

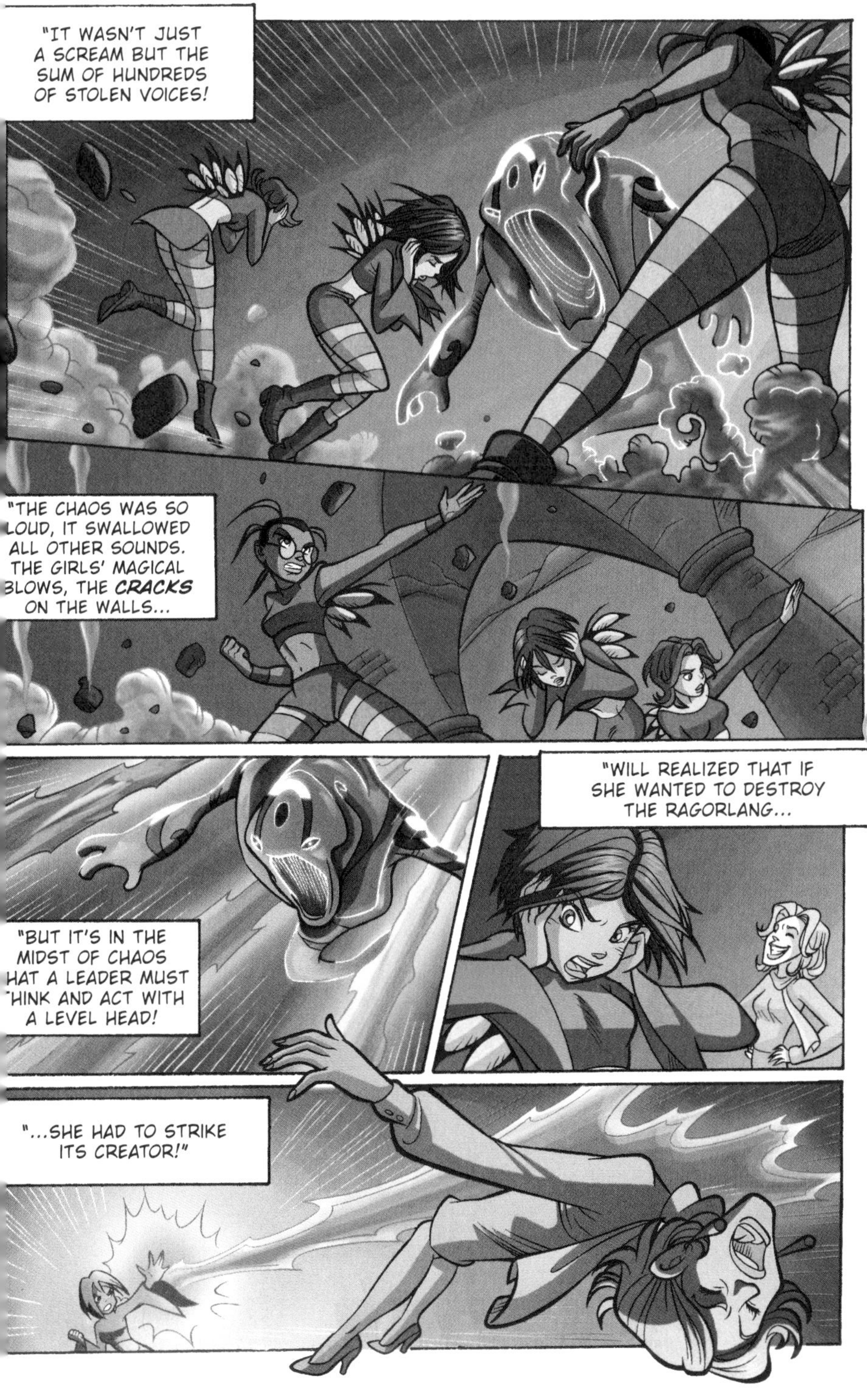
"IT WASN'T JUST A SCREAM BUT THE SUM OF HUNDREDS OF STOLEN VOICES!
"THE CHAOS WAS SO LOUD, IT SWALLOWED ALL OTHER SOUNDS. THE GIRLS' MAGICAL BLOWS, THE *CRACKS* ON THE WALLS...
"BUT IT'S IN THE MIDST OF CHAOS HAT A LEADER MUST HINK AND ACT WITH A LEVEL HEAD!
"WILL REALIZED THAT IF SHE WANTED TO DESTROY THE RAGORLANG...
"...SHE HAD TO STRIKE ITS CREATOR!"

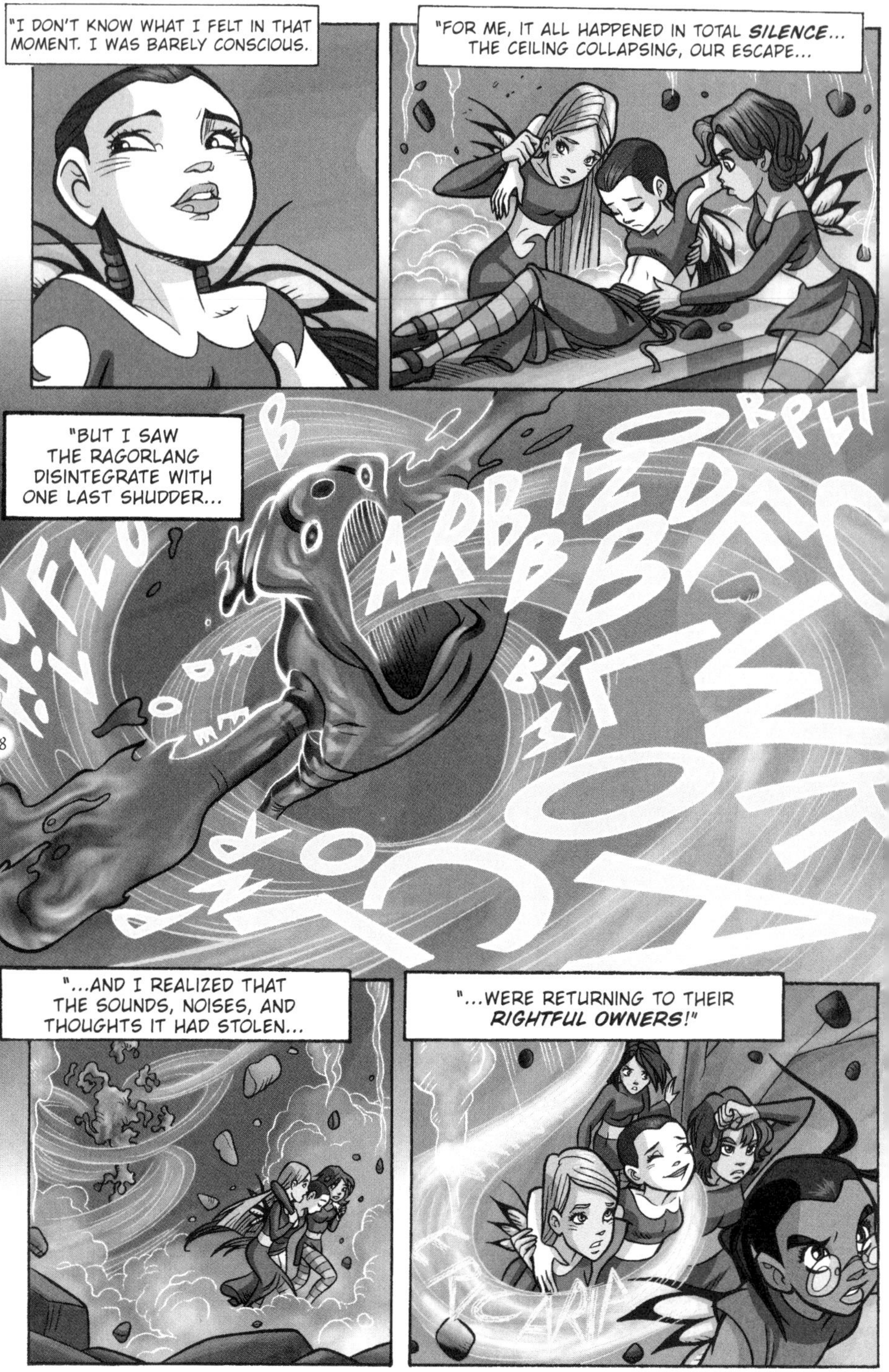
"I DON'T KNOW WHAT I FELT IN THAT MOMENT. I WAS BARELY CONSCIOUS.
"FOR ME, IT ALL HAPPENED IN TOTAL *SILENCE*... THE CEILING COLLAPSING, OUR ESCAPE...
"BUT I SAW THE RAGORLANG DISINTEGRATE WITH ONE LAST SHUDDER...
"...AND I REALIZED THAT THE SOUNDS, NOISES, AND THOUGHTS IT HAD STOLEN...
"...WERE RETURNING TO THEIR *RIGHTFUL OWNERS!*"

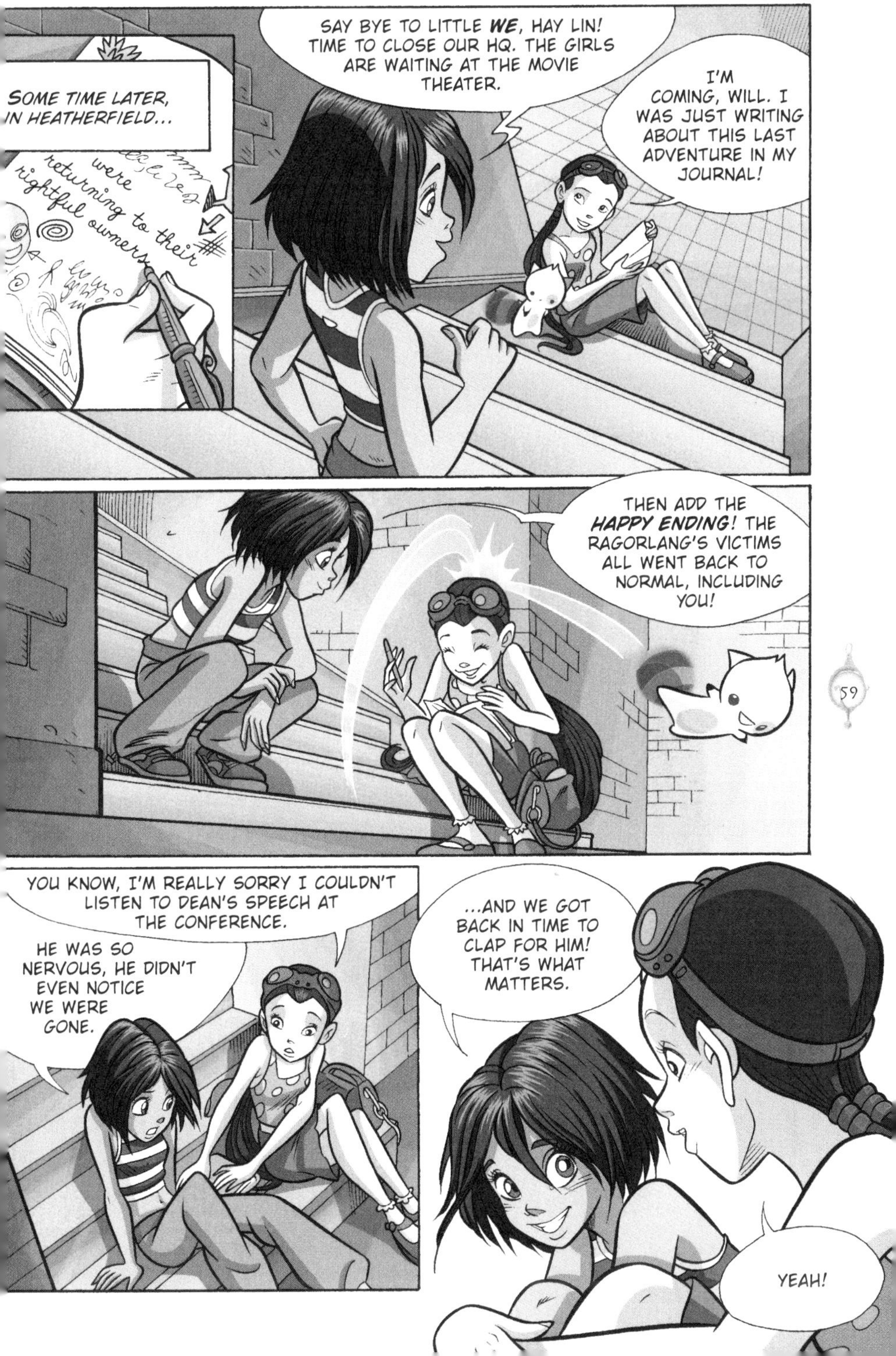
SOME TIME LATER, IN HEATHERFIELD...
were returning to their rightful owners
SAY BYE TO LITTLE **WE**, HAY LIN! TIME TO CLOSE OUR HQ. THE GIRLS ARE WAITING AT THE MOVIE THEATER.
I'M COMING, WILL. I WAS JUST WRITING ABOUT THIS LAST ADVENTURE IN MY JOURNAL!
THEN ADD THE ***HAPPY ENDING!*** THE RAGORLANG'S VICTIMS ALL WENT BACK TO NORMAL, INCLUDING YOU!
YOU KNOW, I'M REALLY SORRY I COULDN'T LISTEN TO DEAN'S SPEECH AT THE CONFERENCE.
HE WAS SO NERVOUS, HE DIDN'T EVEN NOTICE WE WERE GONE.
...AND WE GOT BACK IN TIME TO CLAP FOR HIM! THAT'S WHAT MATTERS.
YEAH!

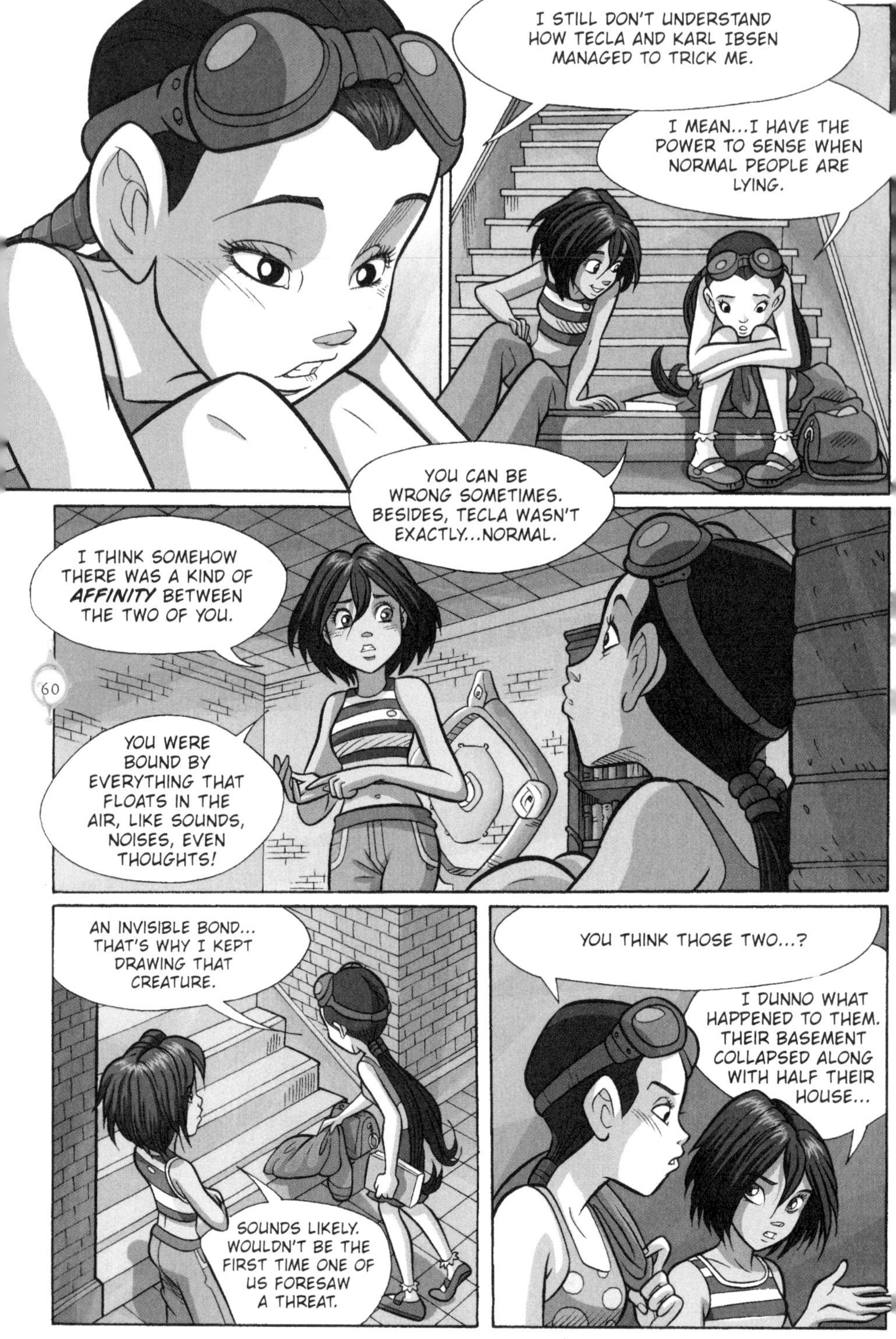
I STILL DON'T UNDERSTAND HOW TECLA AND KARL IBSEN MANAGED TO TRICK ME.
I MEAN...I HAVE THE POWER TO SENSE WHEN NORMAL PEOPLE ARE LYING.
YOU CAN BE WRONG SOMETIMES. BESIDES, TECLA WASN'T EXACTLY...NORMAL.
I THINK SOMEHOW THERE WAS A KIND OF *AFFINITY* BETWEEN THE TWO OF YOU.
YOU WERE BOUND BY EVERYTHING THAT FLOATS IN THE AIR, LIKE SOUNDS, NOISES, EVEN THOUGHTS!
AN INVISIBLE BOND... THAT'S WHY I KEPT DRAWING THAT CREATURE.
SOUNDS LIKELY. WOULDN'T BE THE FIRST TIME ONE OF US FORESAW A THREAT.
YOU THINK THOSE TWO...?
I DUNNO WHAT HAPPENED TO THEM. THEIR BASEMENT COLLAPSED ALONG WITH HALF THEIR HOUSE...

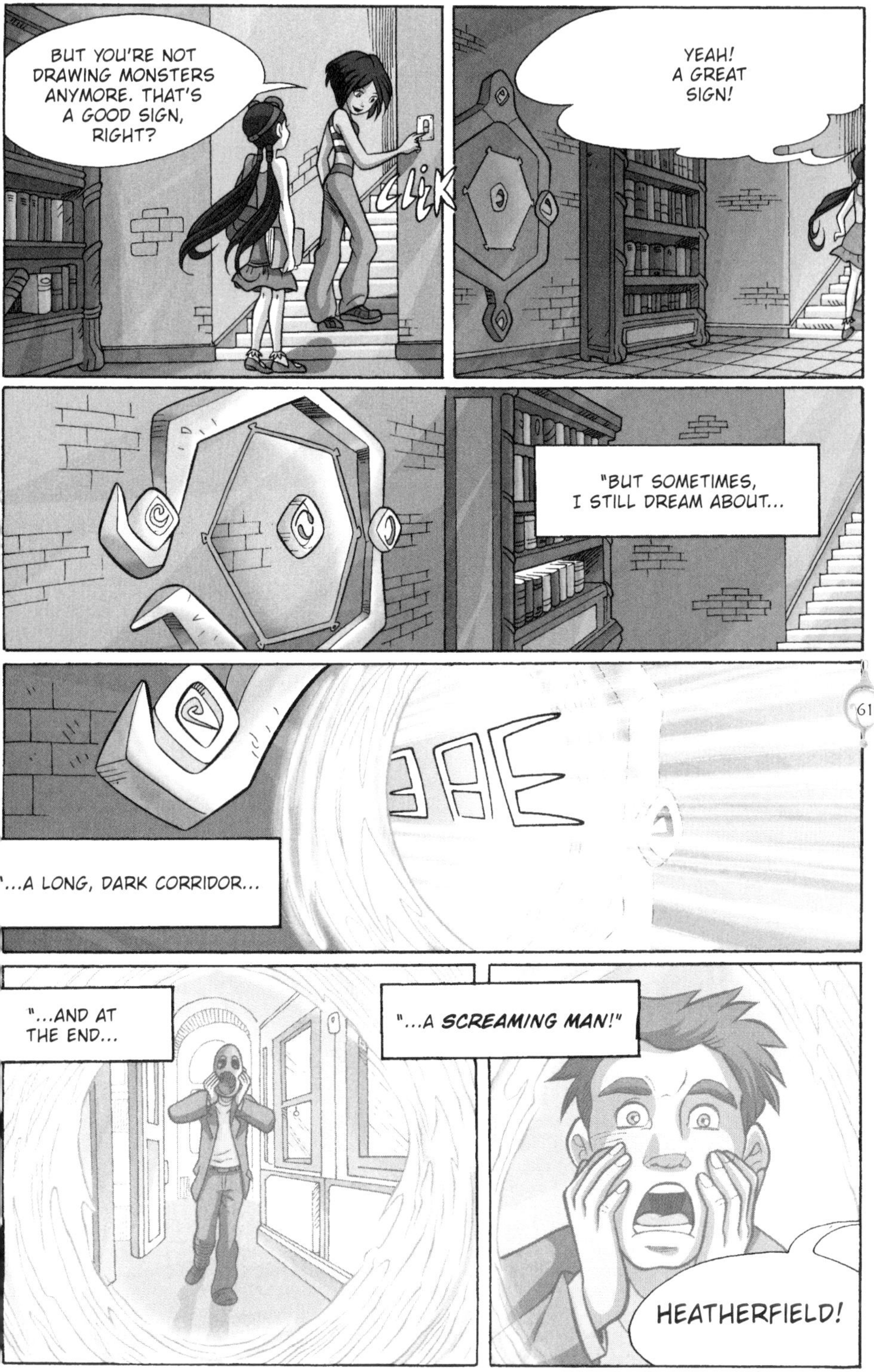
BUT YOU'RE NOT DRAWING MONSTERS ANYMORE. THAT'S A GOOD SIGN, RIGHT?
CLIK
YEAH! A GREAT SIGN!
"BUT SOMETIMES, I STILL DREAM ABOUT...
"...A LONG, DARK CORRIDOR...
"...AND AT THE END...
"...A *SCREAMING MAN!*"
HEATHERFIELD!

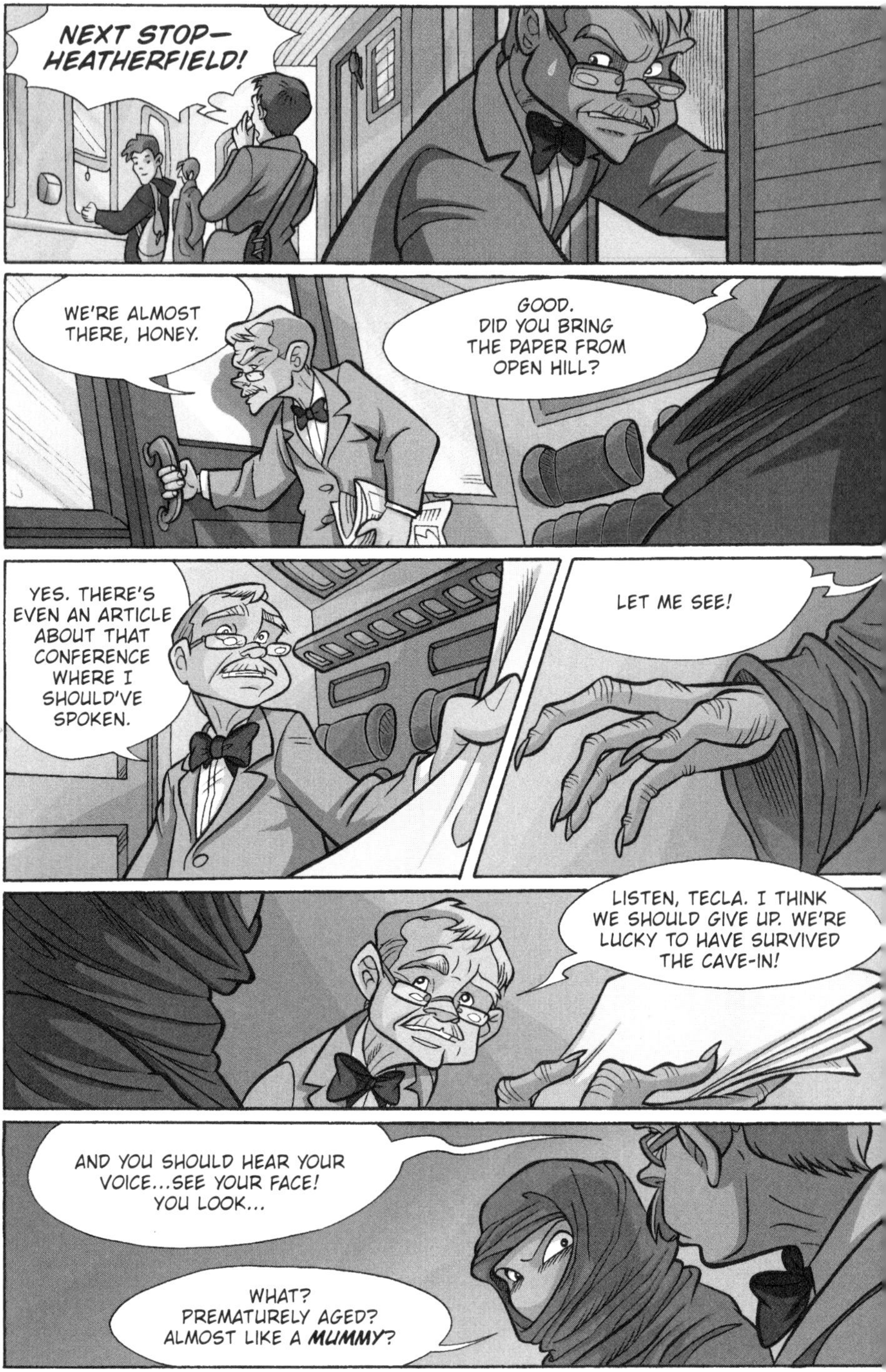
NEXT STOP— HEATHERFIELD!
WE'RE ALMOST THERE, HONEY.
GOOD. DID YOU BRING THE PAPER FROM OPEN HILL?
YES. THERE'S EVEN AN ARTICLE ABOUT THAT CONFERENCE WHERE I SHOULD'VE SPOKEN.
LET ME SEE!
LISTEN, TECLA. I THINK WE SHOULD GIVE UP. WE'RE LUCKY TO HAVE SURVIVED THE CAVE-IN!
AND YOU SHOULD HEAR YOUR VOICE...SEE YOUR FACE! YOU LOOK...
WHAT? PREMATURELY AGED? ALMOST LIKE A MUMMY?

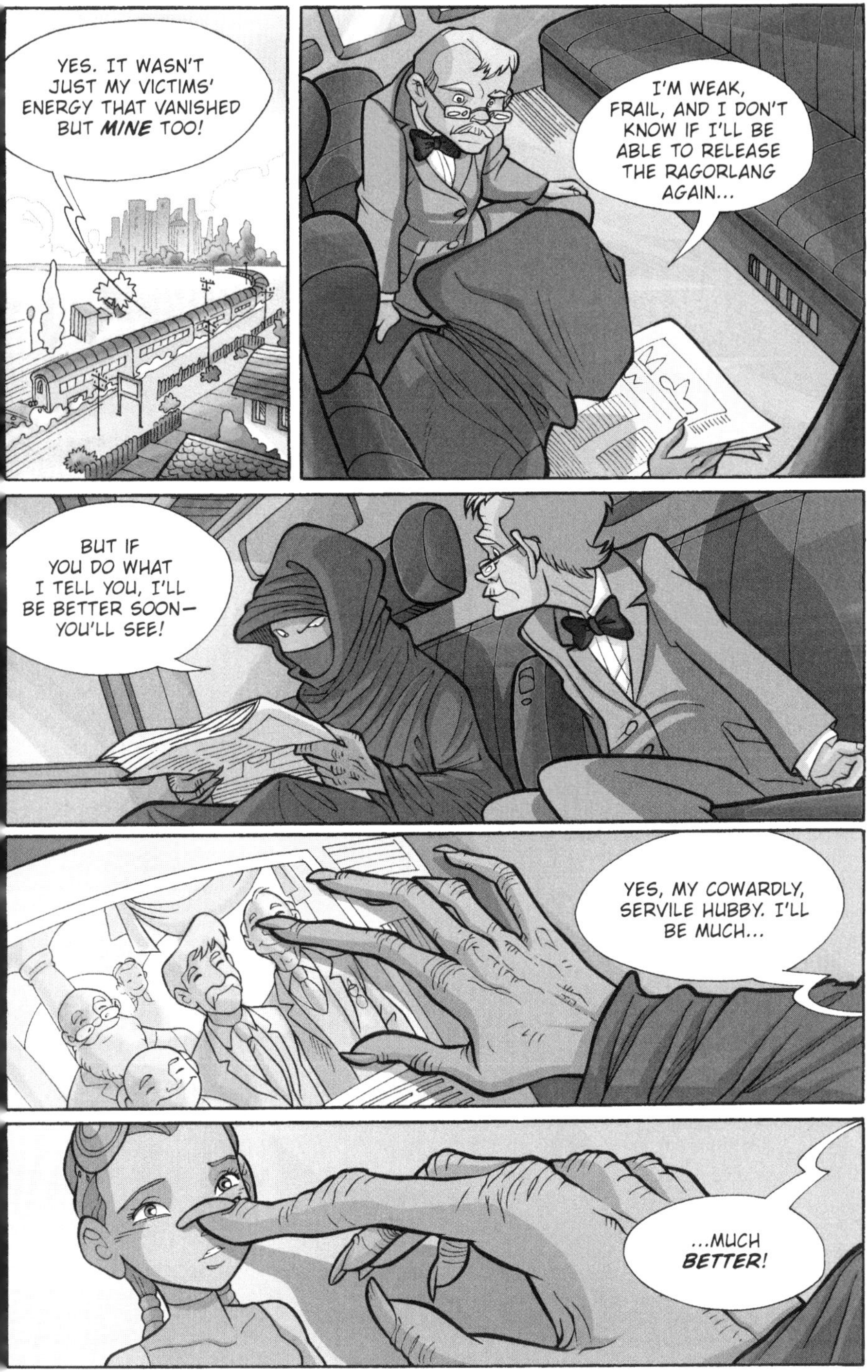
YES. IT WASN'T JUST MY VICTIMS' ENERGY THAT VANISHED BUT ***MINE*** TOO!
I'M WEAK, FRAIL, AND I DON'T KNOW IF I'LL BE ABLE TO RELEASE THE RAGORLANG AGAIN...
BUT IF YOU DO WHAT I TELL YOU, I'LL BE BETTER SOON—YOU'LL SEE!
YES, MY COWARDLY, SERVILE HUBBY. I'LL BE MUCH...
...MUCH ***BETTER!***

END OF CHAPTER 64

Will   Irma   Taranee   Cornelia   Hay Lin

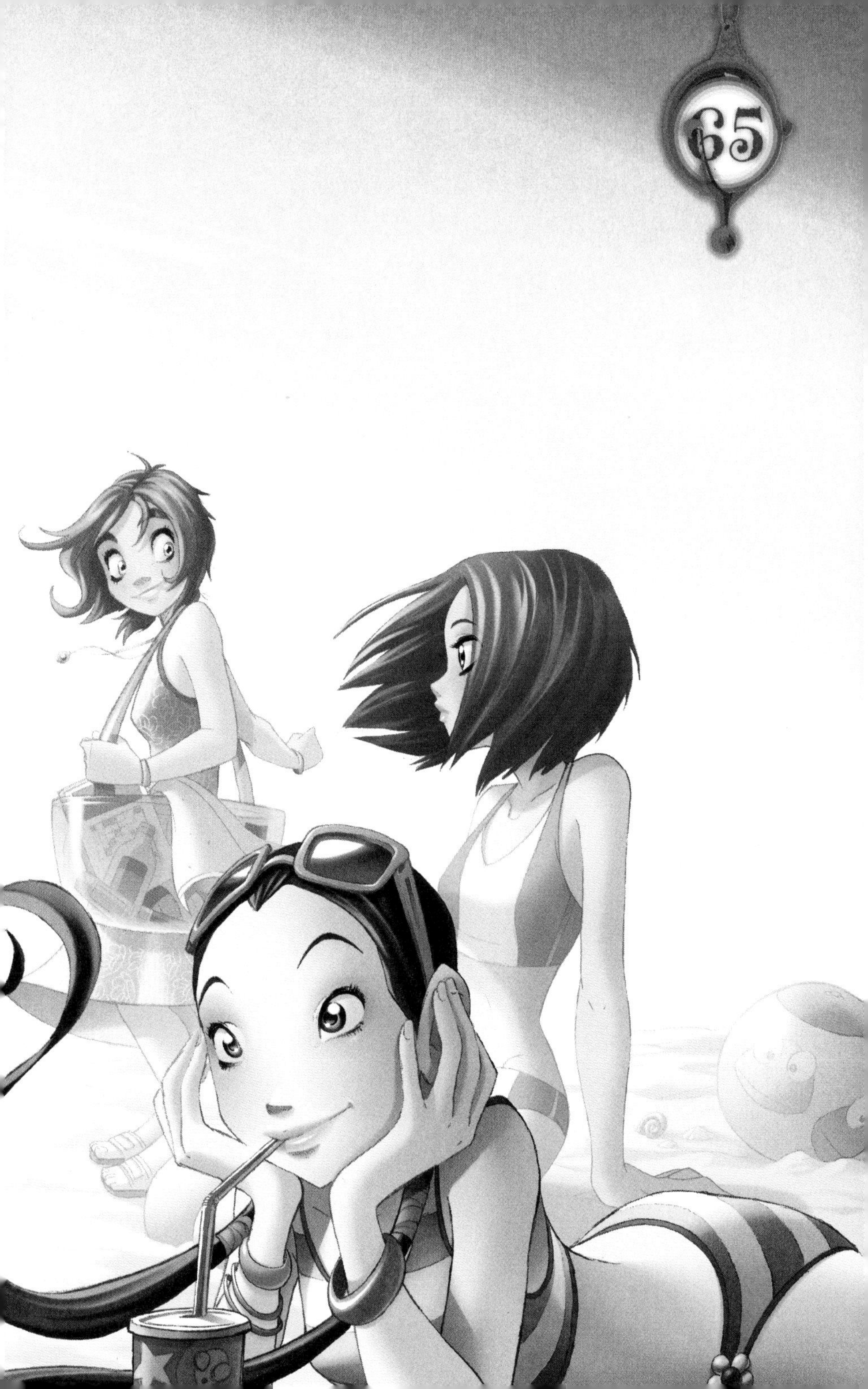
65

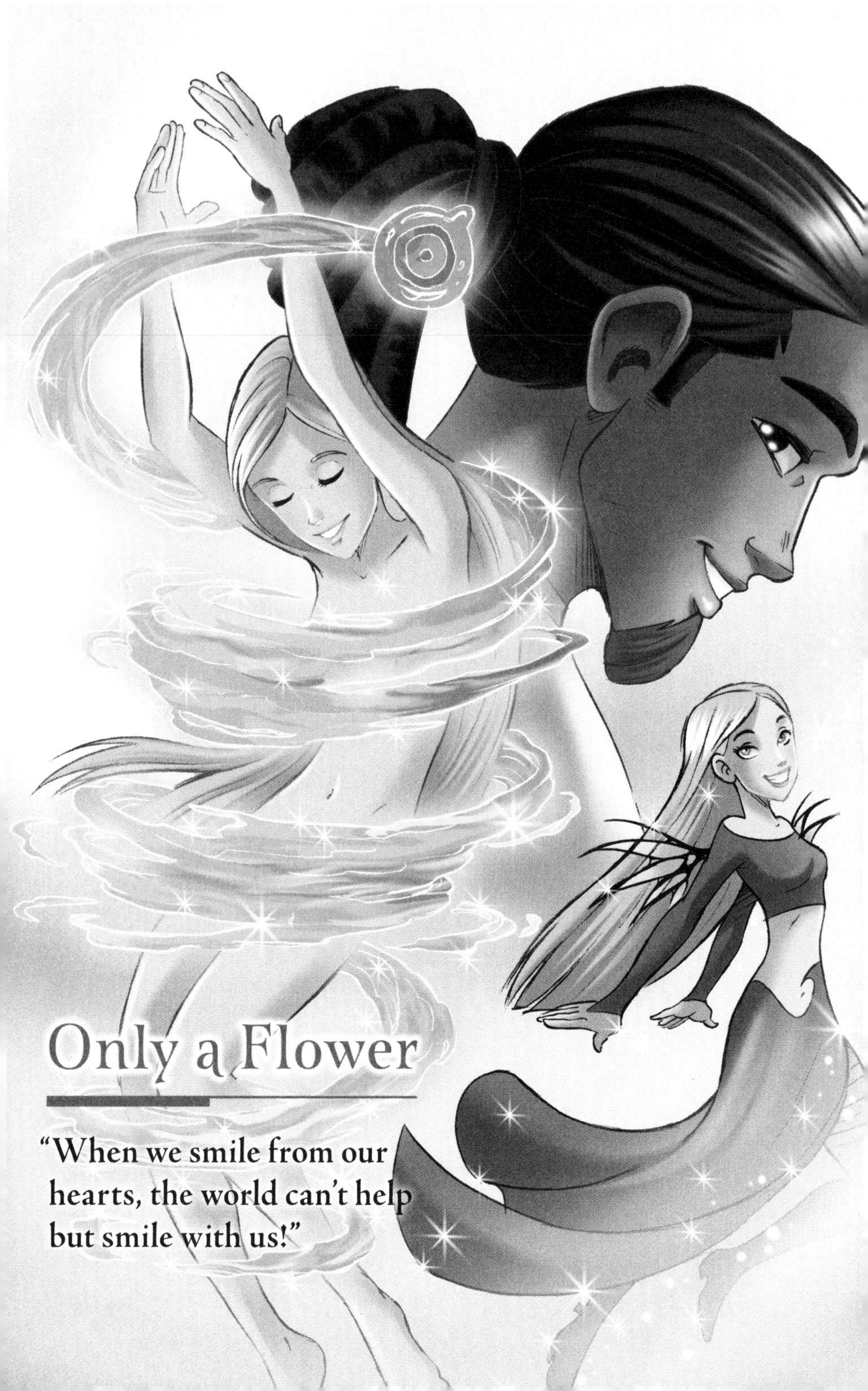

Only a Flower

"When we smile from our hearts, the world can't help but smile with us!"

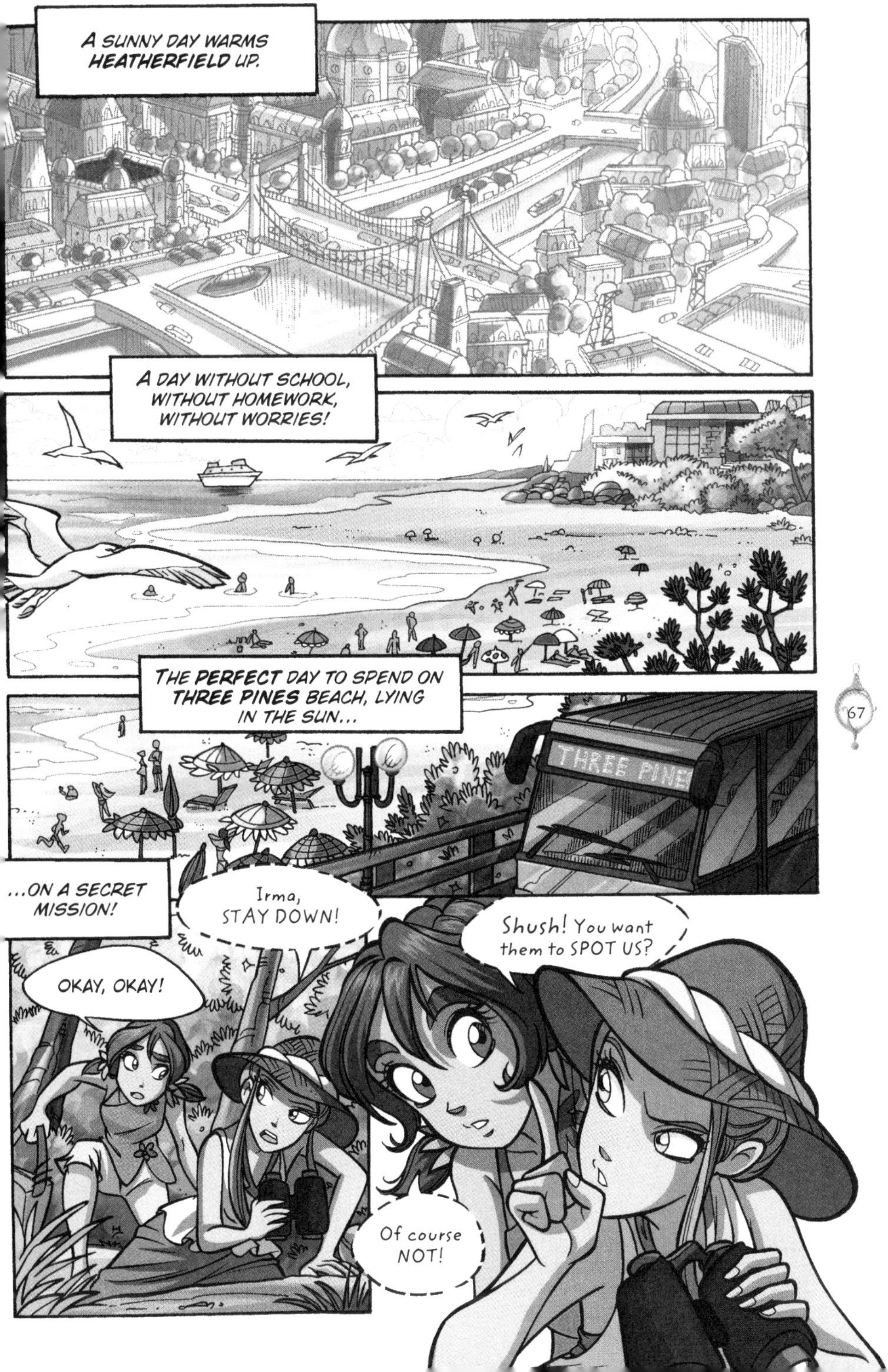
A SUNNY DAY WARMS HEATHERFIELD UP.
A DAY WITHOUT SCHOOL, WITHOUT HOMEWORK, WITHOUT WORRIES!
THE PERFECT DAY TO SPEND ON THREE PINES BEACH, LYING IN THE SUN...
THREE PINES
...ON A SECRET MISSION!
Irma, STAY DOWN!
OKAY, OKAY!
Shush! You want them to SPOT US?
Of course NOT!

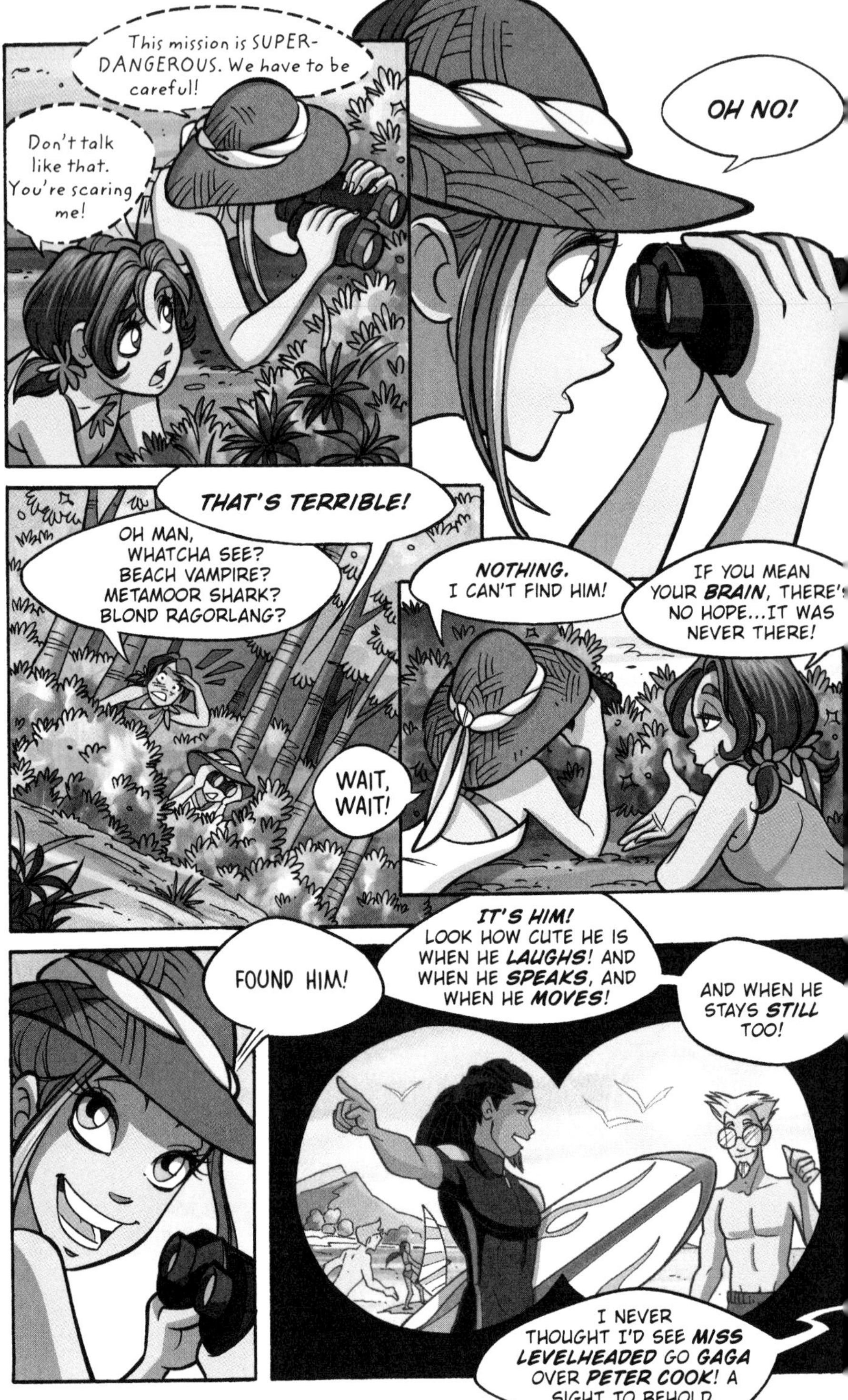

This mission is SUPER-DANGEROUS. We have to be careful!
Don't talk like that. You're scaring me!
OH NO!
THAT'S TERRIBLE!
OH MAN, WHATCHA SEE? BEACH VAMPIRE? METAMOOR SHARK? BLOND RAGORLANG?
WAIT, WAIT!
NOTHING. I CAN'T FIND HIM!
IF YOU MEAN YOUR BRAIN, THERE'S NO HOPE...IT WAS NEVER THERE!
FOUND HIM!
IT'S HIM! LOOK HOW CUTE HE IS WHEN HE LAUGHS! AND WHEN HE SPEAKS, AND WHEN HE MOVES!
AND WHEN HE STAYS STILL TOO!
I NEVER THOUGHT I'D SEE MISS LEVELHEADED GO GAGA OVER PETER COOK! A SIGHT TO BEHOLD.

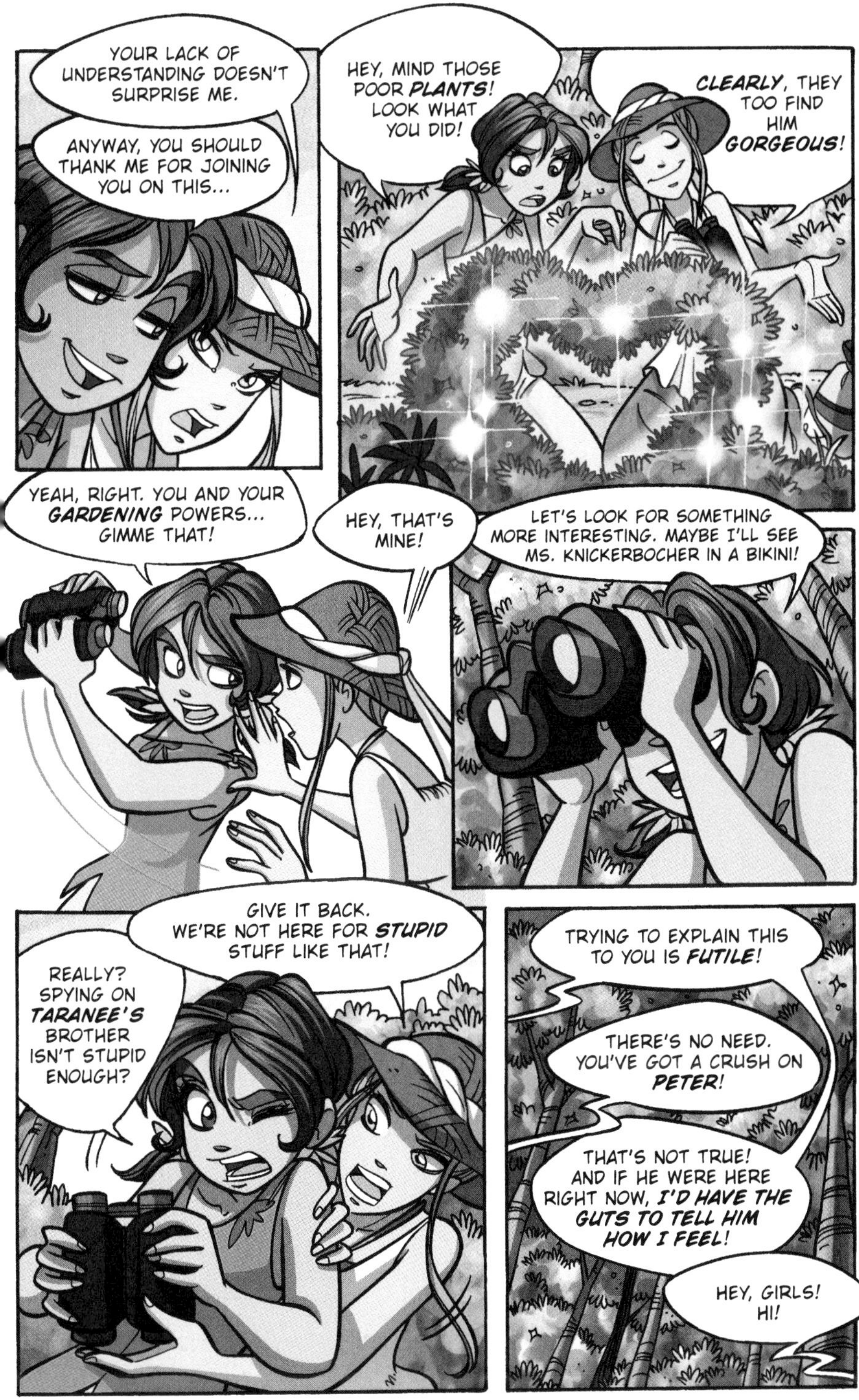
YOUR LACK OF UNDERSTANDING DOESN'T SURPRISE ME.
ANYWAY, YOU SHOULD THANK ME FOR JOINING YOU ON THIS...
HEY, MIND THOSE POOR PLANTS! LOOK WHAT YOU DID!
CLEARLY, THEY TOO FIND HIM GORGEOUS!
YEAH, RIGHT. YOU AND YOUR GARDENING POWERS... GIMME THAT!
HEY, THAT'S MINE!
LET'S LOOK FOR SOMETHING MORE INTERESTING. MAYBE I'LL SEE MS. KNICKERBOCHER IN A BIKINI!
GIVE IT BACK. WE'RE NOT HERE FOR STUPID STUFF LIKE THAT!
REALLY? SPYING ON TARANEE'S BROTHER ISN'T STUPID ENOUGH?
TRYING TO EXPLAIN THIS TO YOU IS FUTILE!
THERE'S NO NEED. YOU'VE GOT A CRUSH ON PETER!
THAT'S NOT TRUE! AND IF HE WERE HERE RIGHT NOW, I'D HAVE THE GUTS TO TELL HIM HOW I FEEL!
HEY, GIRLS! HI!

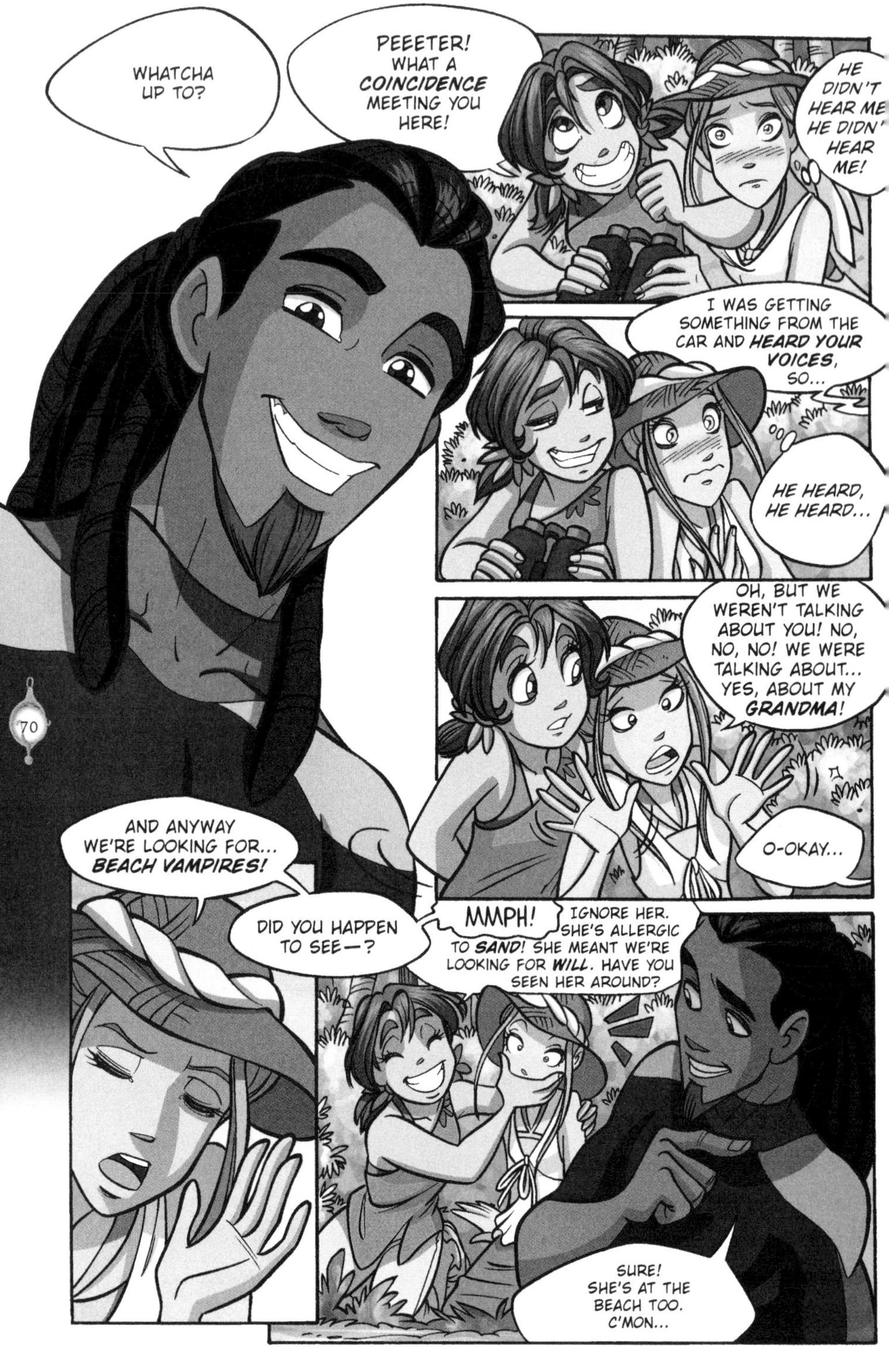
WHATCHA UP TO?
PEEETER! WHAT A COINCIDENCE MEETING YOU HERE!
HE DIDN'T HEAR ME HE DIDN' HEAR ME!
I WAS GETTING SOMETHING FROM THE CAR AND HEARD YOUR VOICES, SO...
HE HEARD, HE HEARD...
OH, BUT WE WEREN'T TALKING ABOUT YOU! NO, NO, NO! WE WERE TALKING ABOUT... YES, ABOUT MY GRANDMA!
O-OKAY...
AND ANYWAY WE'RE LOOKING FOR... BEACH VAMPIRES!
DID YOU HAPPEN TO SEE—?
MMPH!
IGNORE HER. SHE'S ALLERGIC TO SAND! SHE MEANT WE'RE LOOKING FOR WILL. HAVE YOU SEEN HER AROUND?
SURE! SHE'S AT THE BEACH TOO. C'MON...

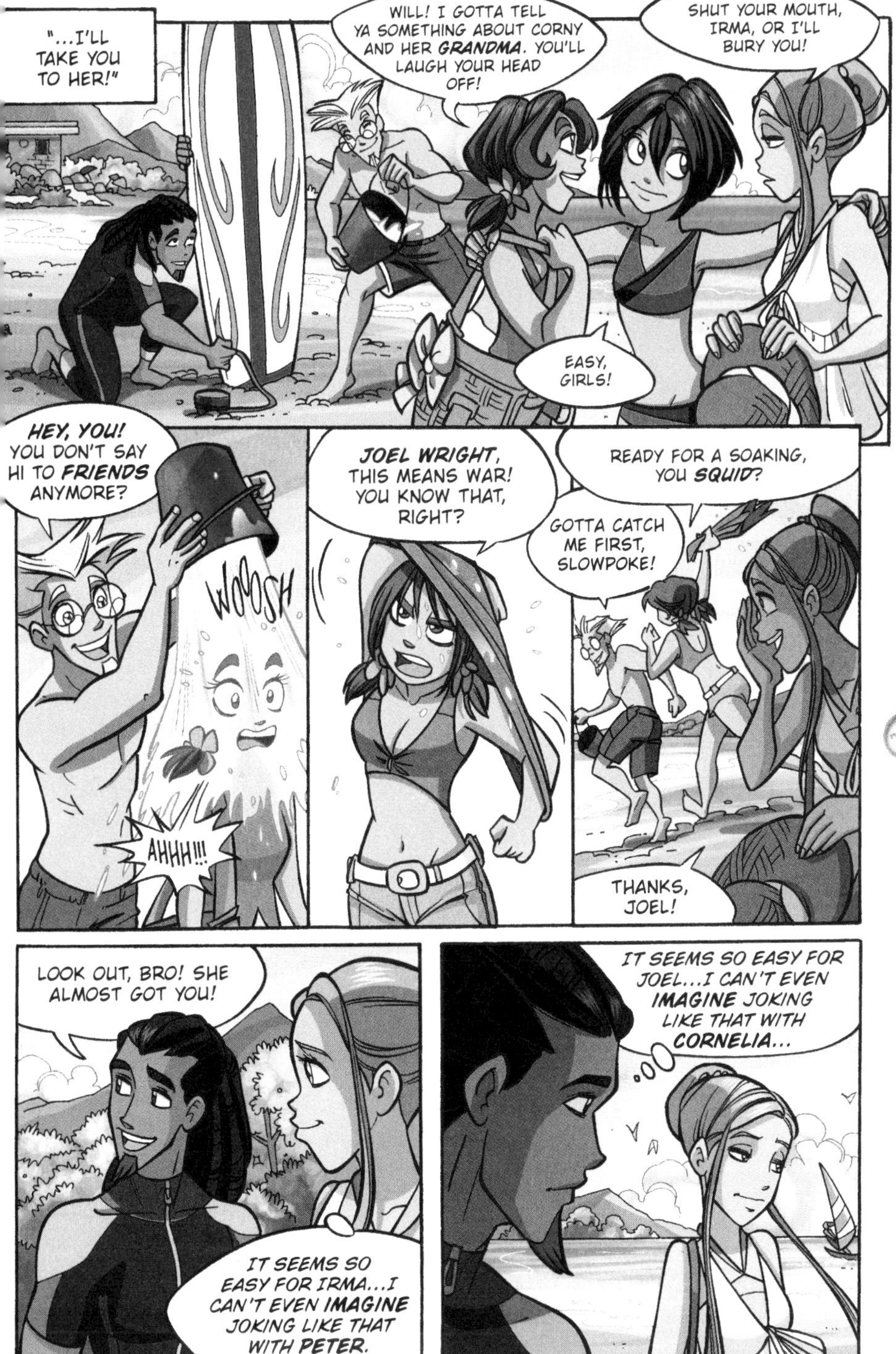
"...I'LL TAKE YOU TO HER!"
WILL! I GOTTA TELL YA SOMETHING ABOUT CORNY AND HER **GRANDMA**. YOU'LL LAUGH YOUR HEAD OFF!
SHUT YOUR MOUTH, IRMA, OR I'LL BURY YOU!
EASY, GIRLS!
HEY, YOU! YOU DON'T SAY HI TO **FRIENDS** ANYMORE?
WOOOSH
AHHH!!!
JOEL WRIGHT, THIS MEANS WAR! YOU KNOW THAT, RIGHT?
READY FOR A SOAKING, YOU **SQUID**?
GOTTA CATCH ME FIRST, SLOWPOKE!
THANKS, JOEL!
LOOK OUT, BRO! SHE ALMOST GOT YOU!
IT SEEMS SO EASY FOR IRMA...I CAN'T EVEN **IMAGINE** JOKING LIKE THAT WITH **PETER**.
IT SEEMS SO EASY FOR JOEL...I CAN'T EVEN **IMAGINE** JOKING LIKE THAT WITH **CORNELIA**...

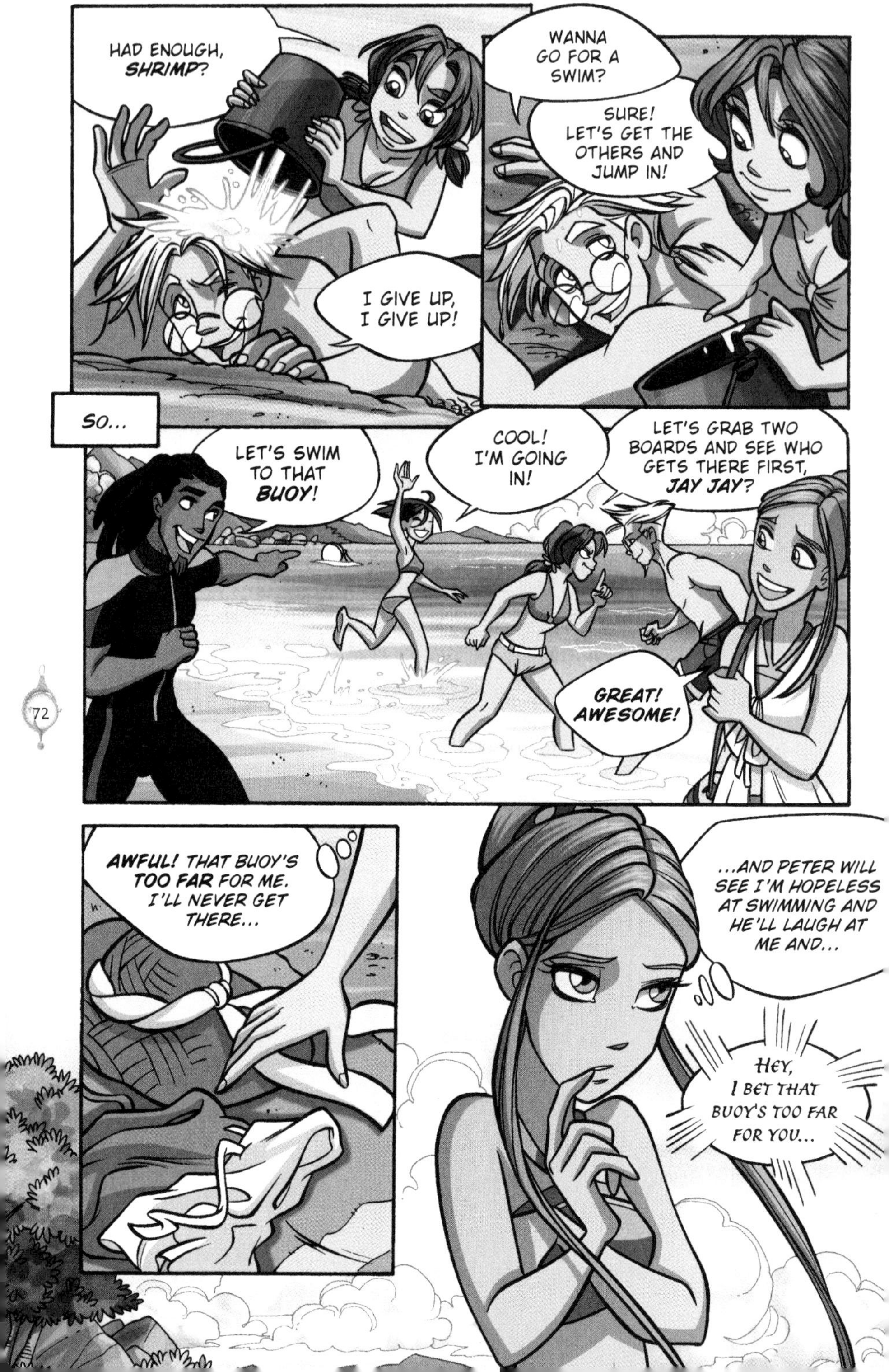
HAD ENOUGH, SHRIMP?
I GIVE UP, I GIVE UP!
WANNA GO FOR A SWIM?
SURE! LET'S GET THE OTHERS AND JUMP IN!
SO...
LET'S SWIM TO THAT BUOY!
COOL! I'M GOING IN!
LET'S GRAB TWO BOARDS AND SEE WHO GETS THERE FIRST, JAY JAY?
GREAT! AWESOME!
AWFUL! THAT BUOY'S TOO FAR FOR ME. I'LL NEVER GET THERE...
...AND PETER WILL SEE I'M HOPELESS AT SWIMMING AND HE'LL LAUGH AT ME AND...
HEY, I BET THAT BUOY'S TOO FAR FOR YOU...

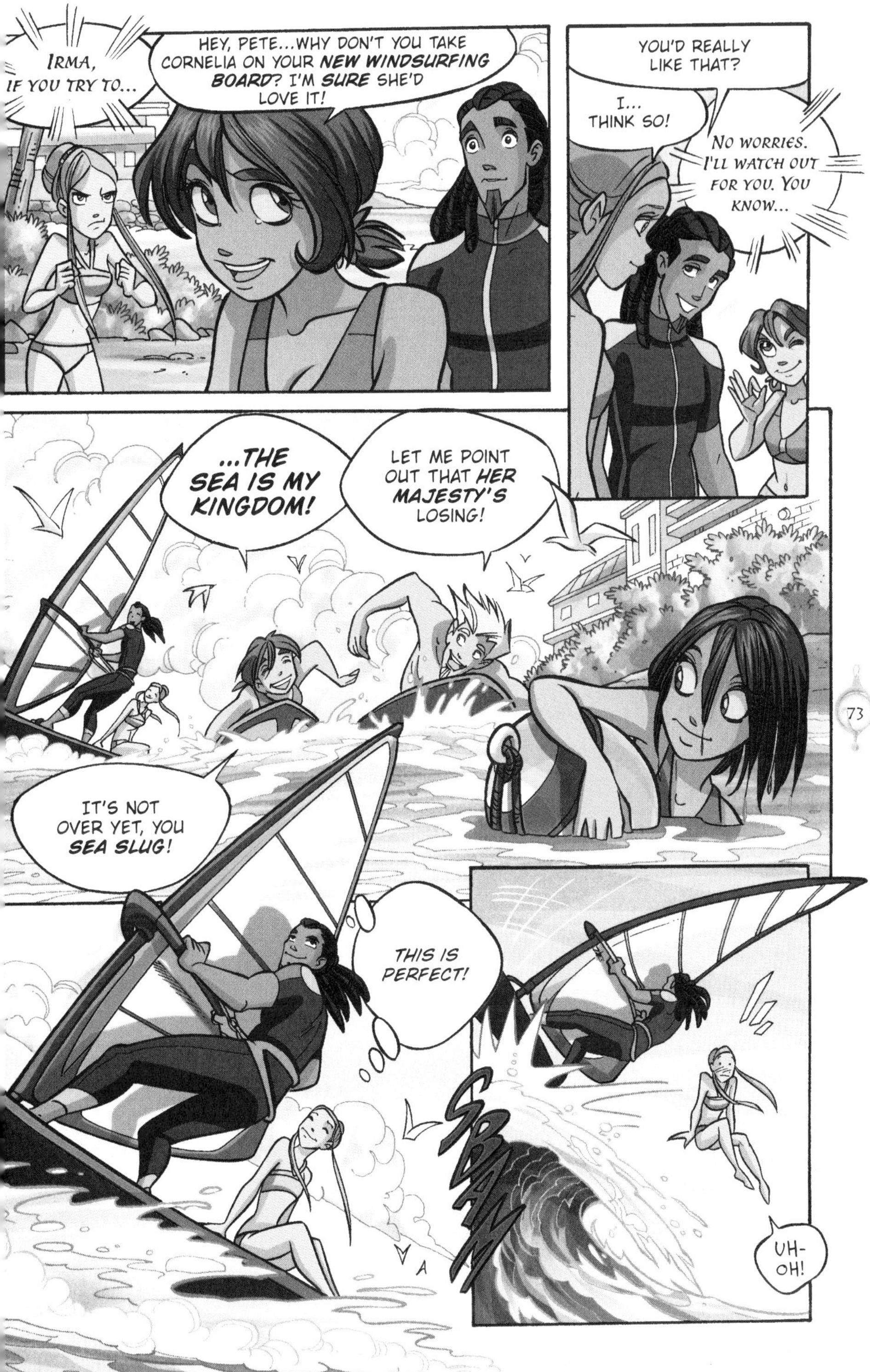
IRMA, IF YOU TRY TO...
HEY, PETE...WHY DON'T YOU TAKE CORNELIA ON YOUR NEW WINDSURFING BOARD? I'M SURE SHE'D LOVE IT!
YOU'D REALLY LIKE THAT?
I... THINK SO!
NO WORRIES. I'LL WATCH OUT FOR YOU. YOU KNOW...
...THE SEA IS MY KINGDOM!
LET ME POINT OUT THAT HER MAJESTY'S LOSING!
IT'S NOT OVER YET, YOU SEA SLUG!
THIS IS PERFECT!
SBAM
UH-OH!

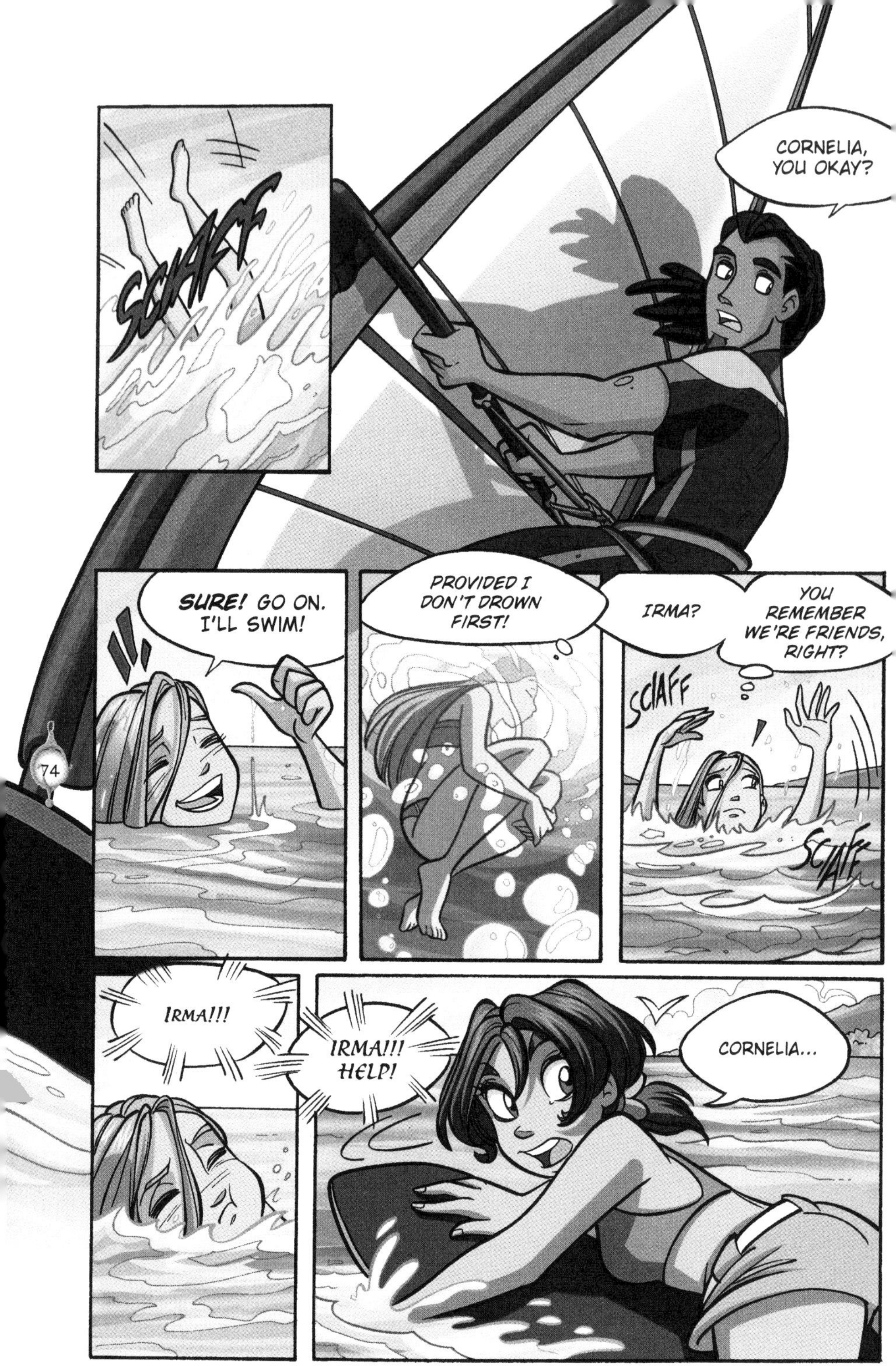
SCIAFF
CORNELIA, YOU OKAY?
SURE! GO ON. I'LL SWIM!
PROVIDED I DON'T DROWN FIRST!
IRMA?
YOU REMEMBER WE'RE FRIENDS, RIGHT?
SCIAFF
SCIAFF
IRMA!!!
IRMA!!! HELP!
CORNELIA...

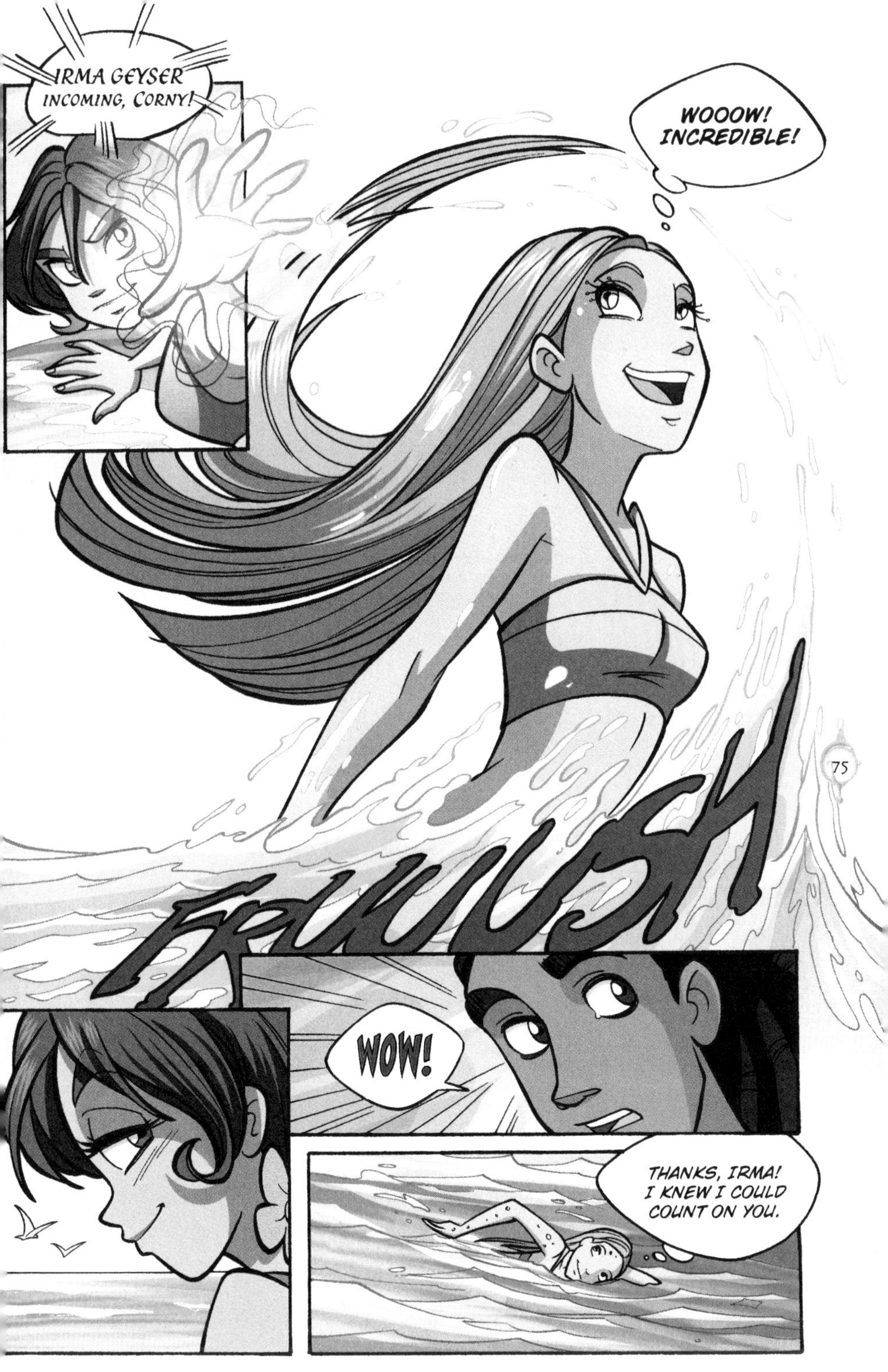
IRMA GEYSER INCOMING, CORNY!
WOOOW! INCREDIBLE!
FRUUUSH
WOW!
THANKS, IRMA! I KNEW I COULD COUNT ON YOU.

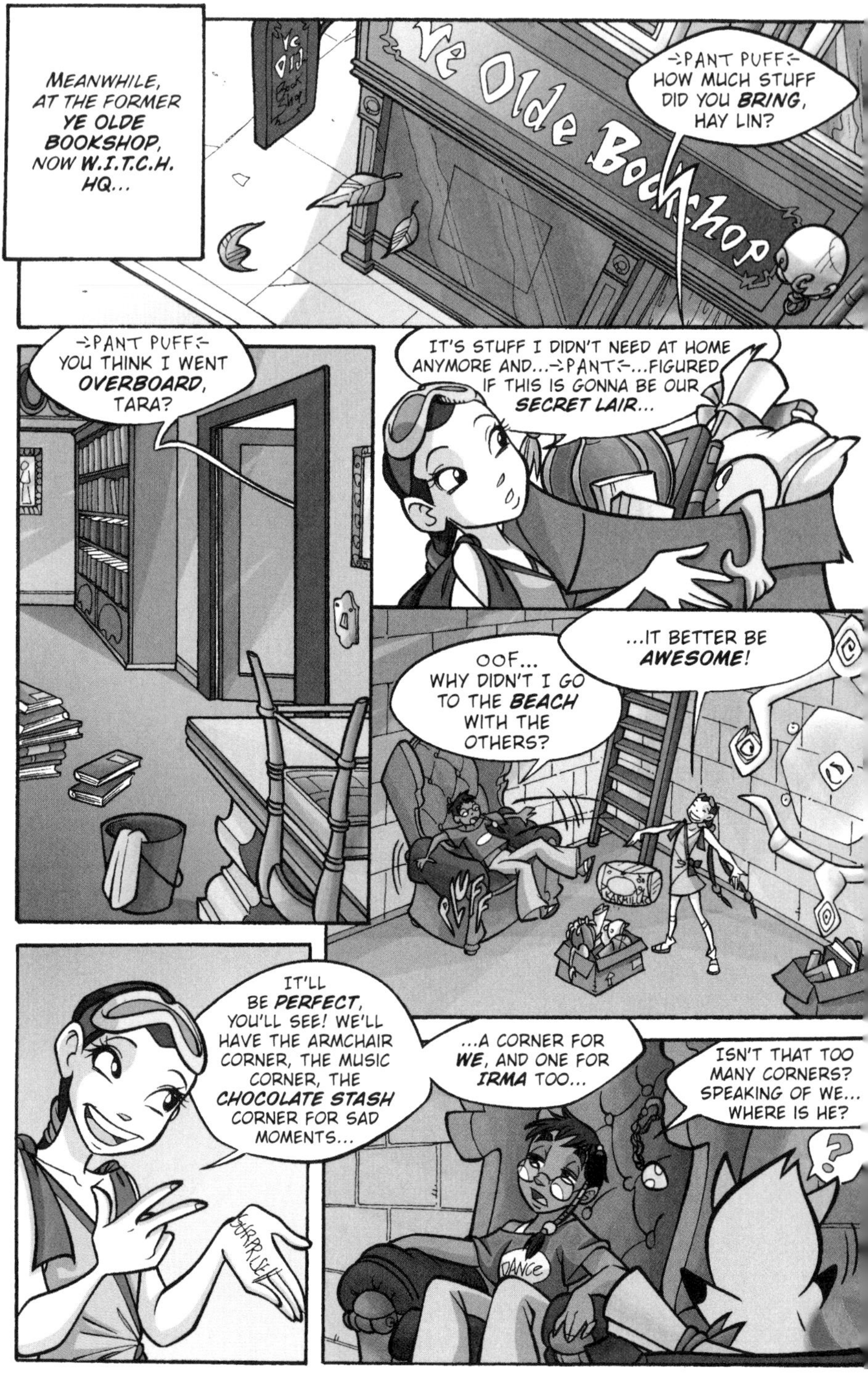
MEANWHILE, AT THE FORMER YE OLDE BOOKSHOP, NOW W.I.T.C.H. HQ...
Ye Olde Bookshop
=PANT PUFF= HOW MUCH STUFF DID YOU BRING, HAY LIN?
=PANT PUFF= YOU THINK I WENT OVERBOARD, TARA?
IT'S STUFF I DIDN'T NEED AT HOME ANYMORE AND...=PANT=...FIGURED IF THIS IS GONNA BE OUR SECRET LAIR...
...IT BETTER BE AWESOME!
OOF... WHY DIDN'T I GO TO THE BEACH WITH THE OTHERS?
IT'LL BE PERFECT, YOU'LL SEE! WE'LL HAVE THE ARMCHAIR CORNER, THE MUSIC CORNER, THE CHOCOLATE STASH CORNER FOR SAD MOMENTS...
...A CORNER FOR WE, AND ONE FOR IRMA TOO...
ISN'T THAT TOO MANY CORNERS? SPEAKING OF WE... WHERE IS HE?
?
SURPRISE!
DANCE

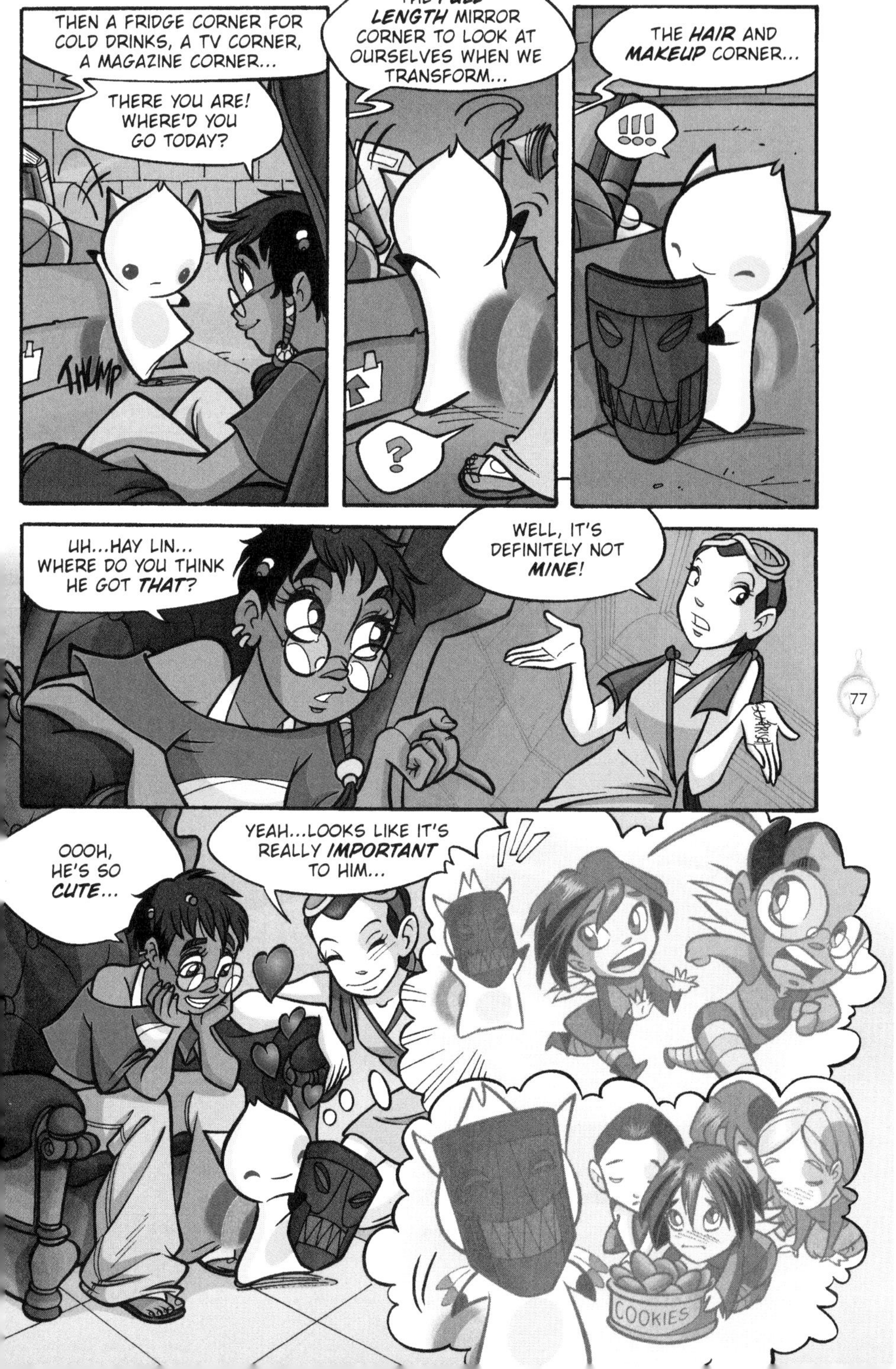
THEN A FRIDGE CORNER FOR COLD DRINKS, A TV CORNER, A MAGAZINE CORNER...
THERE YOU ARE! WHERE'D YOU GO TODAY?
THUMP
THE FULL-LENGTH MIRROR CORNER TO LOOK AT OURSELVES WHEN WE TRANSFORM...
?
THE HAIR AND MAKEUP CORNER...
!!!
UH...HAY LIN... WHERE DO YOU THINK HE GOT THAT?
WELL, IT'S DEFINITELY NOT MINE!
OOOH, HE'S SO CUTE...
YEAH...LOOKS LIKE IT'S REALLY IMPORTANT TO HIM...
COOKIES

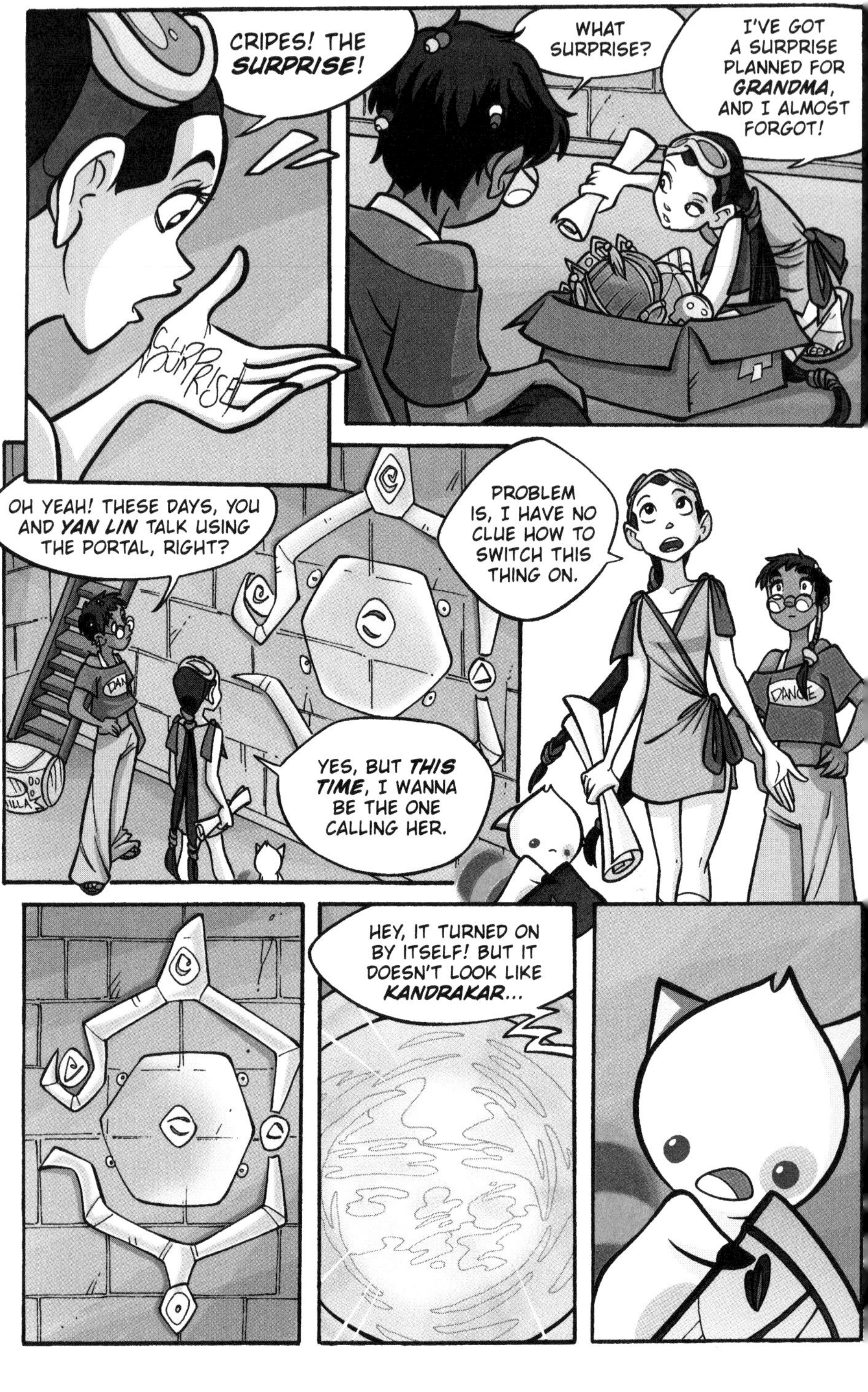
CRIPES! THE *SURPRISE*!
SURPRISE
WHAT SURPRISE?
I'VE GOT A SURPRISE PLANNED FOR *GRANDMA*, AND I ALMOST FORGOT!
OH YEAH! THESE DAYS, YOU AND *YAN LIN* TALK USING THE PORTAL, RIGHT?
YES, BUT *THIS TIME*, I WANNA BE THE ONE CALLING HER.
PROBLEM IS, I HAVE NO CLUE HOW TO SWITCH THIS THING ON.
DANCE
HEY, IT TURNED ON BY ITSELF! BUT IT DOESN'T LOOK LIKE *KANDRAKAR*...

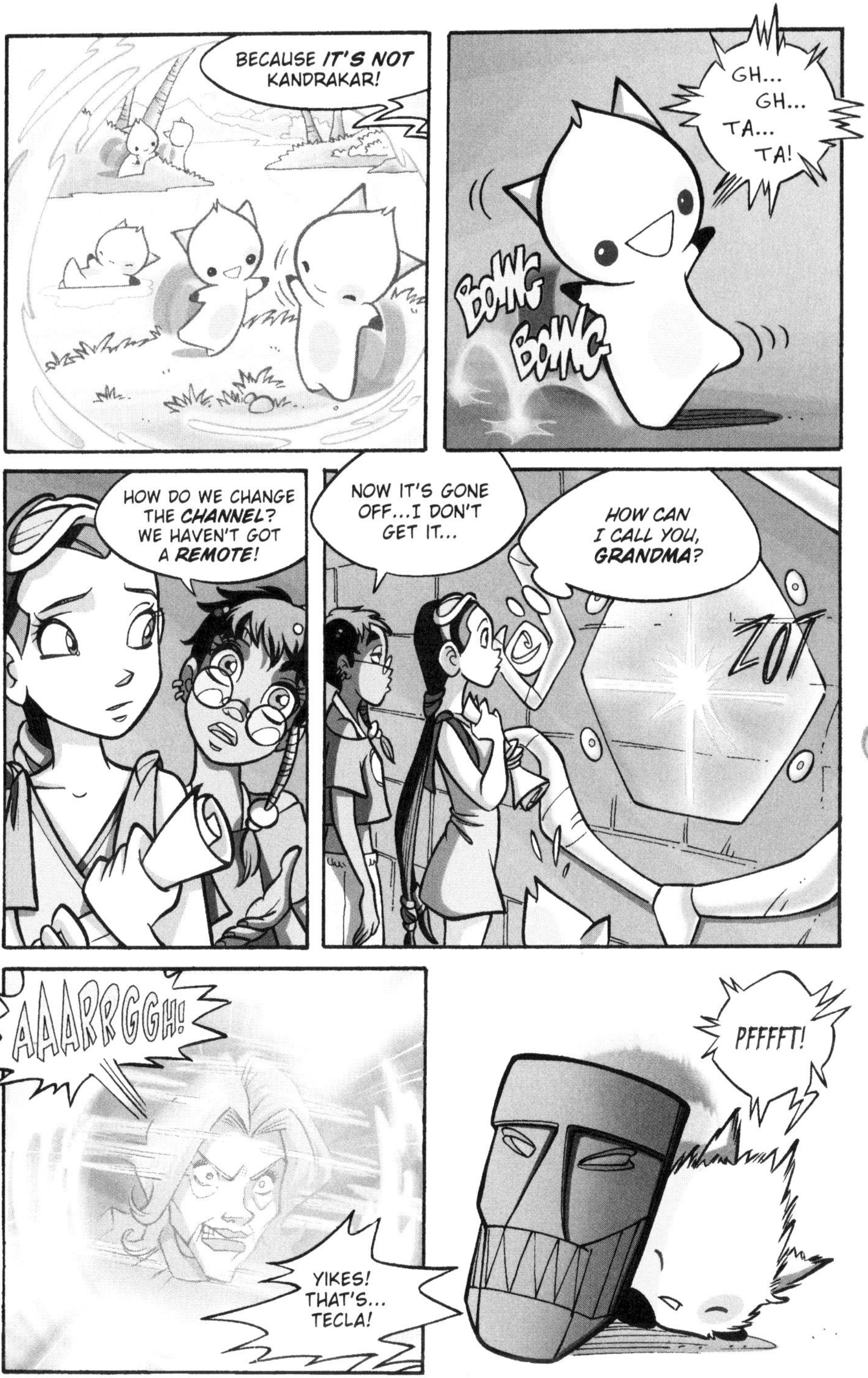
BECAUSE IT'S NOT KANDRAKAR!
GH... GH... TA... TA!
BOING
BOING
HOW DO WE CHANGE THE CHANNEL? WE HAVEN'T GOT A REMOTE!
NOW IT'S GONE OFF...I DON'T GET IT...
HOW CAN I CALL YOU, GRANDMA?
ZOT
AAARRGGH!
YIKES! THAT'S... TECLA!
PFFFFT!

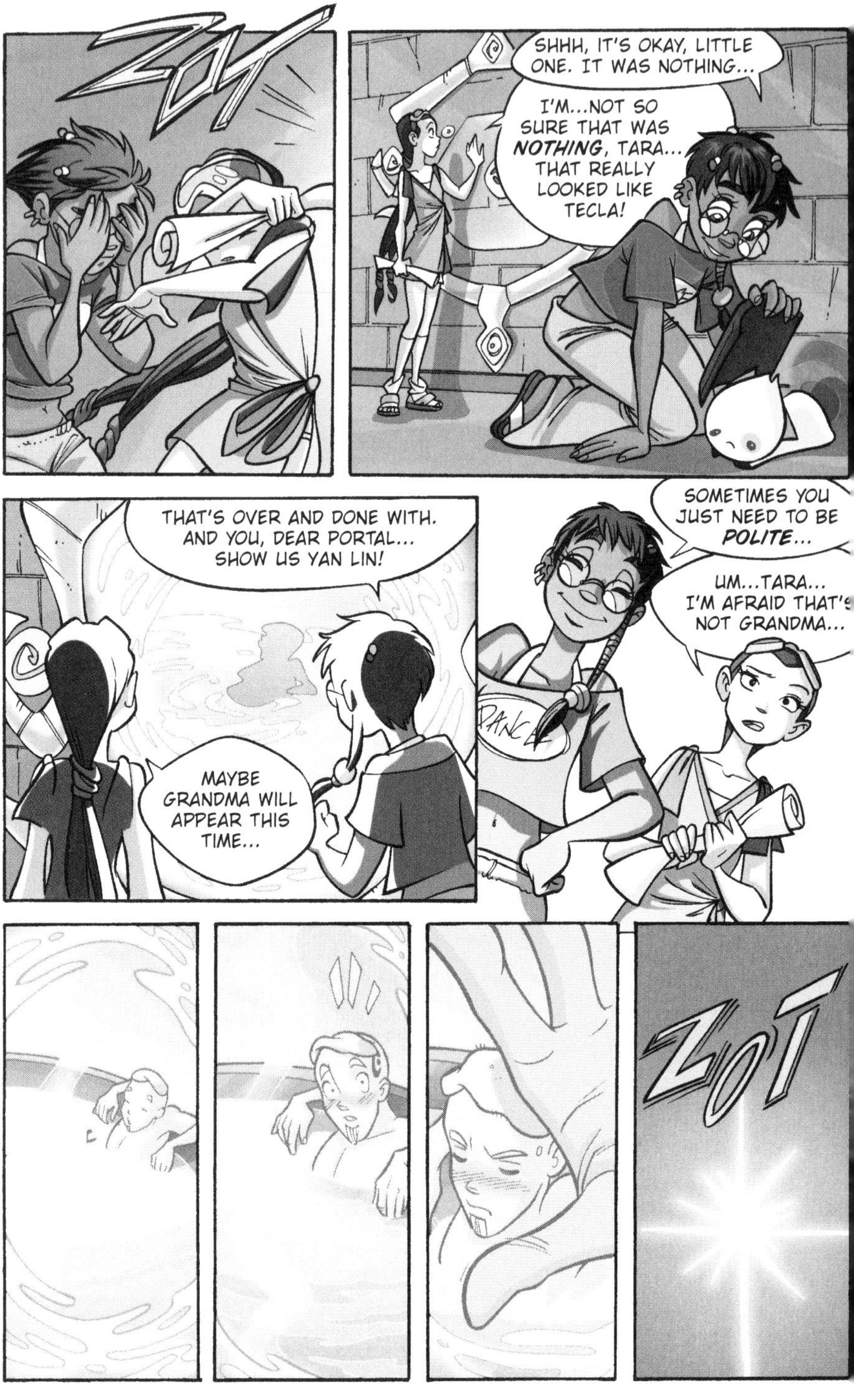
ZOT
SHHH, IT'S OKAY, LITTLE ONE. IT WAS NOTHING...
I'M...NOT SO SURE THAT WAS NOTHING, TARA... THAT REALLY LOOKED LIKE TECLA!
THAT'S OVER AND DONE WITH. AND YOU, DEAR PORTAL... SHOW US YAN LIN!
MAYBE GRANDMA WILL APPEAR THIS TIME...
SOMETIMES YOU JUST NEED TO BE POLITE...
UM...TARA... I'M AFRAID THAT'S NOT GRANDMA...
DANCE
ZOT

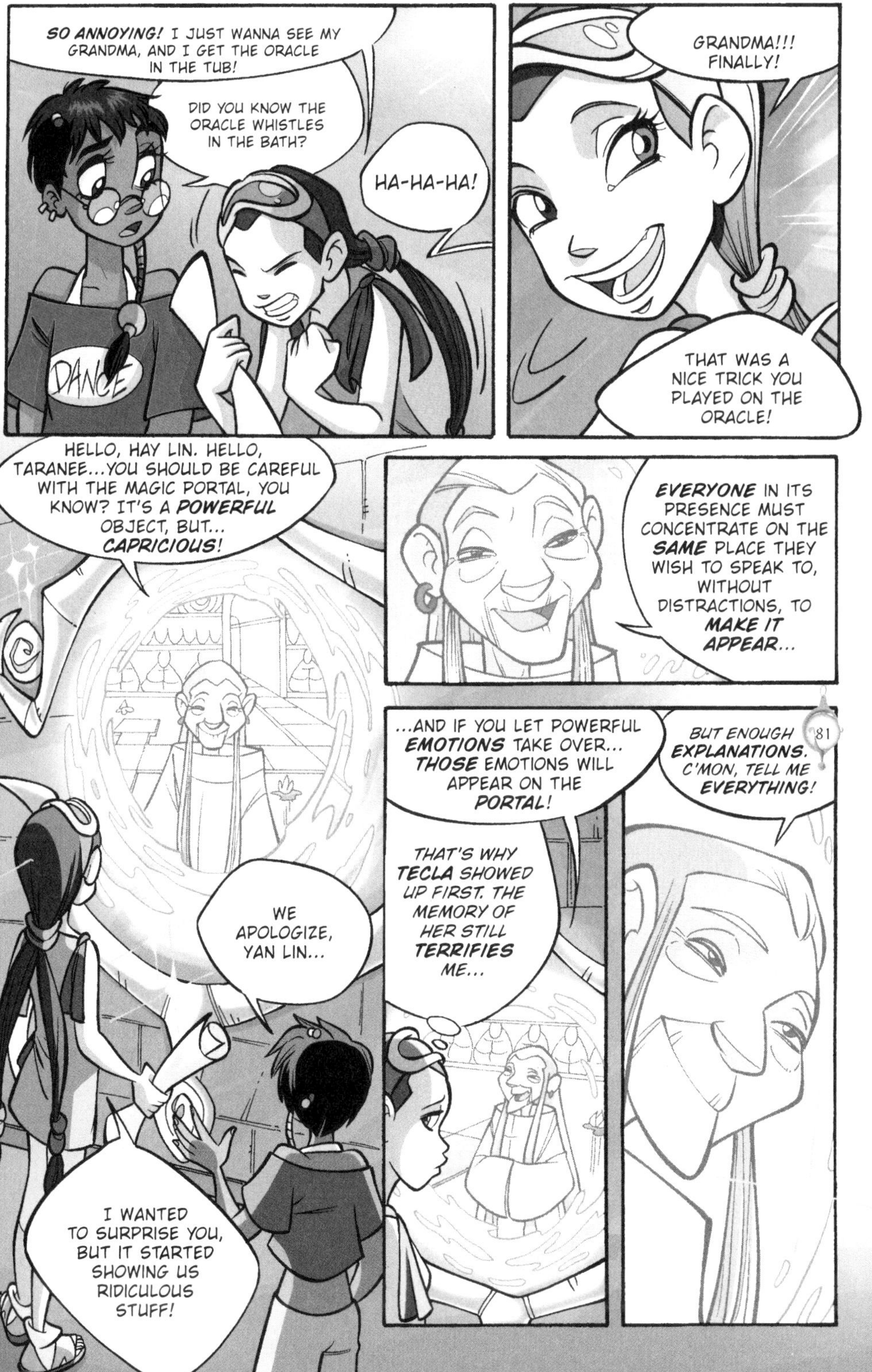
SO ANNOYING! I JUST WANNA SEE MY GRANDMA, AND I GET THE ORACLE IN THE TUB!
DID YOU KNOW THE ORACLE WHISTLES IN THE BATH?
HA-HA-HA!
DANCE
GRANDMA!!! FINALLY!
THAT WAS A NICE TRICK YOU PLAYED ON THE ORACLE!
HELLO, HAY LIN. HELLO, TARANEE...YOU SHOULD BE CAREFUL WITH THE MAGIC PORTAL, YOU KNOW? IT'S A POWERFUL OBJECT, BUT... CAPRICIOUS!
EVERYONE IN ITS PRESENCE MUST CONCENTRATE ON THE SAME PLACE THEY WISH TO SPEAK TO, WITHOUT DISTRACTIONS, TO MAKE IT APPEAR...
WE APOLOGIZE, YAN LIN...
I WANTED TO SURPRISE YOU, BUT IT STARTED SHOWING US RIDICULOUS STUFF!
...AND IF YOU LET POWERFUL EMOTIONS TAKE OVER... THOSE EMOTIONS WILL APPEAR ON THE PORTAL!
THAT'S WHY TECLA SHOWED UP FIRST. THE MEMORY OF HER STILL TERRIFIES ME...
BUT ENOUGH EXPLANATIONS. C'MON, TELL ME EVERYTHING!

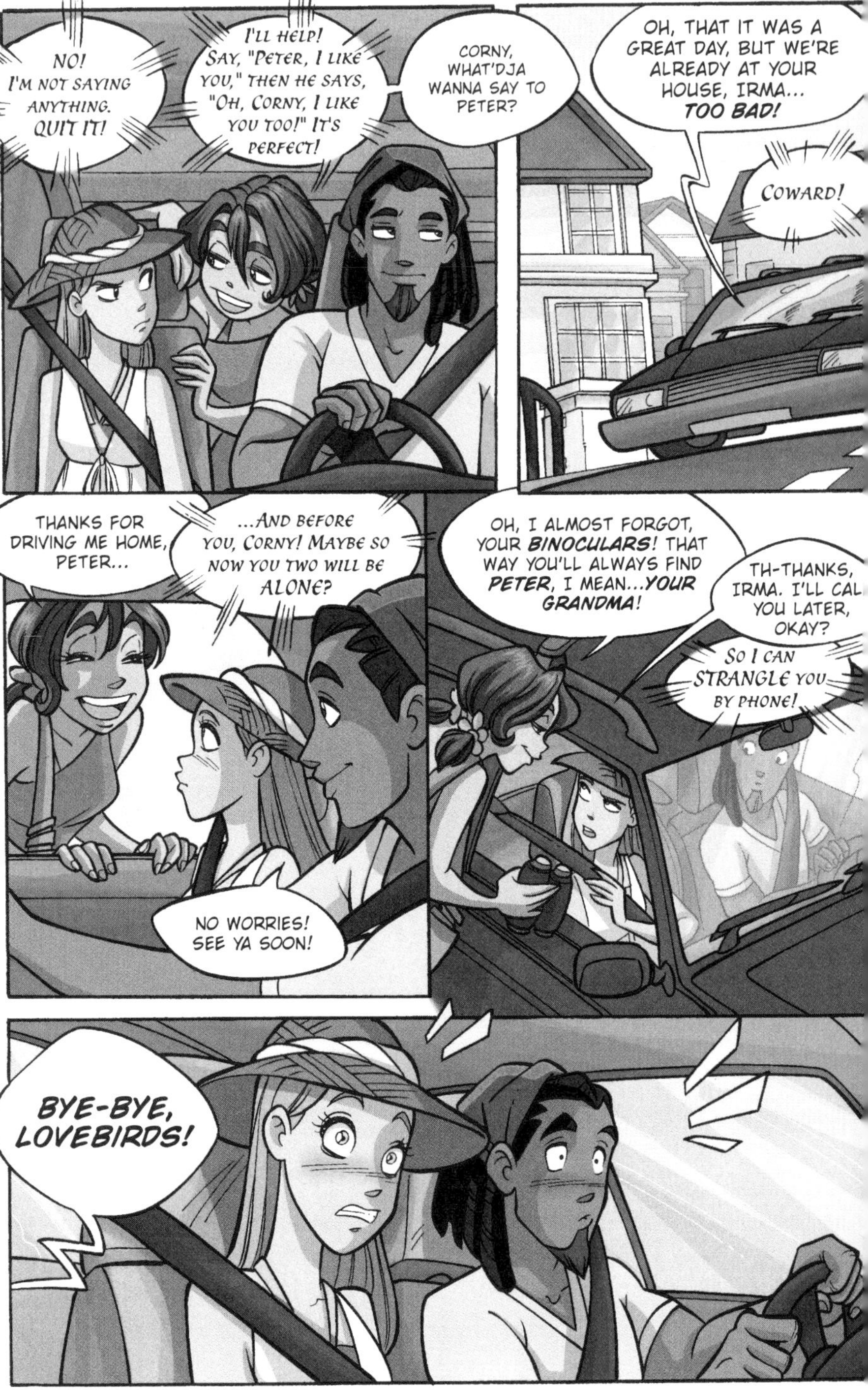
NO! I'M NOT SAYING ANYTHING. QUIT IT!
I'LL HELP! SAY, "PETER, I LIKE YOU," THEN HE SAYS, "OH, CORNY, I LIKE YOU TOO!" IT'S PERFECT!
CORNY, WHAT'DJA WANNA SAY TO PETER?
OH, THAT IT WAS A GREAT DAY, BUT WE'RE ALREADY AT YOUR HOUSE, IRMA... TOO BAD!
COWARD!
THANKS FOR DRIVING ME HOME, PETER...
...AND BEFORE YOU, CORNY! MAYBE SO NOW YOU TWO WILL BE ALONE?
NO WORRIES! SEE YA SOON!
OH, I ALMOST FORGOT, YOUR BINOCULARS! THAT WAY YOU'LL ALWAYS FIND PETER, I MEAN...YOUR GRANDMA!
TH-THANKS, IRMA. I'LL CAL YOU LATER, OKAY?
SO I CAN STRANGLE YOU BY PHONE!
BYE-BYE, LOVEBIRDS!

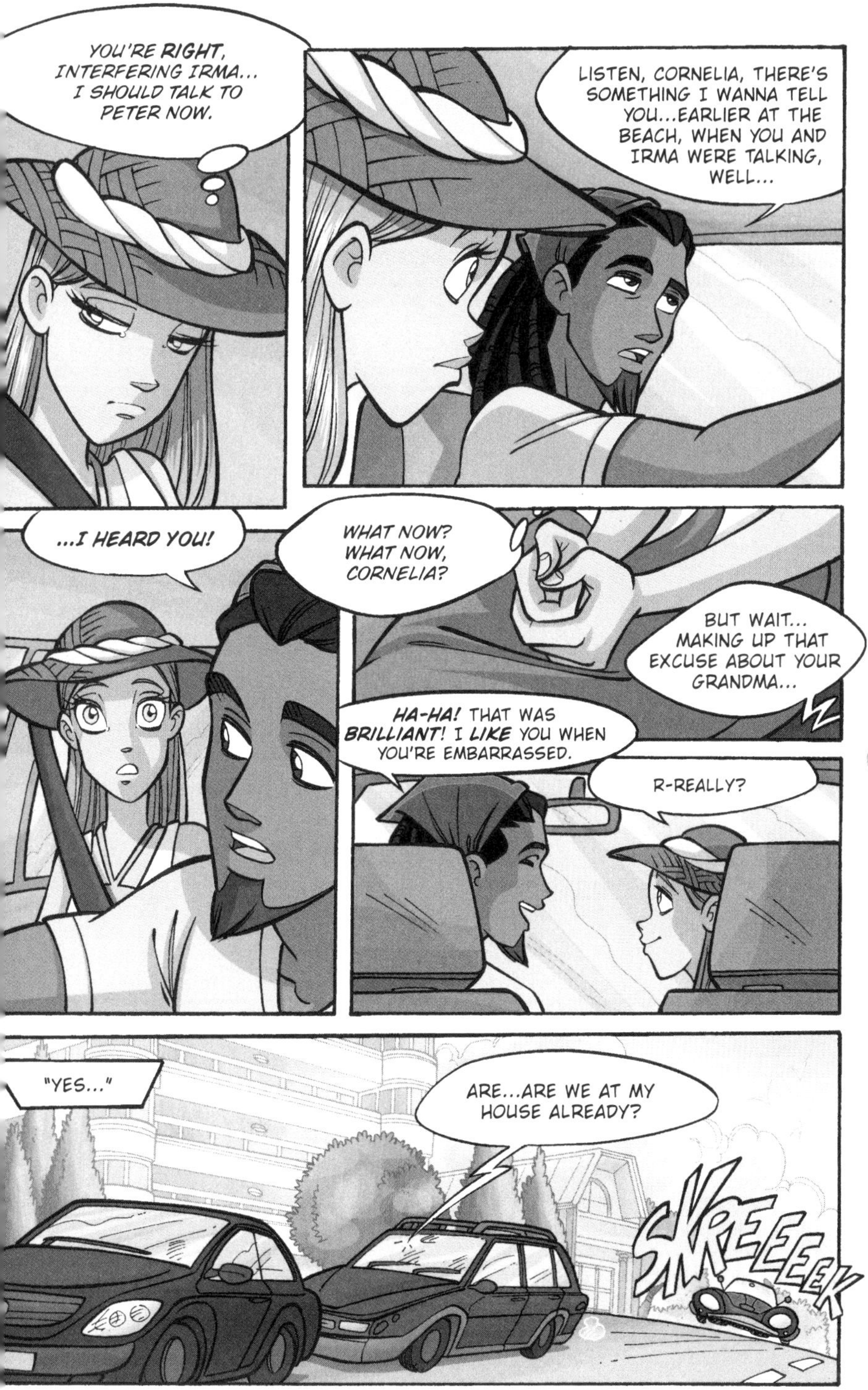
YOU'RE RIGHT, INTERFERING IRMA... I SHOULD TALK TO PETER NOW.
LISTEN, CORNELIA, THERE'S SOMETHING I WANNA TELL YOU...EARLIER AT THE BEACH, WHEN YOU AND IRMA WERE TALKING, WELL...
...I HEARD YOU!
WHAT NOW? WHAT NOW, CORNELIA?
BUT WAIT... MAKING UP THAT EXCUSE ABOUT YOUR GRANDMA...
HA-HA! THAT WAS BRILLIANT! I LIKE YOU WHEN YOU'RE EMBARRASSED.
R-REALLY?
"YES..."
ARE...ARE WE AT MY HOUSE ALREADY?
SKREEEEEK

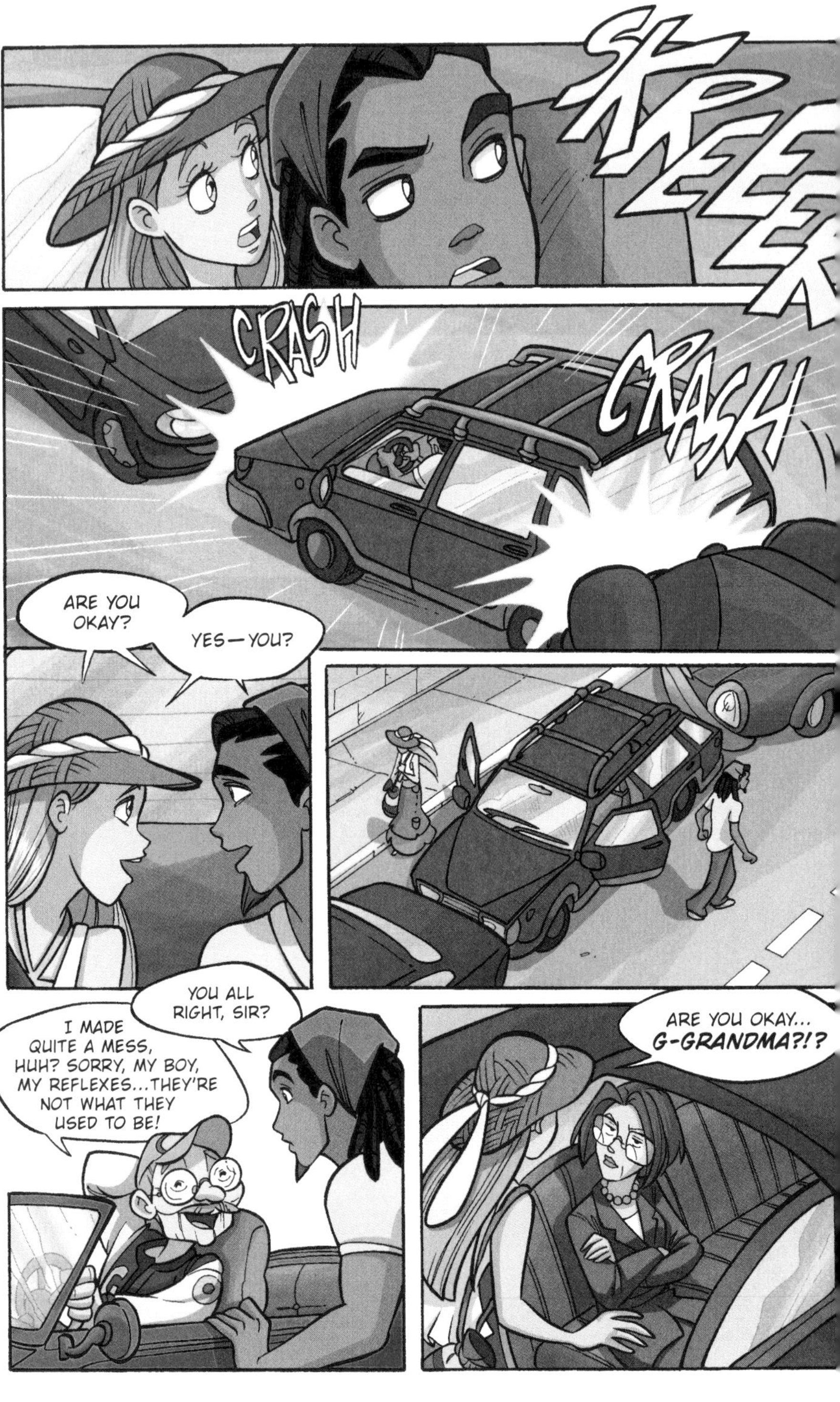
SKREEEK
CRASH
CRASH
ARE YOU OKAY?
YES—YOU?
YOU ALL RIGHT, SIR?
I MADE QUITE A MESS, HUH? SORRY, MY BOY, MY REFLEXES...THEY'RE NOT WHAT THEY USED TO BE!
ARE YOU OKAY... G-GRANDMA?!?

84

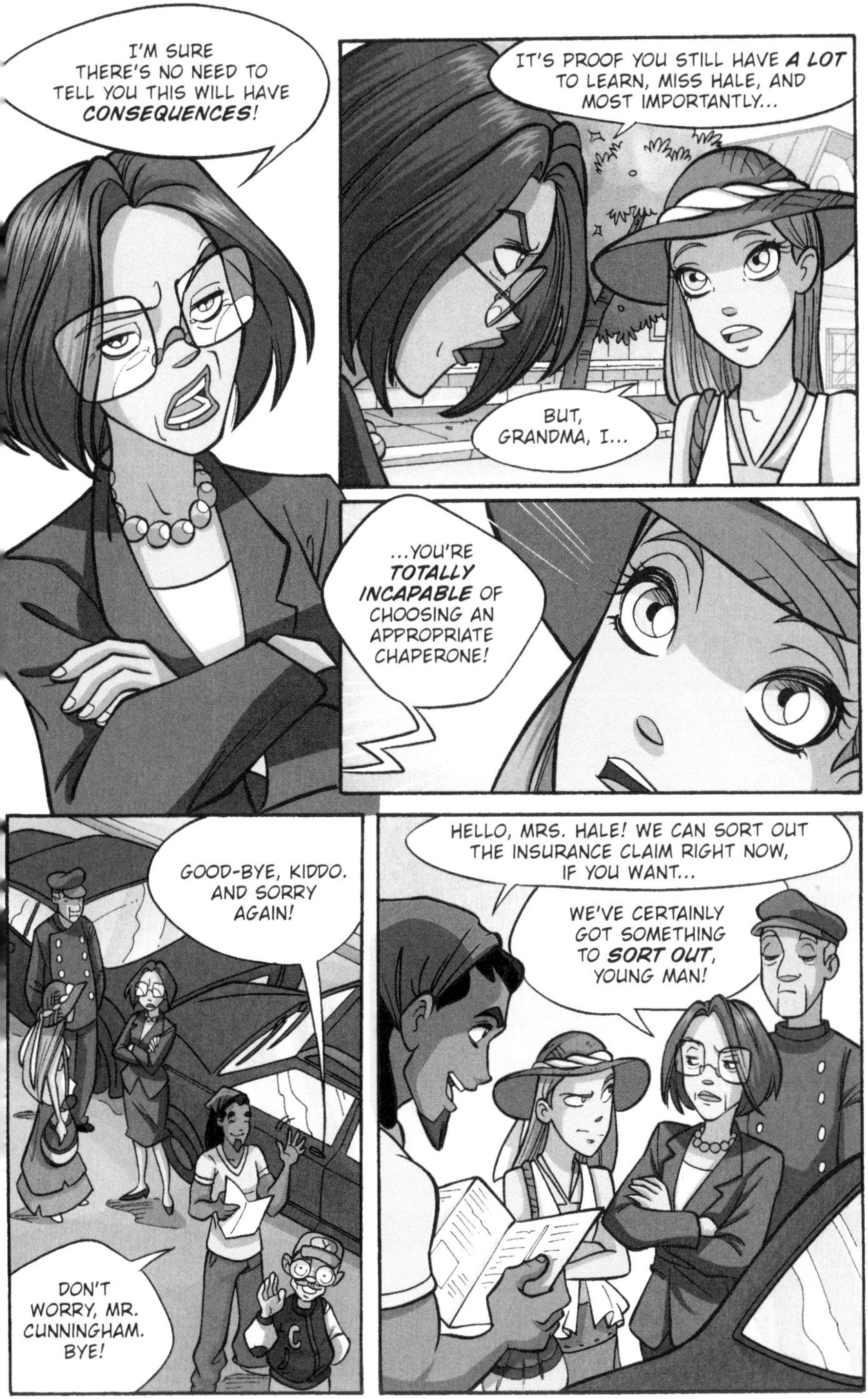
I'M SURE THERE'S NO NEED TO TELL YOU THIS WILL HAVE *CONSEQUENCES*!
IT'S PROOF YOU STILL HAVE *A LOT* TO LEARN, MISS HALE, AND MOST IMPORTANTLY...
BUT, GRANDMA, I...
...YOU'RE *TOTALLY INCAPABLE* OF CHOOSING AN APPROPRIATE CHAPERONE!
GOOD-BYE, KIDDO. AND SORRY AGAIN!
DON'T WORRY, MR. CUNNINGHAM. BYE!
HELLO, MRS. HALE! WE CAN SORT OUT THE INSURANCE CLAIM RIGHT NOW, IF YOU WANT...
WE'VE CERTAINLY GOT SOMETHING TO *SORT OUT*, YOUNG MAN!

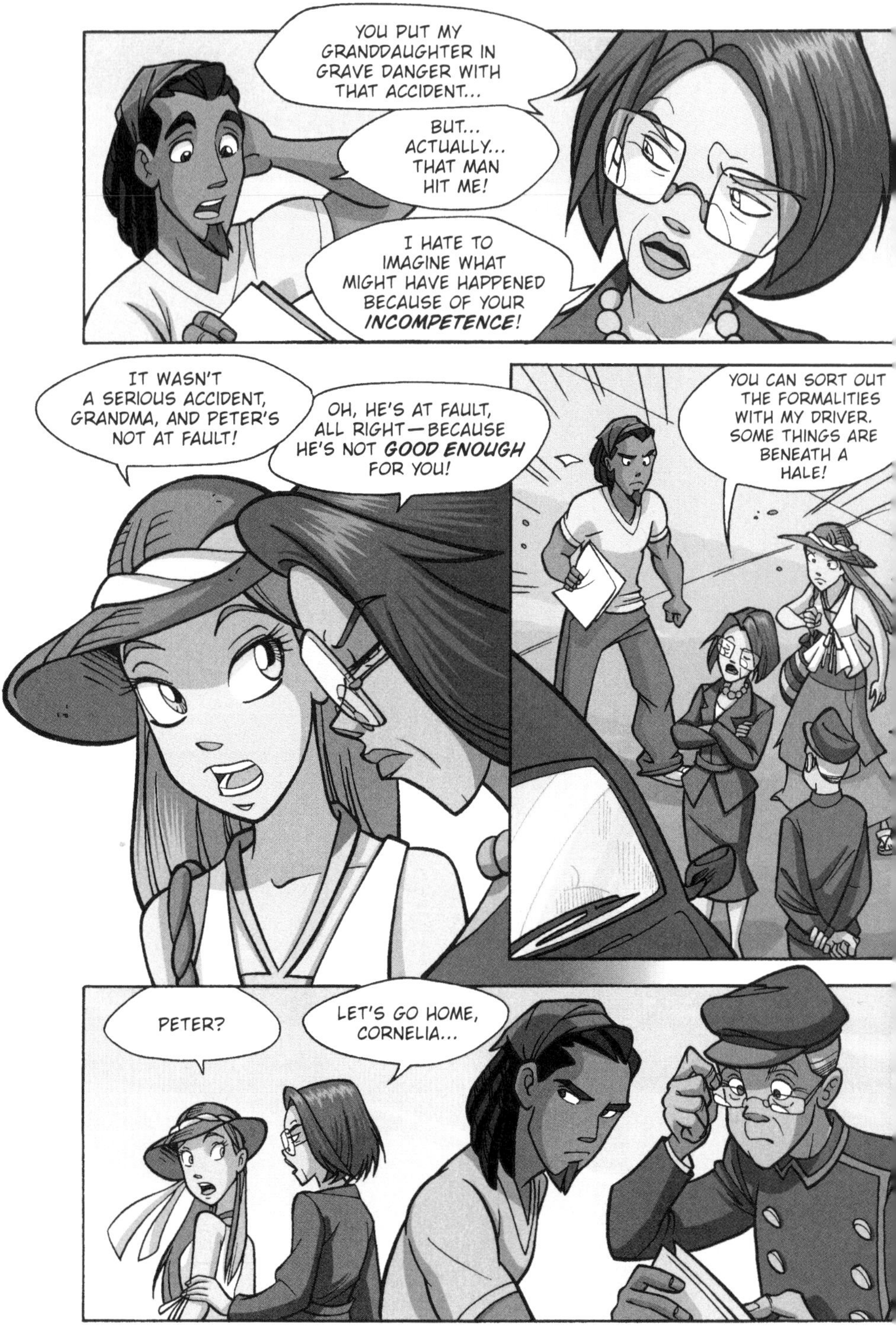
YOU PUT MY GRANDDAUGHTER IN GRAVE DANGER WITH THAT ACCIDENT...
BUT... ACTUALLY... THAT MAN HIT ME!
I HATE TO IMAGINE WHAT MIGHT HAVE HAPPENED BECAUSE OF YOUR *INCOMPETENCE*!
IT WASN'T A SERIOUS ACCIDENT, GRANDMA, AND PETER'S NOT AT FAULT!
OH, HE'S AT FAULT, ALL RIGHT—BECAUSE HE'S NOT *GOOD ENOUGH* FOR YOU!
YOU CAN SORT OUT THE FORMALITIES WITH MY DRIVER. SOME THINGS ARE BENEATH A HALE!
PETER?
LET'S GO HOME, CORNELIA...

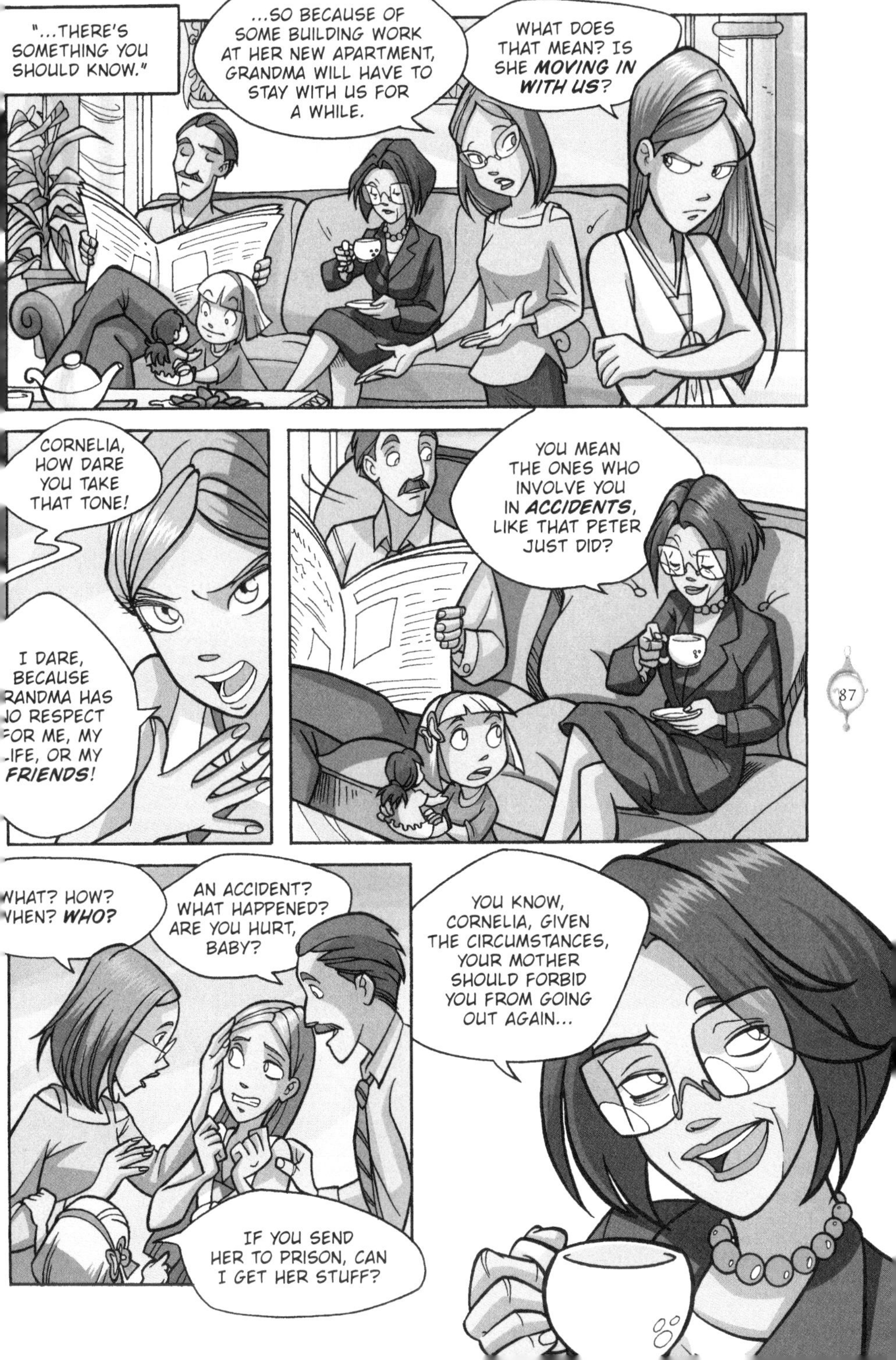
"...THERE'S SOMETHING YOU SHOULD KNOW."
...SO BECAUSE OF SOME BUILDING WORK AT HER NEW APARTMENT, GRANDMA WILL HAVE TO STAY WITH US FOR A WHILE.
WHAT DOES THAT MEAN? IS SHE MOVING IN WITH US?
CORNELIA, HOW DARE YOU TAKE THAT TONE!
I DARE, BECAUSE RANDMA HAS O RESPECT FOR ME, MY IFE, OR MY FRIENDS!
YOU MEAN THE ONES WHO INVOLVE YOU IN ACCIDENTS, LIKE THAT PETER JUST DID?
HAT? HOW? HEN? WHO?
AN ACCIDENT? WHAT HAPPENED? ARE YOU HURT, BABY?
YOU KNOW, CORNELIA, GIVEN THE CIRCUMSTANCES, YOUR MOTHER SHOULD FORBID YOU FROM GOING OUT AGAIN...
IF YOU SEND HER TO PRISON, CAN I GET HER STUFF?

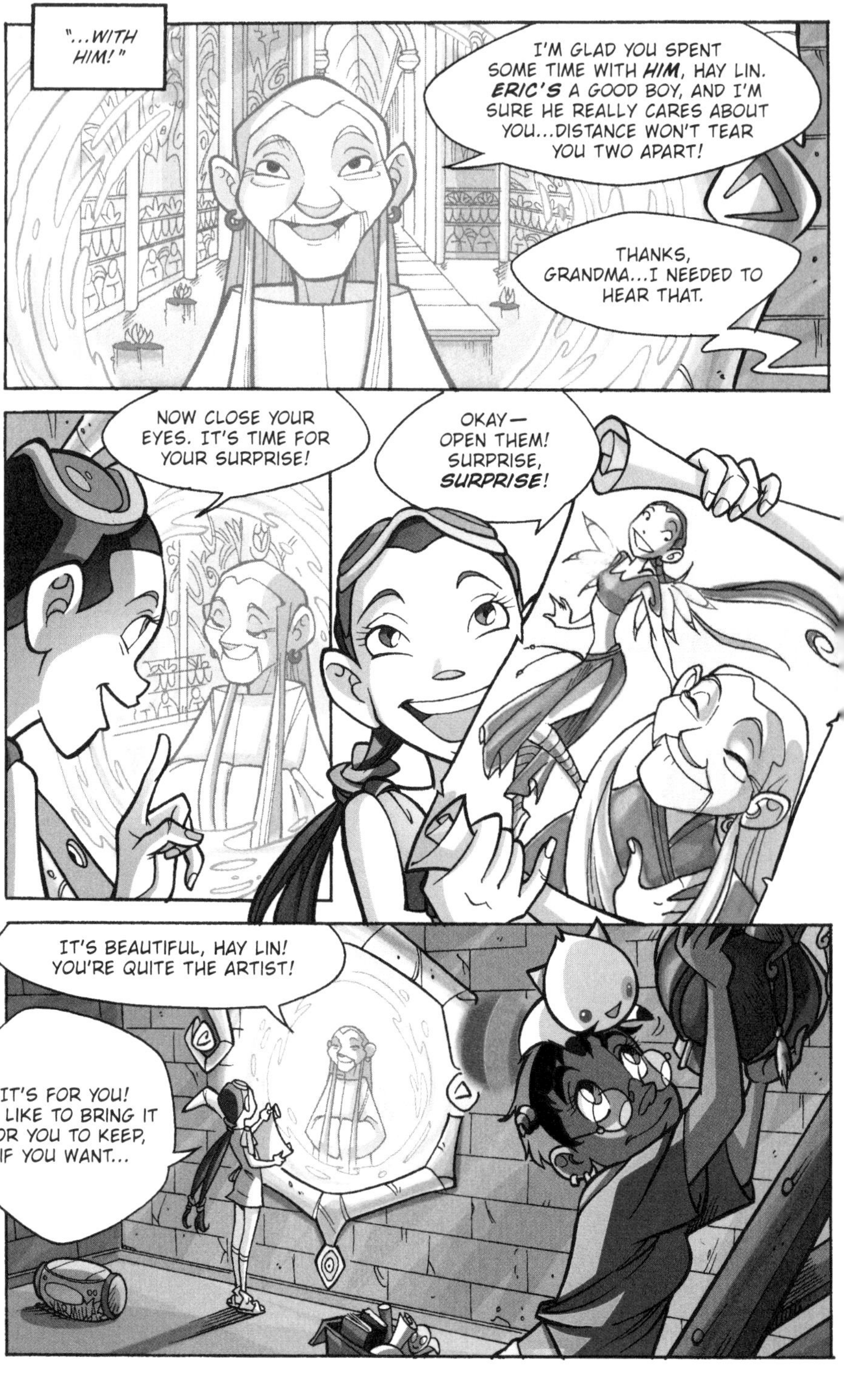
"...WITH HIM!"
I'M GLAD YOU SPENT SOME TIME WITH HIM, HAY LIN. ERIC'S A GOOD BOY, AND I'M SURE HE REALLY CARES ABOUT YOU...DISTANCE WON'T TEAR YOU TWO APART!
THANKS, GRANDMA...I NEEDED TO HEAR THAT.
NOW CLOSE YOUR EYES. IT'S TIME FOR YOUR SURPRISE!
OKAY— OPEN THEM! SURPRISE, SURPRISE!
IT'S BEAUTIFUL, HAY LIN! YOU'RE QUITE THE ARTIST!
IT'S FOR YOU! I'D LIKE TO BRING IT FOR YOU TO KEEP, IF YOU WANT...

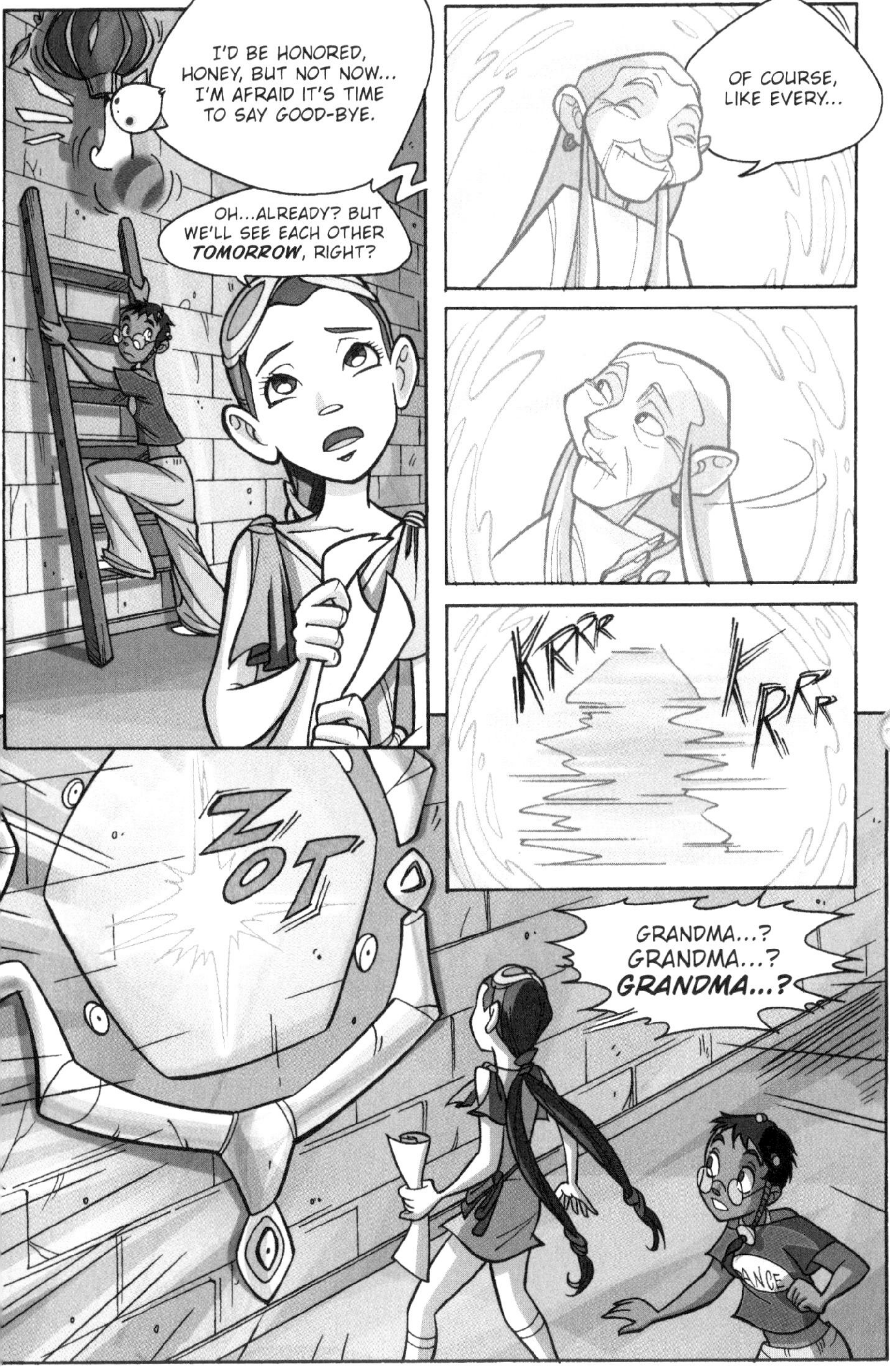
I'D BE HONORED, HONEY, BUT NOT NOW... I'M AFRAID IT'S TIME TO SAY GOOD-BYE.
OH...ALREADY? BUT WE'LL SEE EACH OTHER *TOMORROW*, RIGHT?
OF COURSE, LIKE EVERY...
KRRR KRRR
ZOT
GRANDMA...? GRANDMA...? **GRANDMA...?**

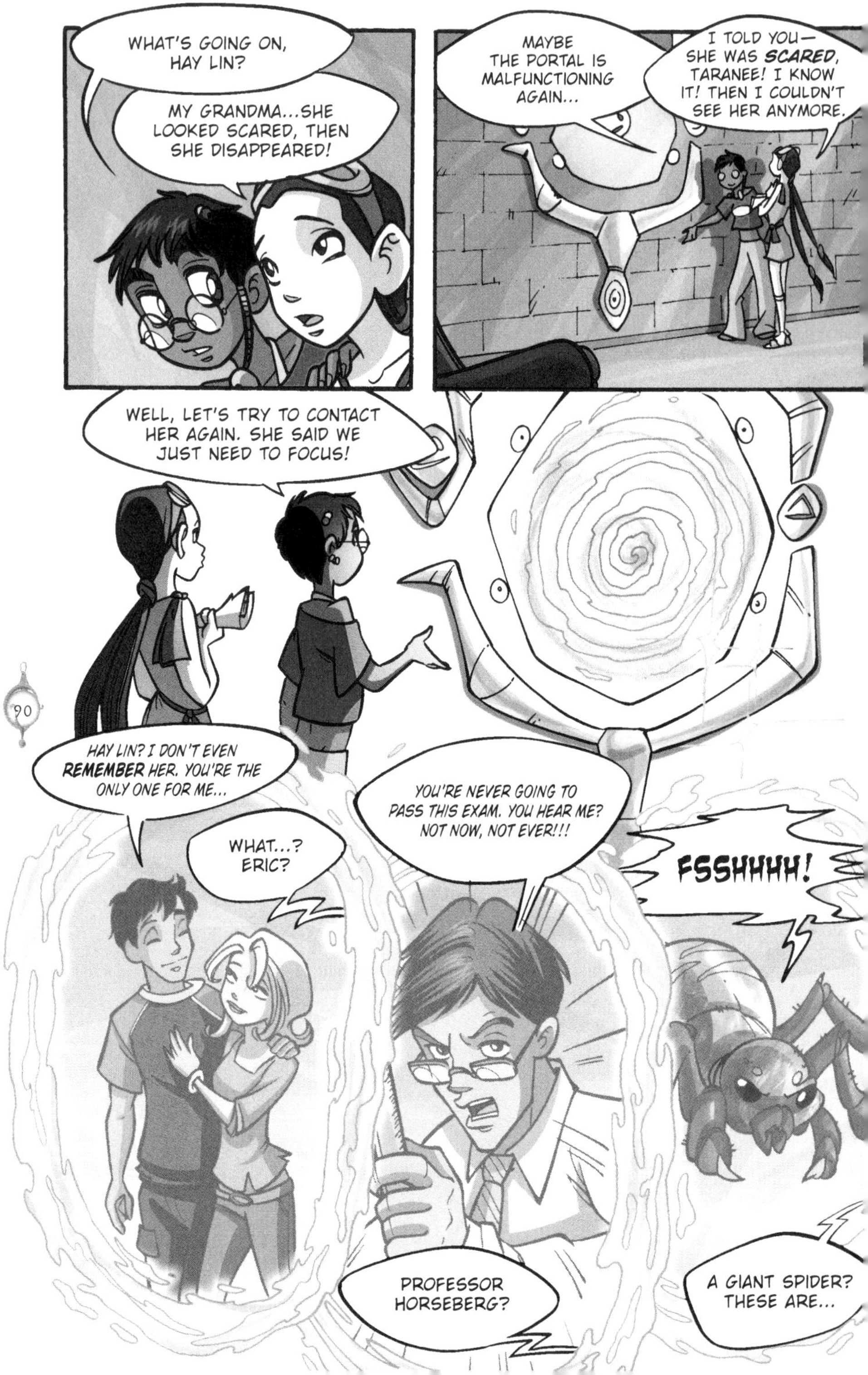
WHAT'S GOING ON, HAY LIN?
MY GRANDMA...SHE LOOKED SCARED, THEN SHE DISAPPEARED!
MAYBE THE PORTAL IS MALFUNCTIONING AGAIN...
I TOLD YOU— SHE WAS SCARED, TARANEE! I KNOW IT! THEN I COULDN'T SEE HER ANYMORE.
WELL, LET'S TRY TO CONTACT HER AGAIN. SHE SAID WE JUST NEED TO FOCUS!
HAY LIN? I DON'T EVEN REMEMBER HER. YOU'RE THE ONLY ONE FOR ME...
WHAT...? ERIC?
YOU'RE NEVER GOING TO PASS THIS EXAM. YOU HEAR ME? NOT NOW, NOT EVER!!!
FSSHHHH!
PROFESSOR HORSEBERG?
A GIANT SPIDER? THESE ARE...

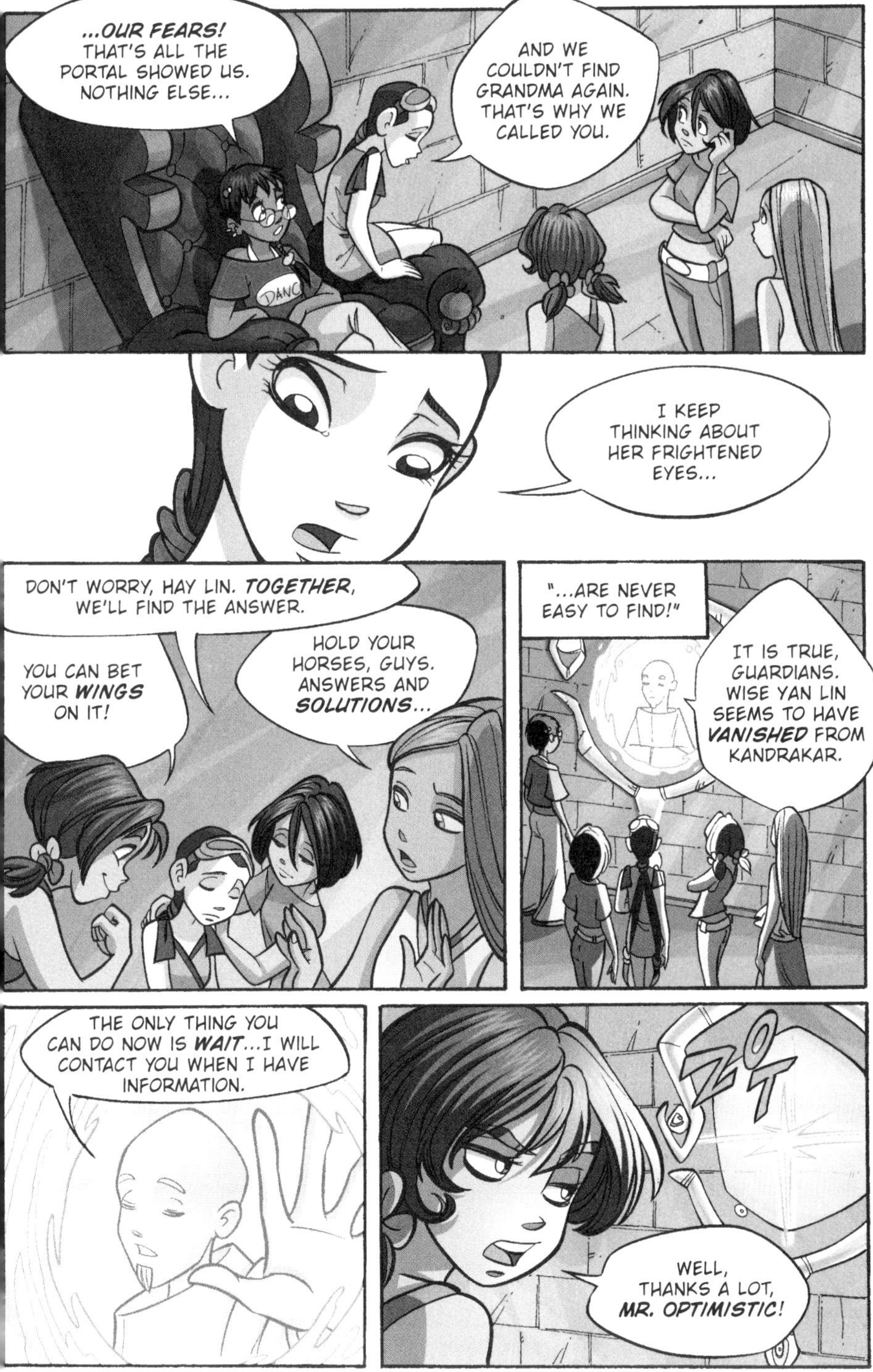
...OUR FEARS! THAT'S ALL THE PORTAL SHOWED US. NOTHING ELSE...
AND WE COULDN'T FIND GRANDMA AGAIN. THAT'S WHY WE CALLED YOU.
I KEEP THINKING ABOUT HER FRIGHTENED EYES...
DON'T WORRY, HAY LIN. TOGETHER, WE'LL FIND THE ANSWER.
YOU CAN BET YOUR WINGS ON IT!
HOLD YOUR HORSES, GUYS. ANSWERS AND SOLUTIONS...
"...ARE NEVER EASY TO FIND!"
IT IS TRUE, GUARDIANS. WISE YAN LIN SEEMS TO HAVE VANISHED FROM KANDRAKAR.
THE ONLY THING YOU CAN DO NOW IS WAIT...I WILL CONTACT YOU WHEN I HAVE INFORMATION.
ZOT
WELL, THANKS A LOT, MR. OPTIMISTIC!

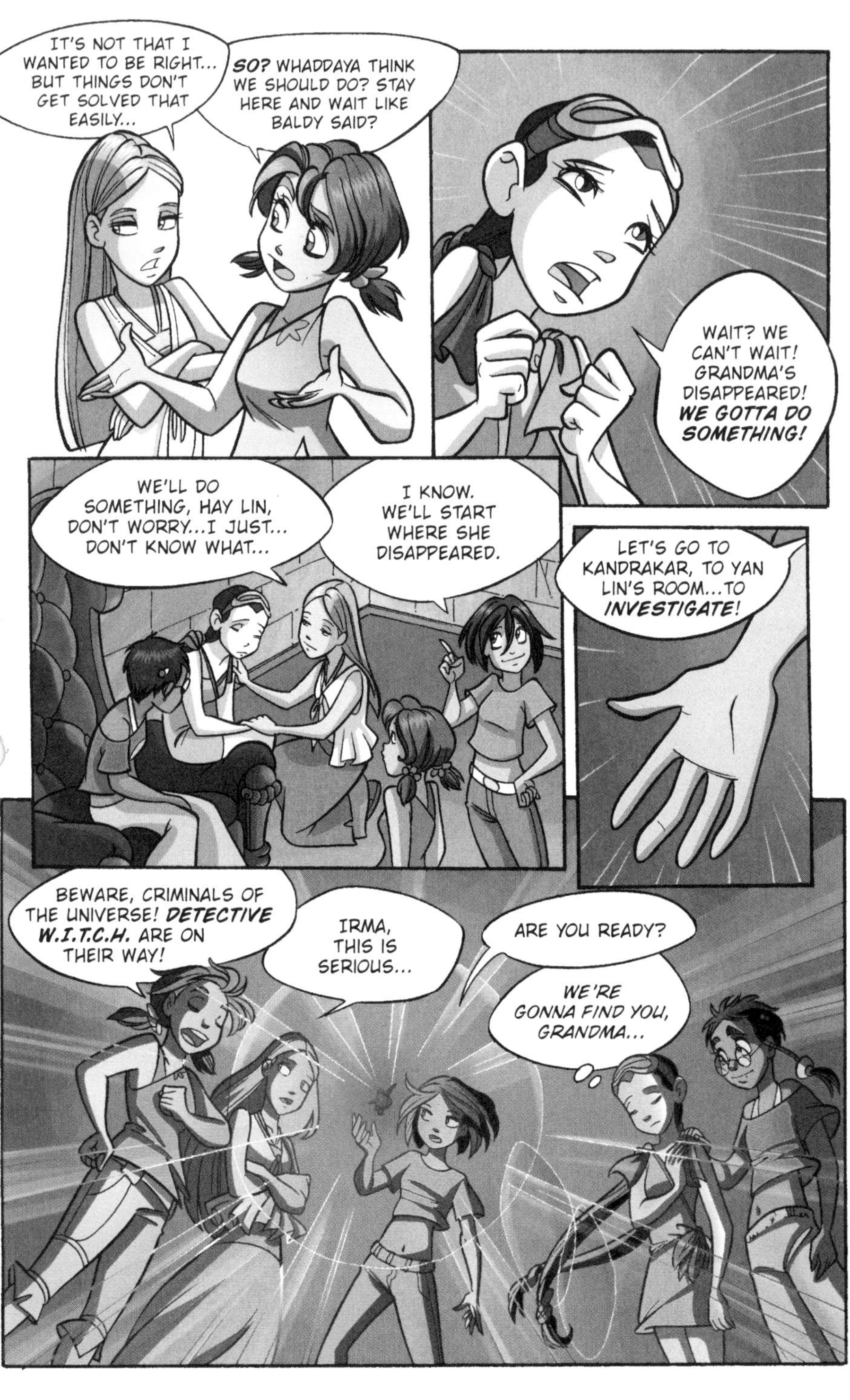
IT'S NOT THAT I WANTED TO BE RIGHT... BUT THINGS DON'T GET SOLVED THAT EASILY...
SO? WHADDAYA THINK WE SHOULD DO? STAY HERE AND WAIT LIKE BALDY SAID?
WAIT? WE CAN'T WAIT! GRANDMA'S DISAPPEARED! WE GOTTA DO SOMETHING!
WE'LL DO SOMETHING, HAY LIN, DON'T WORRY...I JUST... DON'T KNOW WHAT...
I KNOW. WE'LL START WHERE SHE DISAPPEARED.
LET'S GO TO KANDRAKAR, TO YAN LIN'S ROOM...TO INVESTIGATE!
BEWARE, CRIMINALS OF THE UNIVERSE! DETECTIVE W.I.T.C.H. ARE ON THEIR WAY!
IRMA, THIS IS SERIOUS...
ARE YOU READY?
WE'RE GONNA FIND YOU, GRANDMA...

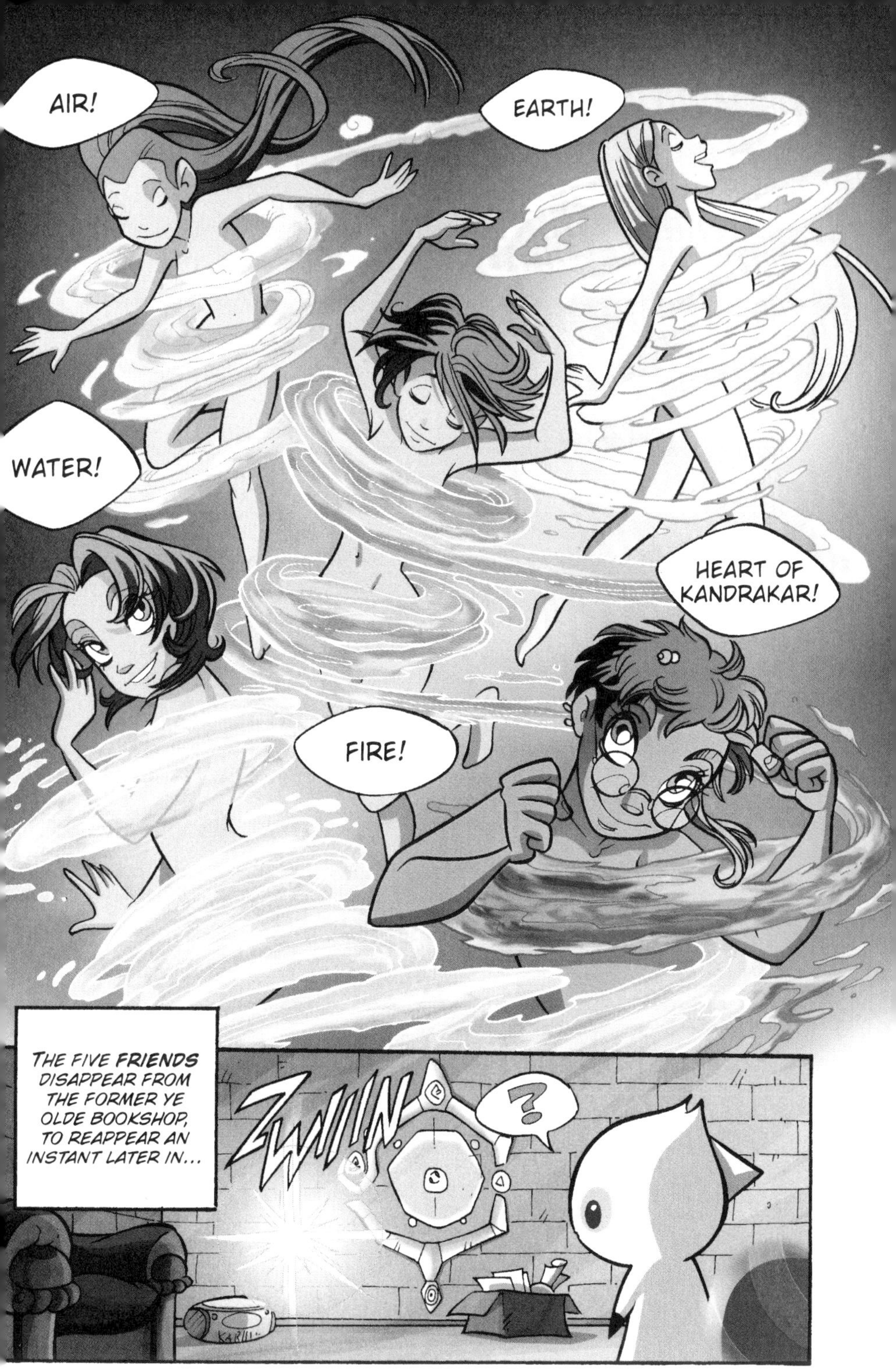
AIR!
EARTH!
WATER!
HEART OF KANDRAKAR!
FIRE!
THE FIVE **FRIENDS** DISAPPEAR FROM THE FORMER YE OLDE BOOKSHOP, TO REAPPEAR AN INSTANT LATER IN...
ZWIIIN
?

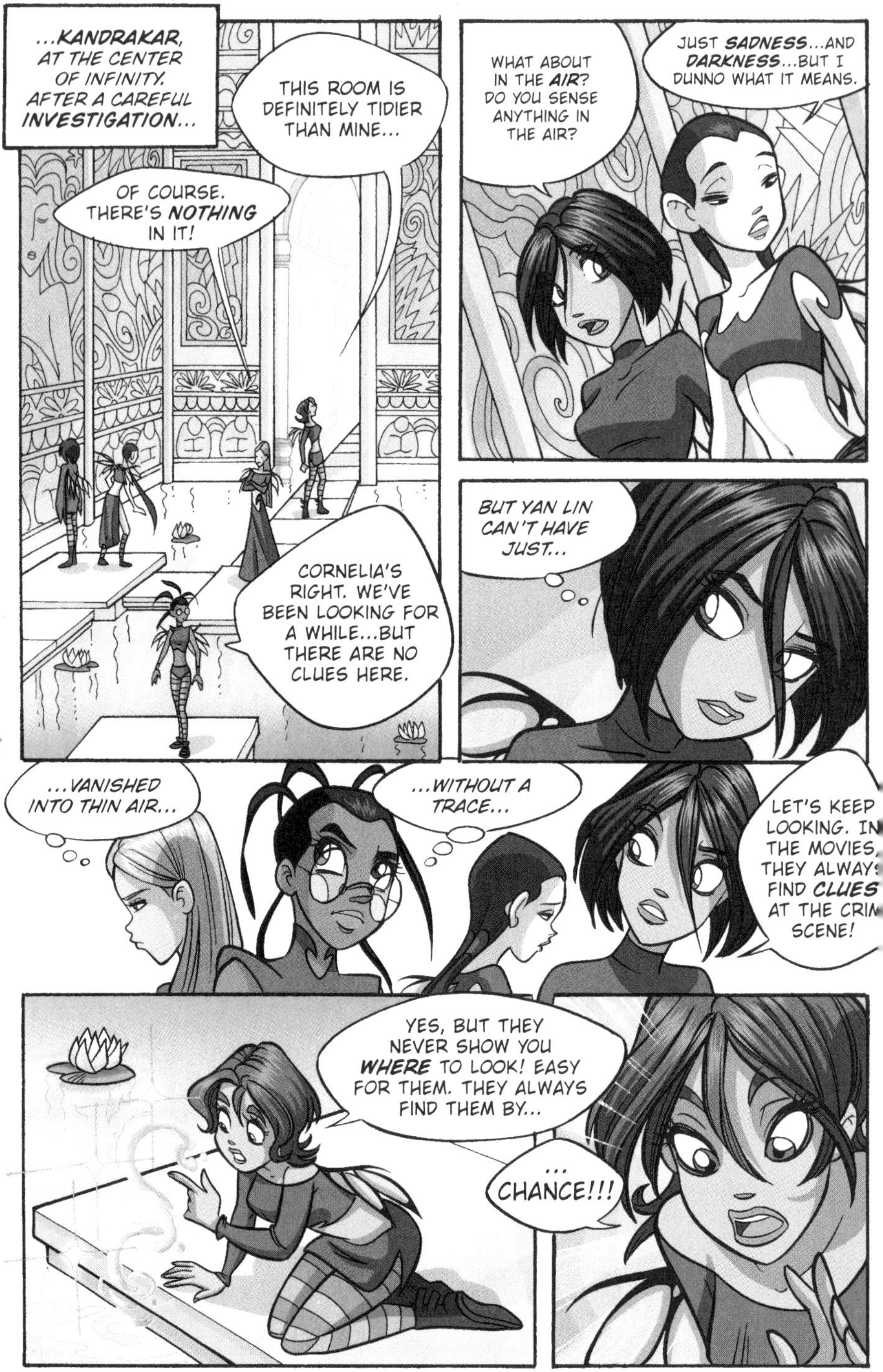

...KANDRAKAR, AT THE CENTER OF INFINITY. AFTER A CAREFUL INVESTIGATION...
THIS ROOM IS DEFINITELY TIDIER THAN MINE...
OF COURSE. THERE'S NOTHING IN IT!
CORNELIA'S RIGHT. WE'VE BEEN LOOKING FOR A WHILE...BUT THERE ARE NO CLUES HERE.
WHAT ABOUT IN THE AIR? DO YOU SENSE ANYTHING IN THE AIR?
JUST SADNESS...AND DARKNESS...BUT I DUNNO WHAT IT MEANS.
BUT YAN LIN CAN'T HAVE JUST...
...VANISHED INTO THIN AIR...
...WITHOUT A TRACE...
LET'S KEEP LOOKING. IN THE MOVIES THEY ALWAYS FIND CLUES AT THE CRIME SCENE!
YES, BUT THEY NEVER SHOW YOU WHERE TO LOOK! EASY FOR THEM. THEY ALWAYS FIND THEM BY...
...CHANCE!!!

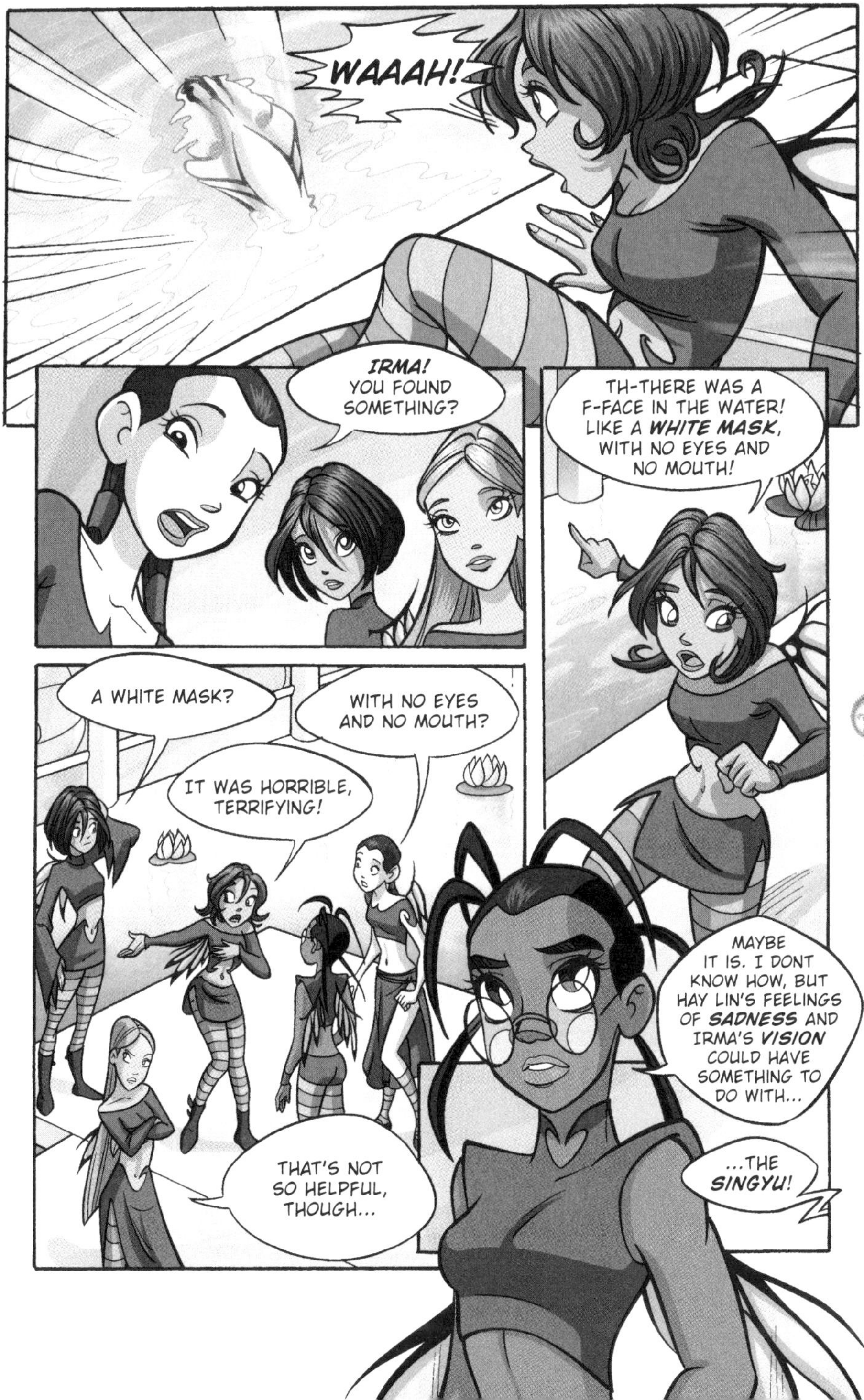
WAAAH!
IRMA! YOU FOUND SOMETHING?
TH-THERE WAS A F-FACE IN THE WATER! LIKE A WHITE MASK, WITH NO EYES AND NO MOUTH!
A WHITE MASK?
WITH NO EYES AND NO MOUTH?
IT WAS HORRIBLE, TERRIFYING!
THAT'S NOT SO HELPFUL, THOUGH...
MAYBE IT IS. I DONT KNOW HOW, BUT HAY LIN'S FEELINGS OF SADNESS AND IRMA'S VISION COULD HAVE SOMETHING TO DO WITH...
...THE SINGYU!

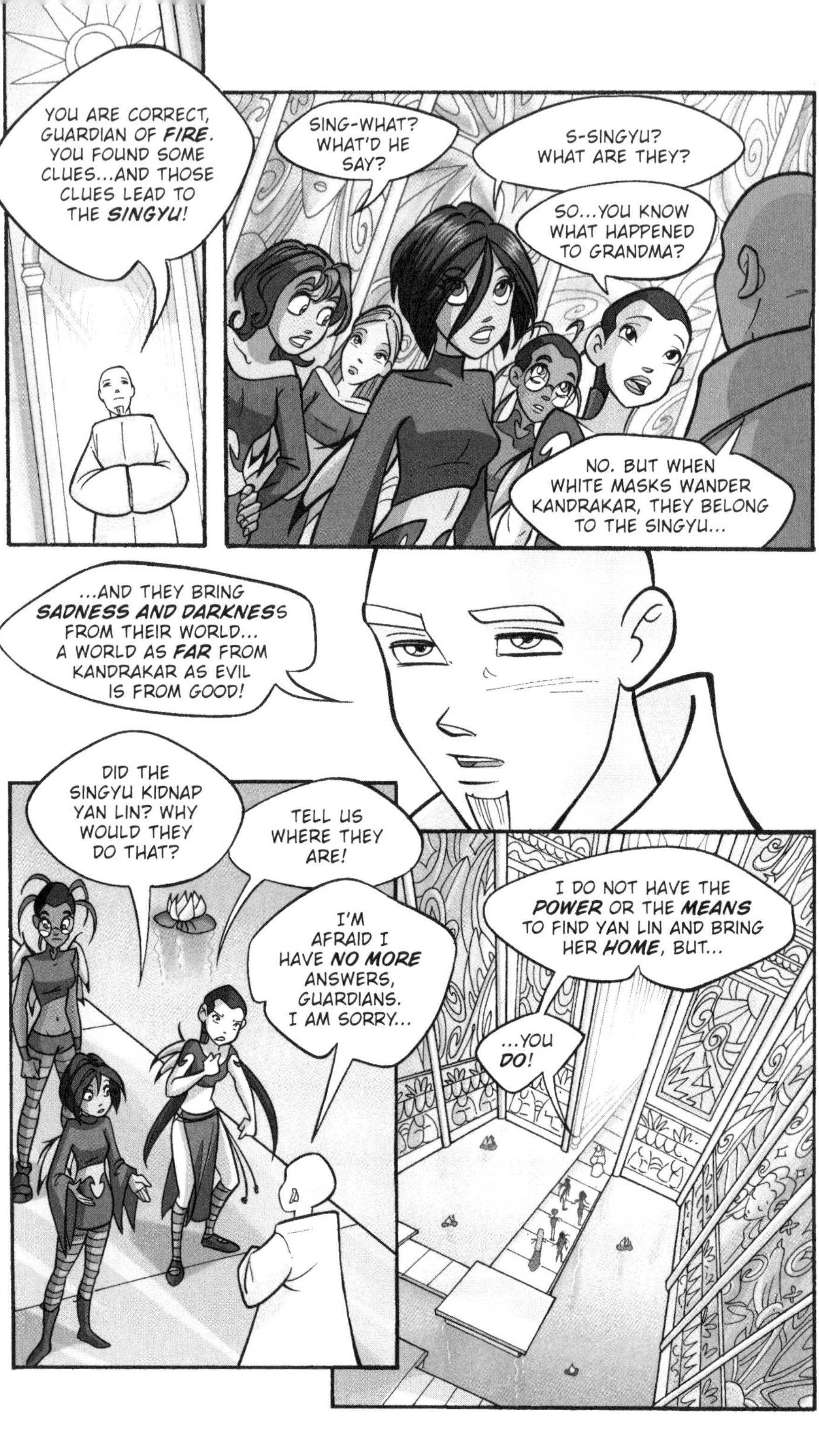

YOU ARE CORRECT, GUARDIAN OF FIRE. YOU FOUND SOME CLUES...AND THOSE CLUES LEAD TO THE SINGYU!
SING-WHAT? WHAT'D HE SAY?
S-SINGYU? WHAT ARE THEY?
SO...YOU KNOW WHAT HAPPENED TO GRANDMA?
NO. BUT WHEN WHITE MASKS WANDER KANDRAKAR, THEY BELONG TO THE SINGYU...
...AND THEY BRING SADNESS AND DARKNESS FROM THEIR WORLD... A WORLD AS FAR FROM KANDRAKAR AS EVIL IS FROM GOOD!
DID THE SINGYU KIDNAP YAN LIN? WHY WOULD THEY DO THAT?
TELL US WHERE THEY ARE!
I'M AFRAID I HAVE NO MORE ANSWERS, GUARDIANS. I AM SORRY...
I DO NOT HAVE THE POWER OR THE MEANS TO FIND YAN LIN AND BRING HER HOME, BUT...
...YOU DO!

W.i.t.c.h.

Will Irma Taranee Cornelia Hay Lin

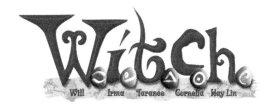

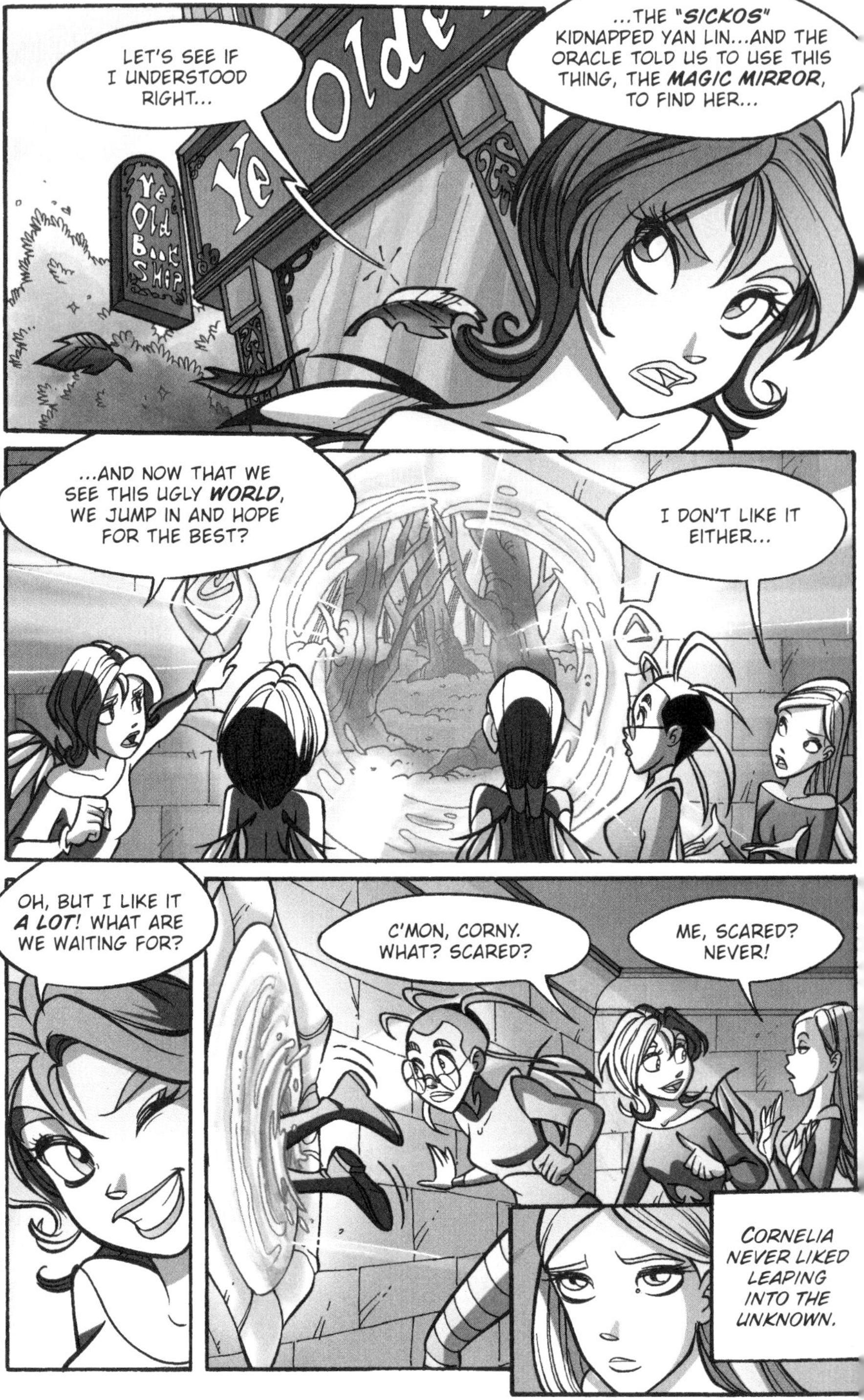
LET'S SEE IF I UNDERSTOOD RIGHT...
...THE "SICKOS" KIDNAPPED YAN LIN...AND THE ORACLE TOLD US TO USE THIS THING, THE MAGIC MIRROR, TO FIND HER...
Ye Olde
Ye Old Book Ship
...AND NOW THAT WE SEE THIS UGLY WORLD, WE JUMP IN AND HOPE FOR THE BEST?
I DON'T LIKE IT EITHER...
OH, BUT I LIKE IT A LOT! WHAT ARE WE WAITING FOR?
C'MON, CORNY. WHAT? SCARED?
ME, SCARED? NEVER!
CORNELIA NEVER LIKED LEAPING INTO THE UNKNOWN.

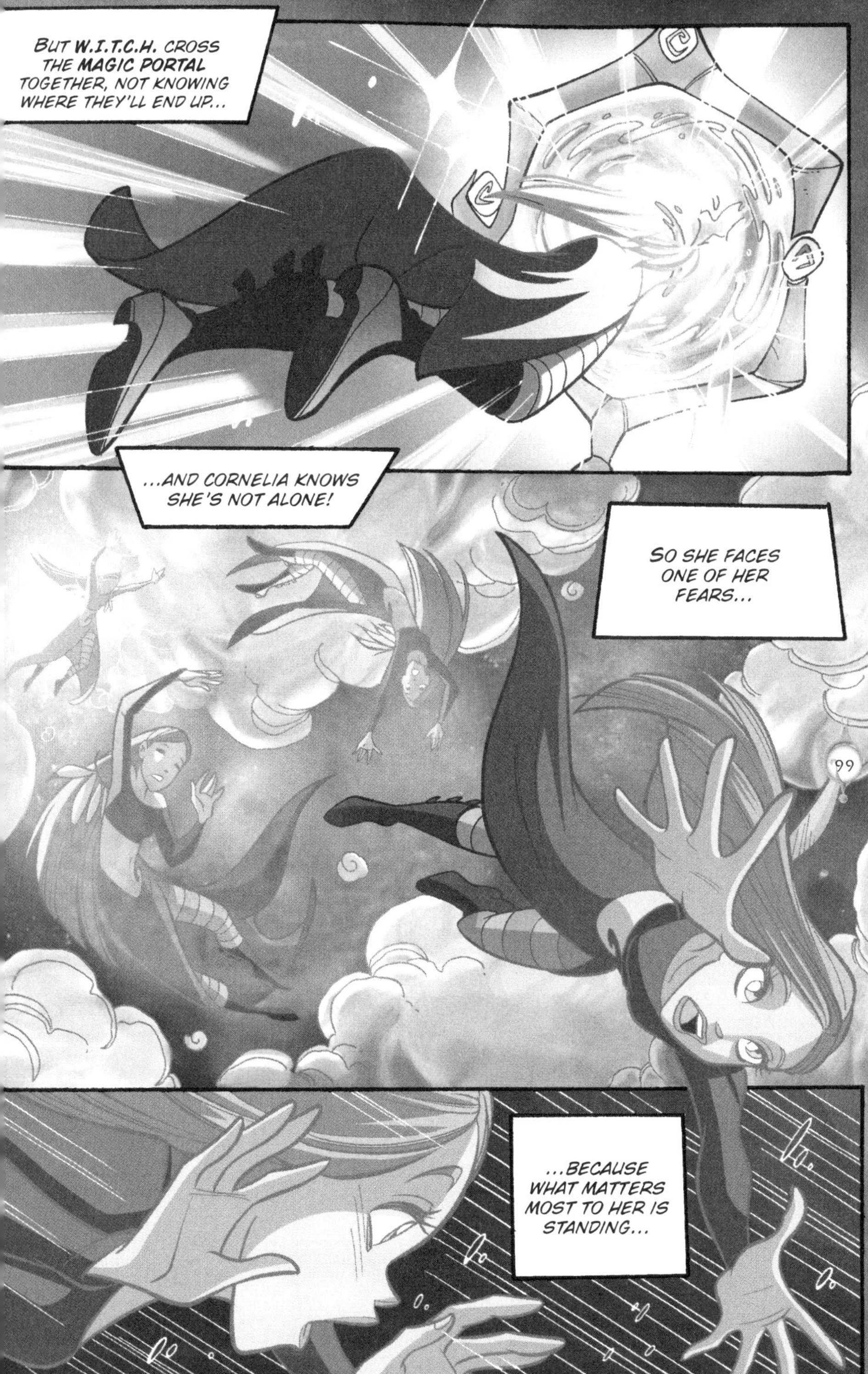

BUT W.I.T.C.H. CROSS THE MAGIC PORTAL TOGETHER, NOT KNOWING WHERE THEY'LL END UP...
...AND CORNELIA KNOWS SHE'S NOT ALONE!
SO SHE FACES ONE OF HER FEARS...
...BECAUSE WHAT MATTERS MOST TO HER IS STANDING...

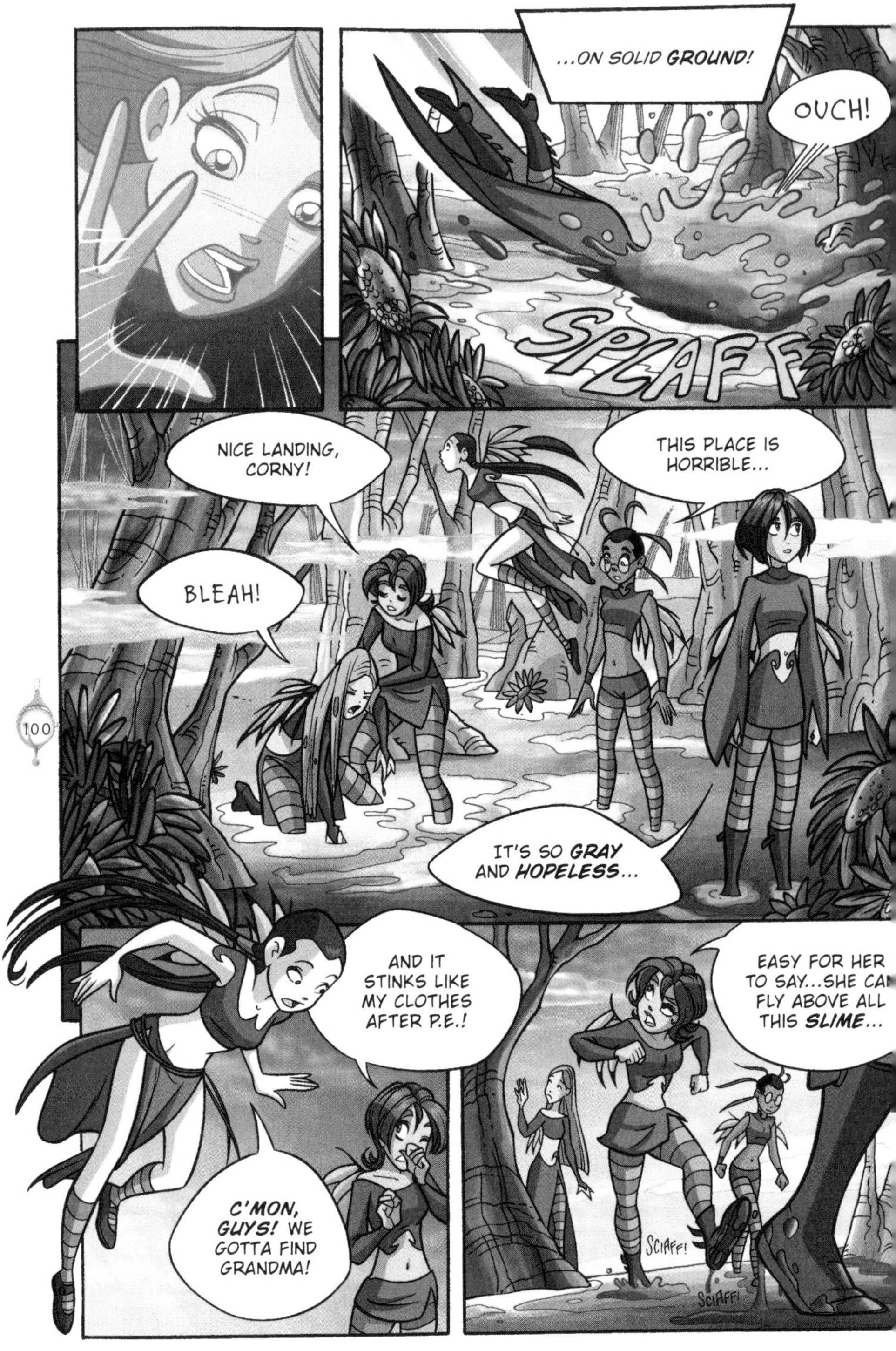
...ON SOLID **GROUND!**
OUCH!
SPLAFF
NICE LANDING, CORNY!
THIS PLACE IS HORRIBLE...
BLEAH!
IT'S SO **GRAY** AND **HOPELESS**...
AND IT STINKS LIKE MY CLOTHES AFTER P.E.!
C'MON, GUYS! WE GOTTA FIND GRANDMA!
SCIAFF!
SCIAFF!

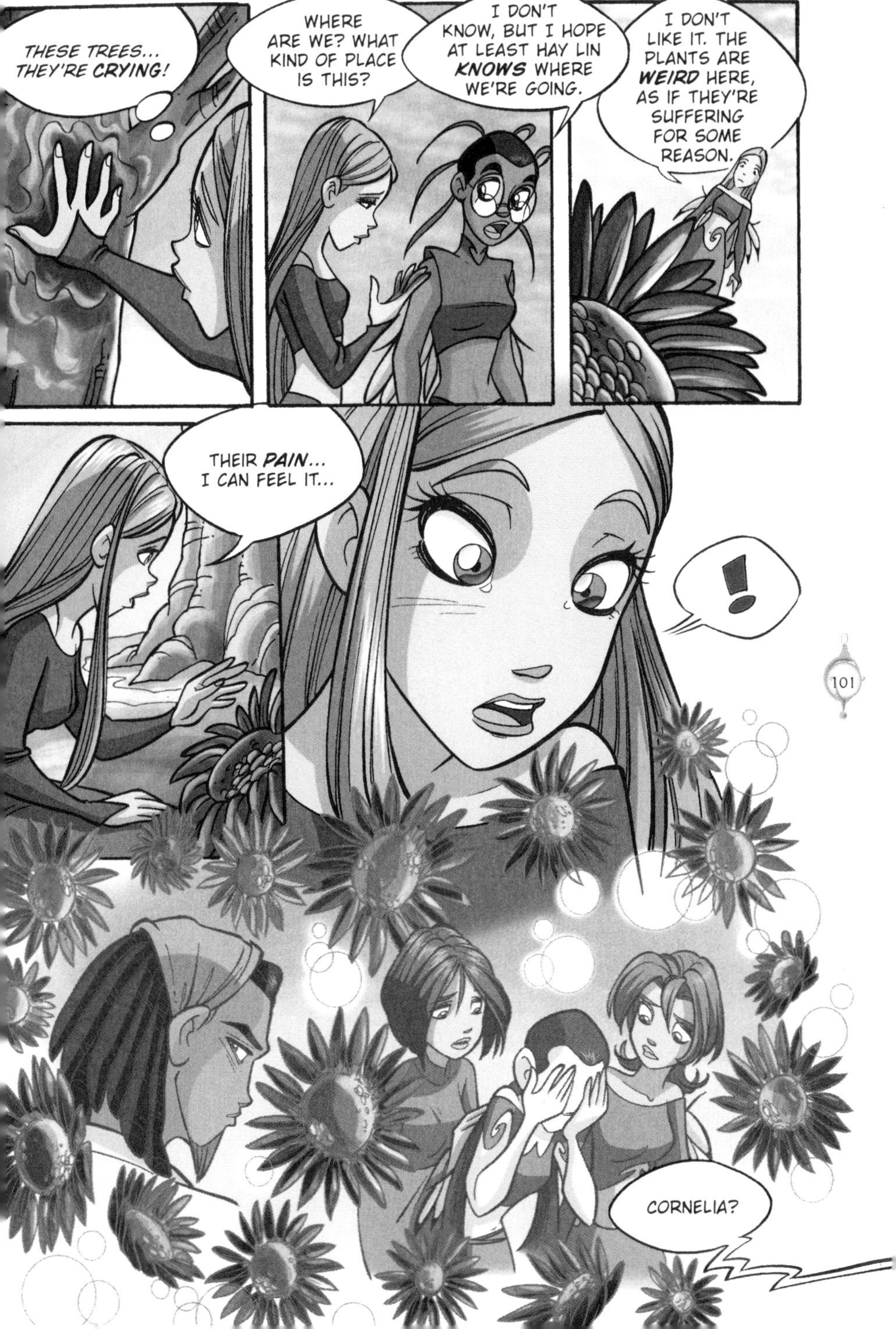
THESE TREES... THEY'RE CRYING!
WHERE ARE WE? WHAT KIND OF PLACE IS THIS?
I DON'T KNOW, BUT I HOPE AT LEAST HAY LIN KNOWS WHERE WE'RE GOING.
I DON'T LIKE IT. THE PLANTS ARE WEIRD HERE, AS IF THEY'RE SUFFERING FOR SOME REASON.
THEIR PAIN... I CAN FEEL IT...
!
CORNELIA?

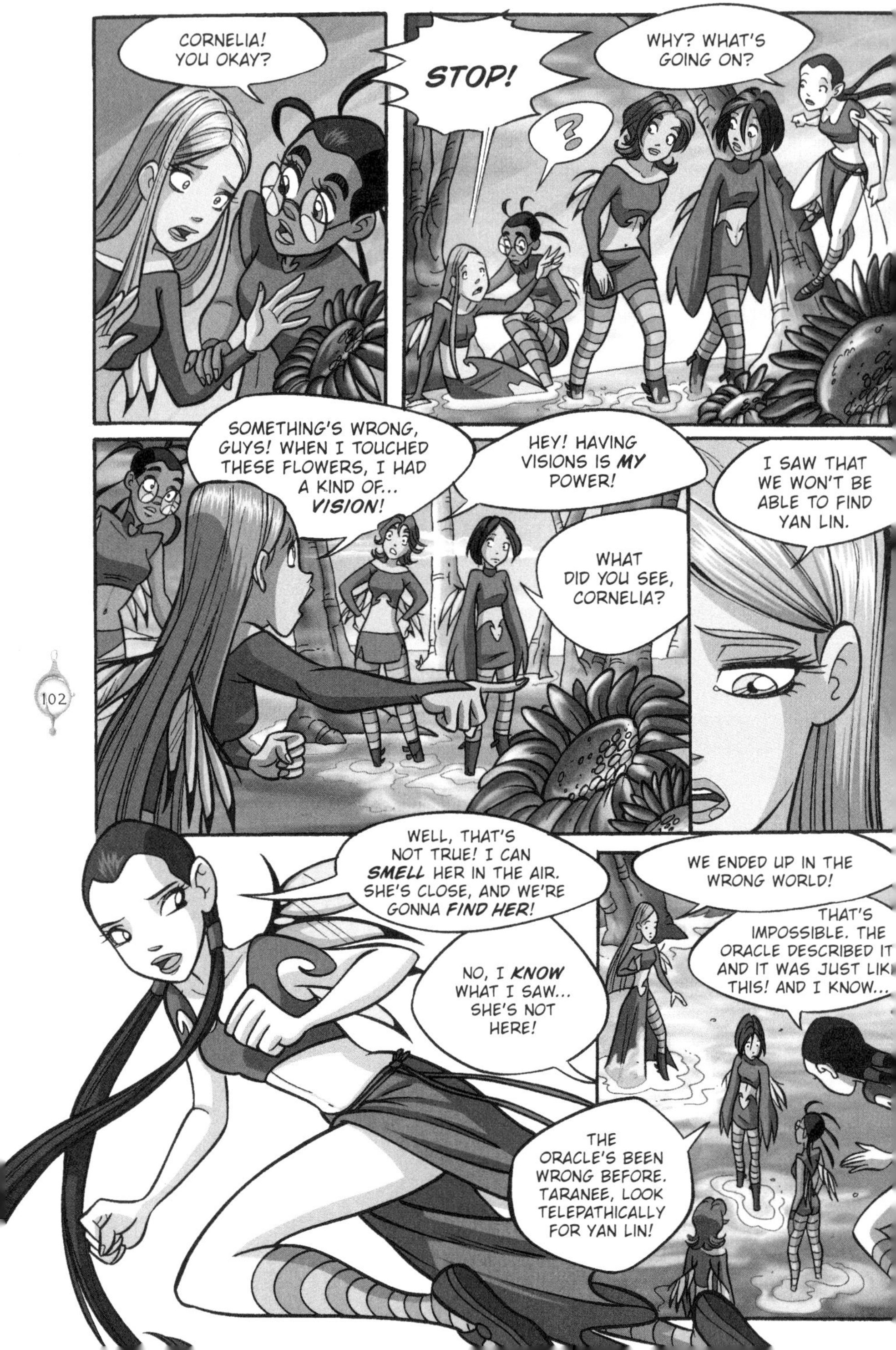
CORNELIA! YOU OKAY?
STOP!
WHY? WHAT'S GOING ON?
?
SOMETHING'S WRONG, GUYS! WHEN I TOUCHED THESE FLOWERS, I HAD A KIND OF... VISION!
HEY! HAVING VISIONS IS MY POWER!
WHAT DID YOU SEE, CORNELIA?
I SAW THAT WE WON'T BE ABLE TO FIND YAN LIN.
WELL, THAT'S NOT TRUE! I CAN SMELL HER IN THE AIR. SHE'S CLOSE, AND WE'RE GONNA FIND HER!
NO, I KNOW WHAT I SAW... SHE'S NOT HERE!
WE ENDED UP IN THE WRONG WORLD!
THAT'S IMPOSSIBLE. THE ORACLE DESCRIBED IT AND IT WAS JUST LIK THIS! AND I KNOW...
THE ORACLE'S BEEN WRONG BEFORE. TARANEE, LOOK TELEPATHICALLY FOR YAN LIN!

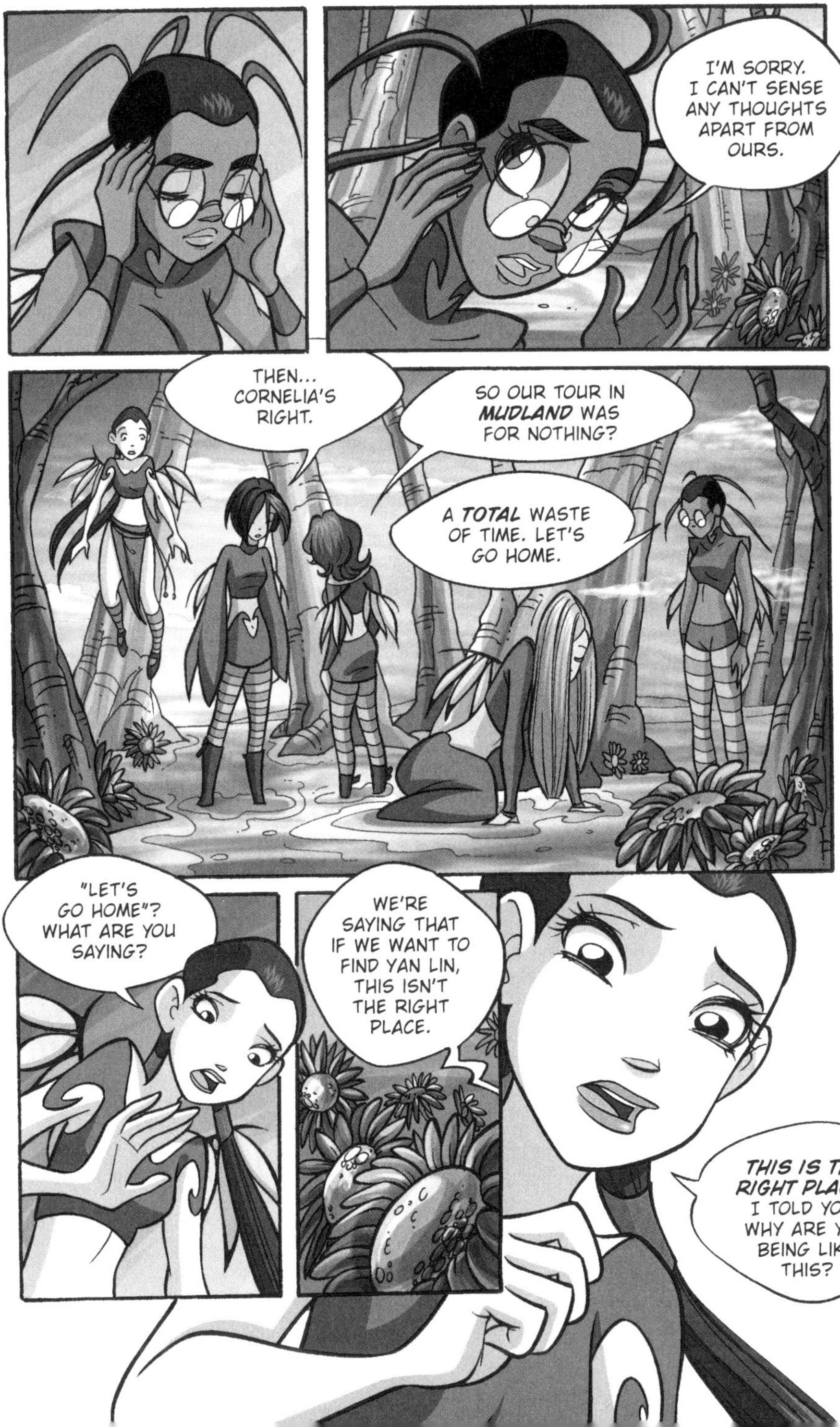
I'M SORRY. I CAN'T SENSE ANY THOUGHTS APART FROM OURS.
THEN... CORNELIA'S RIGHT.
SO OUR TOUR IN MUDLAND WAS FOR NOTHING?
A TOTAL WASTE OF TIME. LET'S GO HOME.
"LET'S GO HOME"? WHAT ARE YOU SAYING?
WE'RE SAYING THAT IF WE WANT TO FIND YAN LIN, THIS ISN'T THE RIGHT PLACE.
THIS IS THE RIGHT PLACE! I TOLD YOU! WHY ARE YOU BEING LIKE THIS?

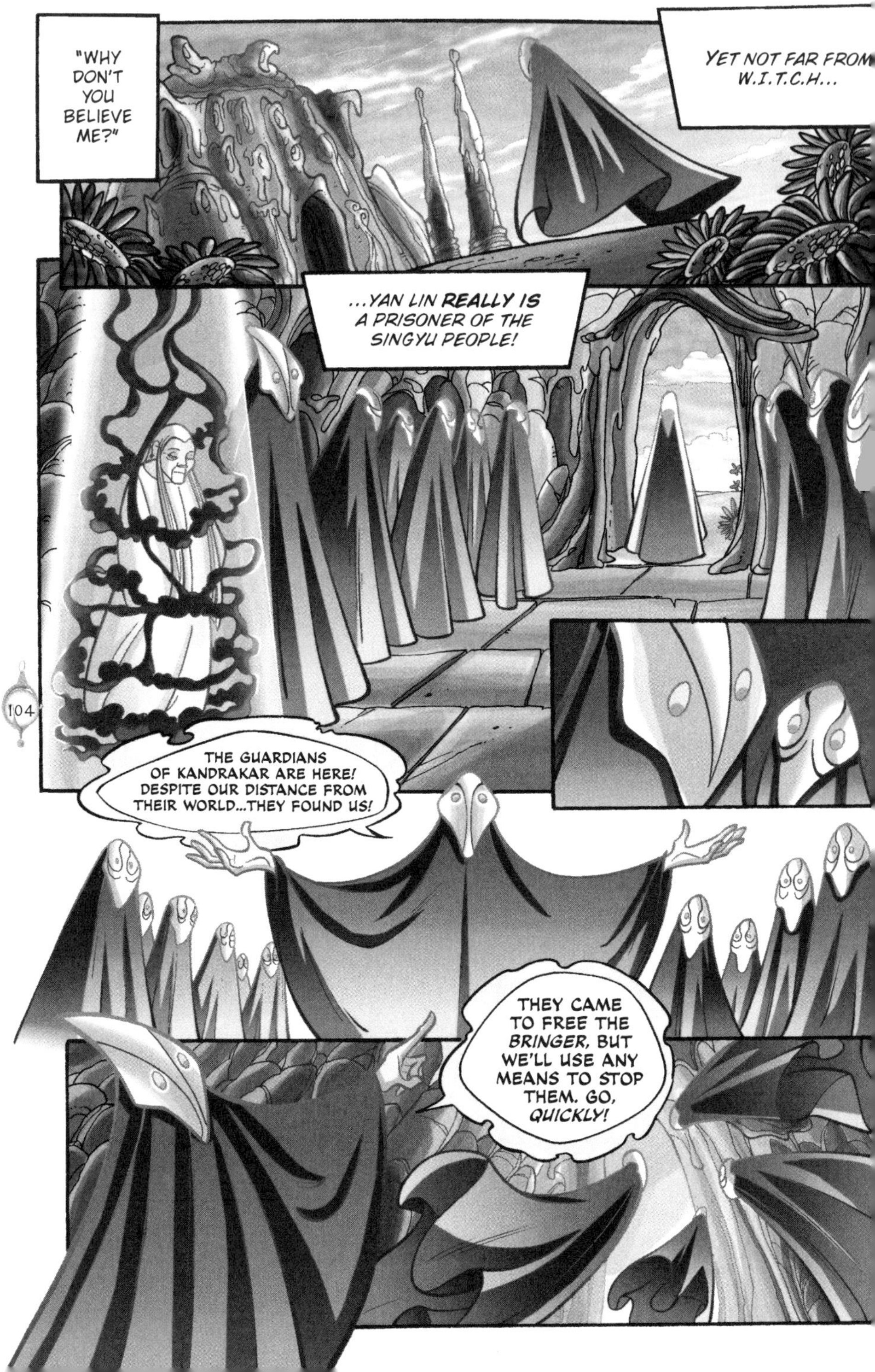

"WHY DON'T YOU BELIEVE ME?"
YET NOT FAR FROM W.I.T.C.H...
...YAN LIN REALLY IS A PRISONER OF THE SINGYU PEOPLE!
THE GUARDIANS OF KANDRAKAR ARE HERE! DESPITE OUR DISTANCE FROM THEIR WORLD...THEY FOUND US!
THEY CAME TO FREE THE BRINGER, BUT WE'LL USE ANY MEANS TO STOP THEM. GO, QUICKLY!

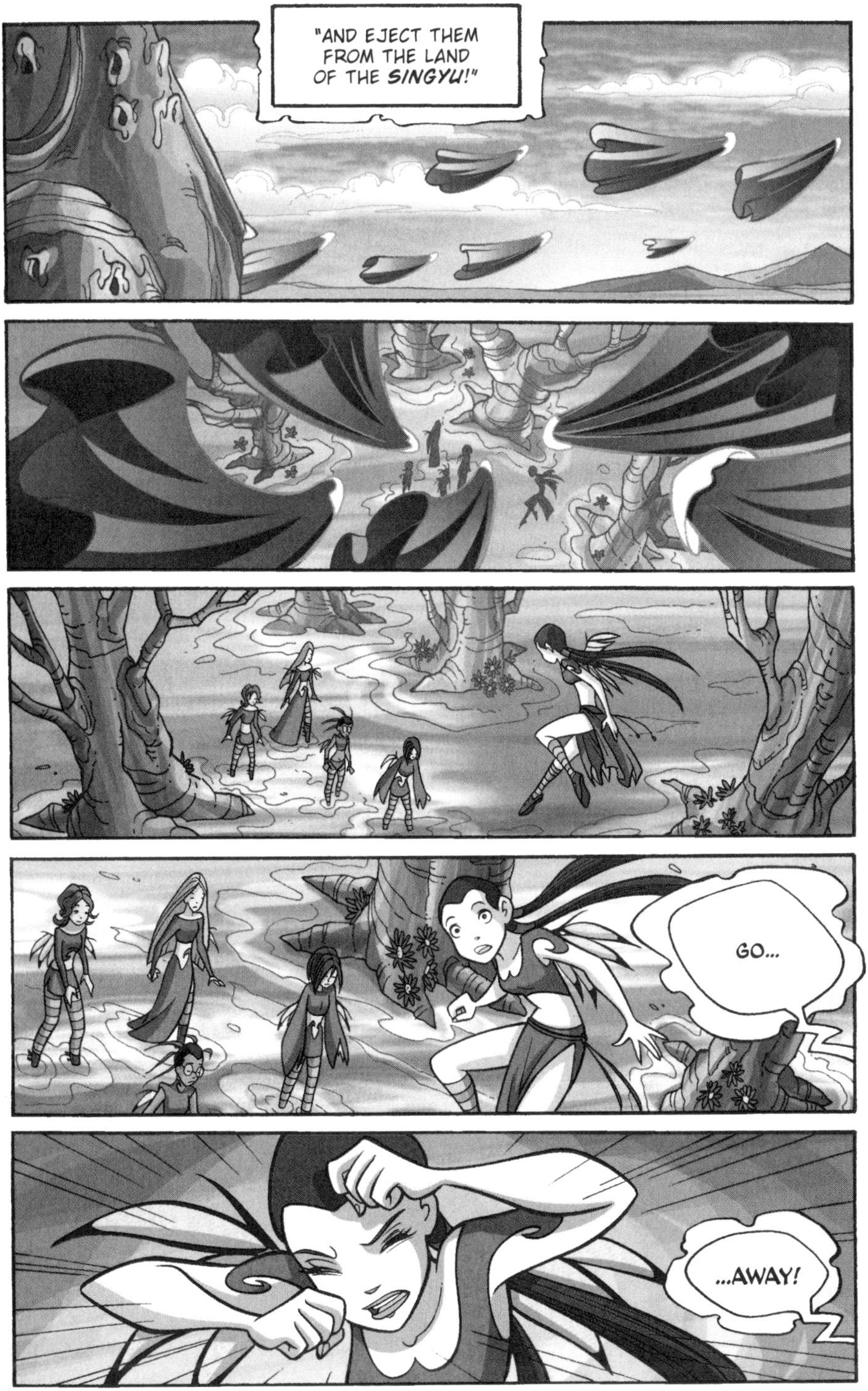
"AND EJECT THEM FROM THE LAND OF THE SINGYU!"
GO...
...AWAY!

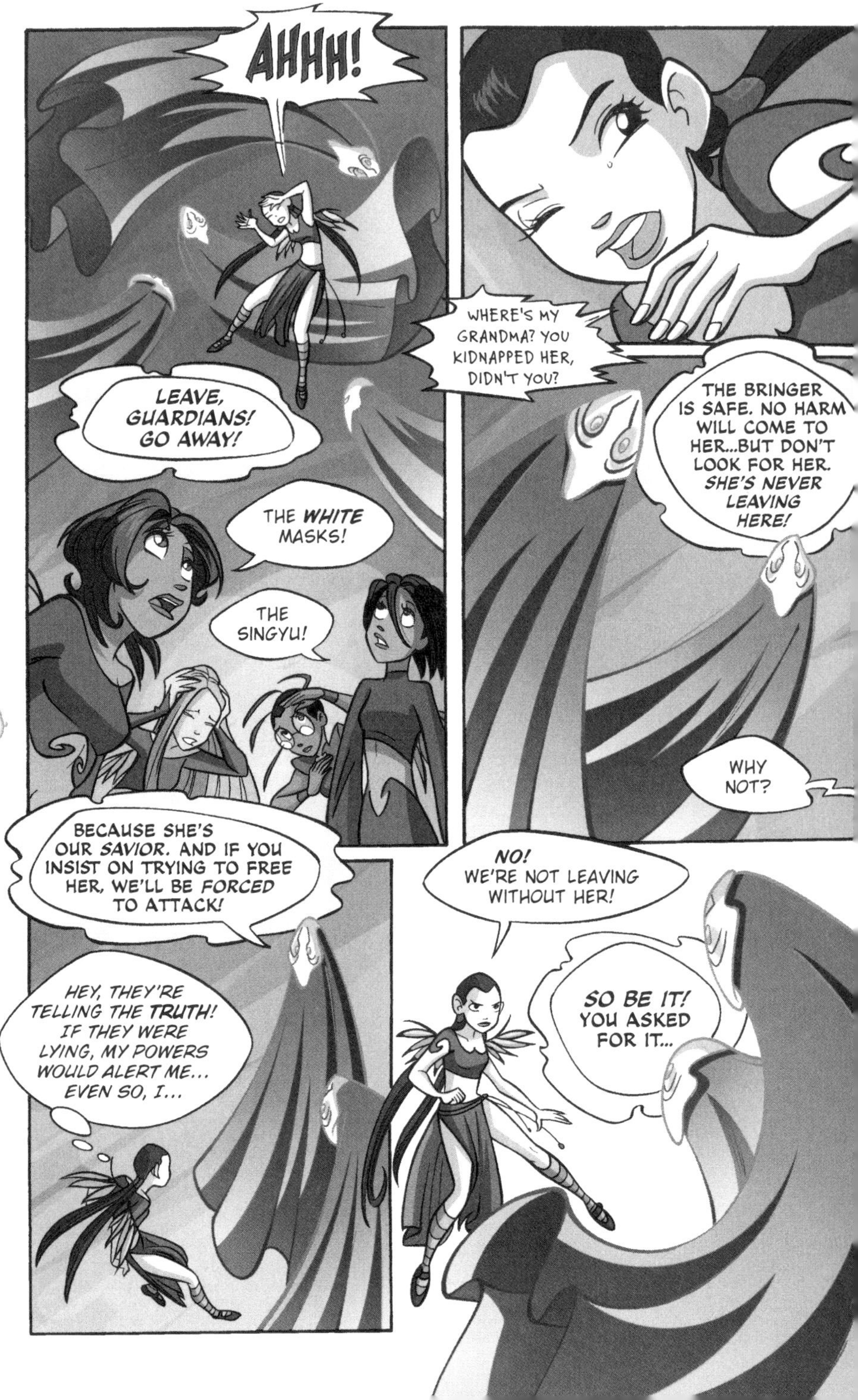

AHHH!
LEAVE, GUARDIANS! GO AWAY!
THE WHITE MASKS!
THE SINGYU!
WHERE'S MY GRANDMA? YOU KIDNAPPED HER, DIDN'T YOU?
THE BRINGER IS SAFE. NO HARM WILL COME TO HER...BUT DON'T LOOK FOR HER. SHE'S NEVER LEAVING HERE!
WHY NOT?
BECAUSE SHE'S OUR SAVIOR. AND IF YOU INSIST ON TRYING TO FREE HER, WE'LL BE FORCED TO ATTACK!
HEY, THEY'RE TELLING THE TRUTH! IF THEY WERE LYING, MY POWERS WOULD ALERT ME... EVEN SO, I...
NO! WE'RE NOT LEAVING WITHOUT HER!
SO BE IT! YOU ASKED FOR IT...

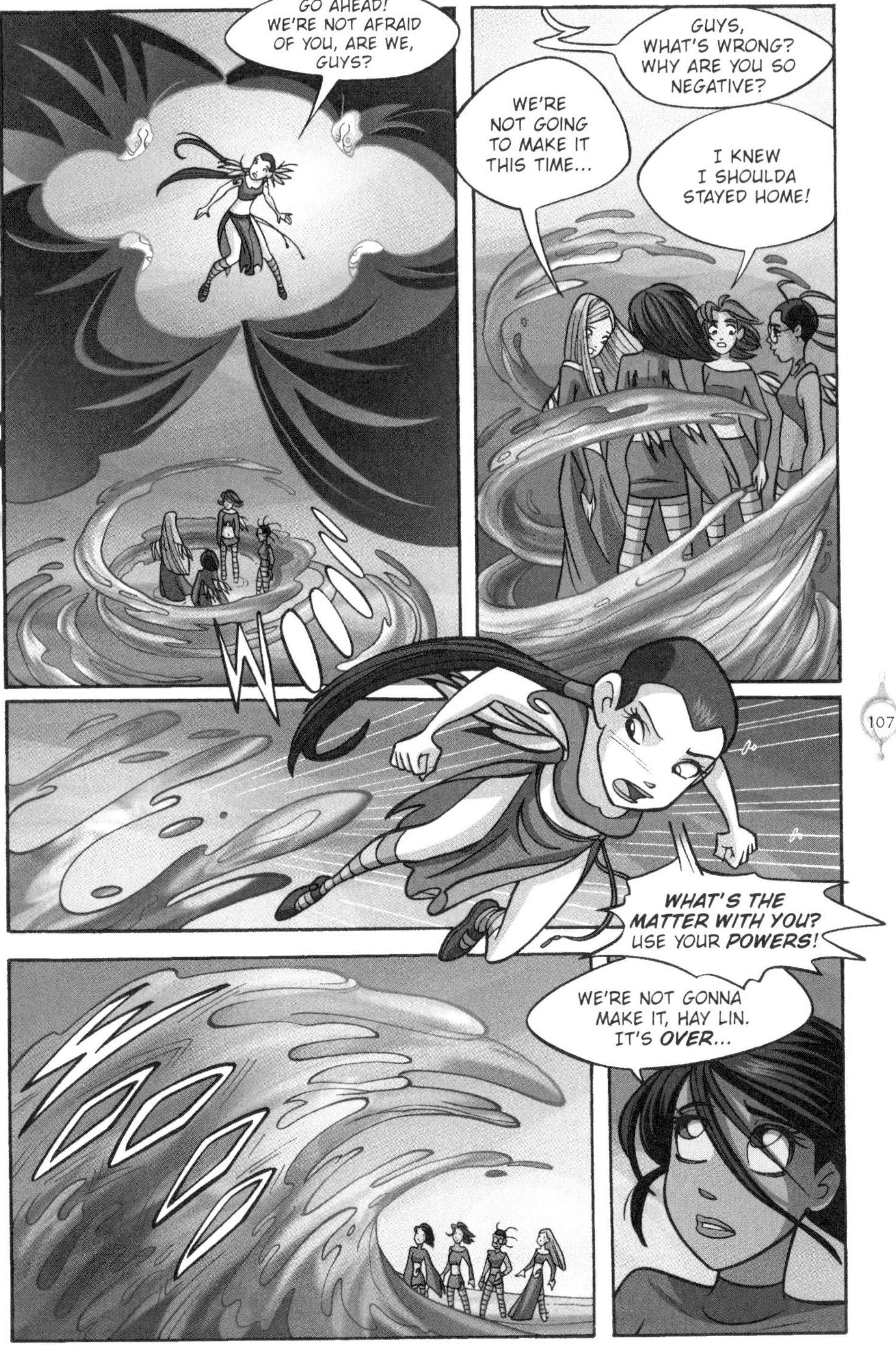
GO AHEAD! WE'RE NOT AFRAID OF YOU, ARE WE, GUYS?
GUYS, WHAT'S WRONG? WHY ARE YOU SO NEGATIVE?
WE'RE NOT GOING TO MAKE IT THIS TIME...
I KNEW I SHOULDA STAYED HOME!
WHOOO
WHAT'S THE MATTER WITH YOU? USE YOUR POWERS!
WE'RE NOT GONNA MAKE IT, HAY LIN. IT'S OVER...

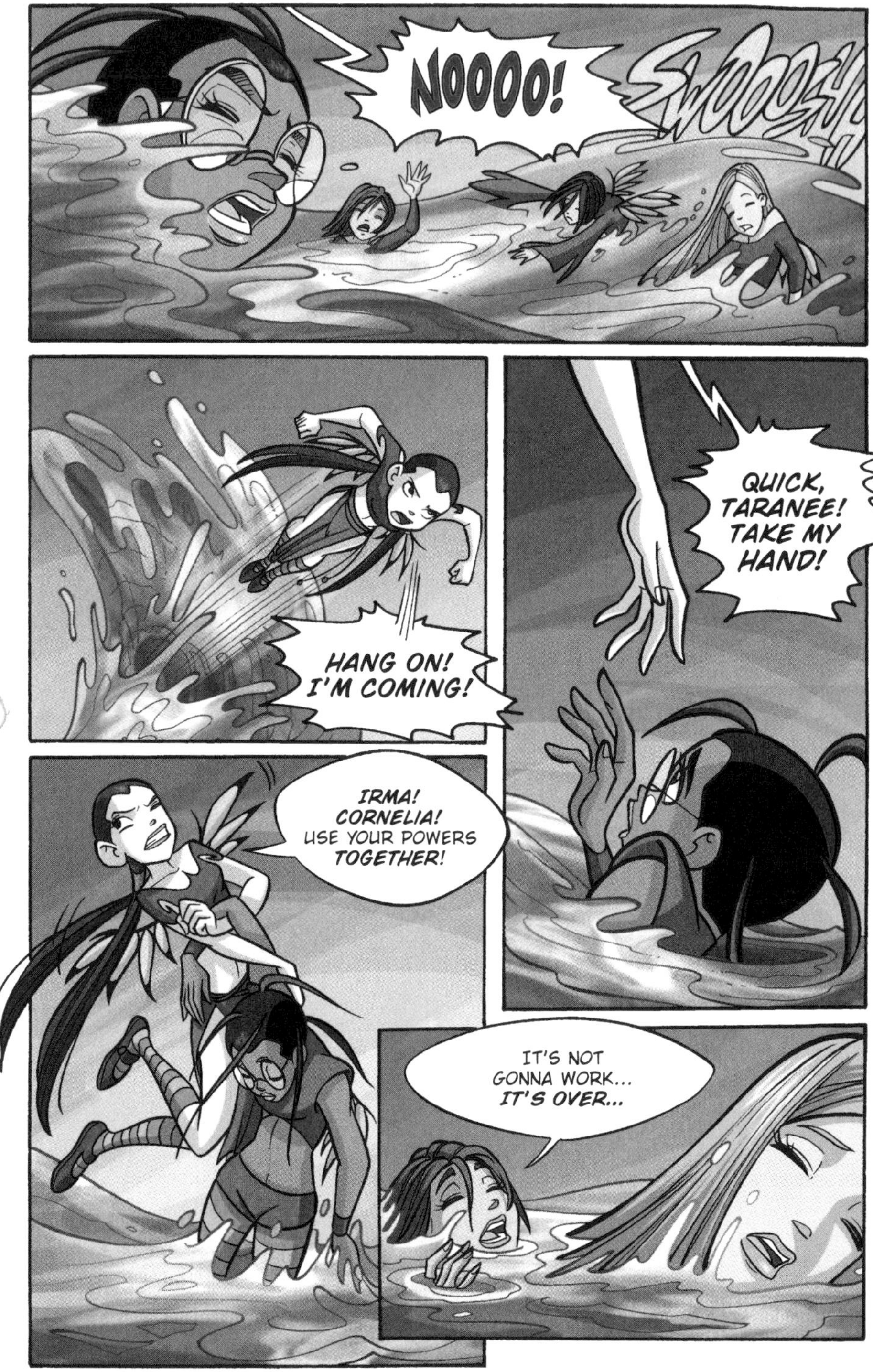
NOOOO!
SWOOSH
HANG ON! I'M COMING!
QUICK, TARANEE! TAKE MY HAND!
IRMA! CORNELIA! USE YOUR POWERS TOGETHER!
IT'S NOT GONNA WORK... IT'S OVER...

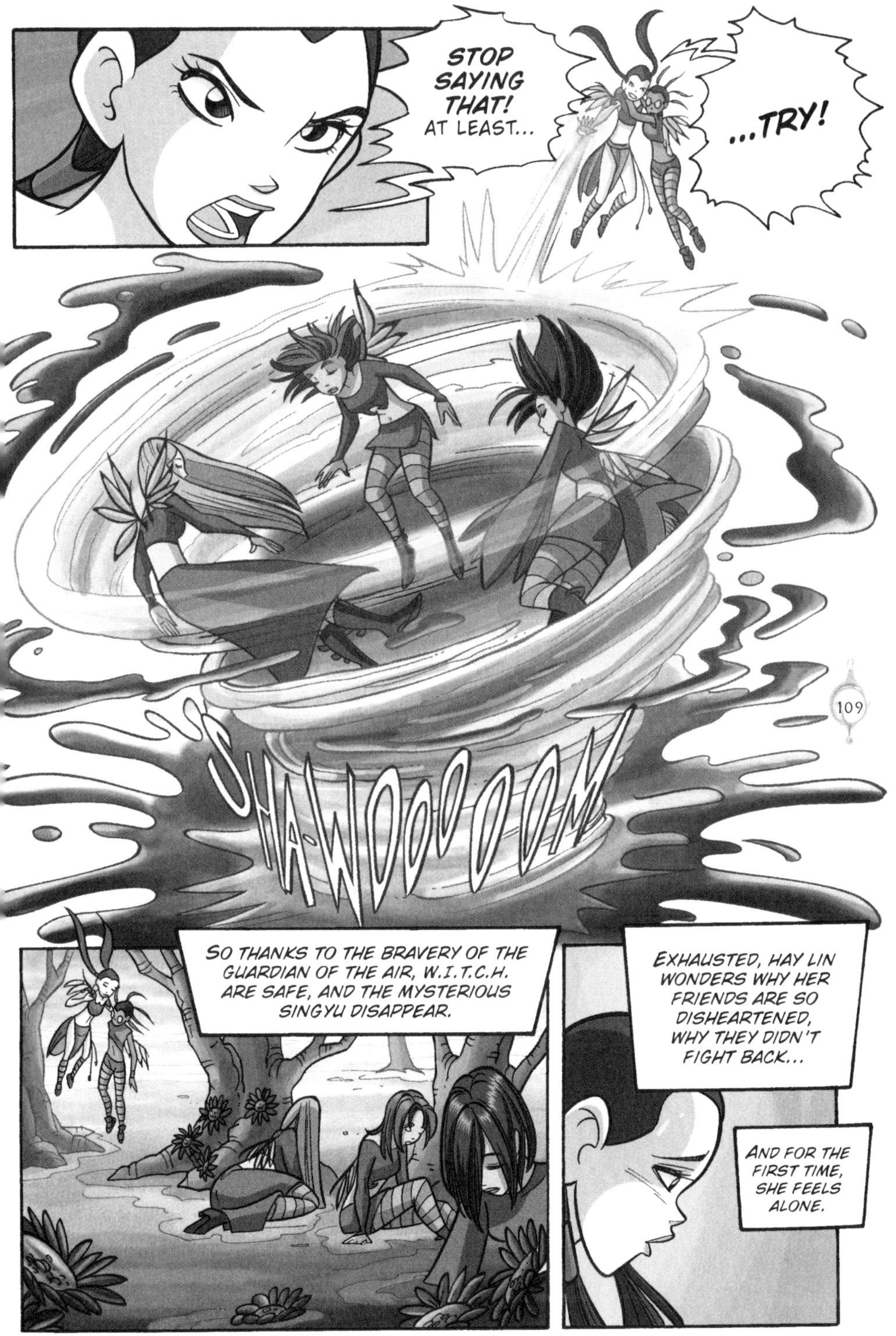
STOP SAYING THAT! AT LEAST...
...TRY!
SHA-WOOOOOM
SO THANKS TO THE BRAVERY OF THE GUARDIAN OF THE AIR, W.I.T.C.H. ARE SAFE, AND THE MYSTERIOUS SINGYU DISAPPEAR.
EXHAUSTED, HAY LIN WONDERS WHY HER FRIENDS ARE SO DISHEARTENED, WHY THEY DIDN'T FIGHT BACK...
AND FOR THE FIRST TIME, SHE FEELS ALONE.

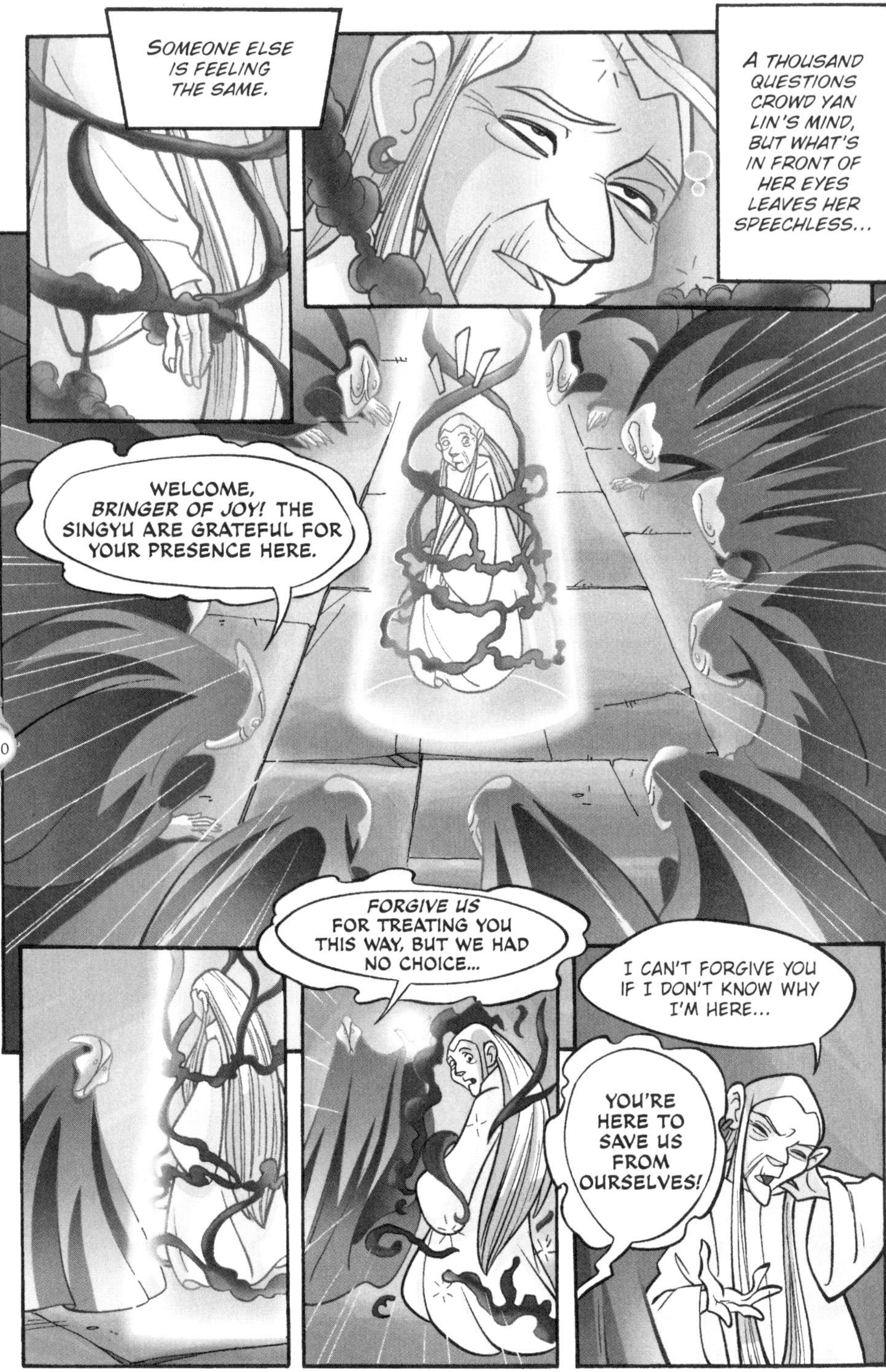
SOMEONE ELSE IS FEELING THE SAME.
A THOUSAND QUESTIONS CROWD YAN LIN'S MIND, BUT WHAT'S IN FRONT OF HER EYES LEAVES HER SPEECHLESS...
WELCOME, BRINGER OF JOY! THE SINGYU ARE GRATEFUL FOR YOUR PRESENCE HERE.
FORGIVE US FOR TREATING YOU THIS WAY, BUT WE HAD NO CHOICE...
I CAN'T FORGIVE YOU IF I DON'T KNOW WHY I'M HERE...
YOU'RE HERE TO SAVE US FROM OURSELVES!

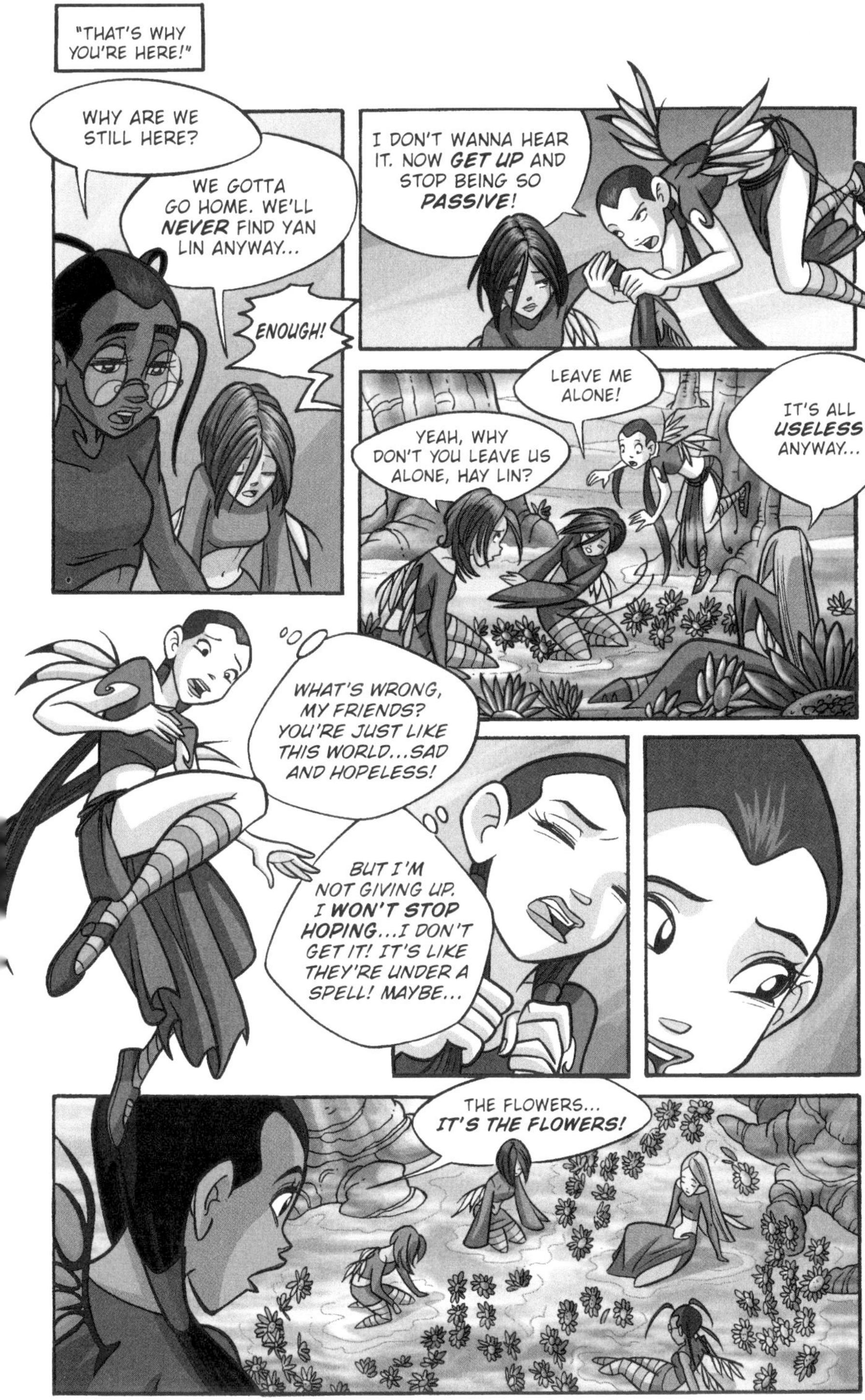
"THAT'S WHY YOU'RE HERE!"
WHY ARE WE STILL HERE?
WE GOTTA GO HOME. WE'LL NEVER FIND YAN LIN ANYWAY...
ENOUGH!
I DON'T WANNA HEAR IT. NOW GET UP AND STOP BEING SO PASSIVE!
LEAVE ME ALONE!
YEAH, WHY DON'T YOU LEAVE US ALONE, HAY LIN?
IT'S ALL USELESS ANYWAY...
WHAT'S WRONG, MY FRIENDS? YOU'RE JUST LIKE THIS WORLD...SAD AND HOPELESS!
BUT I'M NOT GIVING UP. I WON'T STOP HOPING...I DON'T GET IT! IT'S LIKE THEY'RE UNDER A SPELL! MAYBE...
THE FLOWERS... IT'S THE FLOWERS!

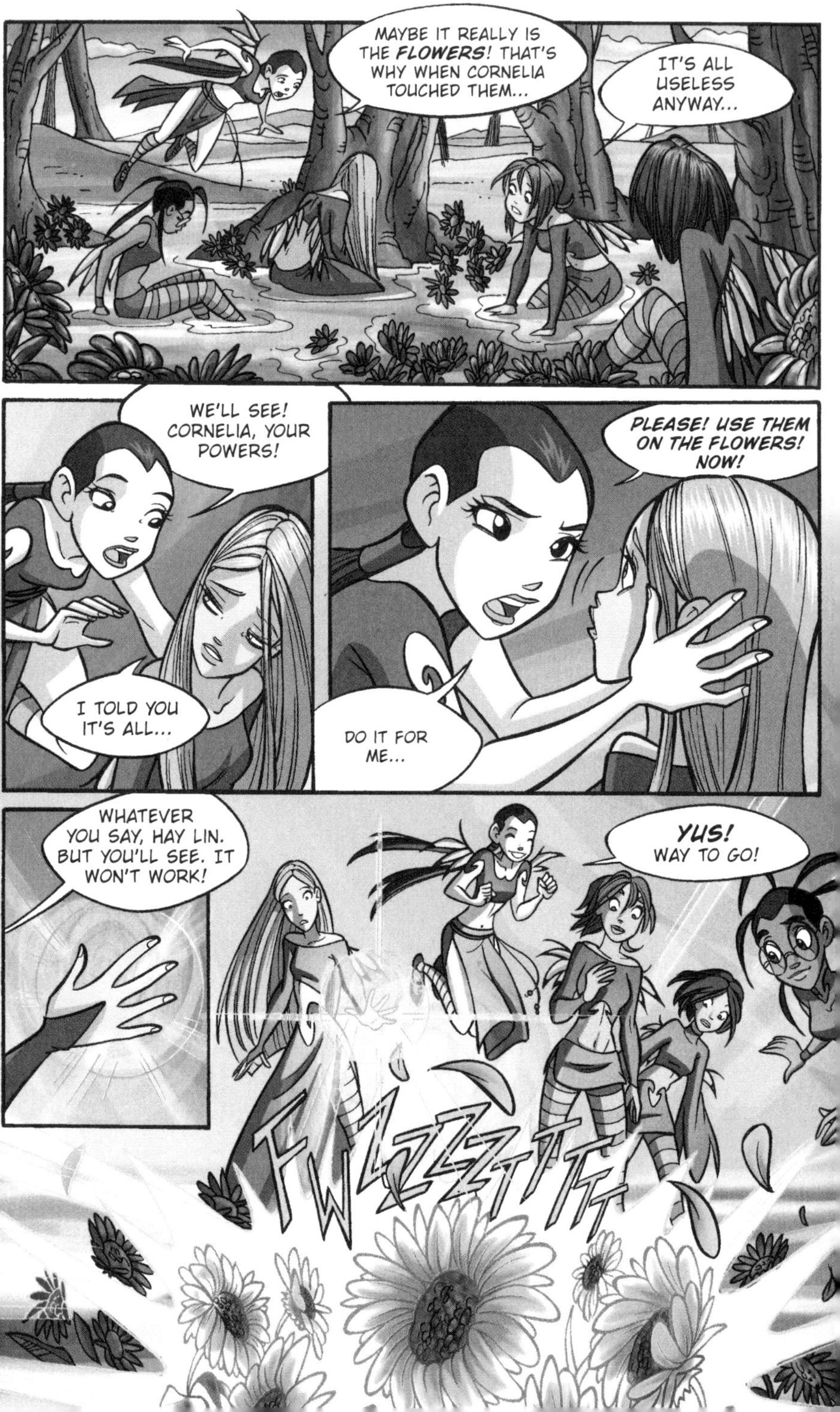

MAYBE IT REALLY IS THE FLOWERS! THAT'S WHY WHEN CORNELIA TOUCHED THEM...
IT'S ALL USELESS ANYWAY...
WE'LL SEE! CORNELIA, YOUR POWERS!
I TOLD YOU IT'S ALL...
PLEASE! USE THEM ON THE FLOWERS! NOW!
DO IT FOR ME...
WHATEVER YOU SAY, HAY LIN. BUT YOU'LL SEE. IT WON'T WORK!
YUS! WAY TO GO!
FWZZZTTTT

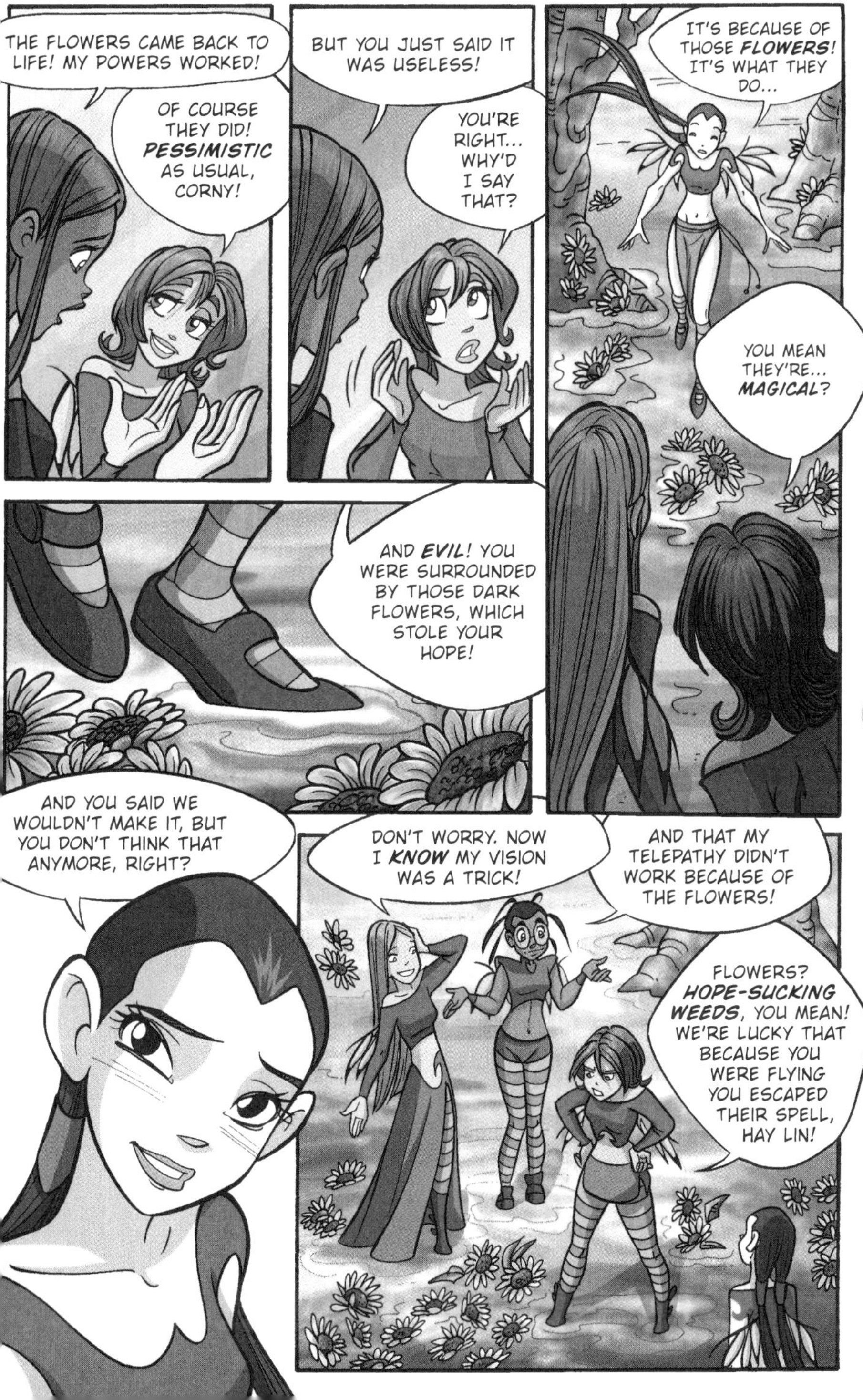
THE FLOWERS CAME BACK TO LIFE! MY POWERS WORKED!
OF COURSE THEY DID! PESSIMISTIC AS USUAL, CORNY!
BUT YOU JUST SAID IT WAS USELESS!
YOU'RE RIGHT... WHY'D I SAY THAT?
IT'S BECAUSE OF THOSE FLOWERS! IT'S WHAT THEY DO...
YOU MEAN THEY'RE... MAGICAL?
AND EVIL! YOU WERE SURROUNDED BY THOSE DARK FLOWERS, WHICH STOLE YOUR HOPE!
AND YOU SAID WE WOULDN'T MAKE IT, BUT YOU DON'T THINK THAT ANYMORE, RIGHT?
DON'T WORRY. NOW I KNOW MY VISION WAS A TRICK!
AND THAT MY TELEPATHY DIDN'T WORK BECAUSE OF THE FLOWERS!
FLOWERS? HOPE-SUCKING WEEDS, YOU MEAN! WE'RE LUCKY THAT BECAUSE YOU WERE FLYING YOU ESCAPED THEIR SPELL, HAY LIN!

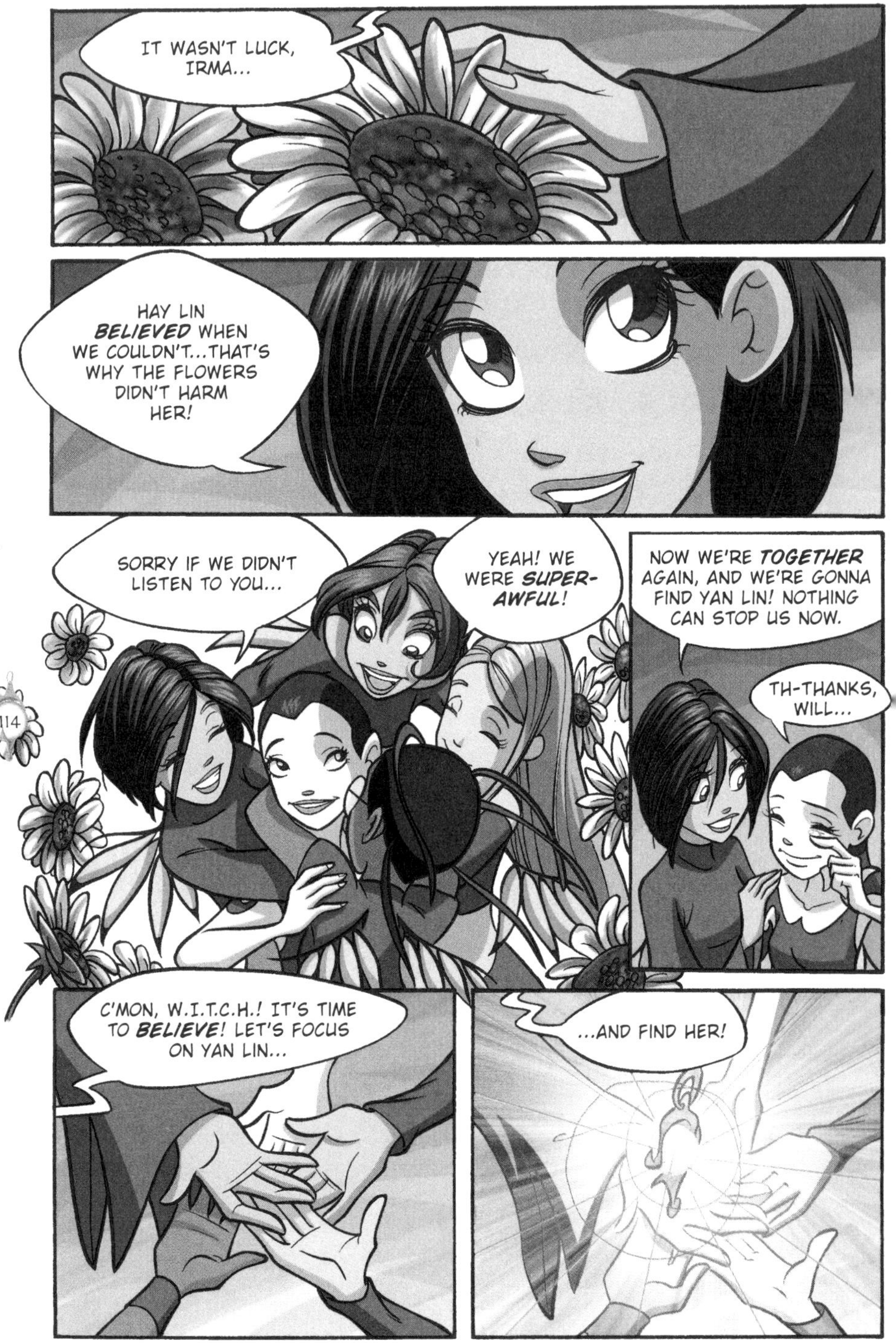

IT WASN'T LUCK, IRMA...
HAY LIN BELIEVED WHEN WE COULDN'T...THAT'S WHY THE FLOWERS DIDN'T HARM HER!
SORRY IF WE DIDN'T LISTEN TO YOU...
YEAH! WE WERE SUPER-AWFUL!
NOW WE'RE TOGETHER AGAIN, AND WE'RE GONNA FIND YAN LIN! NOTHING CAN STOP US NOW.
TH-THANKS, WILL...
C'MON, W.I.T.C.H.! IT'S TIME TO BELIEVE! LET'S FOCUS ON YAN LIN...
...AND FIND HER!

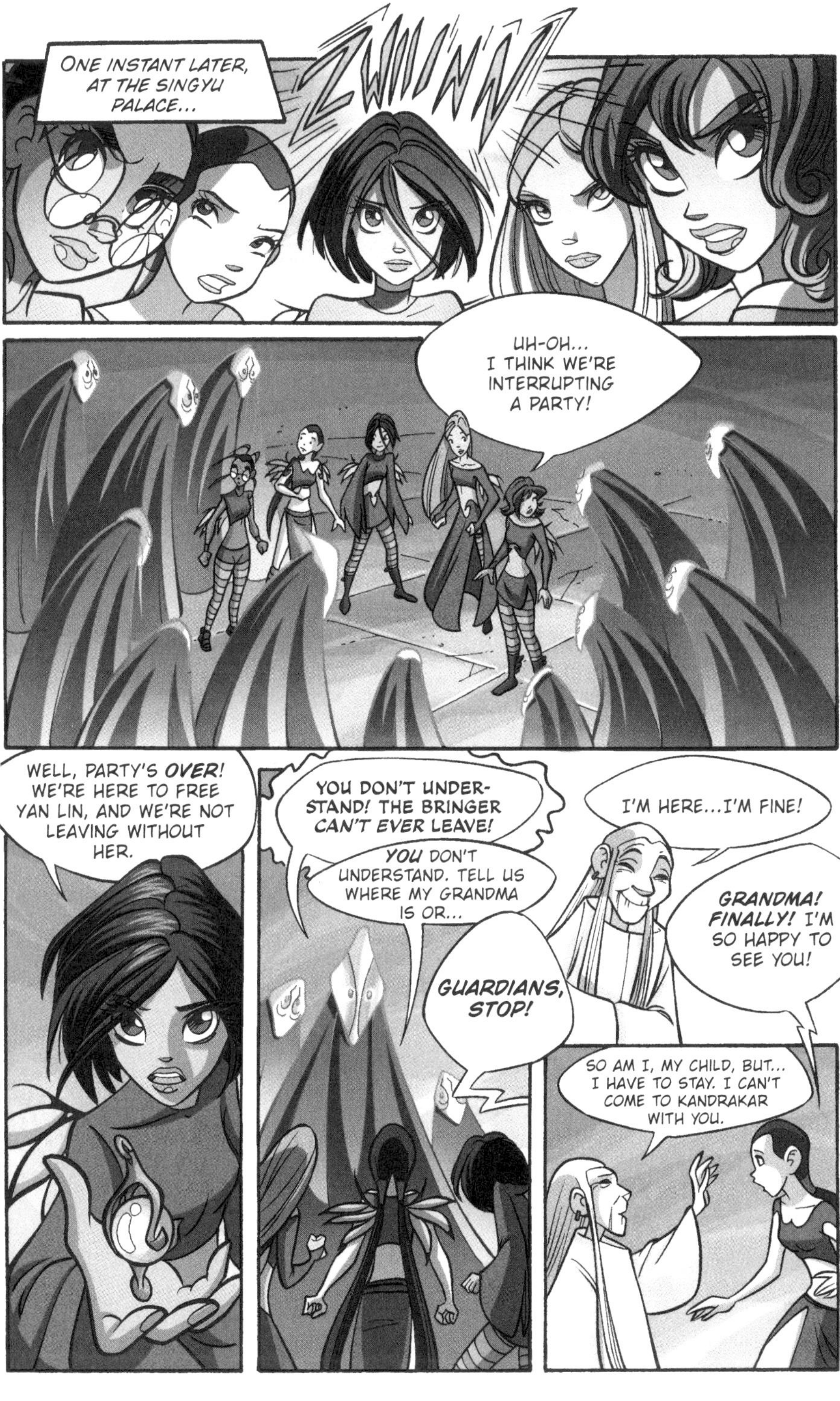

ONE INSTANT LATER, AT THE SINGYU PALACE...
ZWIIINN!
UH-OH... I THINK WE'RE INTERRUPTING A PARTY!
WELL, PARTY'S OVER! WE'RE HERE TO FREE YAN LIN, AND WE'RE NOT LEAVING WITHOUT HER.
YOU DON'T UNDER-STAND! THE BRINGER CAN'T EVER LEAVE!
YOU DON'T UNDERSTAND. TELL US WHERE MY GRANDMA IS OR...
GUARDIANS, STOP!
I'M HERE...I'M FINE!
GRANDMA! FINALLY! I'M SO HAPPY TO SEE YOU!
SO AM I, MY CHILD, BUT... I HAVE TO STAY. I CAN'T COME TO KANDRAKAR WITH YOU.

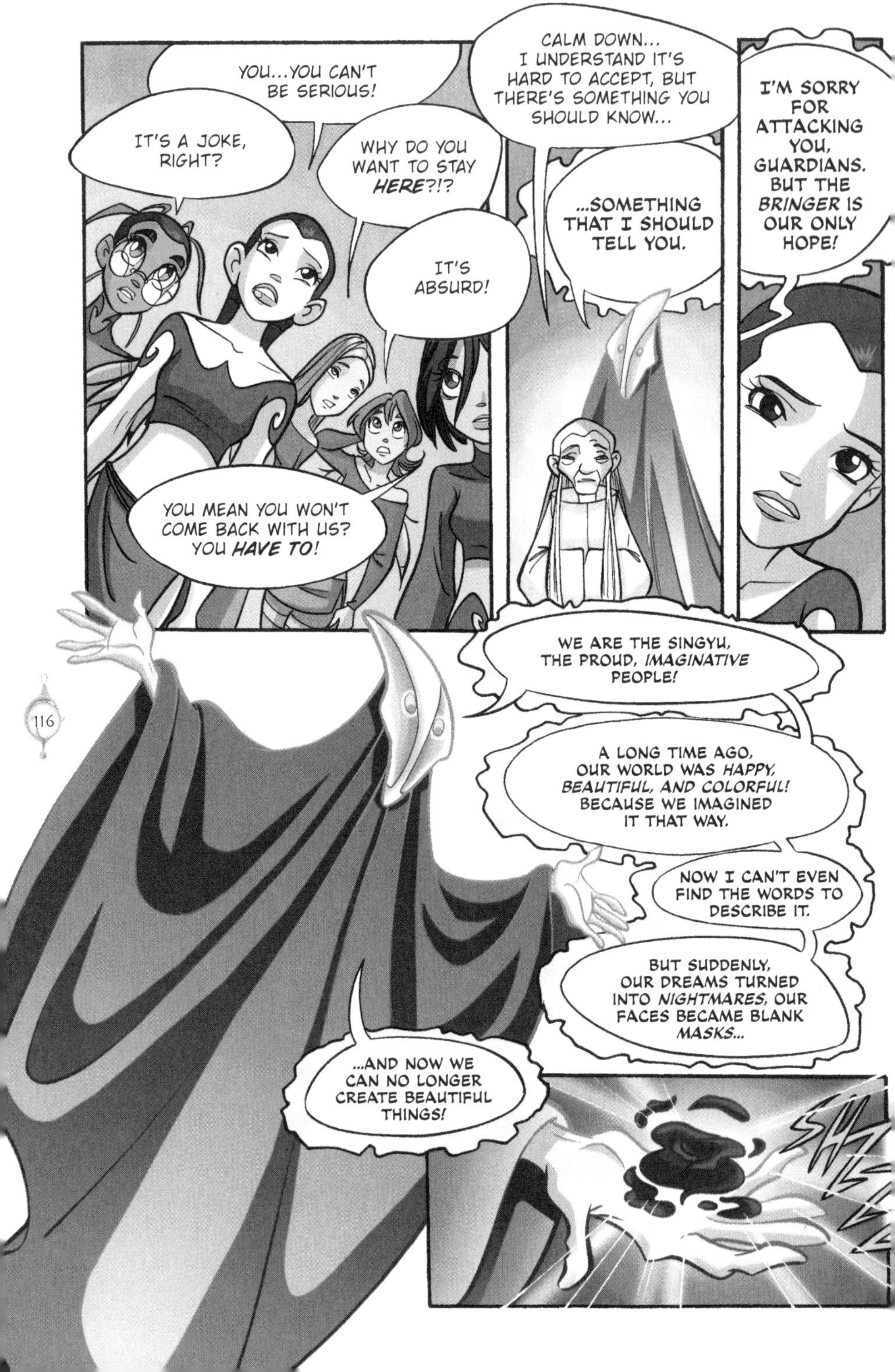
YOU...YOU CAN'T BE SERIOUS!
IT'S A JOKE, RIGHT?
WHY DO YOU WANT TO STAY *HERE*?!?
IT'S ABSURD!
YOU MEAN YOU WON'T COME BACK WITH US? YOU ***HAVE TO***!
CALM DOWN... I UNDERSTAND IT'S HARD TO ACCEPT, BUT THERE'S SOMETHING YOU SHOULD KNOW...
...SOMETHING THAT I SHOULD TELL YOU.
I'M SORRY FOR ATTACKING YOU, GUARDIANS. BUT THE *BRINGER* IS OUR ONLY HOPE!
WE ARE THE SINGYU, THE PROUD, *IMAGINATIVE* PEOPLE!
A LONG TIME AGO, OUR WORLD WAS *HAPPY, BEAUTIFUL, AND COLORFUL!* BECAUSE WE IMAGINED IT THAT WAY.
NOW I CAN'T EVEN FIND THE WORDS TO DESCRIBE IT.
BUT SUDDENLY, OUR DREAMS TURNED INTO *NIGHTMARES*, OUR FACES BECAME BLANK *MASKS*...
...AND NOW WE CAN NO LONGER CREATE BEAUTIFUL THINGS!

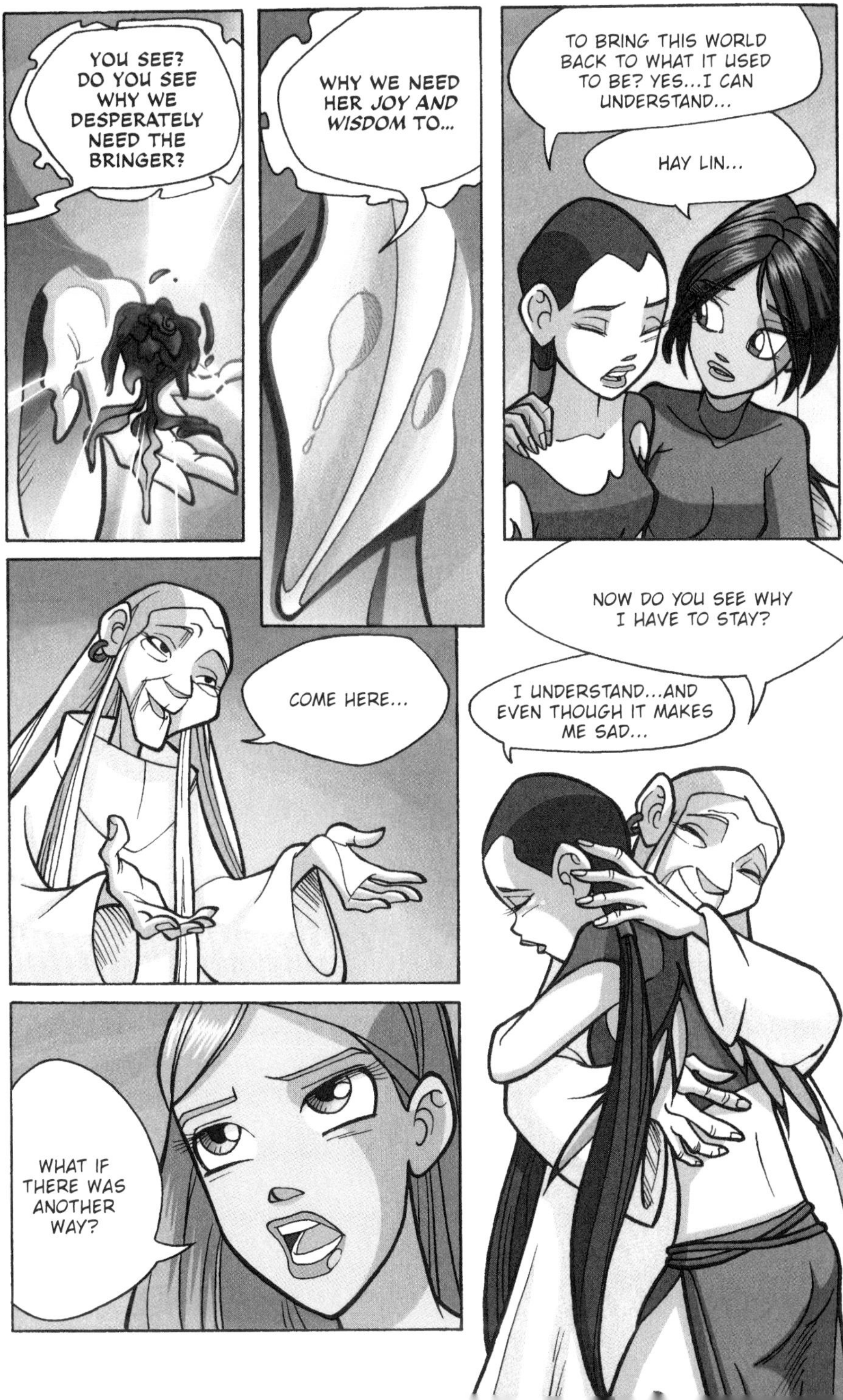
YOU SEE? DO YOU SEE WHY WE DESPERATELY NEED THE BRINGER?
WHY WE NEED HER JOY AND WISDOM TO...
TO BRING THIS WORLD BACK TO WHAT IT USED TO BE? YES...I CAN UNDERSTAND...
HAY LIN...
COME HERE...
NOW DO YOU SEE WHY I HAVE TO STAY?
I UNDERSTAND...AND EVEN THOUGH IT MAKES ME SAD...
WHAT IF THERE WAS ANOTHER WAY?

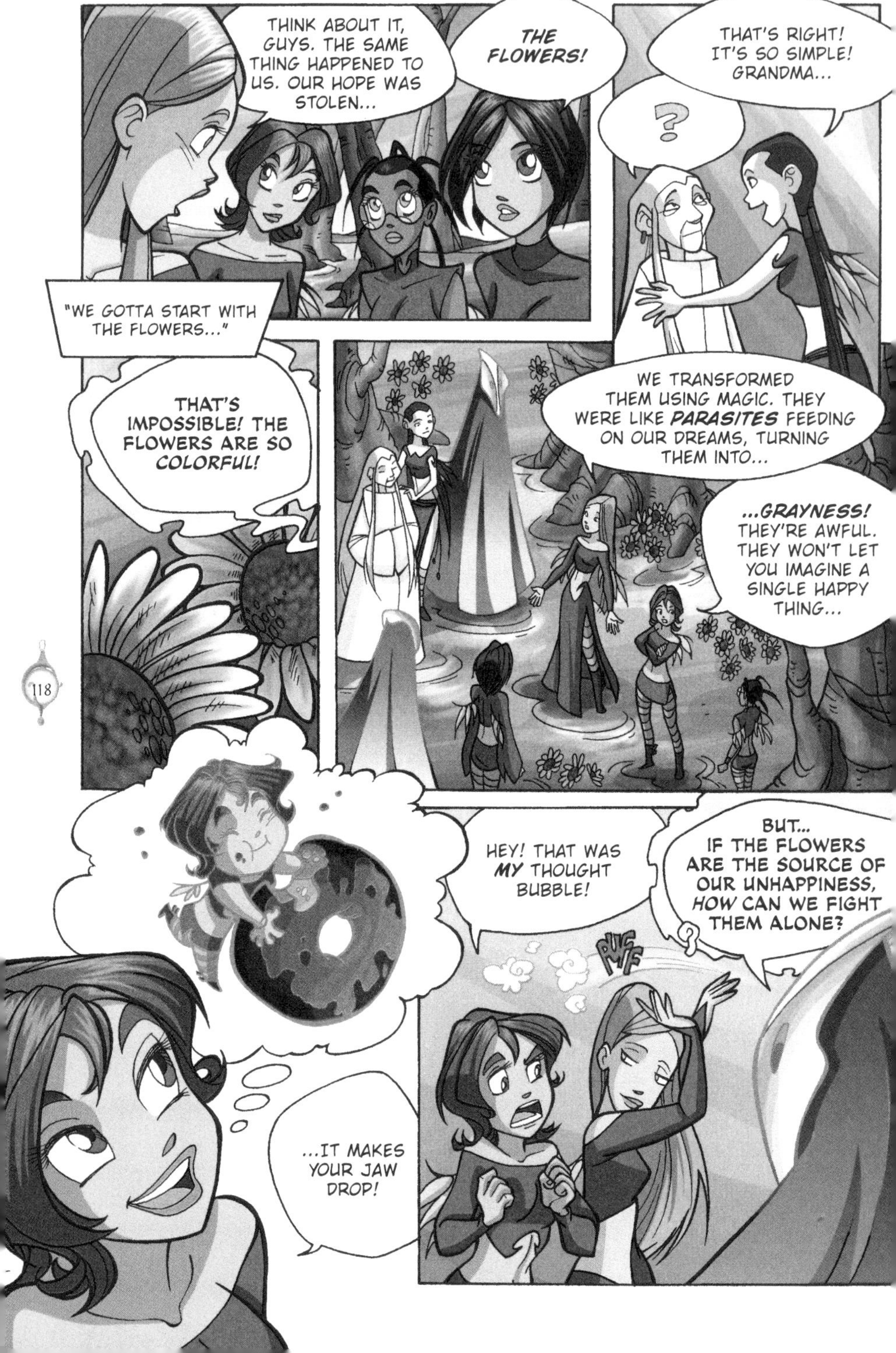
THINK ABOUT IT, GUYS. THE SAME THING HAPPENED TO US. OUR HOPE WAS STOLEN...
THE FLOWERS!
THAT'S RIGHT! IT'S SO SIMPLE! GRANDMA...
?
"WE GOTTA START WITH THE FLOWERS..."
THAT'S IMPOSSIBLE! THE FLOWERS ARE SO COLORFUL!
WE TRANSFORMED THEM USING MAGIC. THEY WERE LIKE PARASITES FEEDING ON OUR DREAMS, TURNING THEM INTO...
...GRAYNESS! THEY'RE AWFUL. THEY WON'T LET YOU IMAGINE A SINGLE HAPPY THING...
...IT MAKES YOUR JAW DROP!
HEY! THAT WAS MY THOUGHT BUBBLE!
BUT... IF THE FLOWERS ARE THE SOURCE OF OUR UNHAPPINESS, HOW CAN WE FIGHT THEM ALONE?
PUFF

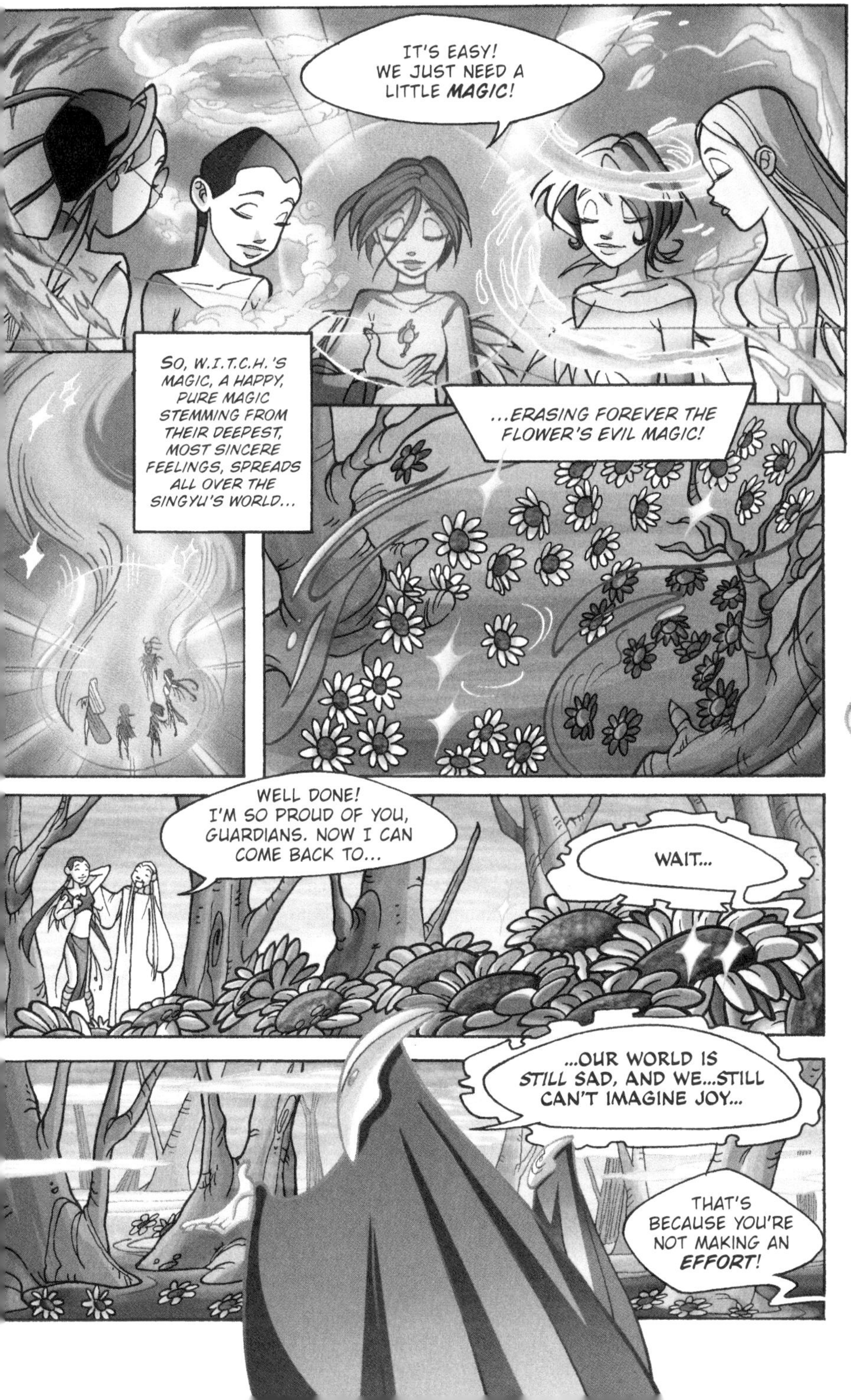
IT'S EASY!
WE JUST NEED A LITTLE MAGIC!
SO, W.I.T.C.H.'S MAGIC, A HAPPY, PURE MAGIC STEMMING FROM THEIR DEEPEST, MOST SINCERE FEELINGS, SPREADS ALL OVER THE SINGYU'S WORLD...
...ERASING FOREVER THE FLOWER'S EVIL MAGIC!
WELL DONE! I'M SO PROUD OF YOU, GUARDIANS. NOW I CAN COME BACK TO...
WAIT...
...OUR WORLD IS STILL SAD, AND WE...STILL CAN'T IMAGINE JOY...
THAT'S BECAUSE YOU'RE NOT MAKING AN EFFORT!

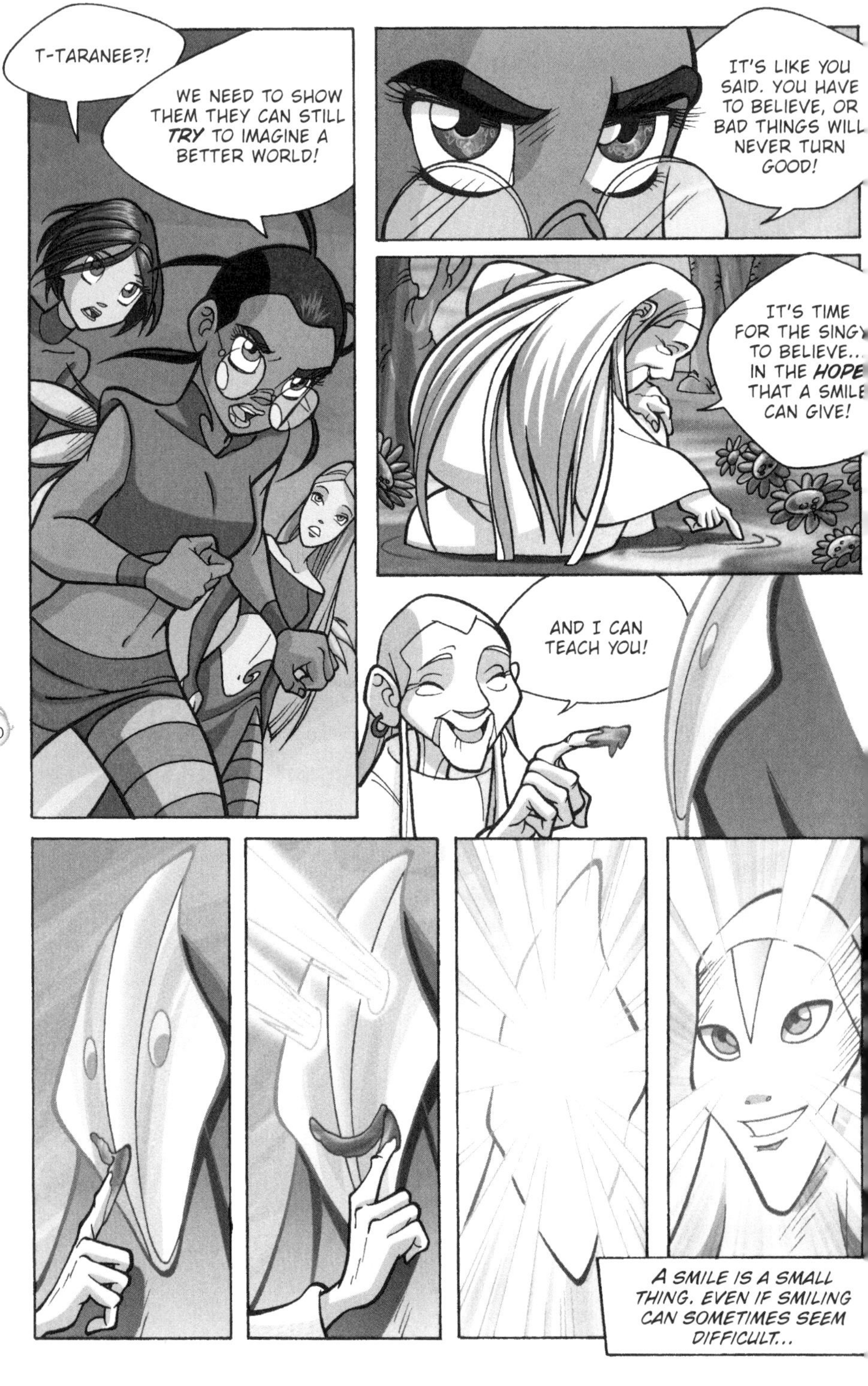

T-TARANEE?!
WE NEED TO SHOW THEM THEY CAN STILL TRY TO IMAGINE A BETTER WORLD!
IT'S LIKE YOU SAID. YOU HAVE TO BELIEVE, OR BAD THINGS WILL NEVER TURN GOOD!
IT'S TIME FOR THE SING TO BELIEVE... IN THE HOPE THAT A SMIL CAN GIVE!
AND I CAN TEACH YOU!
A SMILE IS A SMALL THING. EVEN IF SMILING CAN SOMETIMES SEEM DIFFICULT...

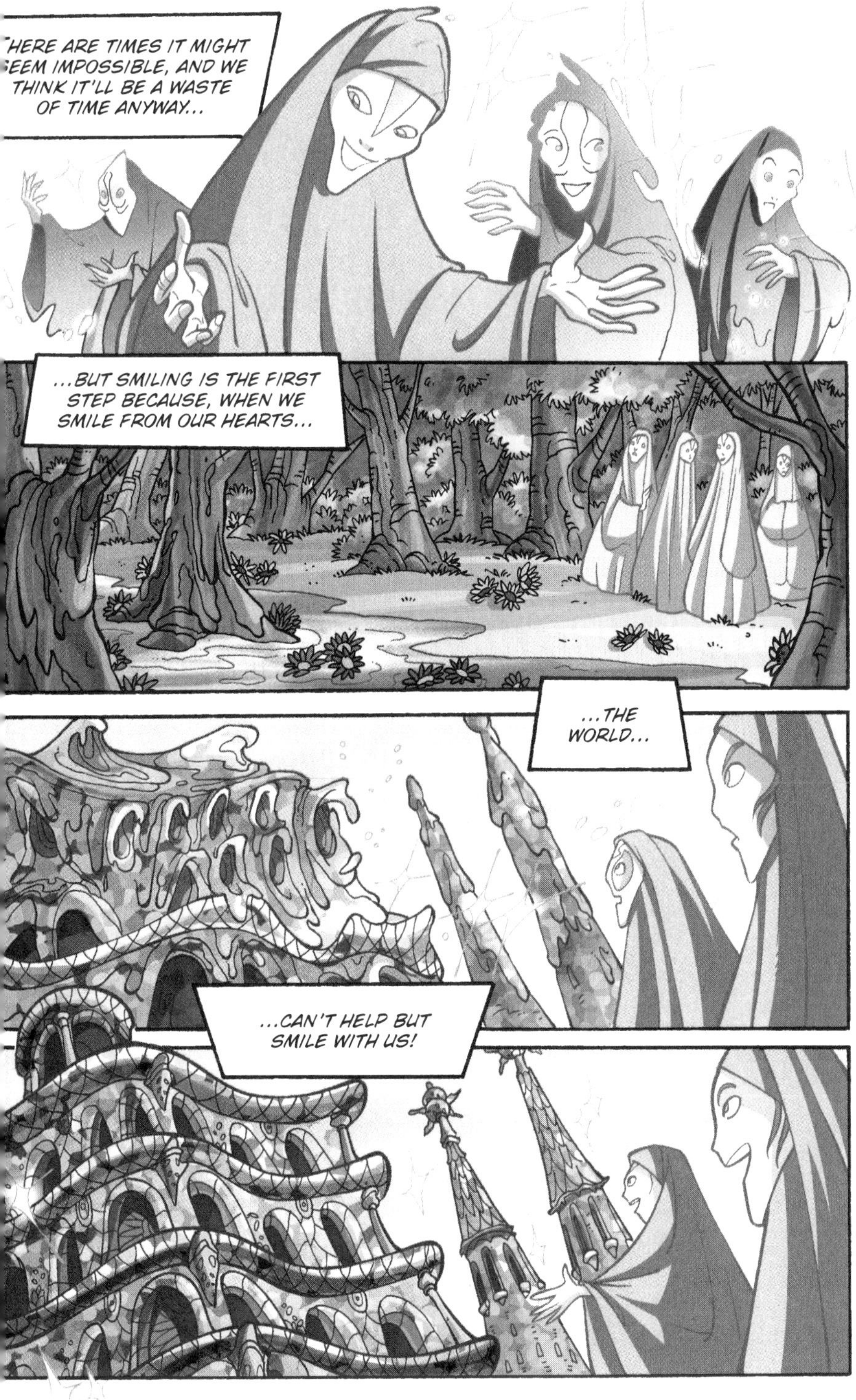
THERE ARE TIMES IT MIGHT SEEM IMPOSSIBLE, AND WE THINK IT'LL BE A WASTE OF TIME ANYWAY...
...BUT SMILING IS THE FIRST STEP BECAUSE, WHEN WE SMILE FROM OUR HEARTS...
...THE WORLD...
...CAN'T HELP BUT SMILE WITH US!

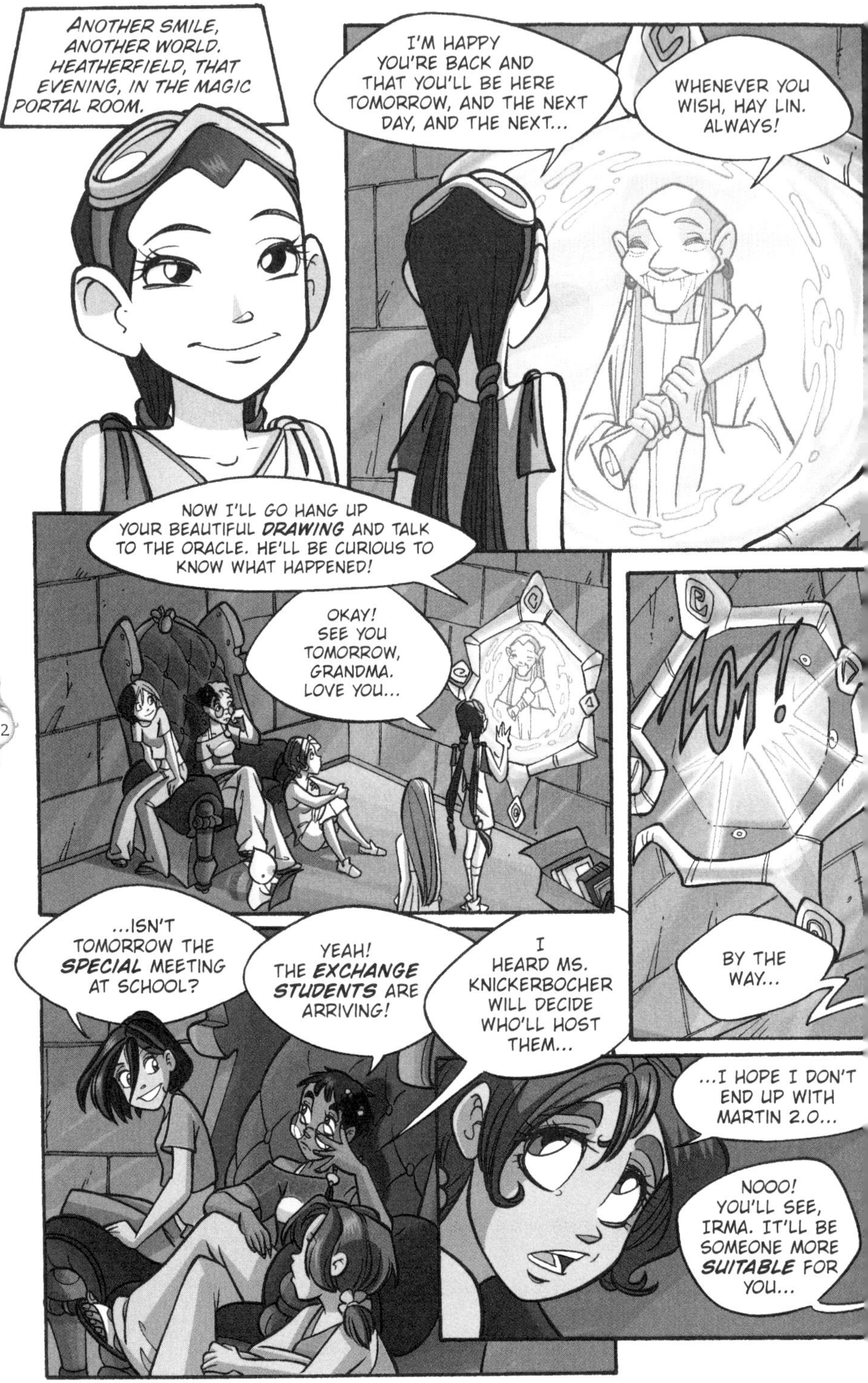
ANOTHER SMILE, ANOTHER WORLD. HEATHERFIELD, THAT EVENING, IN THE MAGIC PORTAL ROOM.
I'M HAPPY YOU'RE BACK AND THAT YOU'LL BE HERE TOMORROW, AND THE NEXT DAY, AND THE NEXT...
WHENEVER YOU WISH, HAY LIN. ALWAYS!
NOW I'LL GO HANG UP YOUR BEAUTIFUL DRAWING AND TALK TO THE ORACLE. HE'LL BE CURIOUS TO KNOW WHAT HAPPENED!
OKAY! SEE YOU TOMORROW, GRANDMA. LOVE YOU...
ZLOT!
BY THE WAY...
...ISN'T TOMORROW THE SPECIAL MEETING AT SCHOOL?
YEAH! THE EXCHANGE STUDENTS ARE ARRIVING!
I HEARD MS. KNICKERBOCHER WILL DECIDE WHO'LL HOST THEM...
...I HOPE I DON'T END UP WITH MARTIN 2.0...
NOOO! YOU'LL SEE, IRMA. IT'LL BE SOMEONE MORE SUITABLE FOR YOU...

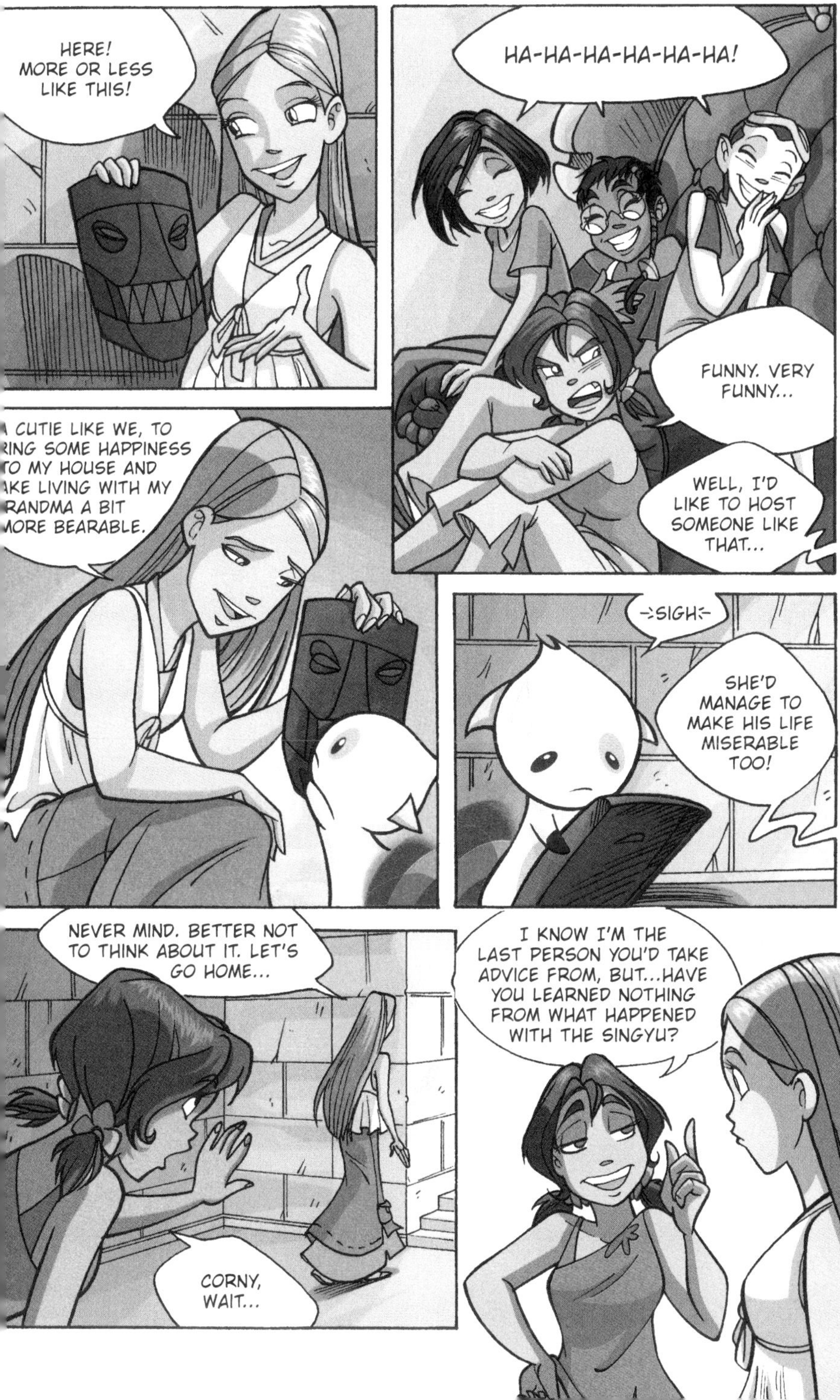
HERE! MORE OR LESS LIKE THIS!
HA-HA-HA-HA-HA-HA!
FUNNY. VERY FUNNY...
CUTIE LIKE WE, TO ING SOME HAPPINESS O MY HOUSE AND KE LIVING WITH MY RANDMA A BIT ORE BEARABLE.
WELL, I'D LIKE TO HOST SOMEONE LIKE THAT...
SIGH
SHE'D MANAGE TO MAKE HIS LIFE MISERABLE TOO!
NEVER MIND. BETTER NOT TO THINK ABOUT IT. LET'S GO HOME...
CORNY, WAIT...
I KNOW I'M THE LAST PERSON YOU'D TAKE ADVICE FROM, BUT...HAVE YOU LEARNED NOTHING FROM WHAT HAPPENED WITH THE SINGYU?

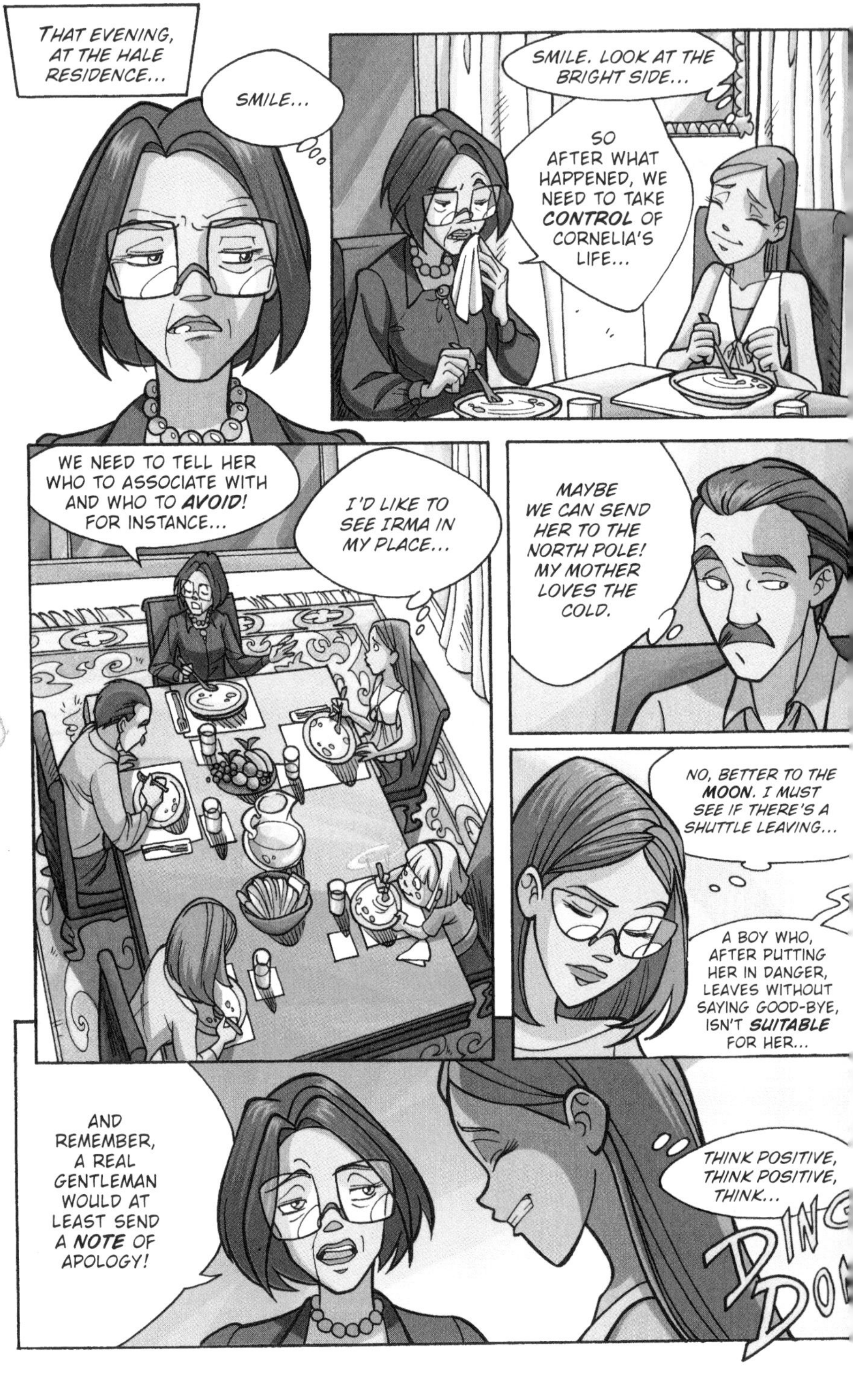
THAT EVENING, AT THE HALE RESIDENCE...
SMILE...
SMILE. LOOK AT THE BRIGHT SIDE...
SO AFTER WHAT HAPPENED, WE NEED TO TAKE CONTROL OF CORNELIA'S LIFE...
WE NEED TO TELL HER WHO TO ASSOCIATE WITH AND WHO TO AVOID! FOR INSTANCE...
I'D LIKE TO SEE IRMA IN MY PLACE...
MAYBE WE CAN SEND HER TO THE NORTH POLE! MY MOTHER LOVES THE COLD.
NO, BETTER TO THE MOON. I MUST SEE IF THERE'S A SHUTTLE LEAVING...
A BOY WHO, AFTER PUTTING HER IN DANGER, LEAVES WITHOUT SAYING GOOD-BYE, ISN'T SUITABLE FOR HER...
AND REMEMBER, A REAL GENTLEMAN WOULD AT LEAST SEND A NOTE OF APOLOGY!
THINK POSITIVE, THINK POSITIVE, THINK...
DING DON

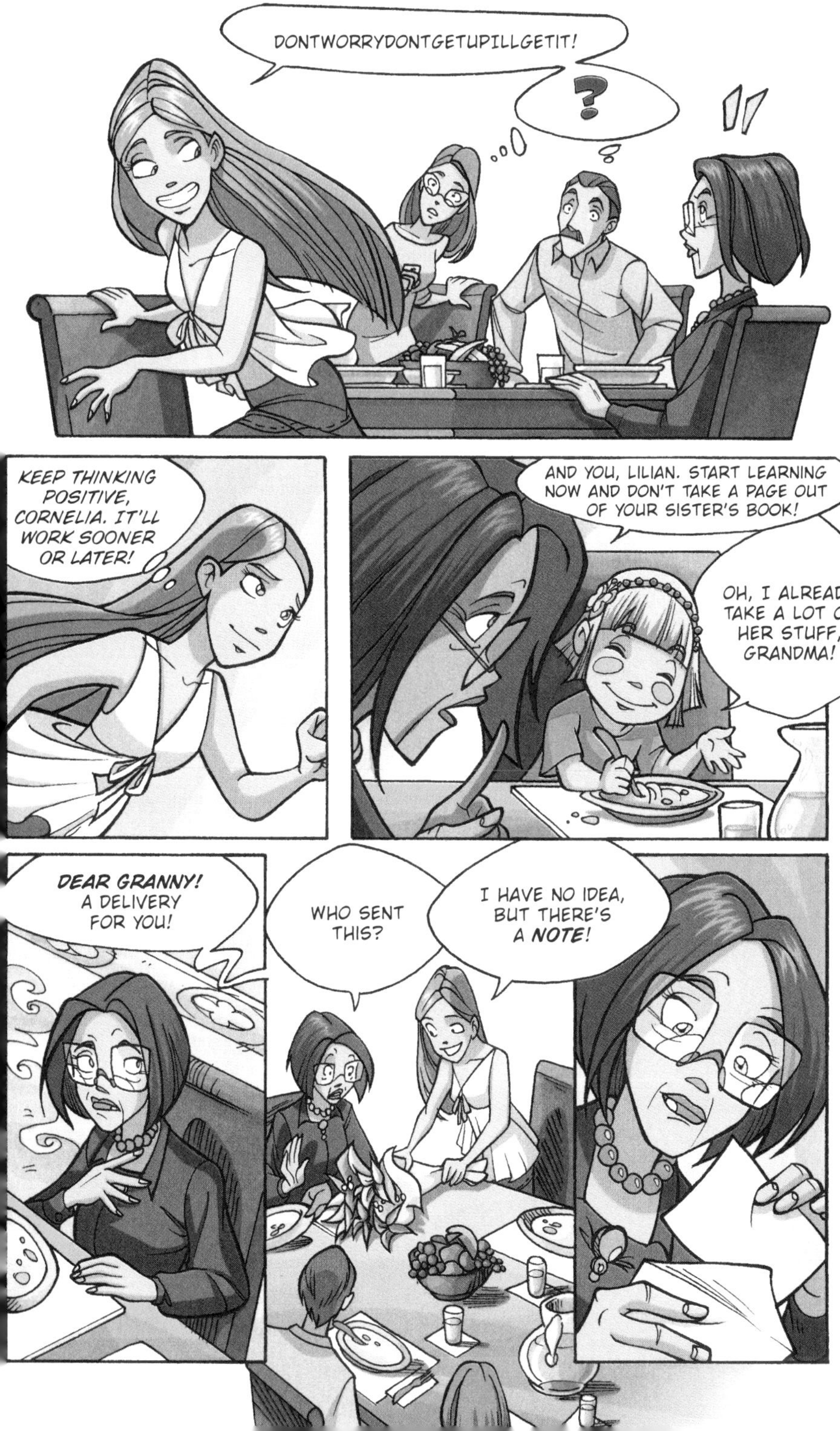
DONTWORRYDONTGETUPILLGETIT!
?
KEEP THINKING POSITIVE, CORNELIA. IT'LL WORK SOONER OR LATER!
AND YOU, LILIAN. START LEARNING NOW AND DON'T TAKE A PAGE OUT OF YOUR SISTER'S BOOK!
OH, I ALREADY TAKE A LOT OF HER STUFF, GRANDMA!
DEAR GRANNY! A DELIVERY FOR YOU!
WHO SENT THIS?
I HAVE NO IDEA, BUT THERE'S A NOTE!

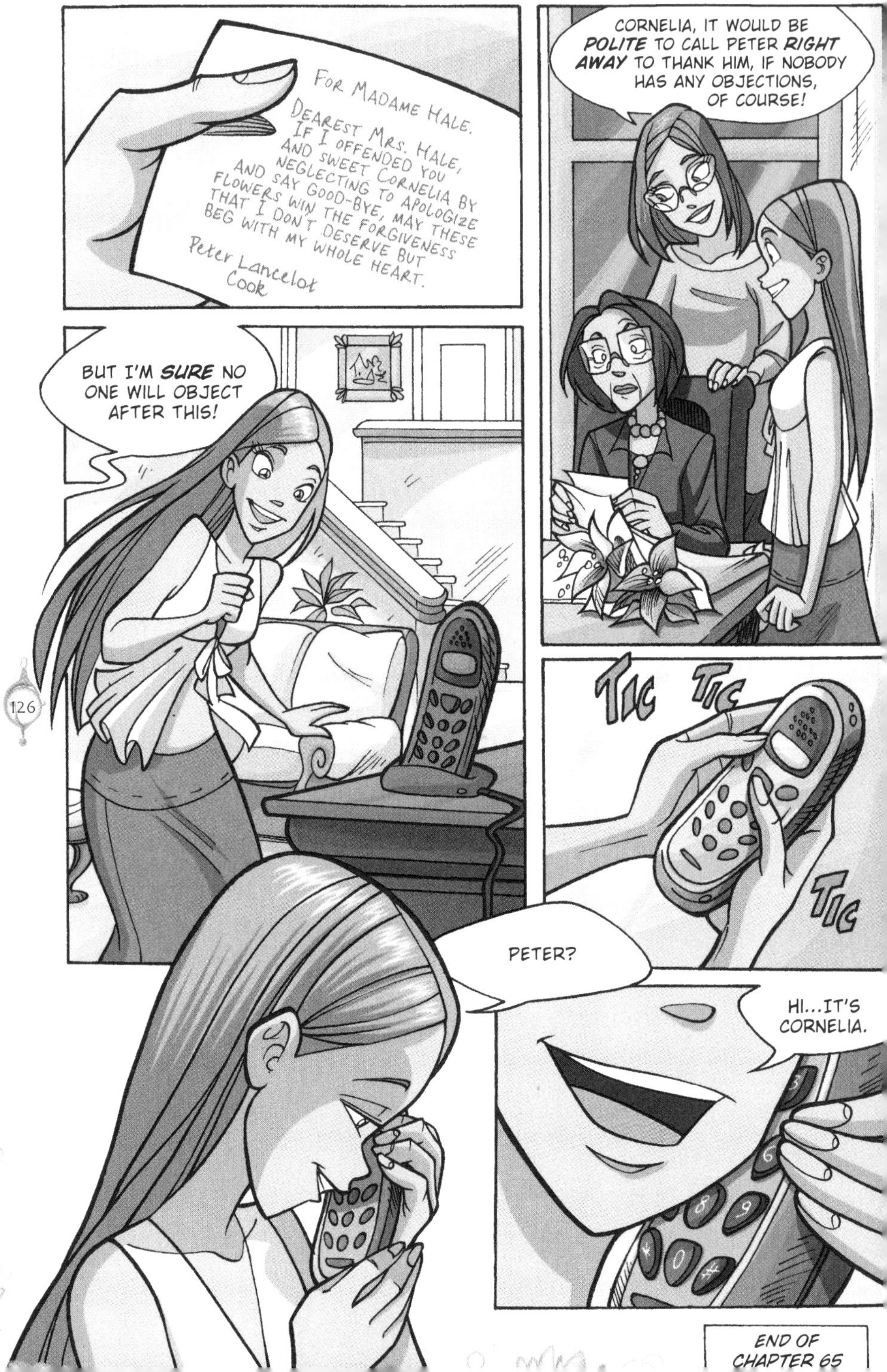
FOR MADAME HALE.
DEAREST MRS. HALE, IF I OFFENDED YOU AND SWEET CORNELIA BY NEGLECTING TO APOLOGIZE AND SAY GOOD-BYE, MAY THESE FLOWERS WIN THE FORGIVENESS THAT I DON'T DESERVE BUT BEG WITH MY WHOLE HEART.
Peter Lancelot Cook
CORNELIA, IT WOULD BE POLITE TO CALL PETER RIGHT AWAY TO THANK HIM, IF NOBODY HAS ANY OBJECTIONS, OF COURSE!
BUT I'M SURE NO ONE WILL OBJECT AFTER THIS!
TIC TIC
TIC
PETER?
HI...IT'S CORNELIA.
END OF CHAPTER 65

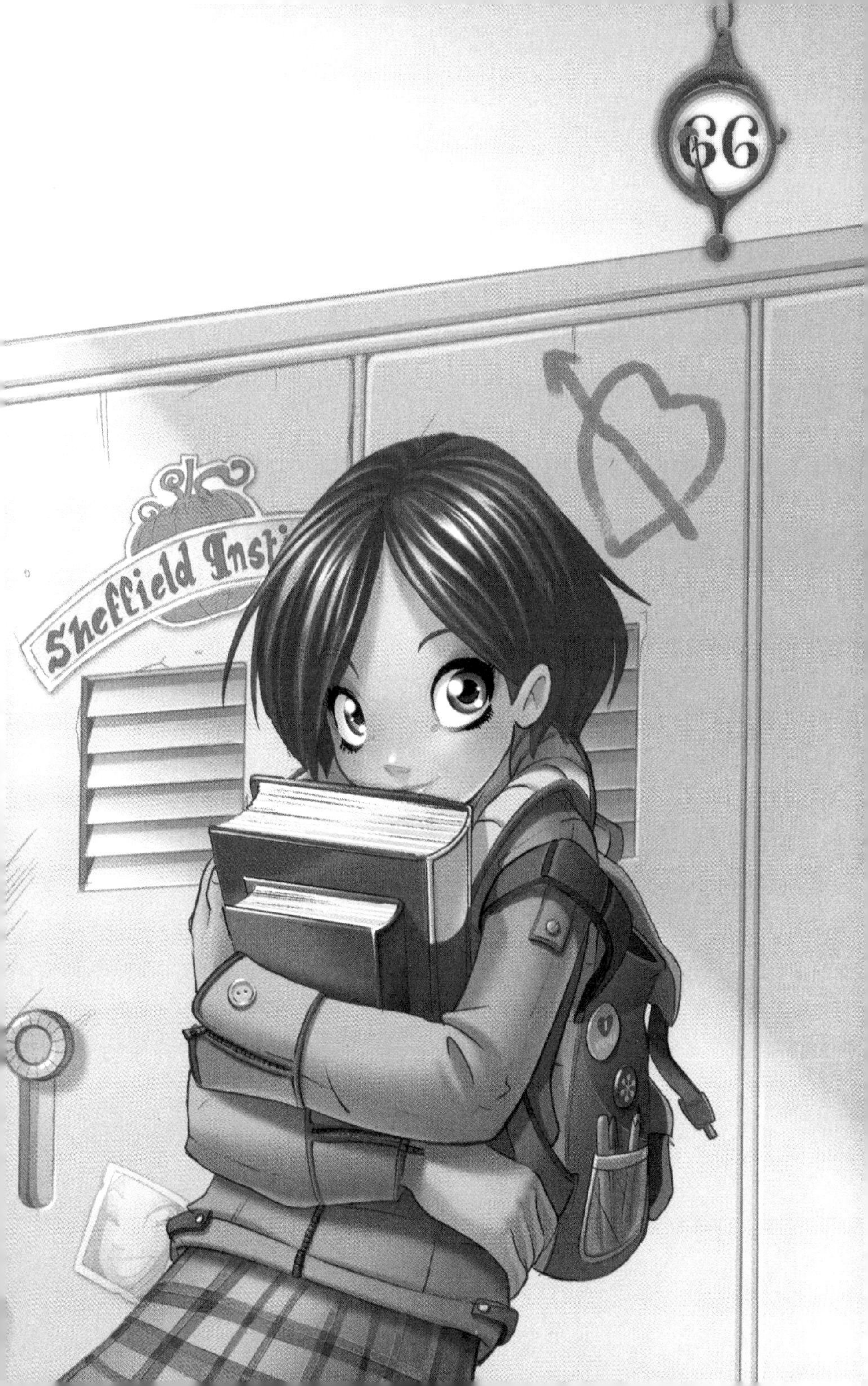
66
Sheffield Insti

Reflected Memories

"Some moments need no words..."

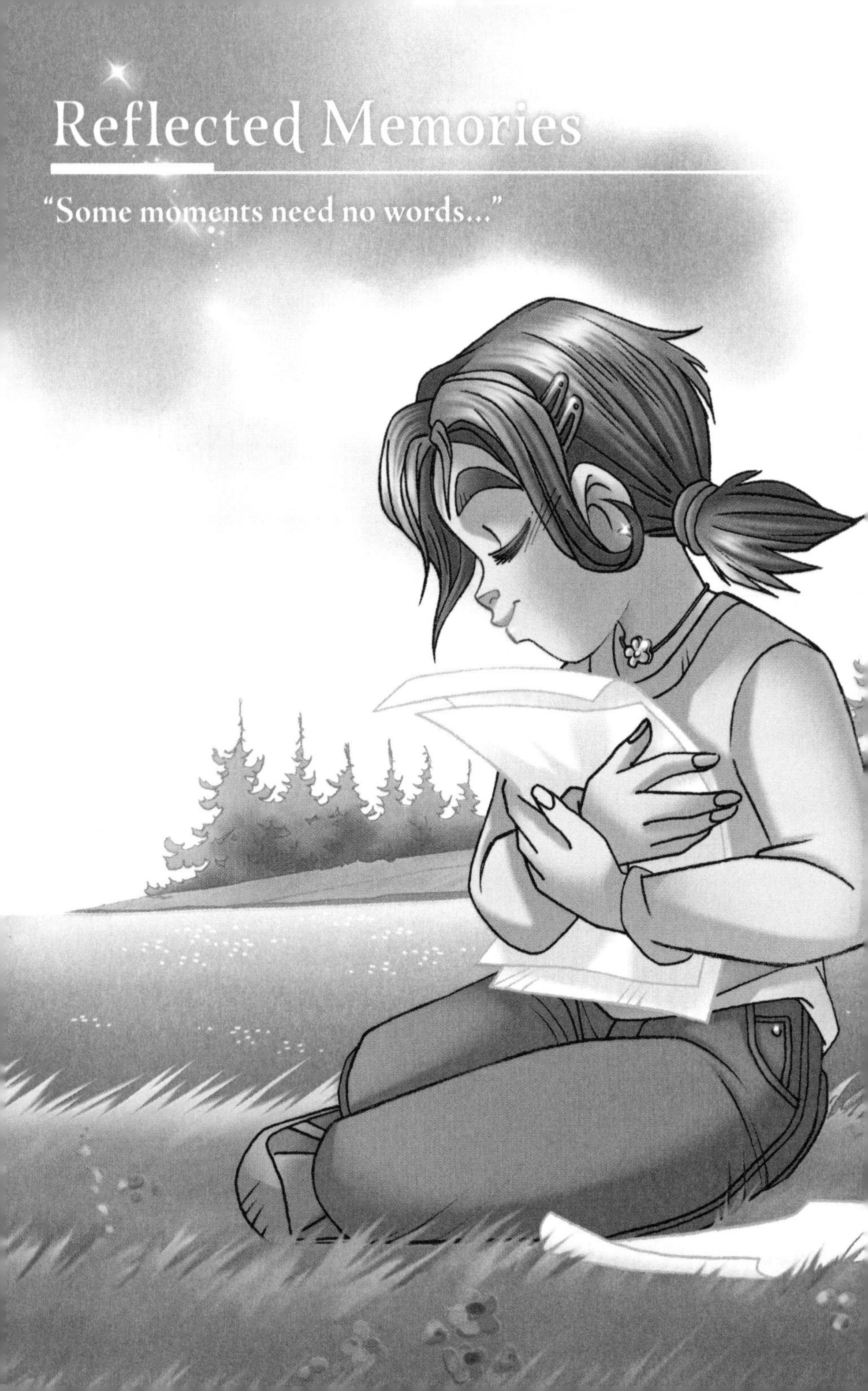

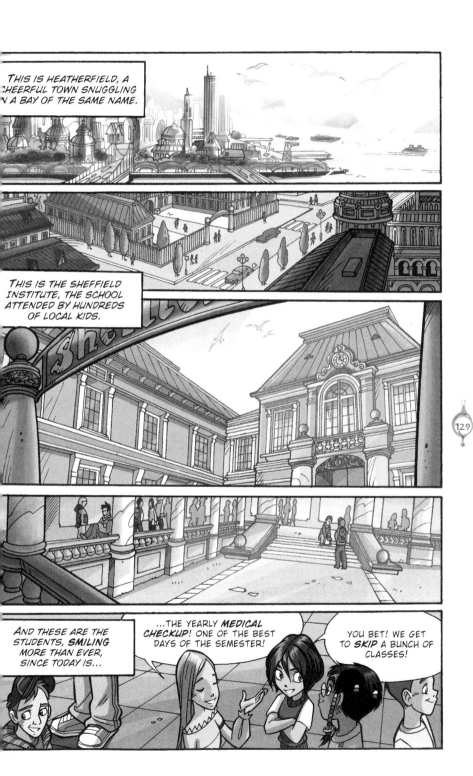

THIS IS HEATHERFIELD, A CHEERFUL TOWN SNUGGLING IN A BAY OF THE SAME NAME.

THIS IS THE SHEFFIELD INSTITUTE, THE SCHOOL ATTENDED BY HUNDREDS OF LOCAL KIDS.

129

AND THESE ARE THE STUDENTS, **SMILING** MORE THAN EVER, SINCE TODAY IS...

...THE YEARLY **MEDICAL CHECKUP**! ONE OF THE BEST DAYS OF THE SEMESTER!

YOU BET! WE GET TO **SKIP** A BUNCH OF CLASSES!

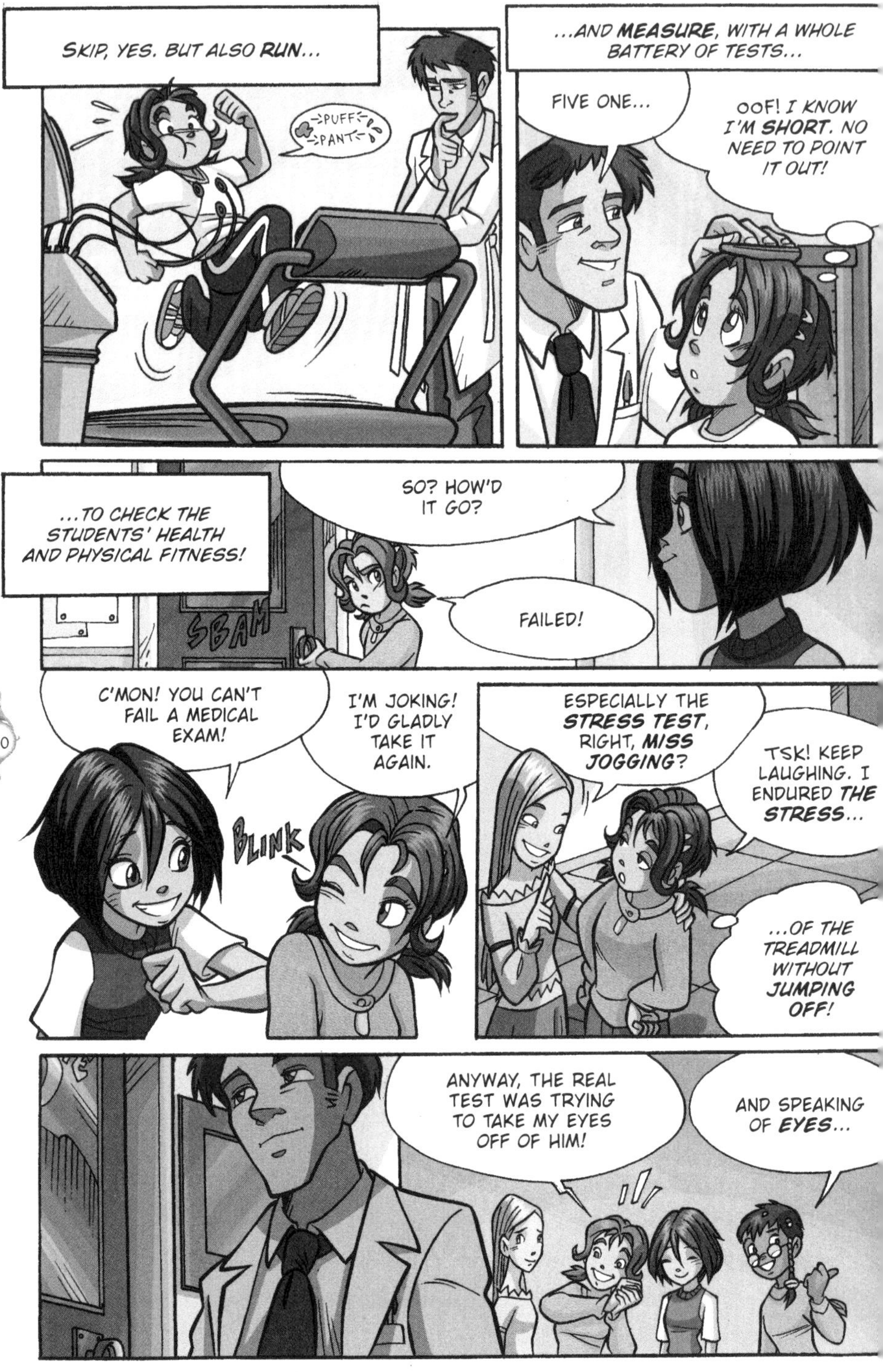
SKIP, YES. BUT ALSO RUN...
PUFF PANT
...AND MEASURE, WITH A WHOLE BATTERY OF TESTS...
FIVE ONE...
OOF! I KNOW I'M SHORT. NO NEED TO POINT IT OUT!
...TO CHECK THE STUDENTS' HEALTH AND PHYSICAL FITNESS!
SO? HOW'D IT GO?
SBAM
FAILED!
C'MON! YOU CAN'T FAIL A MEDICAL EXAM!
BLINK
I'M JOKING! I'D GLADLY TAKE IT AGAIN.
ESPECIALLY THE STRESS TEST, RIGHT, MISS JOGGING?
TSK! KEEP LAUGHING. I ENDURED THE STRESS...
...OF THE TREADMILL WITHOUT JUMPING OFF!
ANYWAY, THE REAL TEST WAS TRYING TO TAKE MY EYES OFF OF HIM!
AND SPEAKING OF EYES...

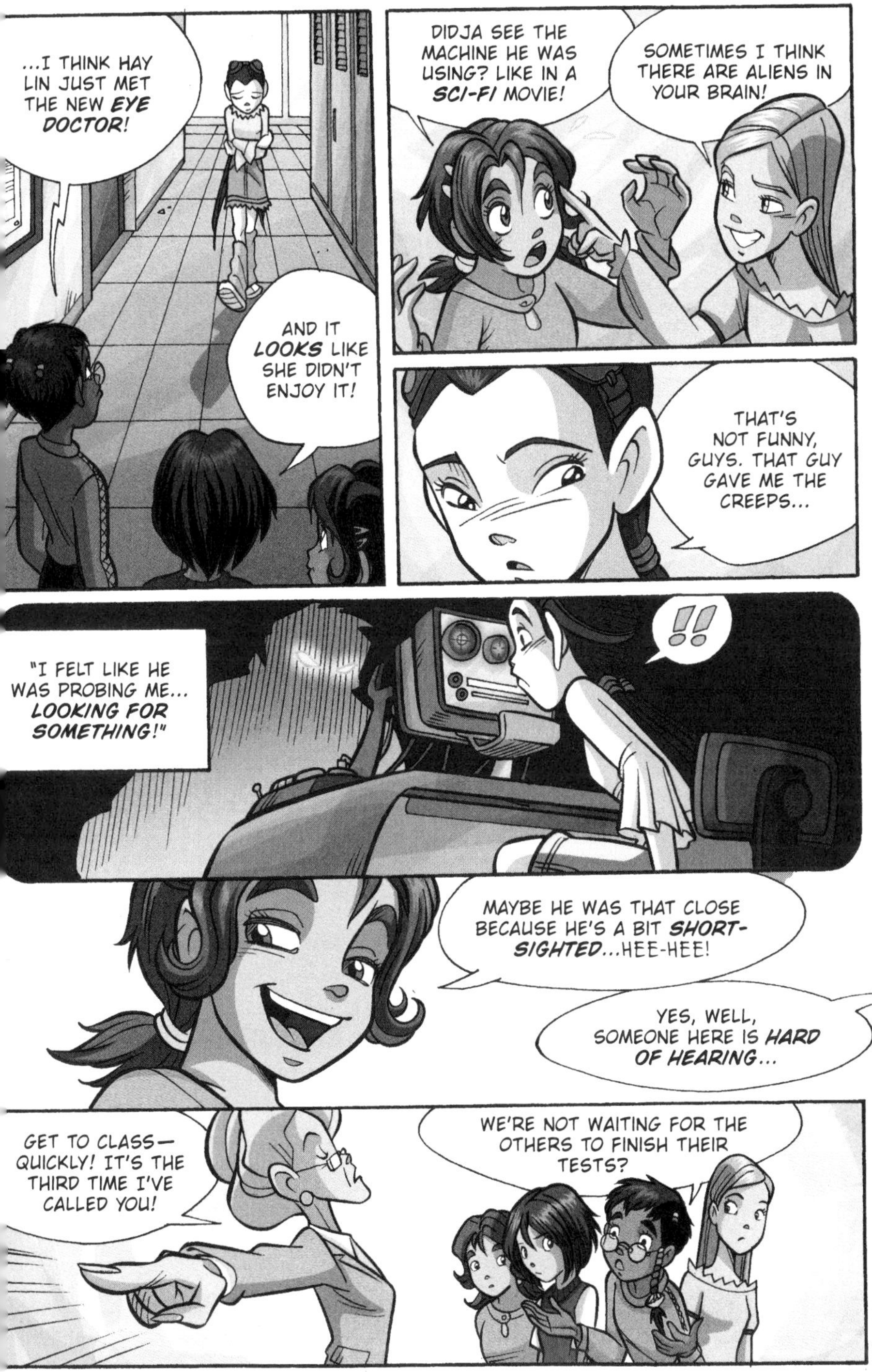
...I THINK HAY LIN JUST MET THE NEW EYE DOCTOR!
AND IT LOOKS LIKE SHE DIDN'T ENJOY IT!
DIDJA SEE THE MACHINE HE WAS USING? LIKE IN A SCI-FI MOVIE!
SOMETIMES I THINK THERE ARE ALIENS IN YOUR BRAIN!
THAT'S NOT FUNNY, GUYS. THAT GUY GAVE ME THE CREEPS...
"I FELT LIKE HE WAS PROBING ME... LOOKING FOR SOMETHING!"
!!
MAYBE HE WAS THAT CLOSE BECAUSE HE'S A BIT SHORT-SIGHTED...HEE-HEE!
YES, WELL, SOMEONE HERE IS HARD OF HEARING...
GET TO CLASS—QUICKLY! IT'S THE THIRD TIME I'VE CALLED YOU!
WE'RE NOT WAITING FOR THE OTHERS TO FINISH THEIR TESTS?

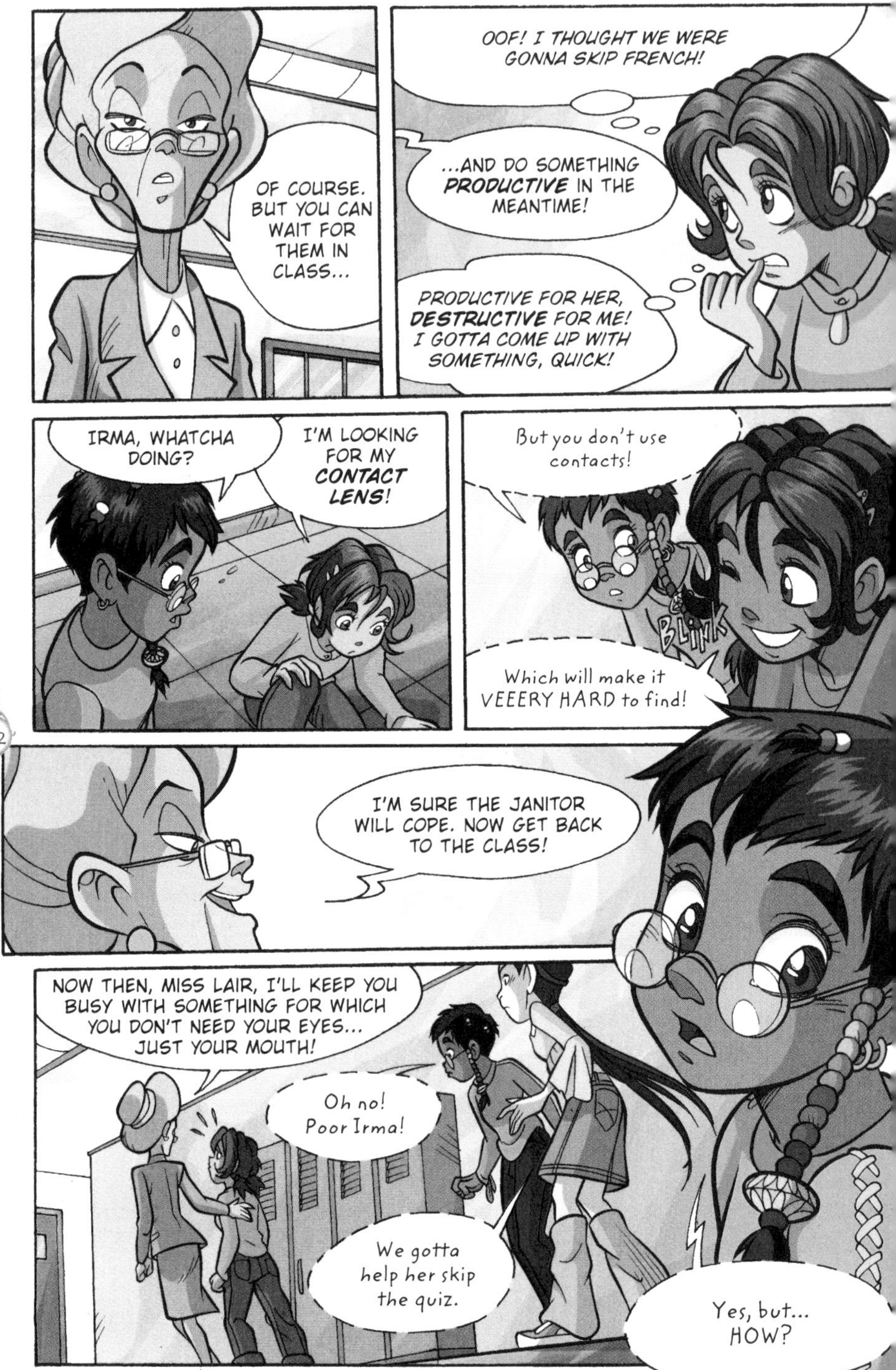
OF COURSE. BUT YOU CAN WAIT FOR THEM IN CLASS...
...AND DO SOMETHING PRODUCTIVE IN THE MEANTIME!
OOF! I THOUGHT WE WERE GONNA SKIP FRENCH!
PRODUCTIVE FOR HER, DESTRUCTIVE FOR ME! I GOTTA COME UP WITH SOMETHING, QUICK!
IRMA, WHATCHA DOING?
I'M LOOKING FOR MY CONTACT LENS!
But you don't use contacts!
BLINK
Which will make it VEEERY HARD to find!
I'M SURE THE JANITOR WILL COPE. NOW GET BACK TO THE CLASS!
NOW THEN, MISS LAIR, I'LL KEEP YOU BUSY WITH SOMETHING FOR WHICH YOU DON'T NEED YOUR EYES... JUST YOUR MOUTH!
Oh no! Poor Irma!
We gotta help her skip the quiz.
Yes, but... HOW?

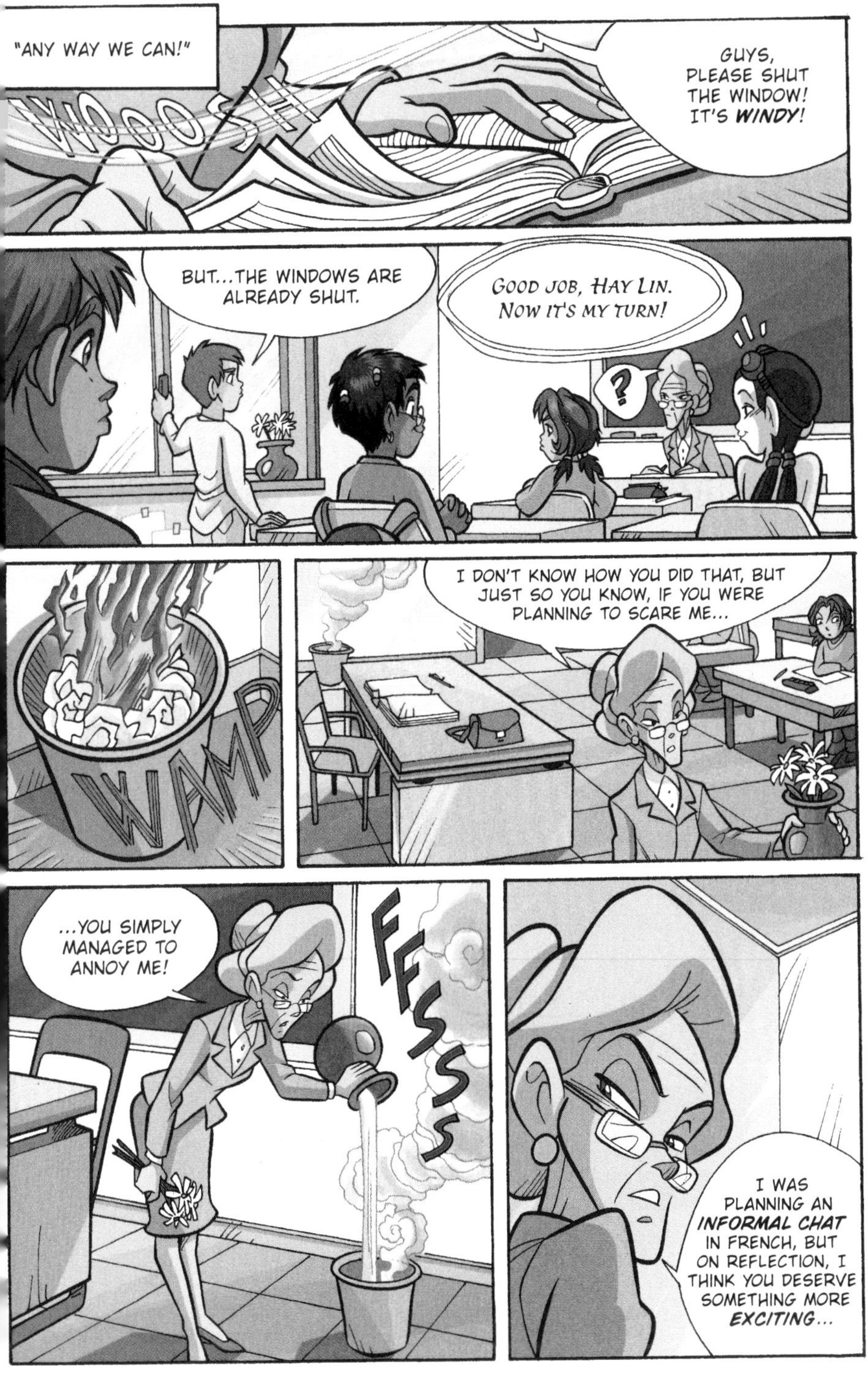
"ANY WAY WE CAN!"
WHOOSH
GUYS, PLEASE SHUT THE WINDOW! IT'S WINDY!
BUT...THE WINDOWS ARE ALREADY SHUT.
GOOD JOB, HAY LIN. NOW IT'S MY TURN!
?
WAMP
I DON'T KNOW HOW YOU DID THAT, BUT JUST SO YOU KNOW, IF YOU WERE PLANNING TO SCARE ME...
...YOU SIMPLY MANAGED TO ANNOY ME!
FFSSS
I WAS PLANNING AN INFORMAL CHAT IN FRENCH, BUT ON REFLECTION, I THINK YOU DESERVE SOMETHING MORE EXCITING...

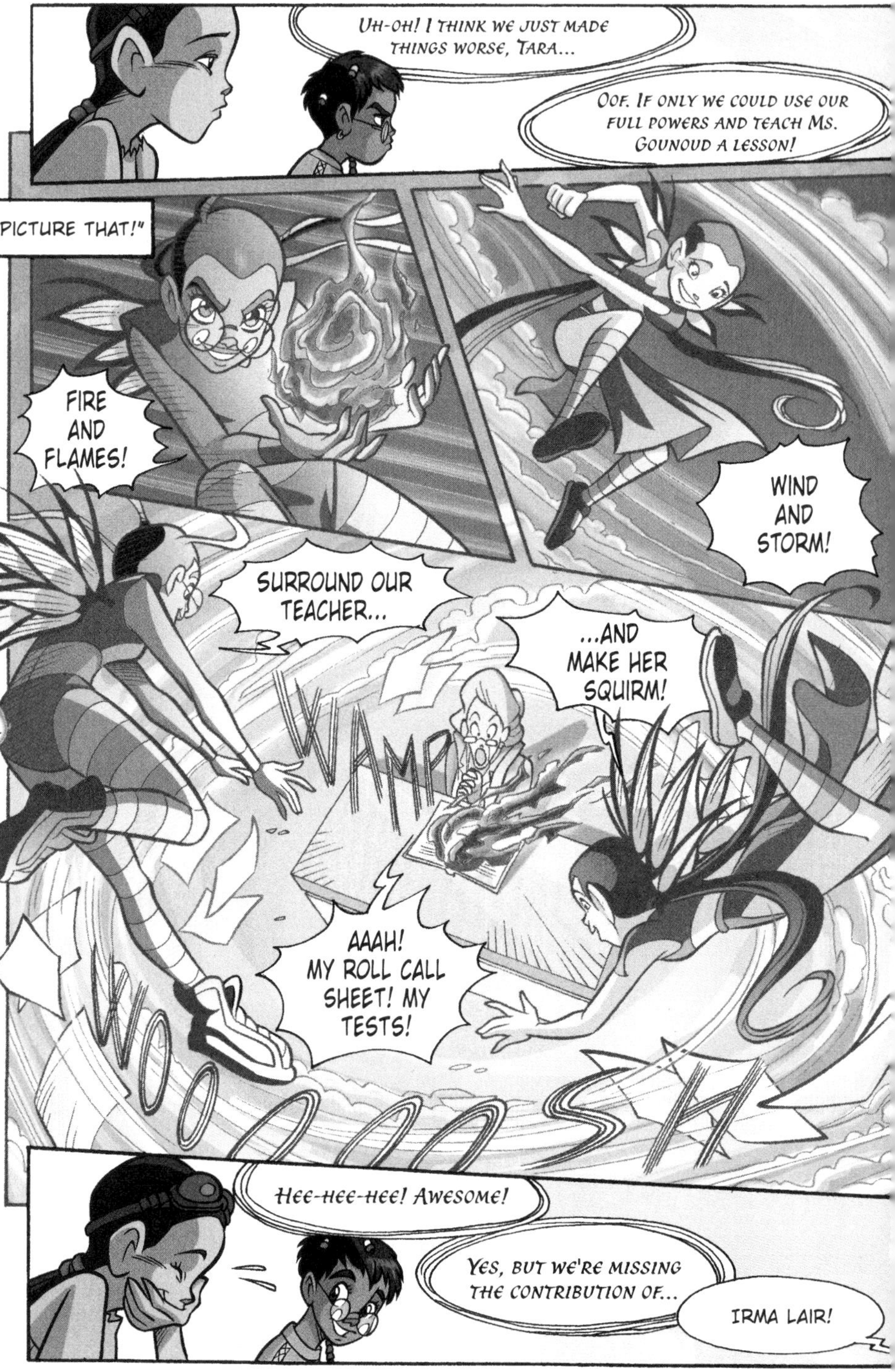

UH-OH! I THINK WE JUST MADE THINGS WORSE, TARA...
OOF. IF ONLY WE COULD USE OUR FULL POWERS AND TEACH MS. GOUNOUD A LESSON!
"PICTURE THAT!"
FIRE AND FLAMES!
WIND AND STORM!
SURROUND OUR TEACHER...
...AND MAKE HER SQUIRM!
WAMP
AAAH! MY ROLL CALL SHEET! MY TESTS!
WOOOOOOSH
HEE-HEE-HEE! AWESOME!
YES, BUT WE'RE MISSING THE CONTRIBUTION OF...
IRMA LAIR!

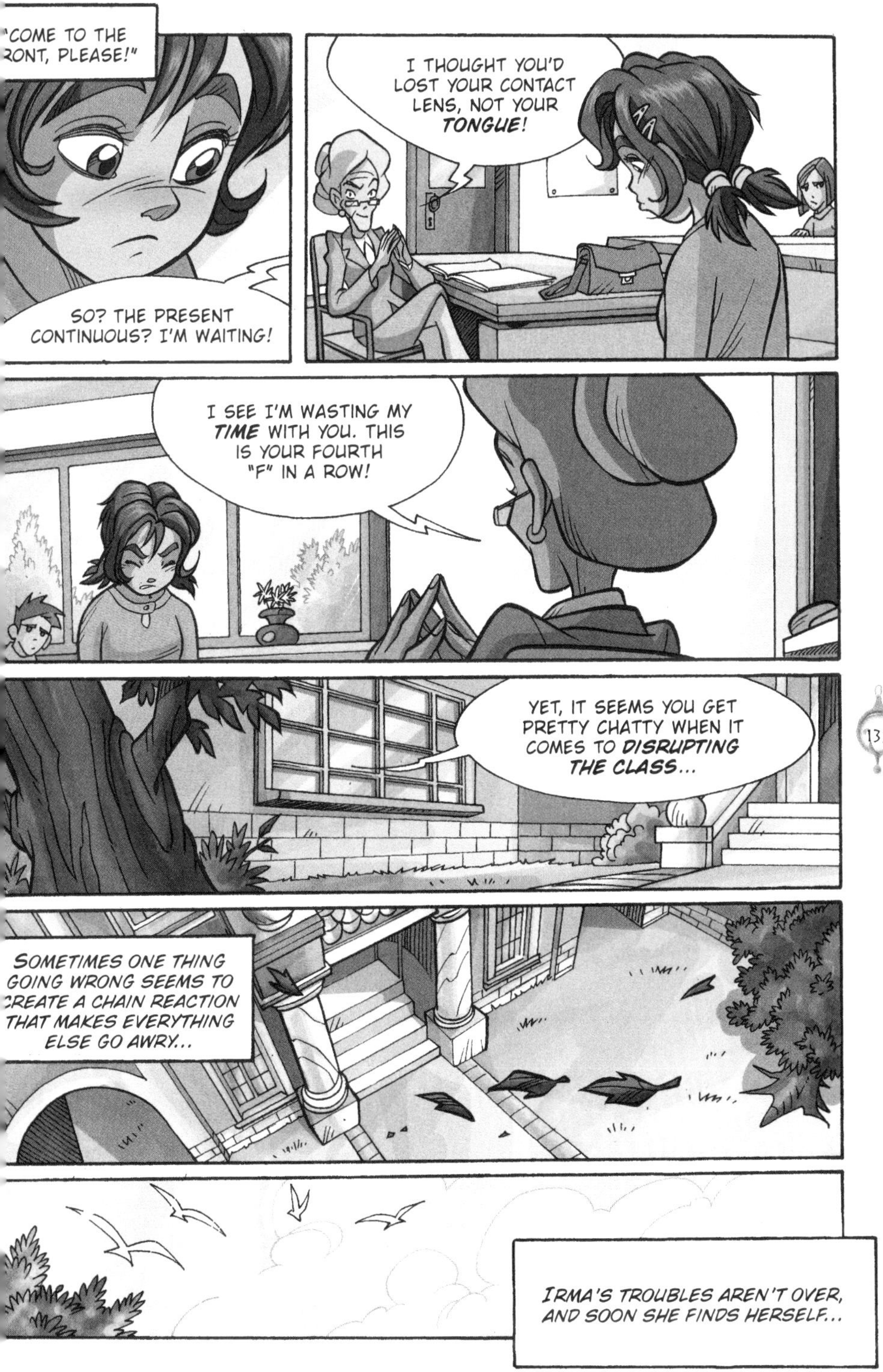
"COME TO THE
FRONT, PLEASE!"
I THOUGHT YOU'D LOST YOUR CONTACT LENS, NOT YOUR TONGUE!
SO? THE PRESENT CONTINUOUS? I'M WAITING!
I SEE I'M WASTING MY TIME WITH YOU. THIS IS YOUR FOURTH "F" IN A ROW!
YET, IT SEEMS YOU GET PRETTY CHATTY WHEN IT COMES TO DISRUPTING THE CLASS...
SOMETIMES ONE THING GOING WRONG SEEMS TO CREATE A CHAIN REACTION THAT MAKES EVERYTHING ELSE GO AWRY...
IRMA'S TROUBLES AREN'T OVER, AND SOON SHE FINDS HERSELF...

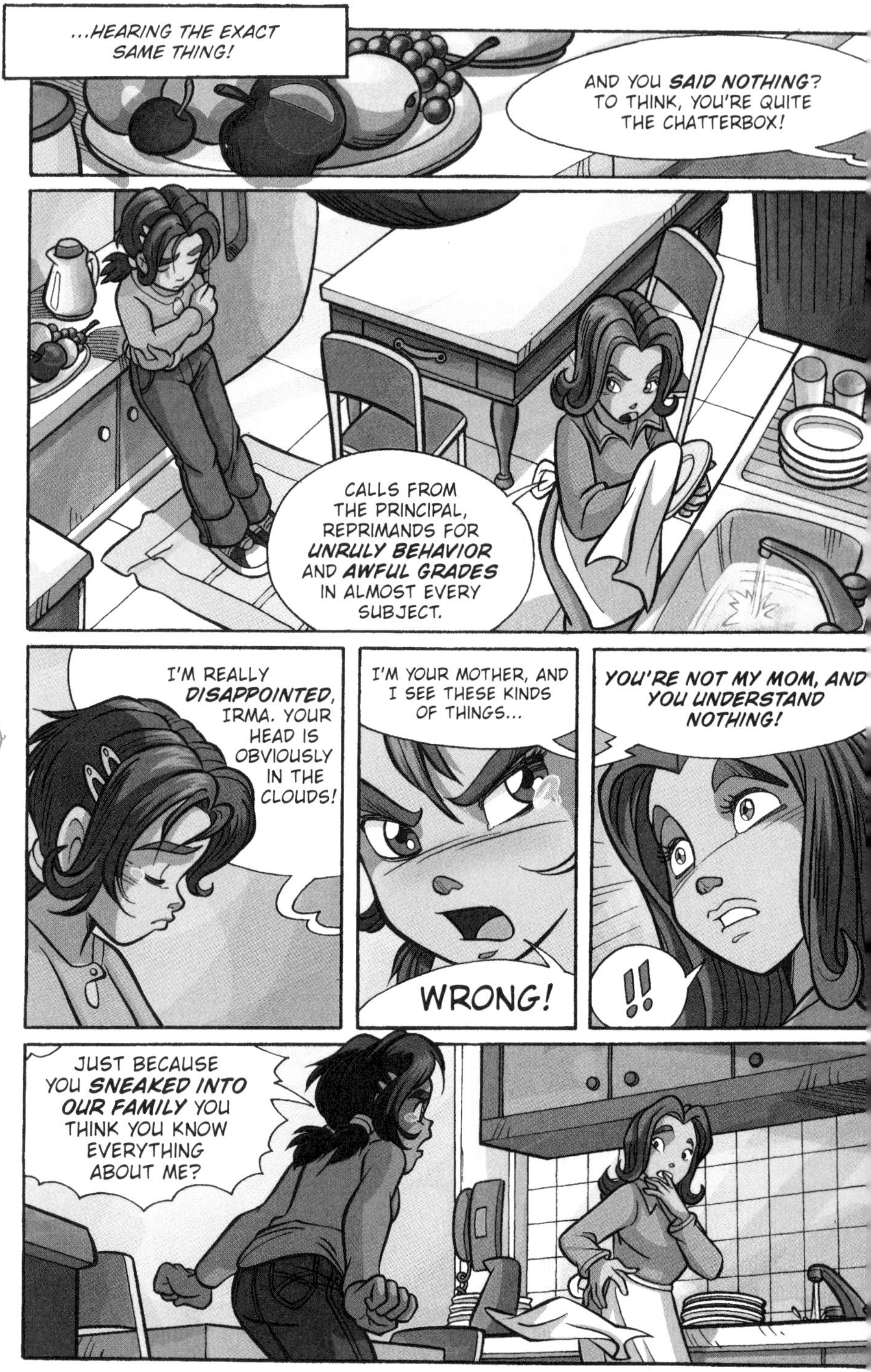
...HEARING THE EXACT SAME THING!
AND YOU SAID NOTHING? TO THINK, YOU'RE QUITE THE CHATTERBOX!
CALLS FROM THE PRINCIPAL, REPRIMANDS FOR UNRULY BEHAVIOR AND AWFUL GRADES IN ALMOST EVERY SUBJECT.
I'M REALLY DISAPPOINTED, IRMA. YOUR HEAD IS OBVIOUSLY IN THE CLOUDS!
I'M YOUR MOTHER, AND I SEE THESE KINDS OF THINGS...
WRONG!
YOU'RE NOT MY MOM, AND YOU UNDERSTAND NOTHING!
!!
JUST BECAUSE YOU SNEAKED INTO OUR FAMILY YOU THINK YOU KNOW EVERYTHING ABOUT ME?

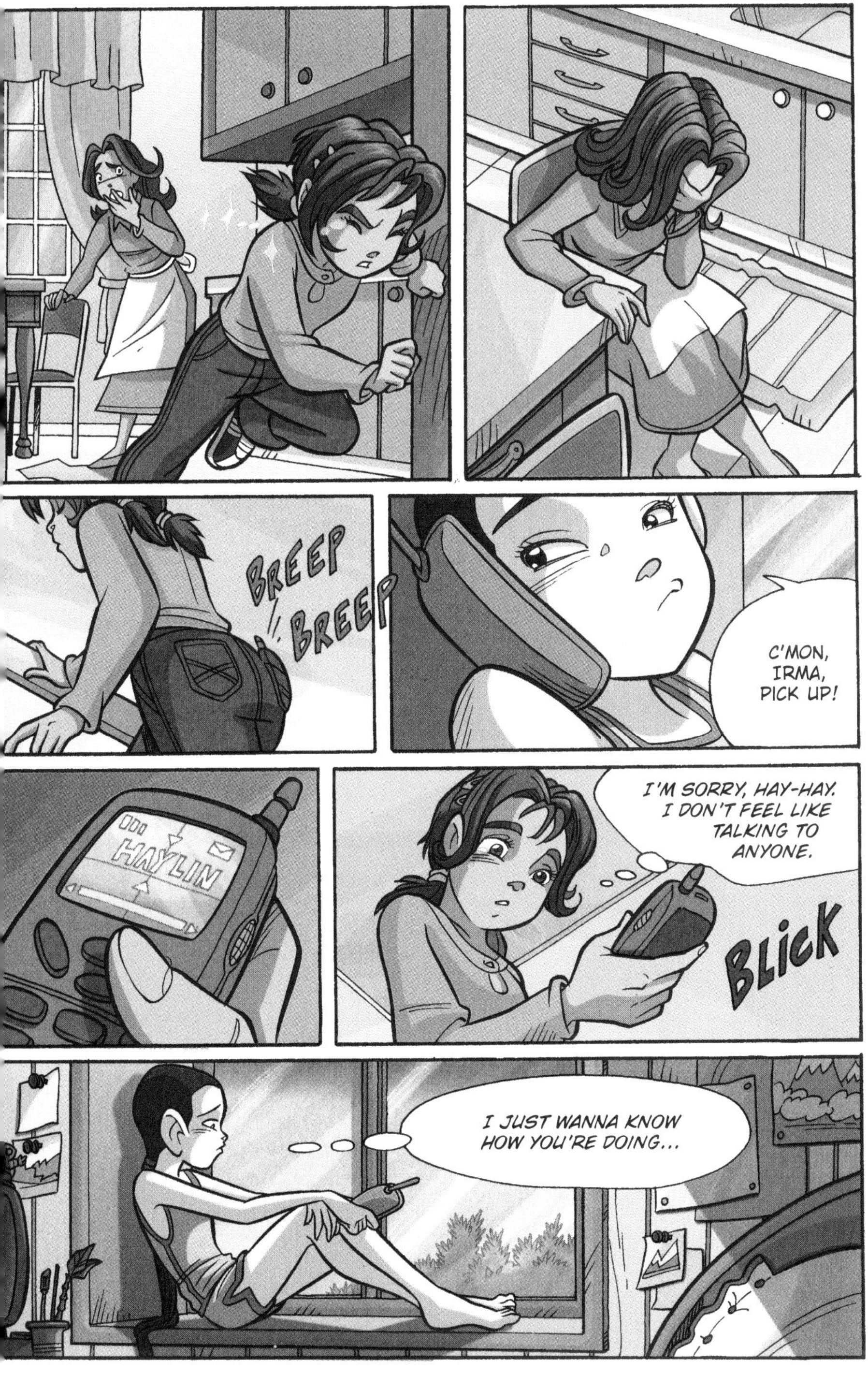
BREEP
BREEP
C'MON, IRMA, PICK UP!
HAYLIN
I'M SORRY, HAY-HAY. I DON'T FEEL LIKE TALKING TO ANYONE.
BLICK
I JUST WANNA KNOW HOW YOU'RE DOING...

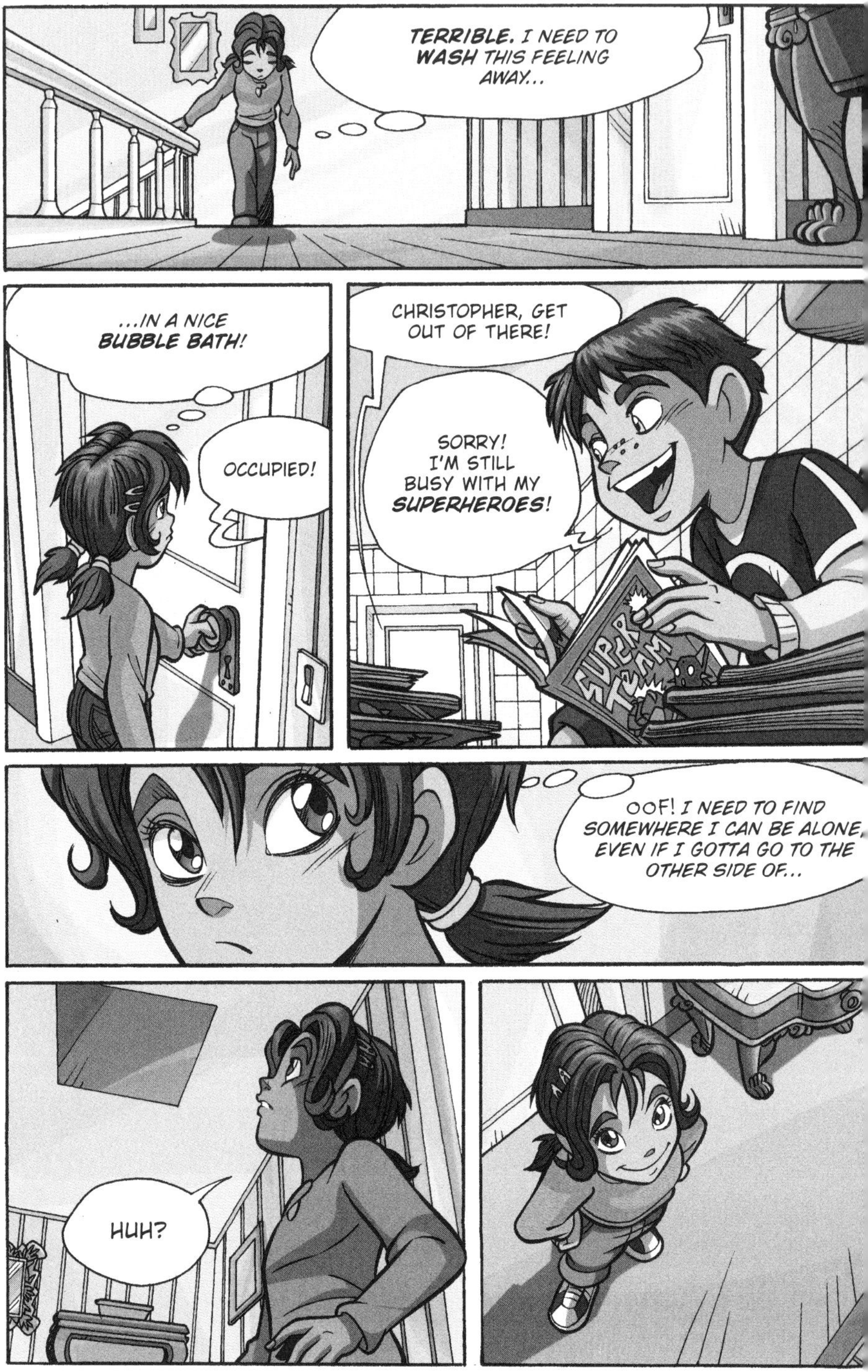
TERRIBLE. I NEED TO WASH THIS FEELING AWAY...
...IN A NICE BUBBLE BATH!
OCCUPIED!
CHRISTOPHER, GET OUT OF THERE!
SORRY! I'M STILL BUSY WITH MY SUPERHEROES!
SUPER TEAM
OOF! I NEED TO FIND SOMEWHERE I CAN BE ALONE, EVEN IF I GOTTA GO TO THE OTHER SIDE OF...
HUH?

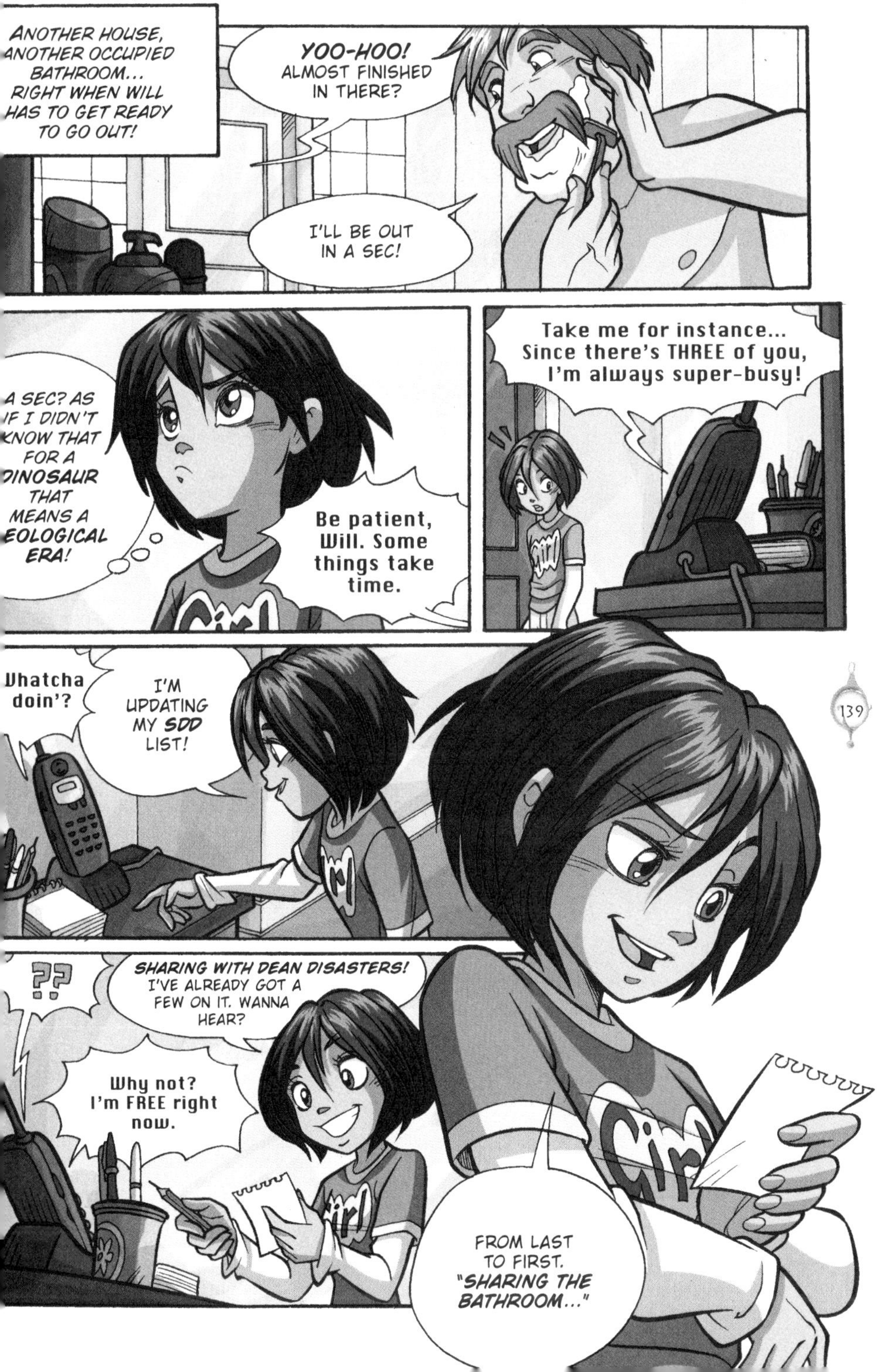
ANOTHER HOUSE, ANOTHER OCCUPIED BATHROOM... RIGHT WHEN WILL HAS TO GET READY TO GO OUT!
YOO-HOO! ALMOST FINISHED IN THERE?
I'LL BE OUT IN A SEC!
A SEC? AS IF I DIDN'T KNOW THAT FOR A DINOSAUR THAT MEANS A EOLOGICAL ERA!
Be patient, Will. Some things take time.
Take me for instance... Since there's THREE of you, I'm always super-busy!
Whatcha doin'?
I'M UPDATING MY SDD LIST!
SHARING WITH DEAN DISASTERS! I'VE ALREADY GOT A FEW ON IT. WANNA HEAR?
??
Why not? I'm FREE right now.
FROM LAST TO FIRST. "SHARING THE BATHROOM..."

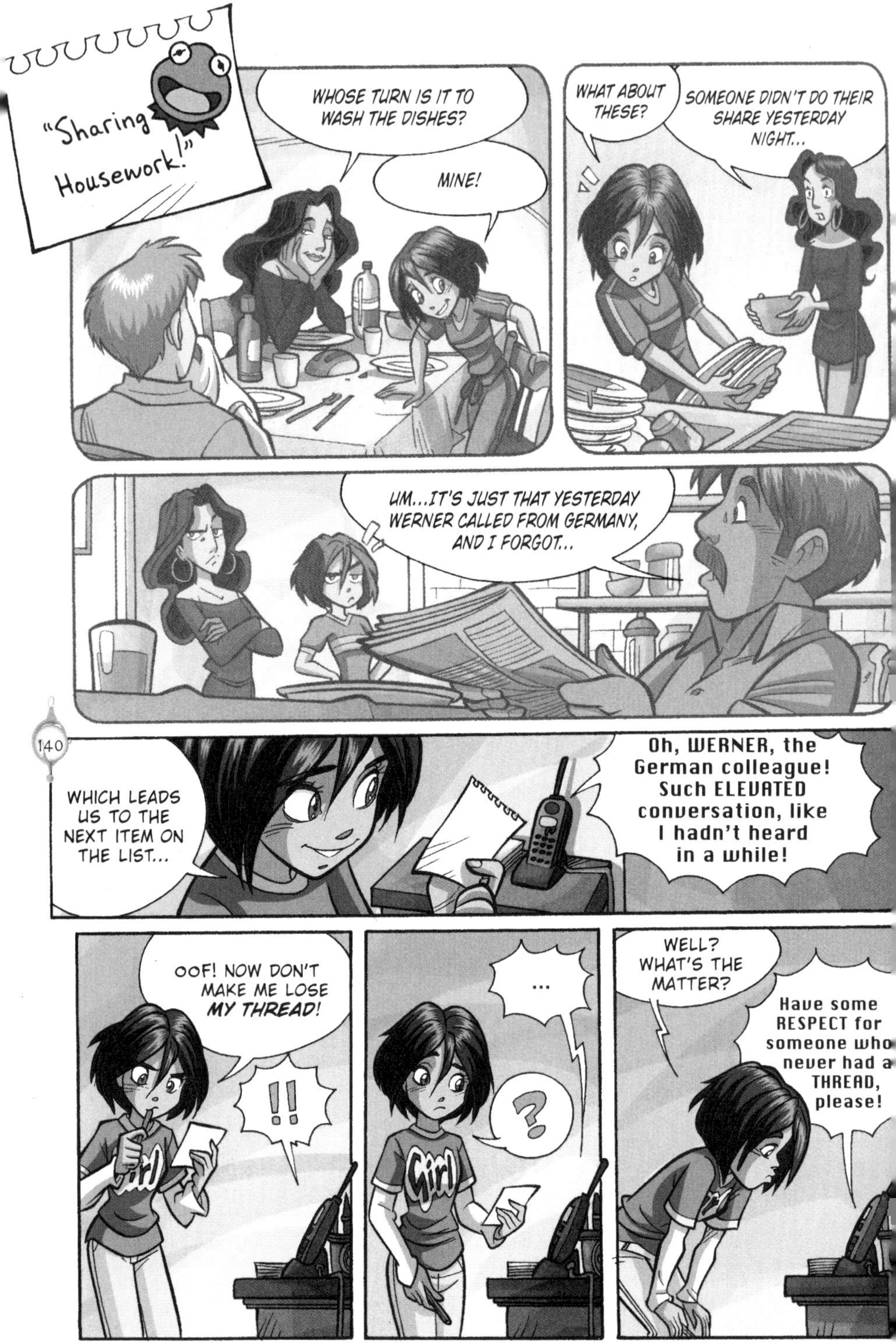
"Sharing Housework!"
WHOSE TURN IS IT TO WASH THE DISHES?
MINE!
WHAT ABOUT THESE?
SOMEONE DIDN'T DO THEIR SHARE YESTERDAY NIGHT...
UM...IT'S JUST THAT YESTERDAY WERNER CALLED FROM GERMANY, AND I FORGOT...
WHICH LEADS US TO THE NEXT ITEM ON THE LIST...
Oh, WERNER, the German colleague! Such ELEVATED conversation, like I hadn't heard in a while!
OOF! NOW DON'T MAKE ME LOSE MY THREAD!
!!
...
?
WELL? WHAT'S THE MATTER?
Have some RESPECT for someone who never had a THREAD, please!

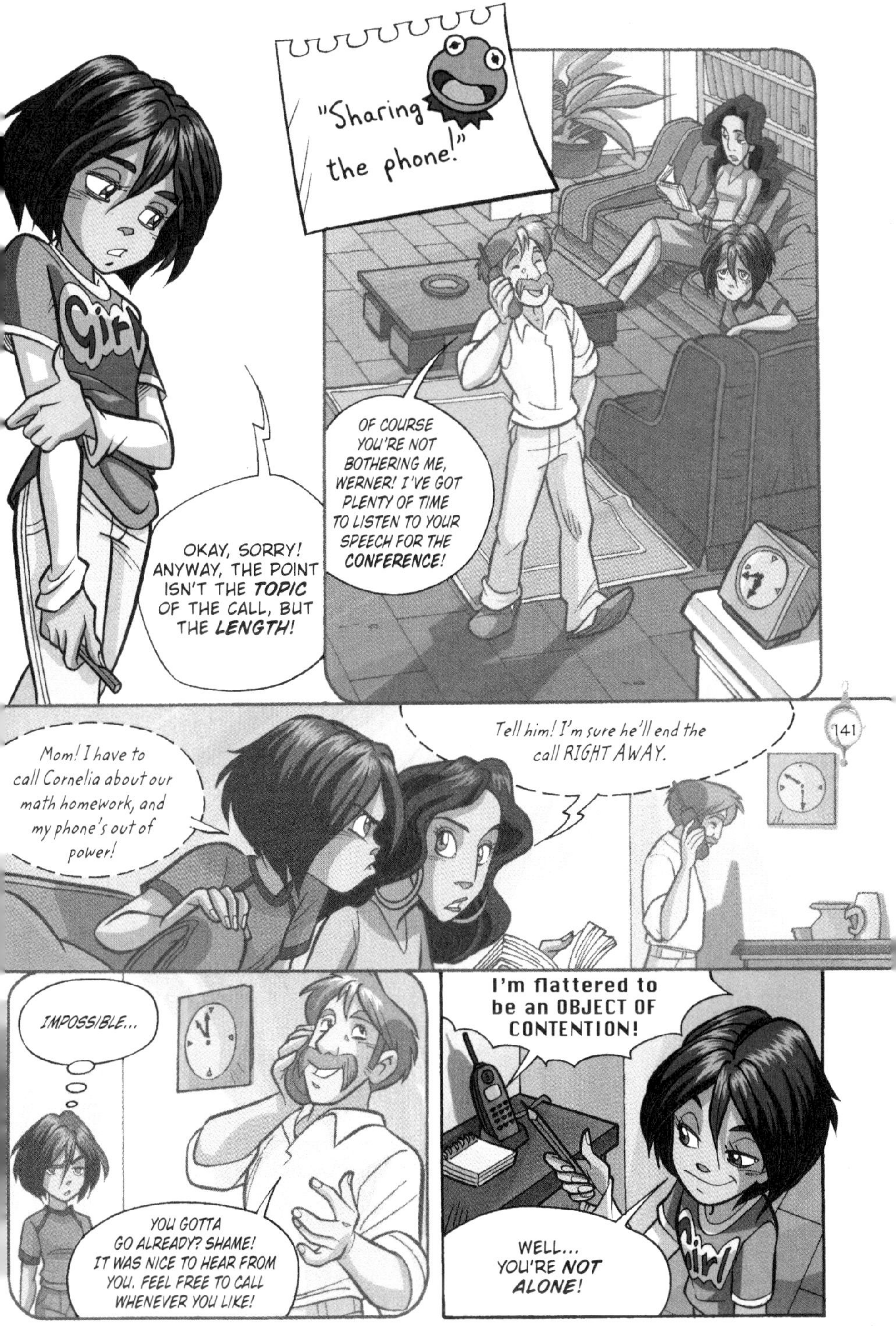
"Sharing the phone!"
OF COURSE YOU'RE NOT BOTHERING ME, WERNER! I'VE GOT PLENTY OF TIME TO LISTEN TO YOUR SPEECH FOR THE CONFERENCE!
OKAY, SORRY! ANYWAY, THE POINT ISN'T THE TOPIC OF THE CALL, BUT THE LENGTH!
Mom! I have to call Cornelia about our math homework, and my phone's out of power!
Tell him! I'm sure he'll end the call RIGHT AWAY.
IMPOSSIBLE...
YOU GOTTA GO ALREADY? SHAME! IT WAS NICE TO HEAR FROM YOU. FEEL FREE TO CALL WHENEVER YOU LIKE!
I'm flattered to be an OBJECT OF CONTENTION!
WELL... YOU'RE NOT ALONE!

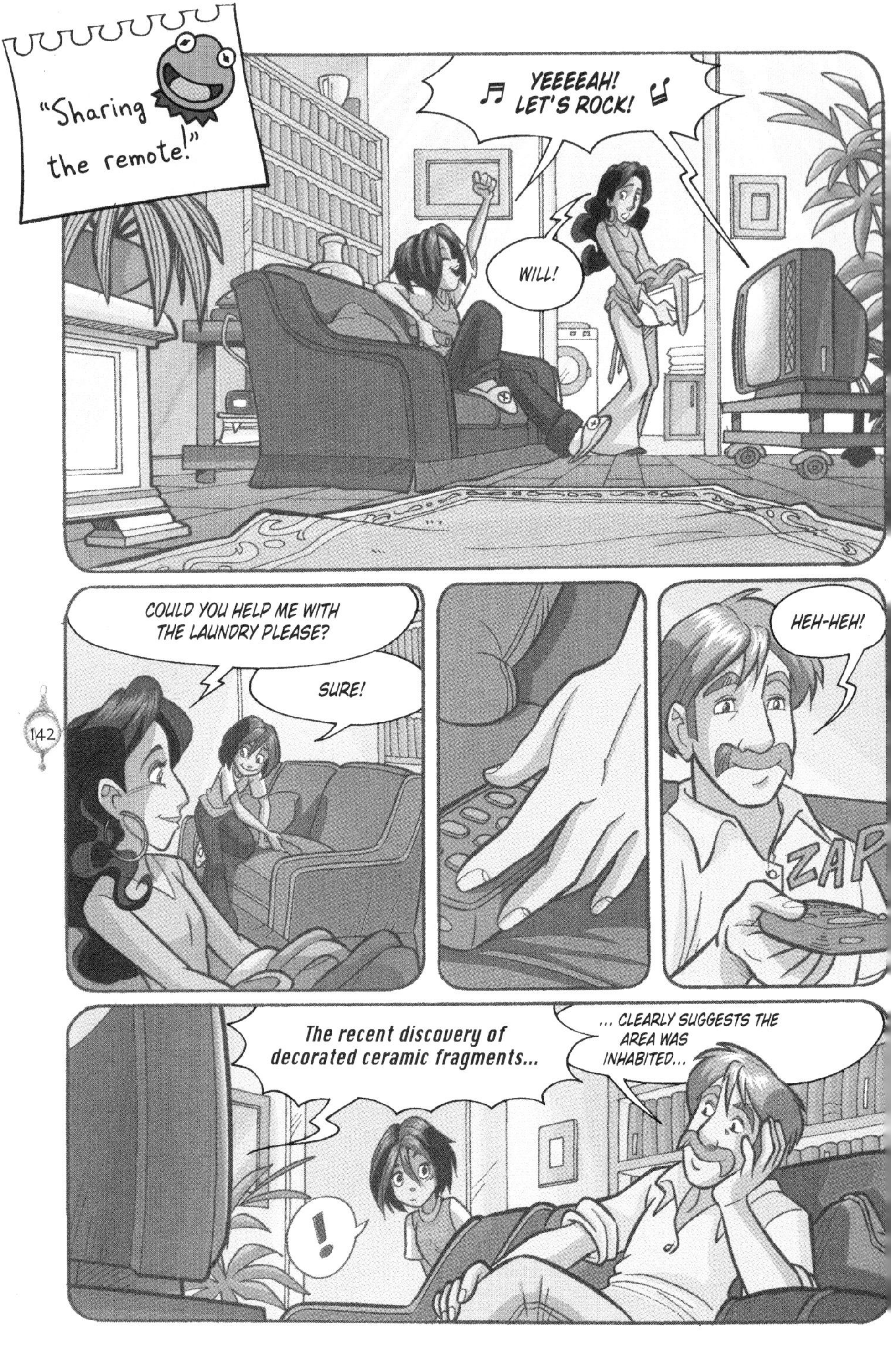
"Sharing the remote!"
YEEEEAH! LET'S ROCK!
WILL!
COULD YOU HELP ME WITH THE LAUNDRY PLEASE?
SURE!
HEH-HEH!
ZAP
The recent discovery of decorated ceramic fragments...
... CLEARLY SUGGESTS THE AREA WAS INHABITED...
!

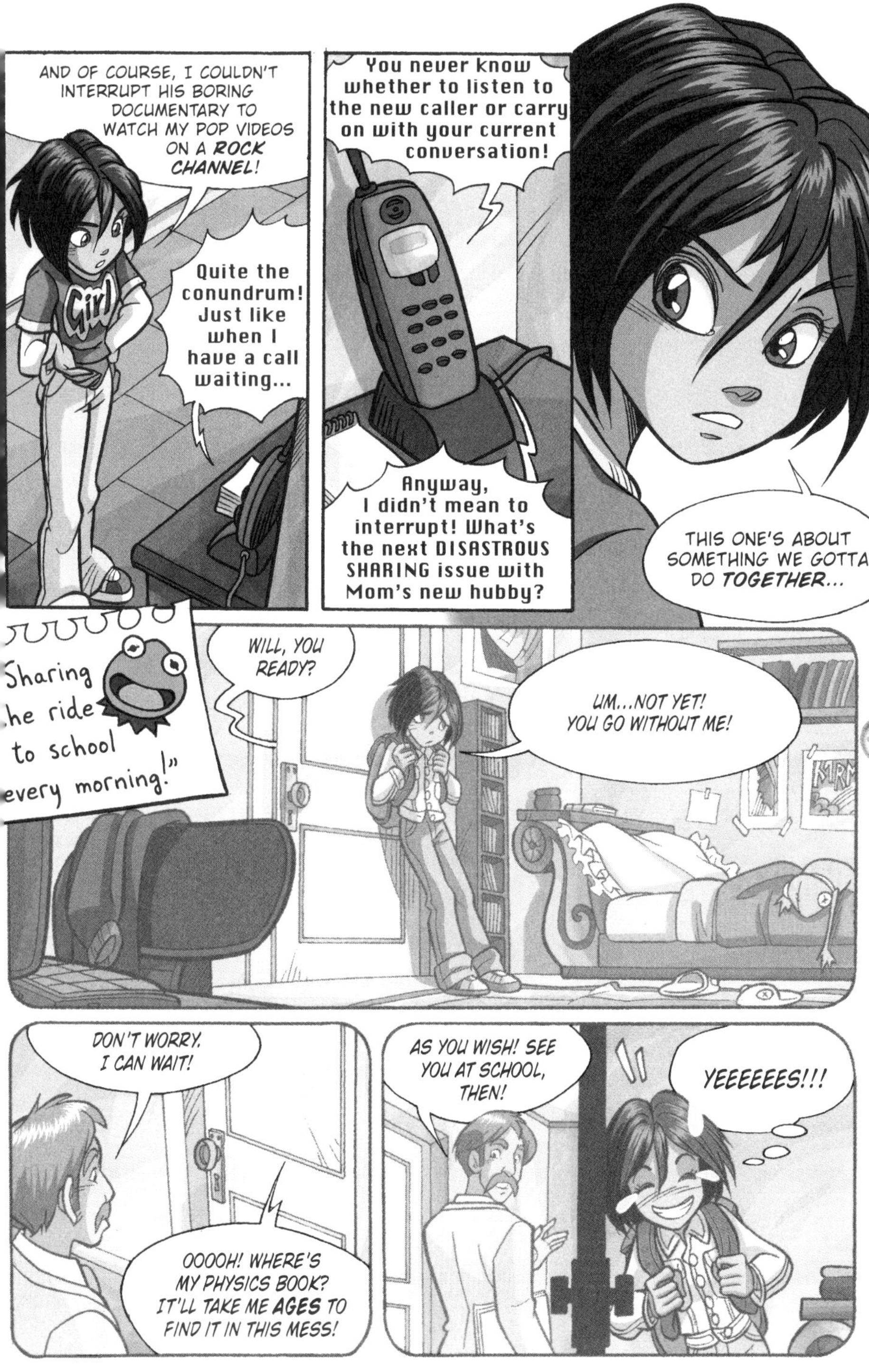
AND OF COURSE, I COULDN'T INTERRUPT HIS BORING DOCUMENTARY TO WATCH MY POP VIDEOS ON A ROCK CHANNEL!
Quite the conundrum! Just like when I have a call waiting...
You never know whether to listen to the new caller or carry on with your current conversation!
Anyway, I didn't mean to interrupt! What's the next DISASTROUS SHARING issue with Mom's new hubby?
THIS ONE'S ABOUT SOMETHING WE GOTTA DO TOGETHER...
Sharing the ride to school every morning!"
WILL, YOU READY?
UM...NOT YET! YOU GO WITHOUT ME!
DON'T WORRY. I CAN WAIT!
OOOOH! WHERE'S MY PHYSICS BOOK? IT'LL TAKE ME AGES TO FIND IT IN THIS MESS!
AS YOU WISH! SEE YOU AT SCHOOL, THEN!
YEEEEEES!!!

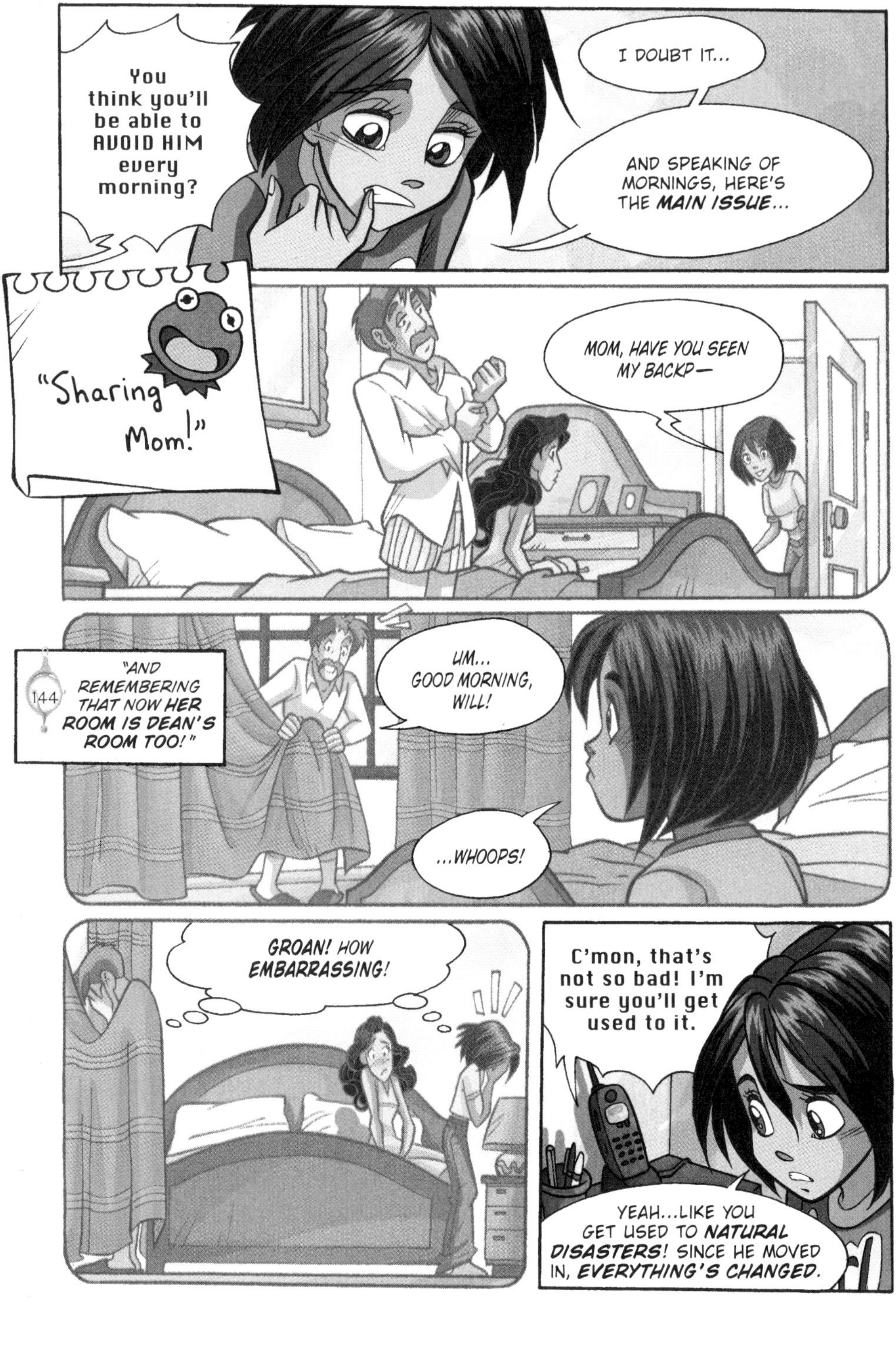

You think you'll be able to AVOID HIM every morning?
I DOUBT IT...
AND SPEAKING OF MORNINGS, HERE'S THE MAIN ISSUE...
"Sharing Mom!"
MOM, HAVE YOU SEEN MY BACKP—
144
"AND REMEMBERING THAT NOW HER ROOM IS DEAN'S ROOM TOO!"
UM... GOOD MORNING, WILL!
...WHOOPS!
GROAN! HOW EMBARRASSING!
C'mon, that's not so bad! I'm sure you'll get used to it.
YEAH...LIKE YOU GET USED TO NATURAL DISASTERS! SINCE HE MOVED IN, EVERYTHING'S CHANGED.

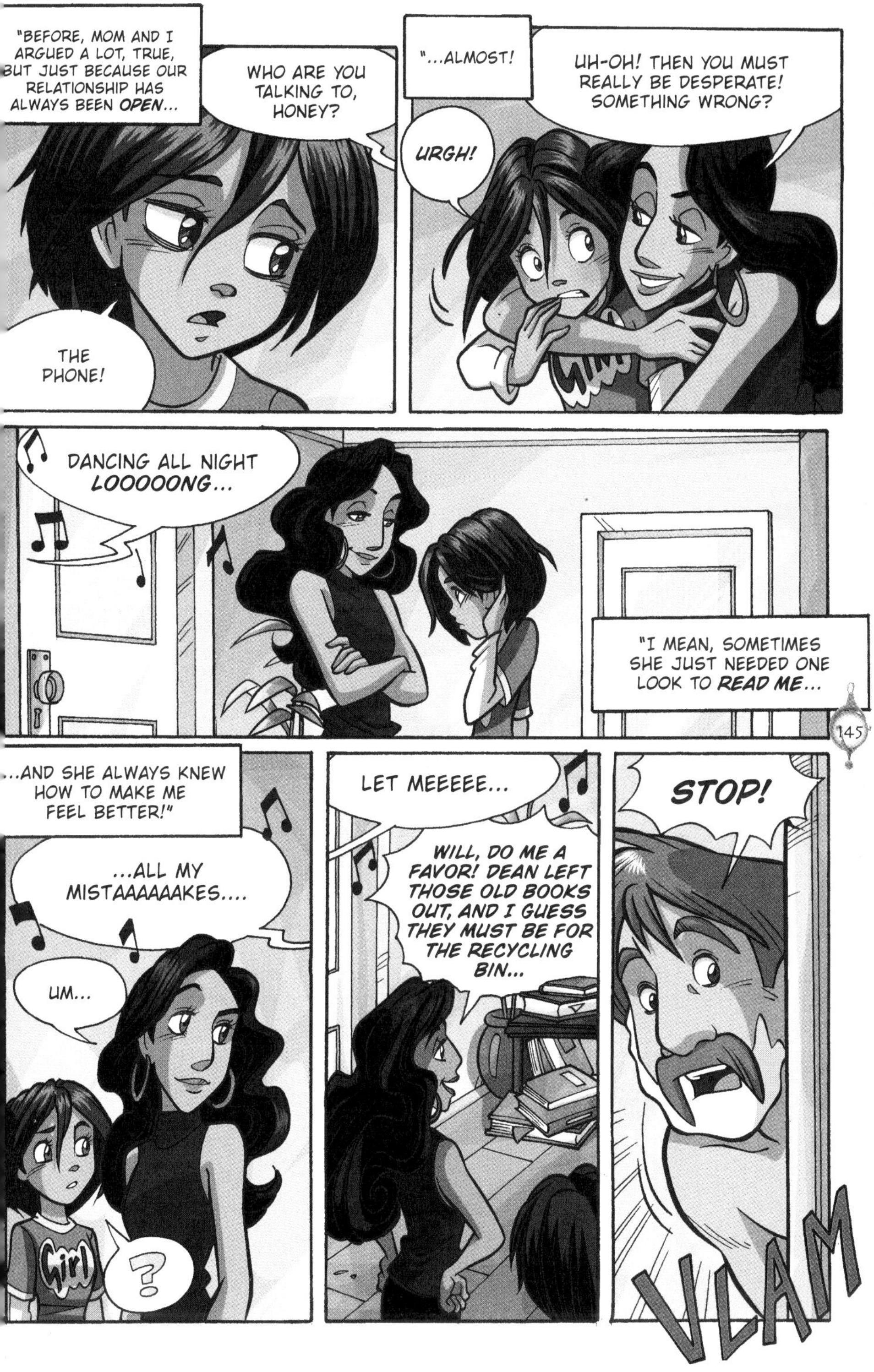
"BEFORE, MOM AND I ARGUED A LOT, TRUE, BUT JUST BECAUSE OUR RELATIONSHIP HAS ALWAYS BEEN OPEN...
WHO ARE YOU TALKING TO, HONEY?
THE PHONE!
"...ALMOST!
UH-OH! THEN YOU MUST REALLY BE DESPERATE! SOMETHING WRONG?
URGH!
DANCING ALL NIGHT LOOOOONG...
"I MEAN, SOMETIMES SHE JUST NEEDED ONE LOOK TO READ ME...
...AND SHE ALWAYS KNEW HOW TO MAKE ME FEEL BETTER!"
...ALL MY MISTAAAAAAKES....
UM...
?
LET MEEEEE...
WILL, DO ME A FAVOR! DEAN LEFT THOSE OLD BOOKS OUT, AND I GUESS THEY MUST BE FOR THE RECYCLING BIN...
STOP!
VLAM

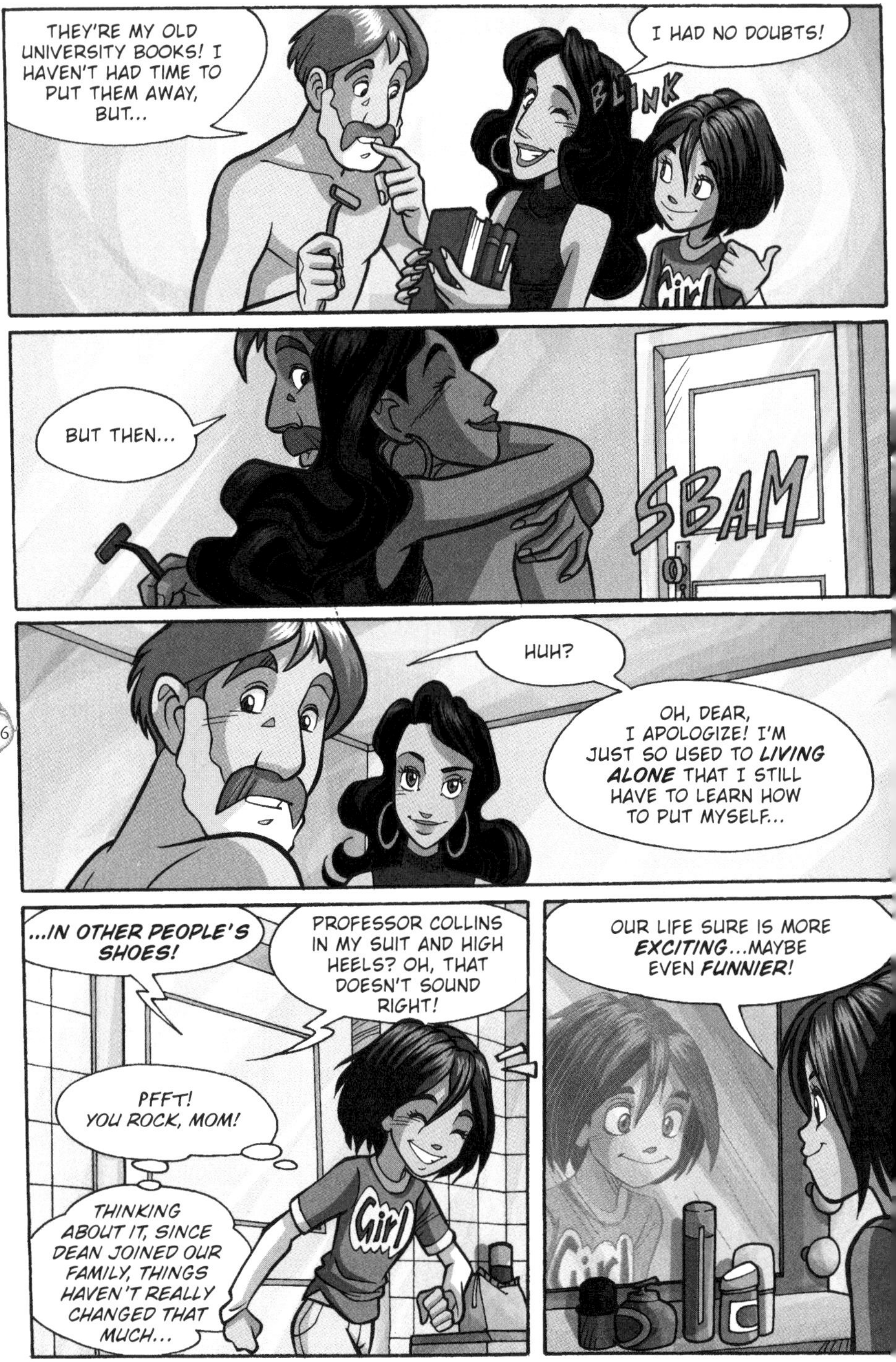
THEY'RE MY OLD UNIVERSITY BOOKS! I HAVEN'T HAD TIME TO PUT THEM AWAY, BUT...
I HAD NO DOUBTS!
BLINK
BUT THEN...
SBAM
HUH?
OH, DEAR, I APOLOGIZE! I'M JUST SO USED TO LIVING ALONE THAT I STILL HAVE TO LEARN HOW TO PUT MYSELF...
...IN OTHER PEOPLE'S SHOES!
PROFESSOR COLLINS IN MY SUIT AND HIGH HEELS? OH, THAT DOESN'T SOUND RIGHT!
PFFT! YOU ROCK, MOM!
THINKING ABOUT IT, SINCE DEAN JOINED OUR FAMILY, THINGS HAVEN'T REALLY CHANGED THAT MUCH...
OUR LIFE SURE IS MORE EXCITING...MAYBE EVEN FUNNIER!

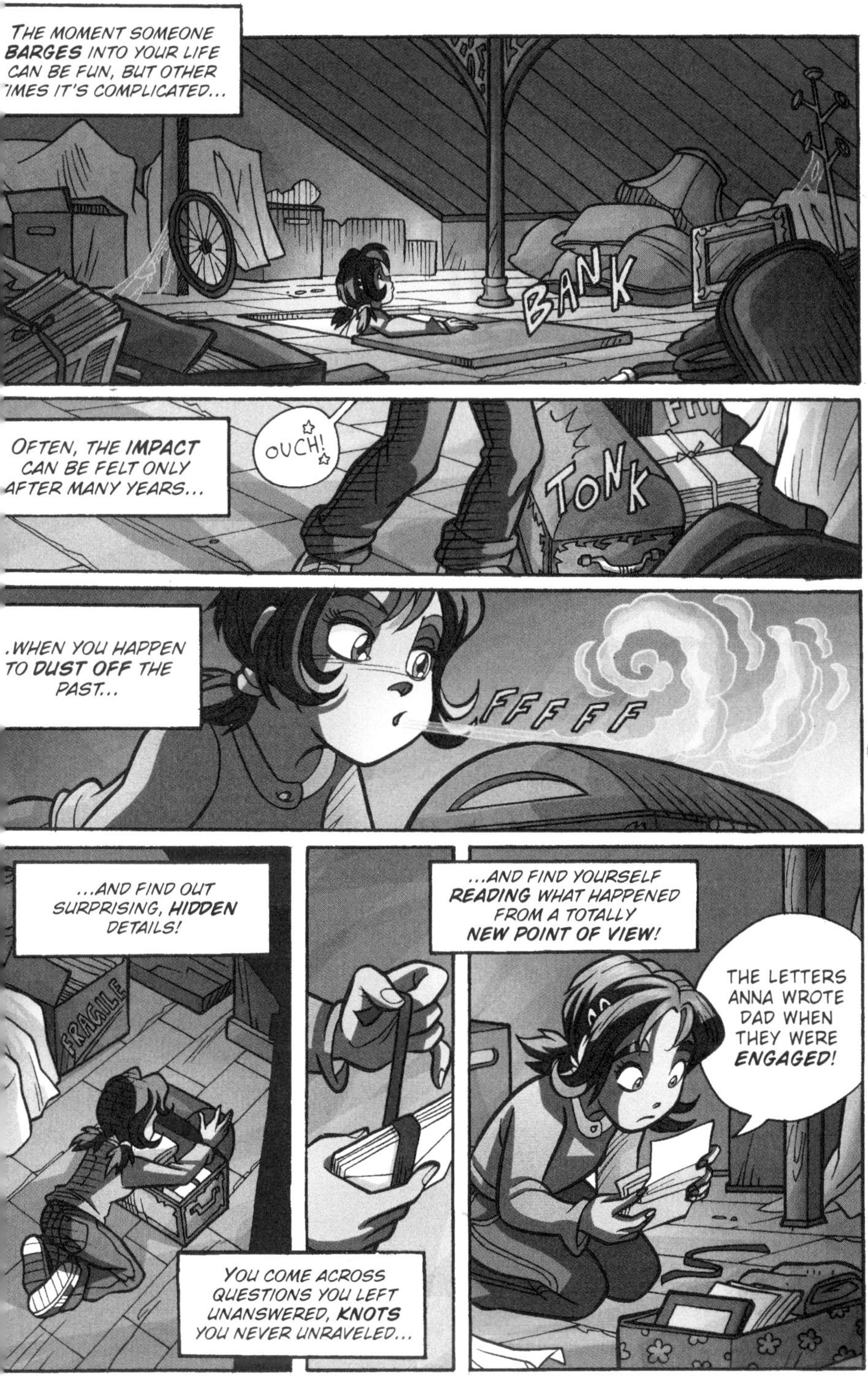

THE MOMENT SOMEONE BARGES INTO YOUR LIFE CAN BE FUN, BUT OTHER IMES IT'S COMPLICATED...
BANK
OFTEN, THE IMPACT CAN BE FELT ONLY AFTER MANY YEARS...
OUCH!
TONK
.WHEN YOU HAPPEN TO DUST OFF THE PAST...
FFFFF
...AND FIND OUT SURPRISING, HIDDEN DETAILS!
FRAGILE
YOU COME ACROSS QUESTIONS YOU LEFT UNANSWERED, KNOTS YOU NEVER UNRAVELED...
...AND FIND YOURSELF READING WHAT HAPPENED FROM A TOTALLY NEW POINT OF VIEW!
THE LETTERS ANNA WROTE DAD WHEN THEY WERE ENGAGED!

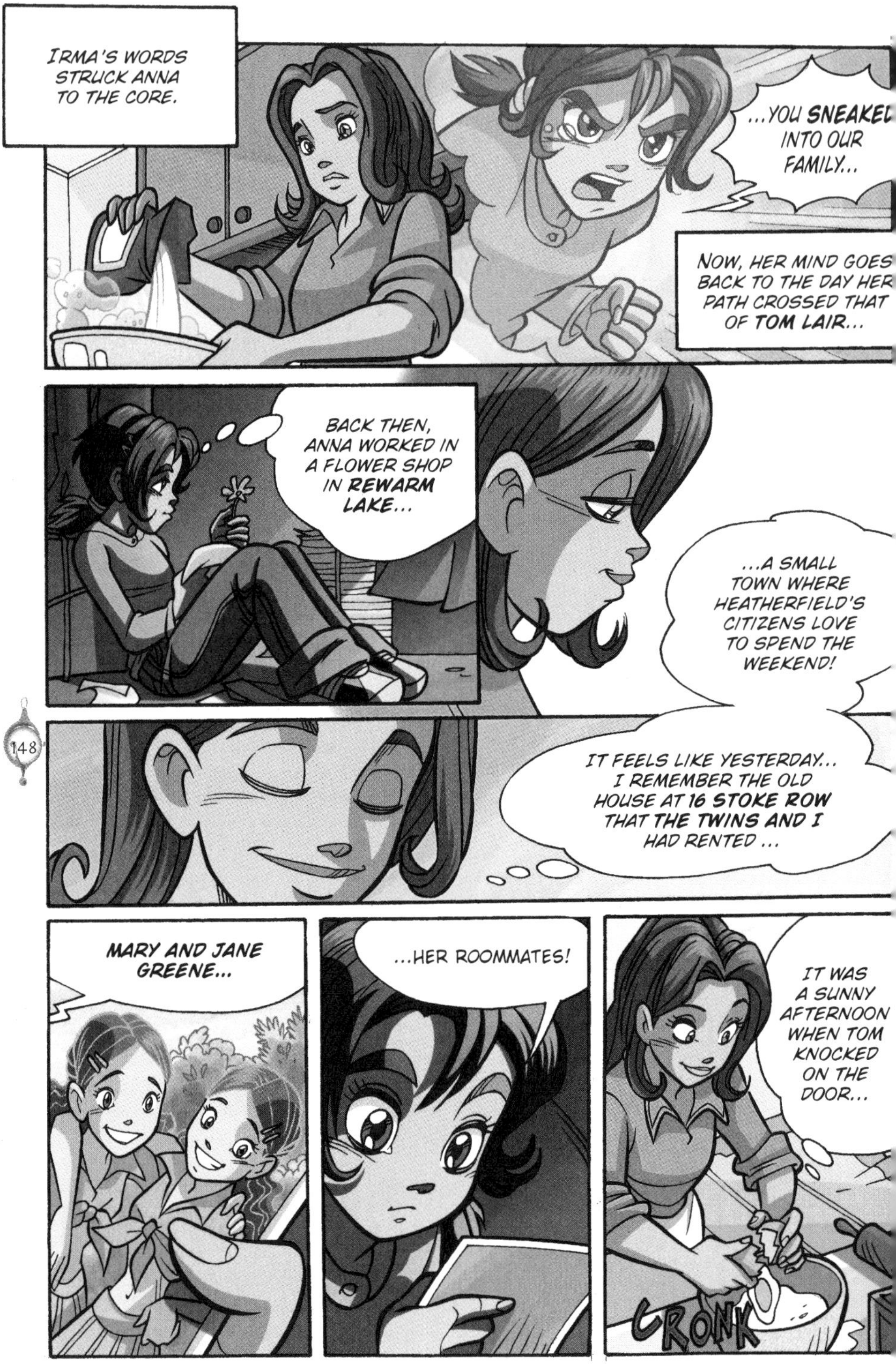
IRMA'S WORDS STRUCK ANNA TO THE CORE.
...YOU SNEAKED INTO OUR FAMILY...
NOW, HER MIND GOES BACK TO THE DAY HER PATH CROSSED THAT OF TOM LAIR...
BACK THEN, ANNA WORKED IN A FLOWER SHOP IN REWARM LAKE...
...A SMALL TOWN WHERE HEATHERFIELD'S CITIZENS LOVE TO SPEND THE WEEKEND!
IT FEELS LIKE YESTERDAY... I REMEMBER THE OLD HOUSE AT 16 STOKE ROW THAT THE TWINS AND I HAD RENTED ...
MARY AND JANE GREENE...
...HER ROOMMATES!
IT WAS A SUNNY AFTERNOON WHEN TOM KNOCKED ON THE DOOR...
CRONK

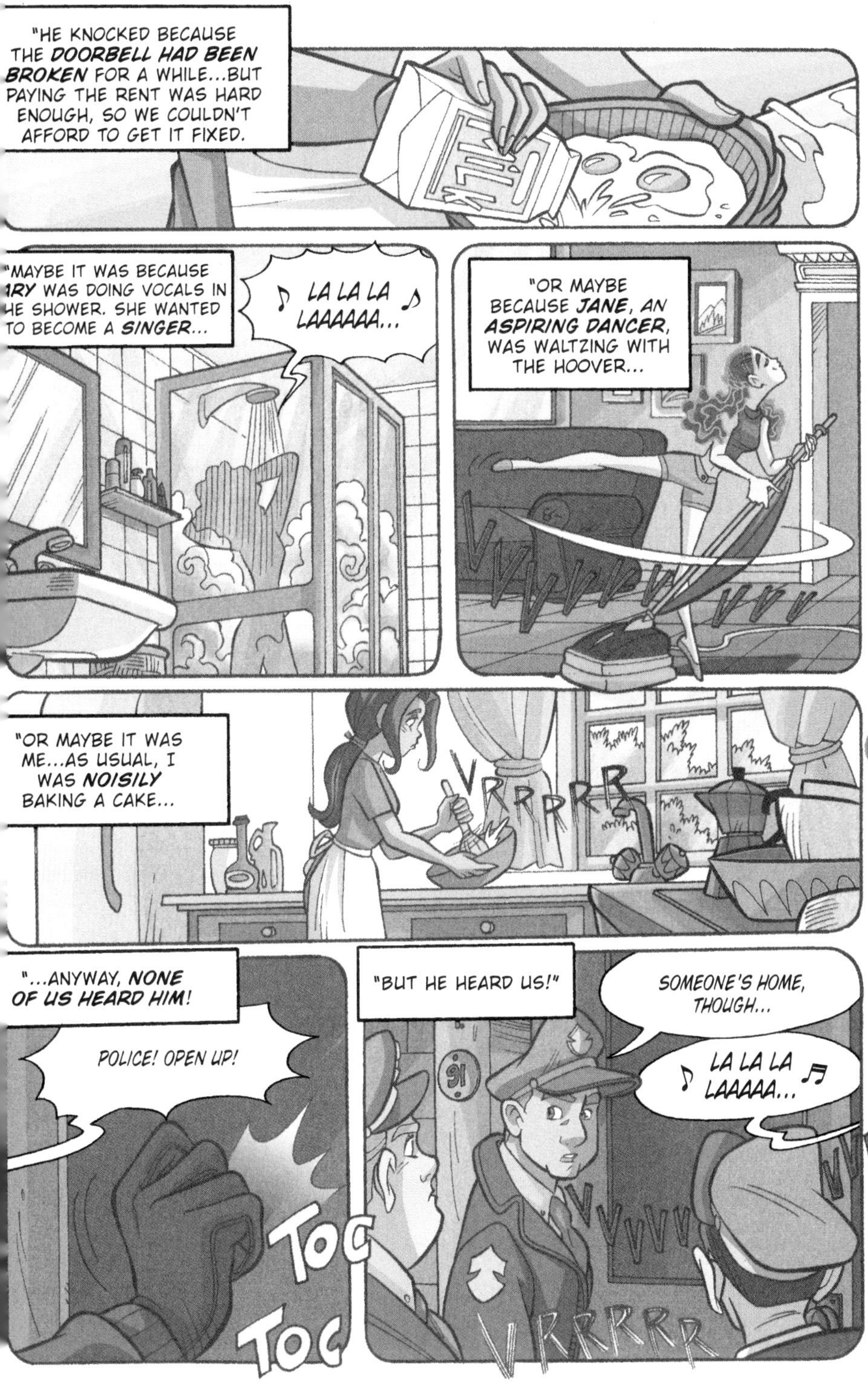
"HE KNOCKED BECAUSE THE DOORBELL HAD BEEN BROKEN FOR A WHILE...BUT PAYING THE RENT WAS HARD ENOUGH, SO WE COULDN'T AFFORD TO GET IT FIXED.
MILK
"MAYBE IT WAS BECAUSE RY WAS DOING VOCALS IN HE SHOWER. SHE WANTED TO BECOME A SINGER...
♪ LA LA LA LAAAAAA... ♪
"OR MAYBE BECAUSE JANE, AN ASPIRING DANCER, WAS WALTZING WITH THE HOOVER...
VVVVVVVVVV VVV
"OR MAYBE IT WAS ME...AS USUAL, I WAS NOISILY BAKING A CAKE...
VRRRRR
"...ANYWAY, NONE OF US HEARD HIM!
POLICE! OPEN UP!
TOC TOC
"BUT HE HEARD US!"
SOMEONE'S HOME, THOUGH...
♪ LA LA LA LAAAAA... ♬
VVVVVVV VVV
VRRRRRR

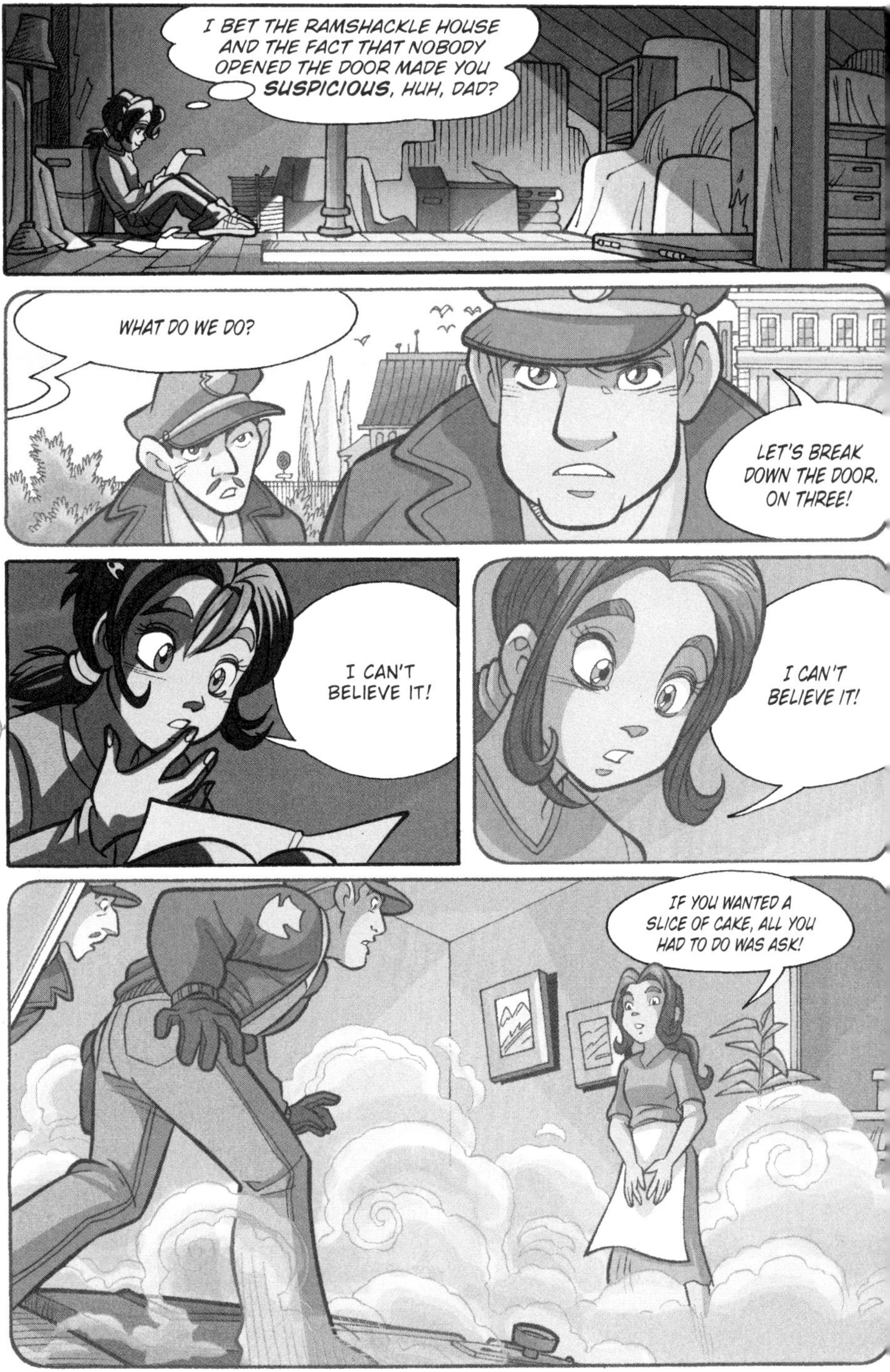
I BET THE RAMSHACKLE HOUSE AND THE FACT THAT NOBODY OPENED THE DOOR MADE YOU SUSPICIOUS, HUH, DAD?
WHAT DO WE DO?
LET'S BREAK DOWN THE DOOR. ON THREE!
I CAN'T BELIEVE IT!
I CAN'T BELIEVE IT!
IF YOU WANTED A SLICE OF CAKE, ALL YOU HAD TO DO WAS ASK!

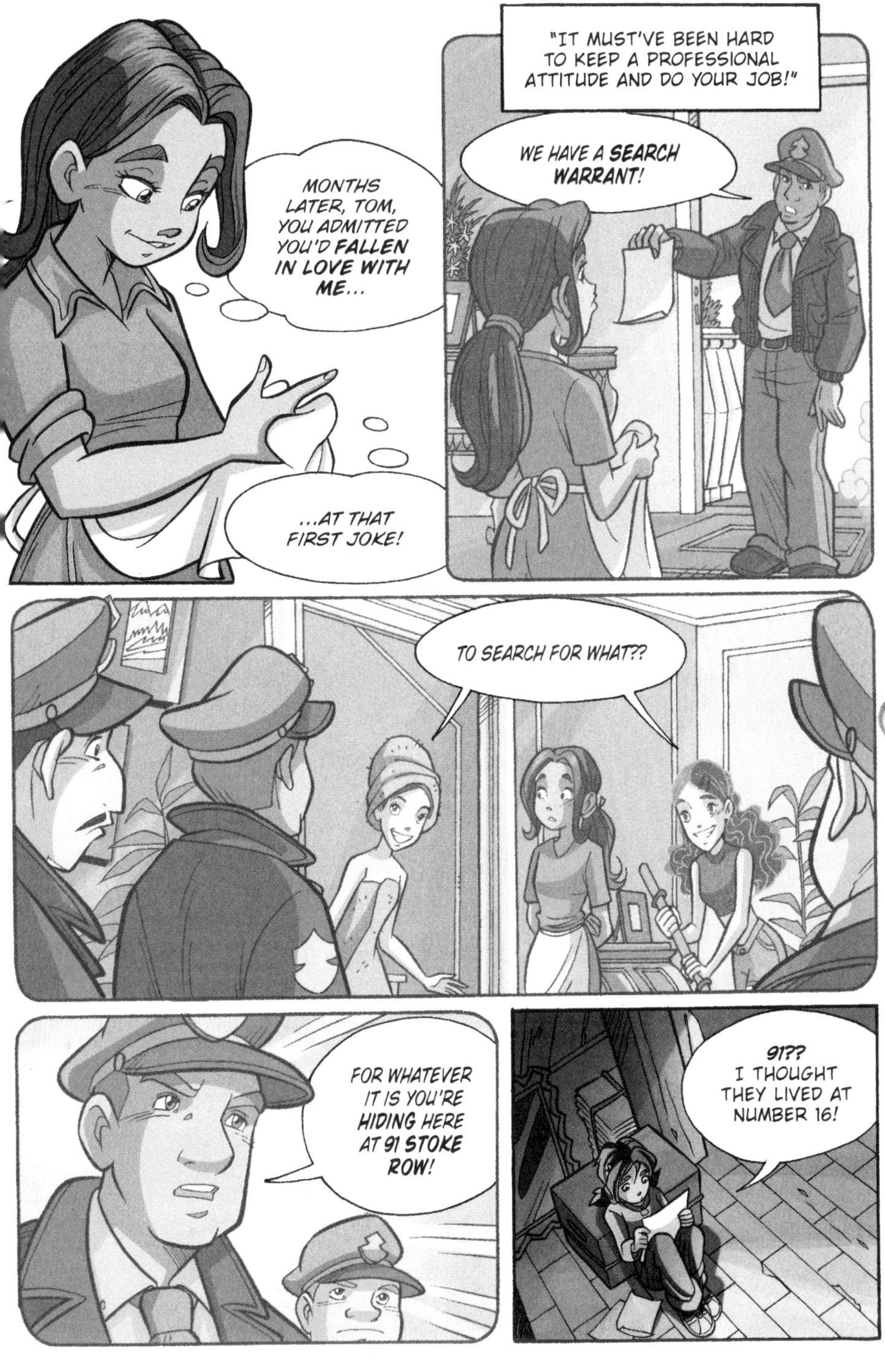
MONTHS LATER, TOM, YOU ADMITTED YOU'D FALLEN IN LOVE WITH ME...
...AT THAT FIRST JOKE!
"IT MUST'VE BEEN HARD TO KEEP A PROFESSIONAL ATTITUDE AND DO YOUR JOB!"
WE HAVE A SEARCH WARRANT!
TO SEARCH FOR WHAT??
FOR WHATEVER IT IS YOU'RE HIDING HERE AT 91 STOKE ROW!
91?? I THOUGHT THEY LIVED AT NUMBER 16!

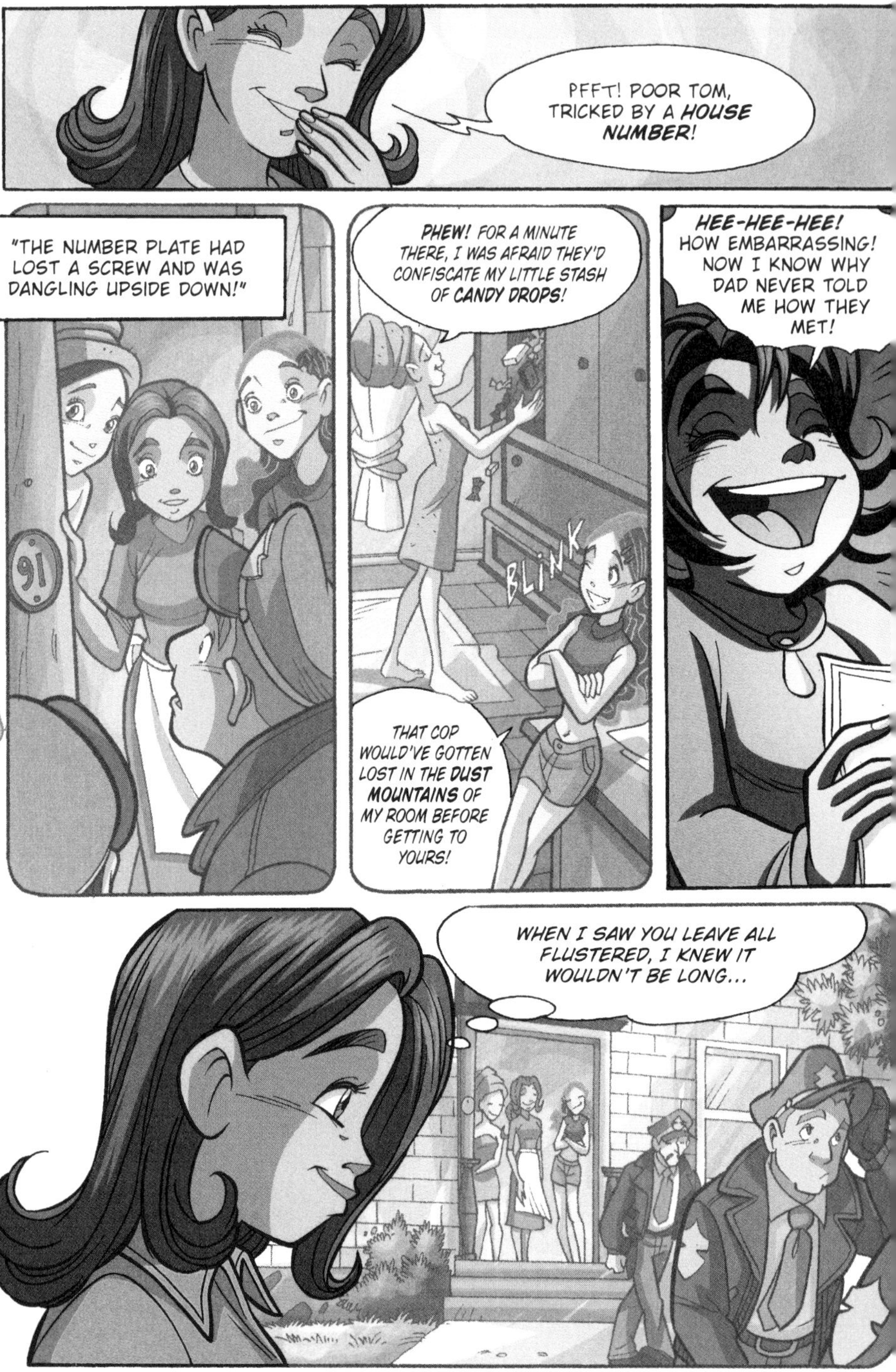
PFFT! POOR TOM, TRICKED BY A HOUSE NUMBER!
"THE NUMBER PLATE HAD LOST A SCREW AND WAS DANGLING UPSIDE DOWN!"
91
PHEW! FOR A MINUTE THERE, I WAS AFRAID THEY'D CONFISCATE MY LITTLE STASH OF CANDY DROPS!
BLINK
THAT COP WOULD'VE GOTTEN LOST IN THE DUST MOUNTAINS OF MY ROOM BEFORE GETTING TO YOURS!
HEE-HEE-HEE! HOW EMBARRASSING! NOW I KNOW WHY DAD NEVER TOLD ME HOW THEY MET!
WHEN I SAW YOU LEAVE ALL FLUSTERED, I KNEW IT WOULDN'T BE LONG...

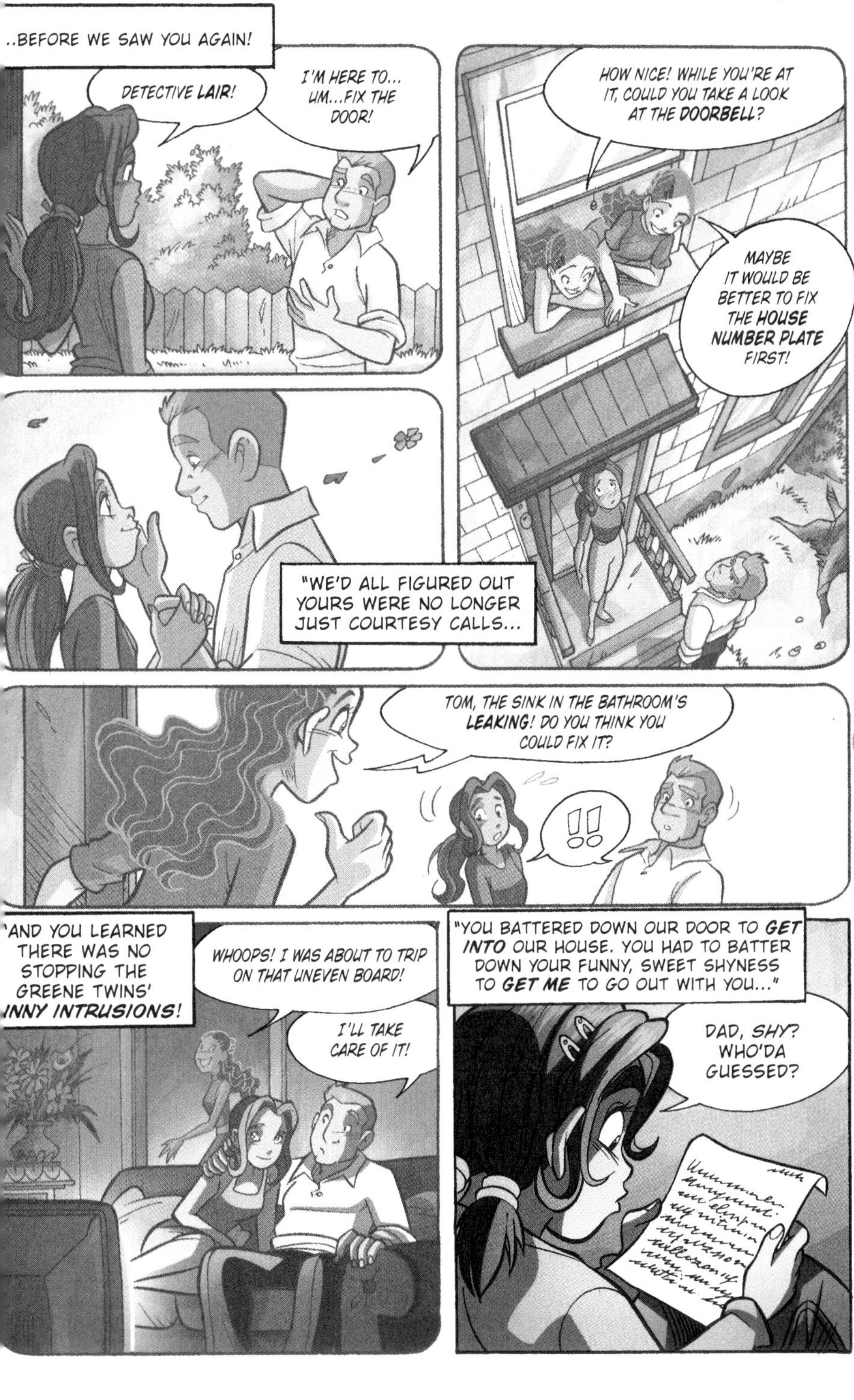
..BEFORE WE SAW YOU AGAIN!
DETECTIVE LAIR!
I'M HERE TO... UM...FIX THE DOOR!
HOW NICE! WHILE YOU'RE AT IT, COULD YOU TAKE A LOOK AT THE DOORBELL?
MAYBE IT WOULD BE BETTER TO FIX THE HOUSE NUMBER PLATE FIRST!
"WE'D ALL FIGURED OUT YOURS WERE NO LONGER JUST COURTESY CALLS...
TOM, THE SINK IN THE BATHROOM'S LEAKING! DO YOU THINK YOU COULD FIX IT?
!!
'AND YOU LEARNED THERE WAS NO STOPPING THE GREENE TWINS' INNY INTRUSIONS!
WHOOPS! I WAS ABOUT TO TRIP ON THAT UNEVEN BOARD!
I'LL TAKE CARE OF IT!
"YOU BATTERED DOWN OUR DOOR TO GET INTO OUR HOUSE. YOU HAD TO BATTER DOWN YOUR FUNNY, SWEET SHYNESS TO GET ME TO GO OUT WITH YOU..."
DAD, SHY? WHO'DA GUESSED?

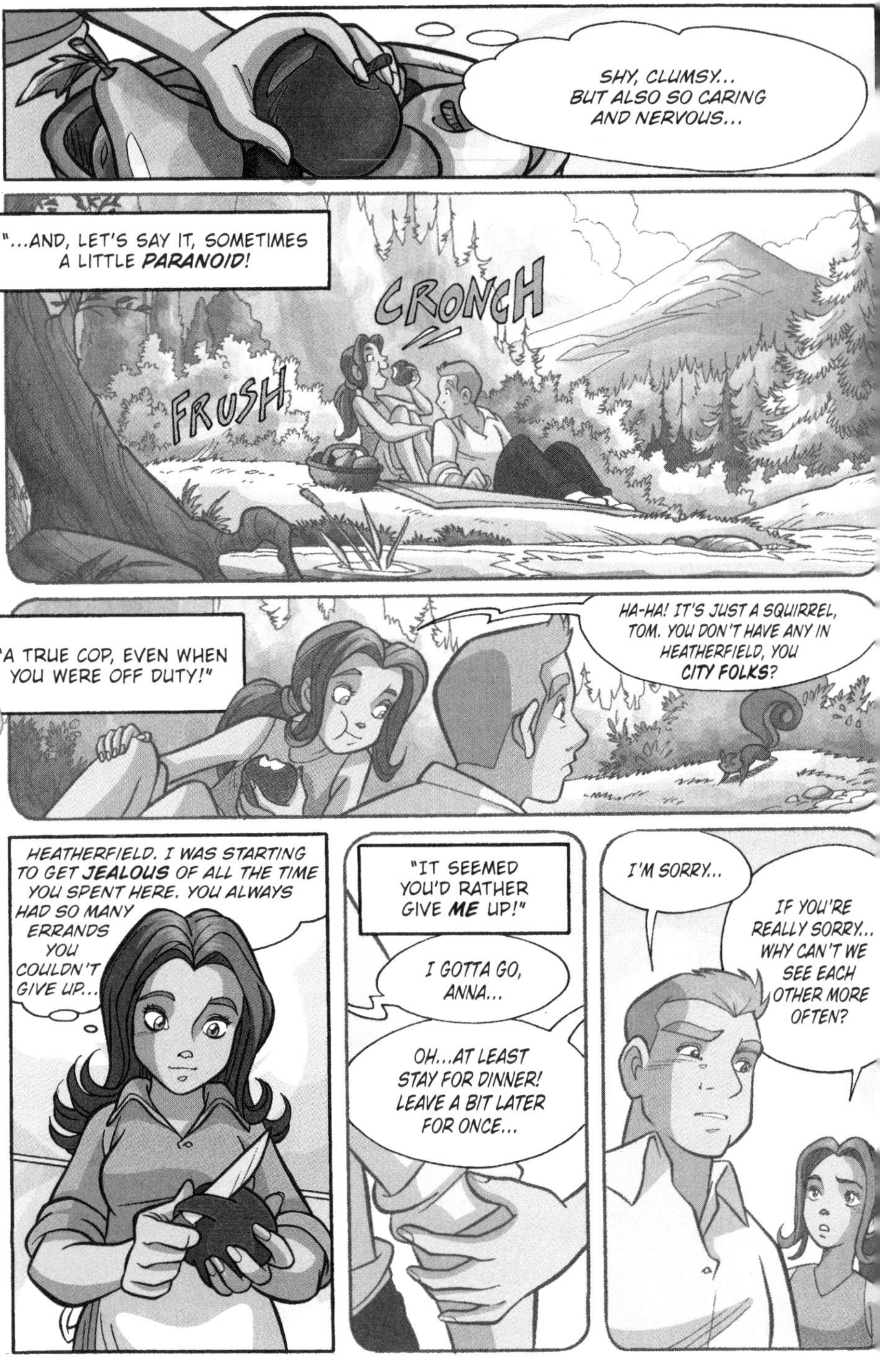
SHY, CLUMSY... BUT ALSO SO CARING AND NERVOUS...
"...AND, LET'S SAY IT, SOMETIMES A LITTLE PARANOID!
CRONCH
FRUSH
"A TRUE COP, EVEN WHEN YOU WERE OFF DUTY!"
HA-HA! IT'S JUST A SQUIRREL, TOM. YOU DON'T HAVE ANY IN HEATHERFIELD, YOU CITY FOLKS?
HEATHERFIELD. I WAS STARTING TO GET JEALOUS OF ALL THE TIME YOU SPENT HERE. YOU ALWAYS HAD SO MANY ERRANDS YOU COULDN'T GIVE UP...
"IT SEEMED YOU'D RATHER GIVE ME UP!"
I GOTTA GO, ANNA...
OH...AT LEAST STAY FOR DINNER! LEAVE A BIT LATER FOR ONCE...
I'M SORRY...
IF YOU'RE REALLY SORRY... WHY CAN'T WE SEE EACH OTHER MORE OFTEN?

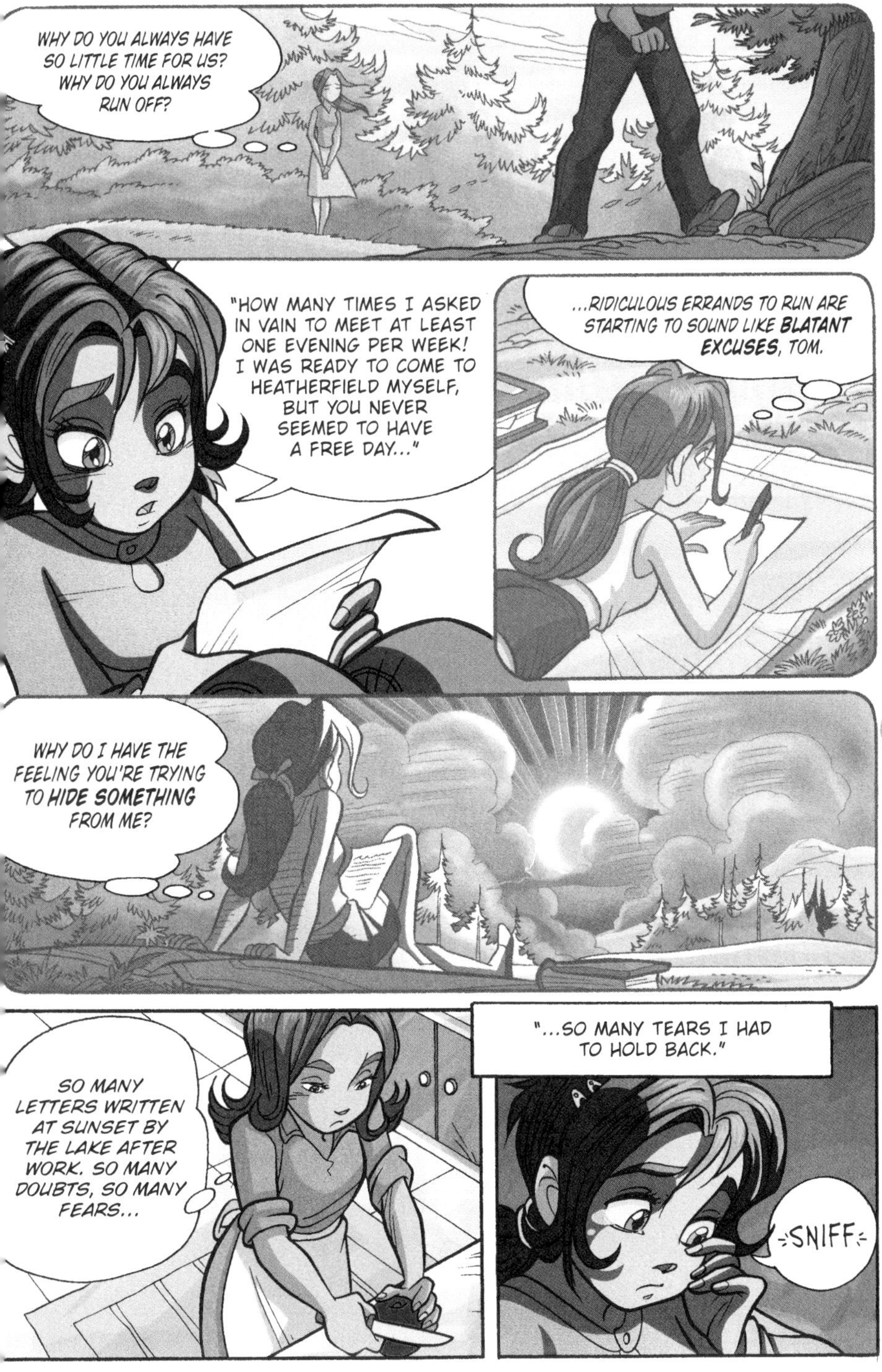
WHY DO YOU ALWAYS HAVE SO LITTLE TIME FOR US? WHY DO YOU ALWAYS RUN OFF?
"HOW MANY TIMES I ASKED IN VAIN TO MEET AT LEAST ONE EVENING PER WEEK! I WAS READY TO COME TO HEATHERFIELD MYSELF, BUT YOU NEVER SEEMED TO HAVE A FREE DAY..."
...RIDICULOUS ERRANDS TO RUN ARE STARTING TO SOUND LIKE BLATANT EXCUSES, TOM.
WHY DO I HAVE THE FEELING YOU'RE TRYING TO HIDE SOMETHING FROM ME?
SO MANY LETTERS WRITTEN AT SUNSET BY THE LAKE AFTER WORK. SO MANY DOUBTS, SO MANY FEARS...
"...SO MANY TEARS I HAD TO HOLD BACK."
SNIFF

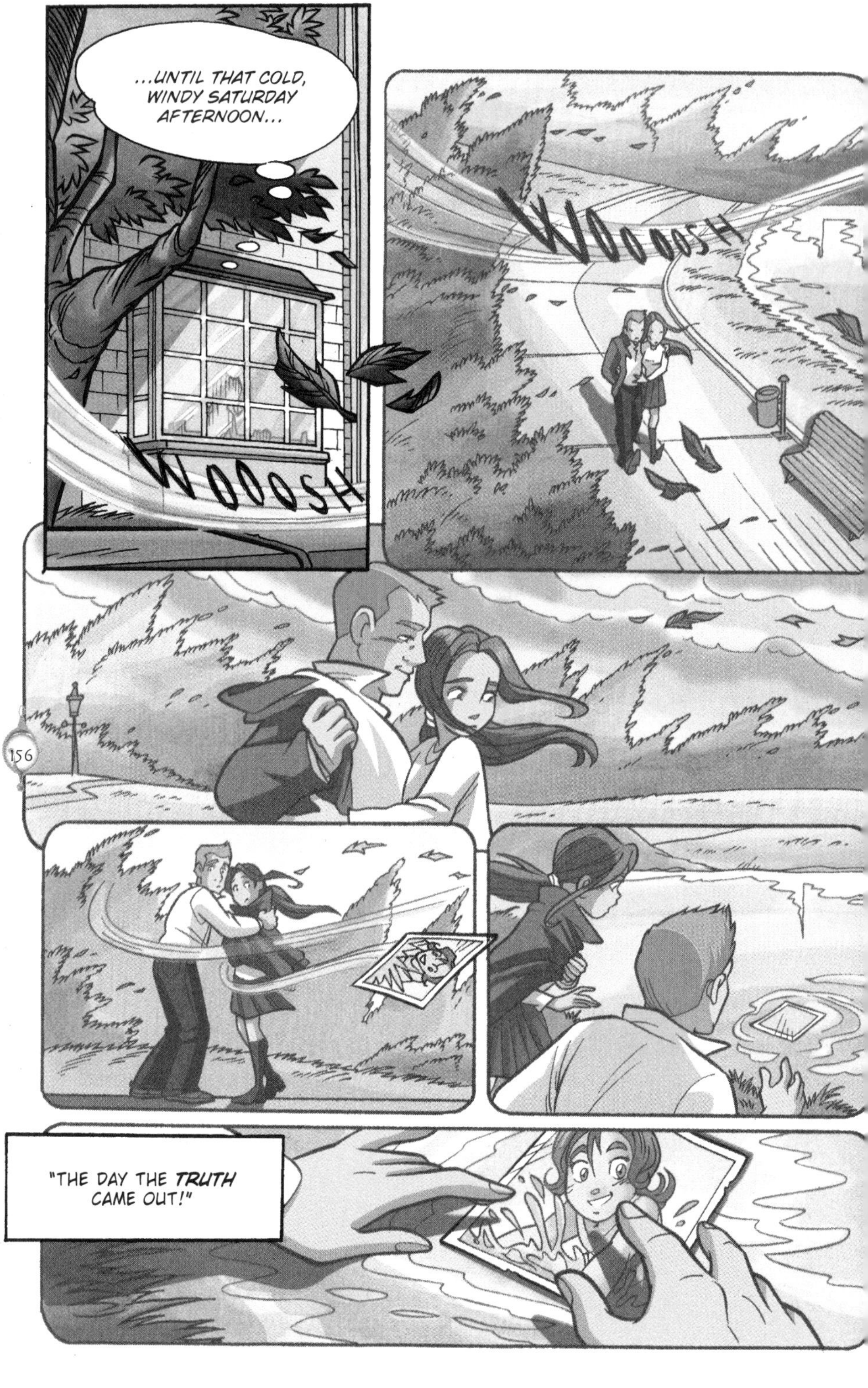
...UNTIL THAT COLD, WINDY SATURDAY AFTERNOON...
WOOOSH
WOOOOOSH
"THE DAY THE TRUTH CAME OUT!"

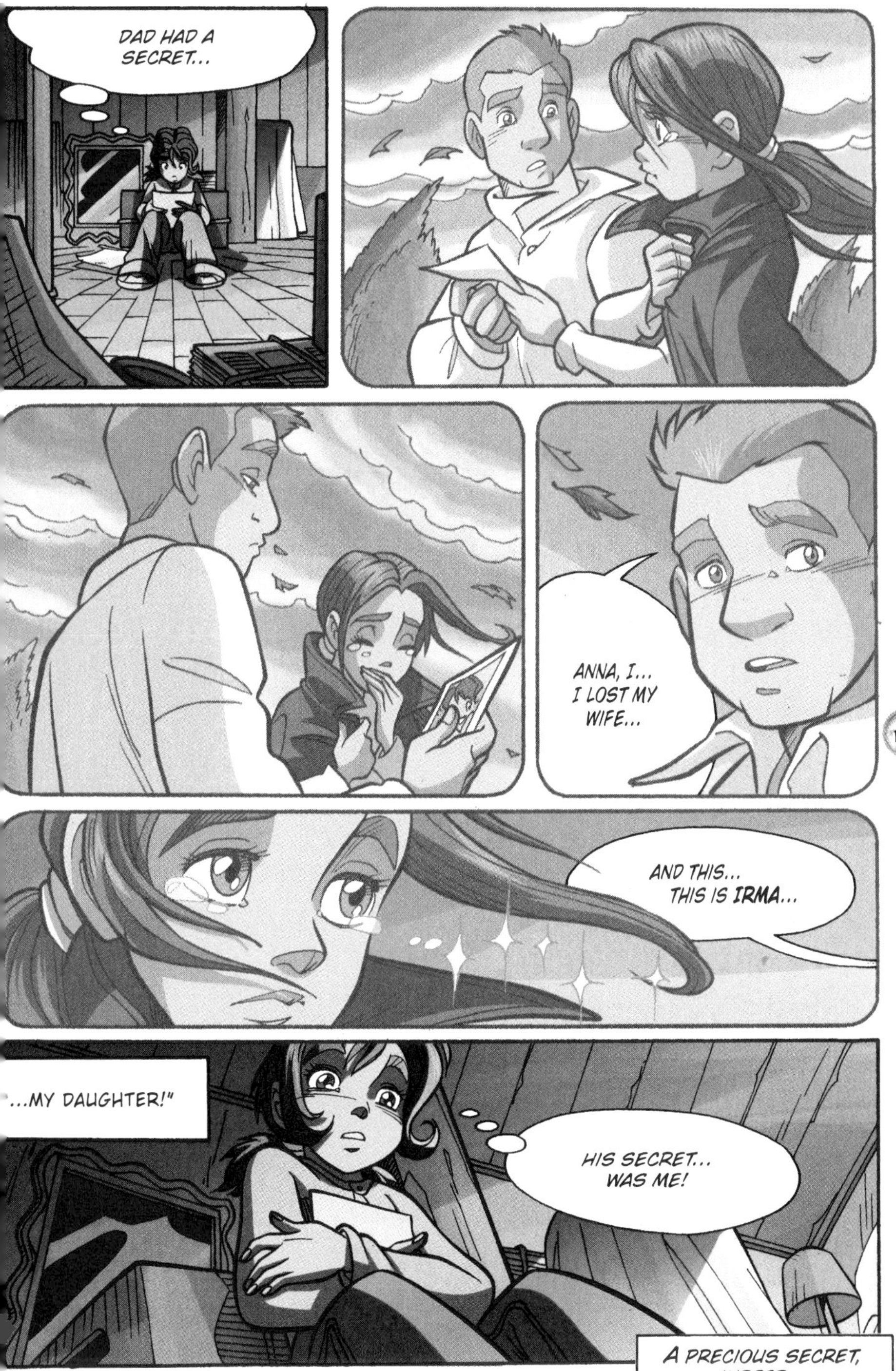

DAD HAD A SECRET...
ANNA, I... I LOST MY WIFE...
AND THIS... THIS IS IRMA...
"...MY DAUGHTER!"
HIS SECRET... WAS ME!
A PRECIOUS SECRET, INDEED...

W.i.t.c.h.

Will Irma Taranee Cornelia Hay Lin

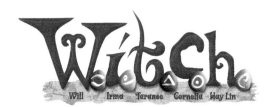

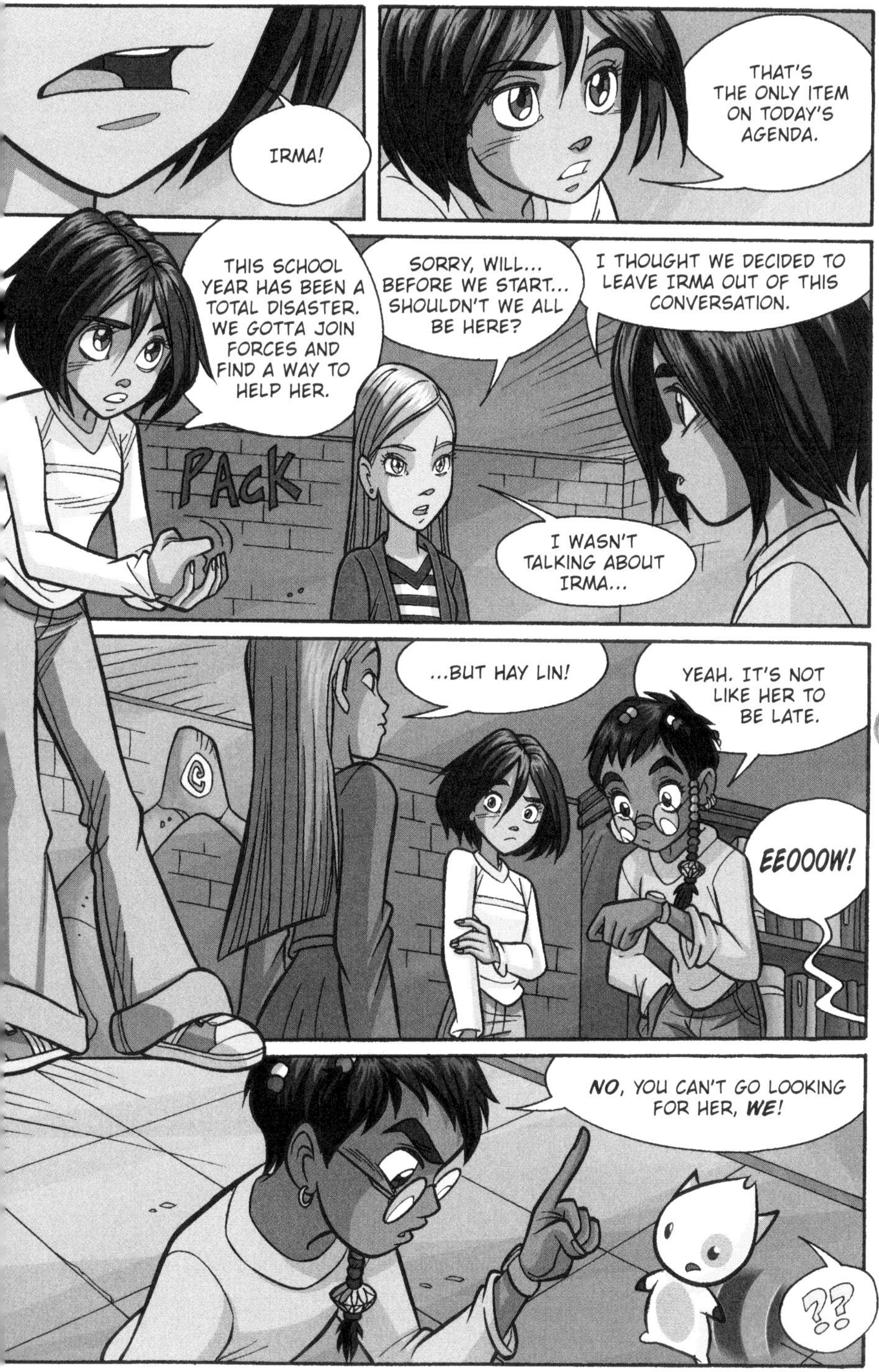
IRMA!
THAT'S THE ONLY ITEM ON TODAY'S AGENDA.
THIS SCHOOL YEAR HAS BEEN A TOTAL DISASTER. WE GOTTA JOIN FORCES AND FIND A WAY TO HELP HER.
SORRY, WILL... BEFORE WE START... SHOULDN'T WE ALL BE HERE?
I THOUGHT WE DECIDED TO LEAVE IRMA OUT OF THIS CONVERSATION.
PACK
I WASN'T TALKING ABOUT IRMA...
...BUT HAY LIN!
YEAH. IT'S NOT LIKE HER TO BE LATE.
EEOOOW!
NO, YOU CAN'T GO LOOKING FOR HER, WE!
??

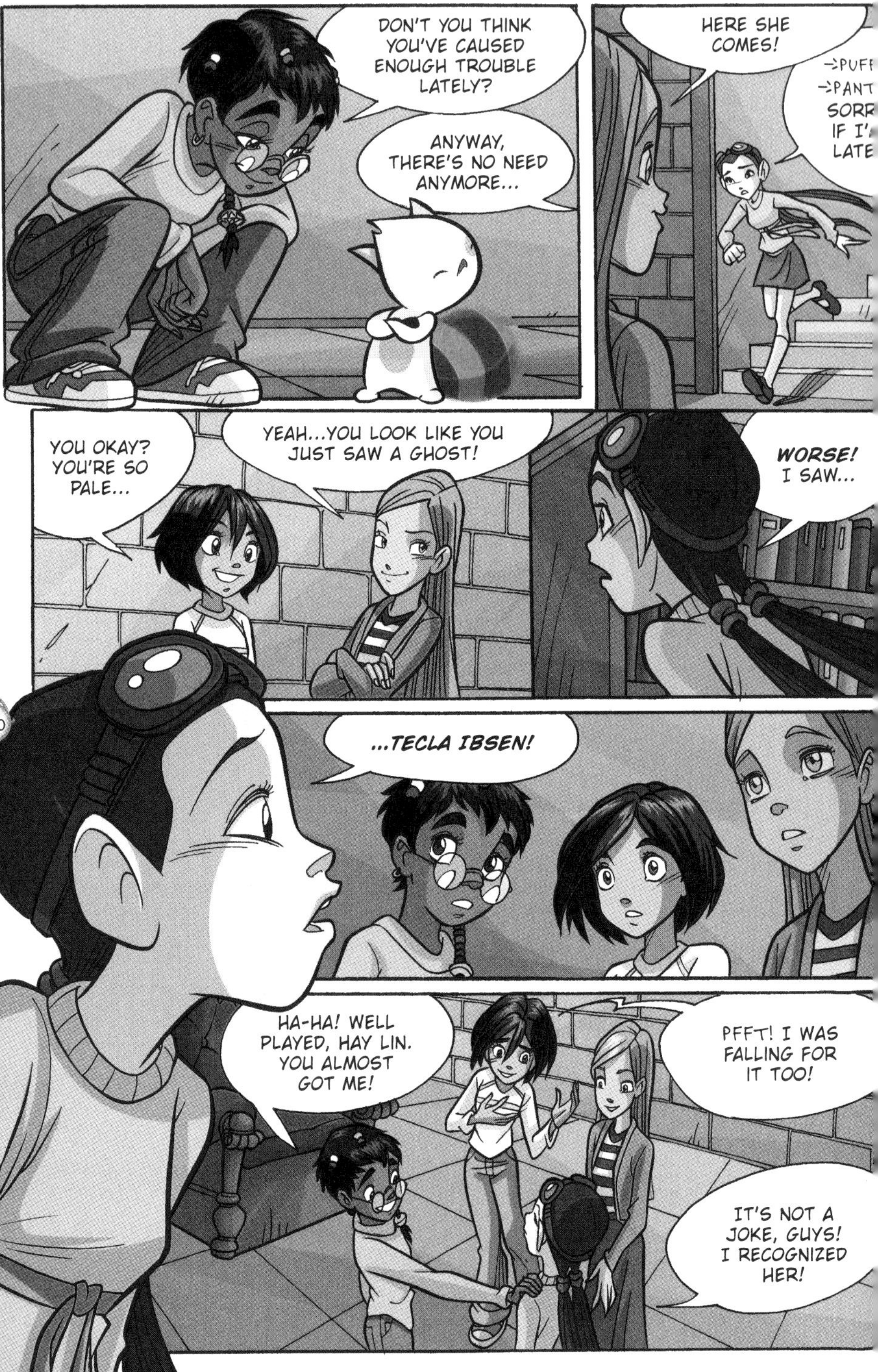
DON'T YOU THINK YOU'VE CAUSED ENOUGH TROUBLE LATELY?
ANYWAY, THERE'S NO NEED ANYMORE...
HERE SHE COMES!
YOU OKAY? YOU'RE SO PALE...
YEAH...YOU LOOK LIKE YOU JUST SAW A GHOST!
WORSE! I SAW...
...TECLA IBSEN!
HA-HA! WELL PLAYED, HAY LIN. YOU ALMOST GOT ME!
PFFT! I WAS FALLING FOR IT TOO!
IT'S NOT A JOKE, GUYS! I RECOGNIZED HER!

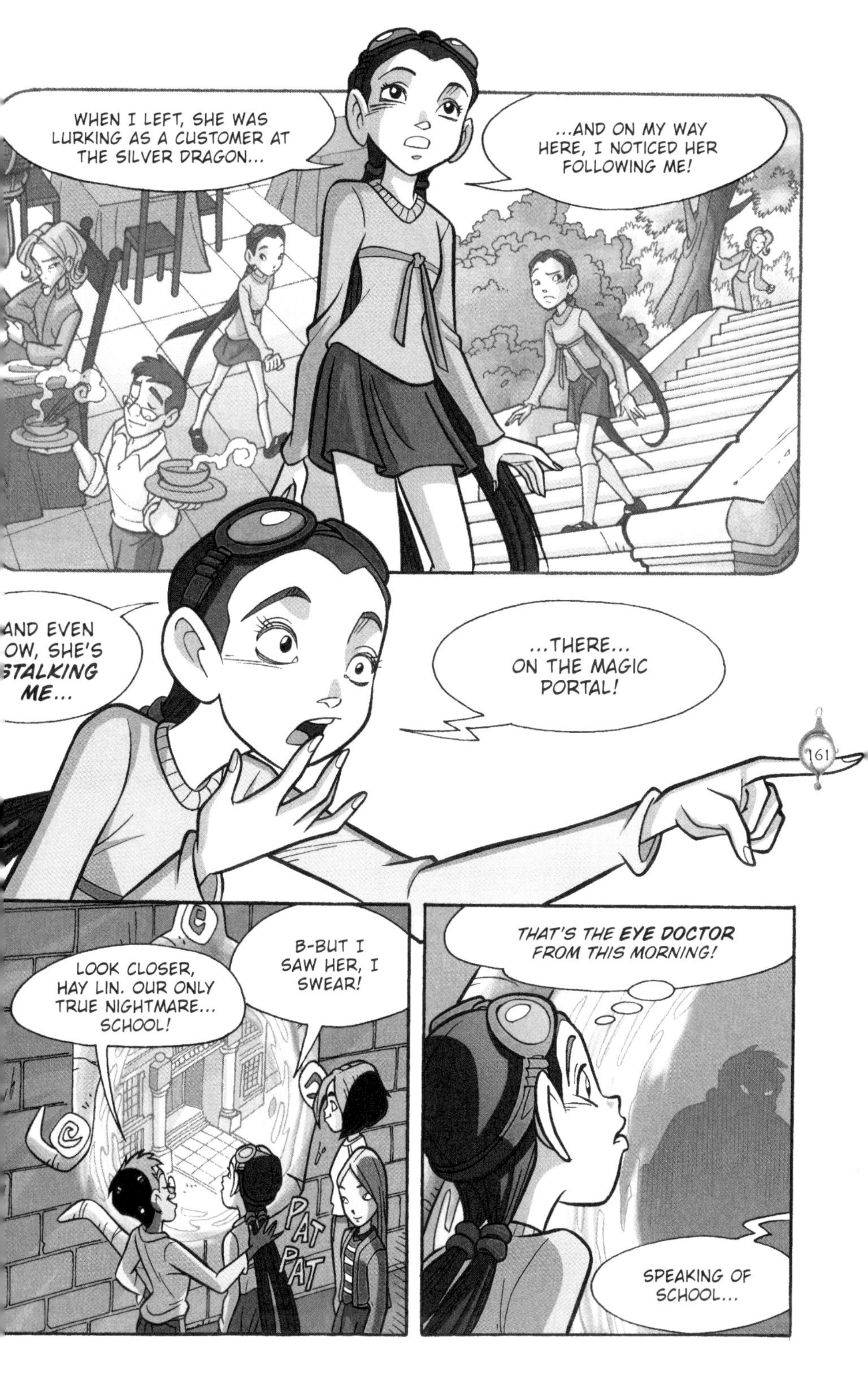
WHEN I LEFT, SHE WAS LURKING AS A CUSTOMER AT THE SILVER DRAGON...
...AND ON MY WAY HERE, I NOTICED HER FOLLOWING ME!
AND EVEN OW, SHE'S *STALKING ME*...
...THERE... ON THE MAGIC PORTAL!
B-BUT I SAW HER, I SWEAR!
LOOK CLOSER, HAY LIN. OUR ONLY TRUE NIGHTMARE... SCHOOL!
PAT PAT
THAT'S THE ***EYE DOCTOR*** FROM THIS MORNING!
SPEAKING OF SCHOOL...

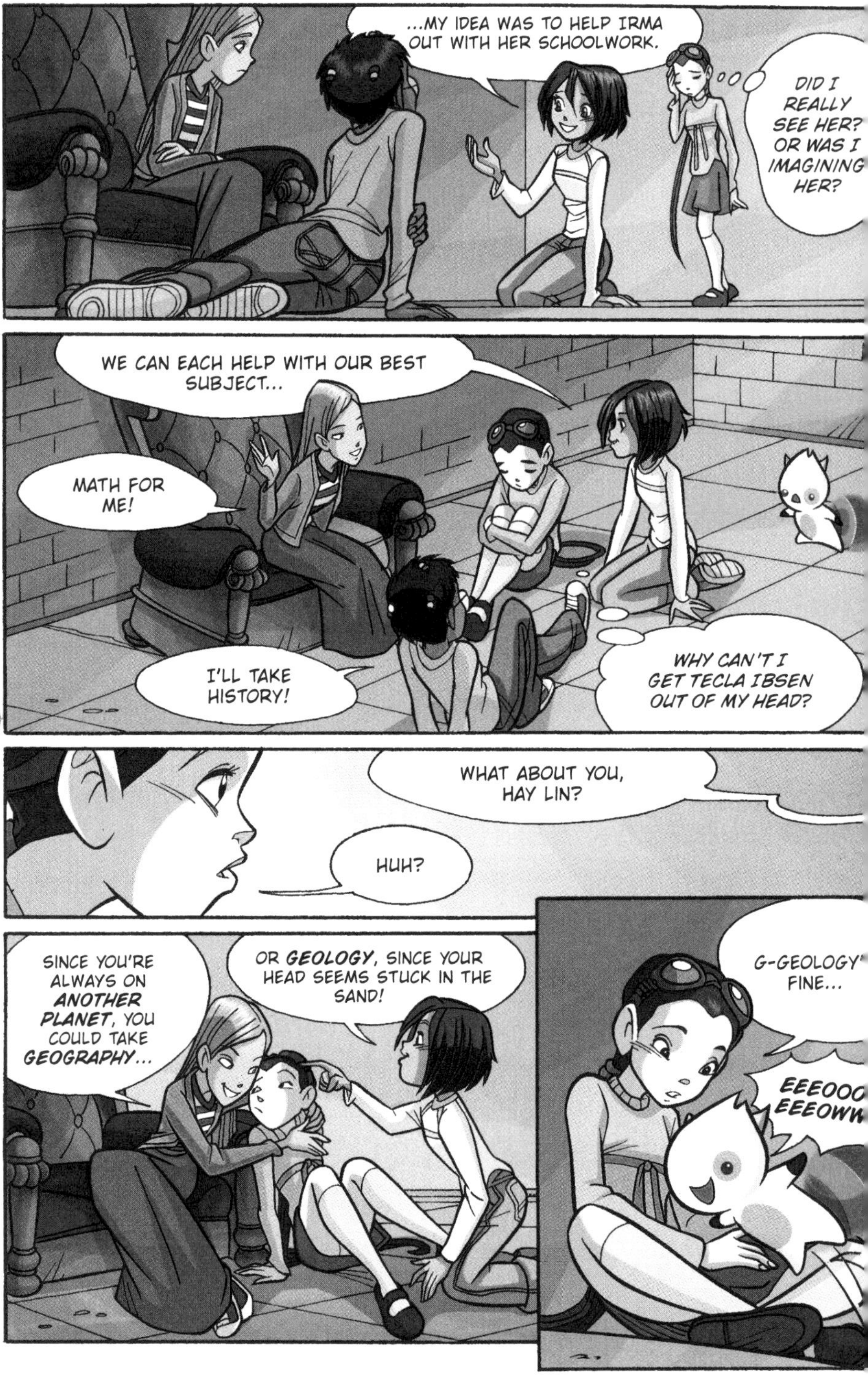
...MY IDEA WAS TO HELP IRMA OUT WITH HER SCHOOLWORK.
DID I REALLY SEE HER? OR WAS I IMAGINING HER?
WE CAN EACH HELP WITH OUR BEST SUBJECT...
MATH FOR ME!
I'LL TAKE HISTORY!
WHY CAN'T I GET TECLA IBSEN OUT OF MY HEAD?
WHAT ABOUT YOU, HAY LIN?
HUH?
SINCE YOU'RE ALWAYS ON ANOTHER PLANET, YOU COULD TAKE GEOGRAPHY...
OR GEOLOGY, SINCE YOUR HEAD SEEMS STUCK IN THE SAND!
G-GEOLOGY'
FINE...
EEEOOO
EEEOWW

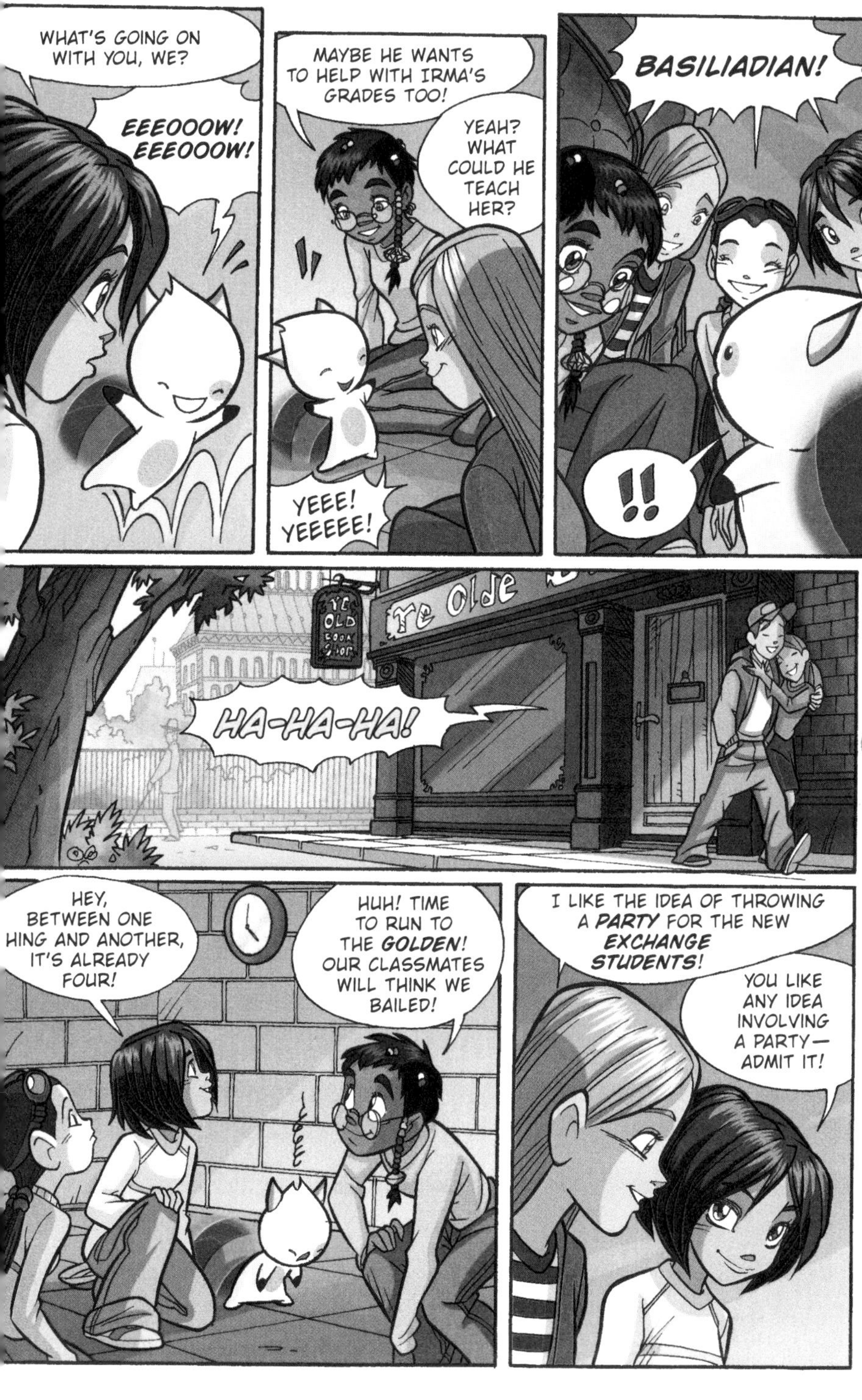
WHAT'S GOING ON WITH YOU, WE?
EEEOOOW! EEEOOOW!
MAYBE HE WANTS TO HELP WITH IRMA'S GRADES TOO!
YEAH? WHAT COULD HE TEACH HER?
YEEE! YEEEEE!
BASILIADIAN!
!!
YE OLD BOOK SHOP
Ye Olde
HA-HA-HA!
HEY, BETWEEN ONE HING AND ANOTHER, IT'S ALREADY FOUR!
HUH! TIME TO RUN TO THE GOLDEN! OUR CLASSMATES WILL THINK WE BAILED!
I LIKE THE IDEA OF THROWING A PARTY FOR THE NEW EXCHANGE STUDENTS!
YOU LIKE ANY IDEA INVOLVING A PARTY— ADMIT IT!

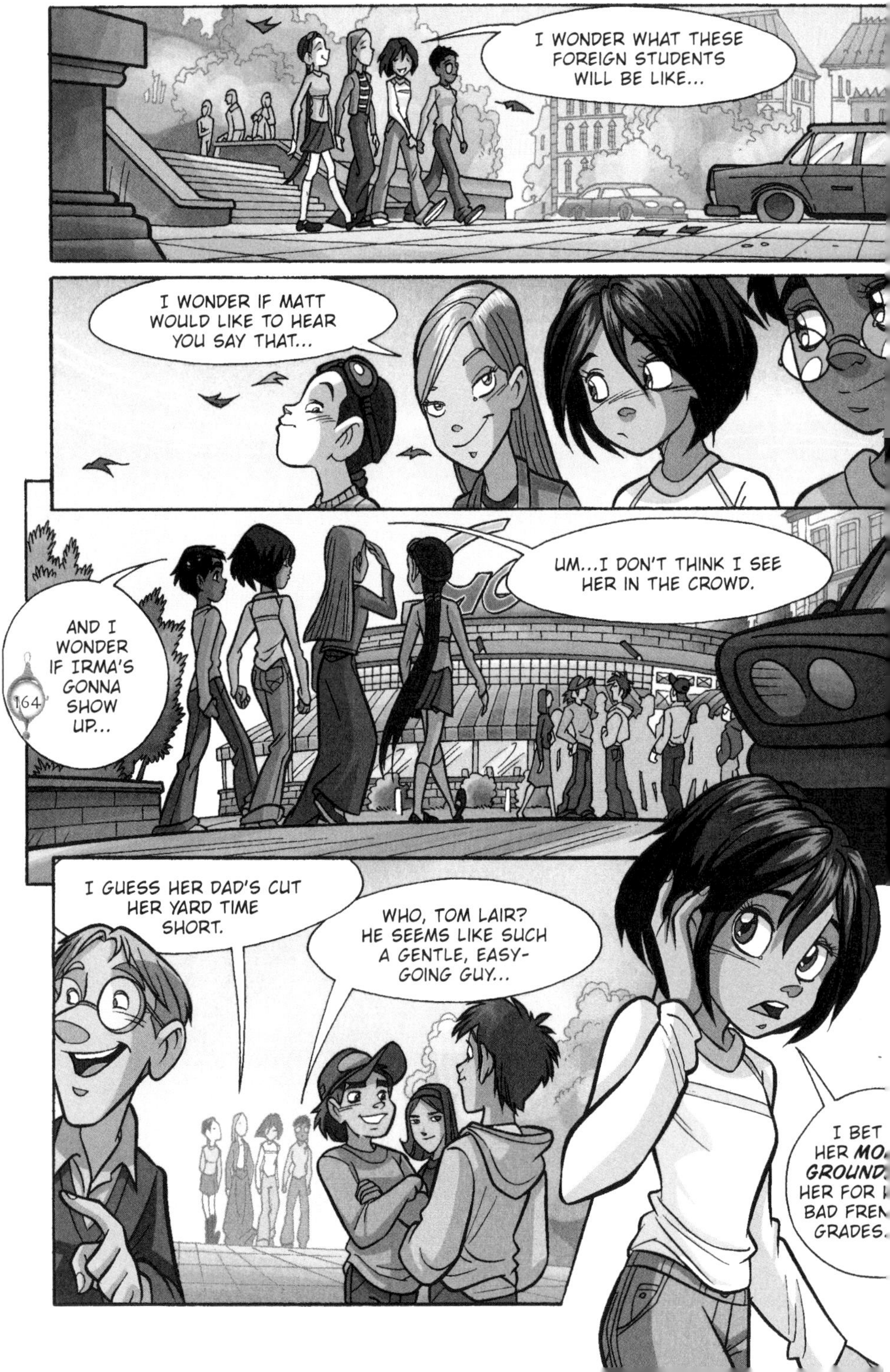
I WONDER WHAT THESE FOREIGN STUDENTS WILL BE LIKE...
I WONDER IF MATT WOULD LIKE TO HEAR YOU SAY THAT...
UM...I DON'T THINK I SEE HER IN THE CROWD.
AND I WONDER IF IRMA'S GONNA SHOW UP...
I GUESS HER DAD'S CUT HER YARD TIME SHORT.
WHO, TOM LAIR? HE SEEMS LIKE SUCH A GENTLE, EASY-GOING GUY...
I BET HER MO GROUND HER FOR BAD FREN GRADES.

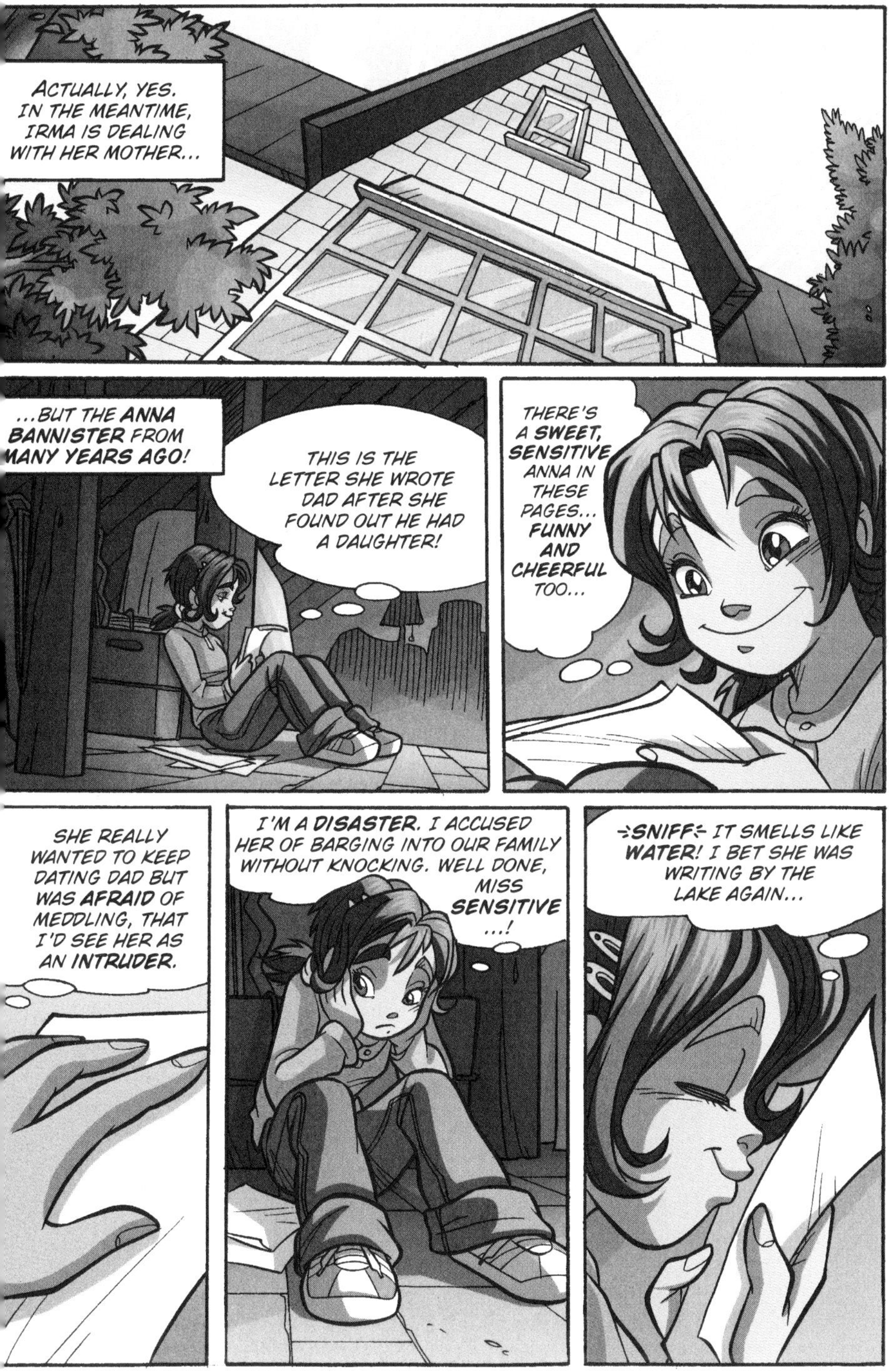
ACTUALLY, YES. IN THE MEANTIME, IRMA IS DEALING WITH HER MOTHER...
...BUT THE ANNA BANNISTER FROM MANY YEARS AGO!
THIS IS THE LETTER SHE WROTE DAD AFTER SHE FOUND OUT HE HAD A DAUGHTER!
THERE'S A SWEET, SENSITIVE ANNA IN THESE PAGES... FUNNY AND CHEERFUL TOO...
SHE REALLY WANTED TO KEEP DATING DAD BUT WAS AFRAID OF MEDDLING, THAT I'D SEE HER AS AN INTRUDER.
I'M A DISASTER. I ACCUSED HER OF BARGING INTO OUR FAMILY WITHOUT KNOCKING. WELL DONE, MISS SENSITIVE ...!
SNIFF IT SMELLS LIKE WATER! I BET SHE WAS WRITING BY THE LAKE AGAIN...

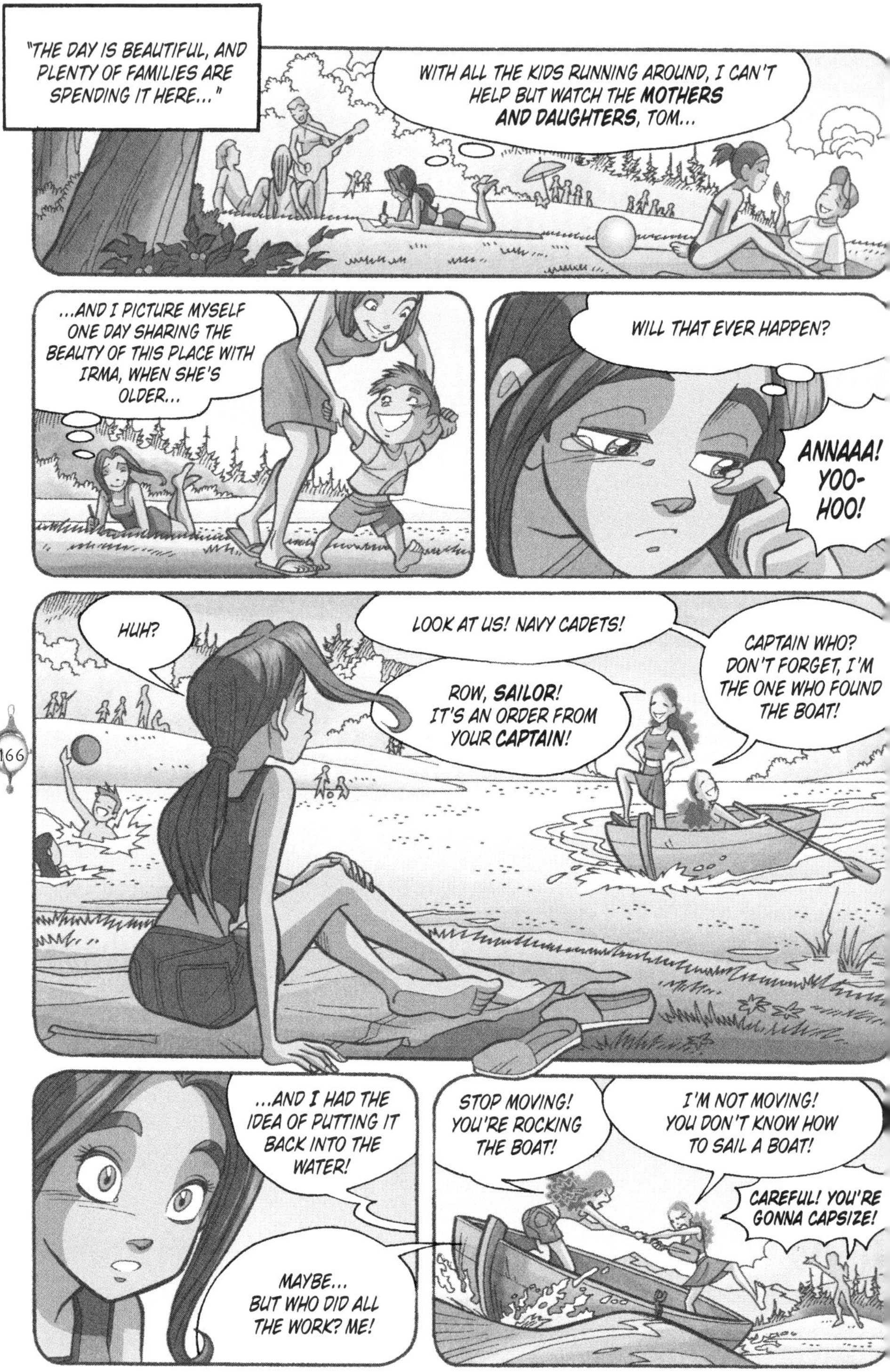
"THE DAY IS BEAUTIFUL, AND PLENTY OF FAMILIES ARE SPENDING IT HERE..."
WITH ALL THE KIDS RUNNING AROUND, I CAN'T HELP BUT WATCH THE MOTHERS AND DAUGHTERS, TOM...
...AND I PICTURE MYSELF ONE DAY SHARING THE BEAUTY OF THIS PLACE WITH IRMA, WHEN SHE'S OLDER...
WILL THAT EVER HAPPEN?
ANNAAA! YOO-HOO!
HUH?
LOOK AT US! NAVY CADETS!
ROW, SAILOR! IT'S AN ORDER FROM YOUR CAPTAIN!
CAPTAIN WHO? DON'T FORGET, I'M THE ONE WHO FOUND THE BOAT!
...AND I HAD THE IDEA OF PUTTING IT BACK INTO THE WATER!
MAYBE... BUT WHO DID ALL THE WORK? ME!
STOP MOVING! YOU'RE ROCKING THE BOAT!
I'M NOT MOVING! YOU DON'T KNOW HOW TO SAIL A BOAT!
CAREFUL! YOU'RE GONNA CAPSIZE!

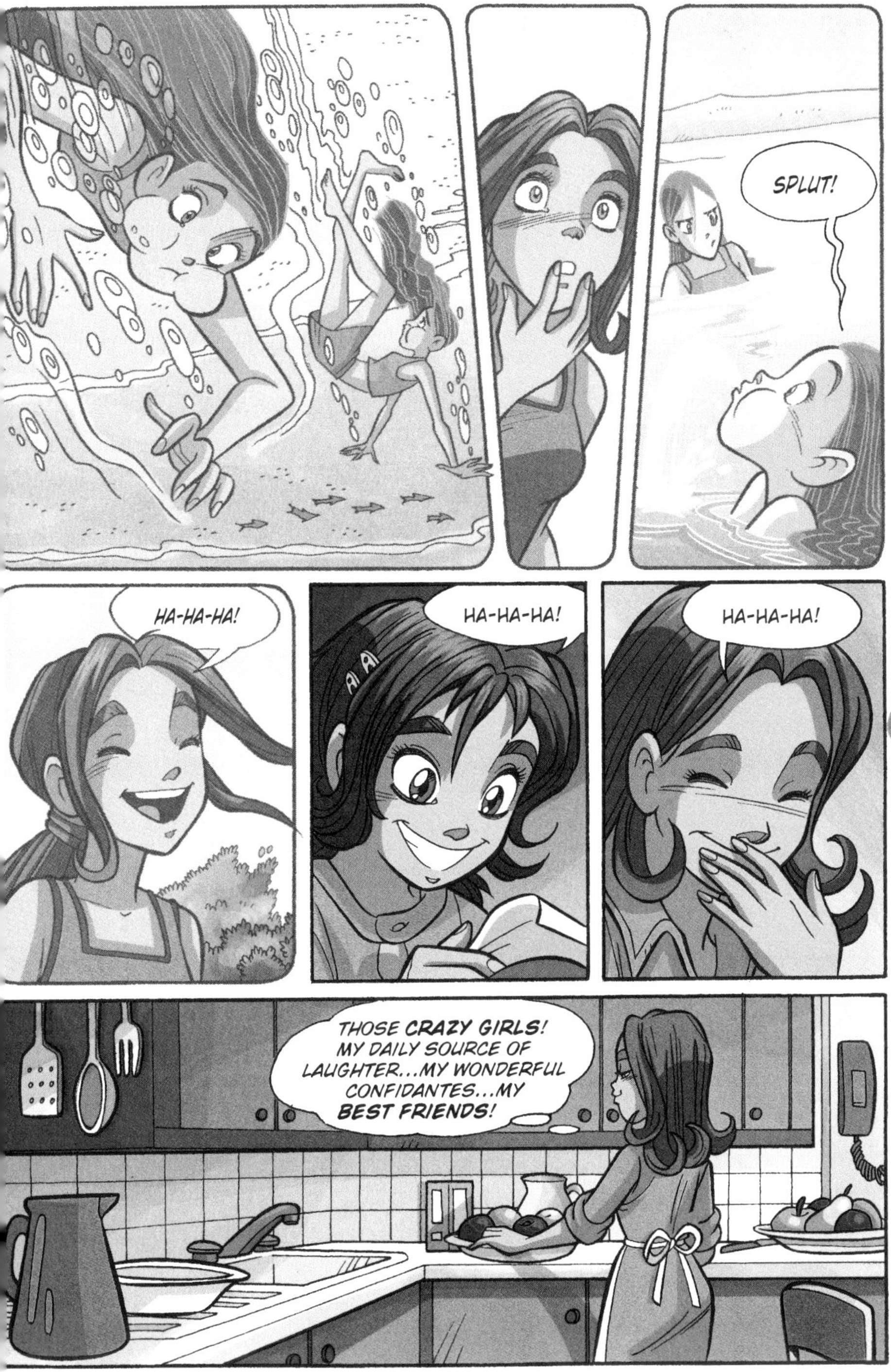
SPLUT!
HA-HA-HA!
HA-HA-HA!
HA-HA-HA!
THOSE CRAZY GIRLS! MY DAILY SOURCE OF LAUGHTER...MY WONDERFUL CONFIDANTES...MY BEST FRIENDS!

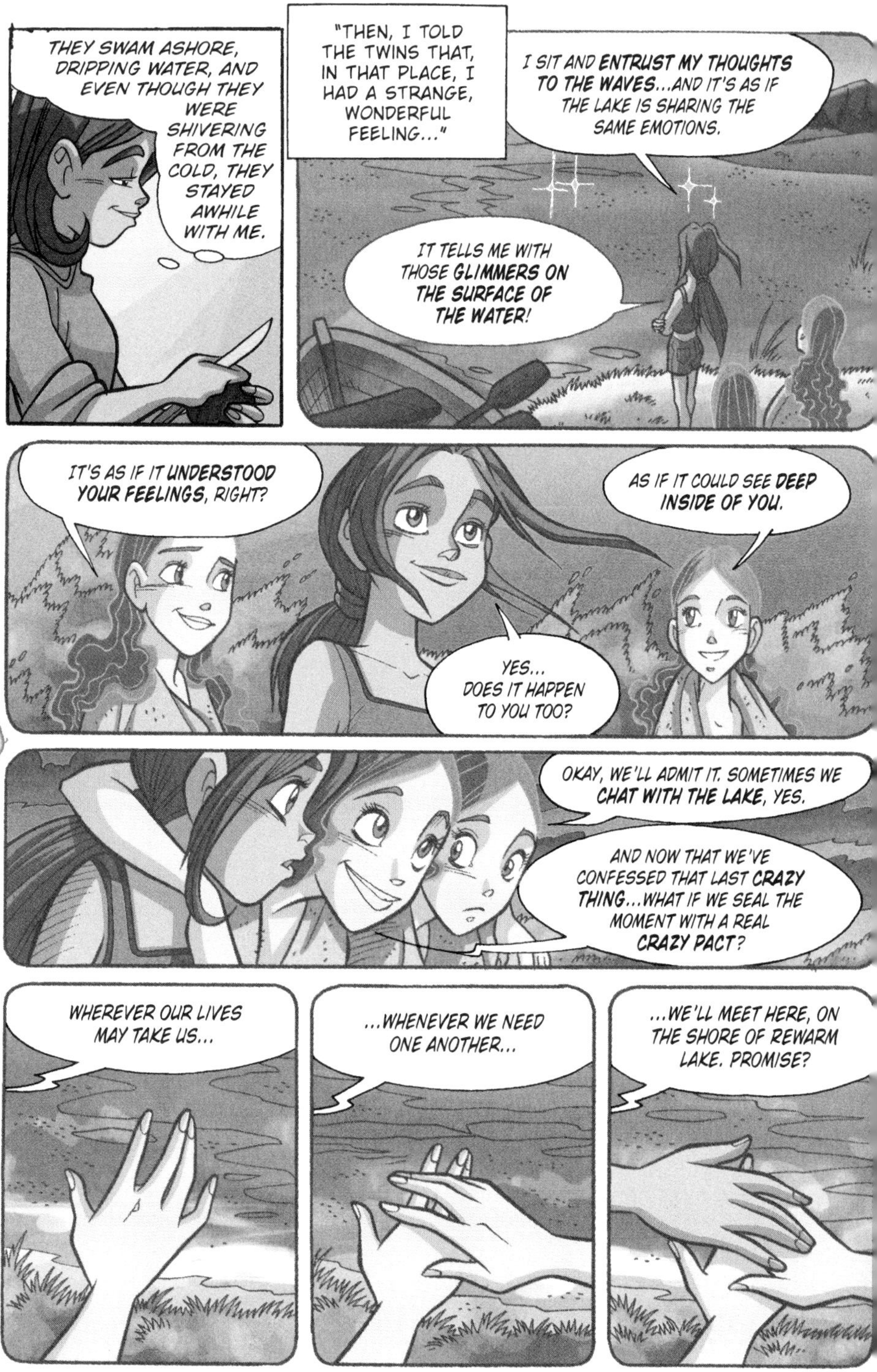
THEY SWAM ASHORE, DRIPPING WATER, AND EVEN THOUGH THEY WERE SHIVERING FROM THE COLD, THEY STAYED AWHILE WITH ME.
"THEN, I TOLD THE TWINS THAT, IN THAT PLACE, I HAD A STRANGE, WONDERFUL FEELING..."
I SIT AND ENTRUST MY THOUGHTS TO THE WAVES...AND IT'S AS IF THE LAKE IS SHARING THE SAME EMOTIONS.
IT TELLS ME WITH THOSE GLIMMERS ON THE SURFACE OF THE WATER!
IT'S AS IF IT UNDERSTOOD YOUR FEELINGS, RIGHT?
AS IF IT COULD SEE DEEP INSIDE OF YOU.
YES... DOES IT HAPPEN TO YOU TOO?
OKAY, WE'LL ADMIT IT. SOMETIMES WE CHAT WITH THE LAKE, YES.
AND NOW THAT WE'VE CONFESSED THAT LAST CRAZY THING...WHAT IF WE SEAL THE MOMENT WITH A REAL CRAZY PACT?
WHEREVER OUR LIVES MAY TAKE US...
...WHENEVER WE NEED ONE ANOTHER...
...WE'LL MEET HERE, ON THE SHORE OF REWARM LAKE. PROMISE?

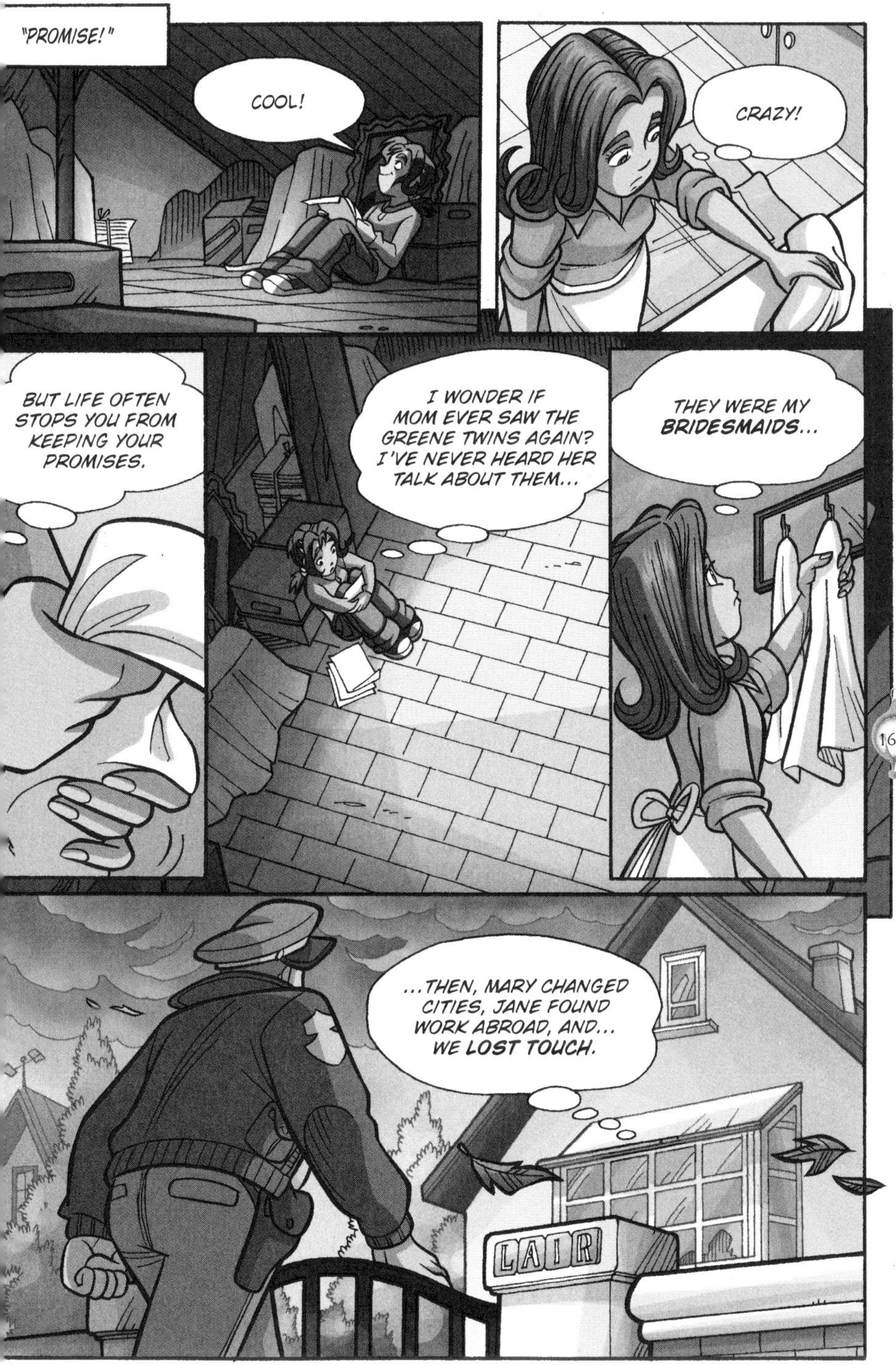
"PROMISE!"
COOL!
CRAZY!
BUT LIFE OFTEN STOPS YOU FROM KEEPING YOUR PROMISES.
I WONDER IF MOM EVER SAW THE GREENE TWINS AGAIN? I'VE NEVER HEARD HER TALK ABOUT THEM...
THEY WERE MY BRIDESMAIDS...
...THEN, MARY CHANGED CITIES, JANE FOUND WORK ABROAD, AND... WE LOST TOUCH.
LAIR

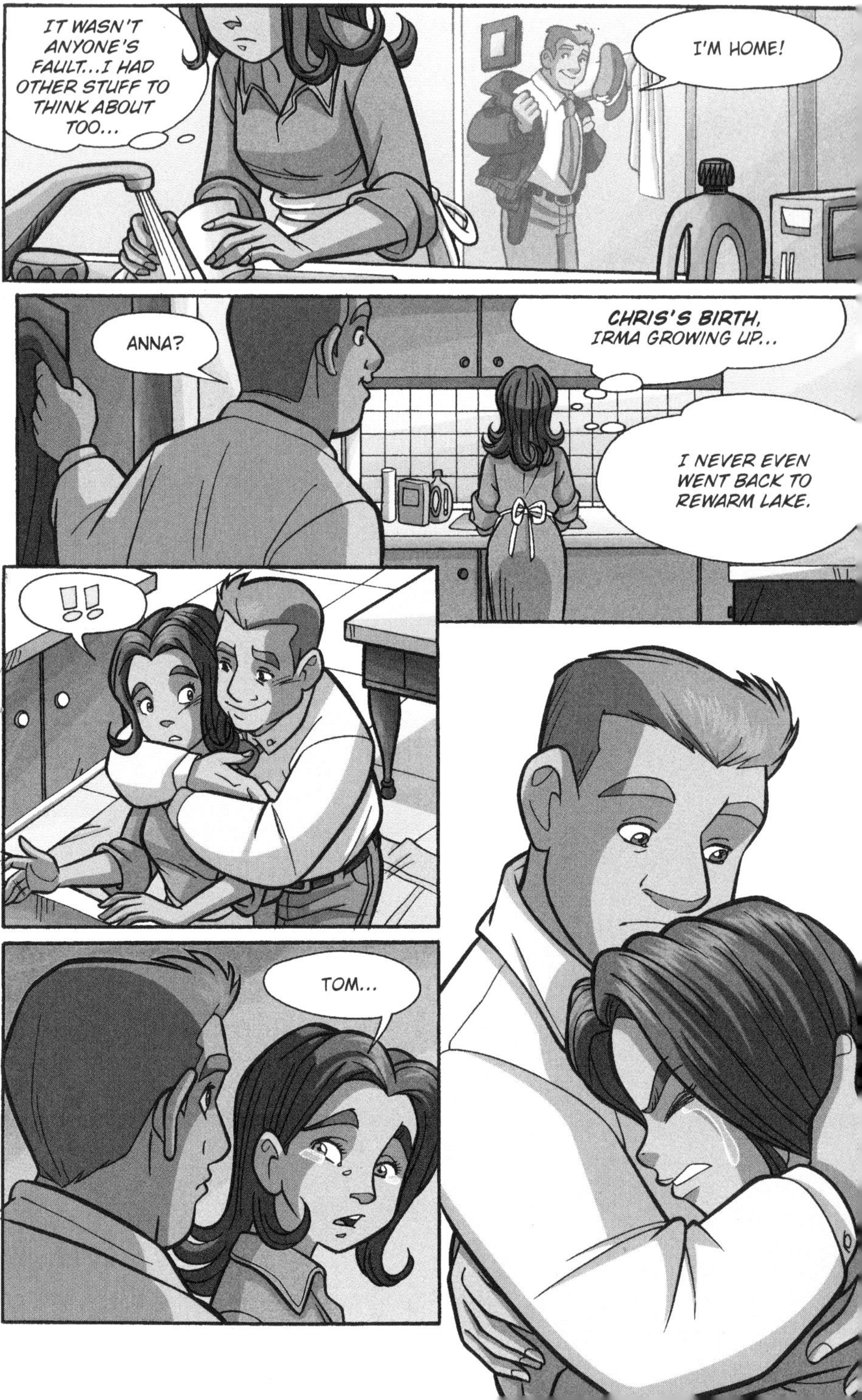

IT WASN'T ANYONE'S FAULT...I HAD OTHER STUFF TO THINK ABOUT TOO...
I'M HOME!
ANNA?
CHRIS'S BIRTH, IRMA GROWING UP...
I NEVER EVEN WENT BACK TO REWARM LAKE.
!!
TOM...

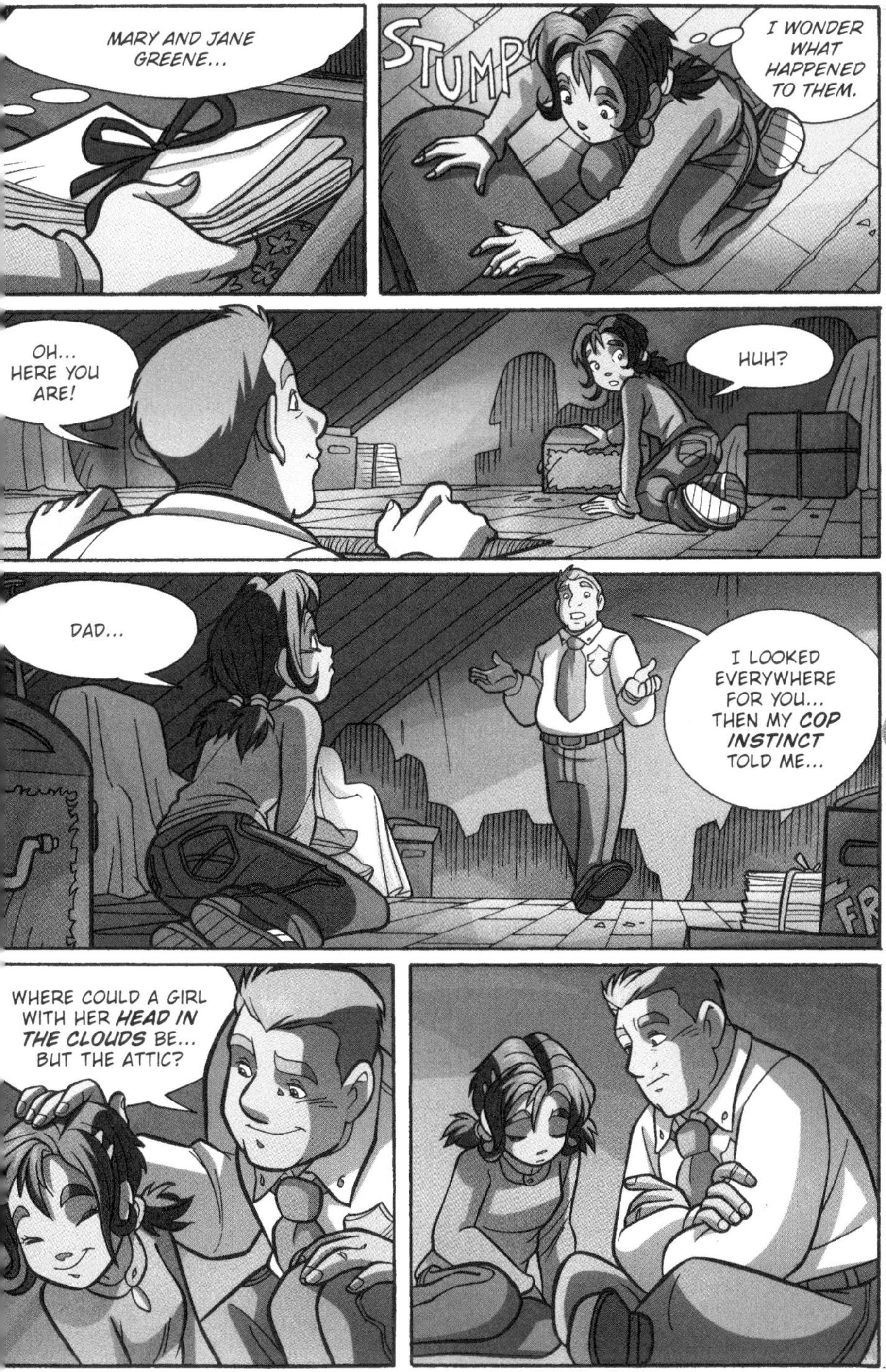
MARY AND JANE GREENE...
STUMP
I WONDER WHAT HAPPENED TO THEM.
OH... HERE YOU ARE!
HUH?
DAD...
I LOOKED EVERYWHERE FOR YOU... THEN MY COP INSTINCT TOLD ME...
WHERE COULD A GIRL WITH HER HEAD IN THE CLOUDS BE... BUT THE ATTIC?

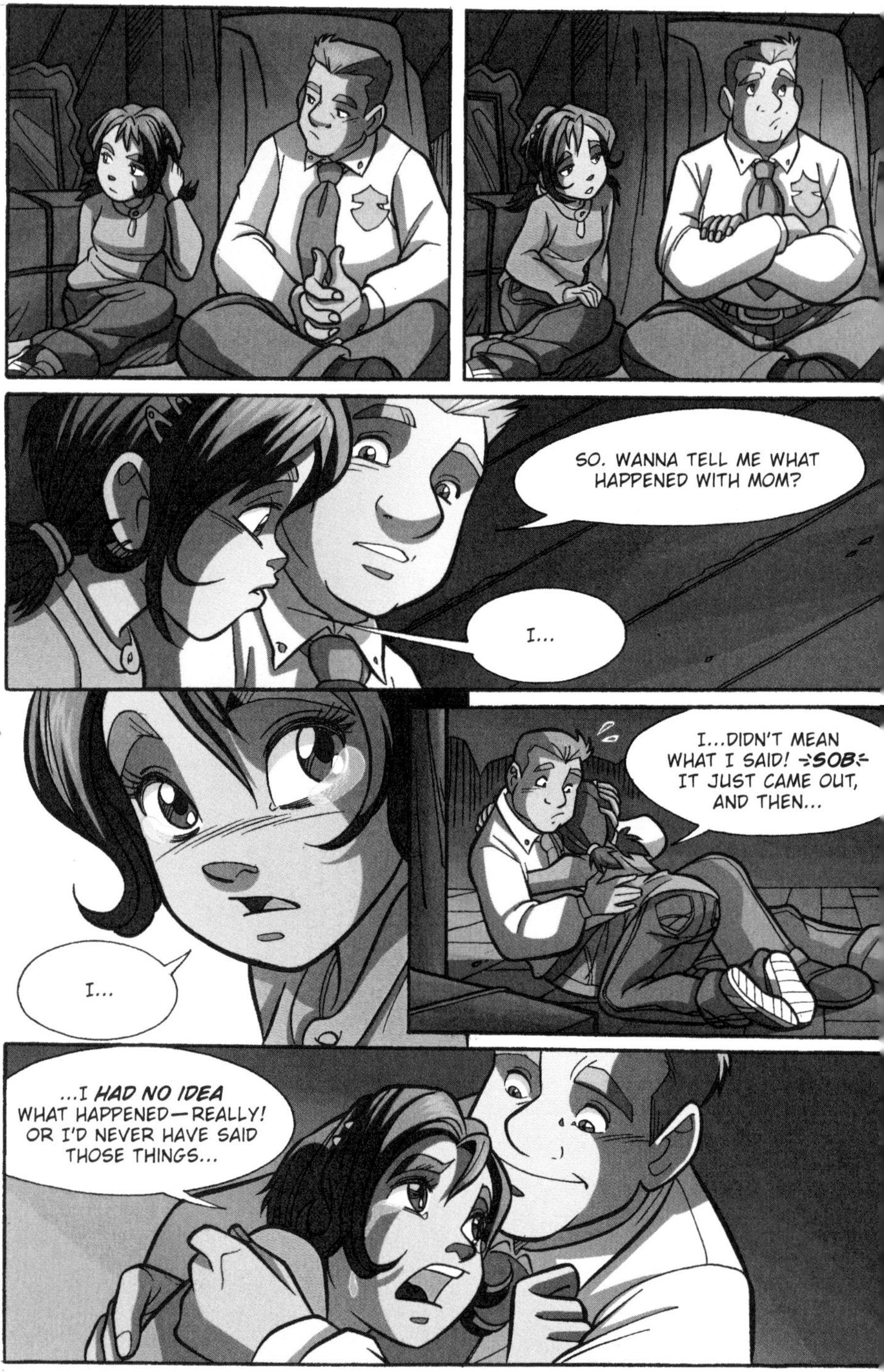
SO. WANNA TELL ME WHAT HAPPENED WITH MOM?
I...
I...
I...DIDN'T MEAN WHAT I SAID! -SOB- IT JUST CAME OUT, AND THEN...
...I HAD NO IDEA WHAT HAPPENED—REALLY! OR I'D NEVER HAVE SAID THOSE THINGS...

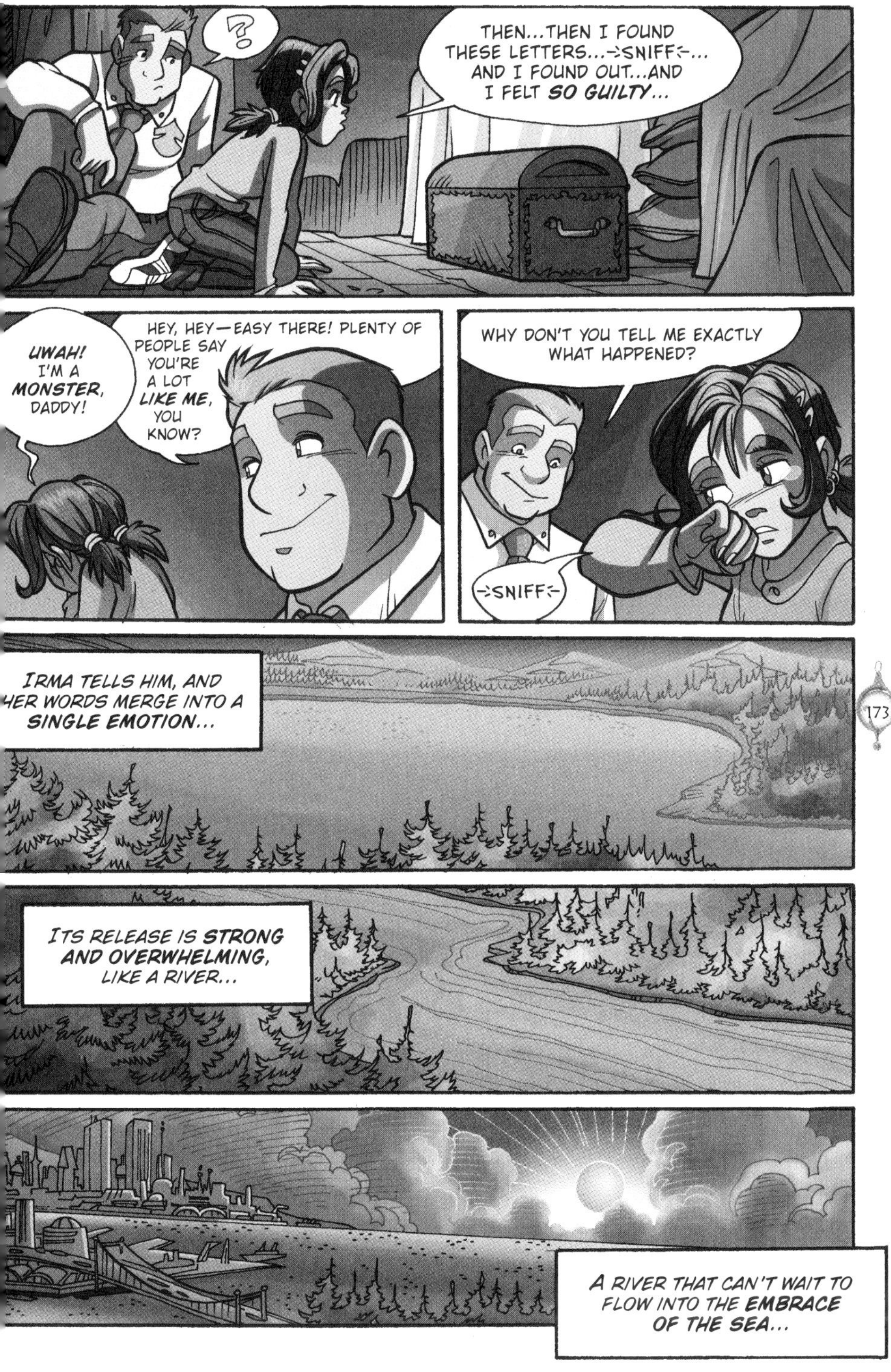
?
THEN...THEN I FOUND THESE LETTERS...⇢SNIFF⇠... AND I FOUND OUT...AND I FELT SO GUILTY...
UWAH! I'M A MONSTER, DADDY!
HEY, HEY—EASY THERE! PLENTY OF PEOPLE SAY YOU'RE A LOT LIKE ME, YOU KNOW?
WHY DON'T YOU TELL ME EXACTLY WHAT HAPPENED?
⇢SNIFF⇠
IRMA TELLS HIM, AND HER WORDS MERGE INTO A SINGLE EMOTION...
ITS RELEASE IS STRONG AND OVERWHELMING, LIKE A RIVER...
A RIVER THAT CAN'T WAIT TO FLOW INTO THE EMBRACE OF THE SEA...

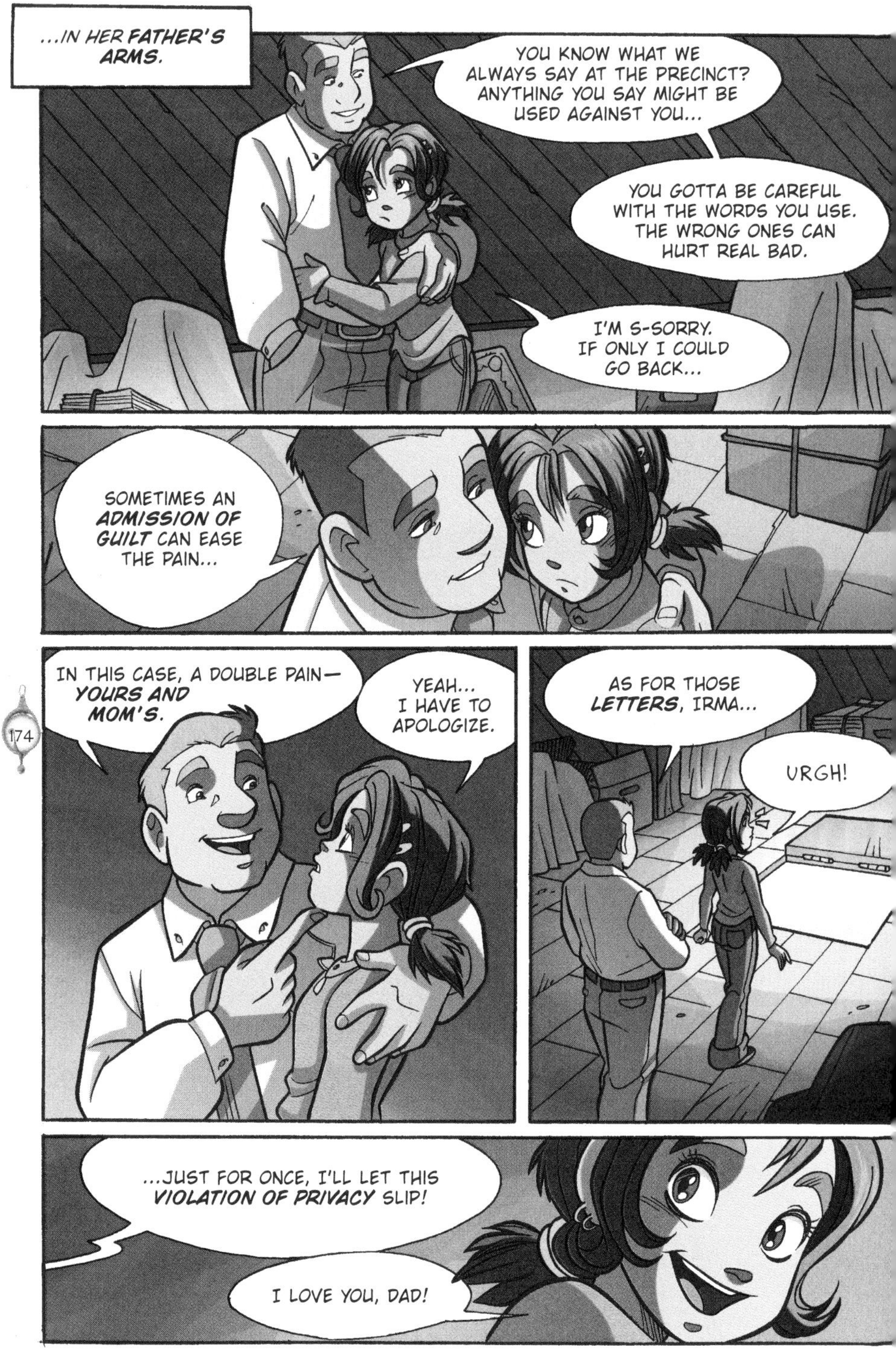
...IN HER **FATHER'S ARMS**.
YOU KNOW WHAT WE ALWAYS SAY AT THE PRECINCT? ANYTHING YOU SAY MIGHT BE USED AGAINST YOU...
YOU GOTTA BE CAREFUL WITH THE WORDS YOU USE. THE WRONG ONES CAN HURT REAL BAD.
I'M S-SORRY. IF ONLY I COULD GO BACK...
SOMETIMES AN **ADMISSION OF GUILT** CAN EASE THE PAIN...
IN THIS CASE, A DOUBLE PAIN—**YOURS AND MOM'S**.
YEAH... I HAVE TO APOLOGIZE.
AS FOR THOSE **LETTERS**, IRMA...
URGH!
...JUST FOR ONCE, I'LL LET THIS **VIOLATION OF PRIVACY** SLIP!
I LOVE YOU, DAD!

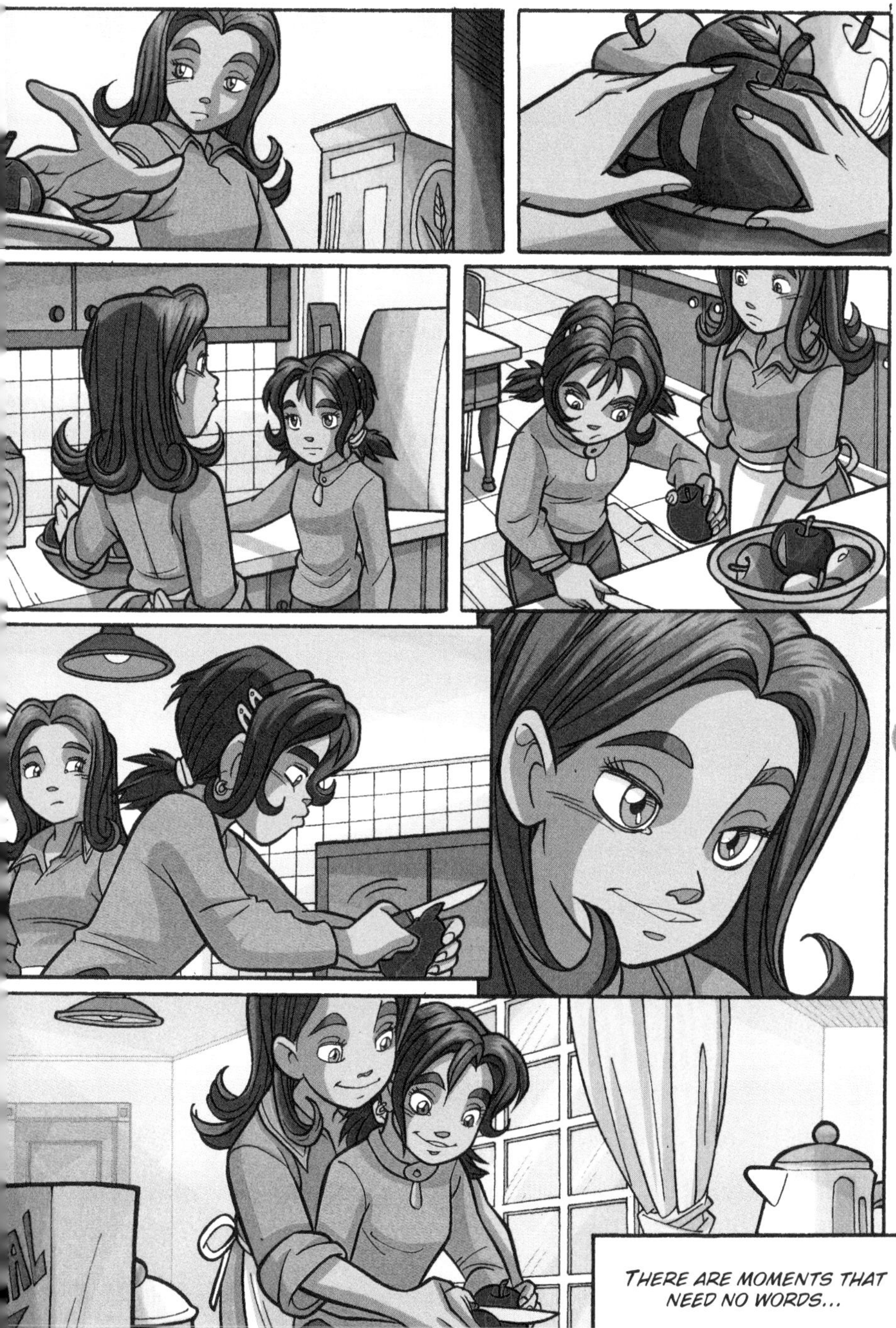
THERE ARE MOMENTS THAT
NEED NO WORDS...

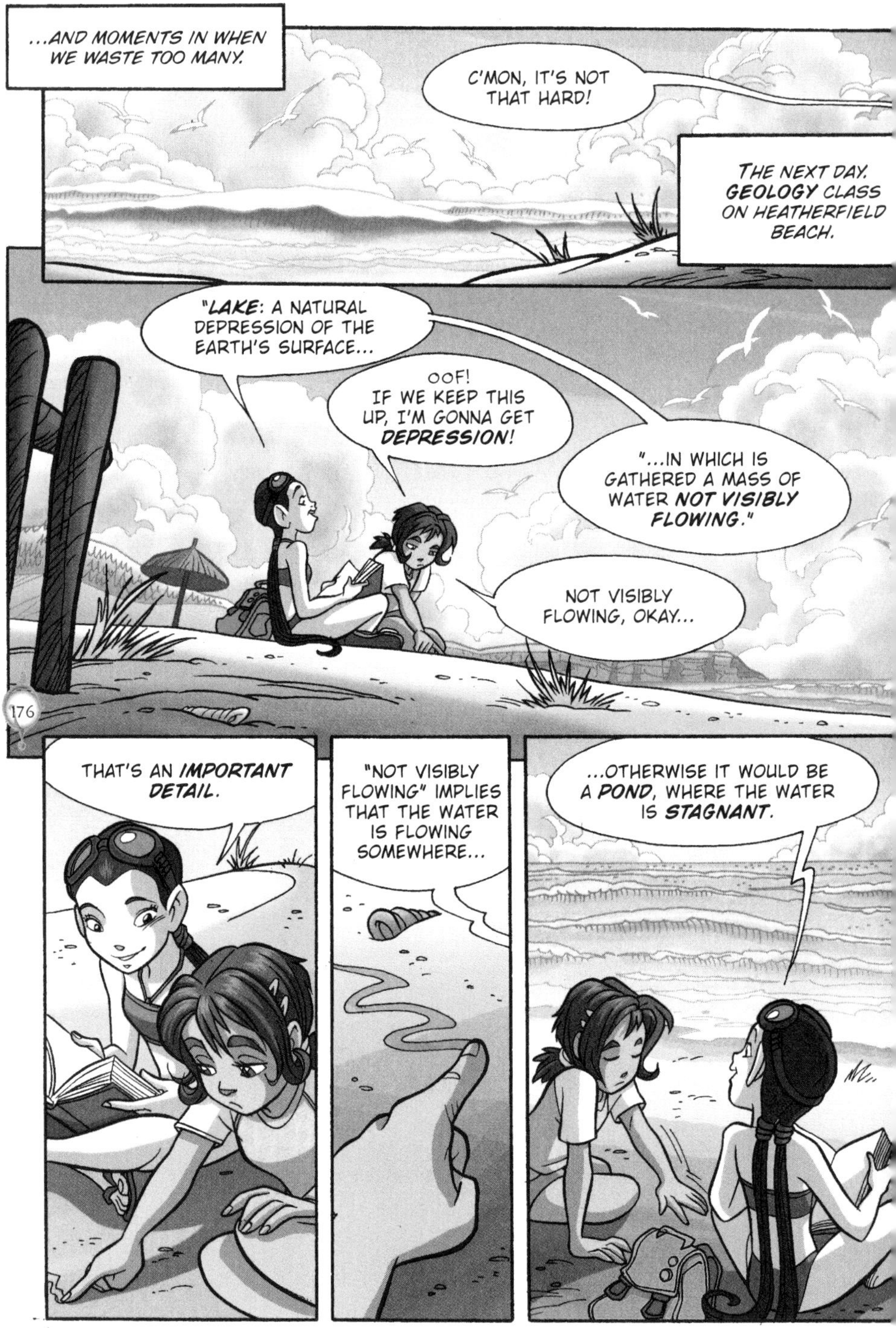

...AND MOMENTS IN WHEN WE WASTE TOO MANY.
C'MON, IT'S NOT THAT HARD!
THE NEXT DAY. GEOLOGY CLASS ON HEATHERFIELD BEACH.
"LAKE: A NATURAL DEPRESSION OF THE EARTH'S SURFACE...
OOF! IF WE KEEP THIS UP, I'M GONNA GET DEPRESSION!
"...IN WHICH IS GATHERED A MASS OF WATER NOT VISIBLY FLOWING."
NOT VISIBLY FLOWING, OKAY...
THAT'S AN IMPORTANT DETAIL.
"NOT VISIBLY FLOWING" IMPLIES THAT THE WATER IS FLOWING SOMEWHERE...
...OTHERWISE IT WOULD BE A POND, WHERE THE WATER IS STAGNANT.

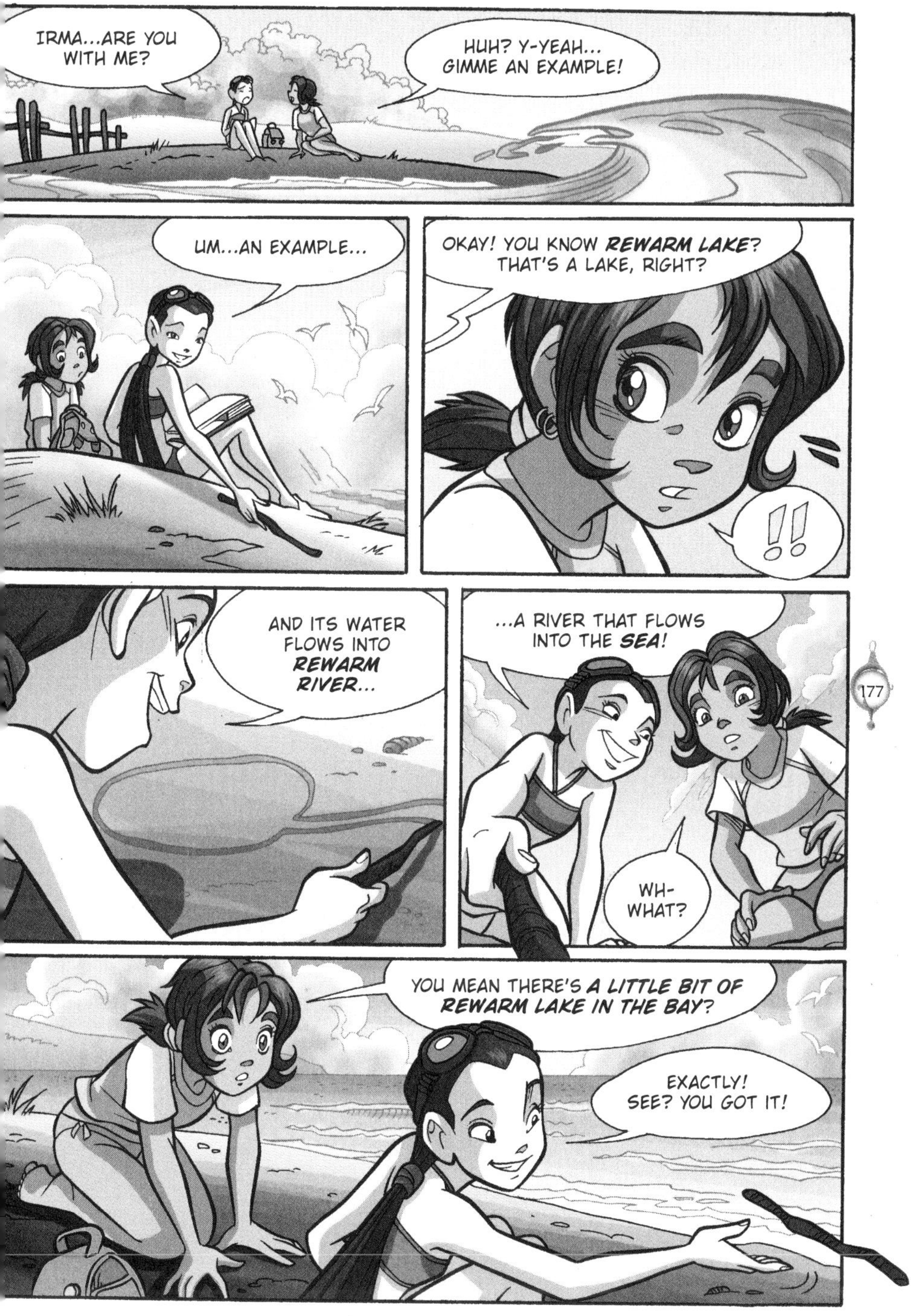
IRMA...ARE YOU WITH ME?
HUH? Y-YEAH... GIMME AN EXAMPLE!
UM...AN EXAMPLE...
OKAY! YOU KNOW **REWARM LAKE**? THAT'S A LAKE, RIGHT?
!!
AND ITS WATER FLOWS INTO **REWARM RIVER**...
...A RIVER THAT FLOWS INTO THE **SEA**!
WH- WHAT?
YOU MEAN THERE'S **A LITTLE BIT OF REWARM LAKE IN THE BAY**?
EXACTLY! SEE? YOU GOT IT!

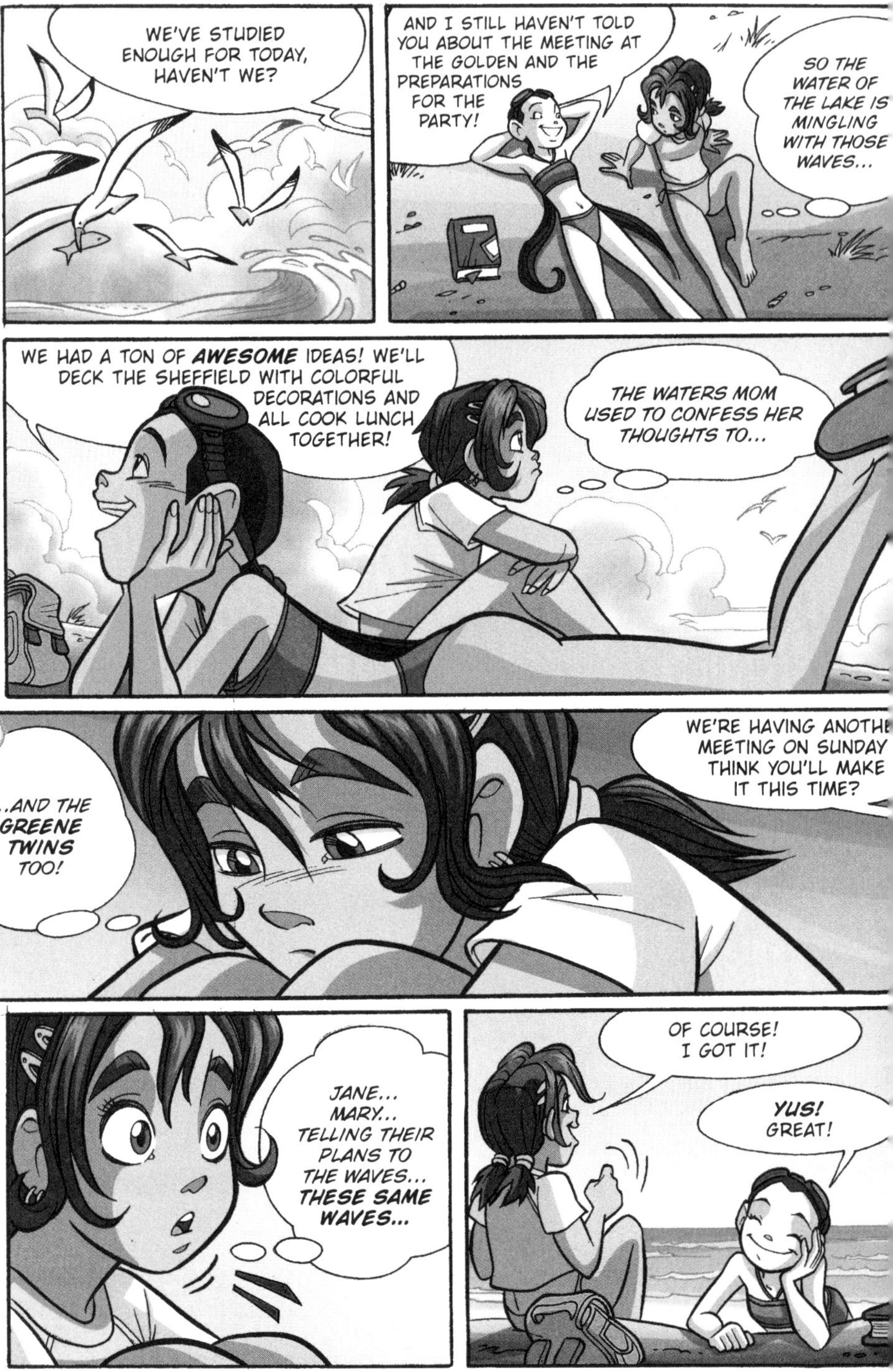
WE'VE STUDIED ENOUGH FOR TODAY, HAVEN'T WE?
AND I STILL HAVEN'T TOLD YOU ABOUT THE MEETING AT THE GOLDEN AND THE PREPARATIONS FOR THE PARTY!
SO THE WATER OF THE LAKE IS MINGLING WITH THOSE WAVES...
WE HAD A TON OF AWESOME IDEAS! WE'LL DECK THE SHEFFIELD WITH COLORFUL DECORATIONS AND ALL COOK LUNCH TOGETHER!
THE WATERS MOM USED TO CONFESS HER THOUGHTS TO...
WE'RE HAVING ANOTHE MEETING ON SUNDAY THINK YOU'LL MAKE IT THIS TIME?
...AND THE GREENE TWINS TOO!
JANE... MARY... TELLING THEIR PLANS TO THE WAVES... THESE SAME WAVES...
OF COURSE! I GOT IT!
YUS! GREAT!

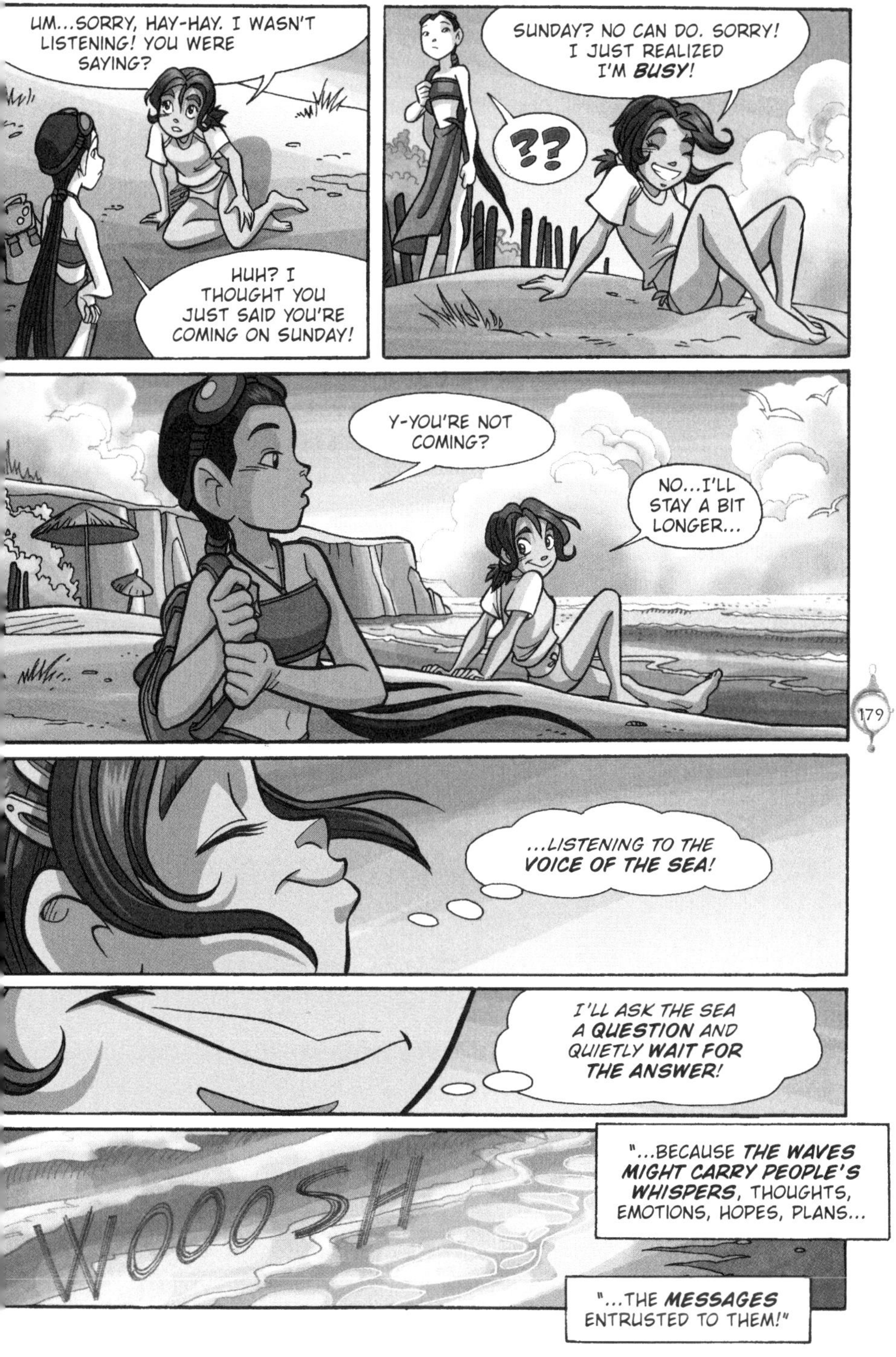
UM...SORRY, HAY-HAY. I WASN'T LISTENING! YOU WERE SAYING?
HUH? I THOUGHT YOU JUST SAID YOU'RE COMING ON SUNDAY!
SUNDAY? NO CAN DO. SORRY! I JUST REALIZED I'M BUSY!
??
Y-YOU'RE NOT COMING?
NO...I'LL STAY A BIT LONGER...
...LISTENING TO THE VOICE OF THE SEA!
I'LL ASK THE SEA A QUESTION AND QUIETLY WAIT FOR THE ANSWER!
WOOOSH
"...BECAUSE THE WAVES MIGHT CARRY PEOPLE'S WHISPERS, THOUGHTS, EMOTIONS, HOPES, PLANS...
"...THE MESSAGES ENTRUSTED TO THEM!"

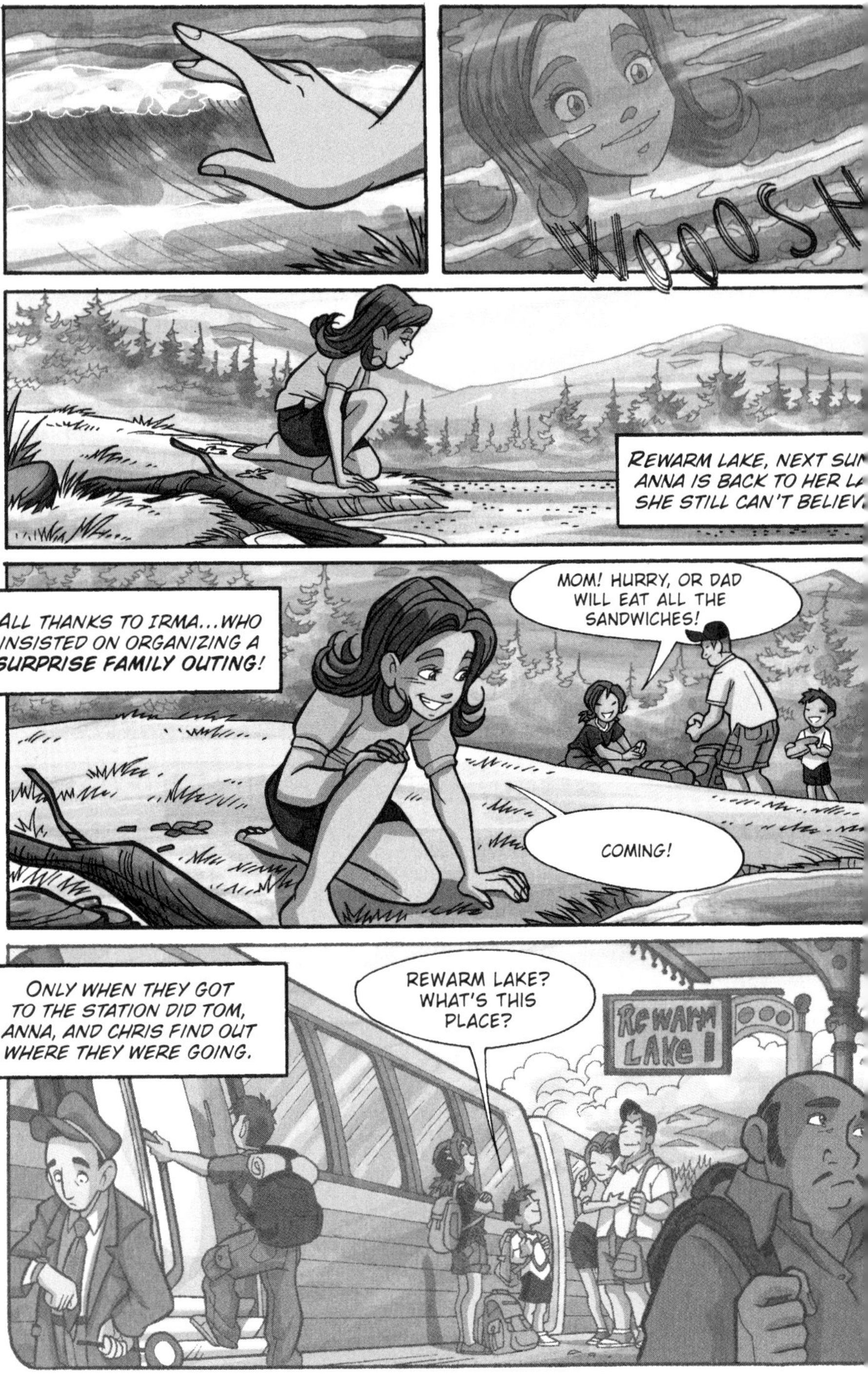
WOOOSH
REWARM LAKE, NEXT SUM
ANNA IS BACK TO HER LA
SHE STILL CAN'T BELIEV
ALL THANKS TO IRMA...WHO INSISTED ON ORGANIZING A SURPRISE FAMILY OUTING!
MOM! HURRY, OR DAD WILL EAT ALL THE SANDWICHES!
COMING!
ONLY WHEN THEY GOT TO THE STATION DID TOM, ANNA, AND CHRIS FIND OUT WHERE THEY WERE GOING.
REWARM LAKE? WHAT'S THIS PLACE?
REWARM LAKE

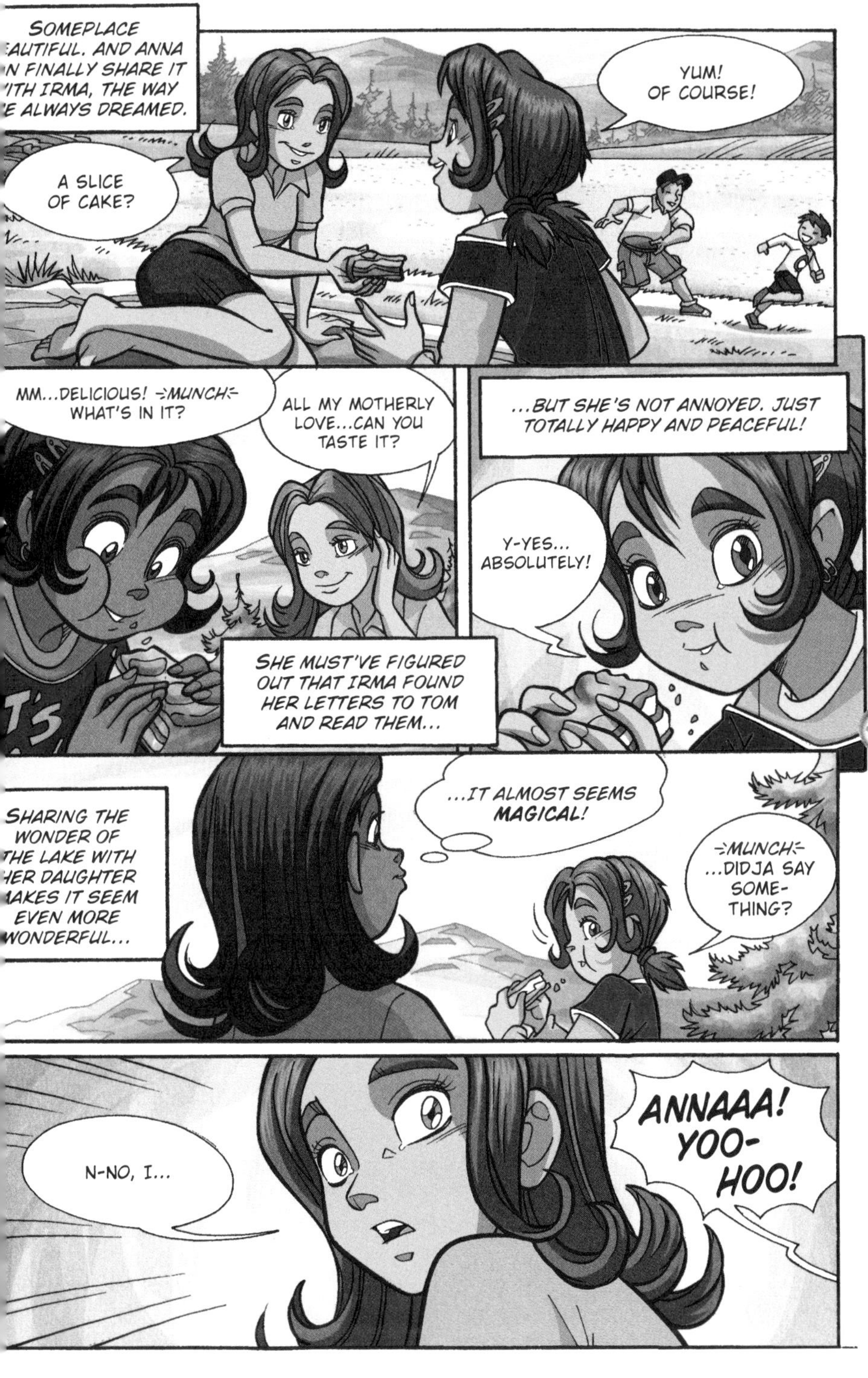
SOMEPLACE
EAUTIFUL. AND ANNA
N FINALLY SHARE IT
ITH IRMA, THE WAY
E ALWAYS DREAMED.
A SLICE OF CAKE?
YUM! OF COURSE!
MM...DELICIOUS! MUNCH WHAT'S IN IT?
ALL MY MOTHERLY LOVE...CAN YOU TASTE IT?
SHE MUST'VE FIGURED OUT THAT IRMA FOUND HER LETTERS TO TOM AND READ THEM...
...BUT SHE'S NOT ANNOYED. JUST TOTALLY HAPPY AND PEACEFUL!
Y-YES... ABSOLUTELY!
SHARING THE WONDER OF THE LAKE WITH HER DAUGHTER AKES IT SEEM EVEN MORE WONDERFUL...
...IT ALMOST SEEMS MAGICAL!
MUNCH ...DIDJA SAY SOME-THING?
N-NO, I...
ANNAAA! YOO-HOO!

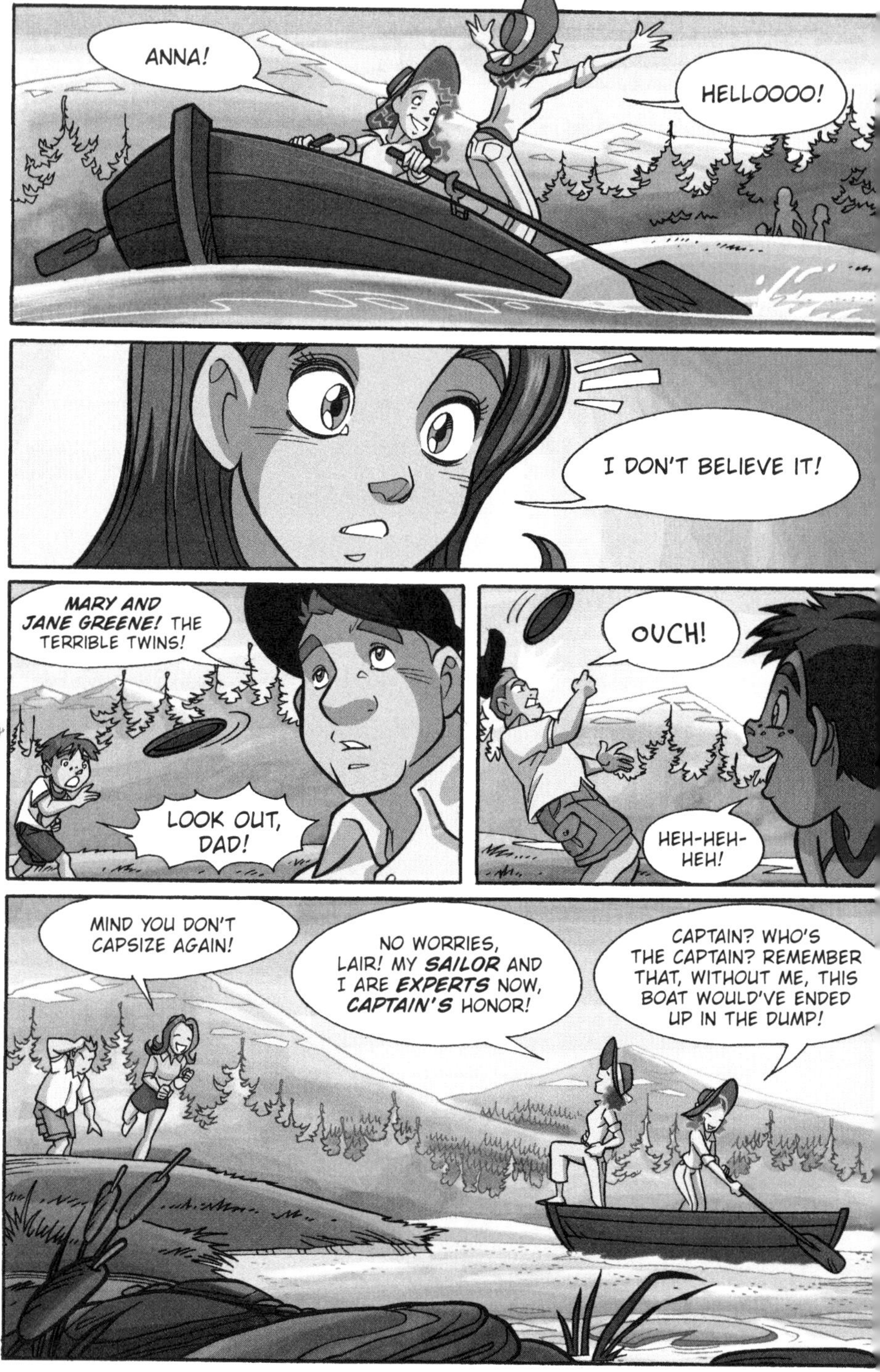
ANNA!
HELLOOOO!
I DON'T BELIEVE IT!
MARY AND JANE GREENE! THE TERRIBLE TWINS!
LOOK OUT, DAD!
OUCH!
HEH-HEH-HEH!
MIND YOU DON'T CAPSIZE AGAIN!
NO WORRIES, LAIR! MY SAILOR AND I ARE EXPERTS NOW, CAPTAIN'S HONOR!
CAPTAIN? WHO'S THE CAPTAIN? REMEMBER THAT, WITHOUT ME, THIS BOAT WOULD'VE ENDED UP IN THE DUMP!

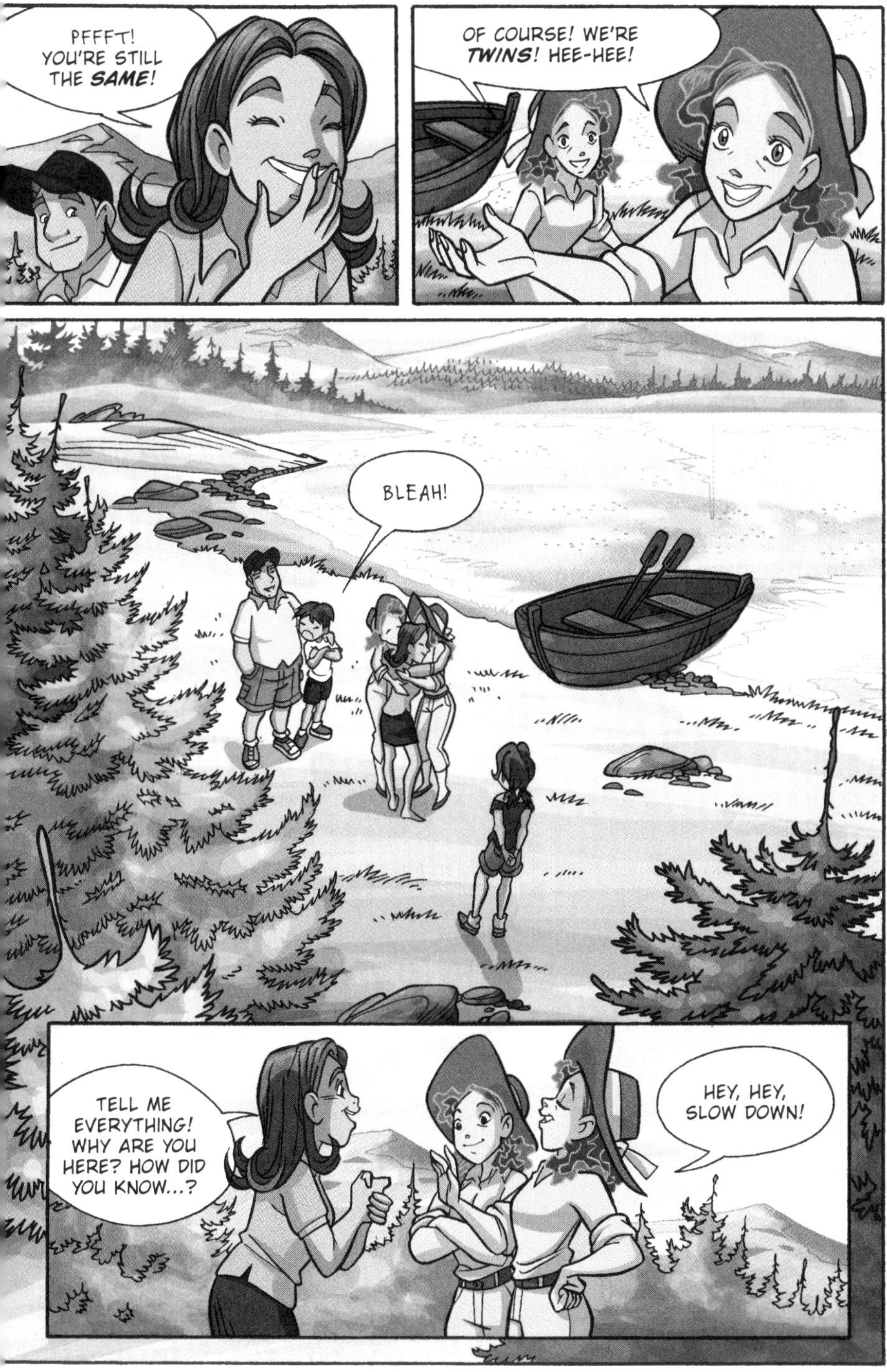
PFFFT! YOU'RE STILL THE **SAME**!
OF COURSE! WE'RE **TWINS**! HEE-HEE!
BLEAH!
TELL ME EVERYTHING! WHY ARE YOU HERE? HOW DID YOU KNOW...?
HEY, HEY, SLOW DOWN!

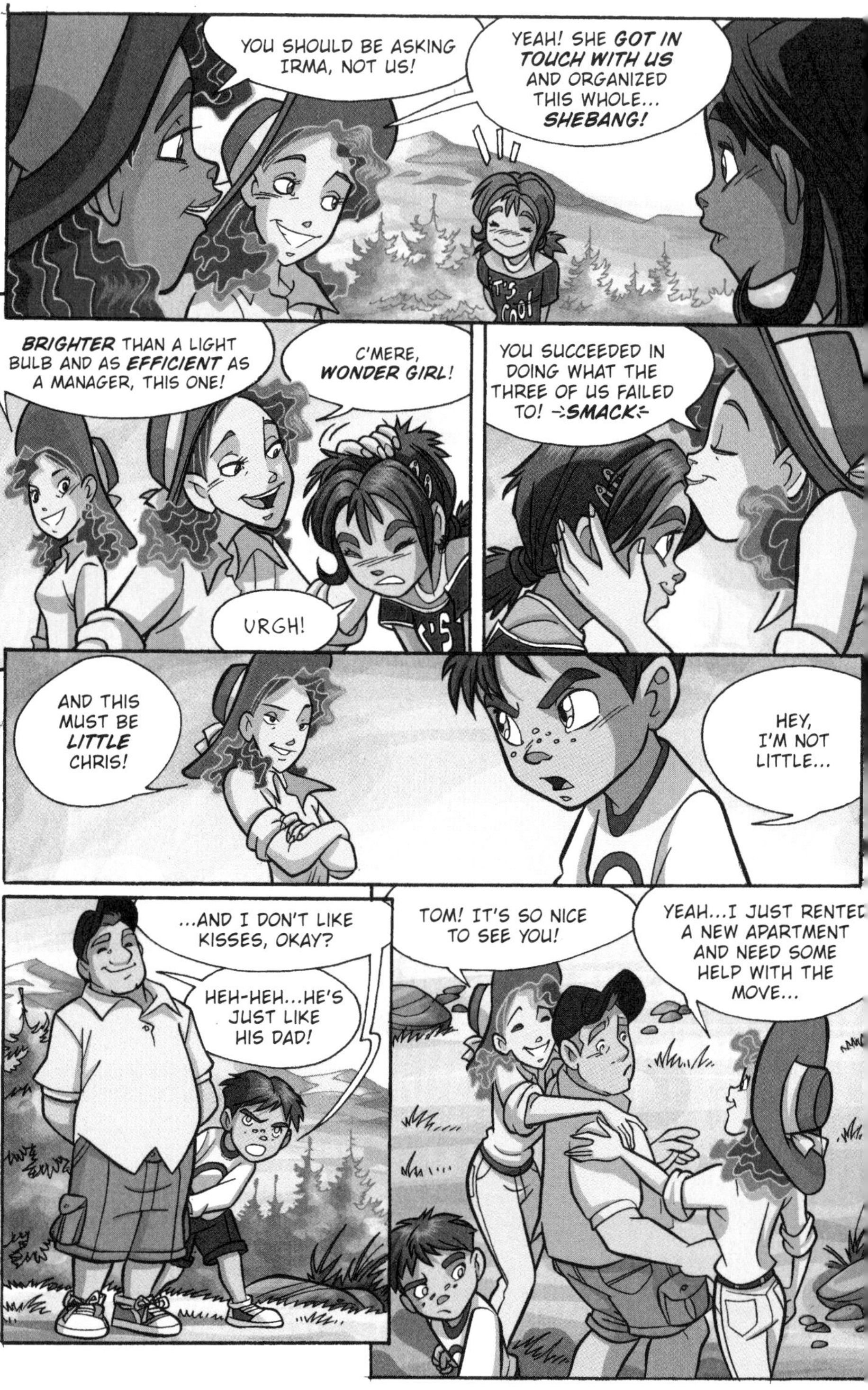

YOU SHOULD BE ASKING IRMA, NOT US!
YEAH! SHE GOT IN TOUCH WITH US AND ORGANIZED THIS WHOLE... SHEBANG!
IT'S COOL
BRIGHTER THAN A LIGHT BULB AND AS EFFICIENT AS A MANAGER, THIS ONE!
C'MERE, WONDER GIRL!
URGH!
YOU SUCCEEDED IN DOING WHAT THE THREE OF US FAILED TO! -SMACK-
AND THIS MUST BE LITTLE CHRIS!
HEY, I'M NOT LITTLE...
...AND I DON'T LIKE KISSES, OKAY?
HEH-HEH...HE'S JUST LIKE HIS DAD!
TOM! IT'S SO NICE TO SEE YOU!
YEAH...I JUST RENTED A NEW APARTMENT AND NEED SOME HELP WITH THE MOVE...

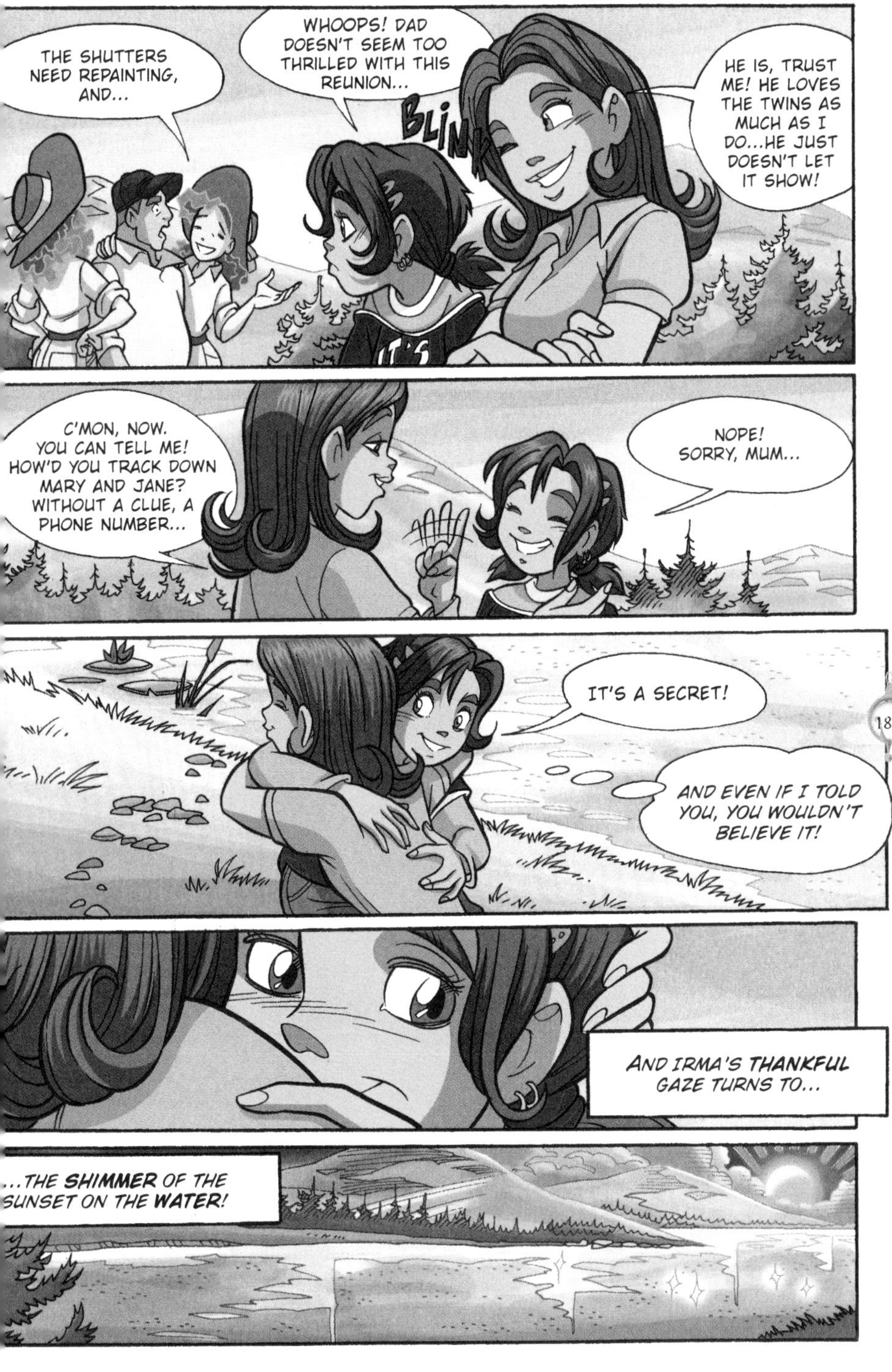
THE SHUTTERS NEED REPAINTING, AND...
WHOOPS! DAD DOESN'T SEEM TOO THRILLED WITH THIS REUNION...
BLINK
HE IS, TRUST ME! HE LOVES THE TWINS AS MUCH AS I DO...HE JUST DOESN'T LET IT SHOW!
C'MON, NOW. YOU CAN TELL ME! HOW'D YOU TRACK DOWN MARY AND JANE? WITHOUT A CLUE, A PHONE NUMBER...
NOPE! SORRY, MUM...
IT'S A SECRET!
AND EVEN IF I TOLD YOU, YOU WOULDN'T BELIEVE IT!
AND IRMA'S THANKFUL GAZE TURNS TO...
...THE SHIMMER OF THE SUNSET ON THE WATER!

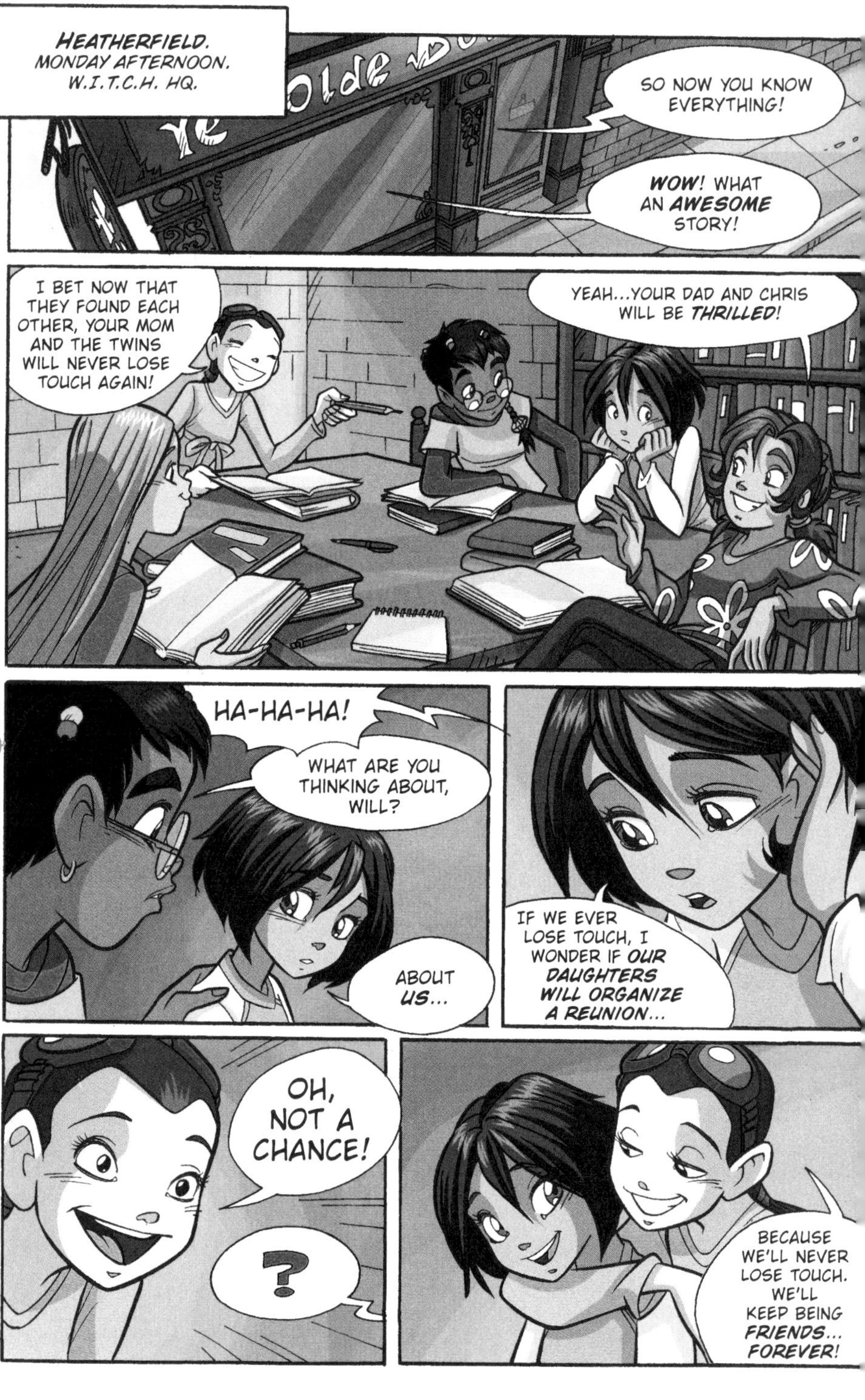
HEATHERFIELD.
MONDAY AFTERNOON.
W.I.T.C.H. HQ.
Ye Olde
SO NOW YOU KNOW EVERYTHING!
WOW! WHAT AN AWESOME STORY!
I BET NOW THAT THEY FOUND EACH OTHER, YOUR MOM AND THE TWINS WILL NEVER LOSE TOUCH AGAIN!
YEAH...YOUR DAD AND CHRIS WILL BE THRILLED!
HA-HA-HA!
WHAT ARE YOU THINKING ABOUT, WILL?
ABOUT US...
IF WE EVER LOSE TOUCH, I WONDER IF OUR DAUGHTERS WILL ORGANIZE A REUNION...
OH, NOT A CHANCE!
?
BECAUSE WE'LL NEVER LOSE TOUCH. WE'LL KEEP BEING FRIENDS... FOREVER!

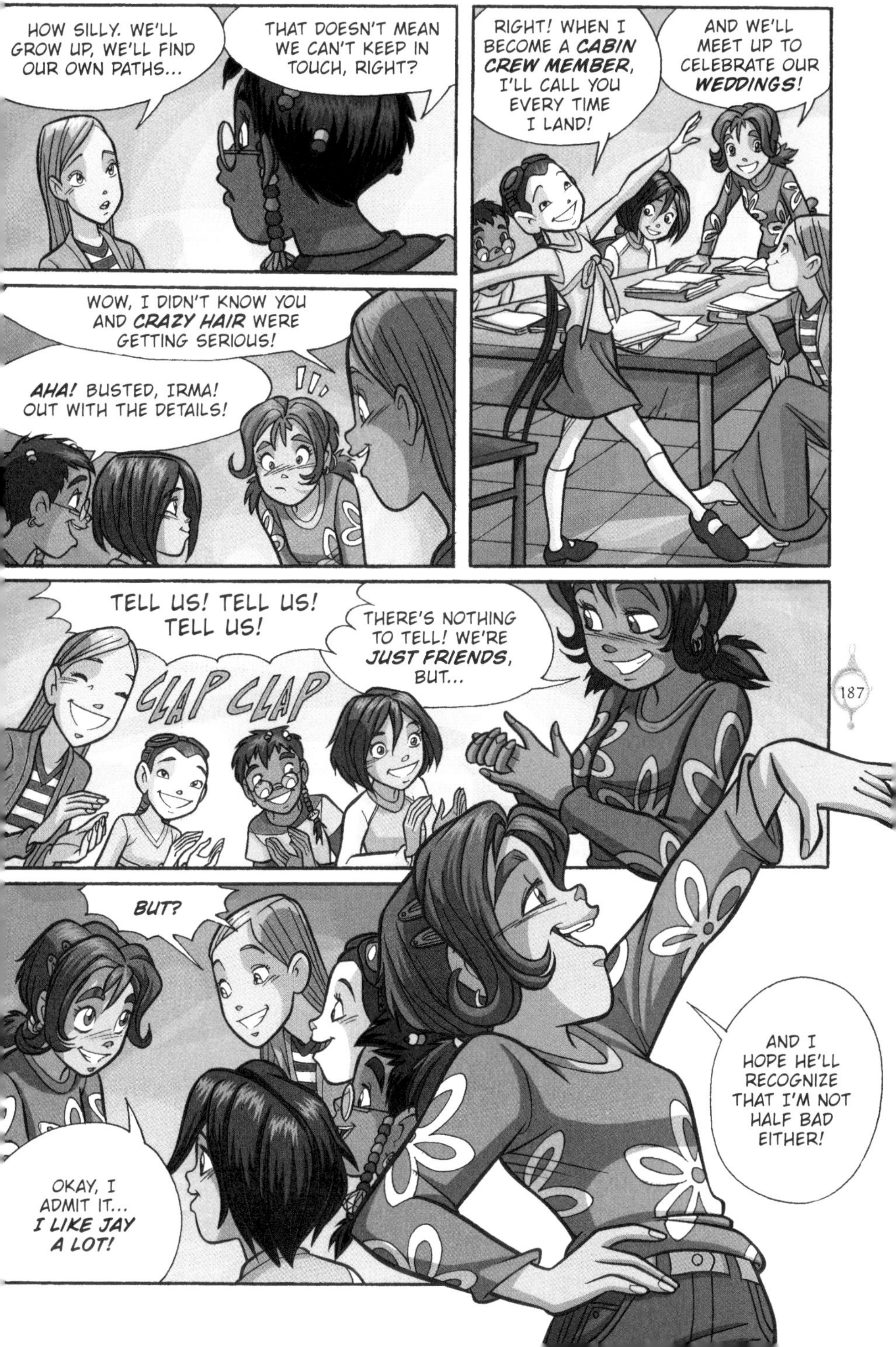
HOW SILLY. WE'LL GROW UP, WE'LL FIND OUR OWN PATHS...
THAT DOESN'T MEAN WE CAN'T KEEP IN TOUCH, RIGHT?
RIGHT! WHEN I BECOME A CABIN CREW MEMBER, I'LL CALL YOU EVERY TIME I LAND!
AND WE'LL MEET UP TO CELEBRATE OUR WEDDINGS!
WOW, I DIDN'T KNOW YOU AND CRAZY HAIR WERE GETTING SERIOUS!
AHA! BUSTED, IRMA! OUT WITH THE DETAILS!
TELL US! TELL US! TELL US!
CLAP CLAP
THERE'S NOTHING TO TELL! WE'RE JUST FRIENDS, BUT...
BUT?
OKAY, I ADMIT IT... I LIKE JAY A LOT!
AND I HOPE HE'LL RECOGNIZE THAT I'M NOT HALF BAD EITHER!

WELL, GUYS, AFTER THIS *SCOOP*, I THINK WE SHOULD MAKE ONE TOO—

?

188

A *CRAZY PACT!* IT WORKED FOR ANNA AND HER FRIENDS.

GREAT IDEA, WILL!

COOL!

WHEREVER OUR LIVES MAY LEAD US...

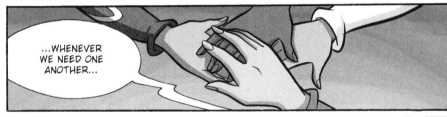

...WHENEVER WE NEED ONE ANOTHER...

...WE'LL MEET HERE IN *HEATHERFIELD!* *YUS!*

PROMISE?

"PROMISE!"

END OF CHAPTER 66

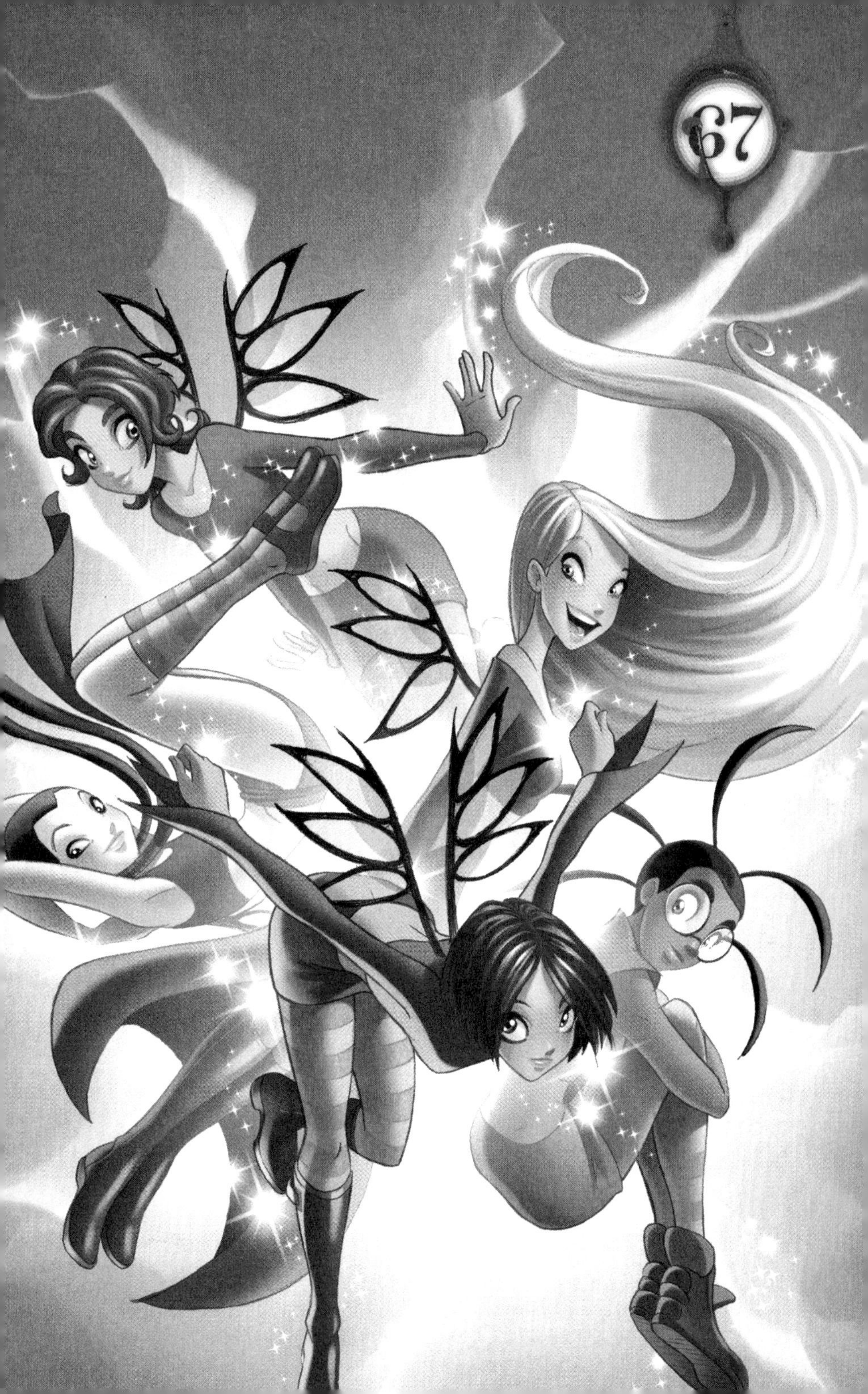
67

On Your Side

"Break their bond. You must sneak into one of the girls' lives..."

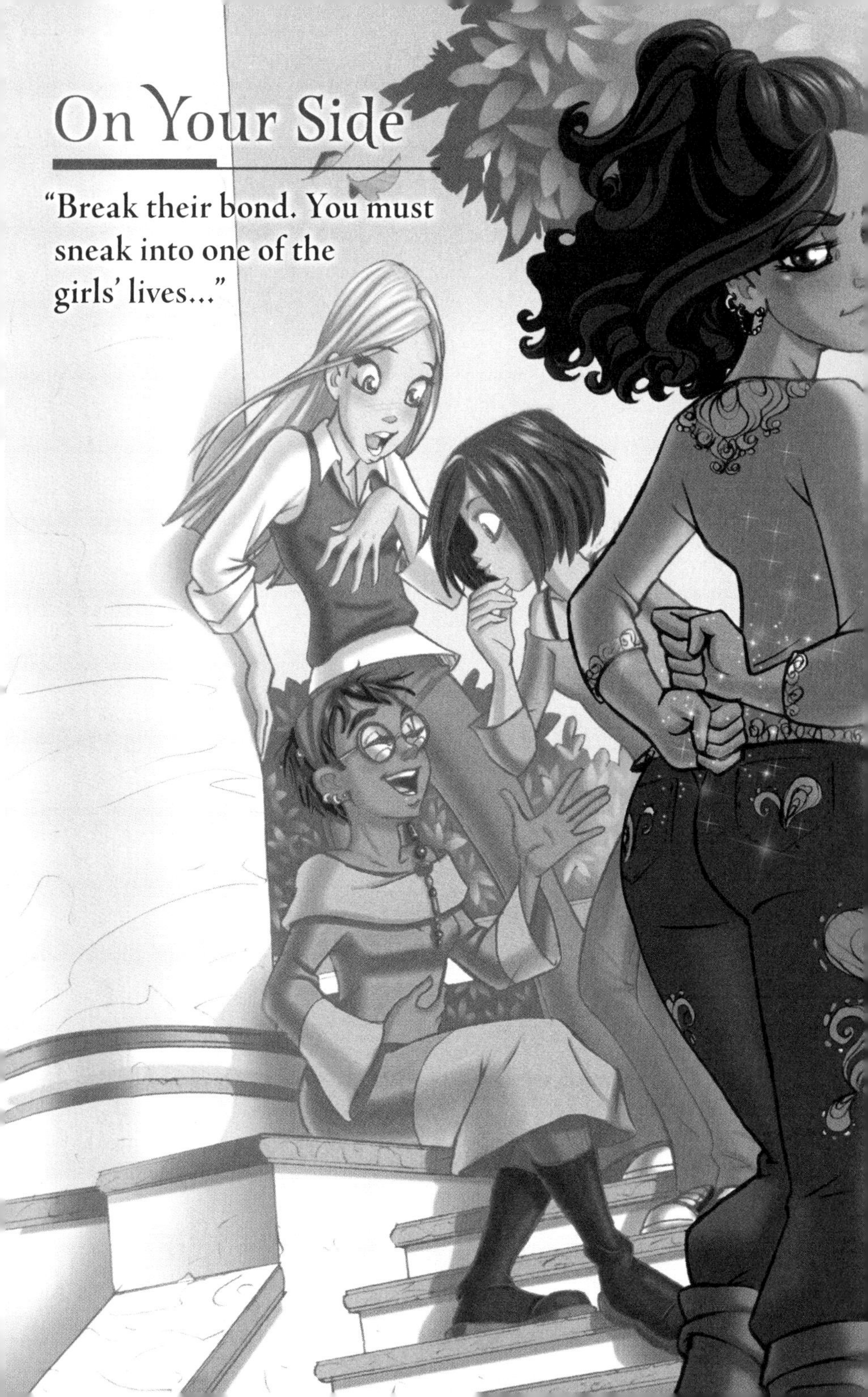

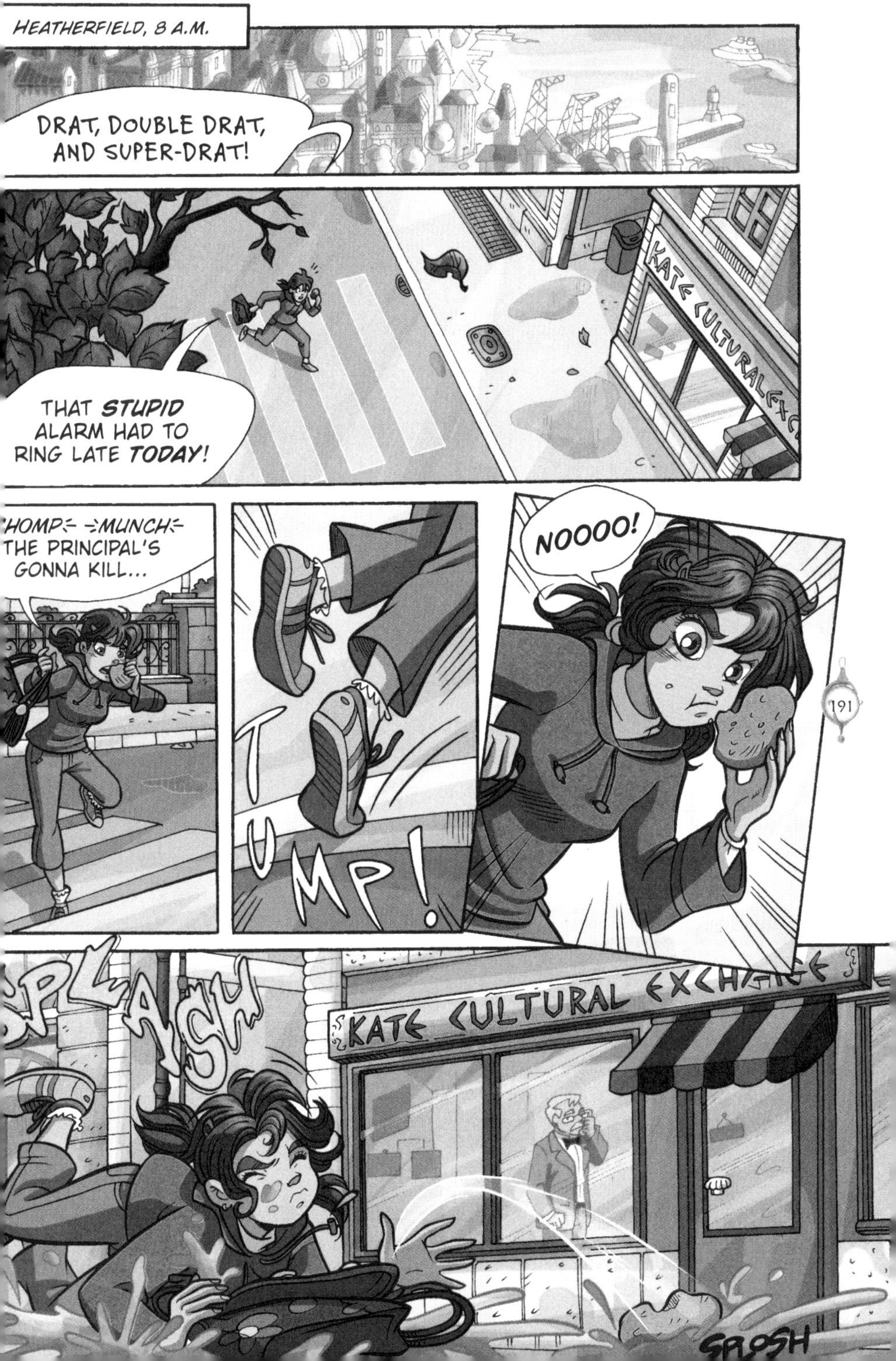
HEATHERFIELD, 8 A.M.
DRAT, DOUBLE DRAT, AND SUPER-DRAT!
THAT STUPID ALARM HAD TO RING LATE TODAY!
HOMP MUNCH THE PRINCIPAL'S GONNA KILL...
TUMP!
NOOOO!
SPLASH
KATE CULTURAL EXCHANGE
SPLOSH

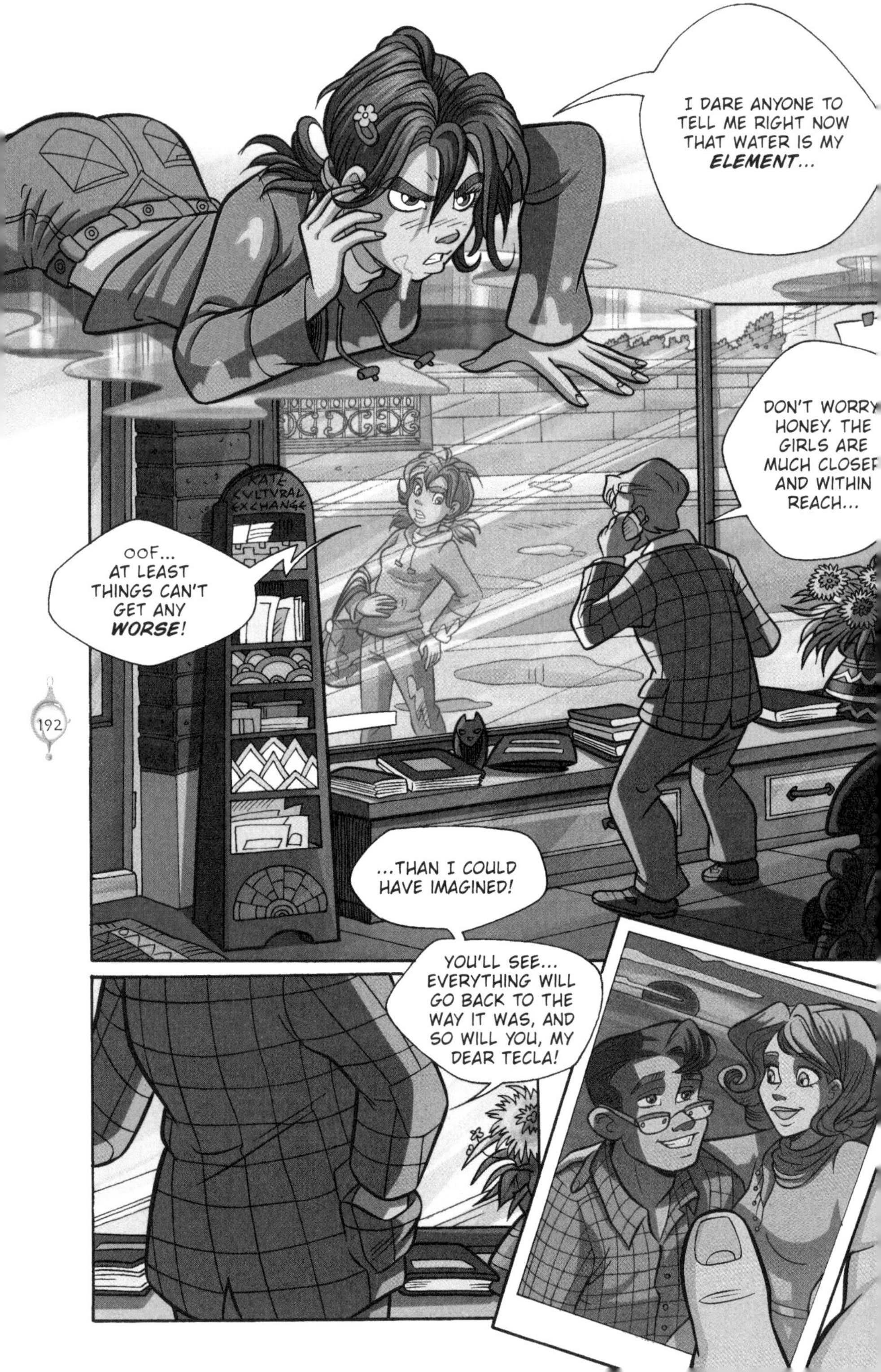
I DARE ANYONE TO TELL ME RIGHT NOW THAT WATER IS MY ELEMENT...
DON'T WORRY HONEY. THE GIRLS ARE MUCH CLOSER AND WITHIN REACH...
KATE CULTURAL EXCHANGE
OOF... AT LEAST THINGS CAN'T GET ANY WORSE!
...THAN I COULD HAVE IMAGINED!
YOU'LL SEE... EVERYTHING WILL GO BACK TO THE WAY IT WAS, AND SO WILL YOU, MY DEAR TECLA!

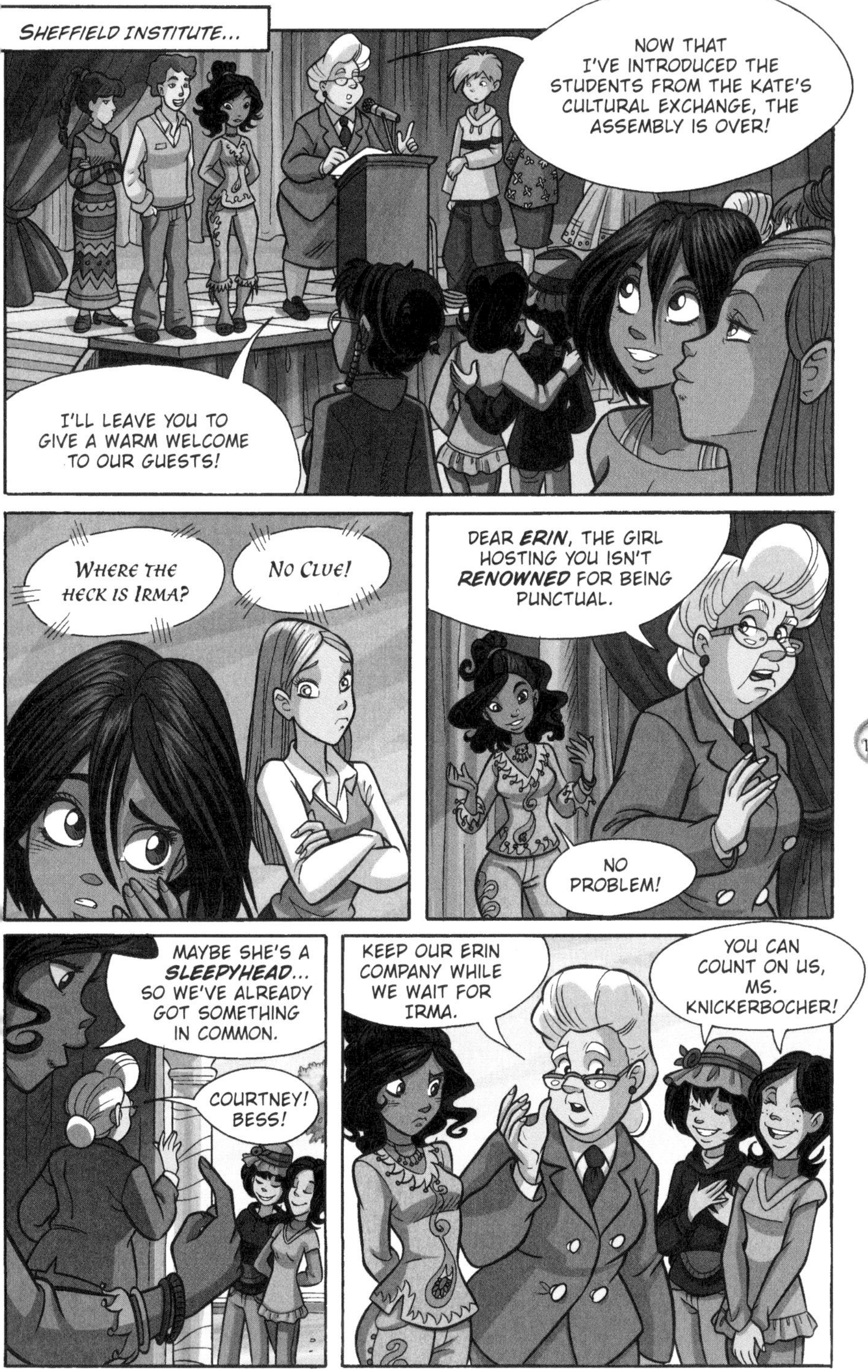
SHEFFIELD INSTITUTE...
NOW THAT I'VE INTRODUCED THE STUDENTS FROM THE KATE'S CULTURAL EXCHANGE, THE ASSEMBLY IS OVER!
I'LL LEAVE YOU TO GIVE A WARM WELCOME TO OUR GUESTS!
WHERE THE HECK IS IRMA?
NO CLUE!
DEAR ERIN, THE GIRL HOSTING YOU ISN'T RENOWNED FOR BEING PUNCTUAL.
NO PROBLEM!
MAYBE SHE'S A SLEEPYHEAD... SO WE'VE ALREADY GOT SOMETHING IN COMMON.
COURTNEY! BESS!
KEEP OUR ERIN COMPANY WHILE WE WAIT FOR IRMA.
YOU CAN COUNT ON US, MS. KNICKERBOCHER!

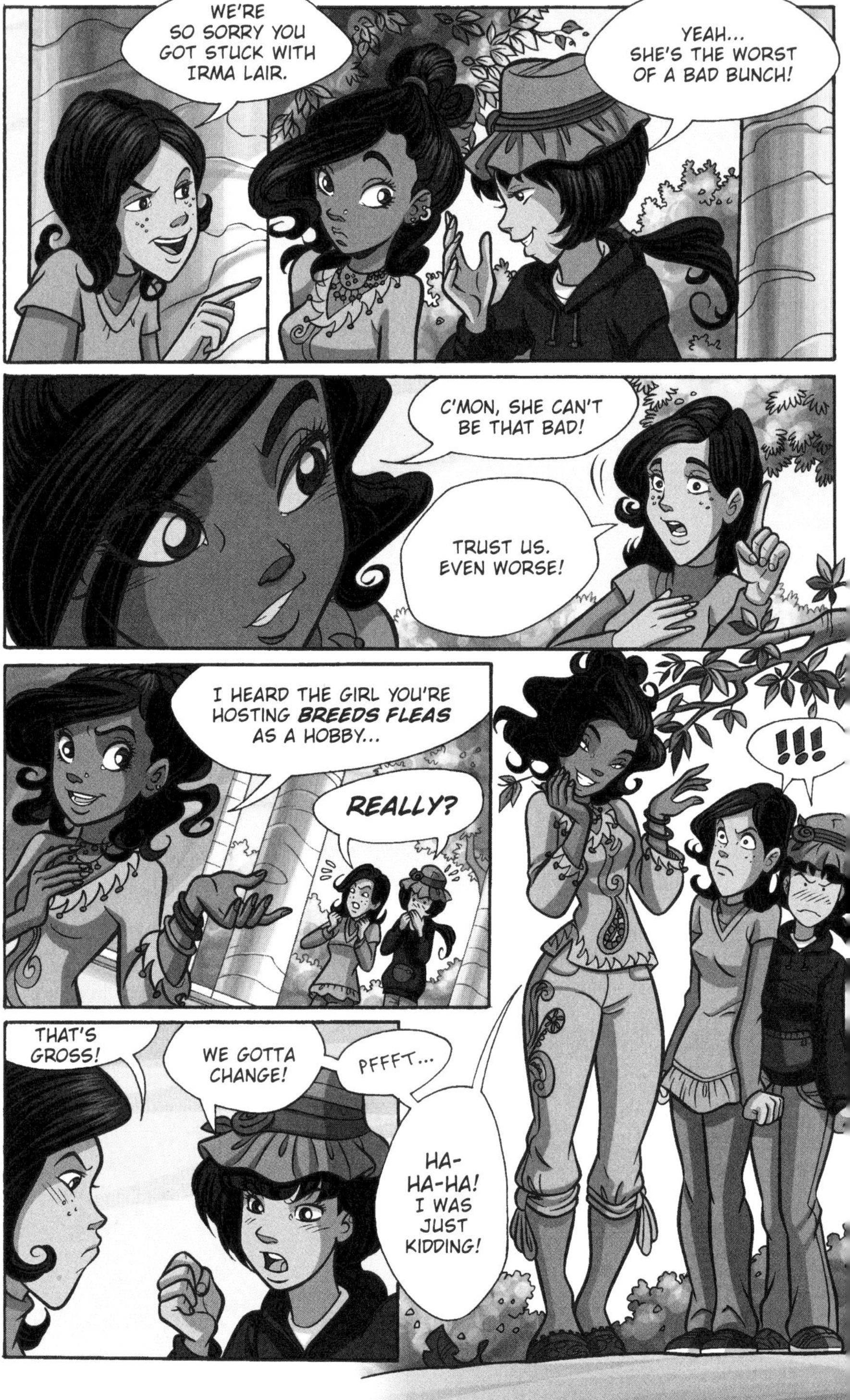
WE'RE SO SORRY YOU GOT STUCK WITH IRMA LAIR.
YEAH... SHE'S THE WORST OF A BAD BUNCH!
C'MON, SHE CAN'T BE THAT BAD!
TRUST US. EVEN WORSE!
I HEARD THE GIRL YOU'RE HOSTING **BREEDS FLEAS** AS A HOBBY...
REALLY?
!!!
THAT'S GROSS!
WE GOTTA CHANGE!
PFFFT...
HA-HA-HA! I WAS JUST KIDDING!

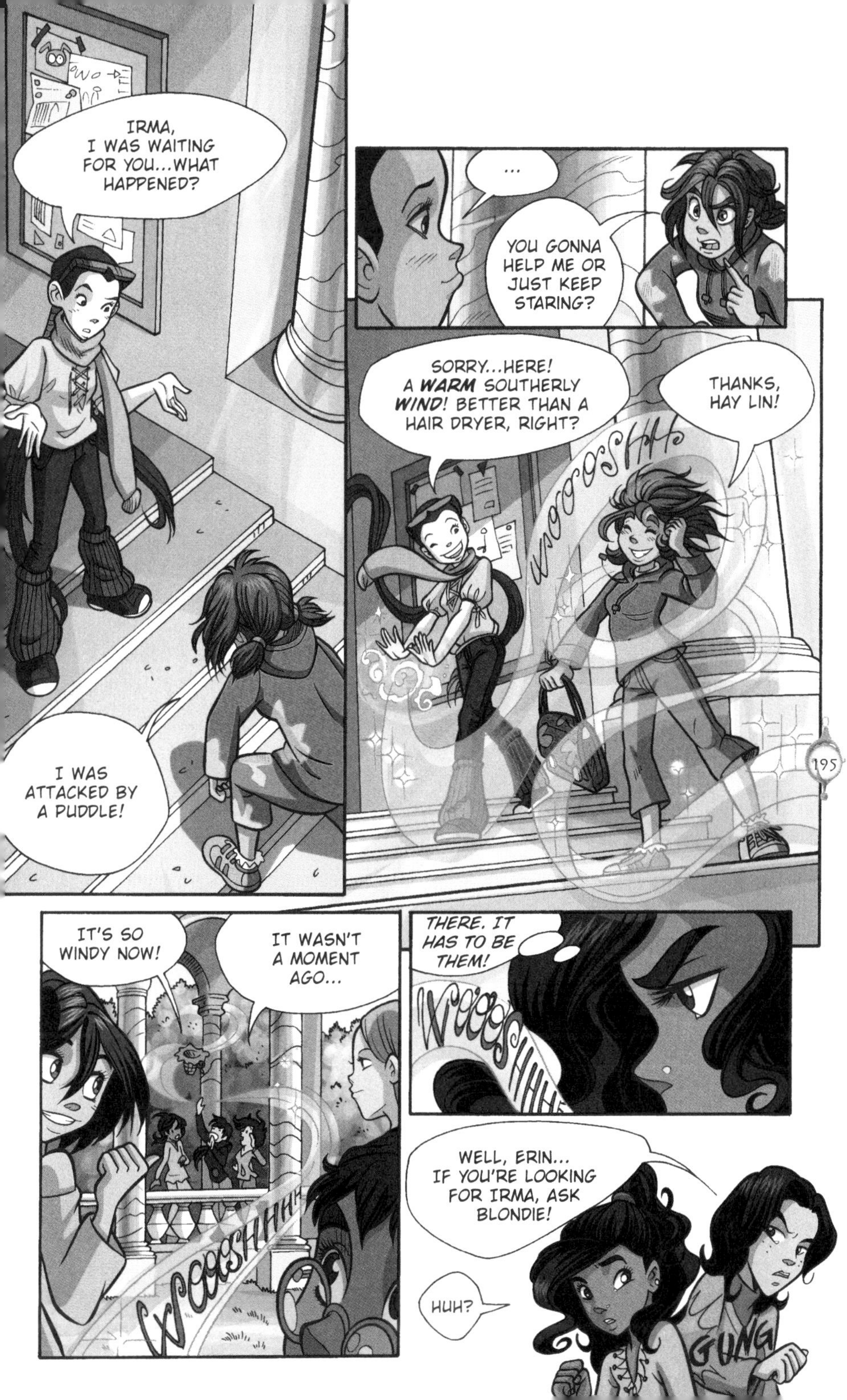
IRMA, I WAS WAITING FOR YOU...WHAT HAPPENED?
I WAS ATTACKED BY A PUDDLE!
...
YOU GONNA HELP ME OR JUST KEEP STARING?
SORRY...HERE! A **WARM** SOUTHERLY **WIND**! BETTER THAN A HAIR DRYER, RIGHT?
THANKS, HAY LIN!
WHOOOOSHHH
IT'S SO WINDY NOW!
IT WASN'T A MOMENT AGO...
WHOOOSHHHH
THERE. IT HAS TO BE THEM!
WHOOOSHHH
WELL, ERIN... IF YOU'RE LOOKING FOR IRMA, ASK BLONDIE!
HUH?
GUNG

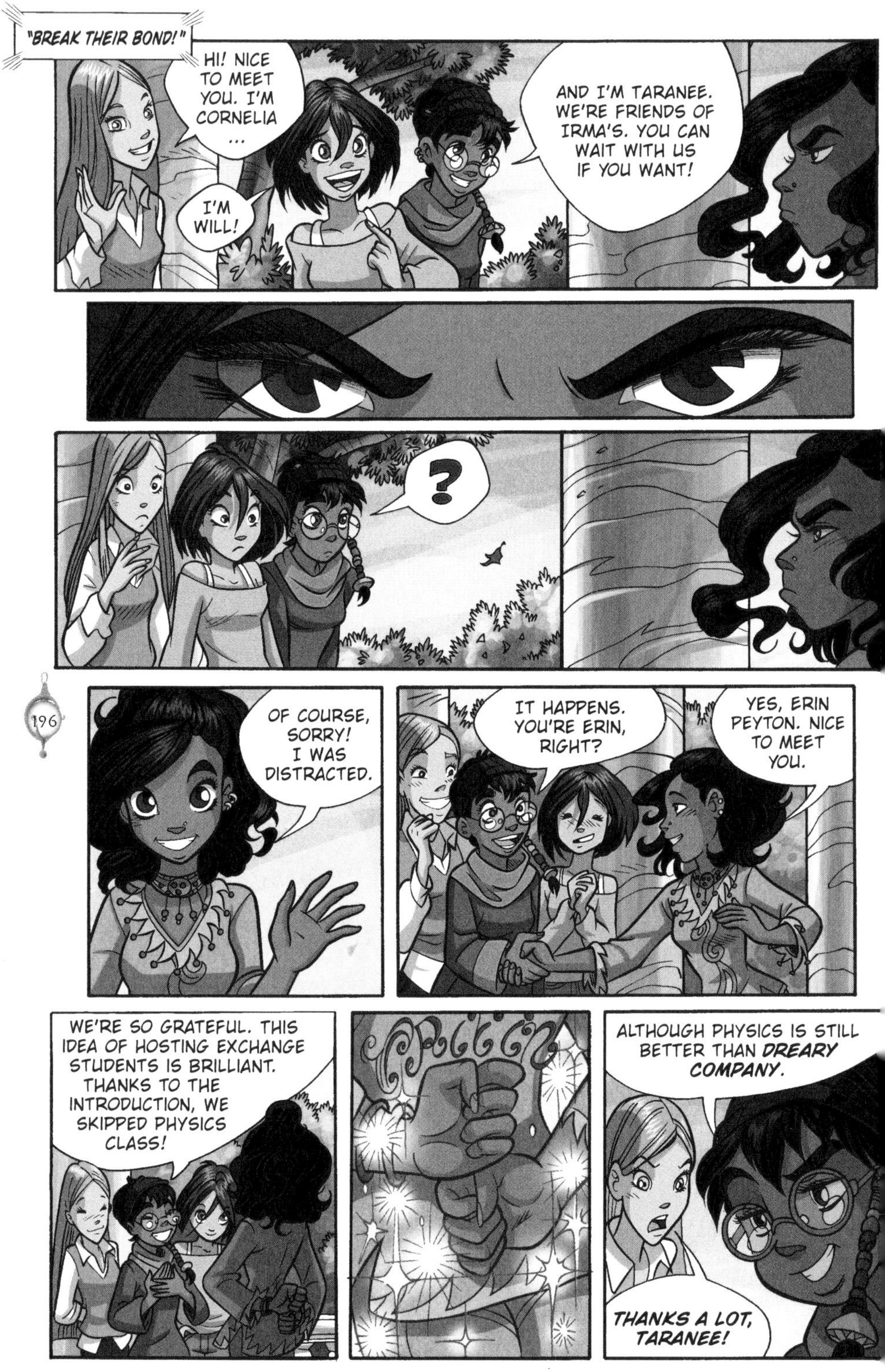
"BREAK THEIR BOND!"
HI! NICE TO MEET YOU. I'M CORNELIA ...
I'M WILL!
AND I'M TARANEE. WE'RE FRIENDS OF IRMA'S. YOU CAN WAIT WITH US IF YOU WANT!
?
OF COURSE, SORRY! I WAS DISTRACTED.
IT HAPPENS. YOU'RE ERIN, RIGHT?
YES, ERIN PEYTON. NICE TO MEET YOU.
WE'RE SO GRATEFUL. THIS IDEA OF HOSTING EXCHANGE STUDENTS IS BRILLIANT. THANKS TO THE INTRODUCTION, WE SKIPPED PHYSICS CLASS!
ALTHOUGH PHYSICS IS STILL BETTER THAN *DREARY COMPANY*.
THANKS A LOT, TARANEE!

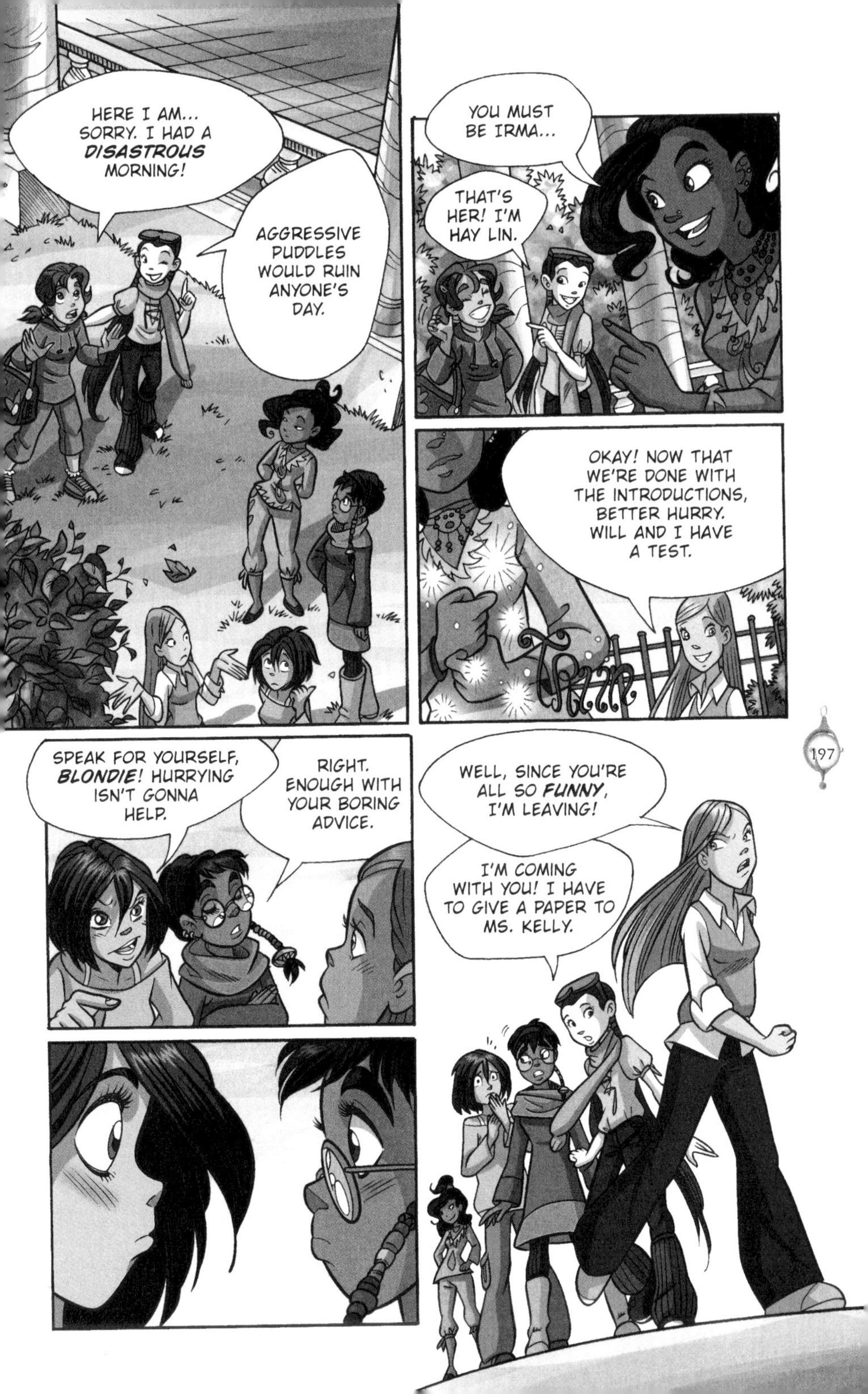
HERE I AM... SORRY. I HAD A DISASTROUS MORNING!
AGGRESSIVE PUDDLES WOULD RUIN ANYONE'S DAY.
YOU MUST BE IRMA...
THAT'S HER! I'M HAY LIN.
OKAY! NOW THAT WE'RE DONE WITH THE INTRODUCTIONS, BETTER HURRY. WILL AND I HAVE A TEST.
SPEAK FOR YOURSELF, BLONDIE! HURRYING ISN'T GONNA HELP.
RIGHT. ENOUGH WITH YOUR BORING ADVICE.
WELL, SINCE YOU'RE ALL SO FUNNY, I'M LEAVING!
I'M COMING WITH YOU! I HAVE TO GIVE A PAPER TO MS. KELLY.

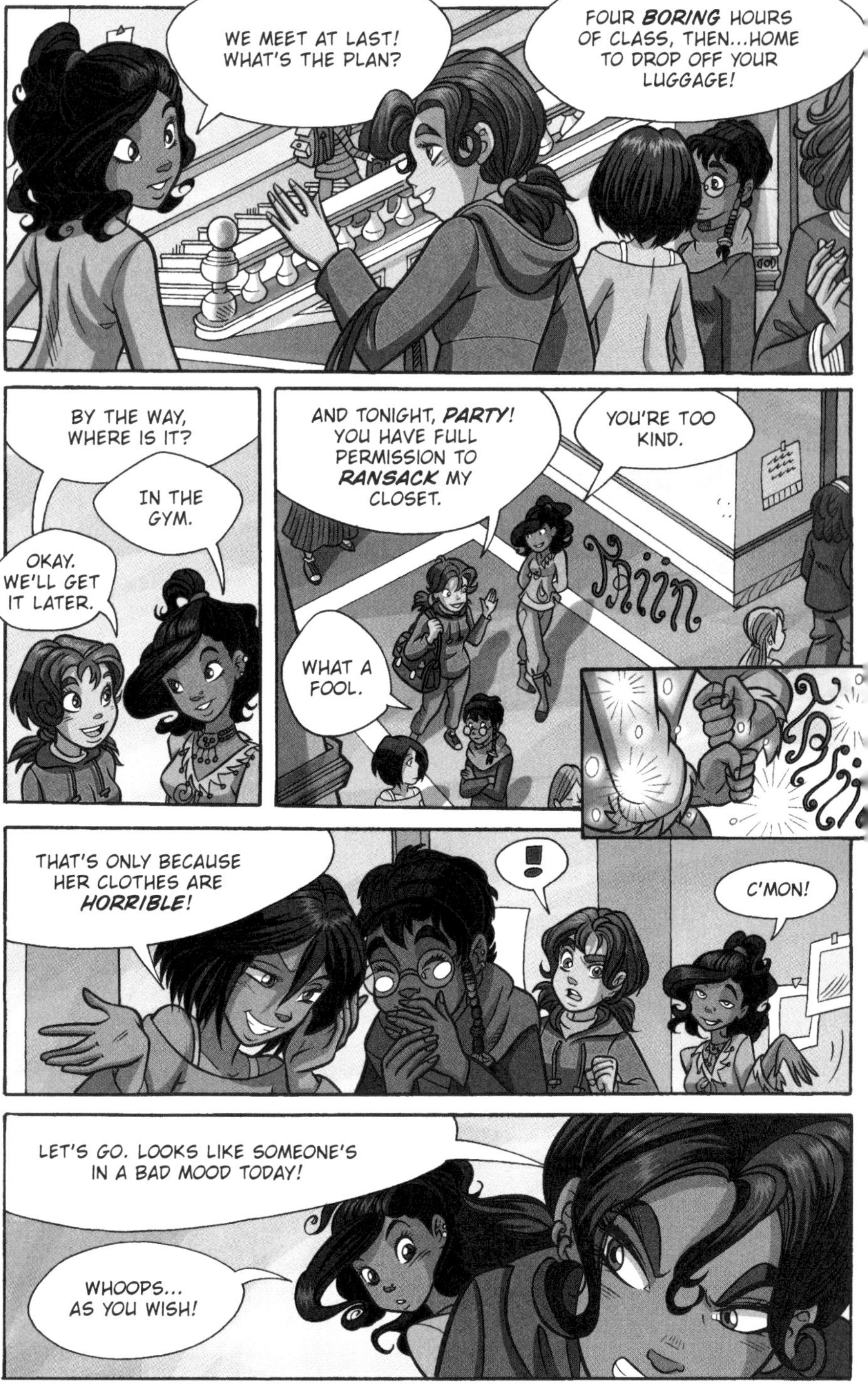
WE MEET AT LAST! WHAT'S THE PLAN?
FOUR BORING HOURS OF CLASS, THEN...HOME TO DROP OFF YOUR LUGGAGE!
BY THE WAY, WHERE IS IT?
IN THE GYM.
OKAY. WE'LL GET IT LATER.
AND TONIGHT, PARTY! YOU HAVE FULL PERMISSION TO RANSACK MY CLOSET.
YOU'RE TOO KIND.
WHAT A FOOL.
THAT'S ONLY BECAUSE HER CLOTHES ARE HORRIBLE!
!
C'MON!
LET'S GO. LOOKS LIKE SOMEONE'S IN A BAD MOOD TODAY!
WHOOPS... AS YOU WISH!

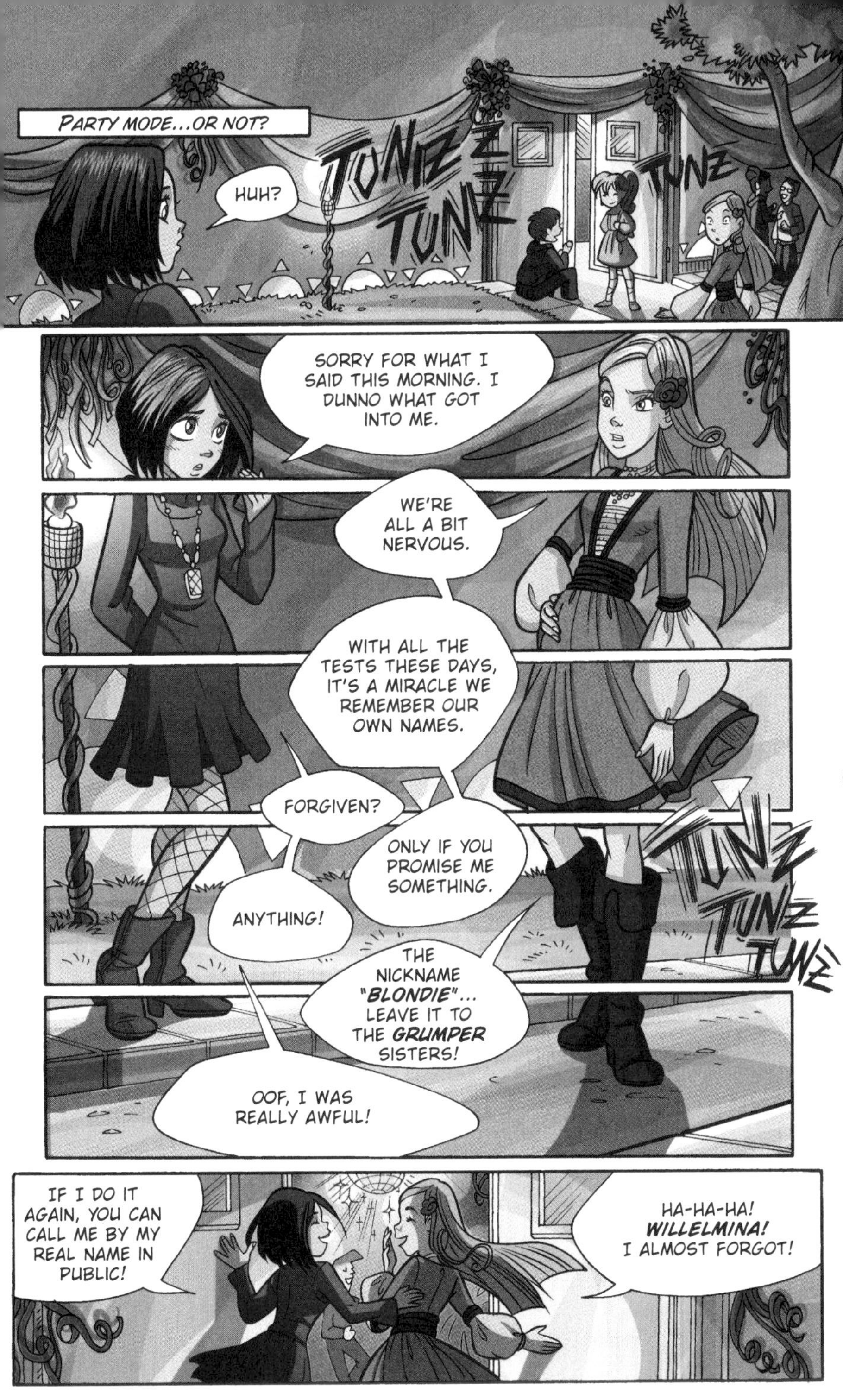
PARTY MODE...OR NOT?
HUH?
TUNZZ TUNZ TUNZ TUNZ
SORRY FOR WHAT I SAID THIS MORNING. I DUNNO WHAT GOT INTO ME.
WE'RE ALL A BIT NERVOUS.
WITH ALL THE TESTS THESE DAYS, IT'S A MIRACLE WE REMEMBER OUR OWN NAMES.
FORGIVEN?
ONLY IF YOU PROMISE ME SOMETHING.
ANYTHING!
TUNZ TUNZ TUNZ
THE NICKNAME "BLONDIE"... LEAVE IT TO THE GRUMPER SISTERS!
OOF, I WAS REALLY AWFUL!
IF I DO IT AGAIN, YOU CAN CALL ME BY MY REAL NAME IN PUBLIC!
HA-HA-HA! WILLELMINA! I ALMOST FORGOT!

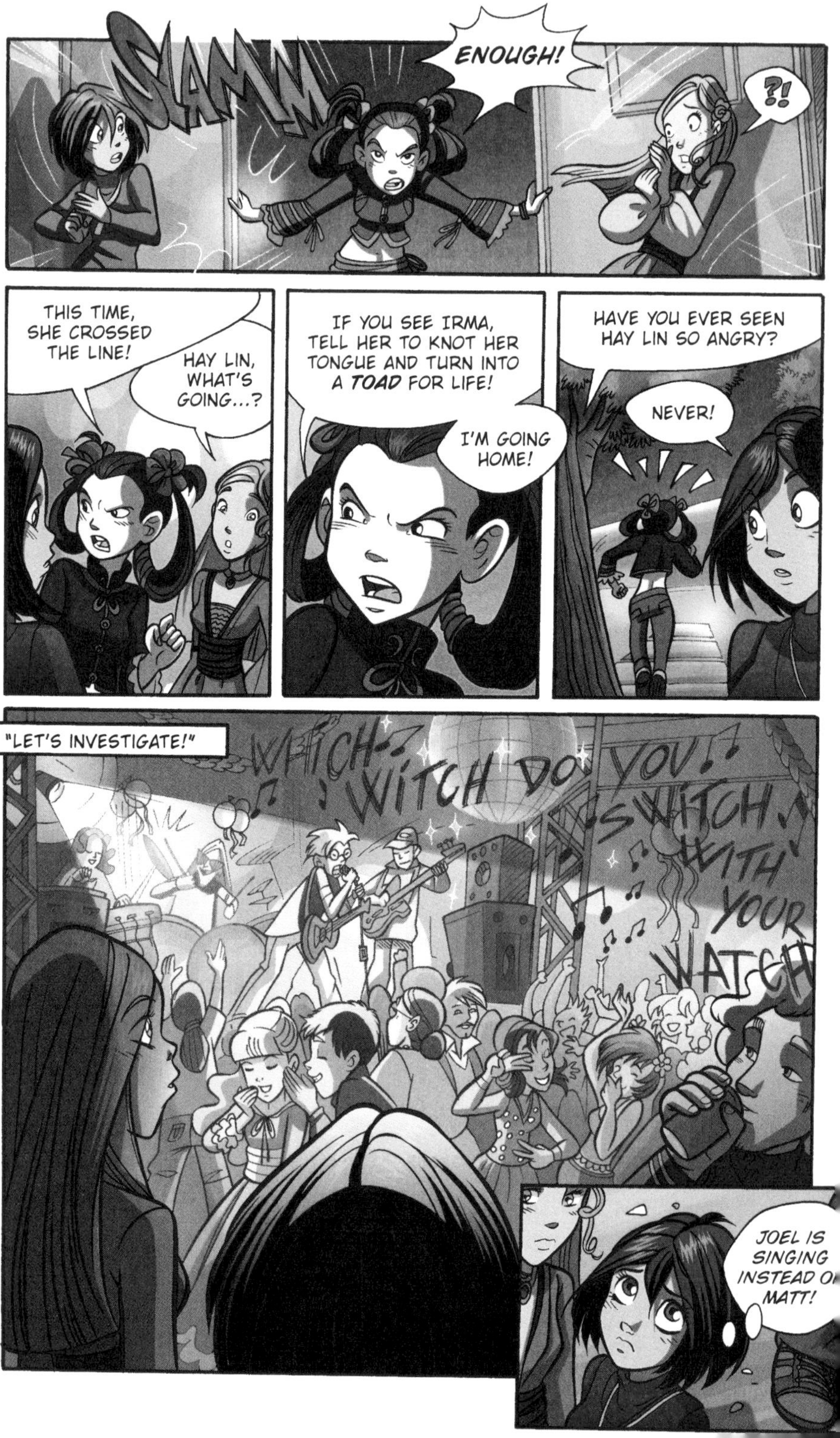
SLAMM
ENOUGH!
?!
THIS TIME, SHE CROSSED THE LINE!
HAY LIN, WHAT'S GOING...?
IF YOU SEE IRMA, TELL HER TO KNOT HER TONGUE AND TURN INTO A *TOAD* FOR LIFE!
I'M GOING HOME!
HAVE YOU EVER SEEN HAY LIN SO ANGRY?
NEVER!
"LET'S INVESTIGATE!"
WITCH-WITCH DO YOU SWITCH WITH YOUR WATCH
JOEL IS SINGING INSTEAD O
MATT!

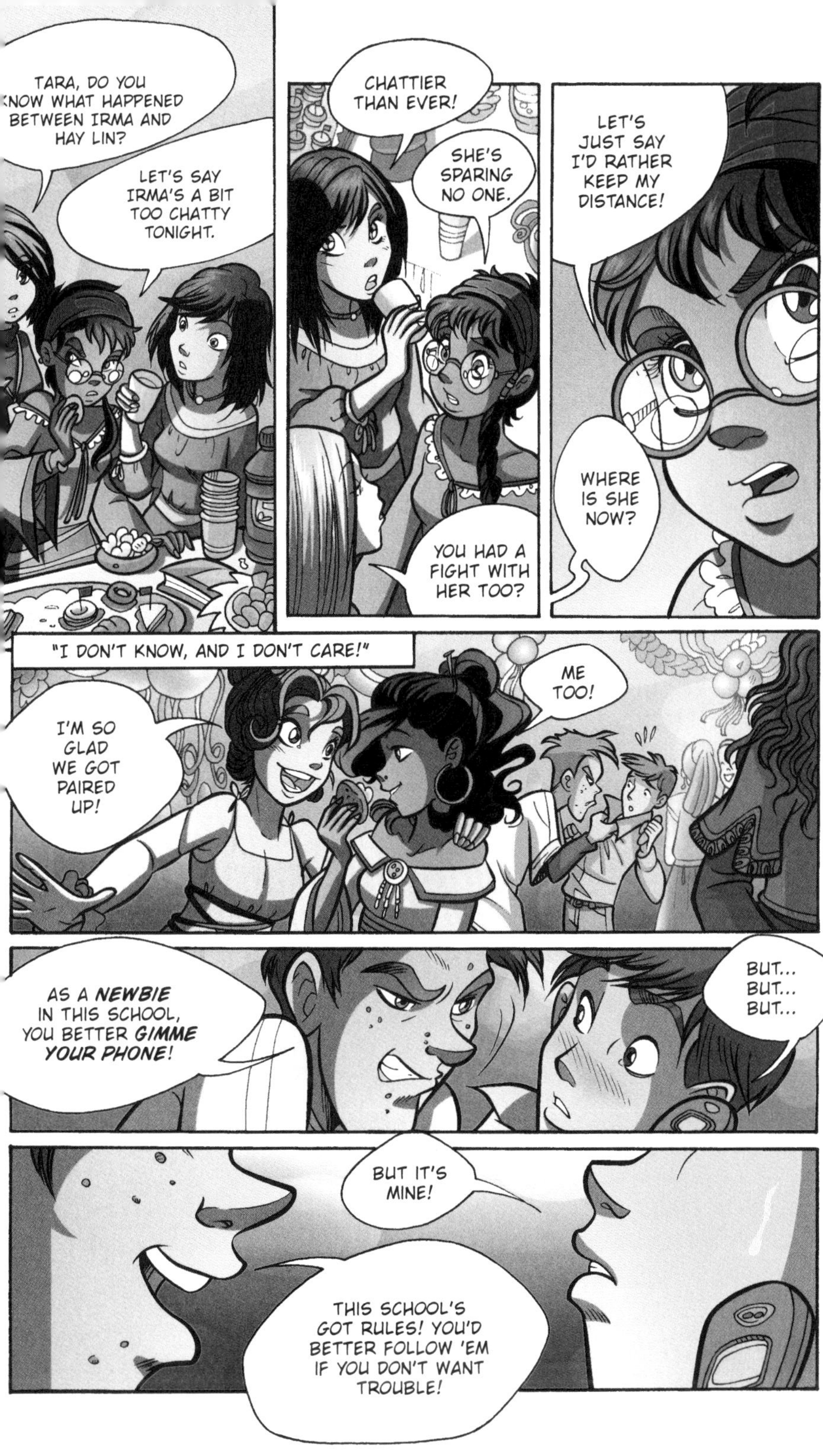
TARA, DO YOU KNOW WHAT HAPPENED BETWEEN IRMA AND HAY LIN?
LET'S SAY IRMA'S A BIT TOO CHATTY TONIGHT.
CHATTIER THAN EVER!
SHE'S SPARING NO ONE.
YOU HAD A FIGHT WITH HER TOO?
LET'S JUST SAY I'D RATHER KEEP MY DISTANCE!
WHERE IS SHE NOW?
"I DON'T KNOW, AND I DON'T CARE!"
I'M SO GLAD WE GOT PAIRED UP!
ME TOO!
AS A NEWBIE IN THIS SCHOOL, YOU BETTER GIMME YOUR PHONE!
BUT... BUT... BUT...
BUT IT'S MINE!
THIS SCHOOL'S GOT RULES! YOU'D BETTER FOLLOW 'EM IF YOU DON'T WANT TROUBLE!

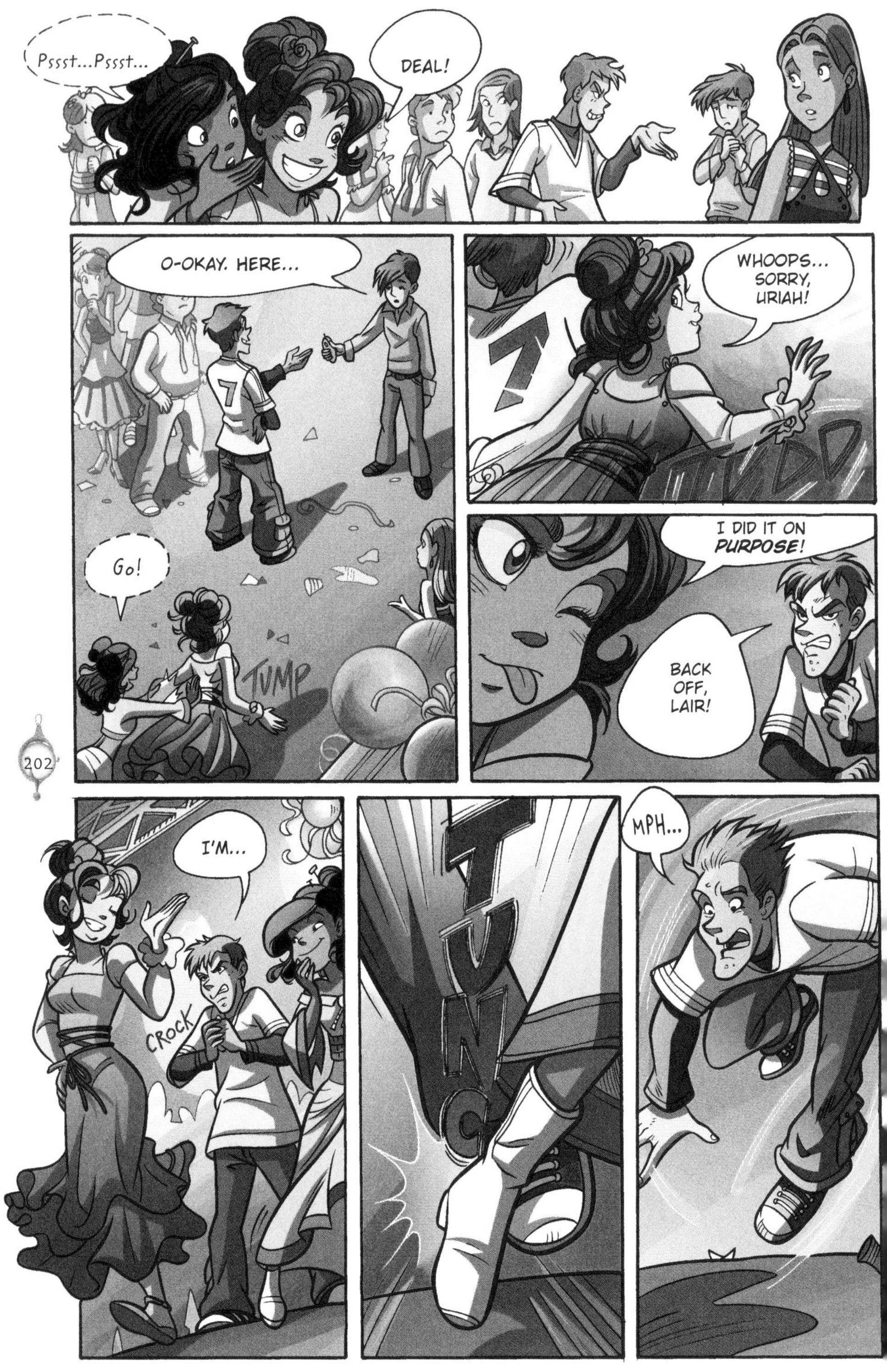
Pssst...Pssst...
DEAL!
O-OKAY. HERE...
Go!
TUMP
WHOOPS... SORRY, URIAH!
TUNDD
I DID IT ON PURPOSE!
BACK OFF, LAIR!
I'M...
CROCK
TUNC
MPH...

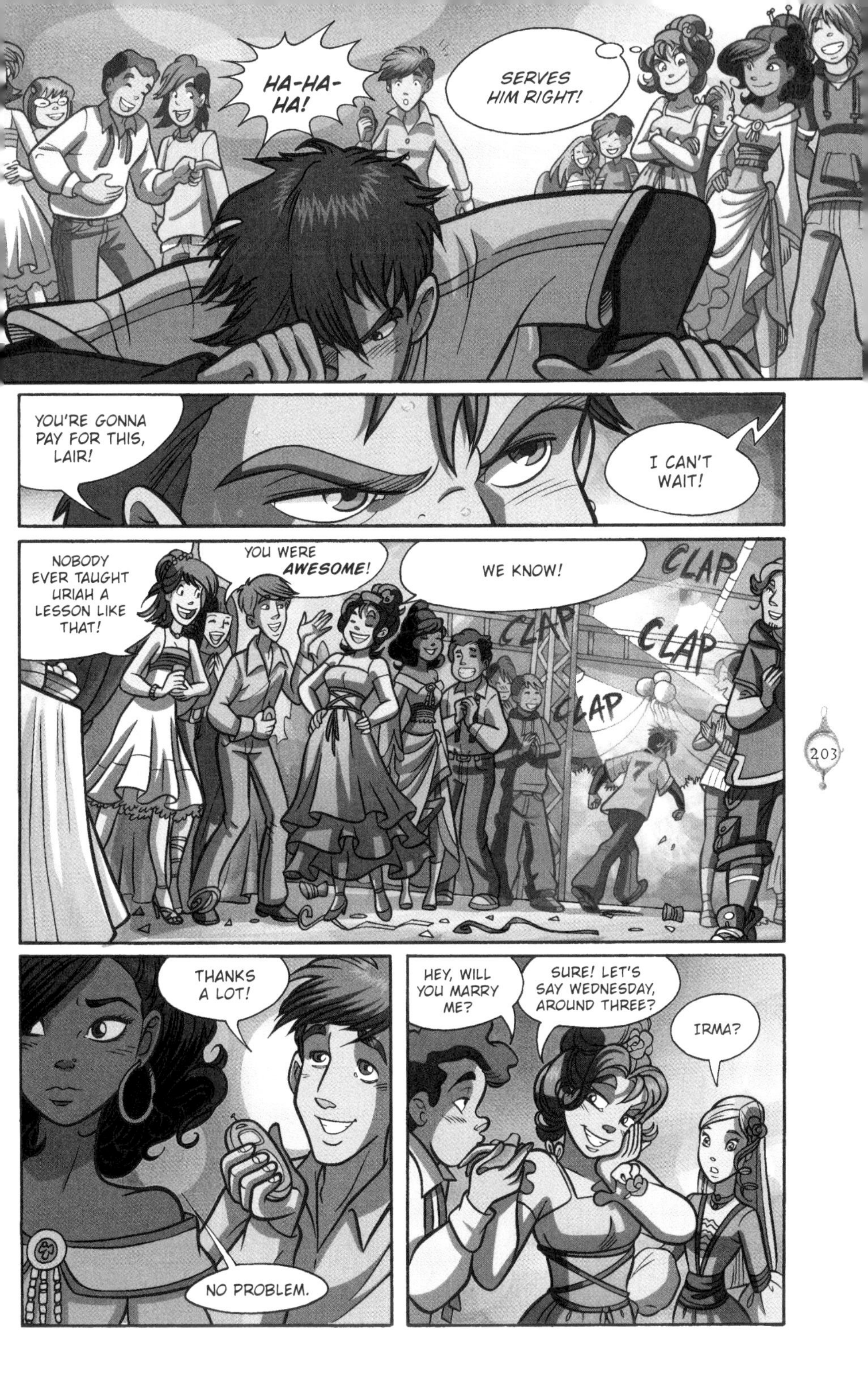

HA-HA-HA!
SERVES HIM RIGHT!
YOU'RE GONNA PAY FOR THIS, LAIR!
I CAN'T WAIT!
NOBODY EVER TAUGHT URIAH A LESSON LIKE THAT!
YOU WERE **AWESOME**!
WE KNOW!
CLAP
CLAP
CLAP
CLAP
THANKS A LOT!
NO PROBLEM.
HEY, WILL YOU MARRY ME?
SURE! LET'S SAY WEDNESDAY, AROUND THREE?
IRMA?

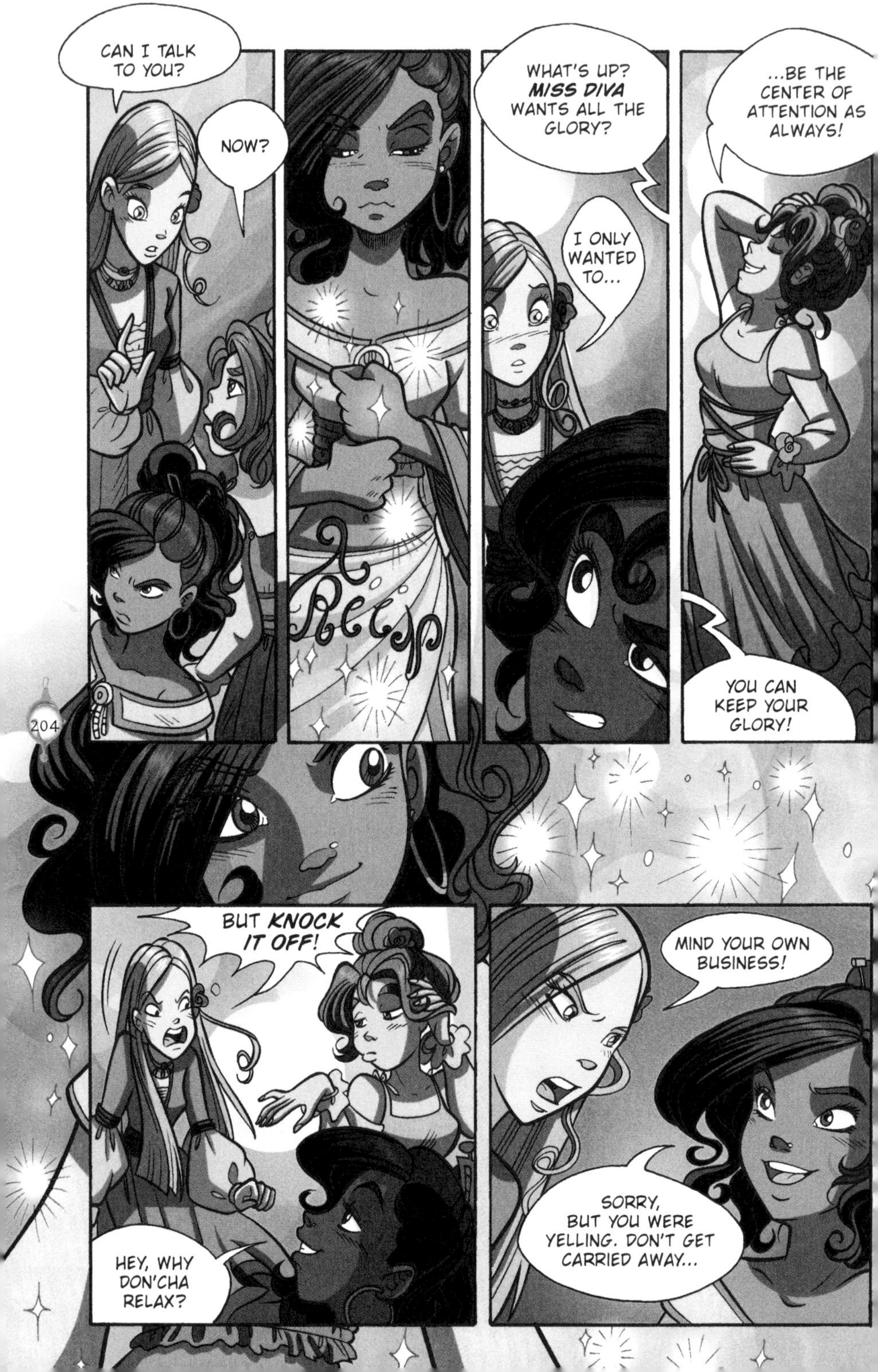

CAN I TALK TO YOU?
NOW?
WHAT'S UP? MISS DIVA WANTS ALL THE GLORY?
I ONLY WANTED TO...
...BE THE CENTER OF ATTENTION AS ALWAYS!
YOU CAN KEEP YOUR GLORY!
BUT KNOCK IT OFF!
HEY, WHY DON'CHA RELAX?
MIND YOUR OWN BUSINESS!
SORRY, BUT YOU WERE YELLING. DON'T GET CARRIED AWAY...

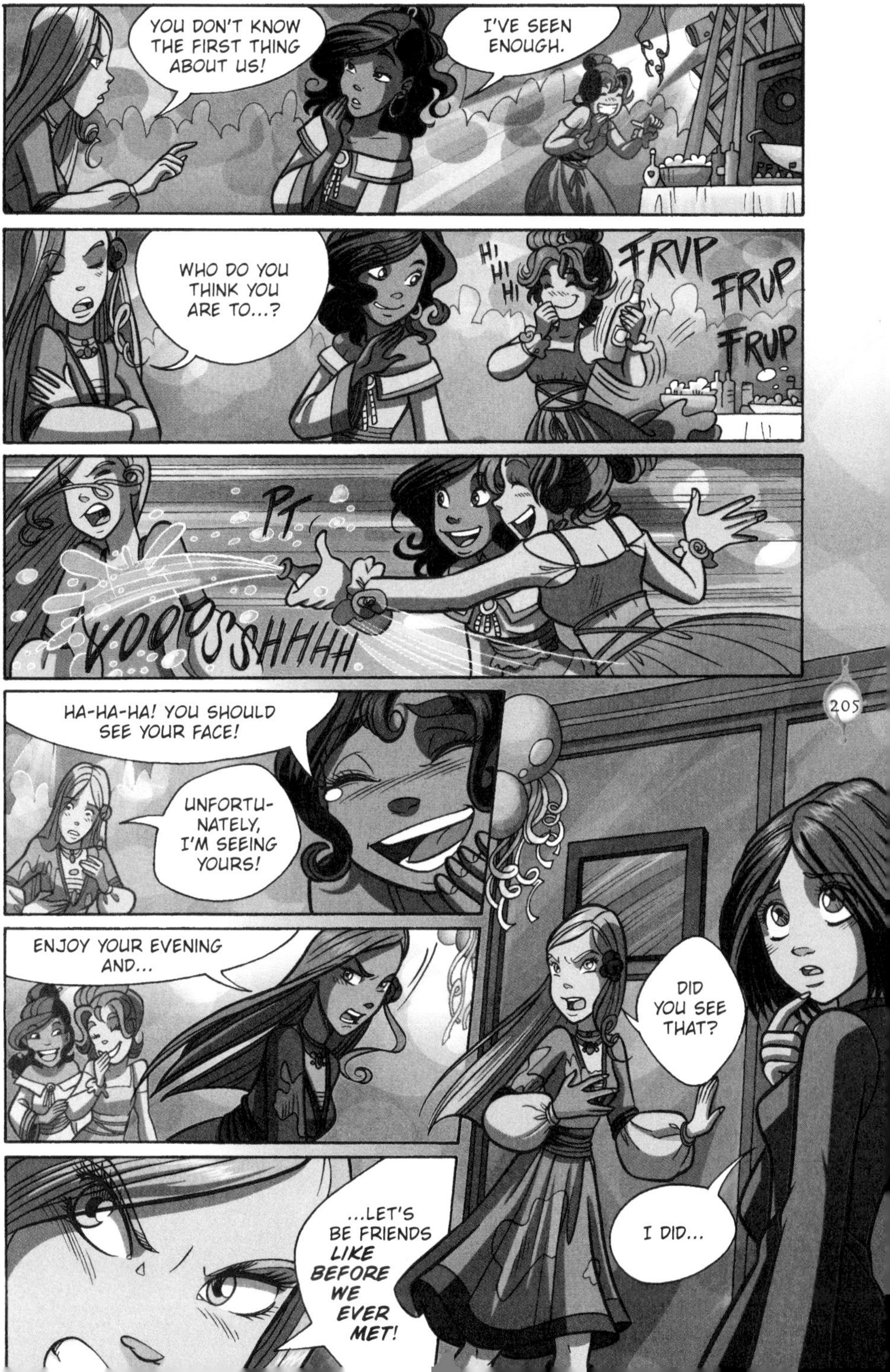
YOU DON'T KNOW THE FIRST THING ABOUT US!
I'VE SEEN ENOUGH.
WHO DO YOU THINK YOU ARE TO...?
HI HI HI
FRUP FRUP FRUP
PT
VOOOSSHHHH
HA-HA-HA! YOU SHOULD SEE YOUR FACE!
UNFORTUNATELY, I'M SEEING YOURS!
ENJOY YOUR EVENING AND...
...LET'S BE FRIENDS LIKE BEFORE WE EVER MET!
DID YOU SEE THAT?
I DID...

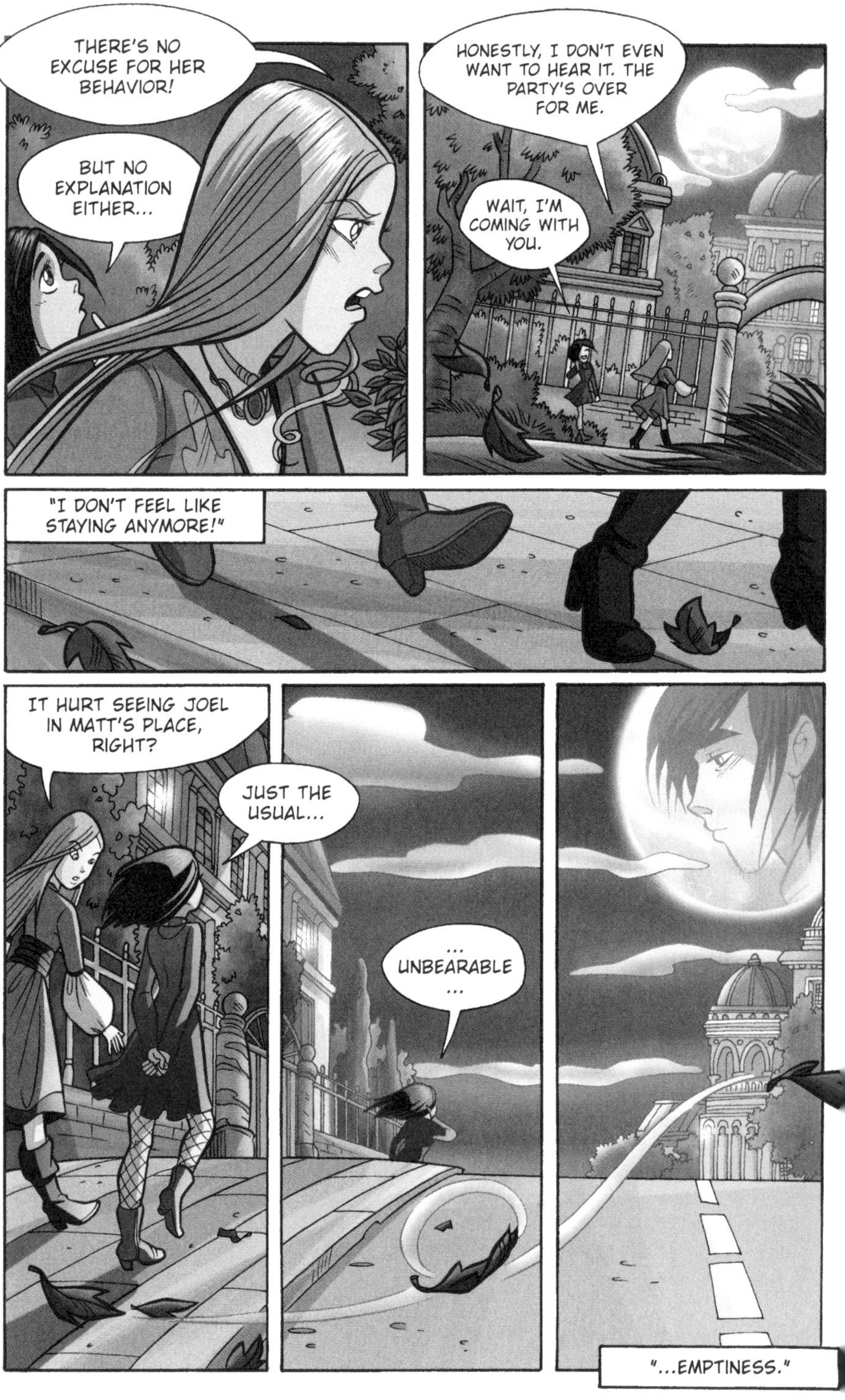
THERE'S NO EXCUSE FOR HER BEHAVIOR!
BUT NO EXPLANATION EITHER...
HONESTLY, I DON'T EVEN WANT TO HEAR IT. THE PARTY'S OVER FOR ME.
WAIT, I'M COMING WITH YOU.
"I DON'T FEEL LIKE STAYING ANYMORE!"
IT HURT SEEING JOEL IN MATT'S PLACE, RIGHT?
JUST THE USUAL...
... UNBEARABLE ...
"...EMPTINESS."

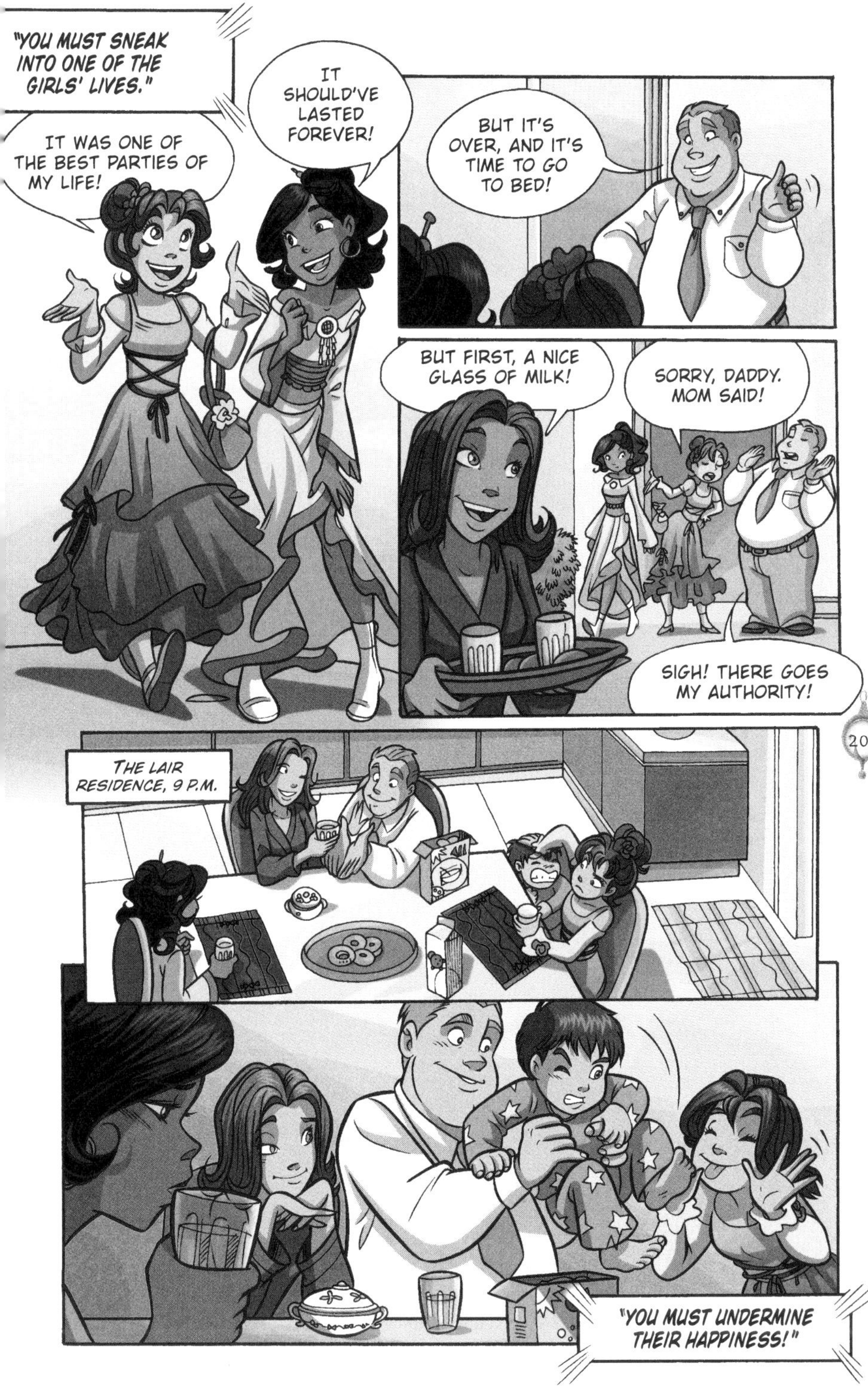
"YOU MUST SNEAK INTO ONE OF THE GIRLS' LIVES."
IT WAS ONE OF THE BEST PARTIES OF MY LIFE!
IT SHOULD'VE LASTED FOREVER!
BUT IT'S OVER, AND IT'S TIME TO GO TO BED!
BUT FIRST, A NICE GLASS OF MILK!
SORRY, DADDY. MOM SAID!
SIGH! THERE GOES MY AUTHORITY!
THE LAIR RESIDENCE, 9 P.M.
"YOU MUST UNDERMINE THEIR HAPPINESS!"

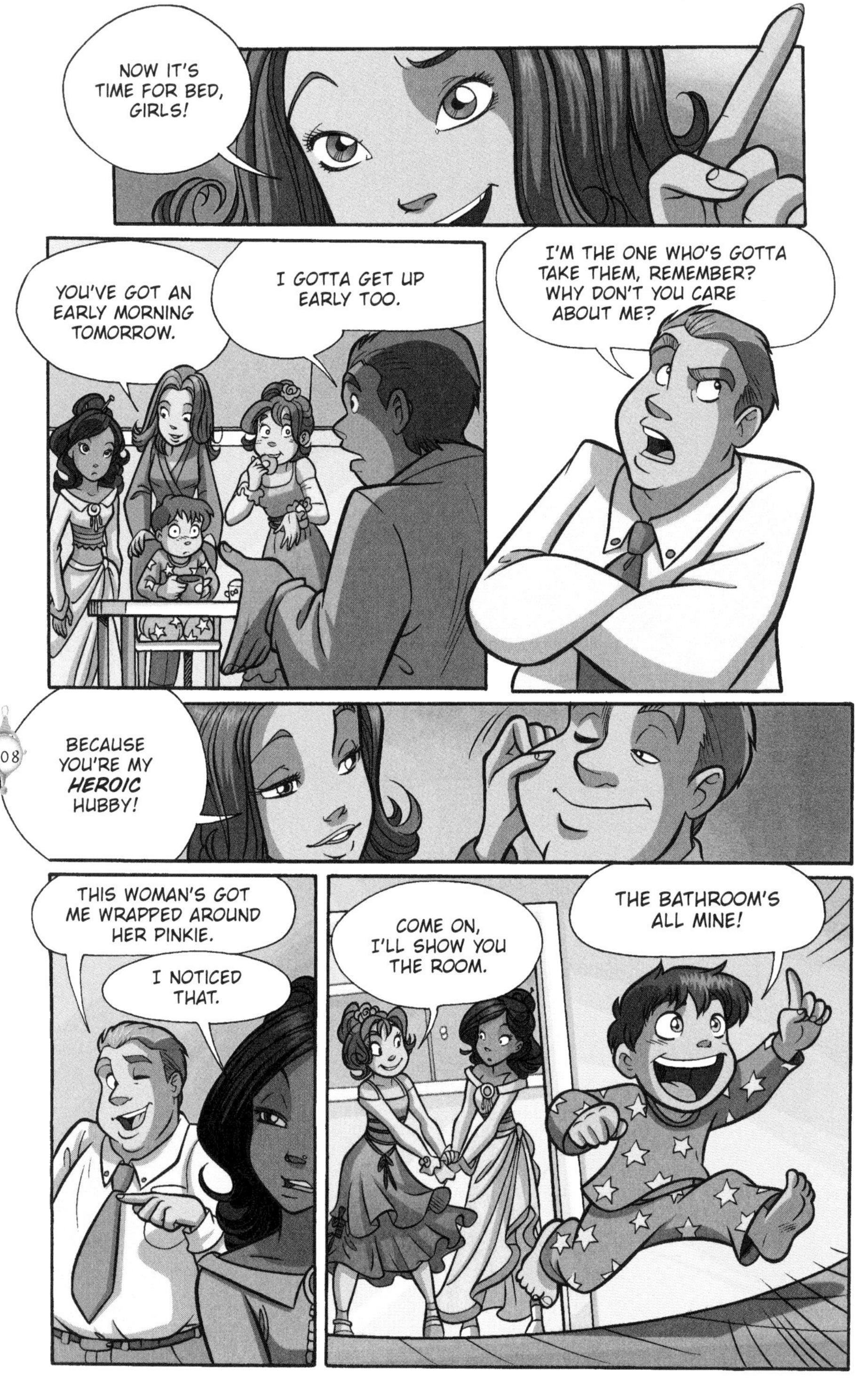
NOW IT'S TIME FOR BED, GIRLS!
YOU'VE GOT AN EARLY MORNING TOMORROW.
I GOTTA GET UP EARLY TOO.
I'M THE ONE WHO'S GOTTA TAKE THEM, REMEMBER? WHY DON'T YOU CARE ABOUT ME?
BECAUSE YOU'RE MY ***HEROIC*** HUBBY!
THIS WOMAN'S GOT ME WRAPPED AROUND HER PINKIE.
I NOTICED THAT.
COME ON, I'LL SHOW YOU THE ROOM.
THE BATHROOM'S ALL MINE!

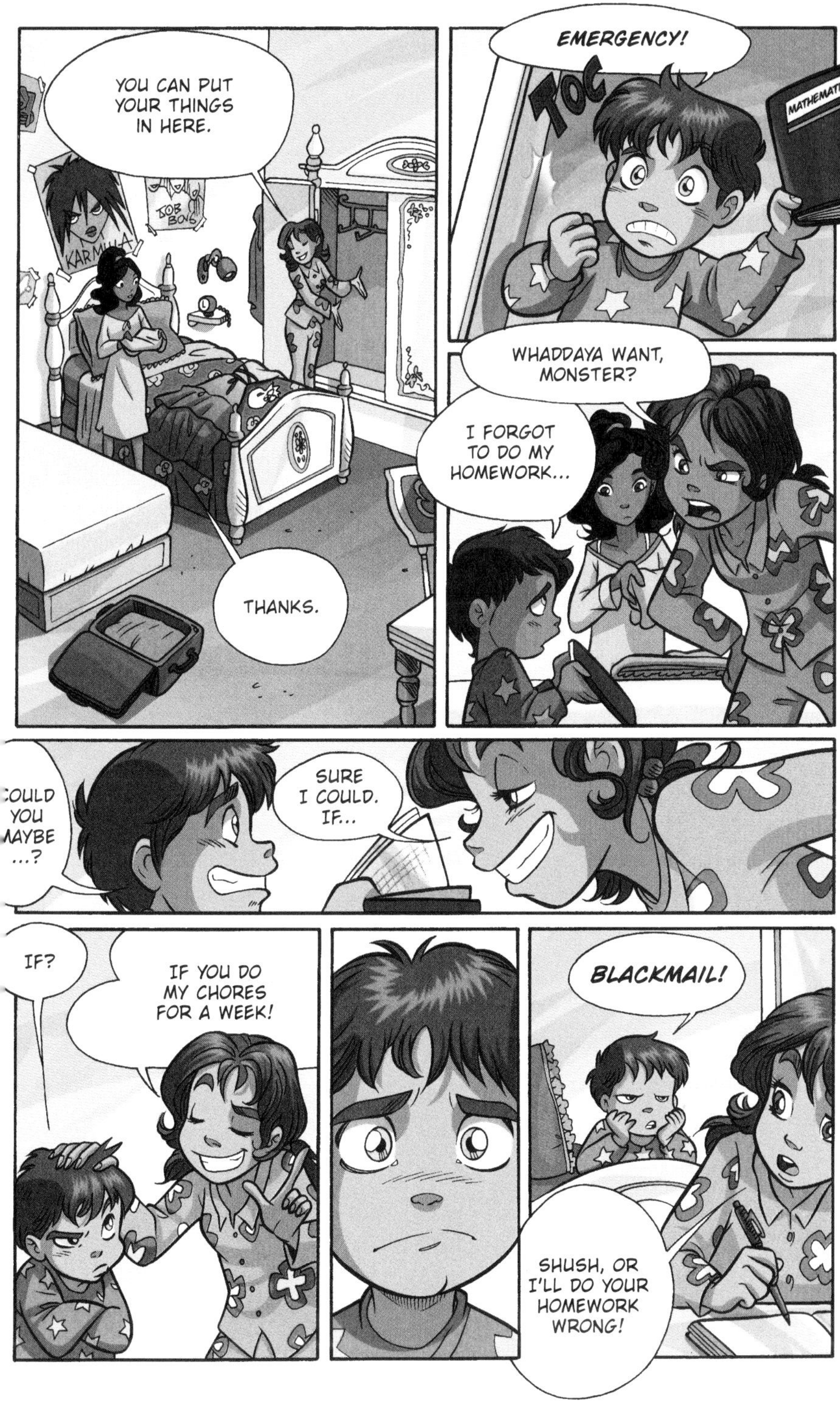
YOU CAN PUT YOUR THINGS IN HERE.
THANKS.
EMERGENCY!
TOC
MATHEMATICS
WHADDAYA WANT, MONSTER?
I FORGOT TO DO MY HOMEWORK...
COULD YOU MAYBE ...?
SURE I COULD. IF...
IF?
IF YOU DO MY CHORES FOR A WEEK!
BLACKMAIL!
SHUSH, OR I'LL DO YOUR HOMEWORK WRONG!

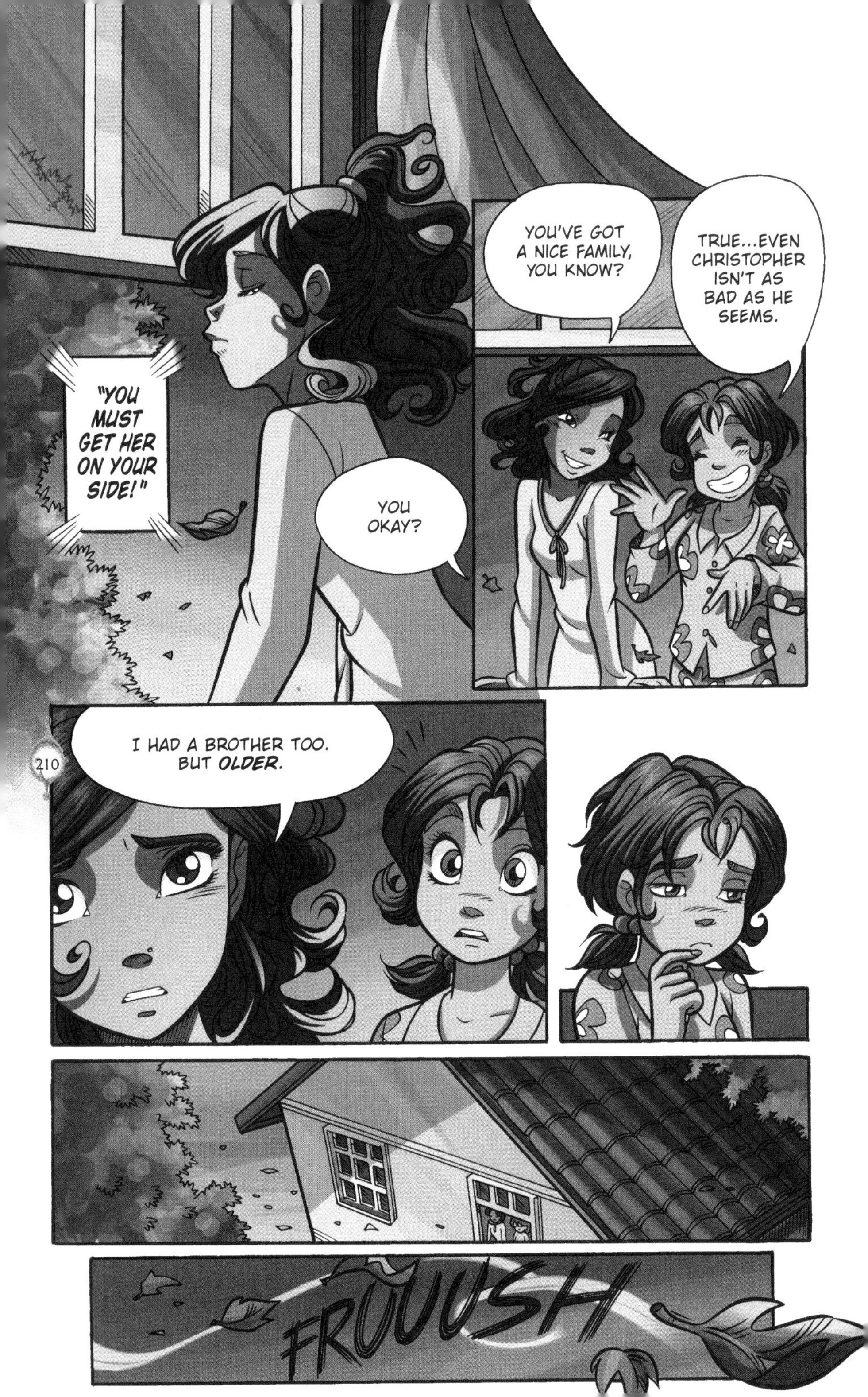
"YOU MUST GET HER ON YOUR SIDE!"
YOU OKAY?
YOU'VE GOT A NICE FAMILY, YOU KNOW?
TRUE...EVEN CHRISTOPHER ISN'T AS BAD AS HE SEEMS.
I HAD A BROTHER TOO. BUT **OLDER**.
FRUUUSH

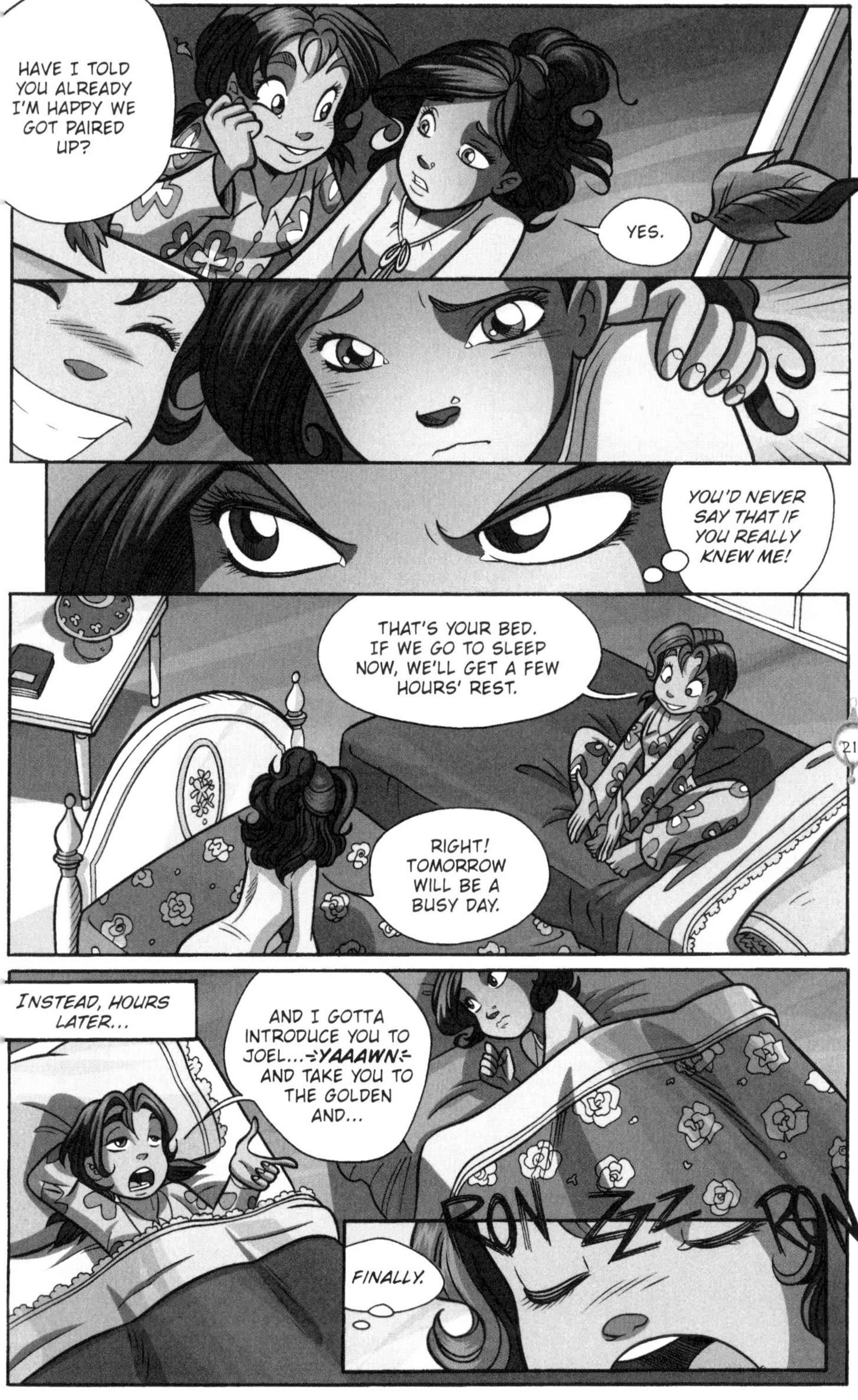

HAVE I TOLD YOU ALREADY I'M HAPPY WE GOT PAIRED UP?
YES.
YOU'D NEVER SAY THAT IF YOU REALLY KNEW ME!
THAT'S YOUR BED. IF WE GO TO SLEEP NOW, WE'LL GET A FEW HOURS' REST.
RIGHT! TOMORROW WILL BE A BUSY DAY.
INSTEAD, HOURS LATER...
AND I GOTTA INTRODUCE YOU TO JOEL... YAAAWN AND TAKE YOU TO THE GOLDEN AND...
RON ZZZ RON
FINALLY.

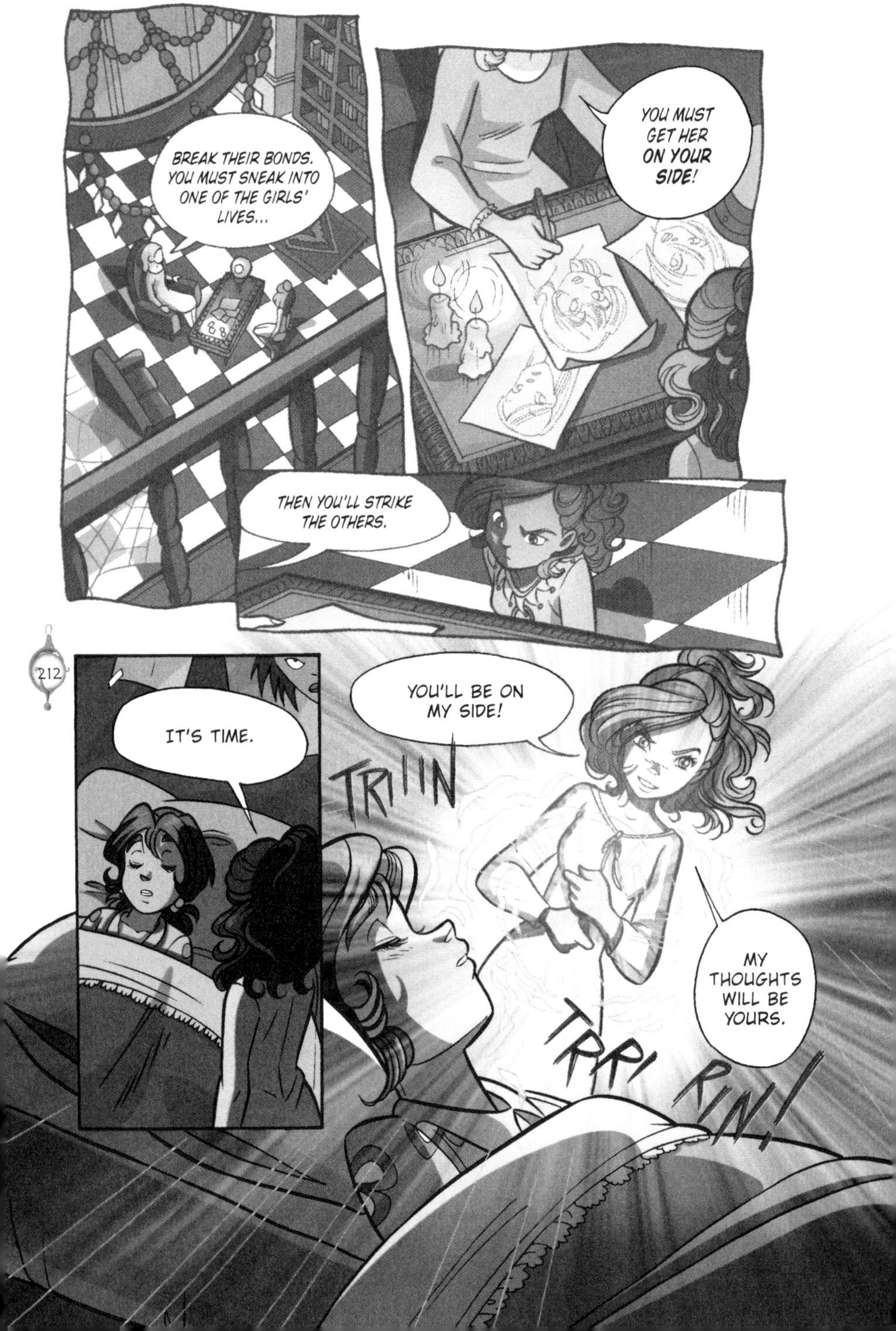
BREAK THEIR BONDS. YOU MUST SNEAK INTO ONE OF THE GIRLS' LIVES...
YOU MUST GET HER ON YOUR SIDE!
THEN YOU'LL STRIKE THE OTHERS.
IT'S TIME.
YOU'LL BE ON MY SIDE!
TRIIN
MY THOUGHTS WILL BE YOURS.
TRRI RIN!

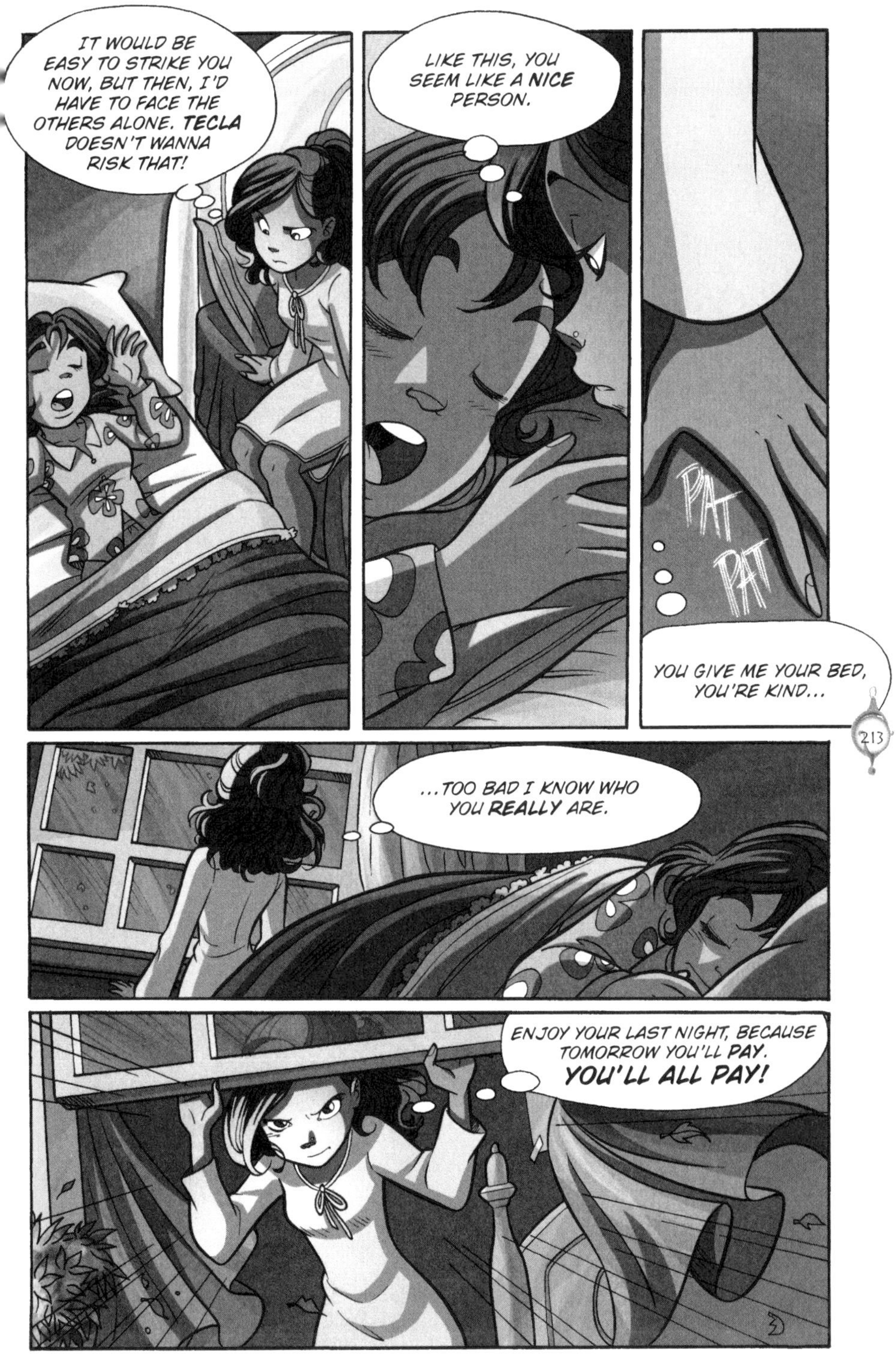
IT WOULD BE EASY TO STRIKE YOU NOW, BUT THEN, I'D HAVE TO FACE THE OTHERS ALONE. TECLA DOESN'T WANNA RISK THAT!
LIKE THIS, YOU SEEM LIKE A NICE PERSON.
PAT PAT
YOU GIVE ME YOUR BED, YOU'RE KIND...
...TOO BAD I KNOW WHO YOU REALLY ARE.
ENJOY YOUR LAST NIGHT, BECAUSE TOMORROW YOU'LL PAY. YOU'LL ALL PAY!

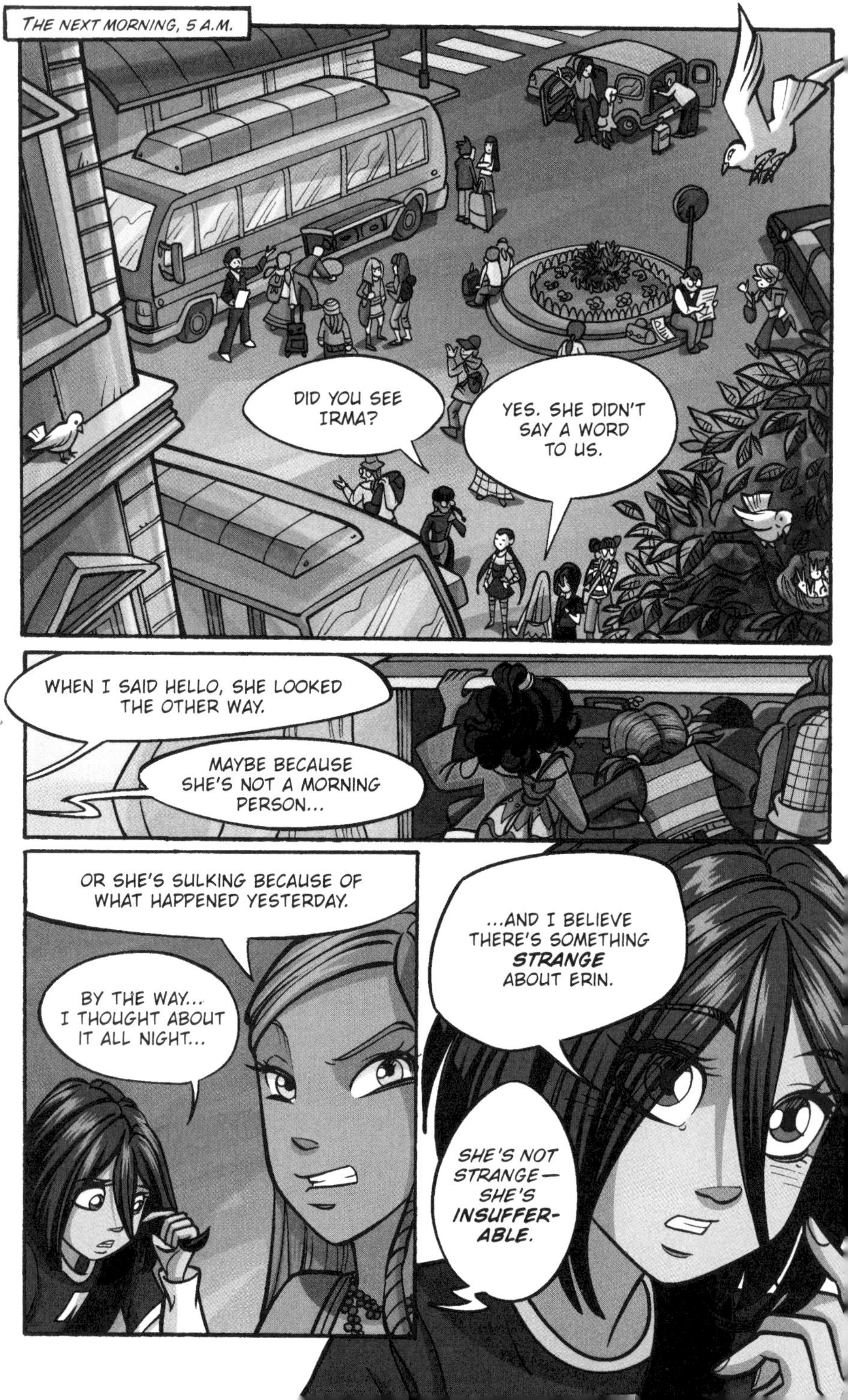
THE NEXT MORNING, 5 A.M.
DID YOU SEE IRMA?
YES. SHE DIDN'T SAY A WORD TO US.
WHEN I SAID HELLO, SHE LOOKED THE OTHER WAY.
MAYBE BECAUSE SHE'S NOT A MORNING PERSON...
OR SHE'S SULKING BECAUSE OF WHAT HAPPENED YESTERDAY.
BY THE WAY... I THOUGHT ABOUT IT ALL NIGHT...
...AND I BELIEVE THERE'S SOMETHING **STRANGE** ABOUT ERIN.
SHE'S NOT STRANGE—SHE'S ***INSUFFER-ABLE.***

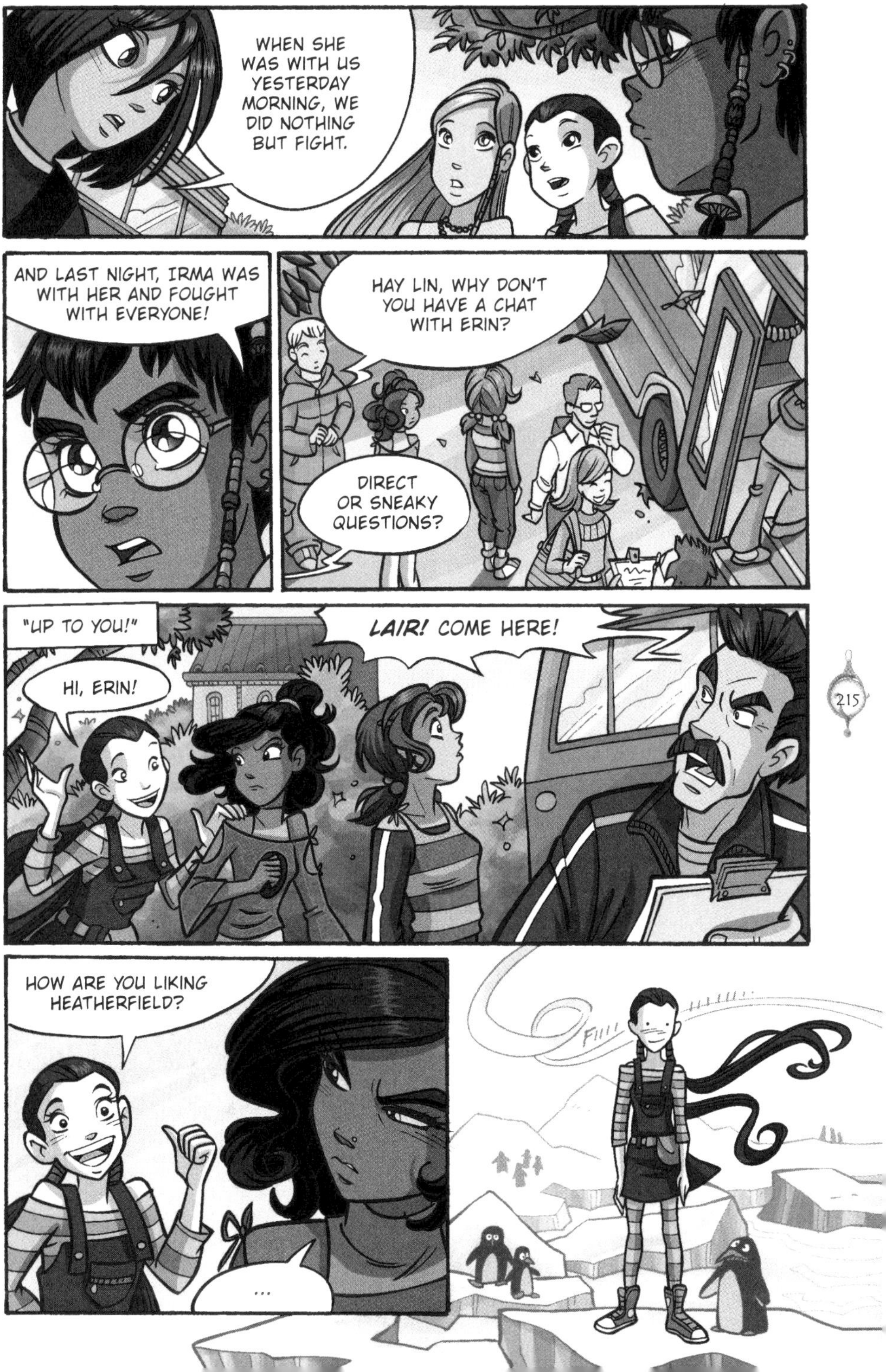
WHEN SHE WAS WITH US YESTERDAY MORNING, WE DID NOTHING BUT FIGHT.
AND LAST NIGHT, IRMA WAS WITH HER AND FOUGHT WITH EVERYONE!
HAY LIN, WHY DON'T YOU HAVE A CHAT WITH ERIN?
DIRECT OR SNEAKY QUESTIONS?
"UP TO YOU!"
LAIR! COME HERE!
HI, ERIN!
HOW ARE YOU LIKING HEATHERFIELD?
...

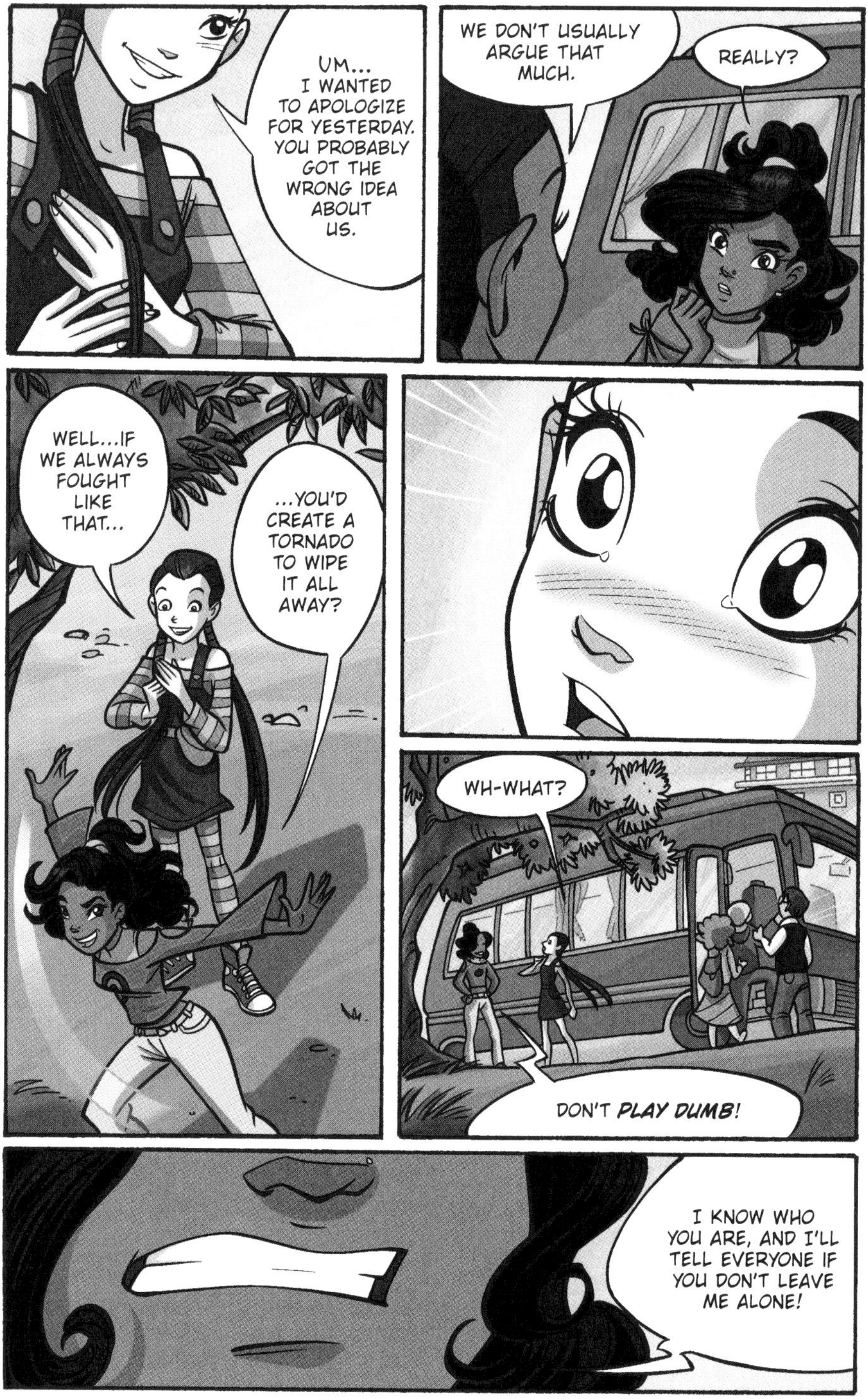
UM... I WANTED TO APOLOGIZE FOR YESTERDAY. YOU PROBABLY GOT THE WRONG IDEA ABOUT US.
WE DON'T USUALLY ARGUE THAT MUCH.
REALLY?
WELL...IF WE ALWAYS FOUGHT LIKE THAT...
...YOU'D CREATE A TORNADO TO WIPE IT ALL AWAY?
WH-WHAT?
DON'T PLAY DUMB!
I KNOW WHO YOU ARE, AND I'LL TELL EVERYONE IF YOU DON'T LEAVE ME ALONE!

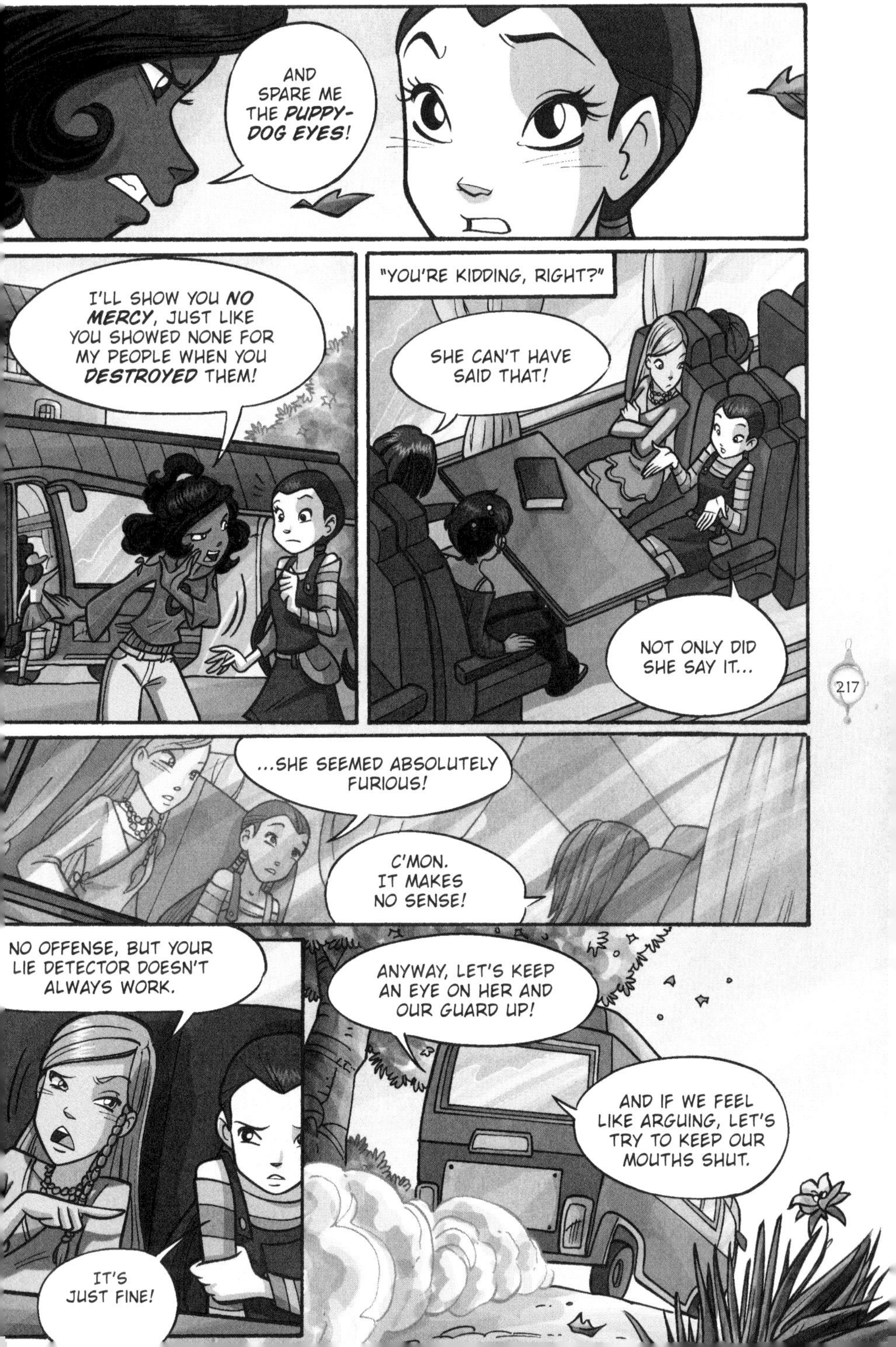
AND SPARE ME THE PUPPY-DOG EYES!
I'LL SHOW YOU NO MERCY, JUST LIKE YOU SHOWED NONE FOR MY PEOPLE WHEN YOU DESTROYED THEM!
"YOU'RE KIDDING, RIGHT?"
SHE CAN'T HAVE SAID THAT!
NOT ONLY DID SHE SAY IT...
...SHE SEEMED ABSOLUTELY FURIOUS!
C'MON. IT MAKES NO SENSE!
NO OFFENSE, BUT YOUR LIE DETECTOR DOESN'T ALWAYS WORK.
IT'S JUST FINE!
ANYWAY, LET'S KEEP AN EYE ON HER AND OUR GUARD UP!
AND IF WE FEEL LIKE ARGUING, LET'S TRY TO KEEP OUR MOUTHS SHUT.

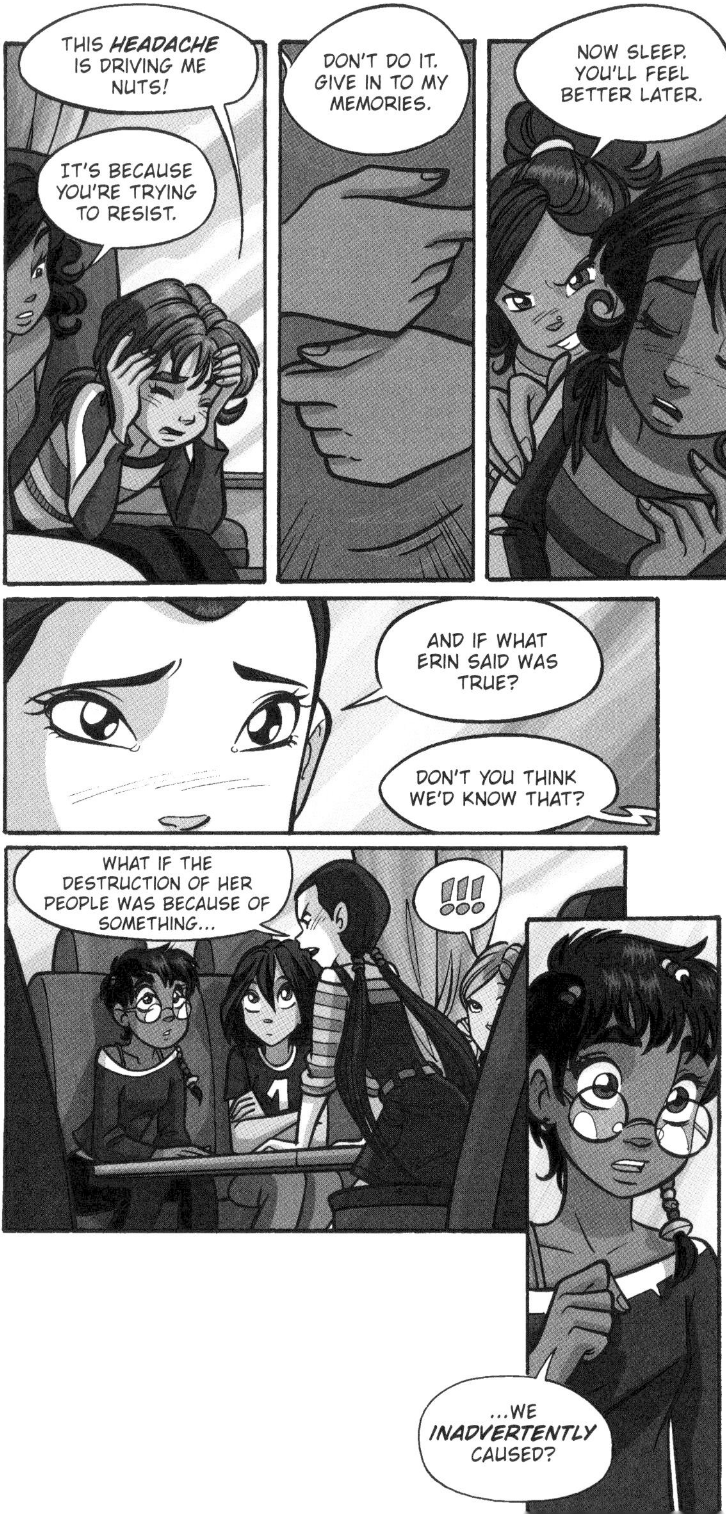
THIS HEADACHE IS DRIVING ME NUTS!
IT'S BECAUSE YOU'RE TRYING TO RESIST.
DON'T DO IT. GIVE IN TO MY MEMORIES.
NOW SLEEP. YOU'LL FEEL BETTER LATER.
AND IF WHAT ERIN SAID WAS TRUE?
DON'T YOU THINK WE'D KNOW THAT?
WHAT IF THE DESTRUCTION OF HER PEOPLE WAS BECAUSE OF SOMETHING...
!!!
...WE INADVERTENTLY CAUSED?

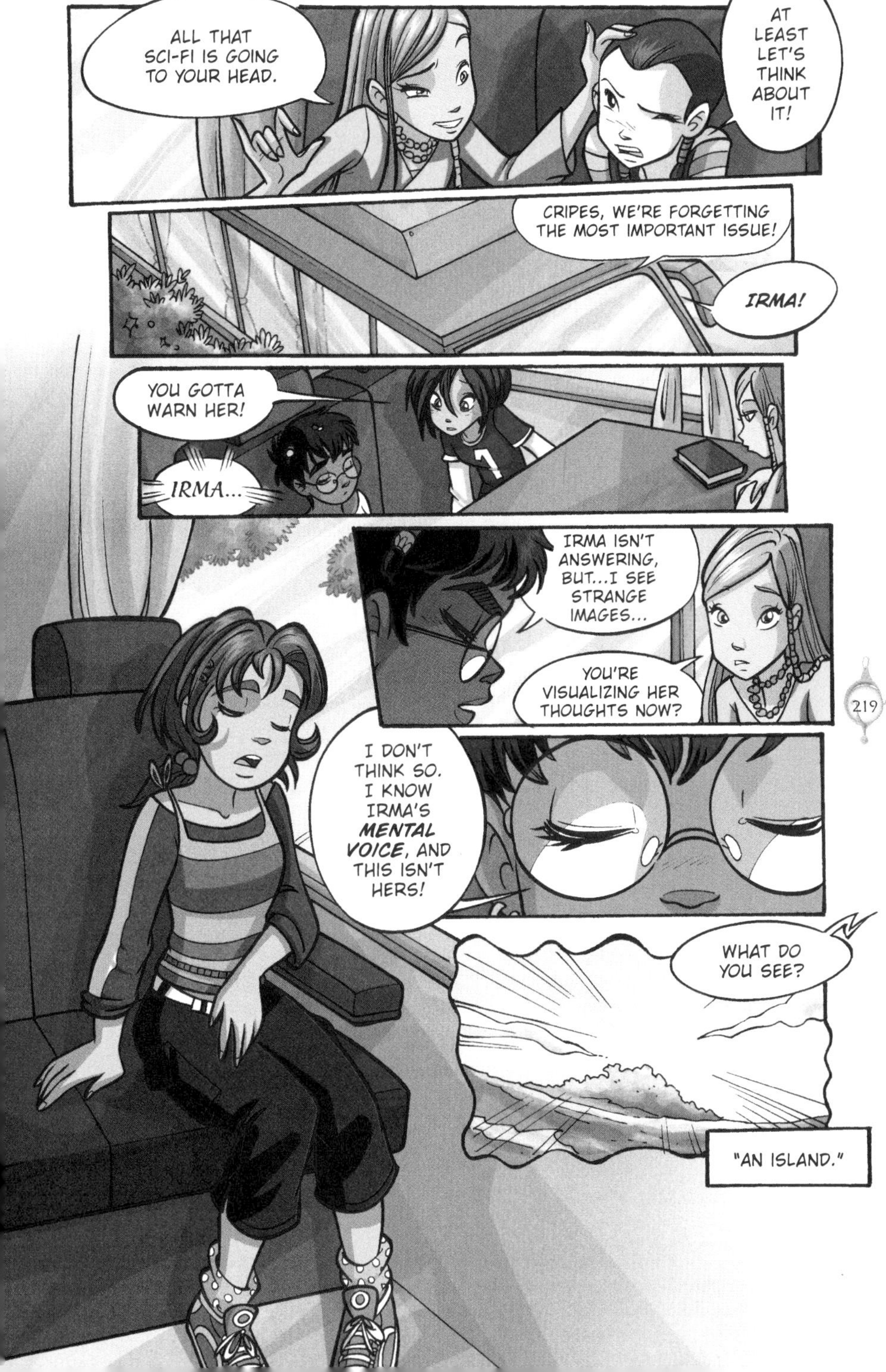

ALL THAT SCI-FI IS GOING TO YOUR HEAD.
AT LEAST LET'S THINK ABOUT IT!
CRIPES, WE'RE FORGETTING THE MOST IMPORTANT ISSUE!
IRMA!
YOU GOTTA WARN HER!
IRMA...
IRMA ISN'T ANSWERING, BUT...I SEE STRANGE IMAGES...
YOU'RE VISUALIZING HER THOUGHTS NOW?
I DON'T THINK SO. I KNOW IRMA'S MENTAL VOICE, AND THIS ISN'T HERS!
WHAT DO YOU SEE?
"AN ISLAND."

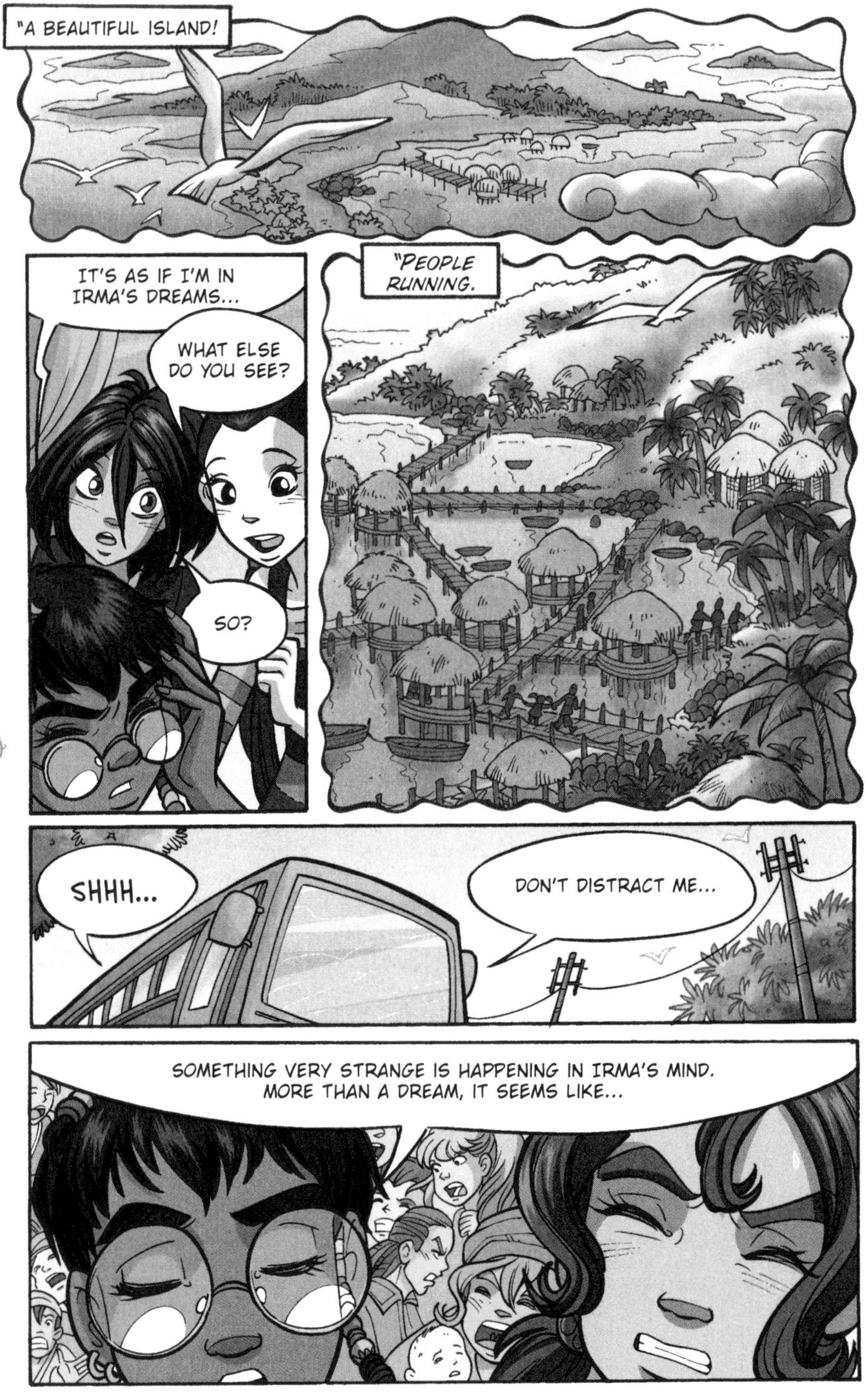
"A BEAUTIFUL ISLAND!
IT'S AS IF I'M IN IRMA'S DREAMS...
WHAT ELSE DO YOU SEE?
SO?
"PEOPLE RUNNING.
SHHH...
DON'T DISTRACT ME...
SOMETHING VERY STRANGE IS HAPPENING IN IRMA'S MIND. MORE THAN A DREAM, IT SEEMS LIKE...

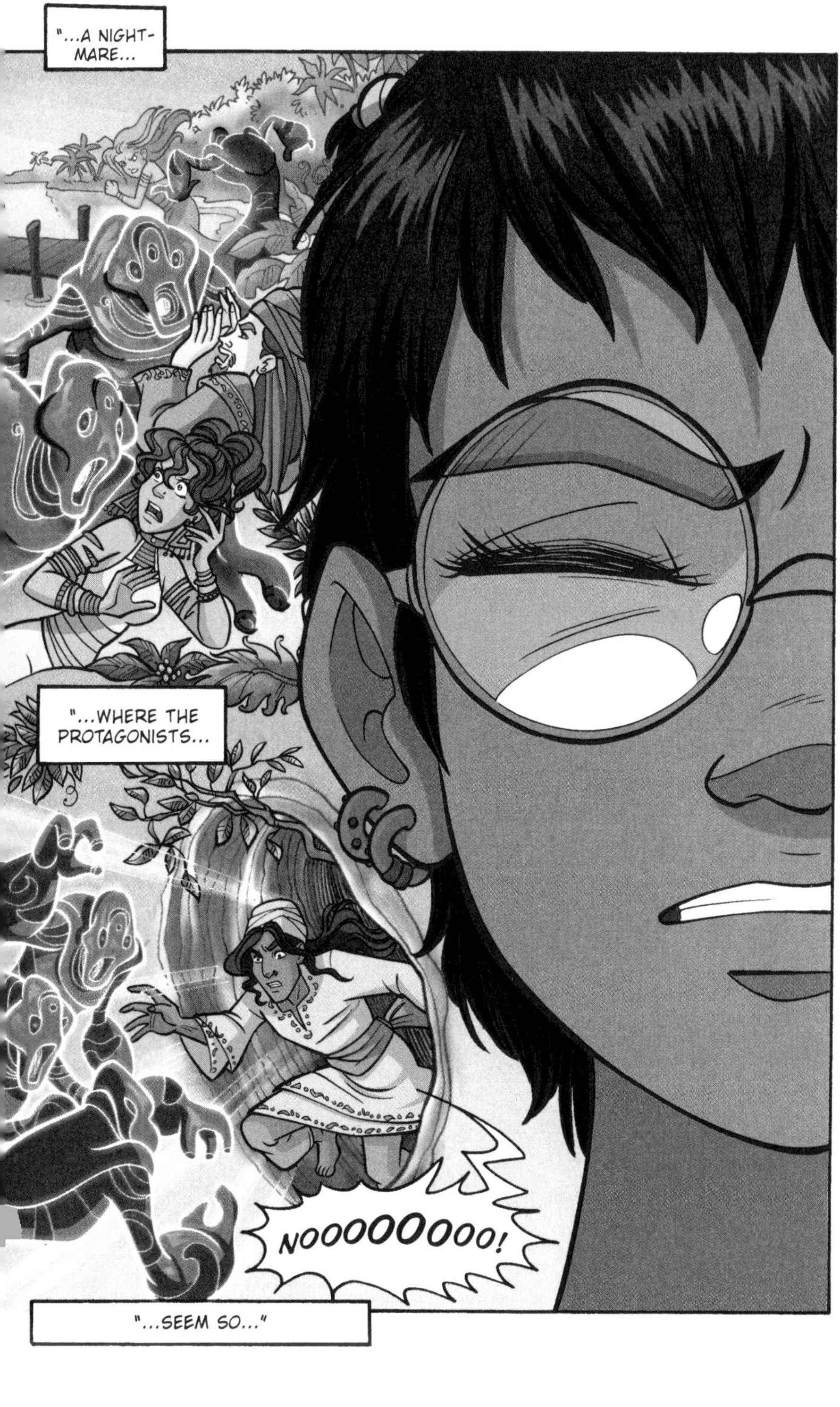
"...A NIGHT-MARE...
"...WHERE THE PROTAGONISTS...
NOOOOOOOO!
"...SEEM SO..."

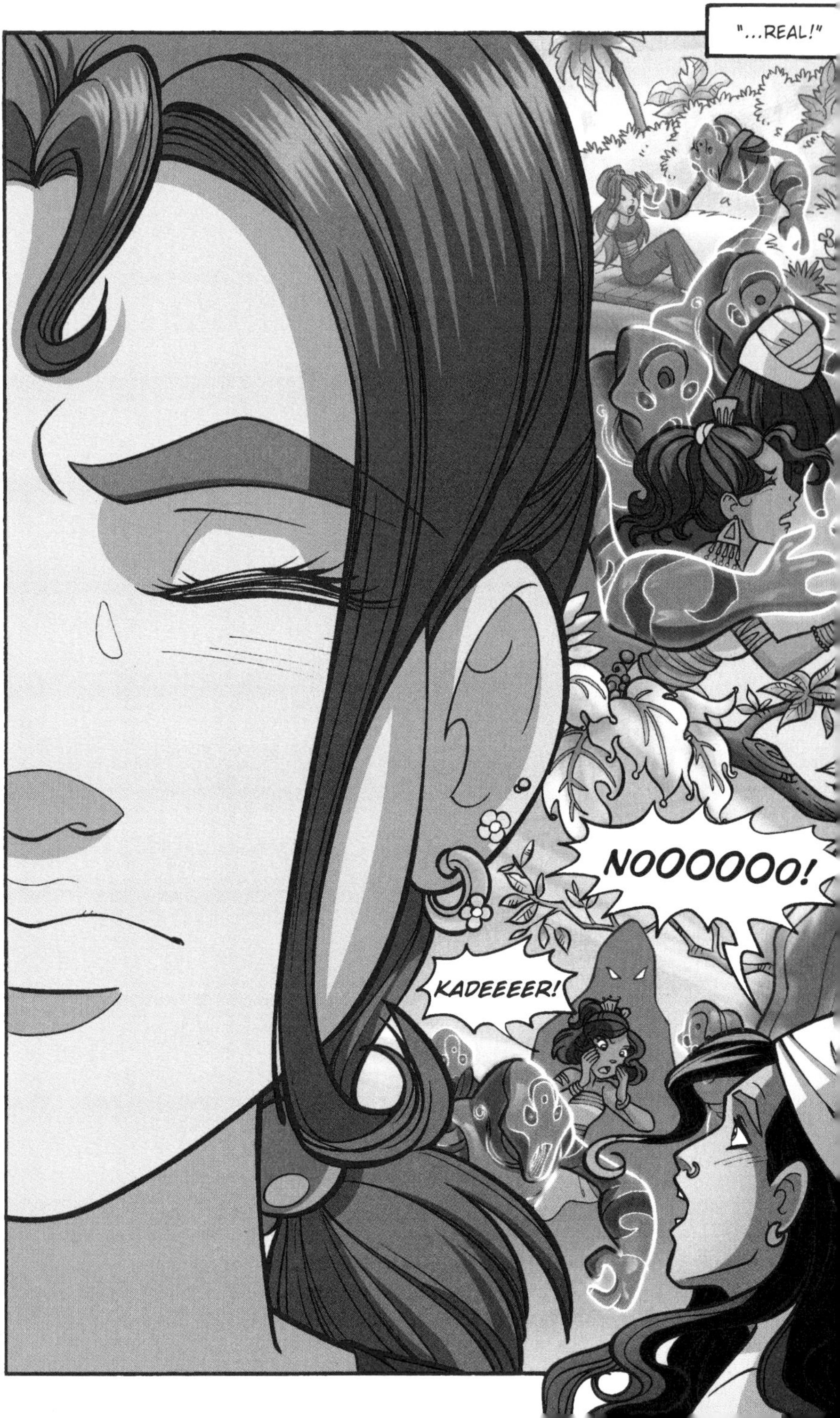
"...REAL!"
NOOOOOO!
KADEEEER!

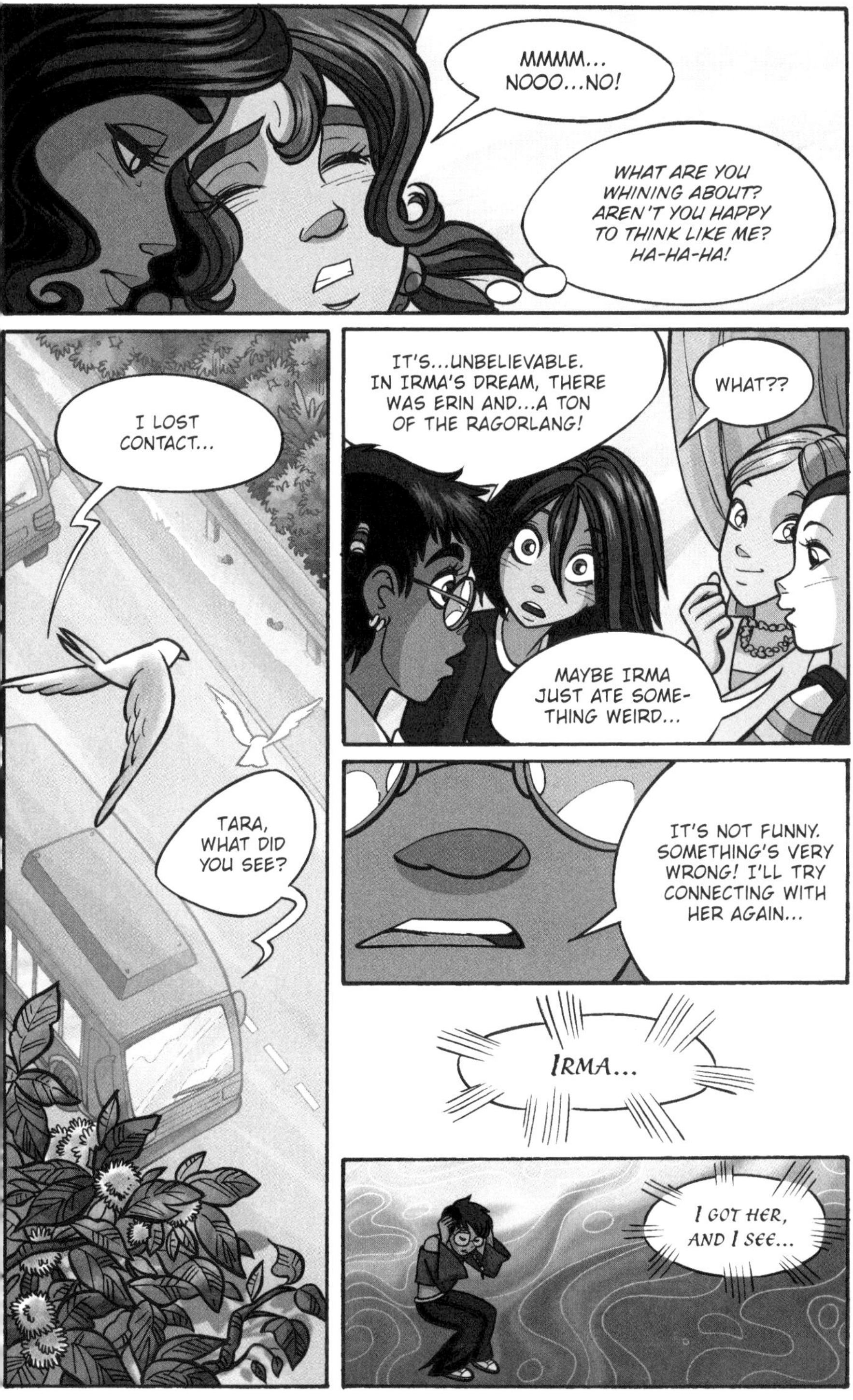
MMMM...
NOOO...NO!
WHAT ARE YOU WHINING ABOUT? AREN'T YOU HAPPY TO THINK LIKE ME? HA-HA-HA!
I LOST CONTACT...
TARA, WHAT DID YOU SEE?
IT'S...UNBELIEVABLE. IN IRMA'S DREAM, THERE WAS ERIN AND...A TON OF THE RAGORLANG!
WHAT??
MAYBE IRMA JUST ATE SOMETHING WEIRD...
IT'S NOT FUNNY. SOMETHING'S VERY WRONG! I'LL TRY CONNECTING WITH HER AGAIN...
IRMA...
I GOT HER, AND I SEE...

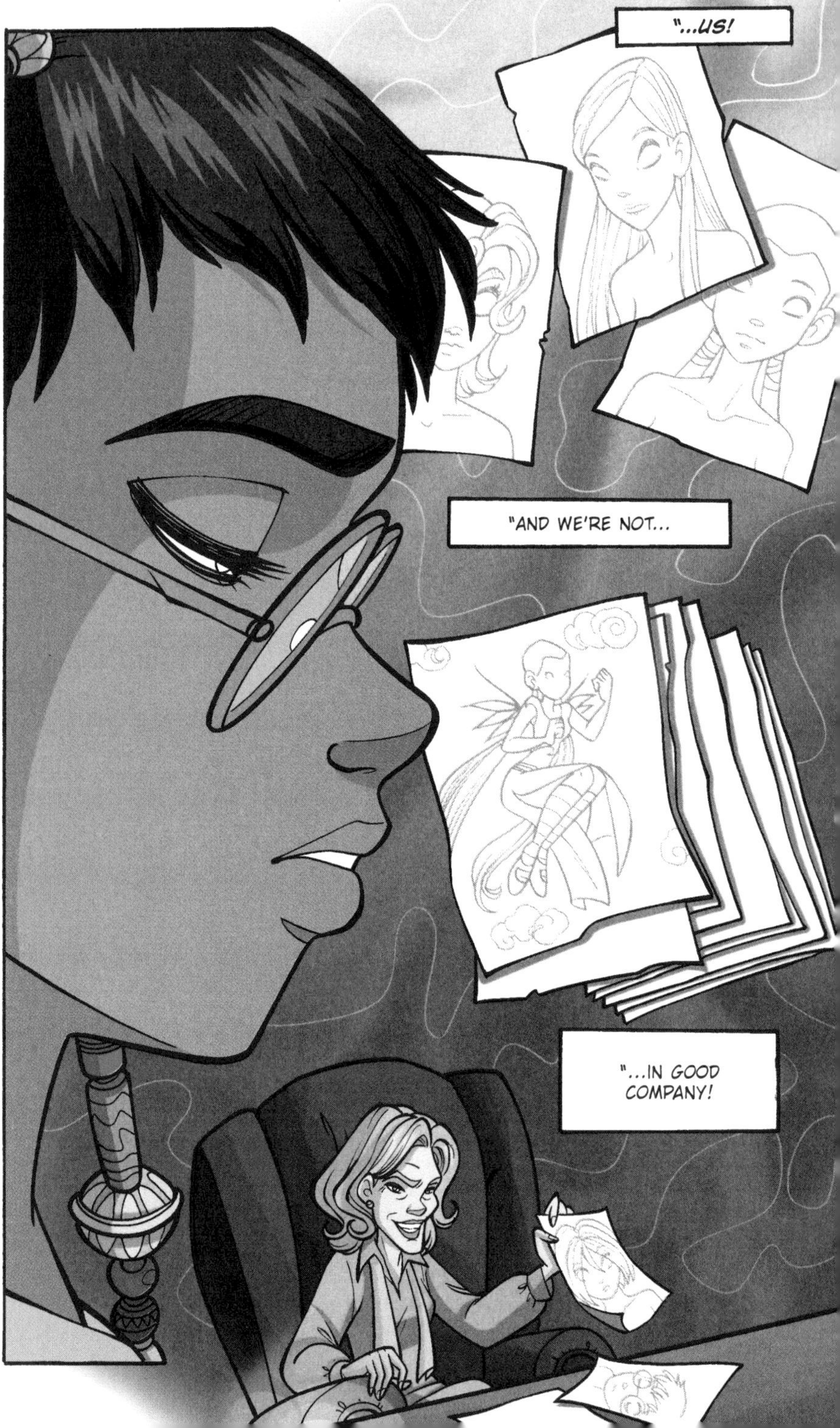
"...US!
"AND WE'RE NOT...
"...IN GOOD COMPANY!

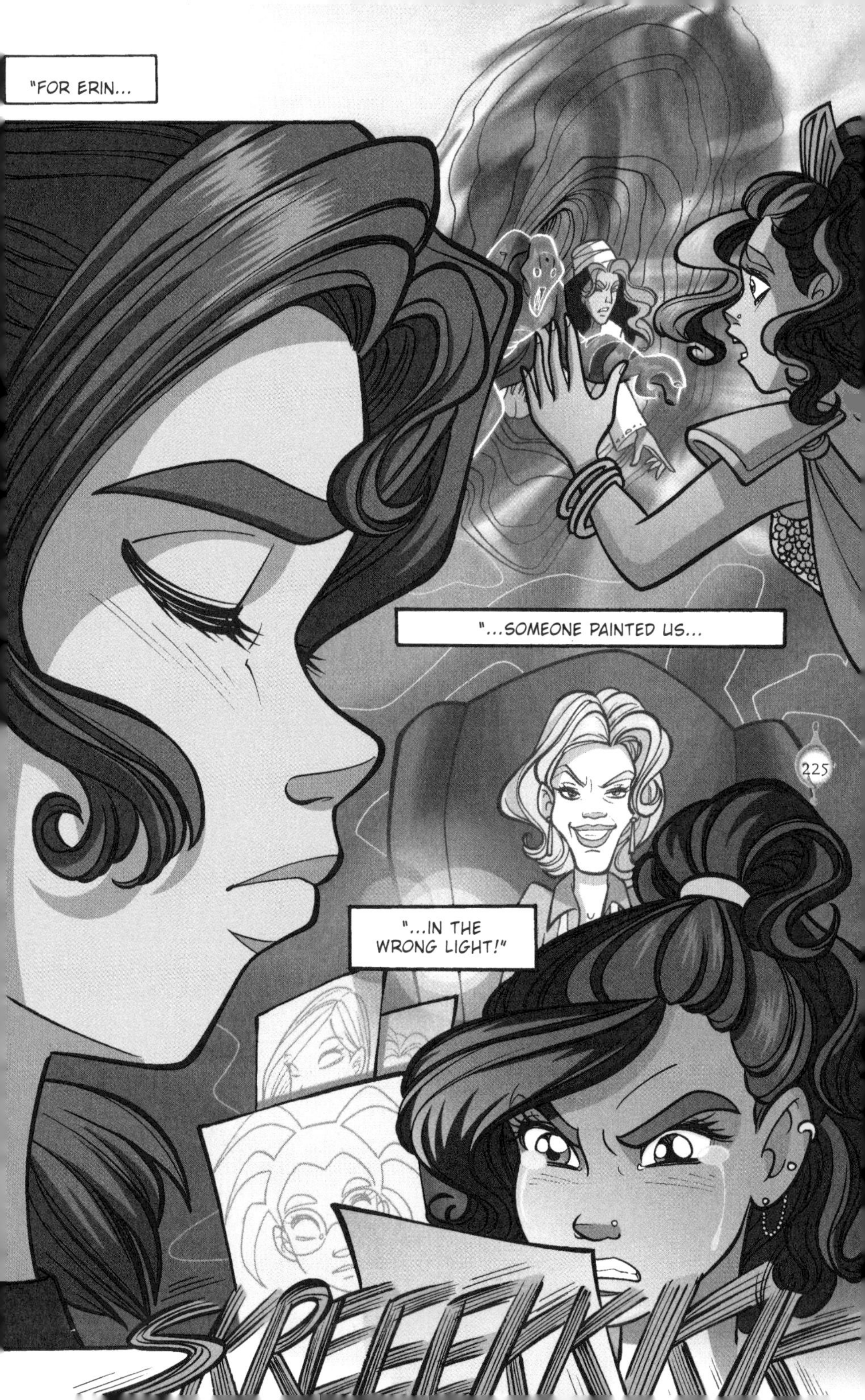
"FOR ERIN...
"...SOMEONE PAINTED US...
"...IN THE WRONG LIGHT!"
SKREEEKKKK

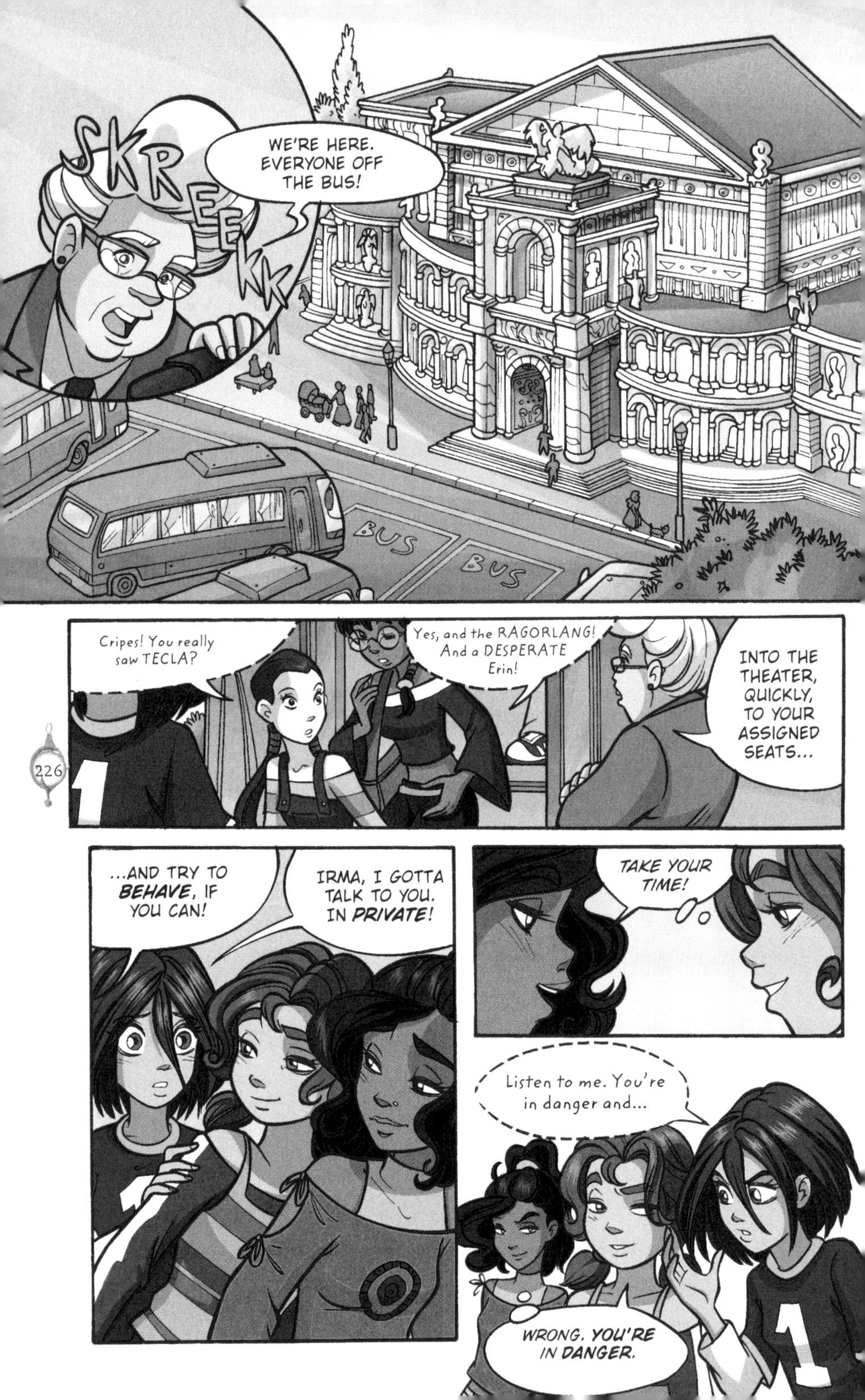
SKREEEKK
WE'RE HERE. EVERYONE OFF THE BUS!
BUS
BUS
Cripes! You really saw TECLA?
Yes, and the RAGORLANG! And a DESPERATE Erin!
INTO THE THEATER, QUICKLY, TO YOUR ASSIGNED SEATS...
...AND TRY TO BEHAVE, IF YOU CAN!
IRMA, I GOTTA TALK TO YOU. IN PRIVATE!
TAKE YOUR TIME!
Listen to me. You're in danger and...
WRONG. YOU'RE IN DANGER.

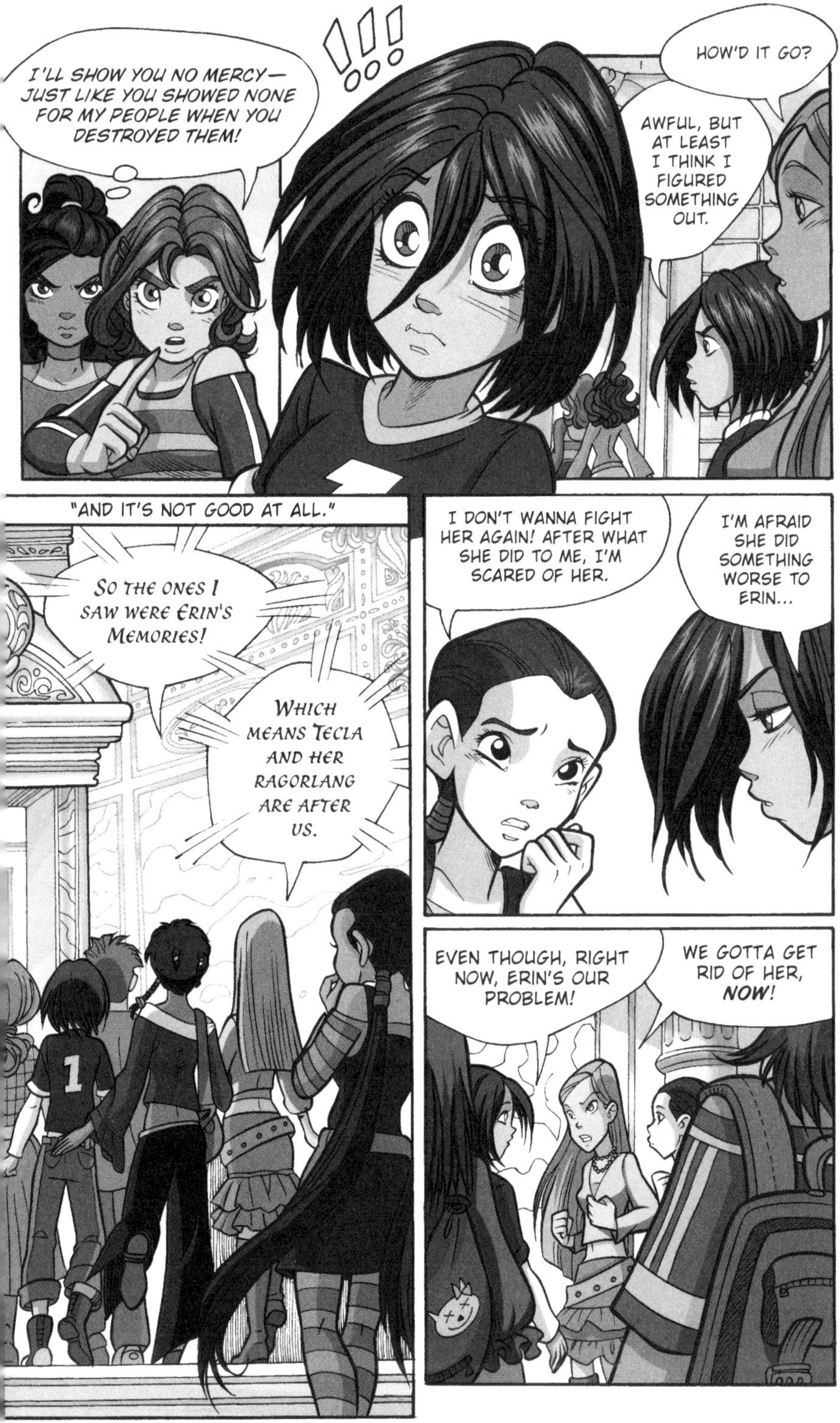

I'LL SHOW YOU NO MERCY—JUST LIKE YOU SHOWED NONE FOR MY PEOPLE WHEN YOU DESTROYED THEM!
!!!
HOW'D IT GO?
AWFUL, BUT AT LEAST I THINK I FIGURED SOMETHING OUT.
"AND IT'S NOT GOOD AT ALL."
So the ones I saw were Erin's Memories!
Which means Tecla and her Ragorlang are after us.
I DON'T WANNA FIGHT HER AGAIN! AFTER WHAT SHE DID TO ME, I'M SCARED OF HER.
I'M AFRAID SHE DID SOMETHING WORSE TO ERIN...
EVEN THOUGH, RIGHT NOW, ERIN'S OUR PROBLEM!
WE GOTTA GET RID OF HER, *NOW*!

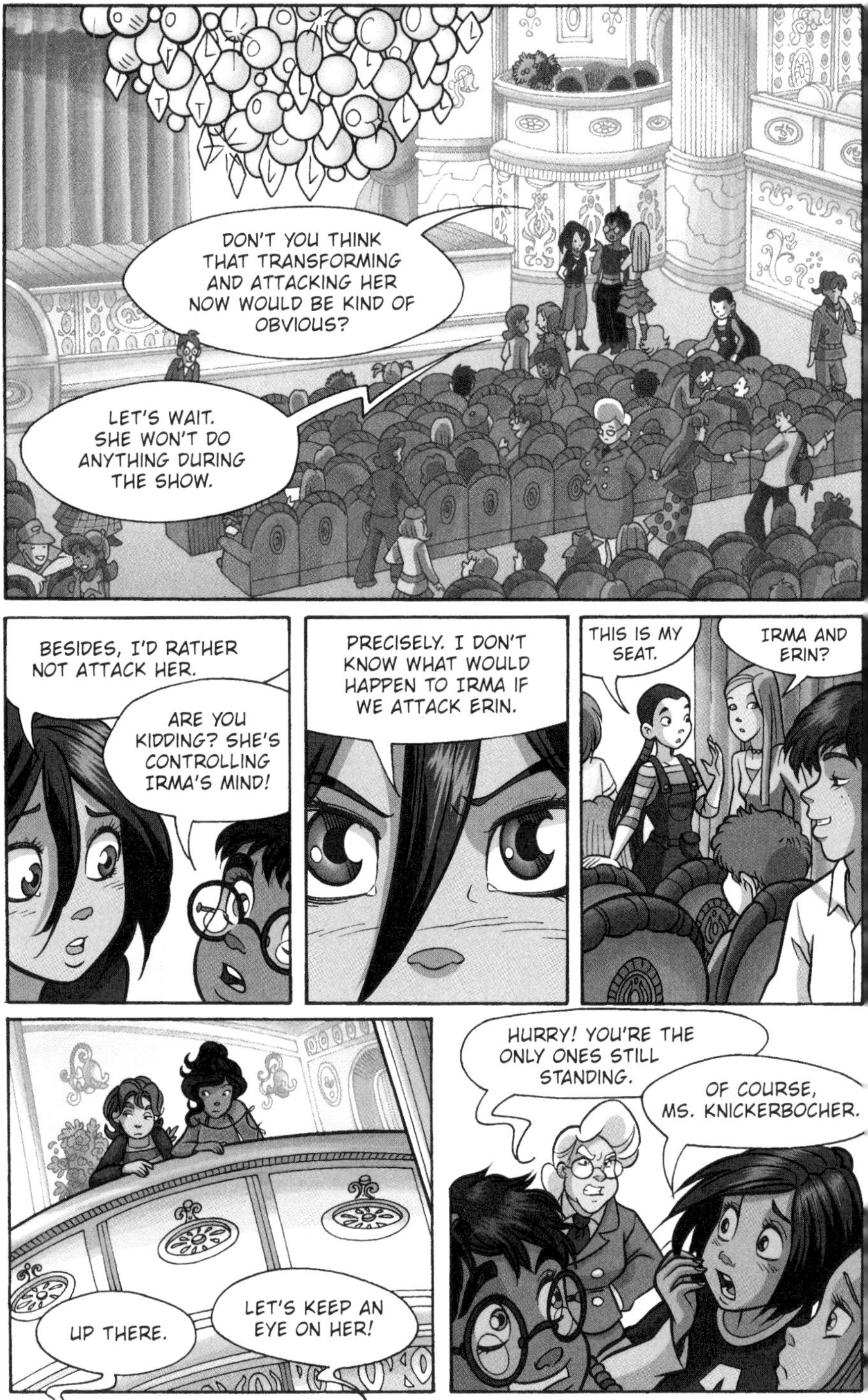
DON'T YOU THINK THAT TRANSFORMING AND ATTACKING HER NOW WOULD BE KIND OF OBVIOUS?
LET'S WAIT. SHE WON'T DO ANYTHING DURING THE SHOW.
BESIDES, I'D RATHER NOT ATTACK HER.
ARE YOU KIDDING? SHE'S CONTROLLING IRMA'S MIND!
PRECISELY. I DON'T KNOW WHAT WOULD HAPPEN TO IRMA IF WE ATTACK ERIN.
THIS IS MY SEAT.
IRMA AND ERIN?
UP THERE.
LET'S KEEP AN EYE ON HER!
HURRY! YOU'RE THE ONLY ONES STILL STANDING.
OF COURSE, MS. KNICKERBOCHER.

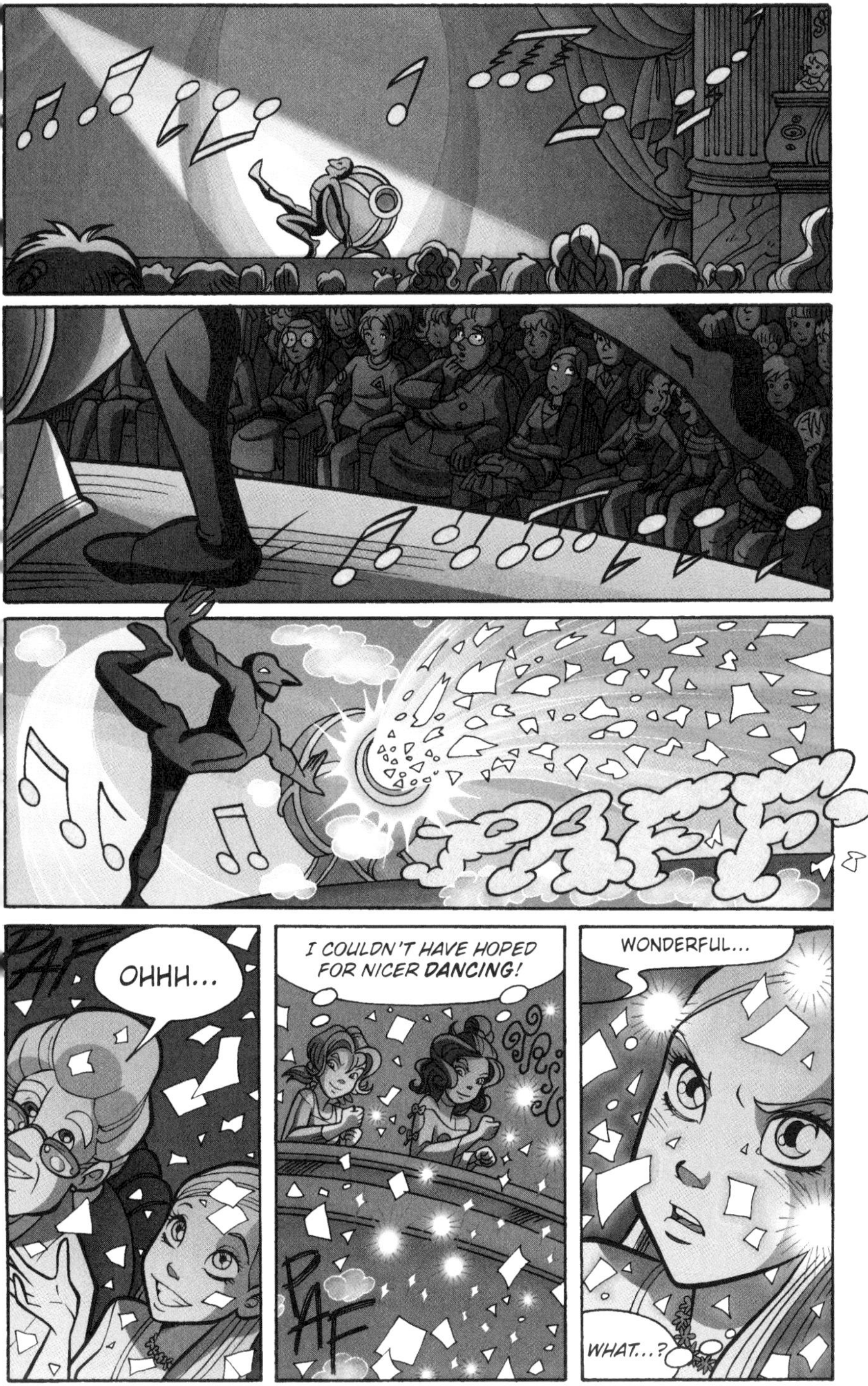
PAFF
PAF
OHHH...
I COULDN'T HAVE HOPED FOR NICER DANCING!
PAF
WONDERFUL...
WHAT...?

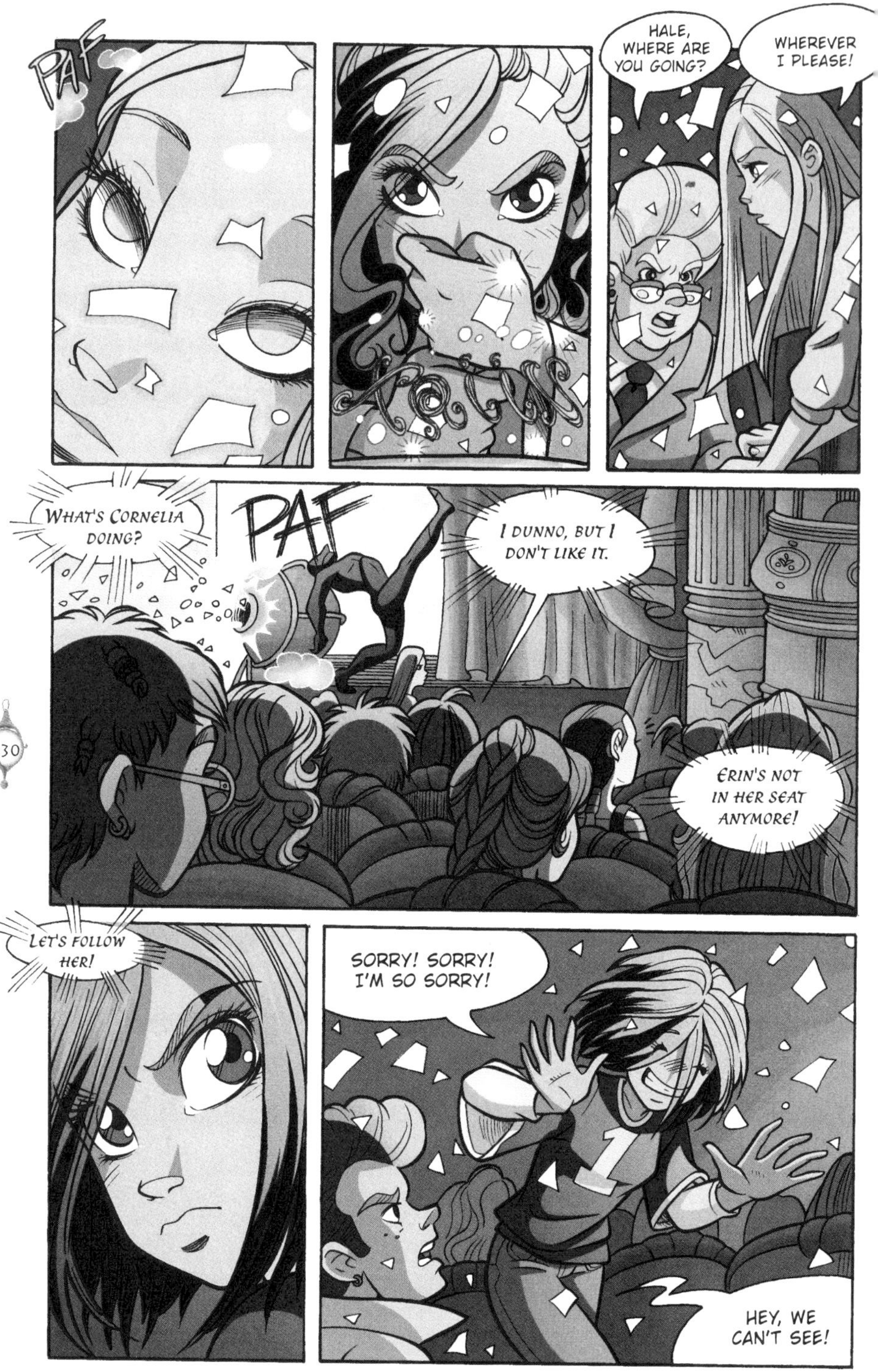
PAF
HALE, WHERE ARE YOU GOING?
WHEREVER I PLEASE!
WHAT'S CORNELIA DOING?
PAF
I DUNNO, BUT I DON'T LIKE IT.
ERIN'S NOT IN HER SEAT ANYMORE!
LET'S FOLLOW HER!
SORRY! SORRY! I'M SO SORRY!
HEY, WE CAN'T SEE!

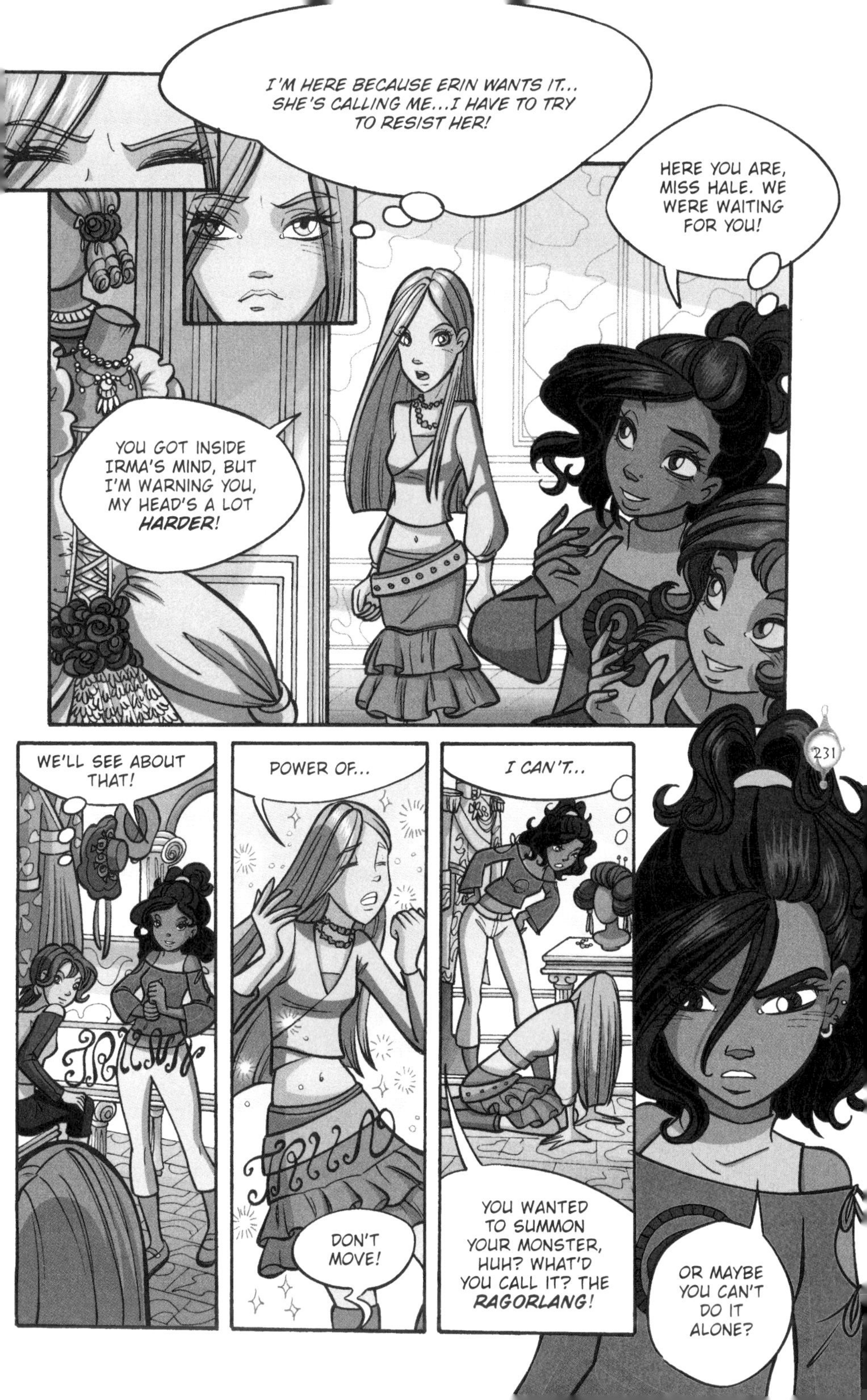
I'M HERE BECAUSE ERIN WANTS IT... SHE'S CALLING ME...I HAVE TO TRY TO RESIST HER!
HERE YOU ARE, MISS HALE. WE WERE WAITING FOR YOU!
YOU GOT INSIDE IRMA'S MIND, BUT I'M WARNING YOU, MY HEAD'S A LOT **HARDER**!
WE'LL SEE ABOUT THAT!
POWER OF...
DON'T MOVE!
I CAN'T...
YOU WANTED TO SUMMON YOUR MONSTER, HUH? WHAT'D YOU CALL IT? THE **RAGORLANG**!
OR MAYBE YOU CAN'T DO IT ALONE?

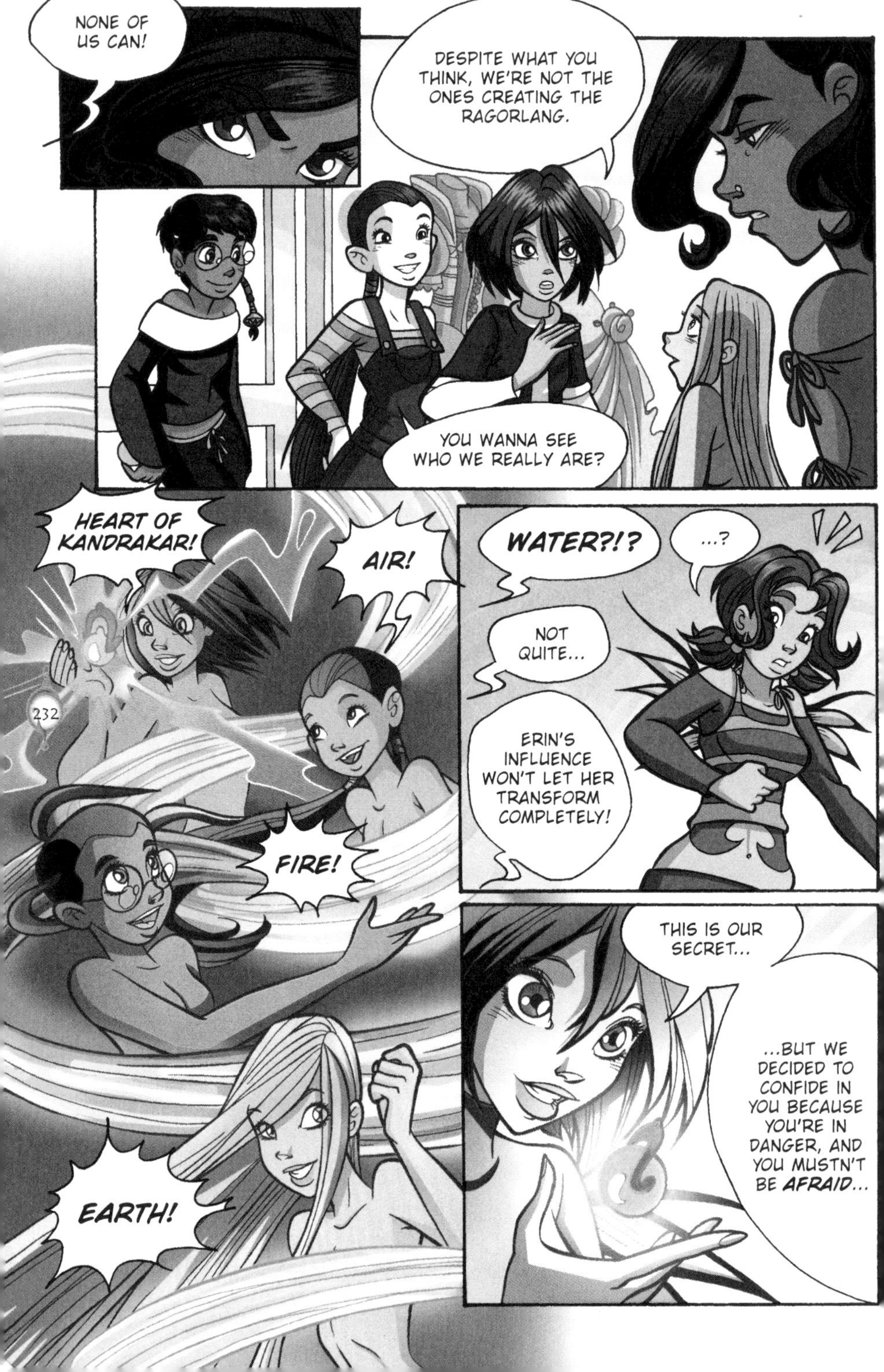
NONE OF US CAN!
DESPITE WHAT YOU THINK, WE'RE NOT THE ONES CREATING THE RAGORLANG.
YOU WANNA SEE WHO WE REALLY ARE?
HEART OF KANDRAKAR!
AIR!
FIRE!
EARTH!
WATER?!?
...?
NOT QUITE...
ERIN'S INFLUENCE WON'T LET HER TRANSFORM COMPLETELY!
THIS IS OUR SECRET...
...BUT WE DECIDED TO CONFIDE IN YOU BECAUSE YOU'RE IN DANGER, AND YOU MUSTN'T BE AFRAID...

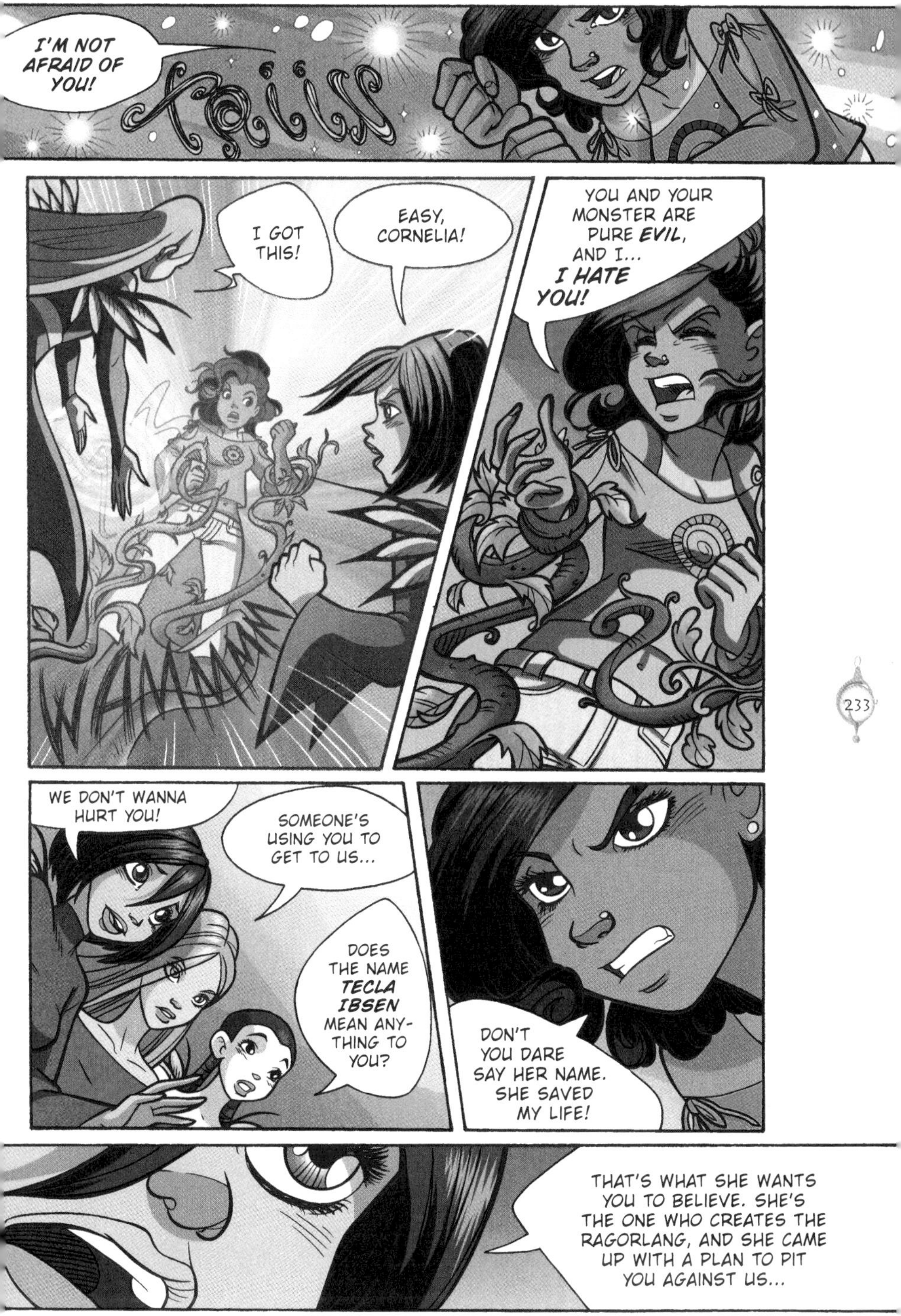

I'M NOT AFRAID OF YOU!
TRILL
I GOT THIS!
EASY, CORNELIA!
WAMMM
YOU AND YOUR MONSTER ARE PURE EVIL, AND I... I HATE YOU!
WE DON'T WANNA HURT YOU!
SOMEONE'S USING YOU TO GET TO US...
DOES THE NAME TECLA IBSEN MEAN ANYTHING TO YOU?
DON'T YOU DARE SAY HER NAME. SHE SAVED MY LIFE!
THAT'S WHAT SHE WANTS YOU TO BELIEVE. SHE'S THE ONE WHO CREATES THE RAGORLANG, AND SHE CAME UP WITH A PLAN TO PIT YOU AGAINST US...

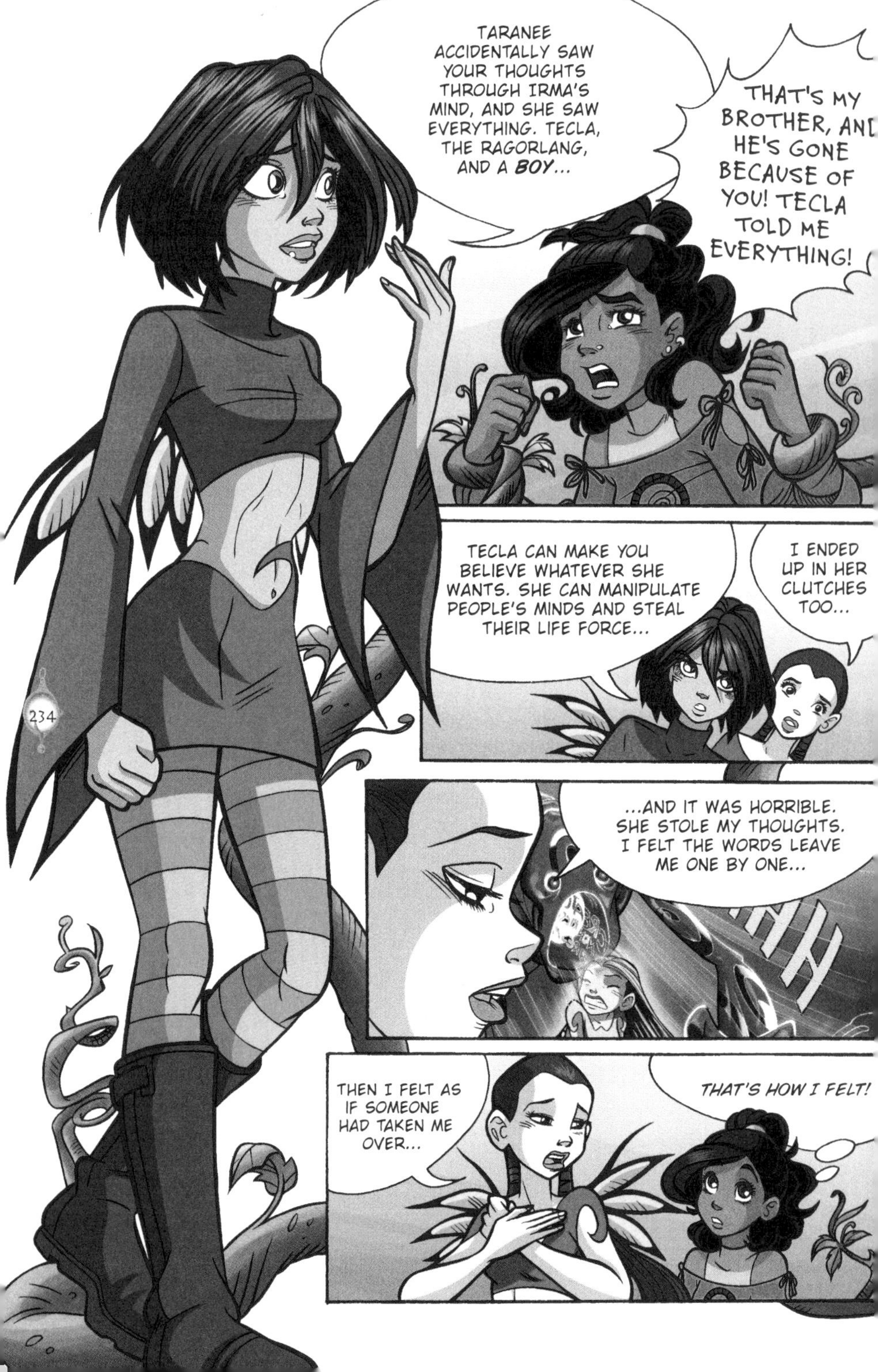
TARANEE ACCIDENTALLY SAW YOUR THOUGHTS THROUGH IRMA'S MIND, AND SHE SAW EVERYTHING. TECLA, THE RAGORLANG, AND A *BOY*...
THAT'S MY BROTHER, AND HE'S GONE BECAUSE OF YOU! TECLA TOLD ME EVERYTHING!
TECLA CAN MAKE YOU BELIEVE WHATEVER SHE WANTS. SHE CAN MANIPULATE PEOPLE'S MINDS AND STEAL THEIR LIFE FORCE...
I ENDED UP IN HER CLUTCHES TOO...
...AND IT WAS HORRIBLE. SHE STOLE MY THOUGHTS. I FELT THE WORDS LEAVE ME ONE BY ONE...
THEN I FELT AS IF SOMEONE HAD TAKEN ME OVER...
THAT'S HOW I FELT!

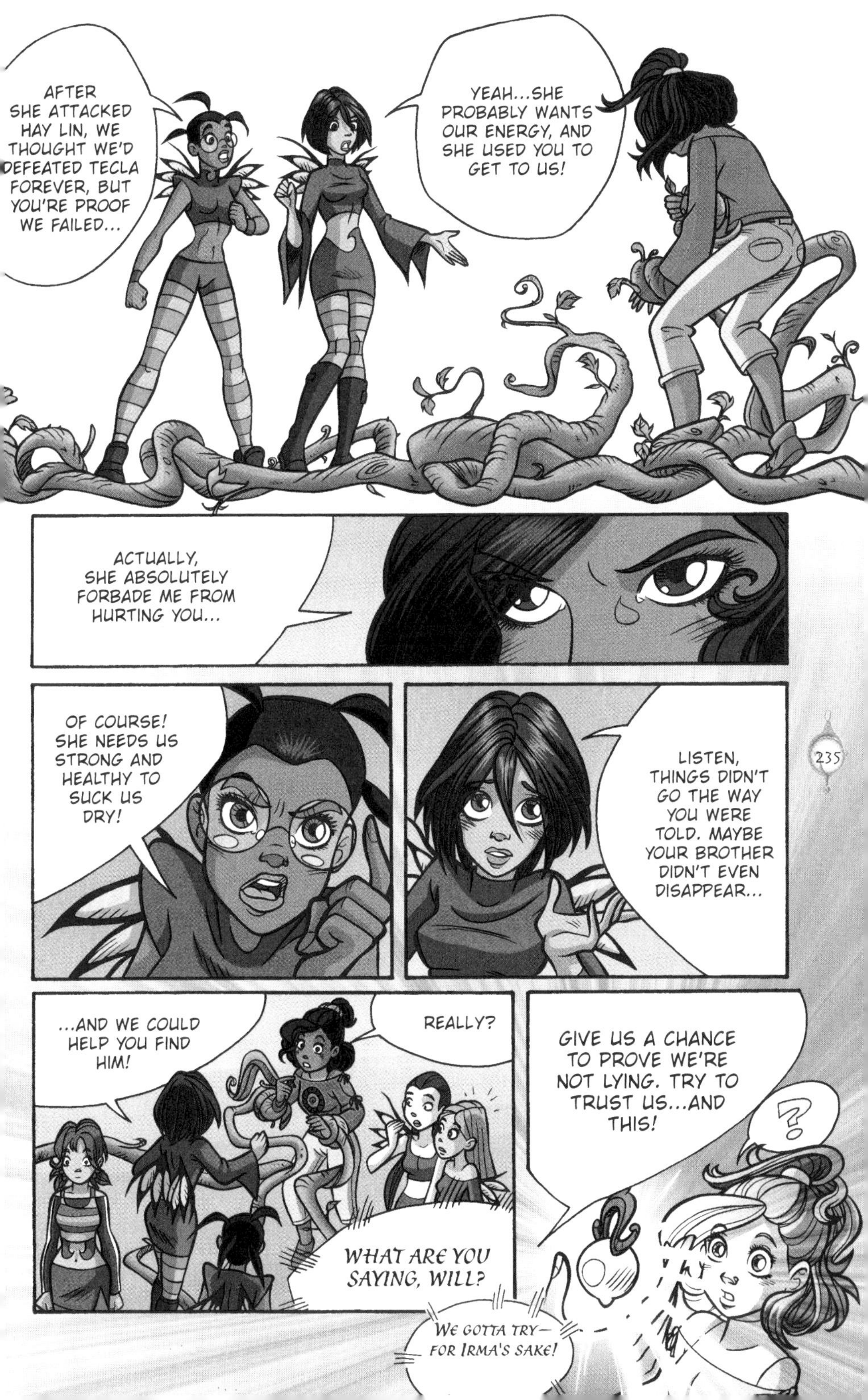
AFTER SHE ATTACKED HAY LIN, WE THOUGHT WE'D DEFEATED TECLA FOREVER, BUT YOU'RE PROOF WE FAILED...
YEAH...SHE PROBABLY WANTS OUR ENERGY, AND SHE USED YOU TO GET TO US!
ACTUALLY, SHE ABSOLUTELY FORBADE ME FROM HURTING YOU...
OF COURSE! SHE NEEDS US STRONG AND HEALTHY TO SUCK US DRY!
LISTEN, THINGS DIDN'T GO THE WAY YOU WERE TOLD. MAYBE YOUR BROTHER DIDN'T EVEN DISAPPEAR...
...AND WE COULD HELP YOU FIND HIM!
REALLY?
WHAT ARE YOU SAYING, WILL?
WE GOTTA TRY— FOR IRMA'S SAKE!
GIVE US A CHANCE TO PROVE WE'RE NOT LYING. TRY TO TRUST US...AND THIS!
?

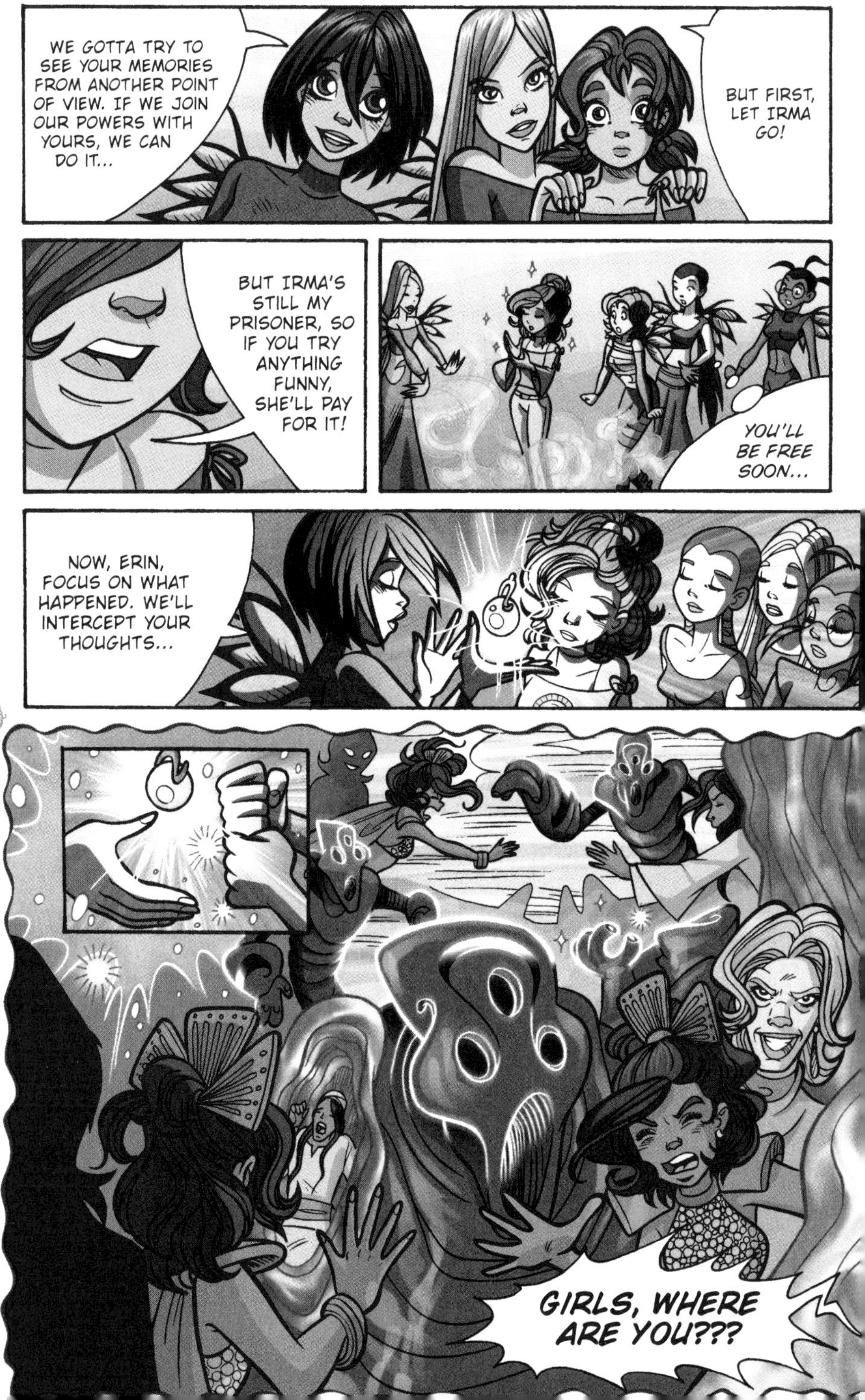
WE GOTTA TRY TO SEE YOUR MEMORIES FROM ANOTHER POINT OF VIEW. IF WE JOIN OUR POWERS WITH YOURS, WE CAN DO IT...
BUT FIRST, LET IRMA GO!
BUT IRMA'S STILL MY PRISONER, SO IF YOU TRY ANYTHING FUNNY, SHE'LL PAY FOR IT!
YOU'LL BE FREE SOON...
NOW, ERIN, FOCUS ON WHAT HAPPENED. WE'LL INTERCEPT YOUR THOUGHTS...
GIRLS, WHERE ARE YOU???

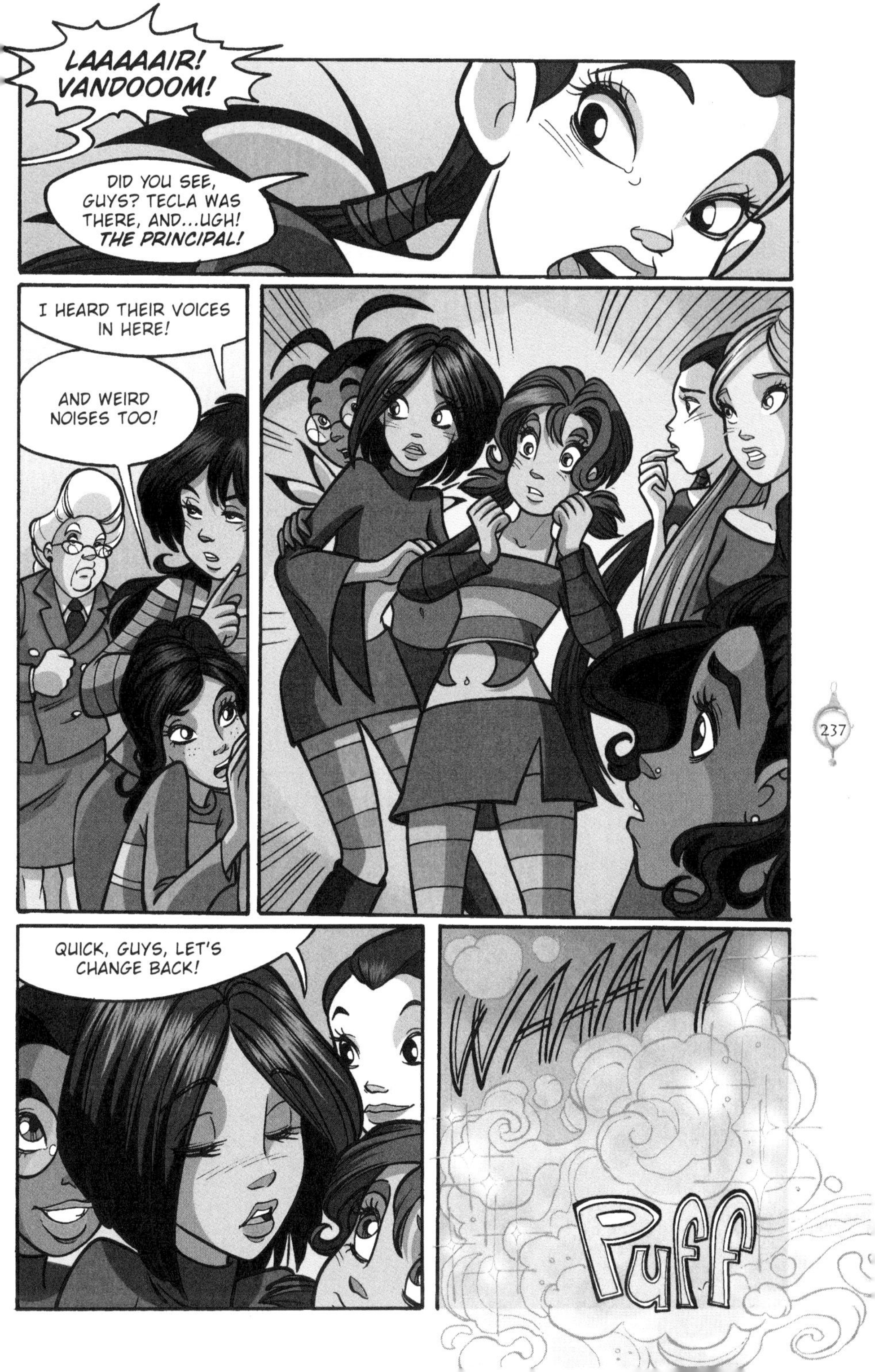
LAAAAAIR! VANDOOOM!
DID YOU SEE, GUYS? TECLA WAS THERE, AND...UGH! THE PRINCIPAL!
I HEARD THEIR VOICES IN HERE!
AND WEIRD NOISES TOO!
QUICK, GUYS, LET'S CHANGE BACK!
WAAAM
Puff

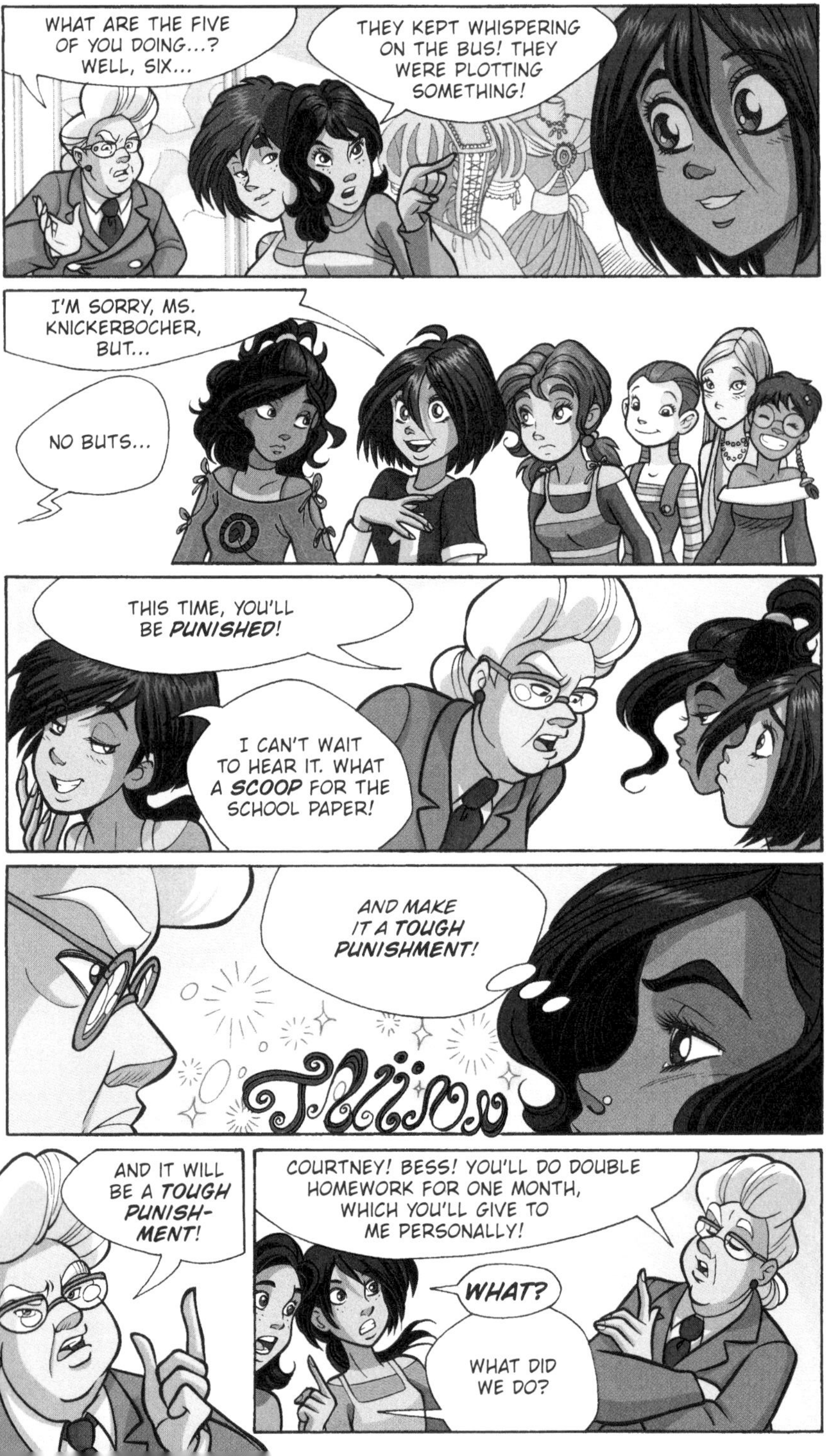
WHAT ARE THE FIVE OF YOU DOING...? WELL, SIX...
THEY KEPT WHISPERING ON THE BUS! THEY WERE PLOTTING SOMETHING!
I'M SORRY, MS. KNICKERBOCHER, BUT...
NO BUTS...
THIS TIME, YOU'LL BE PUNISHED!
I CAN'T WAIT TO HEAR IT. WHAT A SCOOP FOR THE SCHOOL PAPER!
AND MAKE IT A TOUGH PUNISHMENT!
AND IT WILL BE A TOUGH PUNISH-MENT!
COURTNEY! BESS! YOU'LL DO DOUBLE HOMEWORK FOR ONE MONTH, WHICH YOU'LL GIVE TO ME PERSONALLY!
WHAT?
WHAT DID WE DO?

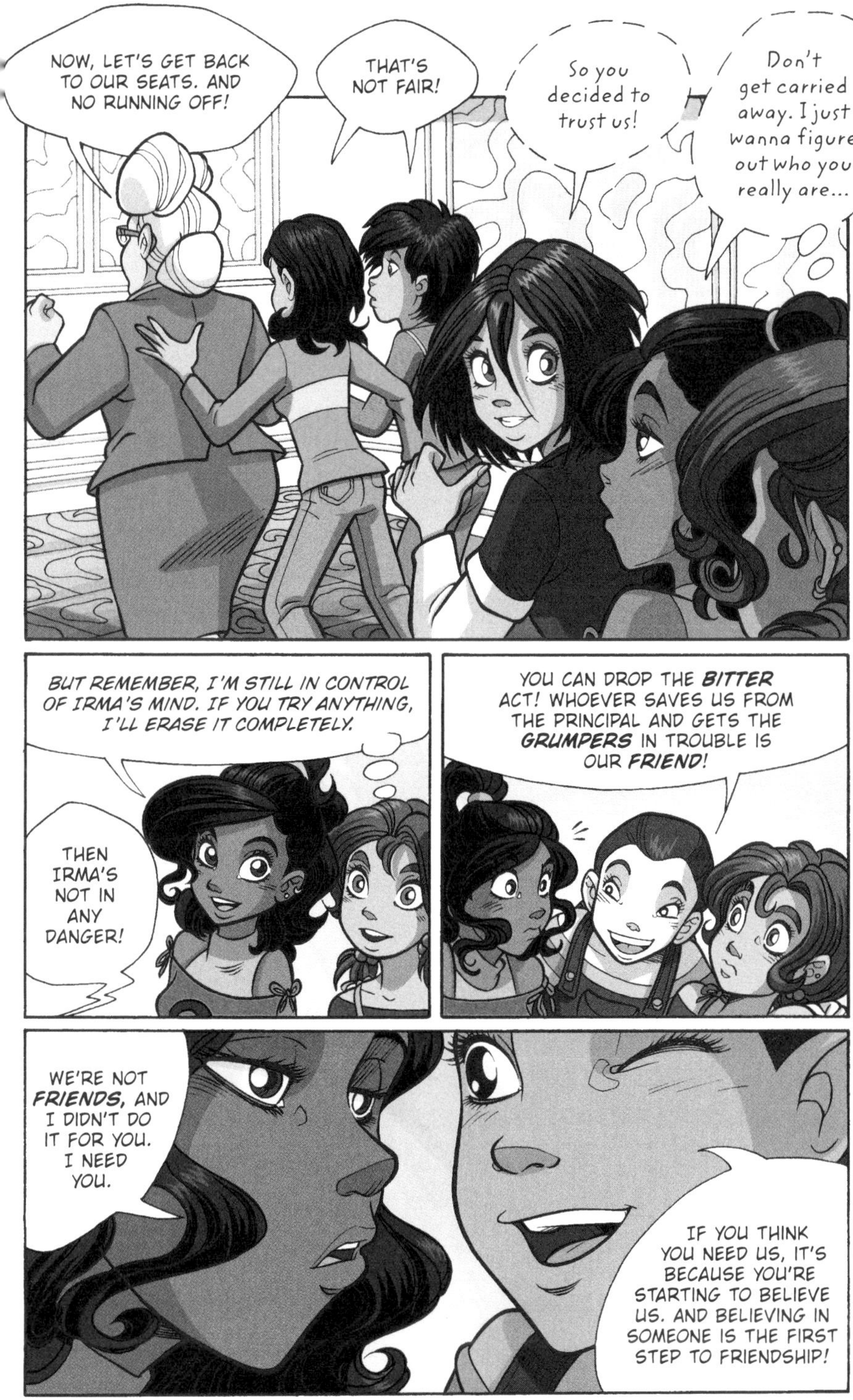
NOW, LET'S GET BACK TO OUR SEATS. AND NO RUNNING OFF!
THAT'S NOT FAIR!
So you decided to trust us!
Don't get carried away. I just wanna figure out who you really are...
BUT REMEMBER, I'M STILL IN CONTROL OF IRMA'S MIND. IF YOU TRY ANYTHING, I'LL ERASE IT COMPLETELY.
THEN IRMA'S NOT IN ANY DANGER!
YOU CAN DROP THE BITTER ACT! WHOEVER SAVES US FROM THE PRINCIPAL AND GETS THE GRUMPERS IN TROUBLE IS OUR FRIEND!
WE'RE NOT FRIENDS, AND I DIDN'T DO IT FOR YOU. I NEED YOU.
IF YOU THINK YOU NEED US, IT'S BECAUSE YOU'RE STARTING TO BELIEVE US. AND BELIEVING IN SOMEONE IS THE FIRST STEP TO FRIENDSHIP!

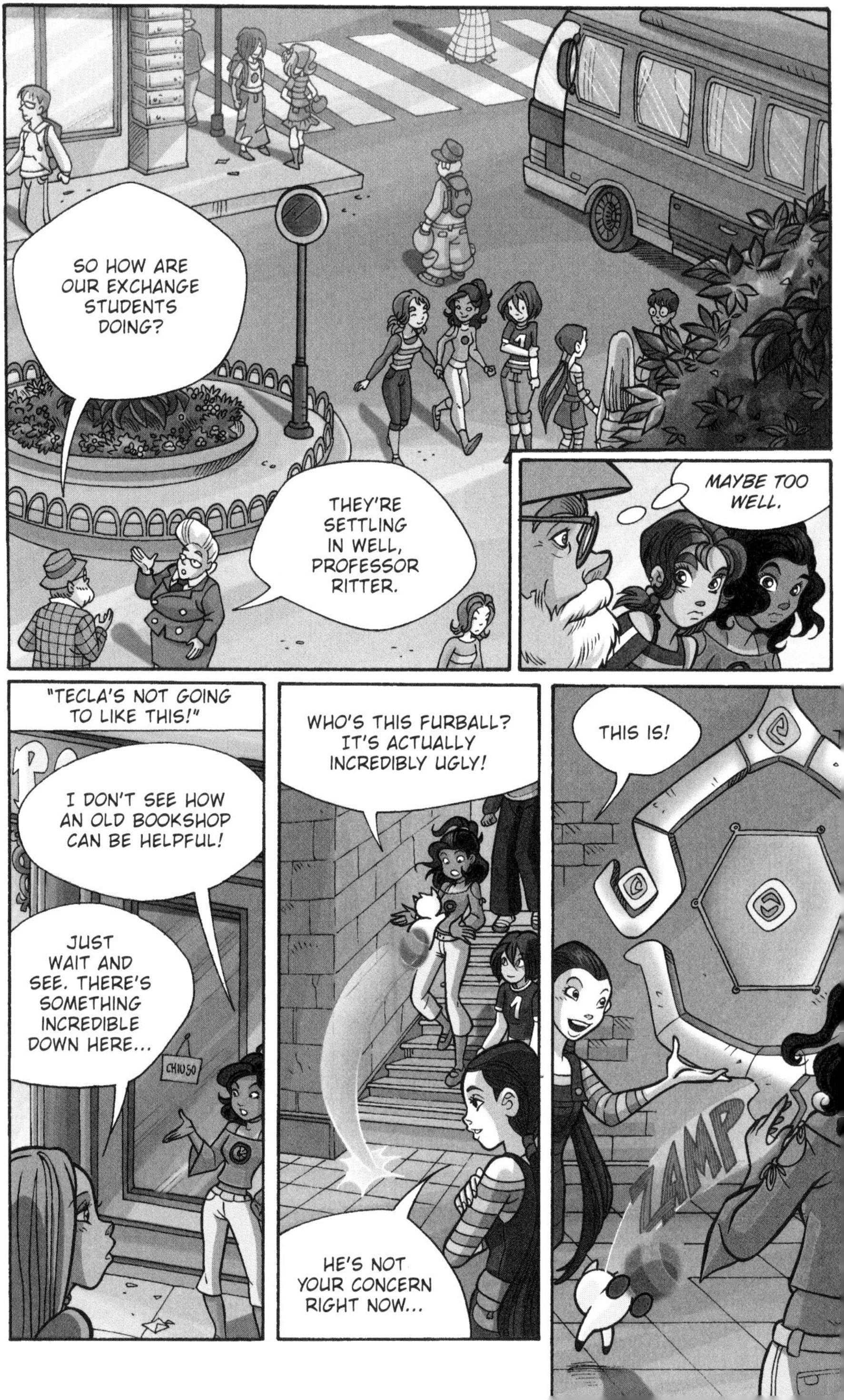
SO HOW ARE OUR EXCHANGE STUDENTS DOING?
THEY'RE SETTLING IN WELL, PROFESSOR RITTER.
MAYBE TOO WELL.
"TECLA'S NOT GOING TO LIKE THIS!"
I DON'T SEE HOW AN OLD BOOKSHOP CAN BE HELPFUL!
JUST WAIT AND SEE. THERE'S SOMETHING INCREDIBLE DOWN HERE...
CHIUSO
WHO'S THIS FURBALL? IT'S ACTUALLY INCREDIBLY UGLY!
HE'S NOT YOUR CONCERN RIGHT NOW...
THIS IS!
ZAMP

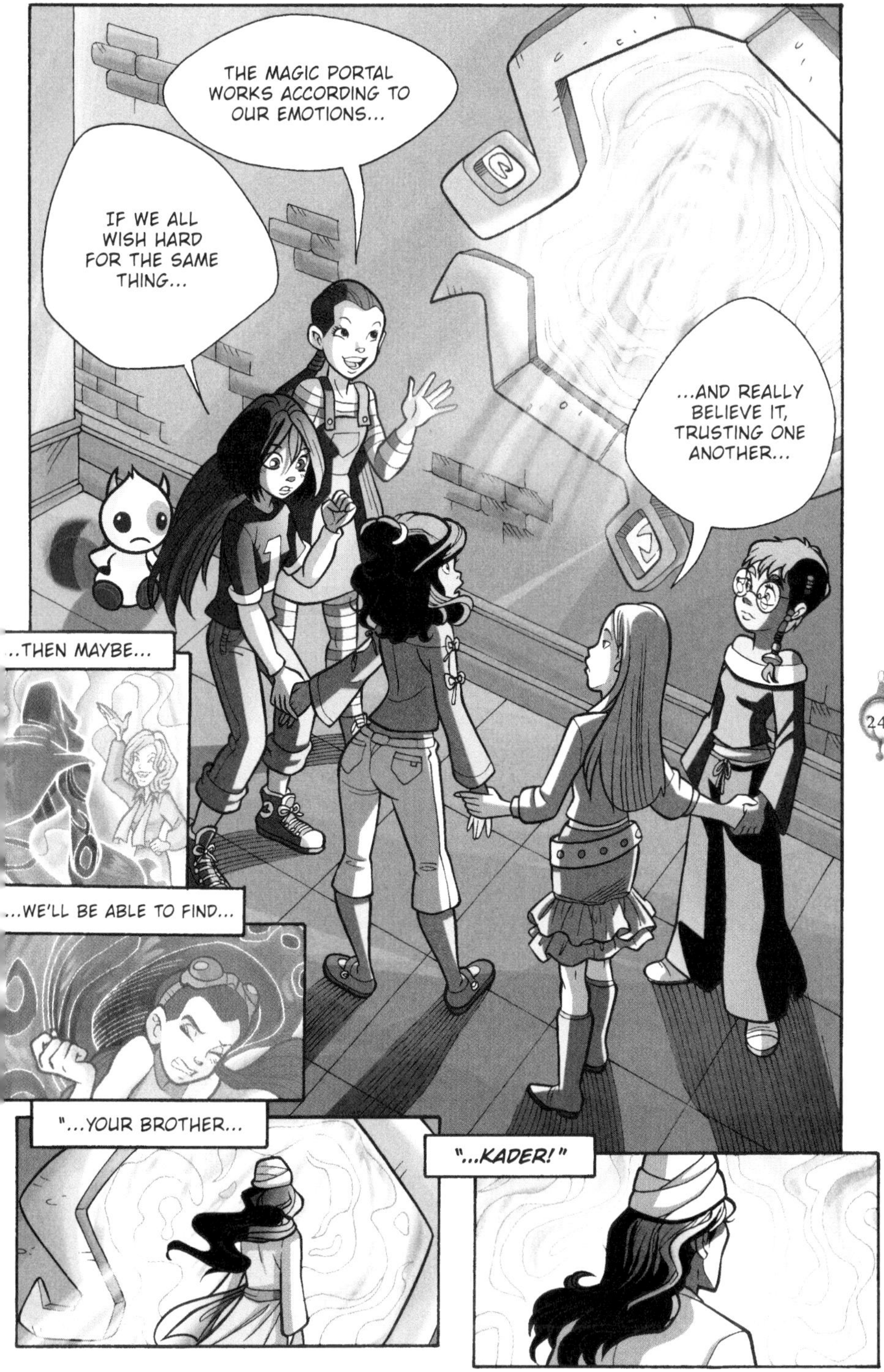
THE MAGIC PORTAL WORKS ACCORDING TO OUR EMOTIONS...
IF WE ALL WISH HARD FOR THE SAME THING...
...AND REALLY BELIEVE IT, TRUSTING ONE ANOTHER...
...THEN MAYBE...
...WE'LL BE ABLE TO FIND...
"...YOUR BROTHER...
"...KADER!"

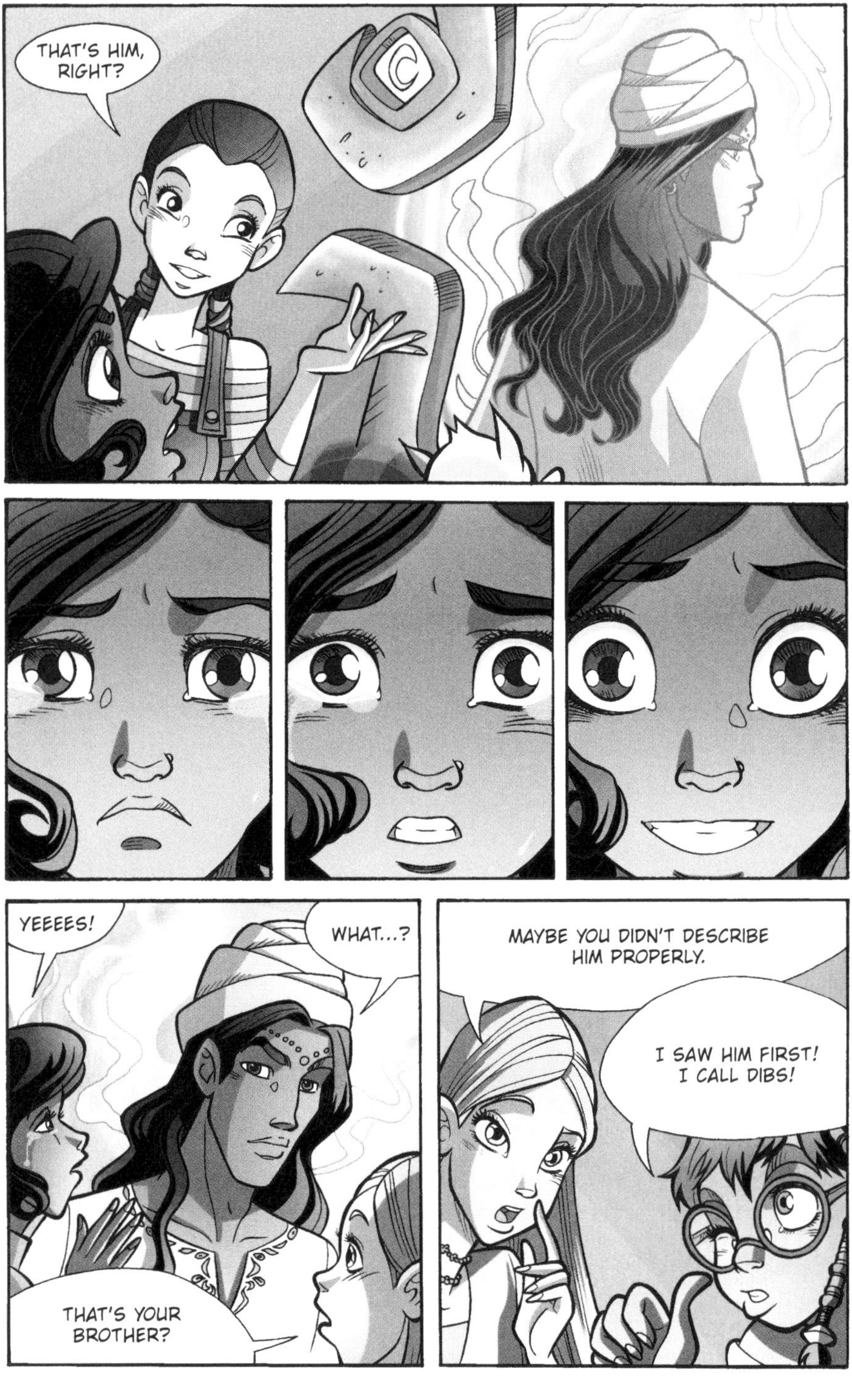
THAT'S HIM, RIGHT?
YEEEES!
WHAT...?
THAT'S YOUR BROTHER?
MAYBE YOU DIDN'T DESCRIBE HIM PROPERLY.
I SAW HIM FIRST! I CALL DIBS!

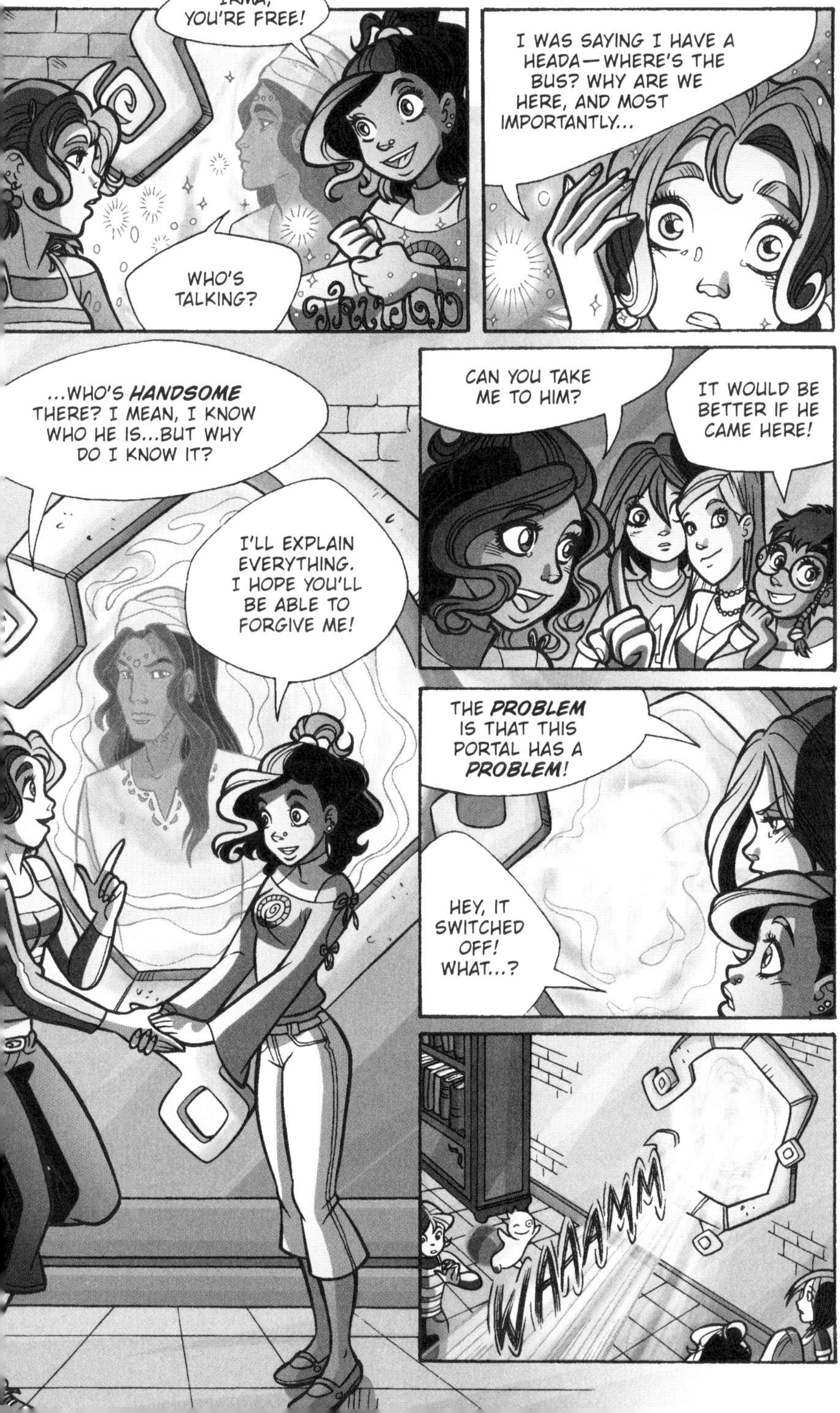
IRMA, YOU'RE FREE!
WHO'S TALKING?
I WAS SAYING I HAVE A HEADA—WHERE'S THE BUS? WHY ARE WE HERE, AND MOST IMPORTANTLY...
...WHO'S HANDSOME THERE? I MEAN, I KNOW WHO HE IS...BUT WHY DO I KNOW IT?
I'LL EXPLAIN EVERYTHING. I HOPE YOU'LL BE ABLE TO FORGIVE ME!
CAN YOU TAKE ME TO HIM?
IT WOULD BE BETTER IF HE CAME HERE!
THE PROBLEM IS THAT THIS PORTAL HAS A PROBLEM!
HEY, IT SWITCHED OFF! WHAT...?
WAAAMM

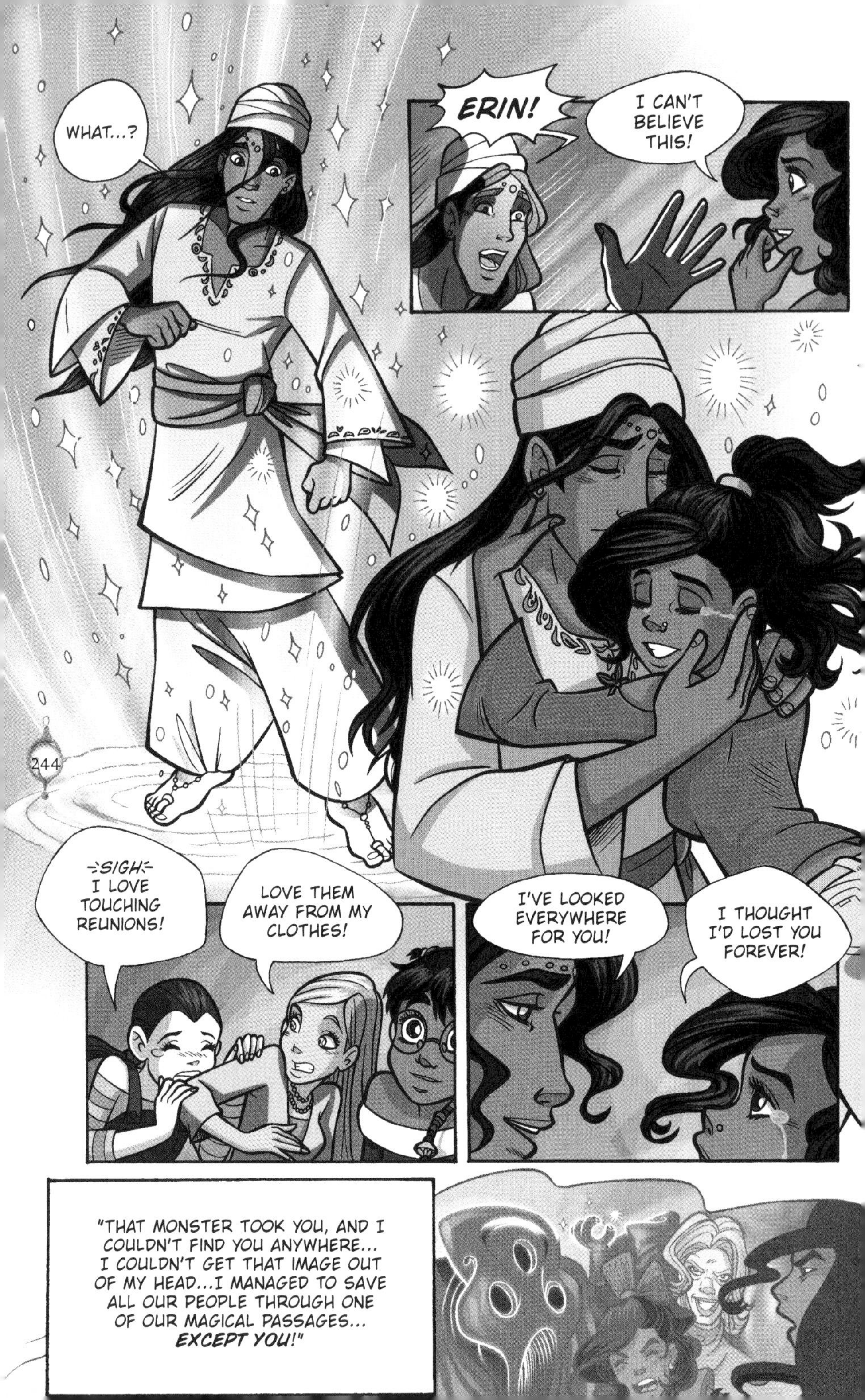

WHAT...?
ERIN!
I CAN'T BELIEVE THIS!
-SIGH- I LOVE TOUCHING REUNIONS!
LOVE THEM AWAY FROM MY CLOTHES!
I'VE LOOKED EVERYWHERE FOR YOU!
I THOUGHT I'D LOST YOU FOREVER!
"THAT MONSTER TOOK YOU, AND I COULDN'T FIND YOU ANYWHERE... I COULDN'T GET THAT IMAGE OUT OF MY HEAD...I MANAGED TO SAVE ALL OUR PEOPLE THROUGH ONE OF OUR MAGICAL PASSAGES... ***EXCEPT YOU!***"

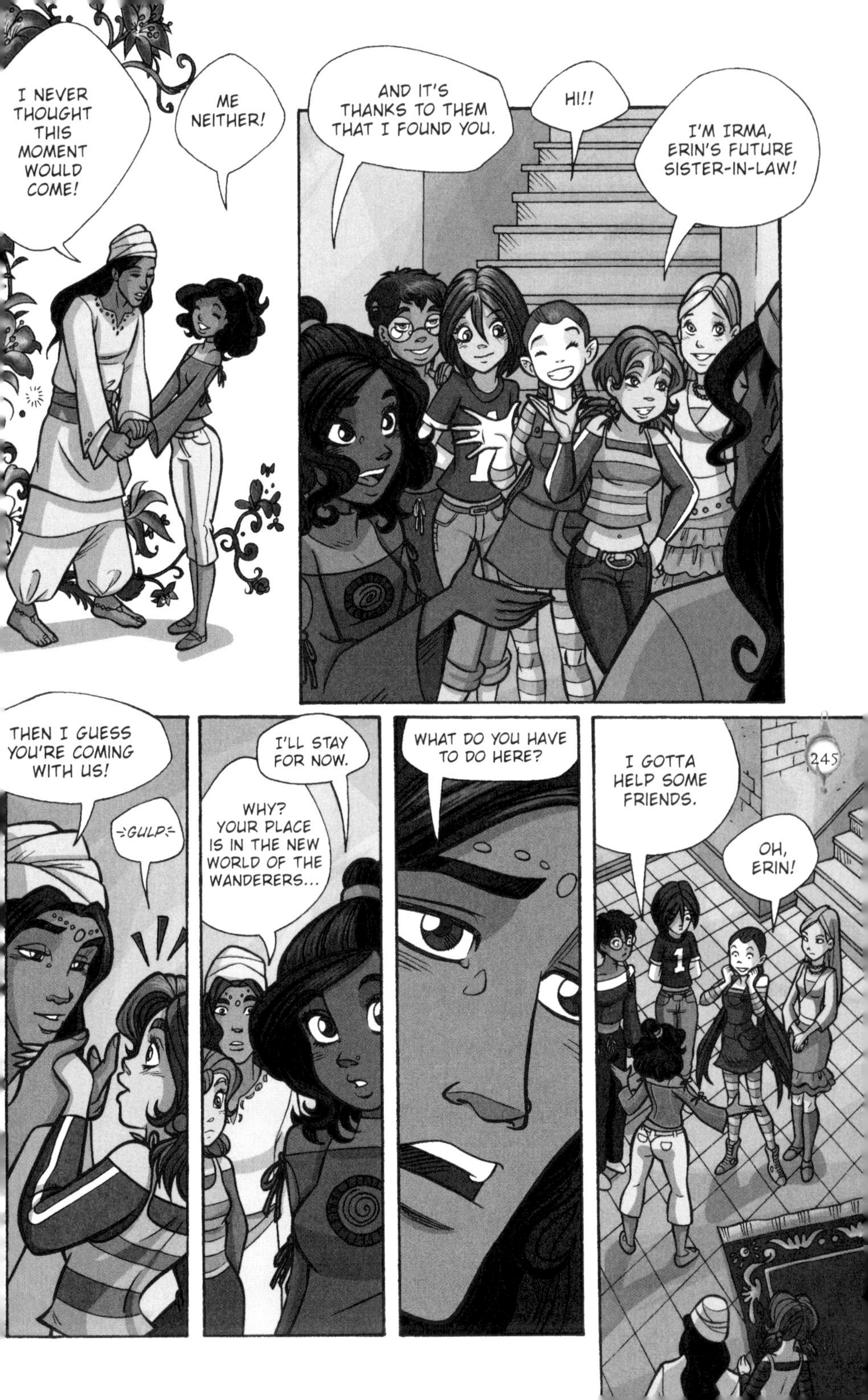
I NEVER THOUGHT THIS MOMENT WOULD COME!
ME NEITHER!
AND IT'S THANKS TO THEM THAT I FOUND YOU.
HI!!
I'M IRMA, ERIN'S FUTURE SISTER-IN-LAW!
THEN I GUESS YOU'RE COMING WITH US!
GULP
I'LL STAY FOR NOW.
WHY? YOUR PLACE IS IN THE NEW WORLD OF THE WANDERERS...
WHAT DO YOU HAVE TO DO HERE?
I GOTTA HELP SOME FRIENDS.
OH, ERIN!
245

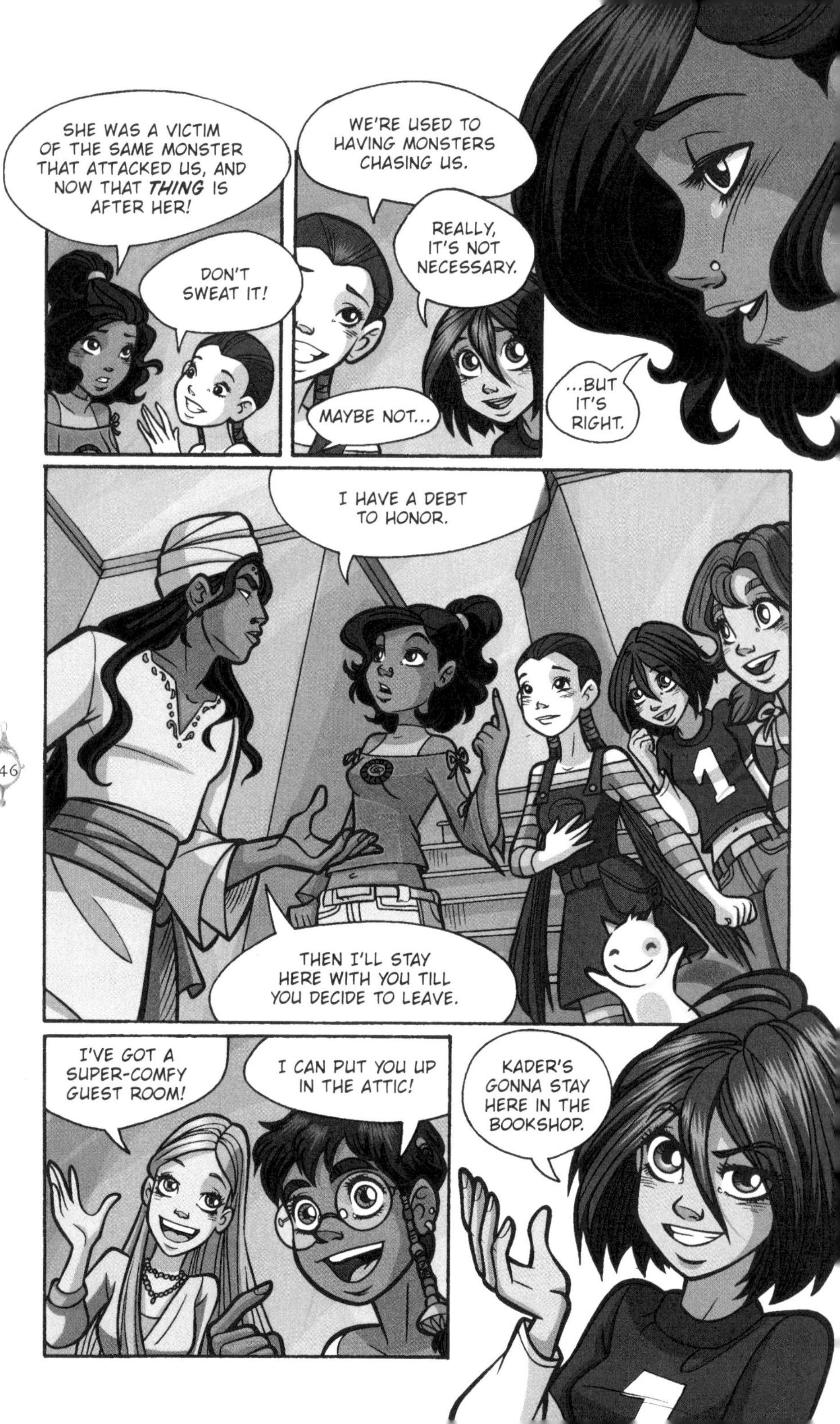
SHE WAS A VICTIM OF THE SAME MONSTER THAT ATTACKED US, AND NOW THAT *THING* IS AFTER HER!
DON'T SWEAT IT!
WE'RE USED TO HAVING MONSTERS CHASING US.
REALLY, IT'S NOT NECESSARY.
MAYBE NOT...
...BUT IT'S RIGHT.
I HAVE A DEBT TO HONOR.
THEN I'LL STAY HERE WITH YOU TILL YOU DECIDE TO LEAVE.
I'VE GOT A SUPER-COMFY GUEST ROOM!
I CAN PUT YOU UP IN THE ATTIC!
KADER'S GONNA STAY HERE IN THE BOOKSHOP.

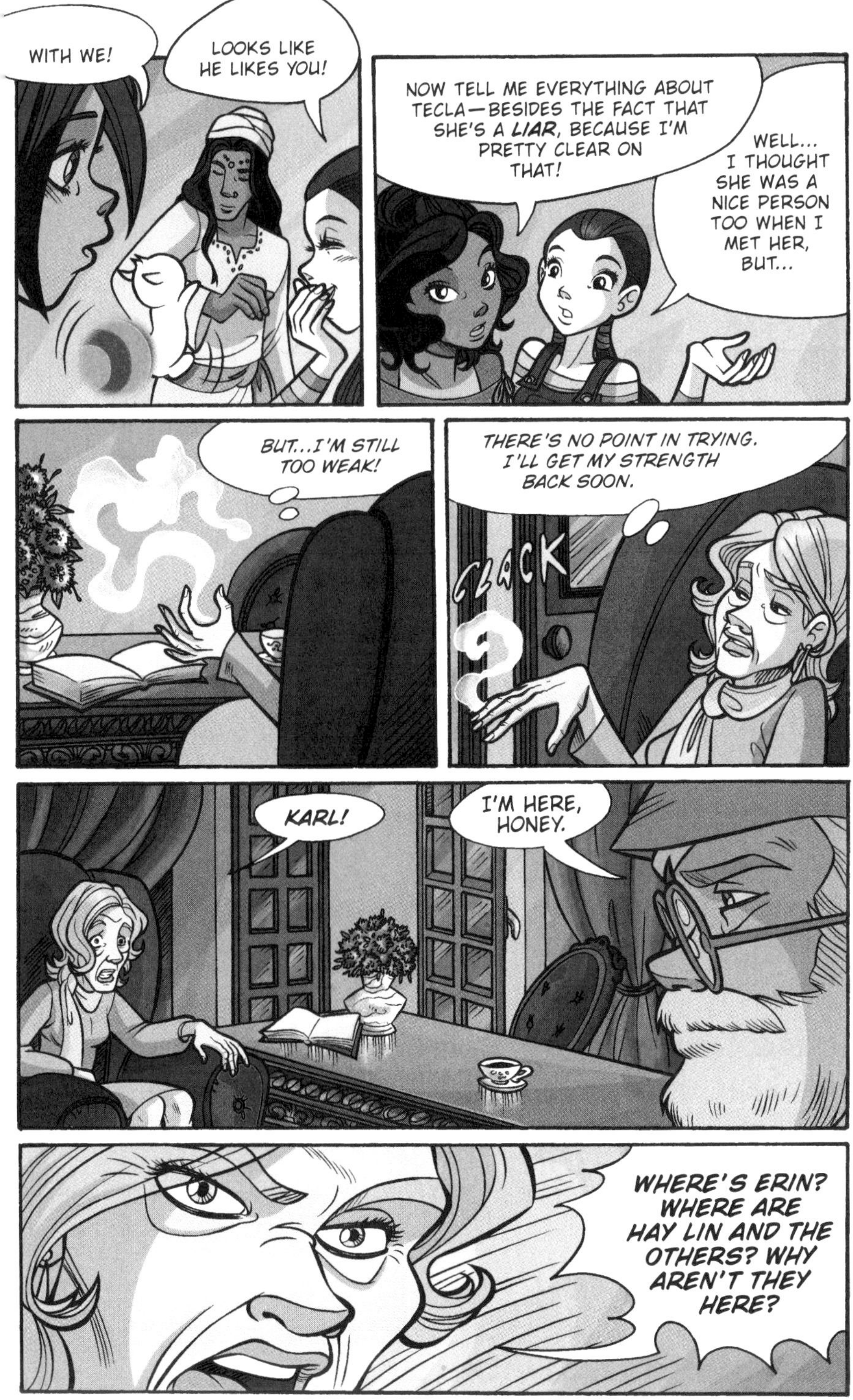
WITH WE!
LOOKS LIKE HE LIKES YOU!
NOW TELL ME EVERYTHING ABOUT TECLA—BESIDES THE FACT THAT SHE'S A *LIAR*, BECAUSE I'M PRETTY CLEAR ON THAT!
WELL... I THOUGHT SHE WAS A NICE PERSON TOO WHEN I MET HER, BUT...
BUT...I'M STILL TOO WEAK!
THERE'S NO POINT IN TRYING. I'LL GET MY STRENGTH BACK SOON.
CLACK
KARL!
I'M HERE, HONEY.
WHERE'S ERIN? WHERE ARE HAY LIN AND THE OTHERS? WHY AREN'T THEY HERE?

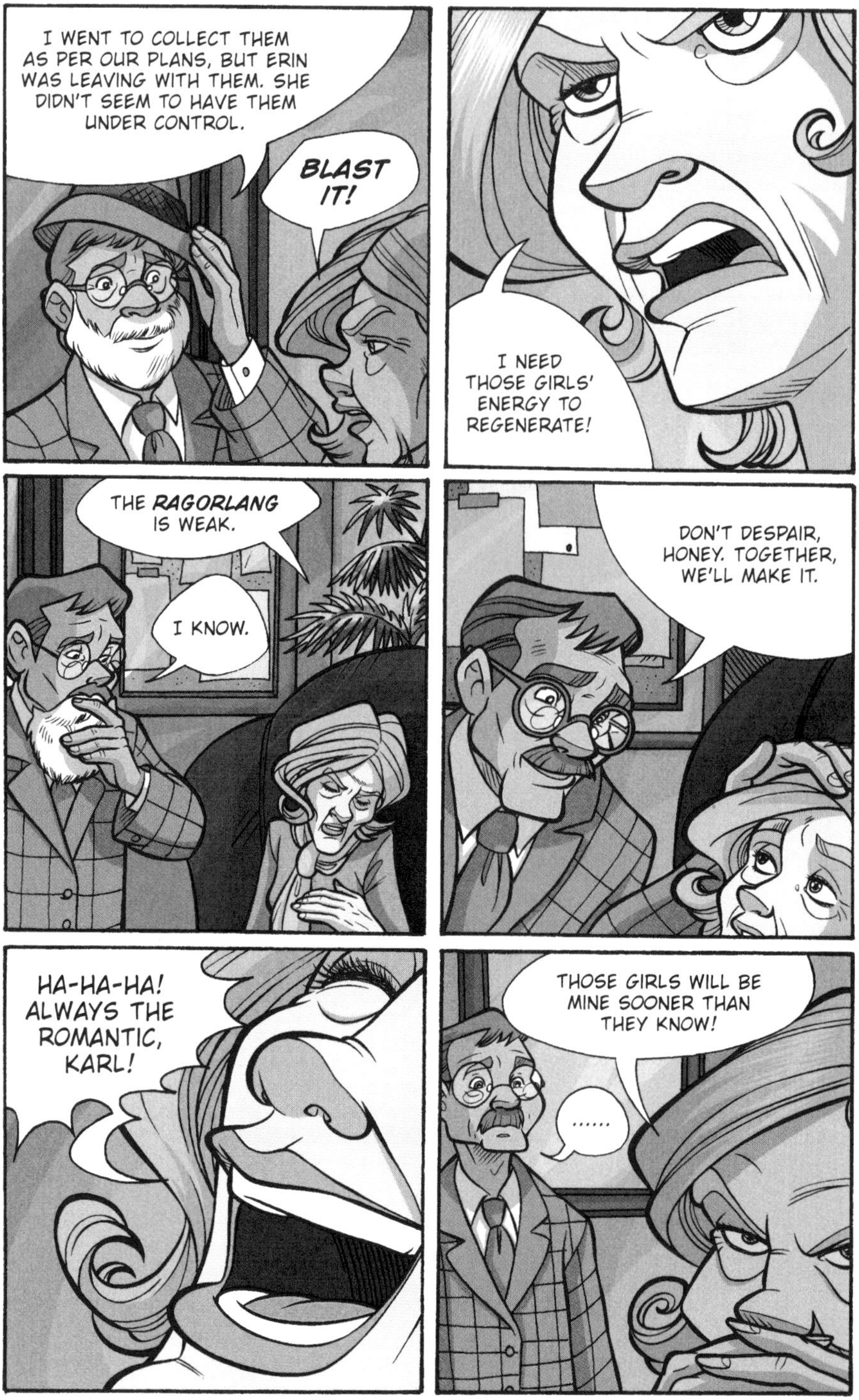
I WENT TO COLLECT THEM AS PER OUR PLANS, BUT ERIN WAS LEAVING WITH THEM. SHE DIDN'T SEEM TO HAVE THEM UNDER CONTROL.
BLAST IT!
I NEED THOSE GIRLS' ENERGY TO REGENERATE!
THE RAGORLANG IS WEAK.
I KNOW.
DON'T DESPAIR, HONEY. TOGETHER, WE'LL MAKE IT.
HA-HA-HA! ALWAYS THE ROMANTIC, KARL!
THOSE GIRLS WILL BE MINE SOONER THAN THEY KNOW!
......

NOT FAR FROM THERE...

HERE WE ARE.

I'LL GO BACK TO THE BOOKSHOP... BE SURE TO GET ME SOME EARTHLY CLOTHES. I WOULDN'T WANT TO ATTRACT ATTENTION!

I'M SO HAPPY TO HAVE FOUND YOU, KADER. I LOVE YOU!

HAVE A GOOD NIGHT, SISTER...

DESPITE EVERYTHING, THIS SEEMS LIKE A QUIET PLACE.

SEE YOU TOMORROW!

IT'S GOOD TO HEAR YOU SAY THAT!

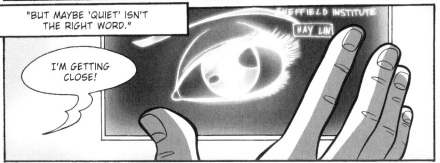

"BUT MAYBE 'QUIET' ISN'T THE RIGHT WORD."

SHEFFIELD INSTITUTE

HAY LIN

I'M GETTING CLOSE!

THE END

Read on in Volume 18!

Tecla Ibsen and...

The secrets of the new threat to W.I.T.C.H.!

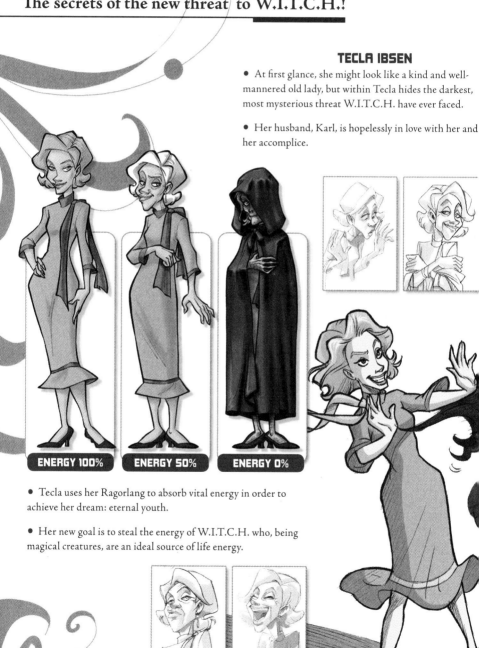

TECLA IBSEN

- At first glance, she might look like a kind and well-mannered old lady, but within Tecla hides the darkest, most mysterious threat W.I.T.C.H. have ever faced.
- Her husband, Karl, is hopelessly in love with her and her accomplice.

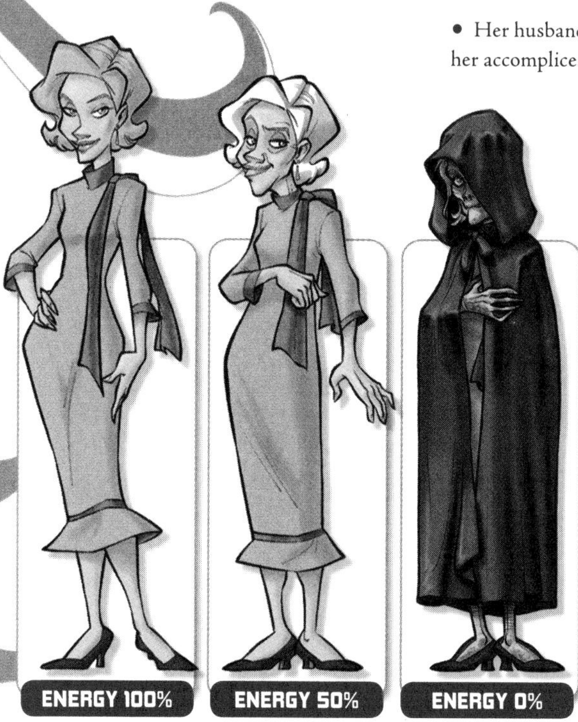
ENERGY 100%
ENERGY 50%
ENERGY 0%

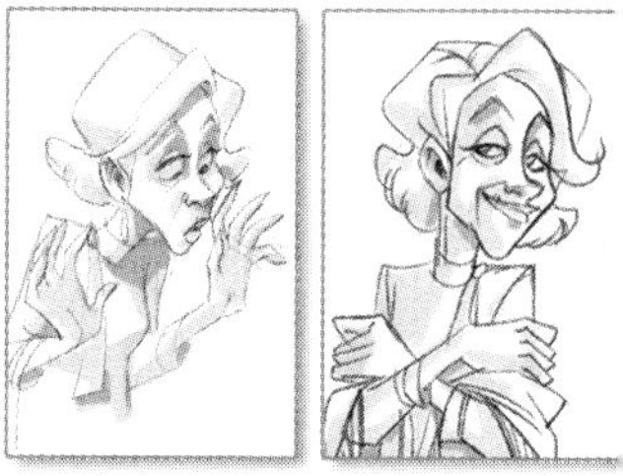

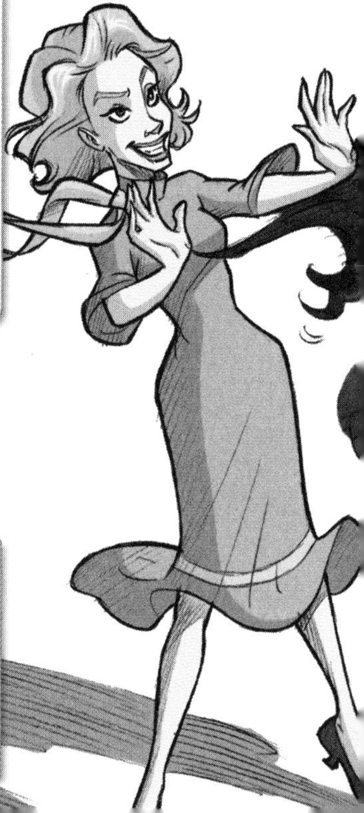

- Tecla uses her Ragorlang to absorb vital energy in order to achieve her dream: eternal youth.
- Her new goal is to steal the energy of W.I.T.C.H. who, being magical creatures, are an ideal source of life energy.

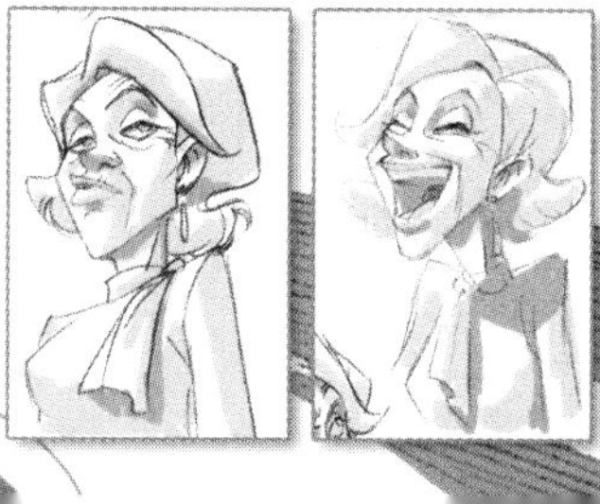

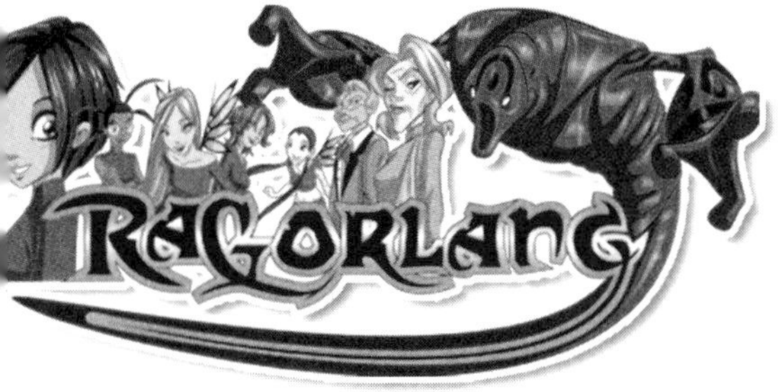
RAGORLANG

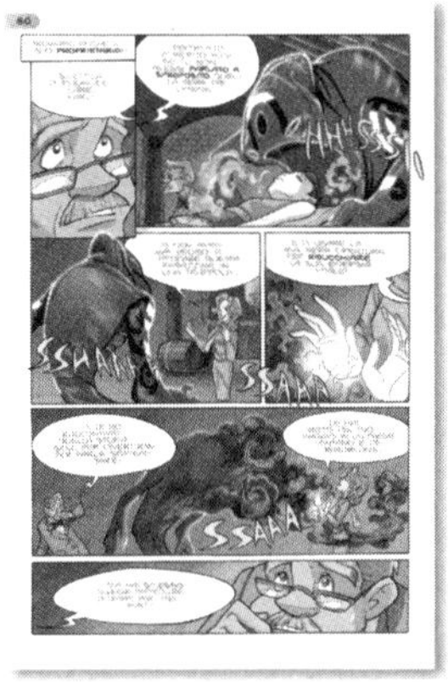

RAGORLANG

• We can't talk about Tecla without mentioning her powerful Ragorlang, a word which sounds like a terrified scream.

• The hideous creature is released by Tecla and acts on her behalf, absorbing energy, words, and thoughts from its victims and leaving them in a catatonic state. The stolen energy is then consumed by Tecla.

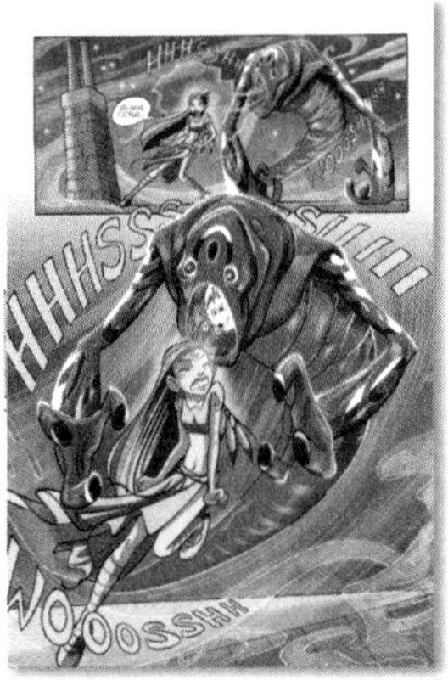

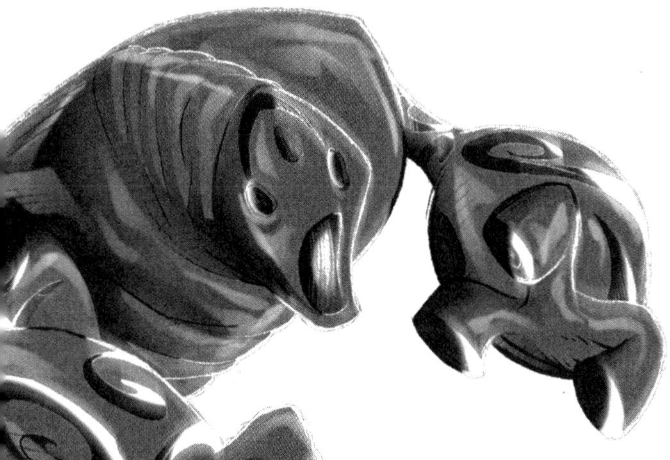

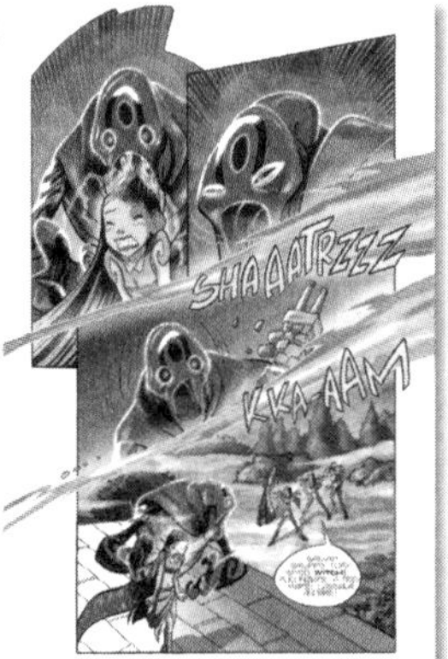

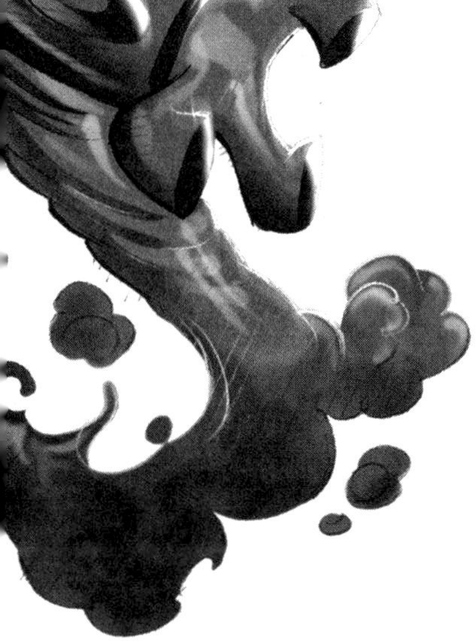

• Hay Lin is the first W.I.T.C.H. to be "marked" by a Ragolang during a trip to visit her friend Eric in Open Hill, where she meets the Ibsens for the first time.

• Old legends about the origins of the Ragorlang describe a seemingly normal human who can split into two, releasing a monstrous shadow.

• When a Ragorlang "marks" its victims, it leaves them completely drained of energy.

Sheffield World

School according to W.I.T.C.H.!

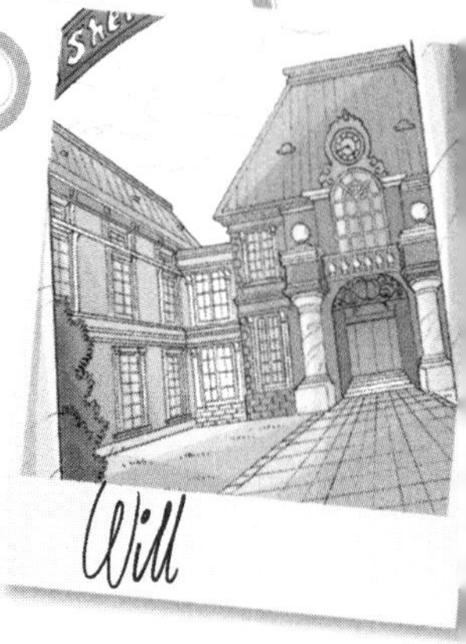

Will

Will spills the beans about the Institute and gives tips on surviving minor school issues! Find out what she hides in her desk, what her favorite place is, and what she thinks about Sheffield Institute.

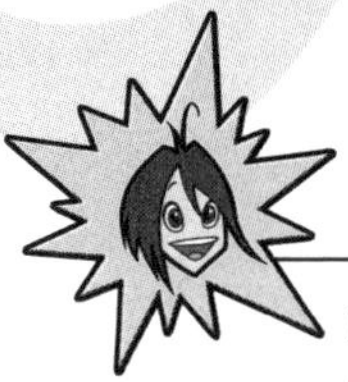

My personal space at the Sheffield

Here's the "PALPITATION STOP," meaning this is my chill-out area! When I arrive at school and get heart palpitations because of a difficult test, I just come to this beautiful portico and feel better right away. It's always a bit crowded, of course, but I barely even notice; I lean against my favorite pillar and...chill out!

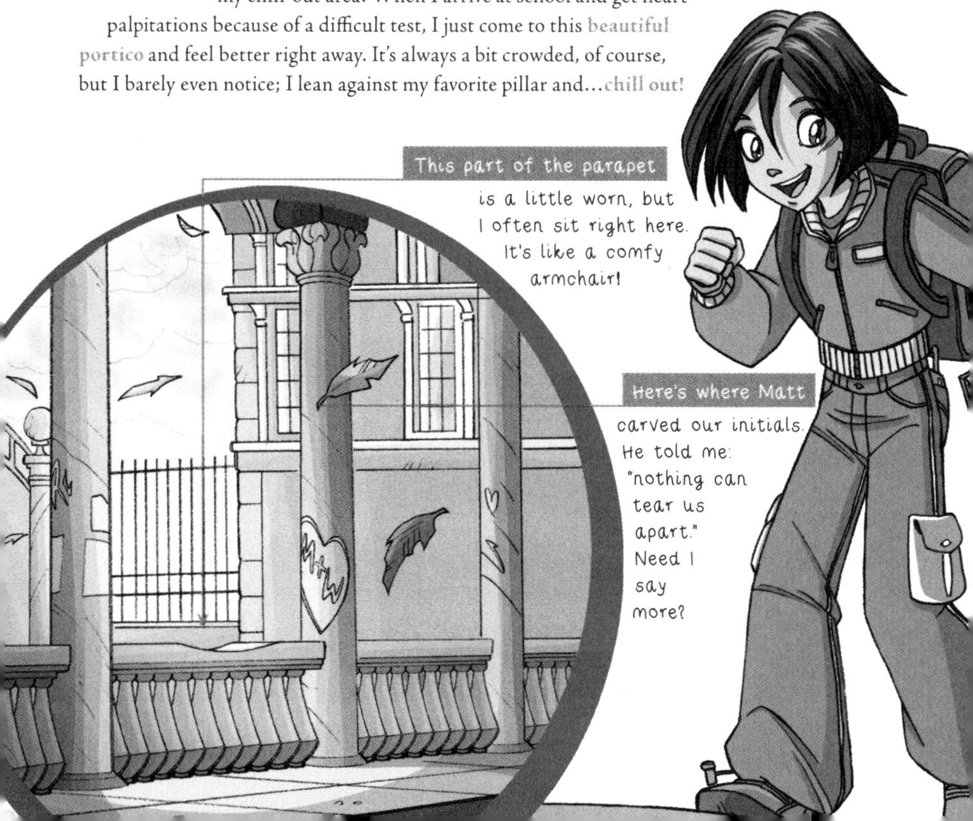

This part of the parapet
is a little worn, but I often sit right here. It's like a comfy armchair!
Here's where Matt
carved our initials. He told me: "nothing can tear us apart." Need I say more?

School according to Will!

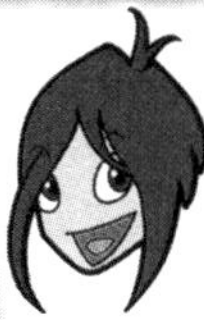

Secrets under the table!

Wanna take a peek in my desk? Go ahead! I stockpile a lot of stuff here, some of it useful, some not so much, but…they keep me company!

My favorite subject is art!

Messy? Who, me? No! I'm just very creative!

My backpack's super-organized. I've always got everything I need for the day!

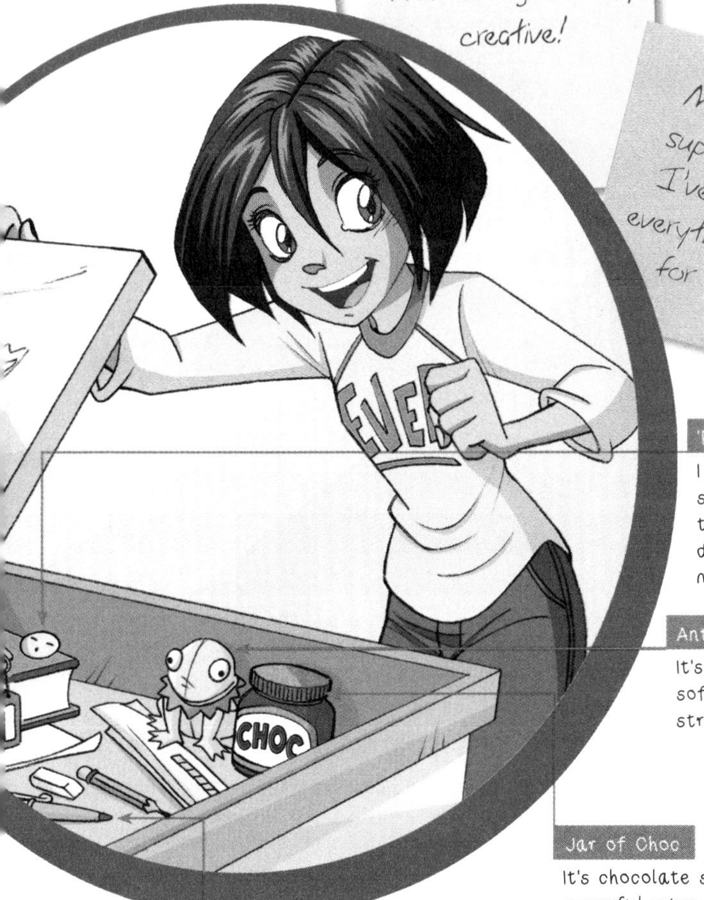

CHOC

'Personalized' planner

I stick different smileys next to my teacher's names, depending on how much I like them!

Anti-stress Frog

It's all squishy and soft, the perfect stress-reliever!

Jar of Choc

It's chocolate spread! I eat a spoonful every now and then to sweeten my day!

Bike lock key

It's a spare! I've already lost too many...

Pen with golden cap

It's my lucky, mega-luxury pen for sparkling results on every test!

Part VI. Ragorlang • Volume I

Series Created by Elisabetta Gnone
Comic Art Direction: Alessandro Barbucci, Barbara Canepa

W.I.T.C.H.: The Graphic Novel, Part VI: Ragorlang
© Disney Enterprises, Inc.

English translation © 2019 by Disney Enterprises, Inc.

JY
150 West 30th Street, 19th Floor
New York, NY 10001

Visit us at jyforkids.com
facebook.com/jyforkids
twitter.com/jyforkids
jyforkids.tumblr.com
instagram.com/jyforkids

First JY Edition: September 2019

JY is an imprint of Yen Press, LLC.
The JY name and logo are trademarks of Yen Press, LLC.

The publisher is not responsible for websites (or their content) that are not owned by the publisher.

Library of Congress Control Number: 2017950917

ISBNs:
978-1-9753-3222-8 (paperback)
978-1-9753-3221-1 (ebook)

10 9 8 7 6 5 4 3 2 1

LSC-C

Printed in the United States of America

Cover Art by Alberto Zanon
Colors by Andrea Cagol

Translation by Linda Ghio and Stephanie Dagg at Editing Zone
Lettering by Katie Blakeslee

THE SCREAMING MAN

Concept and Script by Bruno Enna
Layout and pencils by Davide Baldoni, Lucia Balletti, Federico Bertolucci, Antonella Dalena, Ettore Gula
Inks by Marina Baggio, Danilo Loizzedda, Federica Salfo, Roberta Zanotta
Color and Light Direction by Francesco Legramandi
Title Page Art by Alberto Zanon
with colors by Raffaella Calvino Prina

ONLY A FLOWER

Concept by Paola Mulazzi
Script by Alessandro Ferrari
Layout by Gianluca Panniello
Pencils by Monica Catalano
Inks by Roberta Zanotta and Federica Salfo
Color and Light Direction by Francesco Legramandi
Title Page Art by Alberto Zanon
with colors by Andrea Cagol

REFLECTED MEMORIES

Concept and Script by Teresa Radice
Layout by Ettore Gula
Pencils by Francesco Legramandi
Inks by Marina Baggio
Color and Light Direction by Francesco Legramandi
Title Page Art by Franceso Legramandi

ON YOUR SIDE

Concept and Script by Paola Mulazzi
Layout by Flavia Scuderi and Elisabetta Melaranci
Pencils by Lucia Balletti
Inks by Marina Baggio, Danilo Loizzedda, and Roberta Zanotta
Color and Light Direction by Francesco Legramandi
Title Page Art by Flavia Scuderi
with colors by Ivan Cavero la Torre